The Divine Zetan Trilogy

Martin Lundqvist

Published by Martin Lundqvist, 2020.

This is a work of fiction. Similarities to real people, places, or events are entirely coincidental.

THE DIVINE ZETAN TRILOGY

First edition. June 4, 2020.

Copyright © 2020 Martin Lundqvist.

Written by Martin Lundqvist.

THE DIVINE DISSIMULATION

THE DIVINE ZETAN TRILOGY

MARTIN LUNDQVIST

WHEN GOD DIES,
A VILLAIN TAKES HIS PLACE.

Chapter 1 Introduction

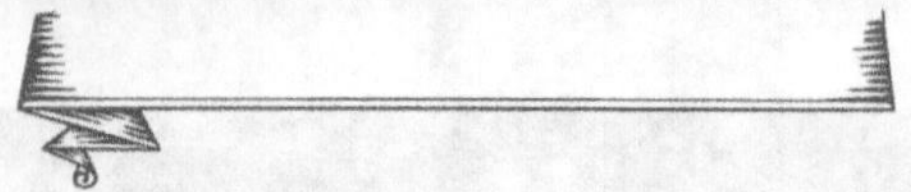

Abraham Goldstein was looking out through the windows of the 3000 meters high Goldstein Tower built in the centre of Antarctica. The Goldstein Tower was the second largest structure on Earth built in a pyramid shape to support its tremendous weight and to make the building secure from attacks. From the top of Goldstein Tower Abraham Goldstein could see all his domains, the lush farmlands, the vast, serene parks, and the residential complexes where his loyal followers lived. Abraham sighed, despite owning all of this he was not satisfied, he wanted to own more, and be more powerful.

Being 250 years old, Abraham hoped that his DNA was possible to regenerate once more so that he would feel like a young man again. Abraham knew there were no guarantees, as he was on the fringes of what was achievable with the DNA regeneration technology. Regardless of what he did death was crawling closer.

Abraham exhaled and relaxed. Tomorrow would be a momentous day, and if he had lived for 250 years, he would survive another day.

Abraham was excited for the next morning because of reports that the Divine Detection program was ready. He had ordered his scientists that he wanted to be the first person to use the innovative technology. Hopefully, it would answer all his questions about God and make him meet the divine being.

The Divine Detection program was the latest marvel of quantum physics and a top-secret project of House Goldstein. It scanned through the dimensional layers of reality, and if it found the Divine Dimension, it could transport the consciousness of the user there, so he could meet the divine beings while still being alive.

Wanting to meet God with a fresh mind, Abraham entered the sleeping pod in his bedroom, set it to four hours, and instantly fell asleep.

Chapter 2: The Solar System In 2785

In 2785 most of the solar system was inhabited. Mars was the major population centre with 4 billion inhabitants. Earth had only 1 billion inhabitants, and they were living their life in abundance as Terran Citizens owned almost everything in the solar system.

Earth's limited population was because the ruling Terran Council in the 23rd century decreed the sterilisation or deportation of everyone who was not rich or had exceptional genes. Most people chose sterilization, living out their lives peacefully while others had left Earth. Since the 24th century, the population of Earth stayed stable around 1 billion, which was the ideal population to avoid civil conflict and resource shortfall.

In 2785 every birth and death on Earth were tightly regulated, and no natural conceptions occurred. Instead, citizens had to apply to have children. If approved, scientific DNA optimisation ensured that every individual had the best possible genes. Individuals who were wealthy could usually apply to have more than one child, while poor people and people with undesired genetics had to leave the planet if they wanted offspring.

The Terran Council controlled the weather on Earth, through launching large mirrors and shades orbiting Earth. The mirrors increased the amount of sunshine on the surface making cold areas such as Antarctica warmer, while the shades decreased the amount of sunshine making the surface cooler in the tropical regions.

Technically, the planet Earth was still divided into different countries, but they had lost their meaning as all the political and economic power was with the major company conglomerates. The five large conglomerates governed Earth via The Terran Council, which consisted of:

- House Goldstein that ruled Antarctica, Australia, and South America;
- House White that ruled North America;
- House Muller that ruled Europe;
- House Rashid that ruled the Middle East and Africa
- House Cheng that ruled most of the Asian continent.

Through the Terran Council, the major factions met and made sure that life on Earth was plentiful and peaceful. There had been peace on Earth through the Pax Terran agreement for 300 years. Outside of Earth, however, the Terran factions were always fighting each other indirectly through supporting different sides in proxy wars on other planets.

All the major population centres on Earth were connected by a network of trains that ran in vacuum tubes and could reach speeds of up to 10,000 kilometres an hour. This way all the major cities could reach each other within an hour or two.

Mars in 2785 was a chaotic poverty-stricken planet full of warring factions. When Mars was terraformed 500 years earlier, it was intended for a maximum of 200 million people, and now it had 20 times more people. The excessive population meant that water and other natural resources were limited. The only things that seemed to exist in abundance were weapons and synthetic drugs.

Despite its imperfections, many of the Martians still loved the Martian lifestyle, as it was freer than the Terran one. On Mars, people could live like they wanted, while everything was tightly regulated on Earth. Freedom came at a price though, as the life expectancy on Mars was 40 years while it was 150 years on Earth. Abraham Goldstein who was 250 years old was the oldest man on Earth as he was wealthy and could get his scientists to extend his life a lot longer than most people.

Life on Mars could have been better if the Terran Council had not feared the Martian way of life, and intentionally kept the planet weak. The trading terms between the planets were extremely unbalanced, and the Terran Council took whatever they wanted from Mars paying next to nothing. The Terran Council extorted the Martians, intimidating them with the superior Terran technology and creating mayhem when the Martians dared to resist.

Export of Terran technology to Mars was not allowed, so most Martians had only access to 500-year-old technology. If the Terran Council wanted to, they could have given Martian population a safe atmosphere protecting them from the toxic stellar background radiation. Instead, these resources were spent on having a massive military fleet orbiting Mars to show the Martians who were the masters of the solar system.

Humans had evolved differently on different planets. The people on Earth were all picture perfect due to the genetic pre-selection. Depending on the culture they could be athletic or lean, but in all cultures, they had ideal complexion and ideal posture. They were highly intelligent humanoids but also highly obedient and non-questioning as that was how the ruling classes liked their subjects. The Martian human genome had defects from radiation and genetic mutation. Most Martians looked sickly and were genetically predisposed for artificial drug addictions. On the flipside, they were radiation, virus, and infection resistant and a lot more resilient than their Terran counterparts.

Because of their radiation resistance, Martians were employed to do dangerous jobs in the solar system such as building and maintaining the automated mining stations on Jupiter's moons and building asteroid mining stations. A lot of them smuggled Terran technology back to Mars, so the expeditions hiring Martians was not allowed to use new technology due to the paranoia of the Terran Council. The Martian laborers were always supervised under close Terran military supervision.

Among other inhabited places in the solar system; Venus was only used for its automated mines and prison camps where condemned prisoners lived in endless darkness and suffering. Life expectancy for anyone residing on Venus was less than 15 years. Likewise, Mercury was too close to the sun to terraform properly for human settlement.

Many of the asteroids were used by wealthy Terrans as holiday houses. This was because the technology existed that could put them in any selected orbit around the sun, with artificial atmosphere and artificial gravity. A lot of asteroids also orbited Earth as holiday houses for wealthy Terrans.

Finally, a few planets orbiting other stars had human colonies. While the technology existed to travel this far, the Terran Council did not see it as viable investments. The fastest travel speed possible with the available technology was $1/10^{th}$ of the speed of light, which meant that it took at least 40 years to reach Alpha Centauri B, the closest star. While it was possible to travel this far by cryogenically freezing the crew before the trip, it was not profitable to do so, as it was impossible to control the inhabitants of colonies on Alpha Centauri as it took four years to send them a message and 40 years to travel there.

Thus, all the colonies outside the solar system, was founded by eccentric trillionaires with no heirs and no better use for their money. These colonies were independent and had very limited contact with Earth.

Chapter 3 The Divine Suicide and Ascension Plan

Abraham Goldstein woke up four hours later. He was full of energy. He took the elevator 800 levels down, to a top-secret research lab 300 meters below ground. It was so secret that not even his family members knew about it.

Abraham met up with Jack Brown, the lead scientist for the project. Abraham:

- Is the machine ready?

Jack:

- Yes, it should be operational now. I must warn you though, we haven't tested the device yet and it might be dangerous.

Abraham:

- And you are not going to test the machine for that matter. I am not spending 80 billion Terran Credits on a scientist's toy; this is MY toy!

The 80 billion Terran Credits devoted to the Divine Detector machine was an absolute fortune. The construction of the entire 3000 meters high Goldstein tower had cost 120 billion Terran Credits, and that was an 800-level building with 16,000 rooms.

Jack:

- Understood, sir! We have scanned the entire spectra of potential dimensions, and we believe that the one you are looking for is located at the coordinates Gamma; Omega; Delta; one; nine; eight; five.

Abraham:

- Excellent, plug me in.

Jack:

- Okay, I'll keep you in the Divine Dimension for just a few seconds. You'll experience it as a lot longer as we predict that time moves very slowly in there.

Jack Brown started the Divine Detector particle accelerator, and Abraham Goldstein could feel that his consciousness left his body. He was travelling through space at speed faster than light. In the blink of an eye, Abraham crashed down into an open courtyard.

Abraham got up and studied the courtyard. It was both beautiful and eerie at the same time. He looked at a pond full of lotus flowers. In the reflection of the pond, he could see the Goldstein Tower below as if he was on a floating structure high up in the sky. Abraham was stunned by fascination, but he snapped out of it. He was here with a purpose; to meet God. Abraham saw a big gate at the end of the courtyard, and his gut feeling told him it was the right way. He walked through the gate, and he entered a throne room. At the far end of the room, there was a golden throne full of gemstones. The gemstones radiated with an intense light.

After marvelling at the beauty of the throne for a while, Abraham saw a dead man in robes lying on the ground; facing down. Abraham approached the lifeless body and turned it around. He looked at it in awe. The corpse belonged to Yahweh the god of his people. But Yahweh was dead? How could this be?

After the initial shock, Abraham knew that he had to find a reason behind Yahweh's death. He searched the clothes of the dead deity, and he found a letter. It was written in an ancient language, but Abraham instinctively understood the meaning of the message. The letter said;

"This is how I end my life, with a knife to my throat. I thought that being the sole ruler of humanity was all I ever wanted, so I expelled the other divines from my palace after murdering Lucifer, my best friend and lover. Unfortunately, I destroyed the portal to Earth in the altercation with the other Zetans. I am lonely and battling with guilt and my demons. Humanity does not need me anymore, and I don't feel the need to live either. This is my end.

Yours Truly

Yahweh

PS. Since you are reading this, humanity obviously needs a god. Take my place! Go to the altar, to the left of my throne and you'll know how."

Abraham got up and he walked to the altar. What he saw fascinated him. On the altar, he saw a blueprint for three different microchips:

- The top chip was the god chip; it allowed the user to connect with and communicate with up to 10,000 followers at a time. It also enabled the user to directly control the actions of anyone with an angel chip implanted. The God chip also had the feature that the one wearing it, could instantly kill anyone with an angel or human chip implanted.
- The middle chip was the angel chip. It allowed the user to connect with up to 100 followers at the time.
- The bottom chip was the human chip. It made it possible for gods and angels to enter the mind of anyone having the chip implanted in their brain and communicates with them.

Abraham memorised the schematics, using the bionic memory enhancing microchip he had implanted in his brain. The world then blurred in front of his eyes, and he was back in the research lab of Goldstein Tower.

Jack Brown approached Abraham as he came back to consciousness:

- Did you find what you were looking for?

Abraham:

- No, but I found something else.
- Can you extract three schematics from my memory?

Jack:

- Yes, wait a second.
- Yes, I got them.
- Do you know what they are?

Abraham:

- Yes, but that is none of your business.
- All I need to know is whether you can make them?

Jack:

- Yes, with our particle replicator machine we can replicate any item we have a blueprint of, including those schematics.

Abraham:

- Good.

- I want one microchip of the top schematic plan and 300 microchips of the bottom plan. Have them done by tomorrow.

- And make sure this stays between us, for your families' sake.

Jack:

- Yes, sir! Consider it done, sir!

Abraham left the room, and Jack sighed. He felt worried. Although he was an agnostic, humans should not try to reach the divine realm. What was the story with these microchips? What had happened when Abraham was connected to the machine? Jack Brown had never seen any microchips like these schematics before, and he could only guess what they would do. Regardless, Jack would do as Abraham had ordered and produce the batch. He owed Abraham that.

A decade earlier, Jack Brown had done the unthinkable and fallen in love with a Martian woman during a House White research expedition on Mars. When Benjamin White, the director of the Mars expedition found out about the love affair, he condemned Jack Brown's entire research team, consisting of 16 researchers and revoked their Terran citizenships. He did this, as House White was the most racist of the Terran factions, and it showed their people on Earth that it was not okay for anyone to have relations with Martians.

Unfortunately for Benjamin White, his move to banish House White's foremost quantum physicists over a race matter was not appreciated by his peers, and he was assassinated later that year. By that time there was no trace of the team, and it took House White years to find out that Abraham Goldstein had hired Jack Brown.

Fortunately, for Jack and his staff; Abraham was more pragmatic than racist, and he offered them safe re-entry to Earth as well as new Terran citizenships if they worked for him. He even promised Jack Brown that he could have children with his Martian wife and that both she and the children would be granted Terran citizenships by Abraham when the project finished.

With no time to waste, Jack gathered his team to make the microchips requested by Abraham. It would be a challenging task, but luckily, they were all experts at using the particle replicator machine, and they had access to every element possible.

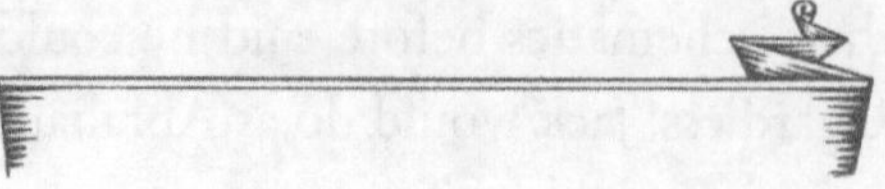

Chapter 4: Abraham Goldstein Makes New Plans.

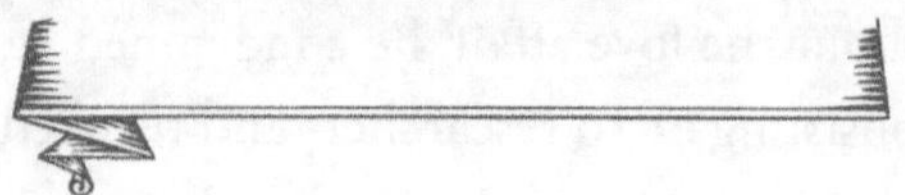

Abraham Goldstein sat in his penthouse reflecting over the past day's event. It was a shame that Yahweh was dead, as Abraham had so much respect for him and wanted to learn everything from the great creator. But Yahweh's death had opened the opportunity for Abraham to reach a higher goal, to be greater than any man before him, to be immortal, to become a god. This was his destiny; it wasn't chance that led him to the Divine Dimension, it was providence. Yahweh wanted Abraham to be his successor and it was his duty to comply.

But first, he had to find out if the divine microchip worked. The god version of the chip was big and bulky as it needed to be able to communicate with up to 10,000 followers at a time. To protect it, Abraham had ordered Jack Brown to forge it into a golden crown. Abraham put on the crown and screamed in pain as the microchip merged with his brain, and the crown was stuck into place. A young and beautiful female servant came rushing in.

Servant:

 - Are you okay sir; I heard a loud scream?

Abraham:

 - I have never been better.

Servant:

- That's excellent sir. May I ask about the golden crown, I have never seen you wear it before?

Abraham:

- You are not paid to ask questions! Be gone!

Abraham clenched his teeth in frustration after the servant left. He used to sleep with his servants when he was younger and more virile. He still wanted to keep up the illusion that he had sex with his servants, so he hired young and beautiful girls to be his aides. The truth was that he had not had sex for the last 100 years. He just could not feel physical attraction anymore. His doctors had told him this was a common side effect of the DNA regenerations technology; that many people could not feel sexual attraction after their natural lifespan ended.

Abraham thought of his former wife, Lillian Goldstein, who died 130 years earlier. She had refused DNA regeneration technology claiming that if God had wanted her to live longer, he would have given her better genes, and artificially extending one's life led to misery. Abraham mourned Lillian's death, and he was unable to love anyone else; thus, he was very lonely.

Abraham got back to the matter at hand. The divine golden crown caused him an excruciating headache, but it didn't give spiritual clarity and supernatural insights. He realised that the purpose of the God chip wasn't to provide in-depth knowledge but merely to control the subjects below him. Thus, he needed to test the Human chip, and fortunately there was a suitable candidate.

Abraham's inner circle, the Angels, had caught a suspected spy from House Cheng earlier in the day. This spy would be the ideal test subject for the human chip, as he would be killed anyway. With no time to waste, Abraham took the elevator down to another basement level of Goldstein tower, to the premises of the Angel program.

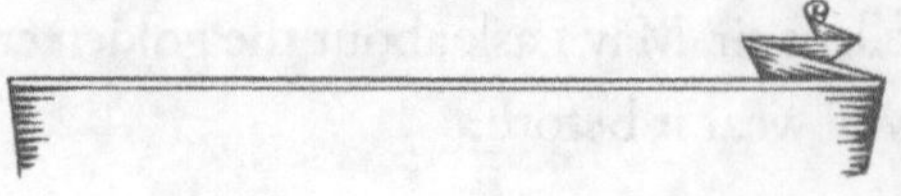

Chapter 5: A Successful Test

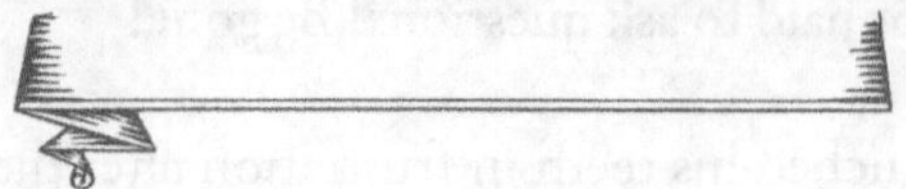

Wilfred Zhang was terrified. He was gravely wounded, and he understood that he would never see his family again. The worst part was that he was completely innocent of the allegations. He had travelled to Antarctica to negotiate a trade deal for a minor independent Chinese company. Suddenly, masked men had knocked him unconscious and moved him to this dark room.

Wilfred looked up. He was surprised when he saw a familiar face in front of him, the face of Abraham Goldstein. Wilfred was baffled; he could never have imagined that the leader of a major faction came down to oversee the torture of a prisoner. Abraham signalled to the guards to hold Wilfred while he pressed something into his ear. After that, they all left without saying a word.

In the next room, Abraham observed Wilfred and felt excited. The Human chip had merged with Wilfred's brain stem. The technology worked; he could feel what Wilfred felt, he could see what Wilfred saw, and he could read his mind. Poor Wilfred; he wasn't a spy just an innocent man petrified of his imminent death. *"Oh well I can sort you out,"* Abraham thought and started transmitting to Wilfred

Abraham (As a voice in Wilfred's head)

- Wilfred, Wilfred can you hear me.
- This is God; I can show you the path out of here.

Wilfred (screaming out loud):

- What? What is this, what are you doing to me?

Abraham:

  - Don't question, just believe, and follow the path

Wilfred:

  - Okay God, please show me the path

Abraham:

  - Good, you'll be rewarded.
  - You'll see your family again, and the pain will be gone.

Having said this, Abraham induced a hallucination into the brain of Wilfred. While hallucinating, Wilfred thought he was at home with his family and the pain was gone. It didn't last for long, as Abraham got distracted when Lucifer and Metatron, from his ANGEL program, talked among themselves:

Lucifer:

  - What the heck is happening? What is he doing?

Metatron:

  - I have no idea

Abraham:

  - Don't worry gentlemen. Everything is working exactly as it should. This man is innocent. I want you to detain him until I instruct you otherwise.

  - Make sure he gets medical attention at once; I don't want him dead.

Abraham left the room, and the flabbergasted Lucifer and Metatron sat quiet for a long time trying to figure out what had just happened.

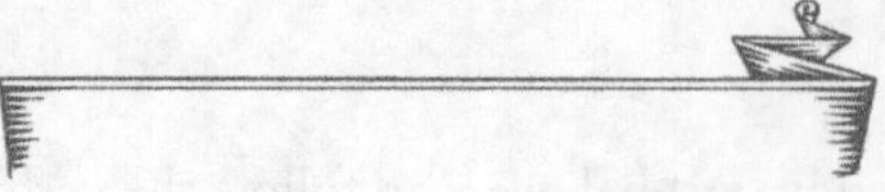

Chapter 6: More Test Subjects Are Acquired

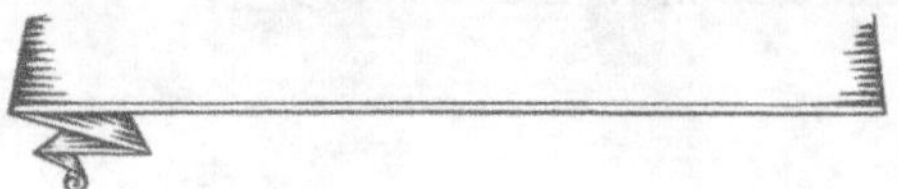

Abraham Goldstein was back in his Penthouse in Goldstein Tower. He marvelled over the day's successful technology test. The Divine Technology was divine inspiration and not imagination nor insanity. Given that divine technology worked, that would imply that everything else he had experienced in the Divine Dimension was also genuine and not a product of his imagination.

Abraham had noticed that he had struggled to focus his mind to control the mind of the person below him. As soon as he got distracted, he lost the connection, and the power over the test subject's mind was lost. While controlling the mind of one individual at the time was useful, it hardly made him a divine being, so he had to step up his performance as the divine chip was meant to control up to 10,000 people at the same time.

The first step would be to connect more test subjects. Abraham was thinking of getting his Angels to acquire new subjects, but he realised that there was a much easier way. His female assistants had a clause in their contracts that they were to satisfy his sexual desires if requested. It was time to activate that clause and give them the time of their lives at the same time. Abraham had eight female assistants, and this evening Jenny Lundberg from Northern Europe was the one on duty. He called her on the intercom asking her to come over in a sexy dress.

A bit later, she arrived in the room. Jenny seemed anxious and reluctant. She had been hired for over three years, and Abraham had during this time never used any sexual innuendo. Asking her to come in a sexy dress was different from his usual self. The Abraham she that knew liked to spend hours reading ancient tomes in solitude and silence.

Abraham Goldstein:

- Hello Jenny. I have summoned you to honour clause 6.6 of your employment contract.

Jenny Lundberg (speaking nervously)

- He-he I don't know what that means. I haven't read the contract since I started.

Abraham Goldstein:

- It means that you and I are going to have sex tonight.
- Come here, I don't like asking twice!

Jenny stood petrified, and she did not know what to do. Abraham decided that he did not have the time to wait, so he walked up to her and pressed the human chip into her ear. She felt a sharp pain, but soon she forgot about the pain as she became head over heel aroused. The next 25 minutes she had sex that was out of this world with the oldest man on the planet. Or at least, that was what Jenny thought. In reality, Abraham was sitting on a couch with an excellent scotch controlling her hallucination.

Although Abraham for the first time in 100 years felt some sexual arousal, he chose not to act on it. His body was an old vessel with not much time left; it would be unwise to risk losing his future immortality trying to please something that was going to disappear soon anyway.

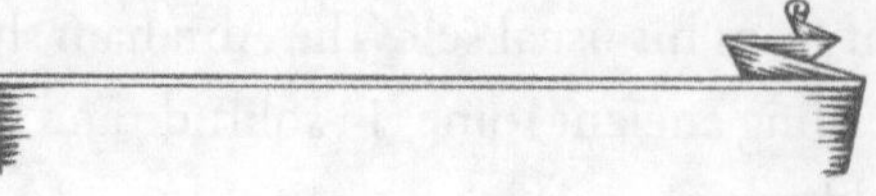

Chapter 7: Abraham Returns to The Divine Dimension

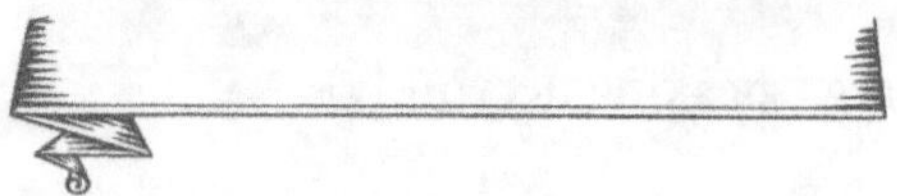

A few days later, Abraham Goldstein was in the basement level where the Divine Detector machine was found. He had managed to implant the human chip into six out of eight assistants. The last two had stormed off when Abraham requested sex and mentioned the contract. It wasn't a big deal; he would just have to fire them.

The purpose of Abraham's trip back to the Divine Dimension was to see if he could control multiple subjects at the same time. An hour in the Divine Dimension was equivalent to a second in the real world so with a bit of luck he would be able to control several subjects at the same time without losing connection. He had arranged so that all his six assistants would be at the spa in his penthouse. They would all get an experience out of this world today. He connected to each of them, and yes, they were all waiting for him in the spa. *"Good girls,"* he thought and smiled.

Jack Brown and few of his team members walked in. Jack approached Abraham:

Jack:

- I brought some more people today.

- 20 minutes in there will feel like 50 days if what you are saying is correct.

Abraham:

- So, I get 50 days from 20 minutes? That sounds like an excellent way to extend my life.

Jack:

- There is one problem, the immense amount of energy that the machine uses.

Abraham:

- I got your memo; I have ordered all non-essential production to shut down for the next 30 minutes.

Jack:

- A lot of people will complain.

Abraham:

- Yes, but that's my problem and not yours.
- I don't have time for more questions.
- Start the machine

A moment later, Abraham arrived in the Divine Dimension. He took a seat under a lotus tree and tried connect with all the subjects at once. Success! From the Divine Dimension, he could Control the minds of several individuals at once. Abraham felt like a god. He invoked himself and his subjects into an orgasmic trance. He could feel how days and nights passed by as he was engulfed by the transcendental feelings of spirituality and desire. In the blink of an eye, he was back in the divine detector lab.

Jack:

- You look blissful...

Abraham:

- Yes...

- Turn on the production again; I don't want my whiny grandson to complain about lost money.

Chapter 8: CEO Meeting with Jake Goldstein.

Jake Goldstein was furious. He had requested an explanation from his grandfather, Abraham Goldstein, why all the production had been stopped earlier during the day. Abraham had nonchalantly told him that he was welcome to swing by his penthouse if he wanted to talk.

As Jake arrived at the elevator, there was a notice saying that the elevator was turned off to save power, but Jake was more than welcome to walk up. As Jake's office was located 20 levels below Abraham's penthouse, it was a lot of stairs to climb. Jake Goldstein was 190 years old and he resembled his grandfather in having almost relentless energy, especially when angered. Huffing and puffing he reached the top level of Goldstein Tower. Abraham was sitting in the spa with one of his assistants and flanked by several bodyguards.

Abraham greeted his grandson arrogantly:

  - Greetings grandson, you don't look to well, did you have a
  nice walk.

After a while, Jake finally caught his breath.

  - You bastard! You made me WALK 20 levels!

Abraham:

  - Yes, exercise is good for you, and besides, I reckoned we
  needed to save power to get our production up.

Jake:

- Ha-ha very funny
- Now tell me why on earth you turned off production for half an hour?
- Do you even realise how expensive that is?

Abraham:

- Is this trivia time? Very well.

- I turned off the production because I needed extra power for my secret research project.

- It costs us 1.2 million Terran Credits per minute to turn off production, so I would say around 36 million for the half an hour.

Jake:

- WHAT is our secret research project? Shouldn't I, the CEO, know what is costing us all this money? We are losing money for the first time in company history.

Abraham:

- Dear Grandson. You are the CEO because you are my oldest living descendant and I can't be bothered with day-to-day operations anymore.

- Our secret research program has made a significant breakthrough, and I will showcase it at the annual general meeting next week.

- I am turning on the elevator for you to save your legs.

- Guards, show Jake to the elevator, please.

After Jake had left the penthouse level, Abraham told his female assistant and security guards to leave him alone. He preferred solitude, so he could think without unnecessary distractions. Abraham had felt compelled to give Jake a display as he hated when people questioned him.

Abraham disliked most of his descendants and extended family members. And there were a lot of them! As Abraham had lived for 250 years, he had ten generations below him. As the Goldstein's were the wealthiest family in the world, they all qualified to have a lot of children, and all these generations, had spouses. In total the living members of Abraham's extended family accounted to 300 individuals, and sadly the only one's Abraham had liked was his wife and his children, and they had all died of age and sickness.

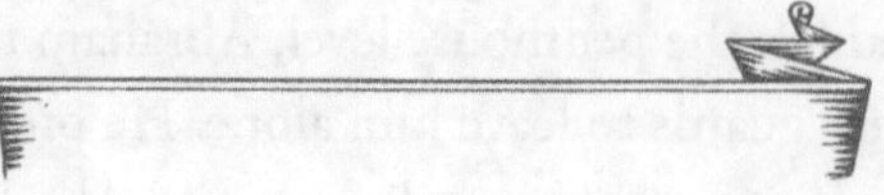

Chapter 9: Annual General of Meeting House Goldstein

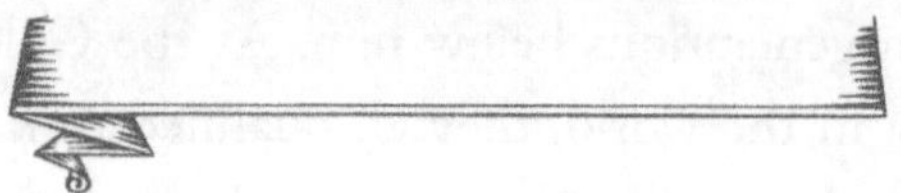

Abraham Goldstein was sitting on the golden throne in the Divine Dimension meditating. Abraham was waiting for the annual general meeting of House Goldstein to begin. The 300 largest shareholders, mostly family members were expected to come for the proceedings, which were held in the main auditorium of Goldstein Tower.

Abraham had a surprise for his family members! The days before the meeting, his Angels had secretly implanted a Divine Technology Human chips into everyone's head. This was done night-time after spraying in in sleep-inducing gas in the rooms of the delegates. As the gas had sedative properties, Abraham hoped that no one had noticed the pain when the chip merged with the brain stem.

For the first time since Abraham found the Divine Dimension, he felt annoyed. Since a second in the real world was equivalent to an hour in the Divine Dimension, it was not an easy waiting for the last stragglers to get to the meeting. Abraham felt like he had been waiting for weeks and this was angering him.

Eventually, everyone had arrived, and Abraham made a unique entry as a mass hallucination:

Abraham:

- Welcome To the 2785 AD Annual General Meeting of House Goldstein.

- I am going to be brief. You have complained about the inflated research budget these last few years.

- The research project has been an enormous success, and I am now speaking to you from the Divine Dimension.

Abraham waited for a reaction from the crowd.
Eventually, Jake Goldstein got up:

- The Divine Dimension! What the hell is that? Are you saying that you are sitting in another room and it's a hologram on the stage? Did you spend 80 Billion Terran credits on improved hologram technology!

Abraham:

- Narrow-minded fool. You are experiencing innovative technology but not hologram technology. You are experiencing divine technology given to ME by Divine Providence.

Jake (Turning towards the crowd):

- As you can hear Abraham has lost the plot. I suggest that we appoint a new chairman and then postpone the rest of the meeting.

A loud murmuring broke out among the delegates. Abraham silenced them with a deafening roar:

- ENOUGH!

- Jake! The scriptures say you shall obey your elders. You have broken against this rule; you shall suffer.

Clap
Abraham clapped his hand, and Jake fell dead to the ground with a brain haemorrhage, as the Divine Technology had chip ruptured his brain stem.
A long silence followed, before a few delegates ran up to Jake Goldstein and tried to resuscitate him. Abraham spoke again:

- It's pointless! He is dead, and more of you will follow if you
don't bow down to me; your new god.

Upon hearing this, Josef Goldstein, a pious man, swallowed his fear
and stood up:

- This is blasphemy. You are no god; you are just a tyrant and
a murderer! There is only one god, Yahweh, and anyone who
says otherwise is not a real Goldstein.

Abraham caught Josef in his gaze. He roared:

- Yahweh is no more!
- For I have seen the throne of God and it is empty!
- Now bow down to me or suffer!

Josef:

- I will never bow to you, you monster.
- You may take my life, but you will never take my soul.
- You'll burn forever in hell for your crimes!

Abraham:

- Very well, so be it

clap
Abraham clapped his hand, and Josef fell dead to the ground.
Abraham raised his hand to silence the petrified delegates, and he
continued his tirade.

- I came here today with peaceful intentions. I came here to
improve our cause. But you defied me! Now more of you will
suffer.

- Lisa Goldstein, you weren't happy with the money we paid
you, so you stole from us, death to you.

- Aaron Goldstein: Despite being married to a beautiful woman your heart longs for men, death to you.

- Chris Goldstein: You fornicated with your brother's wife, Margaret; Death to both of you.

Clap

Abraham clapped his hand, and everyone mentioned fell dead to the ground. He continued talking:

- I AM your new god, and the rest of you are spared if you bow before me.

Everyone in the room threw themselves to the ground bending to Abraham. Satisfied with this, Abraham continued.

- Good, you are spared for now. But beware, I can see your every thought, and if you ever consider moving against me, your death is certain.

- My fifth-generation grandson Isaac Goldstein will be the new CEO, while I will occupy myself with my spiritual matters.

- The company's new aim will be to aid my divine matters. Hence, all future profits will go to my goals and not to your dividends.

- Thank you for listening, ladies and gentlemen, I am leaving now, but I will be watching you.

After finishing talking, Abraham disappeared from the room. After the initial confusion had settled, medics were called into the meeting hall, but they could not do anything to save the victims.

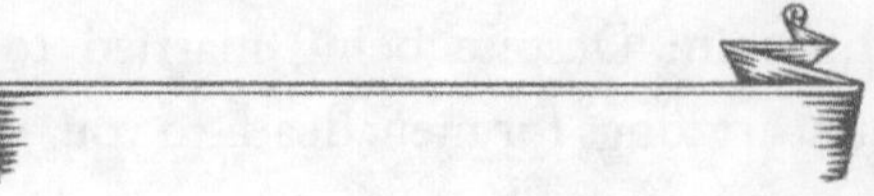

Chapter 10: Abraham Goldstein
Envisions the Eden Project

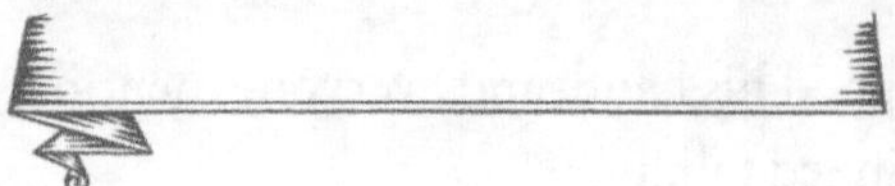

Abraham Goldstein watched the sunrise in his massive private garden. The sunrise and the sunset of Antarctica were two of the greatest moments of the year for him. As Goldstein Tower was located on the South Pole, the sun rose at the spring equinox on the 23rd of September, stayed up for six months, and set at the autumn equinox on the 21st of March. Abraham loved to see the natural sunlight opposed to the artificial one he had to settle for during the winter season.

150 years earlier, before the Goldstein's had colonised Antarctica, they had launched several large orbiting satellites with mirrors to reflect sunlight down to the Antarctic surface to make it inhabitable. By changing the angle of the mirrors, they could control how much sunlight that reached the surface affecting the local climate. The sunlight reaching earth from the mirrors did not look like the sun but resembled several luminous stars. During the summer, the satellites were still reflecting sunlight to the surface, as the Antarctic sun was not strong enough to give the desired temperature.

Abraham felt uneasy and could not enjoy the annual sunrise as much as usual. He had made a lot of enemies, and the only thing that kept them from striking was that they thought that he knew every move they took. In fact, he didn't. In his physical human form, he could only connect with one person at the time, and that took a a lot of focus effectively stopping him from doing anything else.

Abraham reflected on how to move forward. He knew that regardless of external enemies or not his physical years were soon to end, and he needed to be in the Divine Dimension by that time. The best way to stay in the Divine Dimension would be to keep the Divine Detector Machine running, while his body was cryogenically frozen.

Abraham realised that he had moved too fast. There was not enough electricity available to keep both the production facilities and Divine Detector Machine running at the same time. If the production wasn't running, he could not keep the citizens content, and most of them did not have a chip implanted and had nothing to fear from his divine powers. If there was a public uprising against him, no-one would support him, and he would perish without achieving his goals.

The most straightforward solution for Abraham would be to get a few more fusion reactors to get enough power for both the production facilities and the Divine Detector machine. This solution could be implemented in a year and it was achievable. It was also profoundly unsatisfying. This solution would be an extended life where he kept ruling his business empire through intimidating the family members under his control. But, they would not worship him, and eventually, they would find a way to overthrow and kill him.

Abraham wanted to find people that feared him AND worshipped him like a god. Such people had been easier to find in the dawn of the human era when science and technology were less prevalent than mysticism and superstition. But extensive experiments on time travel during the 26^{Th} century had proven that time travel was impossible. But what if he could use memory-wipe technology to completely erase the memories of a group of people and then have them wake up on a terraformed planet, which resembled the Promised Land? They would act like ancient humans did when they first reached self-awareness. And with Abraham's divine direction, they would act like his early ancestors although better, as he would have a stronger grip on them than Yahweh ever had.

But where would he create his Holy Land replica? Abraham could not make it on Earth as his people would eventually wander off and notice the advanced civilisations around them. Awareness of technology was the bane of any divine being, as scientifically minded people had less need for a god to answer for the mysteries of the world. Ideally, he would find a planet in another star system for his plan, although this carried insurmountable difficulties.

Alien planets required advanced technology to be liveable for humans. They could not be terraformed to a degree where humans with only ancient technology could live and thrive. Abraham understood that terraforming a planet in another solar system was beyond his reach.

But, what about an asteroid? Several asteroids with artificial gravity and atmosphere were orbiting earth as luxurious residences for some of the other faction leaders. What if he could do something similar but further away in the Asteroid Belt? All the technology to do it was available:

- He could create gravity through putting fusion thrusters on the bottom of the asteroid to make it rotate.
- A Nanotechnology photon shield generator could be used to stop the atmosphere from dissipating out into space. Refining oxygen from iron and silica oxides could create the oxygen required for the inhabitants.
- Electrifying the iron core of the asteroid would create a magnetic field to protect the inhabitants from dangerous background radiation.
- Satellites with large mirrors would reflect enough sunlight to the surface to make it warm. The Goldstein's had done in Antarctica 150 years earlier.
- The asteroid would need to contain frozen water to start with to save costs, as it was far too costly to transport all the required water from Earth. Once the surface temperature would rise the water would become a liquid, and it would dissipate and come down as rain as on Earth.

Abraham felt inspired and looked through the asteroid database trying to find the perfect rock for his ambitions. After a while he found it, B528A measured 22,072 square kilometres, precisely the same size as the Holy Land. It was orbited by B528B, which measured 100 square kilometres, which was enough to set up his base of operations.

The only problems with the B528A and B528B were that they were co-owned through the Terran Council. But Abraham was convinced that he would not face much opposition from the other factions if he gave them some concessions for them to trade their part of the ownership to him. To most people B528A and B528B were just barren rocks floating through space, but for him they were DESTINY.

Excited with his plan, Abraham set up a proposal to convince the other faction leaders to transfer the ownership of the asteroids to him.

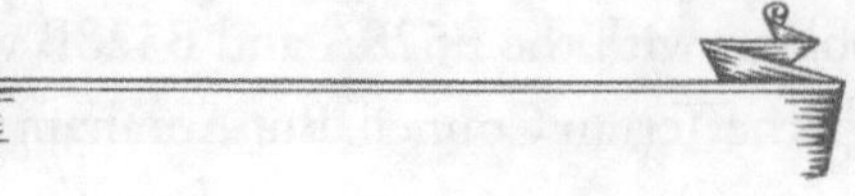

Chapter 11: Abraham Goldstein Travels to the Terran Council Meeting.

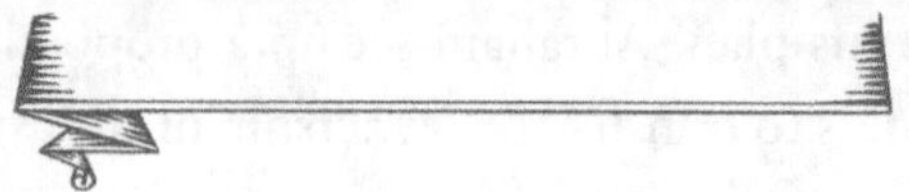

A few weeks later, Abraham Goldstein stepped out of the vacuum tube transport that took him from his headquarters in Antarctica to Hansstadt in Europe. Abraham hated travelling with the vacuum tube trains and usually avoided it. Although the vacuum tubes were considered safe, he was unsettled from travelling under the bottom of the ocean in a confined tube, and the built-in virtual reality entertainment system could not distract him from the claustrophobia he felt.

Hansstadt was the capital of the House Muller faction, and the Terran Council annual general meeting was held there. The Terran Council met monthly, but Abraham Goldstein never attended these due to his age and his dislike of travelling long distances.

Hansstadt was a fascinating mix of old and new, and it was a tax-free zone owned by House Muller. It was built in the Alps, where Europium Tower, built on top of Mount Blanc, constituted the largest building in the world. Built as pyramid it was supported by the mountain with its top 2000 meters over the summit of Mount Blanc. Hansstadt had a comfortable climate averaging 22 throughout the year due to orbital mirrors reflecting down sunlight during the winter months. 30 Kilometres away from Hansstadt was the Muller ski slopes that were always covered in snow because orbital shades were active in the summer which stopped the snow from melting. Around Hansstadt there were many old palaces that were disassembled and then restored to their former glory. This was because the Muller's valued history, and many of their leaders wanted to live in old-fashioned residences outside of Hansstadt instead of staying in the modern dwellings of Europium Tower.

Abraham Goldstein, Isaac Goldstein, and their bodyguards met with Andreas Muller, PR manager of House Muller.

Andreas:

- Good day, Abraham. Is it just you and Isaac today? We assumed you would come with a larger delegation.

Abraham:

- Yes, but it was unnecessary. We have discussed the issues in advance, and I have the board's full confidence to make decisions.

Andreas:

- I see. My condolences on the loss of your grandson, Jake Goldstein, he was a great man and will be missed.

Upon hearing this, Abraham froze for a second. He had taken measures to prevent the deaths from becoming public and yet Andreas Muller knew about it. Abraham concluded that there had to be a spy in his company.

Andreas:

- You look pale Mr Goldstein, is anything wrong?

Abraham:

- No, it's just the sorrow of losing my grandson that is wearing me down.

Andreas:

- I understand. It's a shame the invitation to the funeral was misplaced, House Muller would have liked to take part in the funeral, showing our respects.

Abraham realised that House Muller knew about the other deaths at The Annual General Meeting. He decided to tell them a fabricated story of what had happened.

Abraham:

- I wanted to keep this a secret until after the Terran Council meeting, but since you already know, I am going to tell you the truth.

- I was sick, and I could not make it to the meeting. When I recovered, I found out that five of my family members were poisoned.

- I chose to keep the deaths a secret, as we are conducting an undercover investigation to find the perpetrator.

- Once the deaths are made public, we will have a proper funeral for those upstanding members of our family.

Upon hearing this, Isaac almost exploded but he kept calm. The old monster was twisting reality and feigning grief for his victims. Although Abraham had promoted Isaac, it felt like a punishment as he could feel how Abraham was messing around with his brain using him as a puppet. Abraham tapped Isaac's shoulder.

Abraham:

- Don't get carried away in grief, Isaac. We will find and punish the killers. But for now, let's just focus on the work at hand.

Isaac didn't respond and Andreas Muller spoke:

- Okay, gentlemen. I think it's better that I take you to your rooms. I am sure you need to rest before tomorrow's council meeting.

Andreas led Abraham and his entourage to their rooms. As he left, Abraham told his bodyguards to find and destroy any surveillance equipment in the room, and then he went to sleep.

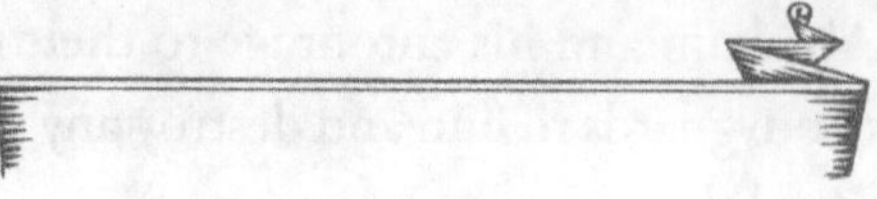

Chapter 12: The Terran Council Meeting.

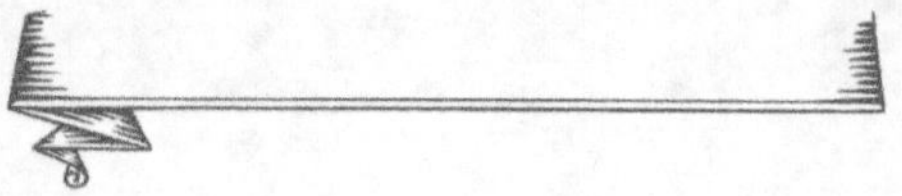

The following day, the Terran Council meeting took place on the top floor of Europium Tower. The top-level was a giant glass dome with a 360-degree vision of the land below. At the height of 7000 meters, the sight range was 300 kilometres in every direction on a sunny day. The glass dome was built to be bullet and explosion proof as House Muller had many enemies among the general population. The levels below the top level were filled with automated defensive weapon systems to shoot down any non-authorized incoming objects.

In the centre of the room was a table made of a type of wood that only existed in the Alpha Centauri system. This was to symbolise that House Muller was the only Terran faction, which had brought things back from other star systems. The room also held several ornamental objects made from materials only available in the Alpha Centauri system to signify that House Muller was peerless when it came to space exploration.

Abraham scoffed at the concept of spending so much time and money bringing wood to Earth. Hans Muller, leader of House Muller and Chairman for the Terran Council, approached him

Hans Muller:

- What's the matter Abraham? You don't seem to appreciate our priceless collection of interstellar materials?

Abraham:

- No. It must have cost a billion Terran Credits to send this stuff back to Earth. Such a waste.

Hans:

- Yes, my great grandfather's legacy was not beneficial to our faction. Colonization of Alpha Centauri cost a fortune, but it has been paid now, and we get to enjoy this marvellous furniture.

- Funny that you complain about the cost of space colonisation as you want to build a new asteroid colony.

Abraham:

- Yes, but I determine that colony to be priceless from a scientific perspective. Science can be worth more than anything in the universe. A table, on the other hand, is just a table

Hans:

- Science is only priceless to a company if they are the sole possessor of that technology. The technologies we developed for the Alpha Centauri expedition are our secrets. This beautiful table, on the hand, is for everyone to enjoy.

Abraham:

- Regardless, my research facilities on Antarctica are more impressive than this table.

Hans:

- The rest of your faction seem unhappy with your research spending. How unfortunate with the murders at your Annual General Meeting

- Regardless, everyone is here, and our meeting is about to begin.

The meeting started, and the delegates were seated around the table. The meeting was filmed, as an edited version was broadcast to the news outlets after the meeting. The cameras went on, and Hans Muller started his opening statement:

- Welcome to the Terran Council Annual General Meeting

- We welcome our distinguished delegates and thank them for giving the council mandate to make decisions that are in the best interest for all Terrans.

- First, I would like to send my condolences to my dear friend Abraham Goldstein for losing five family members during the Annual General Meeting of House Goldstein.

- The council is keen to help finding the heinous criminals behind these murders.

Upon hearing this, Abraham frowned and clenched his teeth. He had kept the deaths a secret, and now they were made public during a television broadcast seen all over the planet. The camera zoomed in on him, and he realised he was meant to say something.
Abraham:

- I am thankful for the condolences. The perpetrators of these heinous crimes will be captured and dealt with. Now let's resume with the issues on hand.

Joachim Muller, the young and progressive CEO for House Muller, started the statement for the next issue:

- Dear delegates. I am Joachim Muller, newly appointed CEO for House Muller. I visited Mars a few years ago, and I noticed how much suffering there was. That is why I am allowing Agnes Bojaxhiu from One Humanity to speak via a hologram link.

A hologram of Agnes Bojaxhiu appeared in the room. She was a peculiar sight wearing dull and worn out clothes looking like a poor Martian. She addressed the delegates with an accusing tone:

- Dear oppressors and fascists in this assembly!

- The Martians are suffering. Their water is toxic, their food is scarce, and their workplaces are unsafe. Many of them even lack basic healthcare. But this can be changed if you sinners stop lining your pockets and instead spend money on helping Mars. With present Terran technology and proper investments, Mars can easily give 4 billion people a good life. It's not too late, repent your sins or burn forever in hell!

Hans Muller was furious and turned off the hologram:

- Joachim, this was not what I expected when I granted you permission to lead this subject. Please leave now. We will talk about this incident later.

Before Joachim Muller had time to respond, security personnel arrived and escorted him out of the room. After a brief pause, Hans Muller spoke again:

- I am sorry, gentlemen. When Joachim asked to make a statement, I could not imagine that THIS was what he had in mind.

Wong Cheng the chairman of House Cheng replied:

- Apology accepted. I assume that Agnes will be deported to Venus straight away?

Hans:

- Yes, she will be detained and severely punished.

- The next speaker is Abraham Goldstein who has made a special request to the Terran Council.

Abraham smiled at Hans and spoke:

- I want that the ownership of the asteroids B528A and B528B. Furthermore, I want an exclusion zone around the asteroids.

- I plan to launch a ground-breaking new asteroid colony there.

Hans:

- The Terran Council can give you the asteroids, but we will not give you the exclusion zone. Mutual intelligence is the best way to keep the peace.

- On behalf of House Muller, I can promise you non-interference with your project as long as you are not a threat to Terran interests

Abraham:

- Since you feel compelled to spy on me, I accept your conditions

- My project will improve conditions in our refugee detention centres on the moon. Resettling people to live on Eden under my supervision is more humane than sending them back to Mars.

Barry White:

- While I am happy for you to acquire some Martian subjects for your project, I am worried about the public reaction.

Abraham:

- My solution soothes the needs of those that want continued space colonisation and the needs of those fools that want us to close the refugee detention centres.

- I don't think many Terrans would care if we resettled some of the Martians elsewhere.

Barry White:

- Very well, you have House White's approval to colonize B528A. Like House Muller, we promise non-interference in your asteroid research project

Hans Muller:

- Very well, if no one has any objections, I declare this meeting finished.

- ...

- Excellent. The Terran Council's media department will have a press release ready by tomorrow. You are all urged to come to our press conference where selected members of the press are going to ask predetermined questions where you give predetermined answers.

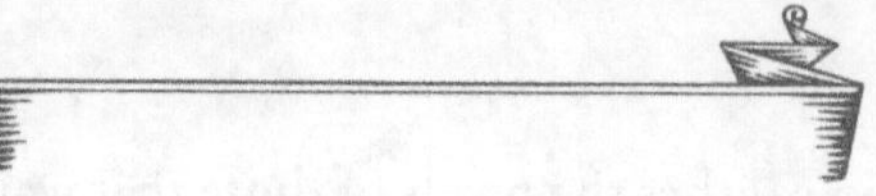

Chapter 13: The Terran Council Charity Ball

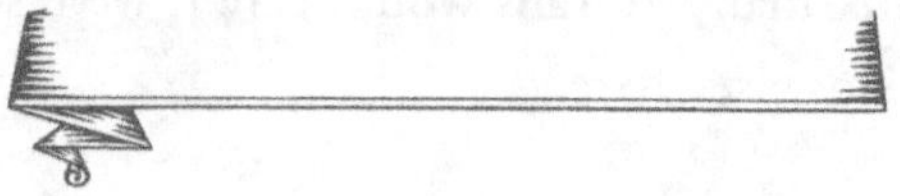

Abraham Goldstein viewed the festivities of the Terran Council's yearly charity ball from his top tiered table with a view of the entire ballroom. The ballroom of Europium Tower was a vast area with six distinct levels where guests could be seated depending on importance. Abraham being the wealthiest man on the planet and leader of a faction was on the top tier so he could look down on everyone and everyone could look up to him. He felt exhausted as his suite did not have the sleep enhancement machine, he was accustomed to. The neural stimulation achieved by a sleep enhancement machine made sleep ten times more efficient reducing the need for rest to an hour or two per day. Without the machine, Abraham felt like zombie due to his advanced age. He could not wait, for this spectacle to be over, so he could go back home.

The background to the charity ball was that The Terran Council had made every country on the planet sign the *"all money to charities tax deductible"* act a few centuries ago to avoid taxes. So, every year the mightiest corporation on Earth gathered for events like this pledging to give most of their profits to charities under their own control with no disclosure obligations to the local governments. This kept the nations broke and powerless while the major corporations could do things the way they wanted.

Sitting in this large crowd, Abraham felt anxious. His actions at the House Goldstein Annual General Meeting had made him many enemies. Due to the divine technology microchips, he could control them and know if they were plotting against him. Here in Europium Tower, it was different. He could not tell if people were plotting against him or not.

The last few weeks, Abraham had grown accustomed to knowing what people around him were thinking, so not knowing scared him.

Apart from the anxiety of sitting in a large room full of potential enemies, Abraham was satisfied with the day. The Terran Council had agreed to his plans, which made them a lot easier to pull through. He was now in full control of his family, but the Terran Council and the other Terran factions were outside of his control. Eventually, Abraham relaxed and enjoyed the rest of the event without any incidents.

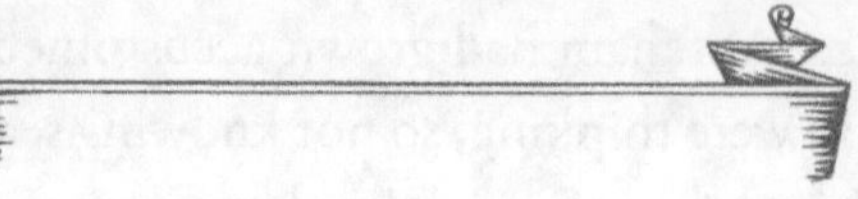

Chapter 14: Abraham Goldstein Leaves Antarctica.

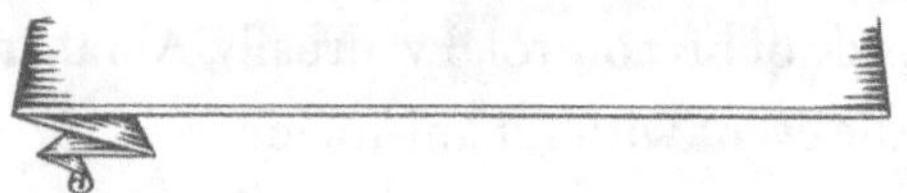

At the beginning of 2786, Abraham decided to leave Antarctica with his luxurious space yacht, The Golden Divine. The destination was the Asteroid B528B where Abraham intended to set up his new command centre for the Eden Project. The crew for the voyage was his personal bodyguards from the ANGEL program, a group of 30 genetically engineered males who were very loyal to Abraham.

Unbeknownst to the crew, Abraham had packed a bag with Divine Technology Angel chips. He planned to implant his inner circle with these chips at the right time. The "Angel" chip was different to the "human" chip, that he had implanted into his disloyal family members some months earlier. The angel chip allowed someone with a god chip to control the actions of the angel directly and not just indirectly.

Abraham felt a bit frustrated to leave Antarctica before his Divine Detector Machine was disassembled and ready for transport. Ideally, his Divine Control Centre at B528B would be ready and fusion-powered before he arrived. However, Because of the resentment from his family it was impossible to stay in Goldstein Tower any longer. Abraham had murdered several more members of his extended family, as he KNEW they were plotting to kill him. Realising that his presence caused so much resentment, he had concluded that he had to leave Earth. His family would have to do his bidding, but they no longer had to see him.

Abraham looked back on Earth, which floated as a blue haven in space, as his yacht flew further away. Knowing that he would never see his home planet again, Abraham felt bittersweet melancholia and did not speak to anyone for days.

Chapter 15: The Angels.

In the 28th century, all the major factions on Earth had programs dedicated to finding genetically gifted individuals and use these individuals for breeding and further improvement of the human genome. House Goldstein was no different and had a project code-named the Angel project.

As these individuals were separated early from their families, their loyalty stemmed directly to the leader of the faction as they were indoctrinated from an early age. While loyalty could never be guaranteed, the 30 men that Abraham Goldstein brought to Eden, was the closest he could get to complete loyalty.

The angels were an awe-inspiring sight. They had tall and athletic bodies with perfect posture. They also had perfect symmetry in their faces, which gave them astounding beauty. They were also intellectually superior and mentally stable. Their only flaw, was their complete emotional detachment, which inhibited their ability to form meaningful relationships with other humans. This was by design as Abraham's angels' emotional detachment made them even more loyal to his cause.

Despite his follower's loyalty, Abraham wanted more control, the Angel chip was his solution. Being able to control the Angels with his mind, they would do his physical bidding when his body had given up.

A month later, Abraham and his crew reached B528B the small asteroid orbiting the much larger asteroid B528A. They were not much to see in their current state just empty dark rocks floating through the vastness of space. But Abraham saw something different; he saw divine providence. These dark and cold rocks would soon be the place for him to rule as a deity.

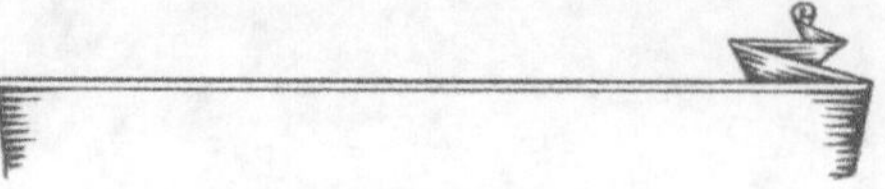

Chapter 16: The Lunar Detention Centres.

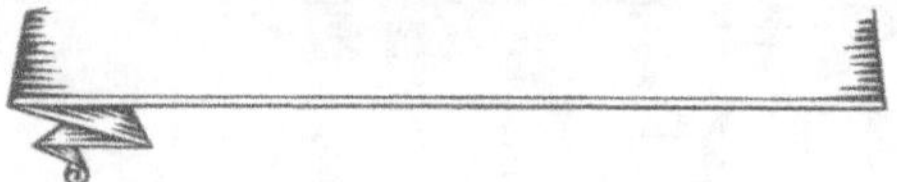

Mars in the 28th century was plagued by eternal wars between its nations, civil wars, and unrest among the civilian population. The major cause for the unrest was the constant lack of resources. The major factions of Earth also often used Mars as a staging ground for their conflicts. While the Terran Council upheld the peace on Earth, there was nothing in its charters that stopped the Terran factions from waging wars by aiding different sides in wars on other planets. In 2785 House White and House Rashid had been stuck in a long-winded proxy-war on Mars for the last decade displacing and killing millions of Martians.

There was a sentiment among many Martians that Earth was the homeworld of all human beings and that it was every person's right to live there in peace and prosperity. Neither the Terran Council nor most Terran citizens shared this notion as Terran citizenship almost guaranteed a happy and wealthy life due to the accumulation of resources and the limited population on Earth. The Terran Council wanted to keep Earth safe and sparsely populated. To ensure this, no Martians could stay on Earth. The Terran Council detained any Martian detected on Earth or en-route to Earth.

Despite this, there was a significant stream of Martians trying their luck moving to Earth. The Martians did this, because large parts of Earth were uninhabited due to the limited population, so there were a lot of places where Martians could live off the land undetected for extended periods of time. Living this way was better than life on Mars, but they got caught eventually, as the Terran Council searched the uninhabited areas regularly.

Life in the detention centres was meant to be rough and inhumane to serve as a warning for everyone thinking of coming to Earth uninvited. Located on the far side of the moon to avoid insight and to stop the refugees from communicating with people on Earth, conditions in the detention centres were deplorable, with starvation, disease, and cramped conditions.

No Terrans worked at the detention centres as it was considered unnecessary, dangerous, and expensive. Instead, the Terran Council occasionally dropped food and provisions from orbit to keep the prisoners alive. There was a military task force stationed close to the Kaguya detention centres to prevent outsiders from helping the prisoners escape.

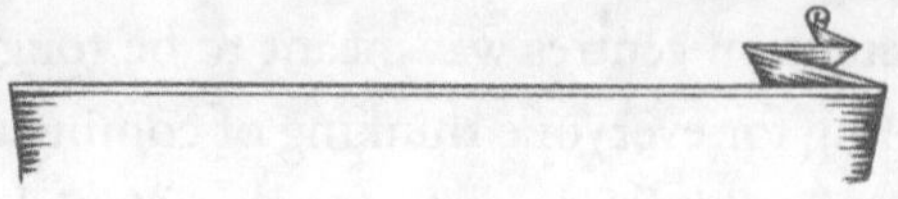

Chapter 17: The Eden Expedition.

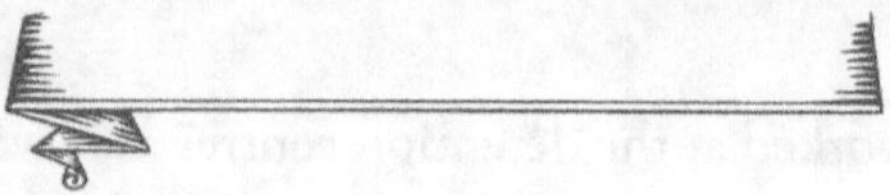

In 2788, three years after receiving Terran Council approval, The Eden project reached its launching stage.

On the 23rd November 2788, 3,000 volunteers from the Kaguya detention centre entered Abraham's spaceships, and they were cryogenically frozen. After taking off from the Moon, the fleet travelled at normal transit speed towards the Eden. The ship flew to B528A where the passengers remained in cryogenic sleep until Abraham and his angels had finished building the colony.

Chapter 18: Abraham Sends Lucifer on a Mission.

Abraham Goldstein walked around on his command ship, The Golden Divine, and inspected his future subjects. They were cryogenically frozen, so they looked like they were sleeping peacefully. Abraham was both fascinated and disgusted by their imperfections. Using Martians instead of Terrans was a choice with both perks and disadvantages. The good thing about using Martians, was that the Terran Council didn't care how Abraham treated them, and they were unlikely to intervene.

To the Terran Council, the Martian refugees were worthless animals; they were nuisances to dispose of. Another advantage of using Martians was that it was more cost-effective. There was no way he could have financed the Eden project if he had to use ships and equipment that were safe for Terrans. Abraham understood that the Terran Council approved the Eden Project because they could not care less if most of its passengers died. With Terran citizens, it was different. Although the Council primarily focused on helping the wealthy and powerful, it still aimed to provide a healthy and safe life for anyone considered worthy of living on Earth.

Another advantage of using Martian humans for the project was that his Angels, the men who were meant to be his physical manifestation on Eden, looked picture perfect compared to his Martian subjects. Abraham had always imagined that the divine should appear infinitely more appealing than the people and his Angels matched these criteria

His future subjects were a sad sight. 500 years of malnutrition and cosmic background radiation had transformed the humans living on

Mars to a mere shadow of their former glory. Natural selection had made their skin thick and warty to protect against radiation, they had a hunched posture from living in burrows underground, they had shorter limbs to survive the icy colds of Martian winter, and they looked sick from adapting to constant malnutrition.

More worrying than the state of Abraham's future subjects was the fact that his family back on Earth seemed to be stalling and delaying his plans. It was January 2789, and it had been three years since he left Earth. Although Abraham knew that the creation of Eden was a long-term project, he needed to get the divine detector quantum physics accelerator up and running as soon as possible so he could transfer his soul and avoid dying. Abraham would turn 254 in a couple of months, and he had the feeling that his family was delaying the project hoping for his age to be his downfall.

Abraham summoned in his favourite Angel, Archangel Lucifer. Abraham had named all the members of the Angel project after the original biblical angels. Unlike the Bible, Abraham hoped that Lucifer would never turn against him. Just like all the other angels, Lucifer had been brought up in the Goldstein talented children program where individuals with favourable genes were indoctrinated to do the bidding of Abraham.

The Goldstein gifted children program admitted both men and women, but Abraham had decided to only bring males for the Eden Project. The purpose of the Angels was to obey him; not to socialise and have their own families. Like all of his fellow angels Lucifer was heterosexual as genes for homosexuality was something that stopped a child from being admitted to the Angel program.

Abraham saw Lucifer as he was approaching; appearance-wise Lucifer was an extraordinary individual. Towering at a height of two meters, Lucifer had a very athletic body with a perfect posture. His face was perfectly symmetrical, and his blue luminescent eyes were shining with energy. He was extremely focused, determined, and intelligent. As a product of his genetics and his very controlled upbringing, he had very bland and controllable personality. He did not seem to have any goals or personal values, and he lived to serve Abraham. Abraham consider Lucifer to be the perfect human, and he trusted him with all his heart.

Lucifer:

- You summoned me, master

Abraham:

- Yes. The wretched unbelievers in my family back on Earth are stalling my plans to reach godhood. I need you to convince them to redouble their efforts and get us back on track.

Lucifer:

- I understand, Master. How do you wish for me to do this?

Abraham Goldstein

- Gather a group of angels and travel to Goldstein Tower on Earth. Intercept their board meeting and meet with my family members.

- Take whatever measures you find necessary. You can kill anyone who resists my divine will but use constraint; we need them to get this done.

Lucifer:

- Understood!

Abraham Goldstein:

- One more thing, during times you might feel that you are losing the connection to me. Do not worry; you know what to do.

Lucifer

- Yes, master. I will take a shuttle and leave at once.

As Lucifer wandered off, Abraham was both relieved and worried. He trusted in Lucifer's loyalty, but he was not convinced of his ability. The Angels' lack of own thoughts and personalities made them particularly useful when they were within his control, but Abraham was not convinced that they were capable of doing things on their own.

A problem that Abraham had faced, since he arrived on Eden, was that the Divine Technology did not have enough range to control and threaten his family members back on Earth. Initially, the shipments had arrived as planned but after a while, his family started stalling deliveries and came up with various excuses to do so. Abraham was not interested in excuses, he wanted results. He hoped that sending Lucifer back to Earth, would convince his family that they needed to do his bidding. Ideally, Abraham would have gone himself, but he understood that his family members would try to kill him if he came. Realising that there was nothing he could do for a couple of months Abraham entered the cryogenic tank and fell into a dreamless sleep.

Chapter 19: An Assault from Above.

A month later, a shuttle with Lucifer and six other angels arrived in orbit around Earth. They chose to stay in orbit over Antarctica so that they could conduct reconnaissance before acting. The shuttle was small, had stealth capabilities and no radio signal activated, so it was difficult for anyone to detect unless they were looking for it. Lucifer had decided that he would not request an audience with the Goldstein leadership. If they were rebelling against his master, they would ambush him and his group as soon as they exited the shuttle. Instead, Lucifer decided to attack the next House Goldstein board meeting.

The Goldstein Building had automated defences, which did not activate when an incoming friendly vessel arrived. The fusion jetpack and advanced exoskeleton armour that the angels had, was produced by Goldstein Corporation, and thus identified as friendly by the AI. There was also a secret escape hatch from Abraham's former penthouse that could open from the outside. From there they could make it to the weekly board meeting, take the board members hostage and ensure that they were cooperating. The mission went according to plan, and the Goldstein board was flabbergasted as the angels stormed in and interrupted the meeting

Isaac Goldstein:

- What is the meaning of this? Security guards should not disrupt board meetings!

Lucifer:

- We are not security guards; we are the angels of the Divine Master Abraham.

- I am Lucifer, leader of the Angels and Abraham's loyal subject

- Abraham is also your master, so why are you disobeying him?

Isaac:

- Disobeying?

- That bloody fool's waste of money is driving the family and our people into bankruptcy.

- I do what is best for the family and the people of Antarctica.

Lucifer:

- Silence peasant!
- Who are you to deny Abraham his divine will?
- I should slay you all for your insolence.

Isaac:

- Do that if you must but realise the death of us will also be the death of you. And I can assure you that our successors will not send any more shipments to your master.

A moment of silence ensued with a lot of tension in the room. Lucifer was cold-sweating trying to figure out how to continue. He wished that he could hear his master's voice, but it was for nothing. Abraham was asleep in his cryogenic tank and his master could not oversee him. Lucifer's predicament was absolved when another angel ,Ishmael, joined in on the conversation:
Ishmael:

- Master Lucifer: It is time to let Isaac know why he cannot defy us.

Thankful for the reminder, Lucifer tried another approach and spoke again:

- Master Isaac. I applause your loyalty to your remaining family and your willingness to sacrifice yourself to protect the rest of the Goldstein family.

- But your actions put your entire clan into immediate danger. You see, we angels can control and kill anyone with mind control as we see fit. So, if you reject our master's demands, we will kill you all.

Lucifer channelled his powers so that the board members could see an illusion of the sun glowing in the centre of the room. The illusory sphere was shining so brightly, so they had to cover their eyes to not damage them. Eventually one of the vice presidents, Elaine Goldstein, screamed out:

- Lucifer is right. Just give Abraham what he wants. Let's not all die here today!

Isaac realised that he didn't want mutually assured destruction and spoke:

- Okay, Lucifer. There is no need to spill any blood today. We will succumb to Abraham's demands and send him the required shipments.

Lucifer:

- Good; you have seen the righteous path. My master will be pleased. Let's hope that no more misunderstandings come in the way between you and Abraham.

Isaac:

- Tell Abraham that his actions are ruining us and that we can't remain a dominant force on Earth if we are fulfil his requirements.

- Abraham worked tirelessly to make House Goldstein the most powerful Terran faction; I am sure he doesn't want us to succumb to mediocrity

Lucifer:

- Earth is no longer important for our master Abraham. Humankind is corrupt and needs a new beginning. Your money will finance this new beginning. Eden is truly marvellous, and Abraham will spend your resources well there.

- Now we must leave. Malphat, Hashmallim, Seraphim, and Ishmael will stay behind to make sure that you fulfil your promises. Do not disappoint us.

Having said this, Lucifer and the two other angels left the building and flew back to their shuttle in orbit. After that, they started their return journey back to Eden. Once they were back on the shuttle, Nuriel spoke up:

- You lied to them, Master Lucifer. We do not have the power to kill humans via mind-control, only Abraham does.

Lucifer:

- Correct, but it helped us complete the mission.

Nuriel:

- An Angel is the bringer of light! An Angel does not lie. Humans lie.

Lucifer:

- True, but even more important than the truth, is being loyal to your master and do his bidding. I showed my loyalty and ability today and so did you.

- You should enter the sleep pod, Nuriel. We have three months of travel ahead of us and we better not waste any of our physical years sitting here doing nothing!

Doubting what Lucifer had said, Nuriel reluctantly walked over to the cryogenic sleep pod and he fell into a dreamless sleep. Lucifer stayed awake for the following months, as he had to keep in contact with the Angels left behind to make sure Isaac Goldstein kept his end of the bargain.

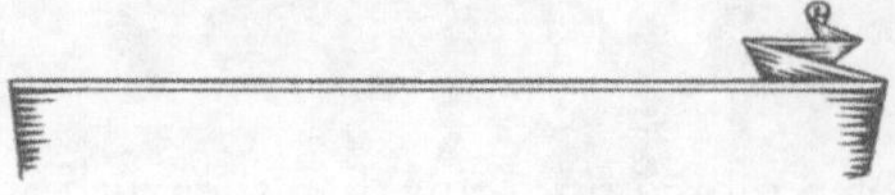

Chapter 20: Supplies Secured.

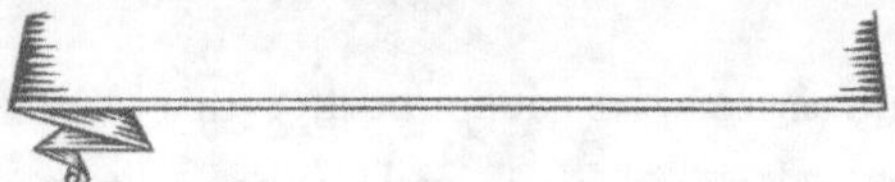

Deceived by Lucifer's lies, the remaining House Goldstein members provided Abraham with all the resources he requested for his Eden project. The shipments to the project ran continuously for 15 years, and the project ruined House Goldstein. Because of the Eden project, House Goldstein lost all their possessions outside of Antarctica, and in the end, they were no longer one of the ruling factions of the Terran Council.

The other factions concluded that the Eden project was not a threat, and watched in bemusement how House Goldstein was torn apart from within. The other factions responded by taking over House Goldstein's holdings in Australia and South America through legal and covert operations.

On B528A and B528B the Angels aided by a myriad of automated drones worked tirelessly creating their master's new world. Abraham connected to the Divine Detector Machine while his body was cryogenically frozen. This transported his mind to the Divine Dimension. In the Divine Dimension he studied the history of the galaxy and the Zetans and this will be the topic for the next chapters.

Chapter 21: The Creation of Eden.

The construction of Eden and the Divine Control Centre began in 2790 after Lucifer's ploy had secured all the required shipments. The angels built the Divine Control Centre on B528B first, as Abraham needed to get the control centre up and running. Abraham felt that his physical years were running out and he wanted immortality through transferring his mind to the Divine Dimension using the Divine Detector machine. Once the device was set up several fusion-powered power plants were built to fulfil the energy requirements for the Divine Control Centre and the Divine Detector Machine.

Since the energy needs of the project was immense, the base consistently needed a supply of fresh hydrogen to provide the fusion reactors with fuel. As there was no water to split into hydrogen and oxygen, Abraham bought a series of automated shuttles transporting compressed liquid hydrogen from the atmosphere of Jupiter to the base. These automated shuttles were sturdy, low-maintenance and were fuelled with the hydrogen collected from Jupiter's atmosphere giving them properties like an infinity machine.

The next step was to create the gravitation on B528A, which was the larger of the asteroids. B528A was meant to be the habitat for the Abraham's subjects. Gravity was created through putting fusion thrusters on the asteroid and making it rotate. Once the gravity was in place, the asteroid was terraformed to resemble the Holy Land 4000 years earlier.

An unsurpassable problem on all the colonised worlds, was to get a fully functional ecosystem on Eden. Even after 700 years of space colonisation, humanity was still not able to replicate the intricate ecosystems found on Earth. Most colonised planets were barren when it came to other life forms except for the mice, the rats, and cockroaches that always followed human societies. Although the technology existed to create worlds that could sustain human life the challenge to develop functioning ecosystems on colonised planets was still an unsolved problem. The challenge was because it difficult to predict what effect the introduction of new species on an alien world would have. Abraham did not intend to get the echo system working on Eden before inhabiting the colony. What better proof could his followers get that he was divine than the fact that he could introduce new species as time went along?

To create the atmosphere of Eden, 20 layers of nanotechnology plates were floating 1 kilometre over the surface of the asteroid and at the edges of Eden. The purpose of these plates was to stop Eden's atmosphere to dissipate into space, and to protect its inhabitants from the harmful background radiation. The plates were kept together by a high-powered electric current and a magnetic field created from several generators on the bottom of the asteroid. The nanotechnology plates, combined with the asteroids magnetic field had the same function as Earth's magnetic field and ozone layer in keeping the surface with a breathable atmosphere, and protection from radiation. To keep the atmospheric pressure breathable, there was continuously pumped in more oxygen and nitrogen so that the atmospheric pressure was similar to Earth even though Eden was a lot smaller.

The water on Eden was found on the asteroid, as it was possible to start pumping up the previously frozen water once the asteroid had warmed up. All the crops and the plants on the asteroid were genetically engineered versions of Terran crops that was designed for the soil and climate conditions on Eden.

Eden was an artificial world, and its climate was always the same. Eden's inhabited side always faced the sun, and it had two mornings, two middays and two evenings every 24-hour day, but never any night. This was because the world was rotating from North to South instead of from East to West as on Earth. Fusion thrusters on the dark side of Eden created the rotation, and it was necessary to maintain rotation to have enough gravity on Eden. The gravity created by the fusion thrusters was equivalent to the gravity on the moon (1.6 meters per second) or roughly one-fifth of Earth's gravity.

The North to South rotation of Eden was a unique feature that did not exist on other human space colonies. The reason for this feature was that the Edenite nights would be too cold to be liveable for humans with Bronze Age technology. Eden was not perfectly spherical which made the curvature and the horizon different from how it was on Earth. From the top of Mount Sinai, the created mountain in the centre of Eden; one could see the vast darkness of space.

The climate around Mount Sinai, in the centre of Eden, where the human settlements was located was around 30 degrees midday dropping to 10 degrees in the evening. Every day, water evaporated in the middle of the day to come down as rain in the evening when it got colder. Closer to the edges of the liveable part of Eden the climate was a lot harsher and erratic. The climate near the edges was harsher; because the Nanotechnology plates that kept Eden's atmosphere was not always 100 per cent airtight. This sometimes led to forceful winds pushing towards the edges of Eden as the pressure difference led to air sipping out to the void outside. Due to the leakage of air, air was constantly pumped in to Eden to keep the desired air pressure.

To make sure that everyone on Eden knew what time and date it was there was also a large hologram displaying the time and date on top of Mount Sinai. Keeping track of time was important as Abraham planned to punish everyone, that did not honour the sacred days.

With everything planned for the Eden project, Abraham left command to Lucifer so he could retreat to the timelessness of the Divine Dimension, where time could not hurt him.

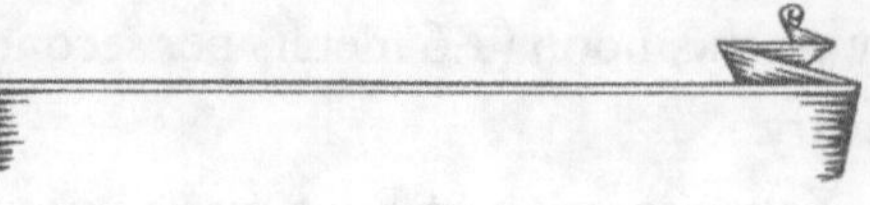

Chapter 22: Abraham Returns to the Divine Dimension.

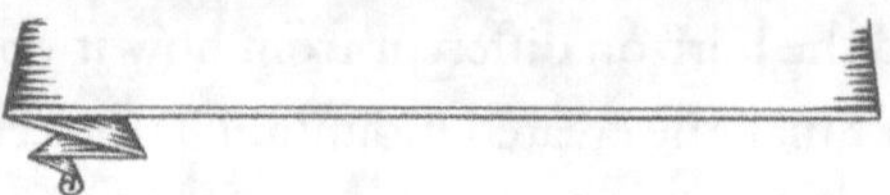

Abraham fell asleep in the cryogenic tank, and his mind was transferred to the Divine Dimension. Satisfied of being back, Abraham didn't intend to ever return to the outside world. Four years had passed since he left Earth and his body had deteriorated.

Ideally, Abraham would have transferred his mind to a neuronal computer so that his digital personality could live on forever. Doing this had been a widespread practice in the past for other prominent Terran leaders. Abraham had never believed in this technology for two reasons:

- The first reason was that it was technically the same as dying and whatever was transferred to the neuronal computer was just a copy and not the original him.
- Secondly, Abraham feared what would happen to his soul if his mind were transferred in the moment of death. There was no conclusive answer to this theological question, and as Abraham was not a man who could let go of control, he had instead invested heavily in life-extending technology, where others' had chosen to have their minds transferred to a neuronal computer when their time was up.

After his first visit to the Divine Dimension, Abraham did not fear Yahweh and what would happen to his soul the day he died. Instead, his fear was a question of a practical nature. The God Chip that he used to control the angels, and the humans was designed to connect to the host's brain. There was no way he could reverse engineer the God chip.

One of the most remarkable aspects of the Divine Dimension was the lack of natural time cycles, which enabled Abraham to manipulate the time in the ordinary dimension to his liking. He could slow down the outside time to an extreme slow-motion which allowed him to control multiple individuals at the same time, or he could speed up the time to the extent where an hour in the Divine Dimension was equivalent to a year outside the Divine Dimension. He could not; however; reverse time to undo things that had already happened.

Abraham predecessor in the Divine Dimension, Yahweh, had suffered from the same limitation, which refuted the claim that he had been omnipotent. For Yahweh's Bronze Age followers; it had seemed unwise to anger him with this detail, thus his unlimited power was written down and described for future generations.

When walking around in his new domain, Abraham came across archives that described the rise of humanity on Earth and how the first gods came to be.

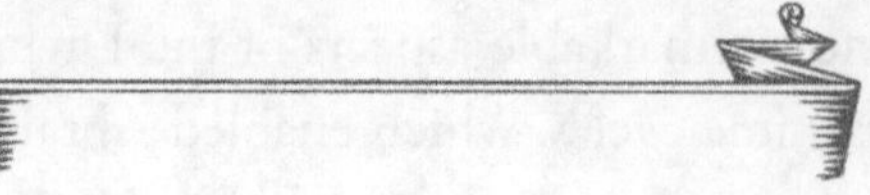

Chapter 23: The Zetans Reach a Technological Singularity.

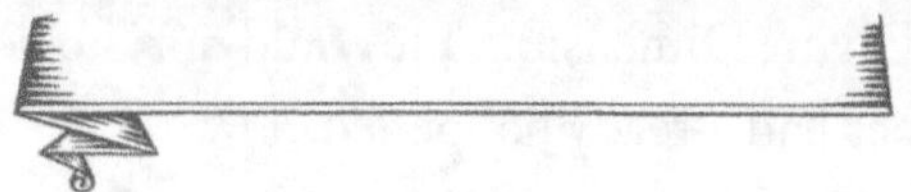

In the centre of the Milky Way Galaxy, there was once an ancient alien race called the Zetans. The Zetans were unique species which had extremely long lifespans, and they had the technology to change their DNA, so they could adapt to living on most planets Their weakness was that their exceptionally long lives also made them the reproduce very slowly. The average Zetan only had one child every 200 years. This weakness stopped them from spreading all over the galaxy.

100,000 years ago, the Zetans reached a technological singularity when they discovered the Divine Dimension, and how to travel there. The discovery of the Divine Dimension was kept a secret, and it was only known and used by a small elite of the species. The Zetans used the timelessness of the Divine Dimension to explore the further reaches of the galaxy, and they found Earth. The Zetan technology opened interdimensional portals that allowed them to move physically into the Divine Dimension.

The Zetan leaders marvelled at the beauty of Earth, and they decided to leave their mark on the world. Since Earth was too far away from Zetan territory to colonise using conventional travel options, and the Zetan leaders had vowed to keep the technology secret, they decided to leave their mark on the planet by altering one species in their image. After vivid discussions, they agreed to alter the human genome to grant humans a superior intellect and awareness. The Zetans chose to alter humanity, as humans reminded them about themselves. The Zetan altered humanity by tripling the size of the human brain, which gave humans heightened intelligence and awareness compared to other species on Earth. Pleased with their work, the Zetans left Earth to move on to the other planets of the Milky Way Galaxy.

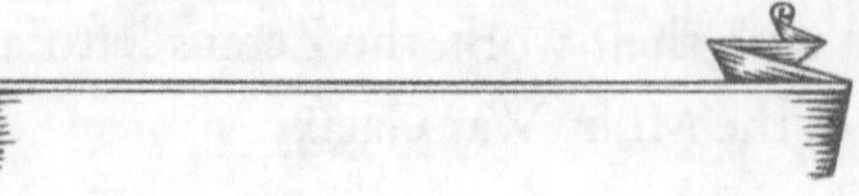

Chapter 24: The Creation and the Physics of the Divine Dimension.

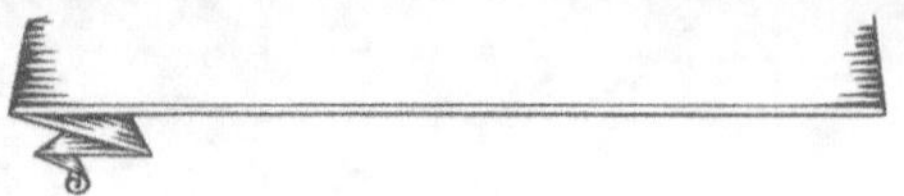

The Divine Dimension was an eternal place, which had always existed, and was filling the gaps between the dimensions in a multiverse. The True Maker, a sentient being residing in the Divine Dimension, governed the laws of physics in each universe. The True Maker was mostly passive, and rarely interacted in the daily lives of the trillions of distinct species that inhabited the Milky Way.

The main purpose of The True Maker was to reset time in dying universes so they were reborn again. The creation of our universe occurred during the Big Bang, 14 billion years ago, and it wasn't the first version of our universe. The distances were shorter in the Divine Dimension than in our universe. The Zetan had used this fact to travel around the Milky Way quickly, through going via the Divine Dimension.

A unique feature with the Divine Dimension was timelessness. Without outside interference nothing would ever change there. But time did exist in the minds of anyone who was inside the Divine Dimension. This meant that the outside time could either be sped up a lot or slowed down to a standstill. The only rule that existed for time in the Divine Dimension was that the outside time could never be reversed, hence it was impossible for anyone except the True Maker, to travel back in time to change something that had already happened.

The True Maker, which was a genderless eternal being, observed the breach created when the Zetans entered the Divine Dimension. The True Maker didn't do anything to stop the Zetans, as its main purpose was to reset the universes that died and set them to specific laws of physics. The True Maker had no interest in managing the lives of the trillions of species that existed in its universes. Technically, the Ture Maker could have destroyed and restarted our universe to stop the breach, but it was an excessive move to stop something that was of little importance.

The True Maker was fascinated by how the Zetans had entered the Divine Dimension. The Divine Dimension had existed for trillions of years with universes dying and being reborn in certain intervals and never had any species managed to traverse to the Divine Dimension. The True Maker concluded that although it was implausible for any species to enter the Divine Dimension, it had finally happened. Following the Zetans through its all-seeing consciousness, the True Maker concluded that they would never pose a threat. Realising this, the True Maker went back to sleep.

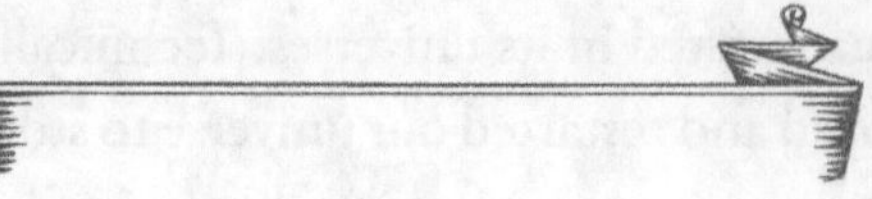

Chapter 25: The Zetans Become Gods on Earth.

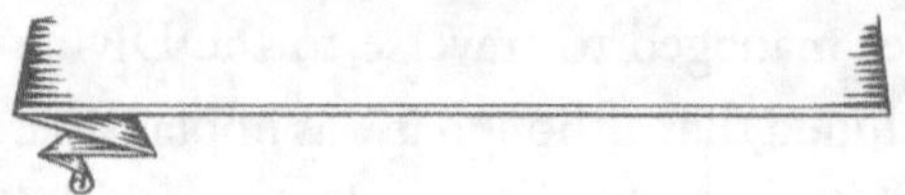

Around 10,000 years ago, the Zetan territory was invaded by an aggressive alien race called the Xenos. The Xenos were one of the many species that had been enhanced by Zetan explorers in the last 100 millennia, but the Xenos was unaware of how they were created. The Xenos were extremely aggressive species, which saw the Zetans as an existential threat, which they had to eliminate. The Zetans, with their superior technology, had no problem repelling the first Xeno attacks on their core worlds. Unfortunately, the Zetan homeworld of Zetani was very far away from the Xeno homeworld Xenora, so the Zetans became bogged down into an unwinnable multi-millennial interstellar war of attrition. The Zetan dilemma was that their incredibly long lifespans and slow life cycles made it impossible for them to rebuild their numbers despite killing hundreds as many enemies as their own losses in every battle.

The Zetan leadership consisting of Brahma, Yahweh, Zeus, and Odin realised that humans from Earth would be excellent as combat troops for the Zetan army. Humans were similar to the Xenos in the regard that they had short lifespans and reproduced quickly. Humans were also intelligent enough to use Zetan equipment while being easy to control.

The next step was recruiting the humans to the Zetan armed forces. Yahweh came up with the solution: The humans seemed to spend a lot of time and effort trying to gain approval from various supernatural beings. What if they could convince the humans that the Zetans were the gods that the humans were trying to communicate with?

The Zetans decided that this was an excellent way to get human volunteers for their armies. The humans seemed to dream about going to heaven after they died. So, why not reverse the order and first go to heaven and then die?

Becoming human gods was easy for the Zetans. Their technology was advanced enough to appear to be magic to the Stone Age humans, and their DNA changing technology made it possible for them to alter their appearances so that they resembled the gods that various human cultures worshipped. Soon, the Zetans learned that Earth was a dangerous place and that human worship could sometimes mean trying to kill their gods. Furthermore, the vast variety of human languages and dialects made it a tedious task trying to communicate with them. The Zetans eventually found a solution; They left prominent humans to work for them on Earth, and they controlled these humans with mind control technology. Through their ability to directly control their human leaders, the Zetans could achieve their goals while staying out of harm's way from the aggressive and unpredictable humans.

The individuals ruling Earth for the Zetans were called angels or demi-gods depending on their culture. They were genetically enhanced by the Zetans to look physically superior to other humans so that they would be admired. The Zetans were not particularly interested in the minuscule details of daily human lives, and they left these details to the Angels. The Zetans had two commands for all their human followers.

1. Be fruitful and multiply as much as you can.
2. Wage constant wars.

These commands were designed to supply the best possible recruits for the Zetan army. Humans needed to procreate quickly to provide enough recruits, and they needed to fight among themselves so that the Zetan could pick the best recruits for their armed forces. Only a small percentage of human warriors were good enough to be enlisted into the Zetan army.

The recruitment process for the Zetan army took place on certain dates that were different in different cultures. The recruitment day was the most significant holiday for a culture. During the recruitment day, the best warriors gathered on top of a building that was visible for the rest of their tribe. On the top of the building was the Zetan or Zetans that were assigned to be gods of that culture. The angels then implanted the human chip in each of their chosen warrior and started to chant. At the height of the ceremony, the ascension process started where everyone started levitating. After that, the Zetans started their machine for dimensional travel and they all disappeared in a flash. The humans landed in a zone of the Divine Dimension where the Zetans had brought weapons and equipment. The human warriors trained in the Divine Dimension until they were ready to go to war. They were teleported the battlefield so they could fight *"the holy war against evil"* for their Zetan masters against the Xenos. Most of these humans died in battle, but a few of them retired on a distant, uninhabited planet that was terraformed to be the ultimate human world.

Chapter 26: The End of the Multi-Millennial War.

The introduction of enlisted humans changed the tide of the conflict. The Zetan weaponry and technology were superior to that of the Xenos, and with the influx of human recruits, the Xenos could no longer capitalise on their superior numbers. The conflict was prolonged because the Xenos was adamantly against the concept of diplomacy and surrendering. The Xeno society held the idea that they were superior species, and they fought to the last individual in every battle instead of surrendering to the stronger Zetan forces.

What made it hard for the Xenos to even considering surrender was that most enemies they saw in battle were humans, a race they considered to be inferior to themselves. While this opinion was factually correct, the humans fighting for the Zetans had superior weaponry and could slowly grind down the Xenos on every planet.

3000 years after the Zetans had introduced human soldiers, their forces reached the Xeno homeworld of Xenora. With the Xenos on the brink of extinction the Xeno leadership finally decided to negotiate with the Zetans. The negotiations dragged on forever, and the delays was a deliberate plan by the Xenos. They Xenos wanted to distract the Zetans from their plan: to send a space shuttle to the star Alpha Omega, the most massive star in the galaxy located close to the centre of the Zetan galactic civilisation. The Xenos blew up Alpha Omega using a secret newly developed technology. This created a massive supernova explosion. The shockwave from this explosion annihilated the Zetan homeworld of Zetani, which signalled the end of the Zetans as a dominant race and galactic civilisation. Enraged by having their homeworld destroyed, the Zetans showed no mercy towards the Xenos and nuked the Xenora to ashes. Combined with their unwillingness to surrender this led to the supposed extinction of the Xeno species and civilization.

For the Zetans the decline came a bit slower, but it was still inevitable. The Zetans had lost their primordial Zeto Crystals, which was divine crystals containing the soul of the True Maker. The Zeto crystals had aided the Zetan abilities and made the pursue the same goal. The power of the Zeto Crystals had united the Zetans and stopped them from fighting each other.

With the Zeto Crystals gone, the Zetan civilisation was split up with every planet on its own. The Zetans on the different planets were very different genetically from each other, and without the Zeto crystals uniting them they started self-determine as separate species, and they started fighting each other. Thus, the centre of the galaxy was still inhabited, but now it was now separate species focusing on their own planets. The remaining humans from the Zetan army resettled on the planet Terra Nova, ended up fighting each other. Eventually faded to obscurity due to the limited amount of females among them.

Chapter 27: The Zetans Fight on Earth.

The Zetan gods became divided when they heard about the destruction of Zetani. They had massive egos and after millennia of praise from their human underlings, but previously the Zeto crystals had ensured that they strived for a common goal. Now that the war had ended, there was no longer any reason for them to stay close to Earth, but there was nowhere else for them to go. Their homeworld was destroyed along with most portals to the Divine Dimension. There were still a few active portals on Earth, but unfortunately, they were challenging to power up without the advanced energy sources that the Zetans had used on Zetani.

Having lost their original purpose, the remaining Zetans in the Divine Dimension got immersed in their roles as human deities. As gods, they started arguing how humans should live their lives, a question that hadn't concerned them before.

One Zetan who was very particular about governing his human followers was Yahweh, who created incredibly detailed rules for how humans should live their lives. The rules were purposefully made to contradict each other so that Yahweh could study the carnage when his followers fought bloody wars about how to interpret the rules. Watching this mayhem kept his life interesting.

As the Zeto crystals no longer unified the Zetans, they started having disagreements and fights among themselves. They chose to settle these arguments on Earth by affecting various human behaviours and betting on the outcome. The primary measure of success for the Zetans stuck in the Divine Dimension was their popularity and dominance on Earth among humanity. By making humans fight wars in their names, separate groups of Zetans could show dominance over other groups without risking the future of their species. This order worked well for the Zetans for thousands of years, until a certain event took place.

Chapter 28: Yahweh Copulates with Humans and Is Knocked Unconscious.

Before the Zetans lost their homeworld, Zetani, their sexual drive was limited and served mostly the utilitarian need to reproduce in enough numbers to keep the species alive. The influence of the Zeto crystals kept them that way as uncontrolled sexuality led to conflicts, diseases and non-optimised offspring. When they lost the Zeto Crystals, the Zetans lost their collective altruism and regressed to their biology. Hence their sexuality became a lot more prominent and with it came associated attributes such as jealousy, egotistical behaviour, and aggression.

Yahweh got obsessed with his sexuality and spent a lot of time condemning sexual behaviour among humans that he secretly craved. Yahweh was bothered by the morality of his homosexual relationship with his assistant Lucifer. The relationship caused Yahweh a lot of grief. He felt guilty for not procreating with the few Zetan women that remained, but unfortunately, they were all taken. In the end it didn't matter, as conception couldn't take place in the Divine Dimension.

Homosexuality was a new concept for the Zetans. They had been governed through the Zeto crystals for as long as records existed and in that collective mindset, sexuality was only for utilitarian purposes, to keep the species alive.

For Yahweh, his sexuality was a big issue. He felt that would eventually die, and he wanted his genetics to survive and remain forever. With no willing females of his species, Yahweh decided to make a radical move. He altered his DNA to be able to procreate with humans and used the portal to go to Earth. Doing this without consent from the other Zetans was forbidden as it took a long time to power up the portals using energy sources available on Earth.

Disobeying the other Zetans did not bother Yahweh. As he saw it, the other Zetans might kill him as retribution, but his genes would live on while theirs would eventually disappear. Once Yahweh reached Earth, he impressed many young and fertile human women with his divine powers. He promised them that that they would give birth to the great Messiah of their people. After a couple of days of non-stop sex on Earth Yahweh decided to go back to the Divine Dimension, as he was disgusted by the humans and had pushed himself hard trying to secure his legacy.

When Yahweh came back, Lucifer was furious with Yahweh's betrayal and he knocked him on conscious.

Chapter 29: The Destruction of the Zetan Portals to Earth.

When Yahweh woke up many years later, he was surrounded by a group of Zetans. Yahweh understood that they were not there because of concerns about his health.

Zeus spoke first:

- Yahweh what have you done? Lucifer told us everything; you went to Earth to have coitus with human females.

- Do you realise how dangerous that is; who knows what diseases you brought back?

Yahweh, who was temperamental, had no intention of apologising to the other Zetans, and instead he lashed out against Zeus.

Yahweh:

- Who are you to judge me? I am just doing what I must keep our genes alive.

- All the other portals are closed, and there are no means for us to travel from Earth to our former home planets.

- None of you have managed to get any offspring. It is impossible in this wretched place.

- I did what I had to do!

Lucifer:

- Your effort only led to one child. A son who was executed before he could father any children of his own. This son became worshipped like a deity after his death, so now the humans have stopped praying to us Zetans.

Yahweh:

- One? That's impossible; there should be many. I took a fertility serum before I went down there copulating with the humans.

Lucifer:

- Well, your plan failed.

Yahweh:

- I NEVER FAIL!

Yahweh was furious and grabbed his lightbringer wand which was an advanced Zetan firearm disguised as an ancient human walking stick. It was so well concealed, so the other Zetans had never realised that it was a weapon. Petrified, they watched Yahweh holding this dangerous weapon, while the rest of them were unarmed. Yahweh shouted in anger:

- Lucifer, we need to talk.
- The rest of you; LEAVE!

The other Zetans quickly left the Divine Palace.

Yahweh turned to Lucifer, who was shaking with fear. Yahweh realised that he needed to act quickly as the others was heading towards the armoury a couple of kilometres away to get their weapons. The Zetans had a rule to not store any weapons at their palaces, and this rule was a blessing for Yahweh who had enough time to execute his plan

Yahweh:

- Move it, Lucifer. We are going to the Divine Portal.

Lucifer:

- Please Yahweh, our portal to Earth is not charged yet, we will never make it to the other side.

Yahweh:

- Shut up and do what I tell you or you'll face an early grave.

Without a word, Lucifer started walking with Yahweh. They walked to the garden of the Zetan Palace. It was a marvellous place that kept beautiful plants from different planets in the Milky Way Galaxy. They walked through the garden and reached the Divine Portal to Earth. The entrance served two purposes. When it was not activated, it was just a regular gate to the vast emptiness of the Divine Dimension. When it was activated, it would teleport the person or object to Earth. They stopped in front of the gate.

Yahweh:

- Activate the portal.

Lucifer:

- Please, Yahweh. The portal is not activated on Earth, and it won't be ready for years. If we step through, we'll get disintegrated in the nothingness and die.

Yahweh:

- I know how the portal works. Just follow my instructions!
- And... Don't speak unless spoken to first!

Lucifer activated the portal, and they stood silent. The Zetan Palace was built on top of a hill and they could overlook the empty wasteland below. Originally, nothing existed in the Divine Dimension, so all the building materials including the hill the palace was built on was teleported there through the millennia by other Zetans. As nothing deteriorated in the Divine Dimension, the palace was as beautiful as when the Zetans built it eons ago.

In the distance, Yahweh could see the other Zetans returning from the armoury. It would take some time before they reached him and Yahweh studied the landscape. He looked the vast training grounds where their human forces had trained before battling the Xenos. He got nostalgic when he saw the big granaries where they had kept the offerings and sacrifices that the humans gave them. Yahweh loved to eat, and he hadn't eaten much lately.

After the destruction of the Zetan home planet, it was difficult to power the portals to Earth for non-essential visits. The portals on Earth could only slowly generate power through absorbing friction energy from Earth's orbit around the sun, but this power was not enough for regular visits. Eventually the other Zetans arrived.

Zeus:

- Yahweh! Why is the portal activated?

Yahweh:

- I am Yahweh; I don't answer to you. This palace is mine and only mine. Go to another palace and spend your time there!

Zeus:

- I don't think so.

- This palace is the only palace that has a working portal to Earth. If you surrender, we'll let you live. We'll lock you up in the Rangda's eternal prison.

Yahweh:

- I will NEVER surrender to you. Go away or I'll kill Lucifer where he stands.

Zeus:

- No one cares about your sodomite friend!
- Zetans, storm the palace and bring Yahweh's head to me!

Yahweh reacted instinctively and shot Lucifer with the force push ability on his staff. This action threw Lucifer straight into the activated Divine Portal where his body disintegrated. Additionally, the energy spike from the force push destroyed the portal, which imploded and created a tiny impassable black hole, stopping the other Zetans from entering the palace, and stopping Yahweh from leaving the palace.

Realising that they couldn't get into the palace, Zeus and the other Zetans decided to leave the Terran Palace for another palace in the Divine Dimension. Yahweh was stuck in his solitude unable to leave his self-made prison or to communicate with anyone. Eventually, he wrote his suicide letter and committed suicide. Thousands of years later, Abraham Goldstein found Yahweh's corpse.

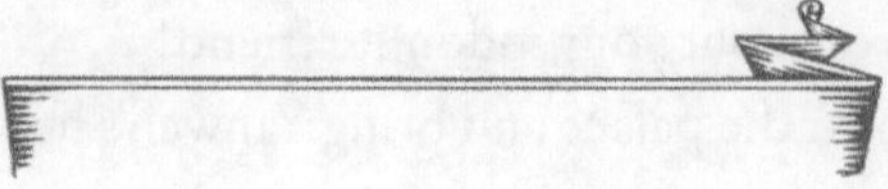

Chapter 30: The Construction of Eden Is Completed.

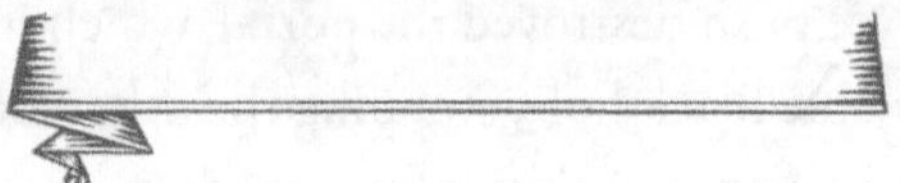

Abraham Goldstein woke up after a long slumber when Lucifer contacted him. Abraham contemplated leaving the Divine Dimension so he could see Lucifer face to face, but he decided against it. His body was old and frail, and every time he woke up in the real world he could potentially die. Speaking telepathically via the divine microchips was safer although it felt less real. Abraham answered Lucifer's call:

- Yes, Lightbringer, what news do you bring me?

Lucifer:

- We have finished our construction work on Eden. It's possible to live on the surface now.

Abraham:

- Eden finalised? How did this happen so quickly?

Lucifer:

- You have been asleep for six months, Master.

Abraham:

- Why didn't you wake me up or contact me during this period?

Lucifer:

- You told me that you needed to sleep Master and that I should only disturb you if I had important news. Eden is finally inhabitable, that is outstanding news.

Abraham felt confused by Lucifer's action. He didn't know if Lucifer had used his directions to his advantage. When Abraham was asleep, Lucifer oversaw The Eden Project, and he shouldn't let this power get to his head. Abraham decided to give Lucifer more exact timelines in the future.

Abraham:

- Very well. So, nothing important happened while I was asleep?

Lucifer cleared his throat and spoke:

- On Eden everything has gone according to plan...

Abraham:

- Spit it out Lucifer, what is not going to plan?

Lucifer:

- House Goldstein have lost control of Australia to House Cheng, they conquered Sydney from us.

- Isaac Goldstein requested to stop deliveries to Eden, so that they could afford to fight back. I let him know that the Eden project was the main priority, and he should find a cheaper way to keep Australia. Apparently, Isaac failed us.

Abraham:

- He didn't fail US, Lucifer; He failed ME. You are not a Goldstein you are my bodyguard. Don't consider yourself a Goldstein; your loyalty should be to me only!

Lucifer:

- I apologise, Master; I will be more thoughtful in the future.

Abraham:

- The loss of Australia doesn't matter. We have left Earth behind us, and Eden is our future. I knew of my relatives' incompetence, and yet the fools have persisted to rebel and question my authority.

- Neither you nor any of the Angels will do the same!

Abraham's last sentence made Lucifer feel worried. He could often feel Abraham messing with his brain and reading his thoughts. Lucifer felt offended by Abraham's lack of trust. He and the other Angels had followed Abraham blindly for decades. Abraham should be courteous enough to ask questions instead of spying on his closest men.

Lucifer's thoughts were interrupted by Abraham who had read his thoughts:

- Don't be angry Lucifer; I am only looking after you and the others. Without the ability to lie to me, your souls are pure, and you can serve a higher purpose.

Lucifer:

- Thank you for showing me the light when doubt clouds my mind.

Abraham:

- Of course, you are the Light-bringer. I need you to show the way to the others.

Lucifer:

- Yes, Master!
- Would you like to wake up and visit Eden with your physical body?

Abraham:

- No, my body is dying. I will see Eden's beauty through your eyes, my son.

Lucifer:

- Agreed, Master. I will travel to the surface at once.

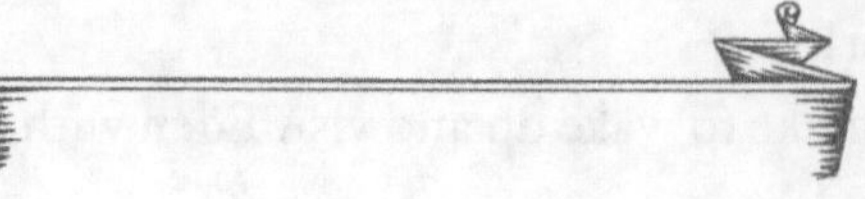

Chapter 31: Lucifer Watches Eden from the Top of Mount Sinai.

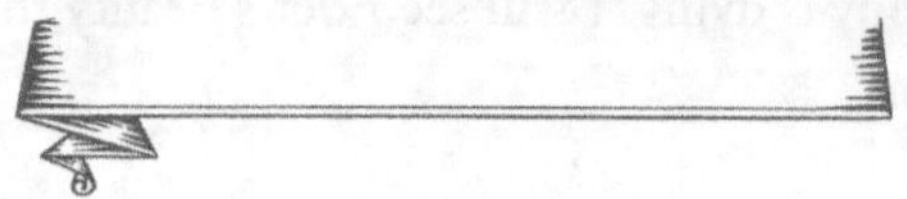

Later that day, Lucifer landed on Mount Sinai, which was a 900-meter high mountain found in the centre of Eden. Mount Sinai was where the ancient people had received their divine laws, and Abraham's followers would receive their religious laws here as well.

A fitting feature for Mount Sinai was that it was impossible to climb without "Divine Providence" This was because the atmosphere of Eden only stretched 1000 meters up. This meant that the atmospheric pressure dropped by 10 % for every 100 meters elevation from the 100 kPA at ground level to 0 kPA at 1000 meters altitude. At the top of the mountain there was only 10% air pressure, so reaching the summit of Mount Sinai without breathing aids was impossible.

Lucifer looked towards the horizon. In every direction, he could see the blackness of space where Eden ended. At surface level, the atmosphere seemed blue like on Earth but on this altitude the sky was dark like in space. Straight above him, he could see the Divine Control Centre in a fixed position 5 kilometres above Eden. In the sky, he could see the seven suns that always kept Eden in comfortable daylight. The suns were the real sun, accompanied by six large orbital space mirrors that reflected light and heat down to Eden. These mirrors could also double up as large orbital lasers that could fire powerful laser beam incinerating anything in seconds. The reason to have several large space mirrors instead of one huge was a failsafe to avoid problems if one of the mirrors got hit by debris from a passing asteroid.

When he looked down on the surface, Lucifer saw a mostly featureless and uniform terrain. Biodiversity was almost non-existent as the focus of the Eden project was to create a liveable world where Abraham could be a god, not to build a realistic replica of Earth. Lack of biodiversity was an issue that existed on all colonised worlds, as it was lot easier to make a planet liveable for humans than to create proper ecosystems.

Lucifer studied the grid-like pattern of canals and dams that would provide the inhabitants of Eden with water. While they lacked the beauty of the rivers and lakes on Earth, they were predictable and functional. There was a certain amount of water on the surface of Eden and evaporated water could not escape the atmosphere so it would always come down as rain.

Around the canals, there was farmland with farm animals and ripe produce. The farm animals had been created from fertilised eggs using synthetic wombs, and the plants was planted and kept by gardening robots. They needed to pack all this advanced technology away and store it on the dark side of Eden out of sight from Eden's future inhabitants. After all, signs of advanced technology could break the illusion of a Bronze Age civilisation honouring their supreme god.

Lucifer returned to the Divine Control Centre. He needed a good sleep, as there were busy days ahead of him. In ten days, Eden was due to be colonised by the Martian captives, and there was a lot of work to be done!

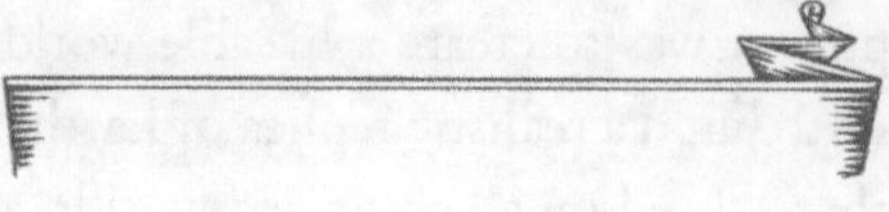

Chapter 32: Genesis.

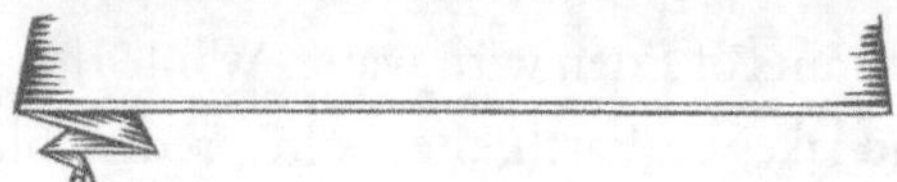

Abraham Goldstein made the final changes to the first chapter of **The Abrahameon** his great religious work that would be the foundation for his religion. Abraham had decided to make Yahweh the great creator in his religion with himself described as Yahweh's successor. Doing this was the least he could do to honour Yahweh, as he admired everything that Yahweh had done. Abraham decided to make Yahweh the only God that was all-powerful. Abraham, as Yahweh's successor would only claim to be powerful. This distinction would not make any difference in the day-to-day life of his followers, as Abraham was still the deity to worship.

Abrahameon first chapter.

In the beginning, the great Divine Yahweh created the heavens and the Earth. After this, he created land and water; He saw that this was good. After a while, his creation started to bore him, so Yahweh created animals and plants to have something to marvel. He marvelled at the beautiful nature for millions of years.

After observing his creation through the Eons, he created humankind in his image. At first, humans were no different from the other mere beasts but eventually; Yahweh induced them with his great spirit to give them consciousness and a soul. He also introduced them to his divine law at Mount Sinai on Earth. This law was to guide them in their lives and keep them aligned to his divine plan. From the start, the foolish humans opposed him trying to live their lives in a way that was opposed to the direction given by the great Yahweh.

Yahweh kept trying to get humanity back to following his divine plan, because he loved them, and because all humans carried a bit of his soul.

Having given away a part of his soul to give humanity consciousness, Yahweh suffered every time someone strayed from the path and broke against the wisdom of his divine law. Eventually, he grew older and lost his enthusiasm because of the vile abominations that humanity took part in, disrespecting his holy will.

Yahweh spoke to his Archangel and closest confidant Abraham: "Why can't I the all-powerful master of the universe get these humans to obey my will when I created them in my image?" Abraham answered: "Because you gave them a piece of your soul to give them consciousness. This part of your spirit also gave them the free will to do as they please, and stray from your path."

Having contemplated Abraham's wise words, Yahweh agreed with Abraham. He had been too kind to these people; they owed him everything, and yet they kept causing him suffering. Yahweh had lived for millions of years in peace, harmony, and bliss before creating humanity. Since he created humankind 7000 years earlier his life was nothing but pain and suffering. He summoned Archangel Abraham and his other Angels.

"I have decided to end myself and humanity." Yahweh said. After a short break, he continued, "I have suffered more these last 7000 years than I did for billions of years before humanity. These beasts have shattered my soul and I will end them, to finally find eternal peace."

The benevolent Archangel Abraham spoke up. "Grandmaster Yahweh, there are still righteous humans left on Earth that follow your divine will. We must not let them suffer" The Great Divine Yahweh answered "Abraham, the goodness of your heart is blinding you from the truth. The good deeds from the few good God-fearing humans is not even close to balance out the vile acts by the others. It is not your soul that is tormented by their actions. You don't feel it like I do" To this, Abraham replied, "You are correct, Grandmaster Yahweh. I am, however, willing to give a piece of my soul to save the worthy people of Earth when you are ready to find eternal peace in death.

Yahweh considered what Abraham had said. He suffered for the last 7000 years, and all he wanted was to end it all so that he could find peace. But destroying the good humans would be an evil deed that could ruin his peace in the afterlife. Yahweh spoke " Benevolent Archangel Abraham; I have decided to give you a year to find the good humans and bind them to your soul. I will put them asleep in a protected vessel. After that, I will kill myself and destroy Earth and everyone on it. You can take my place as the Lord of the Divine Dimension.

Everything happened as Yahweh had said. A year later Earth was destroyed in a massive flash of light. As a last gesture of his greatness, Yahweh had ended all suffering and granted the sinners a peaceful death in the afterlife. Thus, was the end of Yahweh his greatest feat of limitless love and compassion.

Abraham felt guilty as he had only found 3000 individuals on Earth worthy of salvation. Ideally, he would have wanted to give them all a second chance, but he had to follow the guidelines of his wise and all-seeing Master Yahweh. Together with his 30 angels, Master Abraham decided to create Eden as humanity's new home. Abraham promoted Lucifer to be his Archangel and his envoy to Eden while Abraham was overseeing everyone from the Divine Dimension.

The Divine Abraham decided to divide humanity into seven different tribes all living in their territory at the same distance from Mount Sinai. He appointed four angels to oversee each tribe while Archangel Lucifer oversaw all of Eden. To connect with the Divine Abraham, each newborn must have a divine shard infused with Abraham's eternal soul inserted at baptism. The infusion of this shard is the first commandment of Abraham Thy God.

Chapter 33: How Abraham Created the Angels.

Abraham Goldstein studied Lucifer through the eyes of Metatron, as Lucifer was sleeping in a sleep pod. By stimulating the neural signals of the brain during sleep, one could reduce the need to sleep from eight hours to two hours per day without any adverse side effects. Abraham had always used sleep pods, as his restless nature didn't allow him to waste a third of his days sleeping. Most individuals did not like them and preferred to sleep naturally as they needed to sleep and dream.

Lucifer and the other angels had always slept in the sleep pods as they were Abraham's aides and bodyguards, and he didn't like them wasting eight hours on sleeping every day. Abraham studied the features of Lucifer who even in his sleep glowed with charisma and leadership. All the angels had outstanding features, intelligence, and abilities but Lucifer was a man without peers. He was an exceptional individual and his uniqueness also made him potentially dangerous, and Abraham hoped that they would never turn against each other.

The first of the angels had come to be 200 years earlier when Abraham was the new CEO of Goldstein industries back on Earth. Back then it had been a humble and unassuming family business. They had been locally powerful but not omnipresent and not one the ruling houses of the Terran Council. Abraham had dreamt of becoming the wealthiest and most powerful man on the planet but to advance to that stage he needed an edge that took him ahead of his competitors.

The Angel program gave him that edge. Abraham had secretly created individuals with excellent genes and had them conceived in a synthetic womb. These individuals were kept together and isolated from the world. They were indoctrinated to be loyal to Abraham. They were also trained in all the useful skills associated with their line of work.

The Angel program was a highly secret program, and it was secret for several reasons. The most important reasons were the usage of synthetic wombs to create the individuals in the program. Artificial wombs were highly illegal for human reproduction as they created individuals that were thought to lack a soul and individuality. The reason why this happened was debated: Religious people claimed that synthetic wombs was against the divine plan while scientists argued that the issue was the inability to completely recreate the conditions a human uterus. Synthetic wombs were hardly in use on Earth as it was cheaper to create drones to do all the dangerous and monotonous work than to have soulless clones do it.

A legal reason to use synthetic wombs was for raising livestock, as it was less cruel to kill a cow without a soul than killing a cow that potentially had a soul. Artificial wombs were also used to grow body parts using stem cells, where most body parts could be regrown within a matter of weeks.

For Abraham, the lack of ego and individuality in his Angels were desirable. What he got was a group of incredibly talented people who put HIS interests before their own and was ready to give everything including their own lives, to make his will happen. The Angel Program had helped Abraham rise from a locally feared businessperson to the wealthiest and most powerful man on the planet. However, when things had deteriorated with his family, he had still been forced to leave Earth as the angels wasn't enough to protect him when everyone was against him.

Abraham saw Lucifer waking up, and he decided to let Metatron speak for him on this occasion:

Metatron:

- Wake up, Lucifer. Today is the day to populate Eden and start the eternal reign of Grandmaster Abraham.

Lucifer:

- I am ready as always, Metatron. Let's go!

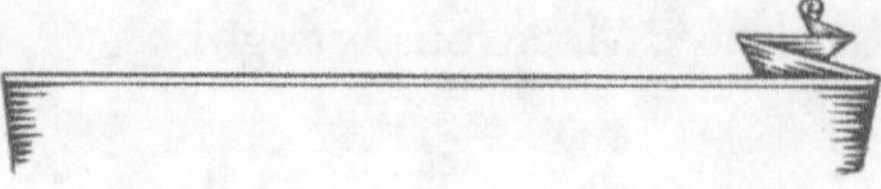

Chapter 34: The First Day on Eden.

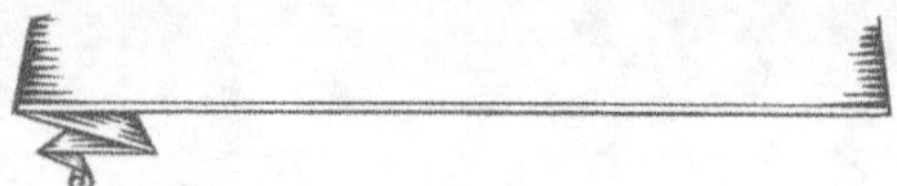

It was 8 AM on the 1st of January 2810, and the people of Eden were to be set awake after being kept asleep for 20 years. Abraham chose to align the calendars with the calendars of Earth and only change the year. The total number of individuals settled on Eden was around 3000, and they had all had their memories wiped, so all they had left was the ability to do basic movements, numeracy and language skills. They were all sleeping in their respective villages, which were replicas of Bronze Age villages from the Holy Land. All the 30 angels of Eden except for Lucifer were stationed in the hamlets under their supervision waiting for Abraham to give the signal to start.

Abraham spoke to all the Edenites through the microchips in their brains:

- Wake up people of Eden!

- You have slept for 20 years.

- You are the chosen ones, the only humans left in existence, after the apocalypse.

- The all-powerful Yahweh has destroyed himself and planet Earth. Before he did, he allowed me; Grandmaster Abraham to take his place on the Divine Throne and lead you to Eden your new home.

- Follow the Angels to Mount Sinai where you will congregate and see your new physical leader, Archangel Lucifer.

Abraham viewed the confused masses get up from their beds and aimlessly walking out. He had expected this. Memory-wiped individuals usually acted confused for a long time after being subjected to the treatment and this was to his advantage. People that were confused were less likely to question him and were easier to influence. Abraham suspected that first generation on Eden would not be easy to control. Even after a memory wipe, individuals tended to get flashbacks from their earlier lives, and these flashbacks would cause some of them to question the world they lived. They would not dare to voice their concerns, however, and after a couple of generations, he would have a group of people that believed in every word he said, through indoctrination and the lack of external stimuli.

Abraham watched the Edenites meet up in their respective villages and slowly make their way to Mount Sinai in the middle of Eden were Lucifer was preparing his speech.

Lucifer was wearing his ceremonial angel outfit while the other angels wore utility outfits. The Angels had three different uniforms depending on the purpose of their visit. They had:

- One ceremonial uniform, which was made to look extravagant, coated in gold and full of diamonds and gemstones attached in intricate patterns. This suit was highly decorative but did not serve any practical purpose except to impress.

- One utility uniform used for peacekeeping, helping villagers or fixing parts of Eden's advanced infrastructure. This suit was light blue and gave moderate protection against the elements and attacks while being mobile, lightly armed, and versatile

- One terror uniform, when Abraham wanted to punish his subjects. This suit was dark and covered the entire body including the face. It had spikes and other ornaments to make it look terrifying. It was heavily armed and designed for destruction and mayhem.

All the uniforms also had angel wings that moved to give the illusion of the angels using their wings to fly. In reality, flight thrusters under the wings gave the momentum, but the biblical angels were portrayed with wings, and Abraham liked this design feature.

The Edenites reached Mount Sinai, and the lights from the seven suns shone on Lucifer, which made him, and his gemstones shine like a beacon with the rest of Eden dimmed. He spoke to the masses, his voice amplified by speakers hidden in the mountain.

Lucifer:

- Welcome to Eden, humans. You are the last remnants of humanity.

- Humanity's terrible sins forced the great Yahweh to destroy Earth. You are alive because of the benevolence of Grandmaster Abraham, your new God.

- I am Lucifer, Abraham's Archangel and emissary on Eden. Grandmaster Abraham speaks directly through me!

- You are expected to follow the commands of Grandmaster Abraham and his angels. Comply and you will be rewarded with an honest good life. Resist and you will suffer.

- Follow the angels to your villages. They will look after you during the transition period.

- Now bow to Abraham, your new God!

As the masses bowed to Lucifer, he experienced mixed feelings; while the rush of power was intoxicating; he would have preferred a role in the background. During all his years on Earth, Lucifer had never attracted any attention. He was just a loyal servant to Abraham. It would take some time getting used to his new role, and Lucifer did not know, if he would like it or not. In the end, it did not matter, Lucifer was loyal to his master, and his master gave him this role.

Chapter 35: Jon, A typical settler on Eden.

Abraham Goldstein observed Jon of the Gad tribe who was sleeping. He could tell that Jon was unwell and confused. Jon woke up cold-sweating next to his wife, Nadia. He had experienced another strange dream that did not make any sense.

In the dream, Jon carried a rod that could fire projectiles and kill people from afar and a gadget that enabled him to speak and look at people that wasn't there. He remembered sitting in a flying ship leaving a reddish planet watching his home blow up. But nothing of this made any sense. None of these things existed, and Jon could also remember that he and Nadia had been together for years as humble farmers on Earth working hard to support their children. But if this was true, why couldn't he feel any connection to his wife nor his kids? Jon contemplated whether he was dead and life on Eden was the afterlife. The memories he had were so shallow and filled with gaps that he couldn't know what was real, and yet they were all that he had. Not finding peace, Jon quickly drank a big tankard of red wine to calm his nerves. As the intoxication took hold of him, he relaxed and fell asleep.

Jon's reaction was typical. When Abraham and the angels had wiped the memories of the first inhabitants of Eden, they had also inserted generic memories to give them a purpose and role in the society. Unfortunately, they had neither the time nor the will to provide all the Edenites with a comprehensive set of unique memories. Erasing and inserting memories was tedious, so instead of creating every individual unique they had just erased everyone's memories and used a few generic templates to create similar memories for all the Edenites. It wouldn't matter anyway; memory erosion and creation technologies could not realistically recreate and destroy a person's memories regardless of how much effort one put in. But after 50 years everyone living on Eden would be born there and all their memories would be real and prove that Abraham was their God.

The disconnection that Jon felt to his wife and children were a natural part of how Eden was set up. Abraham had made sure that all the family units on Eden consisted of individuals with no prior connection to each other. Hence, Jon, Nadia, and their three children were not connected to each other, before they were induced by memories and sent to live together in Eden. Abraham didn't want real family units, as they would share fragmented memories from their earlier lives, and they were more likely to question their current reality. When pairing individuals with no prior connection, they would all have their different memory fragments from before. However, these pieces would not match, and they would instead adapt to reality and hide their emotions.

Jon's drinking was unacceptable to Abraham. Abraham wanted his subjects to live good lives, which included being fruitful and to multiply. If Jon drank to calm his nerves, he would drink himself into an early grave and not be fruitful. If his subjects were not prolific, Abraham would run out of people to rule. Abraham decided to intervene; he activated the human chip in Jon's brain and appeared like a mirage.

Abraham:

- Jon of the Gad tribe, why are you drinking?

Jon:

- Wait, who are you?

Abraham:

- I am Abraham, thy God.

- You are abusing the gift I gave to you! I gave humanity wine, so that you can celebrate together, not to drink away your weaknesses.

Jon:

- I am sorry, Grandmaster Abraham. I repent and beg for forgiveness.

Abraham:

- Good. I forgive you sinful behaviour. For this time.

- Now honour my will and have sex with your consort. I demand you to be fruitful and multiply to praise my name!

Jon:

- I don't mean to be disrespectful, Grandmaster Abraham, but my wife and I have grown distant since you saved us and delivered us to your promised land. We have not engaged in any marital union since we arrived here.

This answer angered Abraham. This insolent human asked for help to fuck his wife. Sexuality was biology and was below his divine work. Abraham wanted to kill the audacious idiot. But that would be a pointless death, and there would be no lessons learned for the rest of the people. The first generation of inhabitants was a complete wreck and Abraham needed people born on Eden with authentic memories to gain better followers. Abraham decided to appear as a mirage to both Jon and Nadia at the same time.

Abraham:

- Wake up, Nadia!

Nadia:

- What, who are you?

Abraham:

- I am Grandmaster Abraham, Thy God!

- Jon told me that the two of you have failed to honour me by not laying together in your marital bed!

- I find this is unacceptable. I command you to have sex tonight!

Abraham made his mirage disappear and he studied Jon and Nadia. They were fumbling a bit, but they were making their way to sex. They would get there eventually; it was only biology.

Abraham concluded that the situation with Nadia and Jon was far from unique. Although he felt it was below him, he would have to face the circumstances and get his subjects to procreate. With 700 couples on Eden, this would keep him bogged down for a while. Life was not all glorious as a god.

Chapter 36: The First Birth on Eden.

Nine months after Abraham's intervention, Jon and Nadia had a baby, which was the firstborn on Eden. Abraham considered whether he should claim credit for this birth or not among the Edenites. He decided not to.

It had taken Abraham weeks to influence every couple on Eden and ensure that their sex lives were flourishing. If people believed that his influence was necessary for them to conceive, they would regularly petition him for help. Being asked for favours was NOT how Abraham wanted to rule as a god. He wanted his subjects to worship, obey and fear him; he had no interest in being a wish-granting genie that was evoked to solve trivial matters in his subjects' lives.

Abraham was relieved that his subjects were able to procreate. Although he had not foreseen any reasons why their reproductive health would be dysfunctional; It was unknown what effects the combination of memory wiping and spending an extended period cryogenically frozen would have on the human reproduction system. There had been earlier expeditions to other star systems where people had procreated once they landed but these expeditions had brought advanced technology aiding human reproduction while his Eden project did not.

Abraham commanded Jon and Nadia to name their firstborn daughter Lillian. Abraham chose this name, to honour his late wife Lillian Goldstein. However, he left this part out of the narrative. It did not fit the story that the divine and eternal Grandmaster Abraham was mourning his dead wife.

Abraham commanded everyone on Eden to attend the baptism of Lillian. As she was the first-born on Eden, her baptism would set the ceremony for all future childbirths. The baptism was led by the Angel Gabriel, who oversaw the Gad tribe. The masses sang a song to praise Abraham for his mercy to save humanity. Gabriel splashed water on the head of the newborn to symbolise that water was the source of all life. After doing this, he inserted a human chip in the newborn so that the Angels and Abraham would able to communicate and read the mind of their new subject. Gabriel described the microchip as a part of the Grandmaster Abraham's soul that he gave all newborn babies to bless them. Finally, Gabriel made a small cut in the child's finger to drop blood on the stone of eternity, which was an advanced DNA analyser disguised as an ornamental rock.

Abraham was satisfied with the ceremony. The baptism ritual went through without any incident, and it solved two practical issues:

- It made sure everyone had a divine technology microchip in
their heads.
- It gathered DNA from every individual.

Collecting DNA from individuals was important for Abraham as it allowed him to further his understanding of how the behaviour of his subjects was linked to their genetics. It also provided him with a framework for how he could utilise selective breeding to alter the features of future generations without using modern technology. The genetics of everyone on Eden was saved in the mainframe for future research.

Chapter 37: The Priests of Eden.

During the first year on Eden, the angels were always at the surface helping and leading the tribes they were supervising. Doing this had a drawback, however, eventually they would age and die. Abraham wanted his Eden project to last for an eternity. For this to happen, the angels needed to be cryogenically frozen most of the time. Abraham estimated that the lifespans of his angels when combining cryogenic sleep and DNA regeneration technology would be thousands of years. With a bit of luck, the rest of humanity would be extinct by then so that Abraham would be the god of all humankind.

Abraham decided to pick the most suitable family of each tribe to become the head priests. Abraham used his DNA database to decide who would be the best head priest for a tribe. Abraham decided that he would not allow female leaders. Female leaders were a poison that he had experienced too much on Earth. The ancients were wise by only allowing male clerics. Allowing female clerics was one of the factors destroying religion back on Earth.

As Eden was a theocracy, the head-priest was the ruler of the tribe. Appointing governors for the tribes saved Abraham time as he could communicate to the leaders to make them do his bidding, instead of talking to every human individually. It was also good to have an earthly power in place to keep some of the mystique around himself and his angels. If a ruler for some reason displeased him, he could always choose to kill them quietly by causing a brain haemorrhage or make a public display by having them executed. No man on Eden, not even the local leaders, were above God, and their life and well-being was dependent on pleasing Abraham and doing his will.

After setting up the religious leadership on Eden, Abraham ordered the angels to return to the Divine Control Centre where they could spend most of their time in suspended animation to extend their lives. Happy with his achievements, Abraham moved to his meditation spot in the Divine Dimension and meditated for ages; letting the humans of Eden govern themselves for a while.

Chapter 38: A Childhood Nightmare.

Lucifer had one of his recurring nightmares. In the dream, he was a young child and today was the day he entered adulthood. Everyone was looking at him when he took the oath that his childhood was over, and he swore to serve Master Abraham for the rest of his life. A man was brought in to him. He was chained and beaten. The man was pleading for mercy. Lucifer's mentor gave Lucifer a loaded gun and told him to kill the prisoner to prove his loyalty. Lucifer felt sick, he had never killed before and he did not know, that this was one his tasks. He searched the room for his best friend, but there were no children in the hall today; only adult Angels screaming for blood. Lucifer raised the pistol and screamed his lungs out as he shot the prisoner with many bullets. With blood on his face, Lucifer caught the gaze of the dying prisoner. Lucifer swallowed the vomit that was coming up from his throat, as he could not allow himself to show weakness.

Lucifer woke up, and he could still see the gaze of the murdered prisoner staring into his soul. His adulthood ceremony had scarred him for life, and he had never shared his feelings with anyone.

For Lucifer, his adulthood ceremony was a shocking revelation on how his life was meant to be. He was brought up in the Angel program, and this was all he knew about, but until that day he was taught mostly physical perfection and science. Lucifer's mentor told him that Master Abraham had selected Lucifer to be one of his guardians which was a fancy title for a bodyguard.

An Angel was considered adult and eligible for active duty at the age of 13 although for practical reasons they usually started active duty when they were around 20. During his years on Earth, Lucifer had killed countless individuals for Abraham, and yet it was always the first murder that came back to haunt him.

What bothered Lucifer was that he never found out why he killed the prisoner on his adulthood ceremony. There was no record explaining why they had killed him. This was often the case as the angels killed on direct orders from Abraham Goldstein, and there was no reason to keep records. After all, too much record-keeping could expose what they were doing. Lucifer never bothered to find out what his other victims had done, but the first one was a splinter in his mind that he could not heal from.

Unable to find peace, Lucifer entered a cryogenic tank and set the timer for six months. Hopefully, such a long time in the tank would get his mind off the matter. Regardless, he was not needed in the day-to-day operation of Eden now that everything was up and running and the others would wake him up if he was needed. Lucifer felt the cold of the helium mixture flowing in before it was a snap, and everything turned dark.

To be cryogenically frozen was like being killed and then resuscitated upon waking up. As no decay could happen on the cellular level in the freezing temperatures of the tank, this was a way to preserve a person indefinitely. While older technologies sometimes failed to resuscitate the user, the technologies used in the 29th century were very safe.

Chapter 39: A Plot Against Abraham.

James Goldstein was a 10th generation descendant of Abraham Goldstein and a low-level manager at House Goldstein. Since he was a Goldstein, he owned a small share of the company and had voting rights at the Annual General Meeting. As James Goldstein was a young child in 2785 when Abraham carried out his coupe, James had no divine technology chip inserted. Thus, his mind could not be read, and Abraham could not kill him remotely. He looked at a picture of his late parents. Abraham had murdered them using the divine technology chip. But James was not driven by revenge; he was motivated by ambition.

James was 29 years old in the year 2812. Abraham murdered James' parents in the year 2786 before he left Earth. Thus, James had very faint memories of them and instead his maternal aunt who was not a Goldstein had raised him. He grew up under humble circumstances far away from the excess and abundance of the Goldstein Tower. While no Terran citizen was poor, James had grown up in relative poverty compared to everyone around him, and he had dreamt about living in the excess and abundance of Goldstein Tower.

Upon reaching adulthood, James was able to access his parent's estate, which was in a trust fund during his childhood. Eager to live a life of luxury and excess, he was thoroughly disappointed once he got to live and work in Goldstein Tower. The place was in shambles with cracks in the walls and old worn out furniture. The food and beverage were not much better than he had received while growing up in poverty and the totality of his parent's estate was not worth more than 100,000 Terran Credits, or ten years of average pay.

James found out that wealth of House Goldstein was depleted due to the excessive spending on the Eden project. James hatched a plan. If he could depose Abraham from power, he could make a move for the top. This plan was counting on a swift and brutal retaliation from Abraham, which would kill off most of the senior members of House Goldstein. By moving in swiftly after their deaths, James planned to grab as much estate as he possible could, while the unprepared descendants of House Goldstein would lose out. This would push James to a position of power in the company or at least to a much higher position.

After spending the last five years finding accomplices, James was ready to make a move for power.

Chapter 40: Breaking News.

Terran Global News 5th August 2812:

A massive explosion occurred today at Goldstein Tower destroying the top five levels of the building and killing dozens on the ground from the debris. The cause of the explosion hasn't been determined, but it is speculated to be a targeted attack aimed to kill the elusive Abraham Goldstein, founder and majority shareholder of House Goldstein who has remained unseen for the last 20 years.

One of the Security Managers for House Goldstein, James Goldstein has confirmed that Abraham Goldstein died in the explosion, and he released a video of Abraham Goldstein conversing with his bodyguards before the bombing.

As the blast vaporised Abraham's body, there is no way to resurrect him. Abraham's death marks the end of 272-year-old stalwart who outlived most of his descendants.

Abraham's death is bad news for House Goldstein that has struggled and lost most of their influence and wealth during the reign of Isaac Goldstein. Analysts speculate about an upcoming and unpredictable power struggle within the company, which could lead to its demise. More updates and commentary on the subject to come!

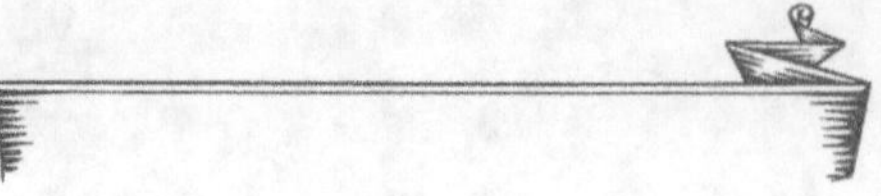

Chapter 41: Abraham's peace is shattered.

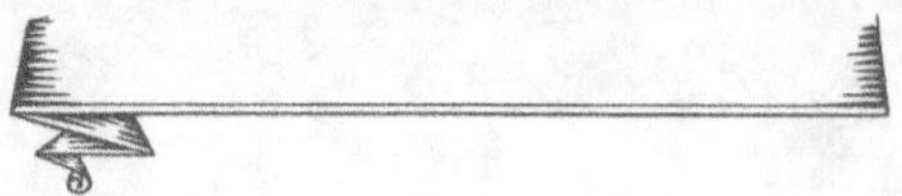

Abraham was meditating under the ever-blooming Lotus Tree in the Divine Dimension. Initially, it had surprised him that he enjoyed the stillness and the vastness of the infinite, more than overlooking his subjects but then it had dawned on him: The old Abraham was no more. The Abraham of Earth had limited time to achieve what he wanted, so he had never allowed himself to let things go. Once Abraham had attained godhood, he got a new outlook on life. With near infinite power over his subjects and unlimited time, control was less important, and he allowed himself to meditate for months on end.

Suddenly, Abraham felt a burning headache that shattered the peace and knocked him to the ground. He screamed his lung out in pain, but no one answered his calls as he was the only one there. Eventually, the pain diminished, and he got back to his senses. The pain reminded him of the insignificant nibbling he felt every time someone on Eden died. But this time it felt a thousand times more intense. Had something happened to one of his angels? He could feel the connection to all the angels on Eden but from the ones on Earth it was only static. Abraham contacted Nuriel:

> - Nuriel I feel a great disturbance in the force. Have you spoken to the Angels on Earth?

Nuriel:

> - I haven't spoken to them, our orbit is too far away from Earth for our telepathic connection to work, and Earth is on the other side of the sun which blocks our encrypted messages.

We received a message from them one week ago, and back then everything was going according to plan

Abraham:

- I see, can you contact them now?

Nuriel:

- No, I can't They will be blocked by the sun's electromagnetic interference zone for another week.

Abraham:

- This is an emergency. Contact them via Spacenet.

Spacenet was the 29th-century interplanetary networks covering every nook and cranny of the solar system. Spacenet consisted of thousands of satellites in different orbits around the sun, and it made it possible to always contact every human settlement regardless of their relative position towards each other. It was developed through the centuries to avoid problems arising when settlements came into radio shadow caused by the sun or other celestial objects. It was rarely used for transmitting sensitive information as it had limited capabilities for secure encryption. This was because the quantum computing power and AI at the time was so advanced, so any encrypted message could be decrypted. The computing power was not an issue in the 29th century, but the speed of light was. Thus, every satellite contained a clone of the entire public part of Spacenet to improve usage speeds. Sending a message to another part of the solar system, however, could take hours, based on the distance between the two colonies.

Abraham navigated Spacenet through the eyes of Nuriel and he checked the distance to Earth. Earth was 45 light minutes away from Eden so the earliest response he could get was in 1.5 hours. Deciding to pass the time, Abraham read the news to find out what was happening on

Earth. Finding out about the explosion at Goldstein Tower and his presumed death was too much for Abraham who passed out from the shock.

Chapter 42: The Resurrected Abraham Faces Problems.

Abraham was floating in the vast darkness of the afterlife. This place was timeless, and he did not mind being here at all. Abraham was dead and with the death came the separation of the ego and the soul. In the distance he could hear the calling *"Master Abraham, can you hear me?"* The calling became louder and eventually Abraham woke up in the Divine Control Centre experiencing excruciating pain. His vision and hearing were blurred, but he perceived that Lucifer and few of his angels were next to his cryogenic tank. Abraham tried to call out, but he could not make a sound. A flash of light struck his eyes, and he was back in the Divine Dimension.

Lucifer:

- Master Abraham, can you hear me?

Abraham:

- Yes, I can hear you. What happened?

Lucifer:

- You died, Master. You have been dead for a year.

Abraham:

- What! How did this happen?

Lucifer:

- Nuriel said that your relatives' betrayal, and the deaths of Malphat, Hashmallim, Seraphim, and Ishmael, was too much for you, so you died from grief.

- When I woke up, your body was beyond saving, but your brain was still preserved due to the freezing cold of the cryogenic tank.

- We had to replace your body with a robotic body, and the only part of you that remains is your brain.

Abraham:

- I see. How come that I have been dead for a year?

Lucifer:

- Because we couldn't get the proper equipment. It would be suicidal to land on Antarctica and asking House Goldstein. We did not dare to approach the other factions, as we were unaware of the current allegiances on Earth. We scouted the black market for the necessary equipment. Eventually, we acquired the hardware needed. As it turned, out we had some untouched bank accounts from our secret operations 25 years ago.

Abraham:

- I see. Thank you very much Lucifer, you are a great man.

Lucifer:

- Thank you, Grandmaster Abraham.

- Unfortunately, there is a complication. We are broke. In your absence, we haven't been able to find a way of funding the

Eden project. Without funding, we will not be able to buy the necessary spare parts to support Eden.

Abraham:

- I feared as much. Leave it with me, Lucifer, I will find a solution. I didn't become the wealthiest man in the solar system for nothing!

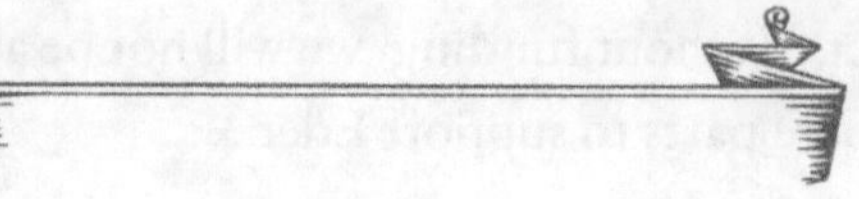

Chapter 43: Abraham Starts Trafficking Children.

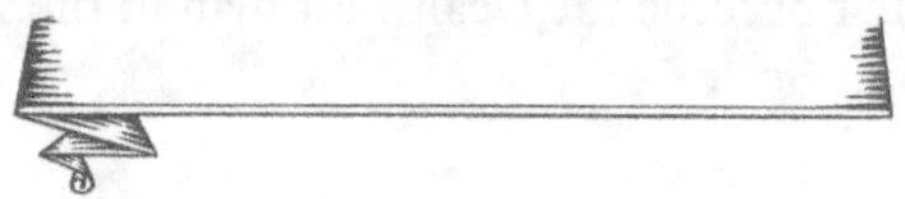

Abraham was sitting on his throne in the Divine Dimension, hoping to come up with a solution to the economic hardship of the Eden project. He was struggling to think clearly as the phantom pains in his body proved hard to disconnect. He had seen his robotic body once, through the eyes of Lucifer, and he did not want to see it again. It was a contraption and an eyesore. While he could stay awake and move around in the regular dimension, he did not want to. The normal dimension was imperfect while the Divine Dimension was perfection. Regardless he could see anything he wanted from there, through controlling his angels and sharing their vision.

Abraham managed to let go off the phantom pains from, and he was struck by frustration instead. The frustration was aimed inwards instead of outwards. Abraham usually blamed everything that did not go according to plans on someone else, but this time it was different. This time he admitted that he had made a critical mistake.

Successfully subduing all the resistance within his own faction, he had failed to account for time and plan long-term. He should have predicted that there would be future Goldstein's, who were not chipped, and had he should have taken precautions against them. Instead, his short-sightedness had put him in a very tricky spot.

Ideally, Abraham would return to Earth proving that he was still alive. Unfortunately, the loss of his physical body meant that he was dead according to Terran law and the division of his assets would have continued.

Abraham realised that he should have hidden enormous amounts of money into slush funds that he controlled. Even when he "died" these assets would not be distributed to his relatives and he could have supported the Eden Project indefinitely. Unfortunately, he had not taken this precaution.

Eventually, it dawned on Abraham what he needed to do. He needed to deal with an old enemy of House Goldstein. As the rest of House Goldstein had turned against him, his former enemy could turn out to be his future friend.

It was a poorly kept secret that the Chairman of House Rashid, Ibrahim Rashid, liked young girls; incredibly young girls. Ibrahim Rashid had been threatened with expulsion from the Terran Council if he did not keep his perverted compulsions at bay. He had agreed to this, knowing that every Terran citizen had a tracking chip implanted so he was unable to spend time with children without this being detected by the Terran Council.

What if Abraham could fund the maintenance of the Eden project by selling unregistered children to Ibrahim Rashid? House Rashid could afford it, as the expensive part was to create Eden, the maintenance was less expensive.

Abraham decided to contact Ibrahim Rashid via the hologram generator. Abraham computer-generated a hologram of himself speaking to Ibrahim, as he did not want not to share his current appearance with his former enemy.

Abraham:

- Ibrahim! Inshallah, it has been too many years since the last time we spoke.

- As you know, my treacherous family destroyed my home at Goldstein Tower and declared me dead to split my assets.

- I am alive, but I have no intention of going back to Earth.

- I need financial aid, and I request a 1 billion Terran Credits interest-free loan to complete the Eden project and regain control over my faction.

- In return, I will provide you with unregistered and very well-maintained young virgins. Please get back to me as soon as possible.

After sending the message, Abraham sat back and relaxed. The message would take 45 minutes to reach Ibrahim Rashid and then the same time to come back. Interplanetary communications were not for the impatient!

A few hours later, Abraham received a response from Ibrahim Rashid:

- Greetings Lucifer of House Goldstein. I did not become the leader of House Rashid by being gullible. Abraham Goldstein has been dead for over 20 years.

- I am considering helping you. But I do request that you are forthcoming with me. I do not know what your agenda is, but it is hurting House Goldstein, which has always been rivals of House Rashid.

- I require that you show yourself. Do this, and we will talk, try to fool me again, and our conversation is over.

At first, Abraham felt angry when he received Ibrahim's message. His ego was offended by the notion that he was dead, and that Lucifer would be shrewd enough to usurp power within House Goldstein. Lucifer had many good qualities, but ambition was not one of them.

After a while, Abraham realised that being "dead" on Earth had advantages. He was disliked on Earth, and yet no other faction had interfered with the Eden project since its inception decades ago. Being 'dead' on Earth was ideal as it left him to focus on his Eden project without interruptions. Abraham summoned Lucifer to the communications room.

Lucifer:

- You summoned me, Master?

Abraham:

- Yes, I need your help to solve our financial problems.
- I need you to call Ibrahim Rashid for me.

Lucifer:

- Ibrahim Rashid? Why would we contact that filthy pae-dophile? The Rashid's have always been our enemy.

Abraham:

- Lucifer! Don't question your Master!

- Ibrahim Rashid is an enemy of House Goldstein. But we are enemies of the remaining Goldstein's'. The enemy of my ene-my is my friend.

- Ibrahim agreed to lend us 1 Billion Terran Credits, which I can invest, to cover the upkeep of Eden indefinitely.

Lucifer:

- I see, and what does that snake want in return?

Abraham:

- He wants to communicate with you. He believes that I am dead and that you are in charge.

- We'll play along with this, but don't get any ideas.

- Tell him your Terran name and show your face to him, he re-quested transparency.

After this conversation, Lucifer connected to the hologram creator to communicate with Ibrahim Rashid. The hologram generators of the 29th century was very advanced as they used Nanotechnology replicating the outer layer of a person to give the feeling that the person was in the room. To verify his identity, Lucifer also attached a sample of his DNA to the message.

Lucifer:

- Dear Mr Rashid.

- This is Terence Lowenstein, known by my operative name, Lucifer. You have requested to communicate with me.

- Please, tell me, what can I do to secure your aid for our project?

When Ibrahim Rashid received the message an hour later, he was a bit perplexed about Lucifer's identity. There was a character match for Terence Lowenstein, but there were almost no records on the activities of Terence Lowenstein. He had left Earth over two decades ago on the same date as Abraham Goldstein. He was back to Antarctica a few years later, to disappear again. He had, however, spent the last six months on Earth and had recently left the planet.

Surprisingly, Terence Lowenstein had no personal assets on Earth or anywhere else in the solar system. If he had siphoned House Goldstein for money, he was either good at hiding his assets, or he was not the one behind internal strife and rapid decline of House Goldstein. But, if supporting Lucifer could bring House Goldstein down, it was worth it, no matter who he was, or what his end goal was. Ibrahim transmitted another message:

- Very well, Terence.

- Although I know who you are, I still don't know your agenda.

- But you are the enemy of my enemy, and as such you are my friend.

- I will issue you an interest-free loan of 1 Billion Terran Credits. To receive the money, you need to assassinate the chairman of House Goldstein, Isaac Goldstein.

- Let me know when it's done.

An hour later, the message reached Eden. Lucifer was about to answer when Abraham stopped him.
Abraham:

- No, Lucifer. We are not killing Isaac Goldstein.

Lucifer:

- But why, Master Abraham? Your body is no longer an issue. You can travel to Earth and kill Isaac with your mind. The money will be yours, and Eden's future will be secured.

Abraham:

- Do you really think Isaac Goldstein was behind the attack at Goldstein Towers?

- The angels at Goldstein Tower could read all the board members minds, and yet they were taken by surprise.

- This means that our enemy us was not chipped and had nothing to fear.

- If we kill the chipped board members, nothing will stop the rest of House Goldstein to send their fleet to annihilate us.

- So, Isaac Goldstein needs to live along with the rest of the board. He is only valuable to us as a hostage.

Lucifer:

- I am sorry, Master Abraham. You are right.

Abraham:

- This I what we will do

- You'll refuse to kill the Goldstein board, as it's unwise to kill the incompetent board members, who bringing the company down.

- You'll also deliver a 9-year-old virgin to Ibrahim's private holiday residence orbiting Earth, as a token of goodwill.

Lucifer:

- What? You want to give a child to that child molester? That's insanely immoral

As this was the second time Lucifer spoke up against him, Abraham lost his temper and he knocked Lucifer to the ground with a psionic blast.

Abraham:

- Silence you fool. I AM YOUR MASTER!

- We need money. Otherwise, Eden will be destroyed, and all our subjects will die.

- Our people need to find their way back to our roots, we are the bearer of Yahweh's legacy, and I am the Chosen One to make it happen.

- Individuals are expendable, it's only the group that matters.

- Now do my bidding.

Lucifer:

- Yes, Master.
- Your will shall be done.

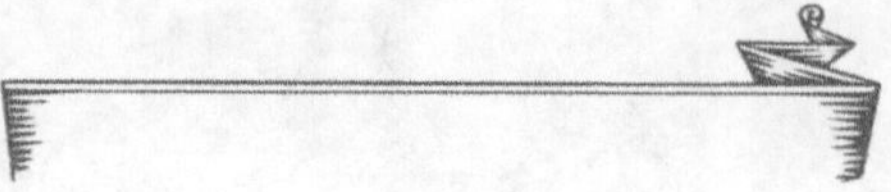

Chapter 44: The agreement between Abraham Goldstein and Ibrahim Rashid.

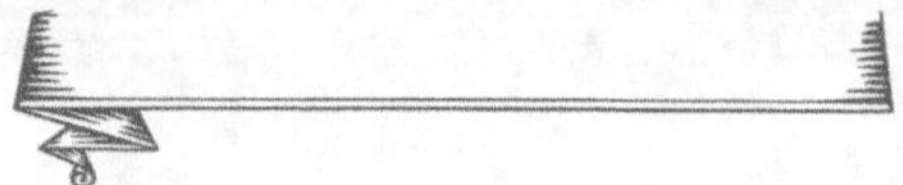

Upon receiving the first child bride, Ibrahim Rashid was overwhelmed with joy. The girl a lot purer than the filth he had ever experienced in the orbiting brothels on the fringes of the solar system. Better yet, she was free from the Martian diseases and radiation issues. Furthermore, as she was not of Terran descent, she was unregistered and not chipped, meaning he could keep her in secret at his orbital vacation residence.

Ibrahim was a bit worried about the Terran Council finding out about the girl, but he shrugged it off. The men working at his private residence was loyal and would not betray him to the ungodly and morally bankrupt other factions. Following the rites of his ancient spiritual guide, Ibrahim Rashid named the girl Alisha and married her according to the old customs of his people. He consummated the marriage later the same day. While the poor little girl was bleeding and crying in the corner, Ibrahim Rashid patted his own fatty belly pleased with himself.

Ibrahim decided to lend Terrence Lowenstein the 1 billion Terran credits that he asked for. The terms agreed was that the loan would run interest-free over 18 years, and instead of paying interest Lucifer would supply Ibrahim with a total of 72 virgins over those 18 years. If the Kaffirs for some reason could not pay back the billion at the end of the loan Ibrahim's armed forces would annihilate them, and Ibrahim Rashid made this clear. Eventually, Ibrahim Rashid dozed off and fell asleep.

Once the money was secured, Abraham invested them and he made enough money to support Eden forever. After all, his greatest strength had always been to predict how the market would develop, and this was how he had created his immense wealth in the first place.

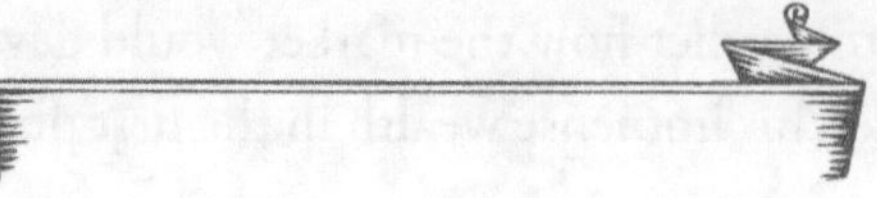

Chapter 45: Of Virgin Blood and Divine Sky.

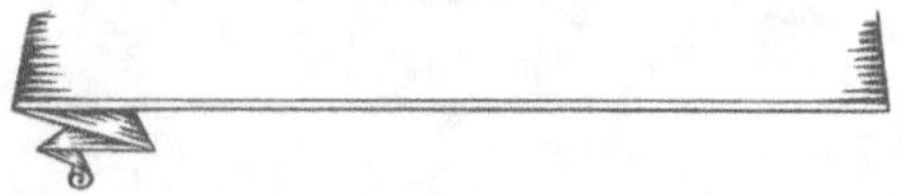

Humankind despite Grandmaster Abraham's effort was still soiled by the ancestor's sins that destroyed our homeworld; Earth.

Master Abraham sayeth: Thou shall slowly cleanse your sin by giving up that, which is pure and loved by all. Bring thy daughters while they are pure untouched by men and have not yet bled. Thy Lord Abraham shall each season pick a bride to bring to his divine realm and slowly cleanse the sin of humanity by forming a union with the virgin. This shall happen until the debt is repaid and the balance is restored.

Abrahameon: Chapter 23 paragraph 7

Lucifer closed the Abrahameon, the holy book for Eden. It was a work in progress. Lucifer was sickened by this chapter, and he strongly disagreed with Abraham' decision to sign a deal with the devil, Ibrahim Rashid. Regardless, there was not much Lucifer could about it. The deal was made, and Ibrahim Rashid had threatened that he would bring his army and destroy Eden if he did not receive what he was promised.

Neither Eden nor the Divine Control Centre was fearsome battle stations. They had enough defences to deter any raiders, pirates, or Martians from daring to approach. But the defences weren't designed to withstand a full-scale attack from a hostile fleet. On the flip side, if they kept House Rashid happy, they were protected from the weakened remains of House Goldstein.

It was time again, time for another innocent girl to be sacrificed for the greater good. Three years had passed, so today's offering would be the 12th to be sent as blood payment to the demented Ibrahim Rashid. Lucifer pitied the girl that would be selected. He tried to avoid thinking about her fate, was it a death sentence or something much worse?

On the selection day, every eligible Edenite girl were summoned to a platform covered in hologram technology or "the blue light of God". They were stripped naked and had to stand that way for the "selection" to take place. This took several hours, as the distance to Earth made transferring the holograms to Ibrahim time-consuming. Once Ibrahim, hade made his decision, all the blue lights was aimed at the selected girl, who was put in a portable cryogenic tank and shipped off to Ibrahim 's private residence.

Lucifer had met Ibrahim Rashid once when delivering one of the unlucky tribute girls. Ibrahim had invited him for a tour of his home, and Lucifer had agreed. Suddenly, Lucifer had been encapsulated in a transparent force field that stopped him from moving. Horrified, Lucifer was forced to watch as the hairy and fat Ibrahim raped his latest victim. During this whole gruesome act, Ibrahim had stared him down to assert his dominance. After completion, the vile monstrosity had dragged the poor girl to another room of the building. After that, Ibrahim's guards evicted Lucifer from the residence. During the two-week trip back to Eden, Lucifer had made plans for revenge and justice. Ibrahim's home was not that well-guarded, and Lucifer and the other angels were trained killers and would be capable of killing Ibrahim and his guards.

Abraham had read Lucifer's mind and reprimanded him. Killing Ibrahim Rashid would kill their only ally and would bring a fleet of House Rashid spaceships to destroy Eden. That was a battle that could not be won. While Ibrahim was a vile man, he was too important to get rid of. The suffering by the few was necessary to bring a good life to the many. Lucifer could not understand how Abraham's action would bring a good life to the people. Abraham replied:

- Do not question, Lucifer. Just dedicate your faith to your Master. You are the jewel of my creation and if you just believe in me and never question, all the answers will come.

Lucifer went to his cryogenic tank and thought back on those words. *"Never question, and all the answers will come".* He had stayed loyal for 30 years on this bloody rock, and Lucifer was none the wiser. Resigning to his fate, he sighed before experiencing the quick chill of the cryogenic tank for a long good sleep.

Chapter 46: The Disconnect Deepens.

Abraham Goldstein was struggling to focus and be satisfied with life. Despite having all the power, he had ever dreamt of he was not satisfied. In fact, he was severely frustrated: Sexually frustrated.

For the last 120 years, Abraham never had sex. It wasn't appealing to him although it was available to him due to his wealth and the right pharmaceuticals. Abraham's physician had explained, that a common side effect of the DNA regeneration technology was the lack of sexual drive once the individual had reached the end of his natural lifespan. It had not bothered Abraham at the time. He was very sexually active during the first 130 years of his life and with the sexual drive gone he could focus his energy on expanding his wealth and power.

Since Abraham had lost his body, Abraham's sex drive had changed, and sex became important again. He realised that this was because his new body made it impossible to have physical sex, and thus it became more important to him. Abraham fulfilled his sexual urges by watching people having sex. This became an addiction to him and filled him with unfulfilled desires. From the Divine Dimension, he could connect to all the humans and watch them have sex. The worst part was of studying people's sex lives were the Sodomites.

Sodomy was very uncommon on Earth during Abraham's lifetime, and it had never bothered him that much. While sodomy was not illegal on Earth, it was uncommon due to laws and regulations surrounding births and conceptions. Every individual on Earth had a set of bionic microchips controlling many aspects of their life. One of these chips acted like a permanent birth control device that prevented unplanned pregnancy.

To get pregnant, an individual needed permission from the authorities, which recommended DNA optimisation for every child. The DNA optimisation gave the child the "best" genetic output based on the parent's DNA. One of the genetics that was usually deselected was the genetic for homosexuality. This meant that only 5 individuals in a million, was gay in the 28th Century. On Mars, where genes were spread naturally, the prevalence of homosexuality was between 5-10 per cent of the population; like the ratio on Earth in the 21st century. Since the Edenites descended from Martians, they also had about 5-10 per cent homosexuals.

Abraham was against homosexuality while his sexual addiction made him fascinated by the concept. He remembered Yahweh's suicide letter, and he realised the dangers that he faced. Abraham decided to do two things:

- He would have a chemical castration drug injected into his brain to get rid of his sexual obsession.
- He would punish the sodomites following the scriptures and the ancient law.

Abraham wanted to justify punishing the homosexuals among the Edenites. Unfortunately, nothing in the Abrahameon stated that homosexuality was a sin or forbidden, as Abraham had been oblivious to the issue. Eventually, Abraham found a way to justify punishment of homosexuals. He contacted Lucifer:

- Lucifer, I am angry with you.

Lucifer:

- Grandmaster Abraham. I don't understand. How have I angered you?

Abraham:

- You have failed to punish the Sodomites for their ungodly behaviour!

Lucifer:

- The Sodomites? What group is that and what have they done?

Abraham:

- The homosexuals, men who lay with men and women with women!

Lucifer:

- Oh...

Lucifer and the other angels were asexual and had little interest in sex. Abraham had designed their DNA this way, to keep them focused on doing the missions he gave them. To be on the safe side, the angels also had microchips that repressed their sexuality. Lucifer had no idea why the homosexuals was an issue or why he was supposed to punish them and he answered Abraham:

- Abraham, I wasn't instructed to keep track of the Edenites' sexual habits and I cannot recall anything in Abrahameon that forbids homosexuality.

Abraham:

- One of my most important commandments in the Abrahameon is "Be fruitful and multiply." Choosing a life of sodomy is a clear intention to break that rule. Hence the culprits need to be punished!

- Gather the angels, dress for punishment and terror; I will make everyone gather at Mount Sinai.

- I will instruct you further, once you are in position. Now go!

Hearing this, Lucifer rushed to get him and the other angels ready for immediate deployment to Eden.

Chapter 47: Death to the Sodomites.

Yehuda was a farmer and a father of eight children. He lived a good life following the decrees of the Abrahameon and to reward this, Lucifer had promoted him to become the high priest for his tribe. While Lucifer and the other angels had been very present during the first years on Eden, their presence became less and less noticeable as the years passed by. 20 years after Yehuda and his family woke up on Eden, the angels were only spotted sporadically. They usually came to solve problems or to collect offerings.

Yehuda had lost one of his daughters in the selection. Her name was Helena, and she had been one of the cutest girls on Eden. Yehuda felt bittersweet about his loss. While it was a great honour that Abraham chose Helena to accompany him in heaven, it was sad to not see her grow up and have a family.

Yehuda often wondered what happened to the chosen girls after the selection. He had asked Lucifer, who had told him that he should be happy for Helena. Grandmaster Abraham had selected his daughter to receive direct entry to heaven while most people had to follow the Abrahameon strictly and live a good life to reach heaven when they died. As Helena was picked while she was still pure, she was saved from the horrors and torment of hell that awaited sinners when they died.

Although this had relieved Yehuda of his worst woes, it also confused him. Lucifer had mentioned that Helena was in paradise with Grandmaster Abraham. But on another occasions, Lucifer had told Yehuda that the enchanted cylinder that selected girls entered before leaving Eden was to prevent them from suffocating.

But if the only way for a human to reach paradise were to die, why would Lucifer bring an enchanted cylinder to stop the selected girls from suffocating? Yehuda concluded that some things were not understandable for ordinary men, and that Grandmaster Abraham had a plan that benefitted everyone on Eden.

While Yehuda missed Helena but was happy for her eternal salvation; Yehuda was concerned about his son Simon. Yehuda had tried to arrange a marriage for Simon so he could be fruitful and multiply. Simon had refused, as he insisted that his true love was a man named Christopher. Simon's homosexuality broke Yehuda's heart, and he hoped that Simon would not face eternal damnation in hell for his desires.

Choosing, a life of sodomy was against the commandment that humans should be fruitful and multiply. Simon had brushed off his father's concern and replied that Grandmaster Abraham wanted everyone to love and be loved, and since he was created this way, there was no way his love could be sinful. Besides, there was no explicit ban on homosexuality in the Abrahameon.

Failing to convince Simon about his mistake, Yehuda still loved him and tried to introduce him to different women, hoping that one of them would trigger his natural desire to procreate. Yehuda had even pleaded with Lucifer to cure Simon's affliction. Lucifer had not shown the issue much interest and had stated that Yehuda's other six children seemed well adapted and with Grandmaster Abraham's blessings Yehuda's bloodline was bound to expand and prosper in the future. Grandmaster Abraham did not expressively forbid sodomy, and Lucifer could not care less how the humans of Eden were directing their sexual energies.

Suddenly, Grandmaster Abraham appeared like a mirage in the room. He commanded Yehuda to gather all the villagers at once and head for Mount Sinai. Once they reached Mount Sinai, they realised that it would not be a friendly announcement. There were fire and smoke around the mountain, and the angels were dressed in terrifying black armour with spikes and blood. Fear and confusion spread among the villagers that had to stand in anticipation until everyone had arrived.

Once everyone was gathered, Abraham appeared as a gigantic illusion standing above the angels. He was wearing his usual robe and cane but to signify the importance of today's assembly he was also wearing his divine crown. Abraham's eyes were burning with anger and his voice shouted out.

- People of Eden. Too many of you engage in ungodly behaviours.

- I have commanded you to be fruitful and multiply, and yet many of you pursue practices that contradict this command!

- Yes, I talk about men who sleep with men, women with women, bestiality and other sick practices that I have witnessed being an all-seeing god

- This must end today. The following people step forward.

Abraham started shouting out names. He was aware of a total of 300 homosexuals out of the current population that had risen to 6000. While it would be convenient to wipe them all out at once, Abraham wanted to instil fear. Besides by outing all the homosexuals and punish some of them publicly, he was sure to get some entertainment later when the religious mobs of Eden made short work of any undesirables.

Abraham instructed the angels to divide the sodomites into two groups. One group consisted of 60 individuals and the other consisted of 240 persons. The 60 were the condemned ones, and Abraham read out the allegations for everyone to hear. Yehuda's son, Simon, was one of them. "*Not only had Simon, son of Yehuda chosen to perform unnatural acts with men, but he had done so against his father's wishes and disregarded all attempts to change his mind and lay with a woman which was the natural thing to do. For such a wicked sinner, there was only one way to go, to be cleansed by fire.*"

The 60 condemned sodomites were placed on an elevated platform surrounded by an invisible forcefield that stopped them from leaving. They were then slowly roasted in front of the crowds by an orbiting laser. The smell of burnt flesh was covering the valley. But Abraham was not going to let them have a swift death. So, the fires were extinguished, and stimulants and oxygen pumped into the area to ensure that everyone was awake and suffering. This process went on for three hours, and eventually Abraham had seen enough. He set the lasers to full effect and killed the condemned.

Abraham:

- Remember this day people of Eden! Every year on this day 60 sodomites will burn on this mountain. You need to deliver them to me. If you do not do so, it's because you are protecting these abominations. If you do more of you will suffer!

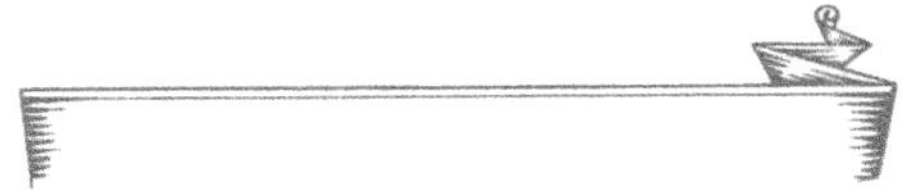

Chapter 48: Lucifer's Dilemma.

Lucifer felt uncomfortable over the things that had happened. Although he understood why Abraham wanted to eradicate the homosexuals the way it had played out was indefensible. The orbital lasers were powerful and could incinerate a man in seconds; it would have been a clean and almost painless death. Instead, Abraham roasted the condemned ones for hours on end for no other reasons than sadistic ones.

The solution was senseless. If Abraham wanted to eradicate the problem, he could have killed all the homosexuals at once. Instead, he murdered one-fifth of them and gave the others a death sentence by proclaiming that 60 homosexuals should be killed every year. The knowledge about their damnation was worse than a swift death, and Lucifer pitied the condemned homosexuals.

Lucifer had answered Yehuda's calls and visited the devastated man afterwards. He was heartbroken and he had cursed Lucifer. Lucifer should have punished Yehuda for this, as disrespecting an angel was a grave crime. But Lucifer chose to not punish the "old man". Fortunately, no outsiders witnessed Lucifer's failure to punish Yehuda, so there was no reason to escalate the matter.

Lucifer pitied Yehuda for his loss and Simon for the way he had died. Simon was a good kid, with his whole life ahead of him. Instead, he was punished with an excruciatingly painful death due to his sexual desires, something that was predetermined by his genes and not controllable from his end. Simon's punishment was very cruel considering he was unaware that he was committing a crime. Lucifer felt guilty for disregarding Simon's homosexuality as a non-issue when Yehuda had begged for his help, but there was nothing that Lucifer could have done about it.

The only "cure" for homosexuality was to change the genetic structure of the individual. This was incredibly difficult to do even on Earth and involved cryogenically freezing the individual to prevent cell death and then individually change every cell. Thus, it took years to alter the genome of an adult individual, and all genetic modification took place on embryos when it was easier to implant desirable human traits.

Lucifer had never understood other humans' obsession with sexuality. The angels had similar genetics when it came to sexuality; they were mostly asexual with a slight inclination towards heterosexuality. For as long as Lucifer had known Abraham, Abraham had not shown much interest in sex. But considering the amount of offspring Abraham had; this was probably age-related. Being 200 years younger than Abraham, Lucifer had never seen him before he started using DNA regenerating technology.

Lucifer was bothered that none of the other angels seemed to be disturbed by the events they had seen. Lucifer did not know whether his colleagues enjoyed taking part in atrocities or whether they feared Abraham's anger. Regardless, Lucifer needed to process what he had seen, but there was no one to talk to. He felt lonely and left out, and even considered leaving Eden and returning to Earth. But what would he do there? Lucifer had never been alone or outside his group of fellow angels. The fear of leaving it all behind was stronger than the fear of what he had become. Lucifer decided to sleep for a long time. The sleep would clear his mind, and the terrors he had seen, would seem less real once he woke up.

Chapter 49: Abraham Looks Ahead.

A few weeks later, a shipment of sexual inhibition medicine arrived, and Abraham instructed an angel to inject it straight into his brain. It caused a sharp pain as the drug was not meant to be administered that way, but the brain was the only part of Abraham's body that had survived. After the initial pain, Abraham felt a profound sense of relief as he could now think clearly without distractions and sexual desires. This enabled him to pursue more constructive goals. The burning of the sodomites made Abraham realise one thing. He now admitted to how much he enjoyed causing suffering and pain to others.

Abraham had never shunned from causing others pain, but he had always justified it with the greater good. He realised that this was because of morals imposed on him by others, but now there was no reason to be dishonest anymore. He had always liked torturing people and causing them pain. Strengthening Abraham's sadistic desires was the fact that he no longer had a human body and he was more machine than man. Before his heart and gut could feel compassion for others but with only the brain left, there was nothing that kept his sadism at bay.

Abraham considered torturing Lucifer for his disobedience. Abraham was aware of Lucifer's treacherous doubts in him. Had any other of the angels dared to question him like Lucifer, that angel would have been tortured and then murdered. But Lucifer was unique, he was created unique, and in this uniqueness laid the difficulty in making him succumb to Abraham's will.

Abraham had lost Lucifer once in the past and that was the darkest day of his life. He did not want to experience this again. Instead, Abraham aimed to form Lucifer in his image, and eventually hand over power to him whenever he was ready for final death.

Abraham felt the need to kill and torture someone. Although he did not need any reason to do so, he still preferred to make up a reason. Fortunately, it was a Saturday, and it was forbidden to work on Saturdays. Although someone always did work. Scanning through the minds of the Edenites he soon found his victim; a village healer who was treating a sick child. The village healer should have known better than doing his job on a Saturday! It was time to punish him.

Unfortunately, Lucifer was sleeping. Although this was for the best, as Abraham had decided against punishing Lucifer, who would object to the task at hand. Instead, he sent the angels Nuriel, Thomas and Michael to do his deed.

Michael who was third in command after Abraham and Lucifer approached the village healer and Abraham spoke through him:

- Greetings Mesaja.

- You are committing a great sin. Do you have anything to say for yourself?

Mesaja:

- Please forgive me, Master Michael. This child is ill and may not survive another day without help.

- I have worked hard to make life better for the villagers, and I try to honour Abraham's glory through my job.

Michael:

- And yet you didn't honour the holy day for him?

- If Grandmaster Abraham intends for this child to die; that is the way things should go.

- Since the child is sick on a Saturday, it is a sign to leave the child's fate into Abraham's hands.

- In his great mercy, Abraham will grant this child the gift of life while you shall suffer and die, for your sins.

Michael took out a vial of medication and injected it into the child. It was a fast-acting cure, and within minutes the child had recovered from his ailment. Michael spoke again:

- Behold people of Eden! Honour Abraham and pray for his mercy and he might grant it to you. Dishonour his glory and you shall suffer.

- Villagers, I'll leave it to you to carry out the punishment. Drag this wretched unbeliever to the village square and stone him to death.

Michael then injected Mesaja, with a stimulant that would keep him conscious for longer and increase his sensation of pain throughout the stoning. The villagers dragged Mesaja to the village square and they stoned him to death. Michael spoke again:

- Fantastic job, Edenites. You have proven your faithfulness to Abraham by killing this wretched man. Now tear his body into pieces and send to the other villages as a warning. No one disrespects Grandmaster Abraham unpunished!

When Michael returned to the Divine Control Center, Abraham congratulated him on a job well done. Not only had he shown that no one could break the holy laws in the Abrahameon but curing the child on the spot had proven that it was beneficial for the people of Eden to put their blind faith into the hands of Abraham.

Abraham would not often intervene and save sick children, because that would take away the miracle of the act and people would start expecting him to protect them. That idea was preposterous. They existed to please him and not the other way around. Then again, a miracle every now and then gave hope, and people that had hope for a better life were less likely to rebel, than individuals who had given up on hope and were ready to die.

Satisfied with the day's events Abraham went back to his throne room in the Divine Dimension. Abraham entered the trance-like state of meditation where he spent most of his time.

Chapter 50: The Selections Continue.

A few years later, Abraham awoke Lucifer from a session of cryogenic sleep. Lucifer felt confused and reckoned that Abraham must have stopped the cryogenic tank before the date it was programmed to.

Lucifer had felt very depressed the last decade, as he had lost his faith in Abraham's vision for Eden. Since he did not know what to do, he chose to sleep for months on end and only take part in special events and public holidays. Lucifer needed to talk to someone, but there was no one to speak to. If he spoke to Abraham about his concerns, he would be punished. If he spoke to the other angels, he would be met with disinterest, and if he was talking about his ethical issues with the Edenites, Abraham would him kill for exposing their lies.

Abraham contacted Lucifer:

- Wake up, Lucifer.
- You have a work obligation today.

Lucifer:

- Apologies, Master Abraham. But I cannot remember what that would be?

Abraham:

- Bah, all that extra sleep is bad for your brain. Today is the 1st of March, the first day of spring. You know what a new season means!

Lucifer:

But I thought the December girl was the 72nd offering, and that the debt with Ibrahim Rashid was settled?

Abraham:

- You are right, she was the 72nd, and the debt is paid.

- But I realised two things:

- Firstly: how do we stop the tradition? How do we tell the people of Eden that an appreciated and well-working tradition is no longer valid?

- Secondly: There is a fortune to be made in selling unregistered, healthy young virgin brides to wealthy buyers.

Lucifer:

- But I thought you had enough money to cover the upkeep of Eden?

Abraham:

- Don't be silly, Lucifer. There is no such thing as enough money in the world.

- I did not become the wealthiest man on Earth by limiting my vision.

Lucifer:

- Apologies, Grandmaster Abraham. I will gather a crew and do your bidding.

Lucifer was disappointed, but he refrained from saying anything. He could almost feel the pain in his head. The pain that Abraham had caused him throughout the years when Lucifer had disagreed with him. Lucifer felt old and he was indeed old, although he still looked like in his prime due to the time spent in cryogenic sleep and the massive usage of DNA regeneration technology.

Meanwhile, on Eden, a girl named Susanna planned to do something that had never happened before. She planned to volunteer to be selected. Technically, Susanna who was 14 years old and had reached puberty was not eligible. To be eligible one had to be a virgin and prepubescent. But Susanna was brave, inquisitive and she wanted to get away from Eden. Susanna wanted to leave because she was betrothed to a disgusting old man. She did not care that he was rich and would be able to support her and the many children to come. To multiply wasn't her life goal, and no matter what Abraham and Lucifer said, she would pursue her own independence.

Susanna had concluded the selected girls were not killed. She had seen many executions during her 14 years on Eden, but during the selection, the angels seemed very keen to not hurt the selected girl.

For this season's selection, Abraham chose a new approach. This time, he had set up an encrypted bidding platform where an auction took place. The girl that received the highest bid would be this season's selection.

Lucifer supervised the selection. He felt lacklustre and uninspired, but as the second in command of Eden he had to take part in the ceremony. Suddenly, Susanna walked up onto the podium where the young girls were displayed.

Lucifer:

- Stop!
- Step down from the podium woman, what is the meaning of this?

Susanna:

- I volunteer to be this season's selection.

Lucifer had a quick look a Susanna. He identified her as Susanna, and a brief moment later he had her biography uploaded into his brain.
Lucifer:

- Susanna, that is NOT how the selection works. The selection is not about volunteering; it's about being selected. Besides, you are not eligible.

Susanna:

- Eligible? I am a virgin, and I am sure that you know it, Lucifer.

Susanna's response baffled Lucifer. Usually, the Edenites were very respectful to him and his fellow angels. Sometimes people were begging and pleading to him which was difficult because Lucifer could not help everyone. With Susanna, things were different, she was breaking against convention by volunteering for the selection, and her tone of voice was sarcastic and mocking of Lucifer. Lucifer replied.

- You are not eligible because you have had your first bleeding.
- Now be gone, or I'll have you flogged

Susanna:

- Oh, come on, everyone knows what the selection is for. You must be feeling lonely with no female angels up in your floating palace. I am ready for you; these other girls are not.

Lucifer blushed. Despite living for almost 100 years, he had never been with a woman and he hadn't felt the urge to. As such he was not accustomed to this kind of language, and he hadn't heard anything like it since he left Earth 50 years earlier. He shouted back:

- That's enough!
- Guards, expel this woman and have her flogged!

Through a strange twist of fate, Susanna was saved. Mahmoud Rashid, Ibrahim's grandson, watched the auction and Susanna stole his heart. as she was beautiful and had a fiery personality. He placed a large bid for Susanna to save her life and make her his. As Abraham received the bid of 50 million Terran Credits, he commanded the angels to declare Susanna as the selection of the spring season.

Michael pushed Susanna into a portable cryogenic tank and flew back with her to the Divine Control Centre where she was shipped off to Mahmoud Rashid. Lucifer was stuck on Eden. He felt dumbfounded and speechless about what had happened. Eventually, he took off and left Eden for the Divine Control Center.

As for Susanna and Mahmoud, it was love at first sight. Although for Susanna the love was more based on the gratitude that Mahmoud paid a lot of money to have her taken off Eden, so she could experience all the wonders of the modern world and get away from Abraham's tyranny.

Unfortunately, their good times did not last long as Ibrahim Rashid was furious at his grandson for spending 50 million credits on a bride without his permission. The couple had to escape to Mars to avoid Ibrahim's wrath. Unfortunately, Mahmoud was weak and timid. He struggled to live on Mars and he perished after a decade

Susanna however, adapted to the times. Susanna's wits, intelligence and bravery made her a prominent smuggler and adventurer. She raised her and Mahmoud's daughter, whom she named Keila Eisenstein.

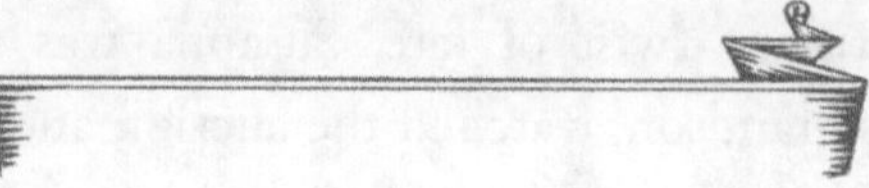

Chapter 51: Abraham Demands Sacrifices.

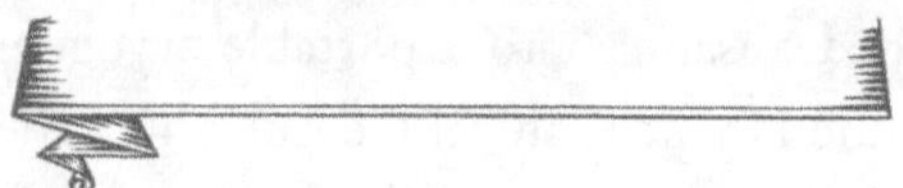

At the end of 2842, Abraham was crunching the numbers and calculating his total wealth and power. This year, the task that usually filled him with joy and bliss turned into anger and frustration. Looking back, he had been the wealthiest and most powerful, man in the solar system back in 2785 before he took upon himself to be Yahweh's successor

Back in 2785, Abraham had amassed the highest individual wealth ever known in the history of humanity. His influence had reached every nook and cranny of the solar system. His army had been the most efficient fighting force in the solar system due to their technological advantage. In 2842 his wealth was a fraction of what it had been and it totalled less than a billion Terran Credits. His reach and military might was non-existent outside of Eden. He felt like he had gone from a king to a chieftan of a small tribe living on a mostly empty and awfully expensive rock. The creation of Eden had totalled over 5 trillion Terran credits, and it was by far the costliest space colony ever built.

The reason Eden was so painfully expensive to create was because of the specifications Abraham chose for it. Eden was the most advanced space colony ever, and the first of its kind where someone could walk around with regular clothes and no technological aids whatsoever and still thrive. Another issue that drove up the cost was that all the machinery and technology that maintained Eden was hidden from the plain eye. Instead of having a visible water purification plant, Eden had an advanced chain of processing that replicated the water cycle from Earth with water evaporating and coming down as rain. The size of Eden also added to the costs. It would be much cheaper to terraform a smaller rock, but Abraham wanted to replicate Yahweh's work as closely as possible, so he picked an asteroid that replicated the size of the Holy Land. Adding to Abraham's woes, Eden did not produce anything of value, which could otherwise, had justified the cost. The Edenites were a bunch of freeloaders who did not appreciate Abraham's sacrifices for them. Abraham decided that the Edenites needed to make more sacrifices.

Abraham decided that those that benefitted the most from his rule were the ones who should make the sacrifice. This was not the angels as they had sacrificed a better life back on Earth for a life of celibacy and hardship helping him rule Eden. No, the real parasites were the high priests of each tribe! They benefitted from Abraham's reign as they were in positions of wealth and power based on his benevolence.

The population of Eden was divided into seven tribes although there was an 8th group of people that lived outside of the villages. Each of these tribes had a high priest that was appointed for life. While being appointed for life seemed helpful, it was a disadvantage as it meant an increased risk to be killed by Abraham from afar if he was dissatisfied with the high priest's performance. Once a high priest was dead the angels, would choose another villager to lead the town. Thus, the position of high priest was not hereditary although one could amass wealth for one's family that lasted after the high priest's death.

The Edenites gathered around Mount Sinai. The angels were dressed in their white ceremonial armours covered in gemstones. They were sparkling under the sun and the clear blue sky. Although people would die today, this was not a day of fear but a day to celebrate. Once they were all gathered, Lucifer spoke:

- Welcome Edenites, for our New Year's Eve celebration.

- Today we celebrate the year that has passed, and the year to come.

- But before we celebrate, I command all the high priests and their families to come up, as Grandmaster Abraham has an announcement to make.

While the high priests and their families were making their way up to the platform, the people were setting up the food and drink stations. The New Year celebration was a celebration of peace as the tribes were putting aside their differences for this celebration. The angels that supervised the celebrations made everyone think twice about causing any disturbances. Once the high priests were on the platform, they were all handed a glass of 'divine wine'. These were wines that had been bought from the finest wineries on Earth, which tasted better than the wines that the Edenites usually drank. The high priests praised the wine and wished everyone a happy new year to the sound of the cheering crowd. Suddenly, a hologram of Abraham appeared on top of the mountain.

Abraham:

- People of Eden. Happy New Year.

- I have a request for you.

- I request that your high priests make a sacrifice to honour my sacrifice.

- As you know the reason that you are living here in joy and happiness, is the sacrifice I made when I saved you from Yahweh's wrath. By protecting you, I gave up my place next to Yahweh in the spiritual afterlife.

- Instead, I am here, working tirelessly to support you by making it rain, making the air you breathe clean and making your crops grow. It is time for you to repay my sacrifice.

- High priests of Eden, you are the most fortunate of the Edenites. Today, I am giving you the opportunity to show your dedication and faith in me.

- At the altar, there is a sacrificial blade. Slit the throat of your firstborn, and you shall be closer to my glory.

Among the high priests, was Yehuda, who had lost one of his daughters to the selection and one of his sons in the purges against homosexuals. Now he was to be tested again, and this time he was supposed to be the one carrying out the horrible deed. Yehuda made a choice; he would not let another one of his children die or disappear. It was the time to sacrifice his own life and say no to Abraham.

Yehuda:

- Grandmaster Abraham. I am grateful for your sacrifices, but I cannot do it. My children are everything to me, and I cannot bear the thought of losing another one before me. Take my life instead.

Before Abraham had the time to answer, Yehuda's oldest son, Jamal, spoke:

- Father, why are you doing this? You cannot deny Grandmaster Abraham his request.

- Abraham is the one granting us life. He deserves to decide when it is our time to go. I am honoured to die on his command.

Yehuda:

- But Jamal, your children are still young, they need you!

Jamal:

- My offspring will be fine. Grandmaster Abraham will look after them.

Having said this, Jamal walked up to the sacrificial altar. Yehuda walked after him slowly and with shaky legs. Yehuda cut Jamal's throat, and as the blood was pouring out of Jamal's dying body, Yehuda collapsed and started crying. Abraham spoke:

- Jamal set us an example for today. He will be granted a place
in heaven for his will to give up his life to honour my name.

- I am asking the rest of the high priests to make the same sacrifice and do it gracefully and with joy in your hearts as thy
firstborns will be granted a secure passage to heaven if you honour me.

The other high priests followed Abraham's command, and half an
hour later the altar was covered in blood, with seven lifeless bodies next
to it. Abraham spoke again:

- Rejoice Edenites, for tonight you have seen seven brave souls
getting passage to heaven for their faith, dedication, and sacrifice.

- High priest Yehuda, you angered me by your lack of commitment, and the ungraceful way you dealt with Jamal's glorious
sacrifice.

- I expel you and your family from the village. You must live
in the wilderness near the edge of Eden without contact with
other people. This is the only way your crime and debt can be
repaid.

Yehuda, his five surviving children, and his grandchildren were gathered and led out in the desert by the angels Michael and Gabriel. They
walked for many hours until they reached the edge of Eden, to a small
cave facing the edge of space. Looking out one could only see the vast
darkness of space. Michael injected Yehuda with a shot of DNA preserv-
ing serum. He spoke to the group.

- Family of Yehuda: This will be your new home. You're all cast
out facing the abyss for the sins of your patriarch Yehuda, who
dared to question Grandmaster Abraham.

- You shall live here, working twice as hard as the rest of your kind for half of the gain.

- Yehuda you shall face the biggest curse. You shall outlive all your children. Age and regret shall torment you, but you shall not die until Abraham lets you.

After saying this, Michael and Gabriel flew back to the Divine Control Centre and left the miserable Yehuda and his family cast out into the wilderness. In an act of desperation Yehuda leapt towards the edge of Eden to jump into the abyss. This failed as he collided with the nanotechnology layer that covered Eden. Yehuda was electrocuted and knocked unconscious. Once Yehuda woke up, he accepted his fate and he led his family's colonisation of this isolated part of Eden.

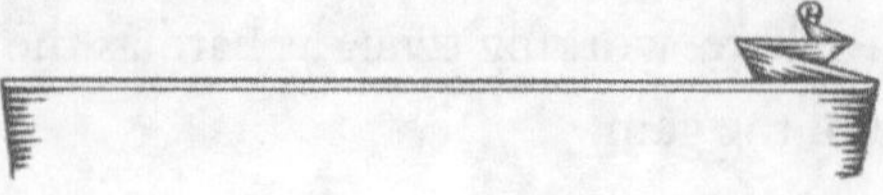

Chapter 52: Lucifer Falls from Above.

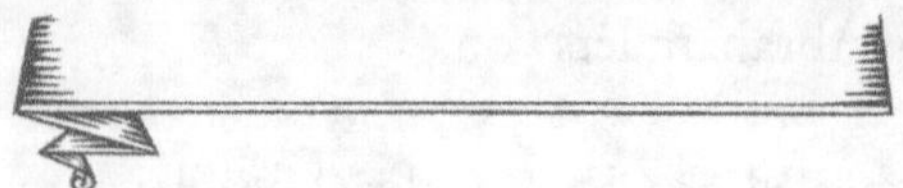

Lucifer felt demoralised and heartbroken. On Abraham's orders, he had conducted the latest atrocity against the Edenites. The victims were two young lovebirds who had gone against their families wishes and had rejected the arranged marriages their parents had organised so that they could be together.

With so many breaches against his divine law, Abraham wanted blood, and a public display. Lucifer was appointed to carry out the gruelling task. The young lovers had first had each fingernail pulled off one by one. They were then whipped with 50 lashes each. When Lucifer received the order to cut off the genitals of the victims with a rusty knife, he had enough. He pulled up his glowing plasma sword, the Dawn Bringer, and he decapitated the two lovers granting them a swift death.

Abraham was displeased but not furious with Lucifer. Abraham had opted to make this execution a display of Lucifer's power. Abraham sometimes sat back without showing himself to the Edenites and instead made it seem like the punishment was the will of a specific Angel. Lucifer was the figurehead while it was Abraham who pulled the strings speaking as a voice inside Lucifer's head. As Lucifer had not publicly disobeyed Abraham's orders, Abraham would not punish him.

Lucifer's plasma sword the, Dawn Bringer, was a modified version of the plasma knife that was standard equipment in the Terran military. It was a battery-powered device with a blade that could be superheated, and this way cut through any material with ease. A thin heat-resistant layer, that was held together by a magnetic field, covered the blade. This way the immense heat from the sword, did not spread to the surroundings but only to the parts cut, with surgical precision. While the Dawn

Bringer was an impractical weapon, it looked impressive, and it spread fear and awe among the Edenites. As the Dawn Bringer could cut through an angels' armour, it had a DNA activation technology that made Lucifer the only one who could wield it.

Lucifer decided to go back to the Divine Control Center. He would get scolded, and then he would get a few months of sleep. They were all going to sleep, as they were running low on medical supplies as well as spare parts for their angel suits. The shortage was because the infamous space pirate, Morgan Henry, had raided their latest shipment. It was not a big deal, space was vast, and the likelihood of facing space pirates was minimal.

Suddenly, Lucifer felt a collision and an electric shock. He realised that he had forgotten to open Eden's magnetic field and thus he had collided with it. The electric shock knocked him unconscious and he fell slowly to the ground.

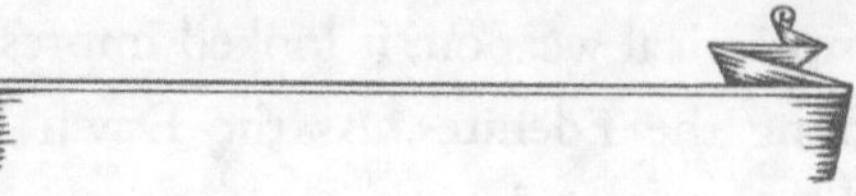

Chapter 53: Lucifer Is Confused and Injured in the Wilderness.

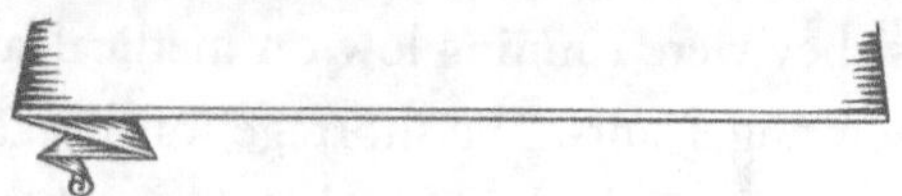

Lucifer woke up. He was in pain and unable to move. His vision was blurry, and nothing made any sense to him. His head was pounding. Was he dead? Lucifer recalled that being cryogenically frozen was just like being dead, except that he wouldn't wake up from being dead. He was present and in pain hence he could not be dead but just injured. Lucifer tried to self-diagnose, he could wiggle his fingers and toes. Thus, his spine could not be broken, so why couldn't he get up?

Lucifer realised the answer. He couldn't get up because his armour was broken. Lucifer's angel suit was controlled by a chip in his brains and felt like a second skin, despite being heavy and requiring built-in motors to move. Thus, with the armour broken but that chip still active, Lucifer had believed that he was crippled when it was only his armour that broke. Lucifer got out of his angel armour.

Lucifer stood up, and for the first time in his life, he saw the world with his own eyes. Like the other members of the angel program, Lucifer had had a multitude of nanotechnology microchips inserted into his brain. These chips changed his perception of the world through enhancing colours, giving detailed information about every object, immediate facial recognition, his current location and his current objective, etc. Without the heightened perception of the world, Lucifer felt crippled. However, he also noticed something he had never felt before, he felt free, and he wanted to explore this brave new world.

But what would he do next? He was stuck in the wilderness, injured and thirsty. His freedom would be short-lived if he was to die out here. Lucifer was quite sure that the emergency beacon on his angel suit would still be functional. He could use it to get airlifted out to safety. Lucifer decided against activating the beacon. While it would save his life, it would also lead to the loss of his newfound freedom.

Lucifer looked around. He saw a hill in the distance and he decided to make his way there. From a hilltop, he would be able to scout the countryside and find a suitable place to find food and shelter. Securing a water supply was paramount, as he would not last long without it. He left his broken angel suit and most of his weapons. The weapons were too heavy and they had limited usefulness. Lucifer hoped that any human or animal he met had friendly intentions. It was pointless to resist if the Edenites were hostile towards him. Lucifer would rather die than take any more innocent lives. Lucifer opted to bring The Dawn Bringer sword, so that he could prove his identity.

Lucifer reached the hilltop and looked around for settlements and other points of interest. Lucifer felt that the angel chips in his brain was activated. Lucifer expected that Abraham had learned of his accident and was going to send help but instead something unexpected happened. Lucifer started seeing the world through Abraham's eyes. Lucifer understood that he was not meant to look at this, but he could not help himself. He needed to know about what was in Abraham's mind. He needed to see the truth to make sense of things.

What Lucifer saw shocked him. Things were not the way that Abraham had told him. Abraham had told Lucifer that Yahweh had met Abraham when Yahweh was on his deathbed. Yahweh had appointed Abraham to be his successor and create a new promised land called Eden. Lucifer had believed in this, and it had kept him going for all these years despite feeling that Abraham's action was wrong and evil.

Lucifer saw the truth. Yahweh was one out of many extra-terrestrials that had used superior technology to manipulate humans into believing he was a god. He had done so, to make them fight his wars. Yahweh was never interested in humanity's happiness; he had only aimed to use and exploit them. Lucifer realised that Abraham had done the same thing, and that he was an accomplice in Abraham's atrocities. Lucifer felt a sickened realising what he had done, but the worst part was when he had a glimpse into Abraham's soul. There was nothing but anger, contempt and insatiable lust for power and control. Abraham did not keep the people Eden alive because he loved them but only because he needed them to fulfil his desire for power. Injured from the electric shock and the fall Lucifer passed out again.

Chapter 54: A Wounded Stranger in the Wilderness.

The siblings Sara and John were foraging in the wilderness when they came across the injured Lucifer. They did not recognise him. He was wearing a blue tracksuit covered in blood and he did not look like the archangel without his angel armour. They were scared and did not know what to do. The Abrahameon did not mention what to do when one came across an injured stranger in the desert. Regardless of what they did, their tyrannical Grandmaster Abraham, could find a reason to punish them.

They had experienced this irrational vengefulness when their uncle Simon was tortured and killed because he was a homosexual. Back then, homosexuality was not a sin, but Abraham had insisted that Simon should have understood that it was a sinful act. The reason that they lived in isolation at the fringe of Eden was that their grandfather, Yehuda, had shown reluctance to sacrifice their other uncle Jamal. Eventually, Sara decided that they should try to save the stranger. She told her brother to go home and get some help.

Sara had a closer look at the wounded stranger. He looked familiar, like one of the angels. She could not tell for sure since she rarely saw the angels. The wounded man was handsome, way better looking than any of the men in her household. She felt a bit of shame, as lust was a sin and sin had destroyed humanity's homeworld and condemned the few survivors to Eden. Copulation was essential for the survival of the species, but it should only happen within the wedlock, and she shouldn't yearn for it. The Abrahameon was very particular of this. The fact that it was forbidden to crave sex, made Sara want it more. She went down on her knees and she started dressing Lucifer's wounds. Sara got startled when Lucifer opened his eyes.

Lucifer was confused when he woke up. He couldn't remember where he was or how he had got there. He could not check his vitals, as all the chips in his brain were broken. He looked to his side, and he saw a beautiful woman sitting next to him. Dead or not dead, he was not in hell. Lucifer spoke:

- Am I dead? Are you an angel?

Sara:

- Don't be silly; all the angels on Eden are men.
- You look familiar, are you an angel.

Lucifer:

- I don't know; I used to be.

Sara:

- What happened?

Lucifer:

- I fell.

Sara:

- I understand

Neither of them said anything else. There was no need to say anything. They were enchanted by each other. For Lucifer, it was the first time that he saw the world with his own eyes, and Sara was the most beautiful woman he had ever seen.

Because of his implants, Lucifer had never appreciated beautiful women and never had any interest in sex. He could feel his desire towards

Sara, but he had no energy to pursue it, so they both sat there in silence enchanted by each other. Eventually, John came back with his horse cart and brought the wounded Lucifer back to his house where Sara nursed him back to health. When Lucifer recovered, he and Sara had each other, over and over, their desire for each other was overwhelming.

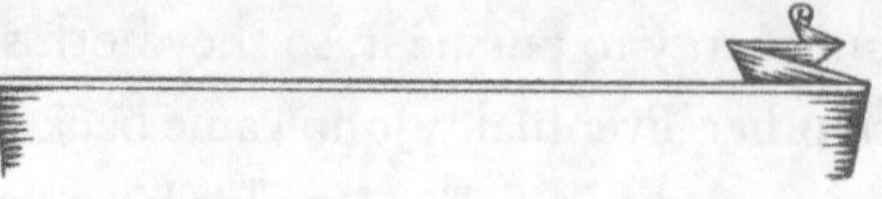

Chapter 55: Yehuda's Dilemma.

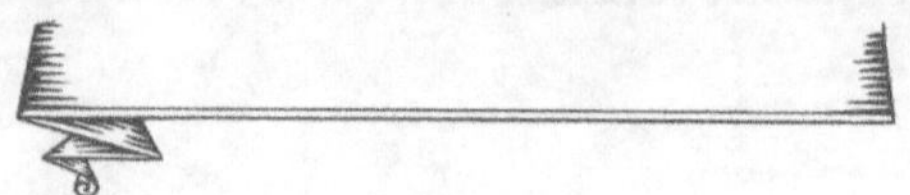

Due to the DNA Regeneration technology that he was exposed to a decade earlier Yehuda had reached the age of 80, and he had witnessed the death of all his children. Seeing the death of all his children had not left him lonely and miserable as he had a dozen grandchildren ranging in age between 20-40 years old, to look after.

Lucifer had not waited long before fornicating with Yehuda's granddaughter, Sara. After that, he had asked Yehuda for Sara's hand in marriage. Since they had already fornicated, it was a mortal sin for them not to get married. But Yehuda did not know why Lucifer fell and what would happen if the former angel stayed with his family. He decided to discuss the matter with Lucifer.

Yehuda:

- Lucifer, why are you here, why did you fall from heaven?

Lucifer:

- Call me Terrence. Lucifer is my employee name, and I am no longer working for Abraham Goldstein.

Yehuda:

- Okay Terrence. Why did you fall from heaven?

Lucifer

- I forgot to deactivate the electromagnetic field surrounding Eden and I got electrocuted. The collision broke my equipment, I passed out, and I crashed onto the surface of Eden.

Yehuda:

- Nothing of this makes any sense. You look like Lucifer, but you don't act like Lucifer. If it weren't for your eyes, I would take you for an imposter.

Lucifer had luminescent blue eyes. Having glowing eyes was a fashion trend for newborn babies on Earth the previous century. Mixing the human eye colour DNA with DNA from animals with luminous eyes created glowing eyes in humans. It did not noticeably change an individual's vision, and Lucifer's enhanced eyesight had been dependent on implanted microchips that allowed him to see the ultraviolet and the infrared part of the spectrum.

Lucifer decided to come clean and expose the truth to Yehuda. There was no reason to lie, and Lucifer was a doomed man regardless of what he did. Lucifer knew that Abraham would not be merciful to him this time. It didn't matter. Lucifer accepted his fate, and his only regret was that he had helped Abraham's atrocities.

Although, Lucifer had questioned Abraham at times, he had never tried to stop him. Instead, he had kept his doubts to himself and carried out his duties. The accident had changed everything. When his bionic microchips broke, Lucifer experienced what it felt like to be human for the first time; to love and be loved.

Yehuda:

- So, you are saying that Earth is still around? That we are living in the future and that Eden is a deception by an evil madman?

Lucifer:

- You could sum it up like that.

Yehuda:

- It sounds crazy, but I believe you, Lucifer.
- So, how do we stop Abraham's tyranny and win our freedom?

Lucifer:

- We cannot stop Abraham, that's impossible.

Yehuda:

- If Abraham and the angels are humans, then they can be stopped.

Lucifer:

- Yehuda, you don't understand. Abraham can read your mind and kill you at any time via the microchip in your brain. If he couldn't do that, he could destroy all life on Eden by turning off the electromagnetic field that keeps the atmosphere in place. Resistance to him is futile.

Yehuda:

- He can kill me if he wishes. I would welcome my death. Abraham killed several of my children, and then he extended my life so that I would see my other children die of natural causes. I am ready to die for a worthy cause.

Lucifer:

- Well, I am over a century old, so I guess I am ready to go as well.
- What do you suggest?

Yehuda:

- You need to make me untraceable to Abraham and the other angels. These microchips that you are talking about; can I remove them?

Lucifer:

- I always thought they were irremovable. But the accident proved that they can be deactivated through using the electromagnetic field surrounding Eden.

Yehuda:

- Excellent. I know what you are talking about. I tried to jump off the edge of Eden when Abraham condemned me. I experienced excruciating pain and I woke up feeling burnt.

Lucifer:

- Yes, you were lucky to survive.

Yehuda:

- A blessing and a curse! Anyways, can you help this old man win his freedom?

Lucifer:

- I believe that I can Yehuda. Keep in mind, if I am wrong, you'll die.

Yehuda:

- That's a risk that I am willing to take. Let's go.

Lucifer and Yehuda walked to where Lucifer had left his broken angel suit. Once Lucifer had found the broken angel armour, he took the parts needed to deactivate Yehuda's chip. Lucifer cut off some electrical cables, and he also took one of the gloves to insulate. Unwittingly, while helping Lucifer to gather the parts, Yehuda activated the silent emergency switch on Lucifer's armour alerting Abraham that Lucifer was in danger.

Lucifer and Yehuda headed towards the edge of Eden. Once they reached the edge, Lucifer connected one part of the electrical cord to Yehuda's ear. This was close to where Yehuda's human chip was attached to his brain stem. Lucifer put on the insulating glove and led the cable to the electromagnetic field covering Eden. Yehuda emitted a sharp scream before passing out. Lucifer hesitated for a second. He did not know if he had killed Yehuda or if everything was going according to plan.

Lucifer pulled out the Dawn Bringer, cut an opening in Yehuda's skull, and removed the chip. Lucifer felt observed and he turned around. He saw a group of angels lead by Michael.

Michael:

- What are you doing, Lucifer?

- You destroyed your suit; you weren't waiting for emergency pick up, and instead you killed this old man here at the edge of Eden. Explain yourself.

Lucifer felt paralysed and was out of words. If they knew what he had done he would face the death penalty for treason. But they did not know. Lucifer's microchips were fried, and Yehuda was most likely dead and would not expose him.

Michael:

- Answer me, Lucifer!

Lucifer decided to fake amnesia and replied:

- Lucifer who is that? I am Terrence Lowenstein. I am a Terran Citizen and senior security operative for House Goldstein. Who are you?

Michael signalled Nuriel, who shot Lucifer with a tranquiliser dart. They put Lucifer put in a life support unit, and they travelled back to the Divine Control Center.

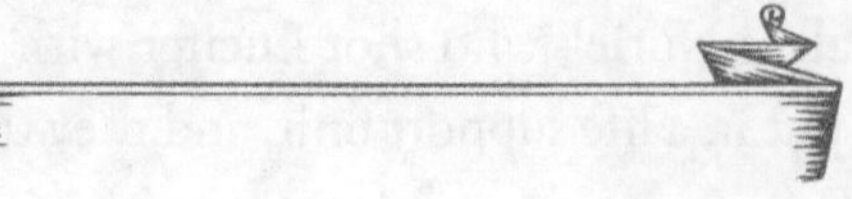

Chapter 56: Abraham Doubts Lucifer and Decides His Fate.

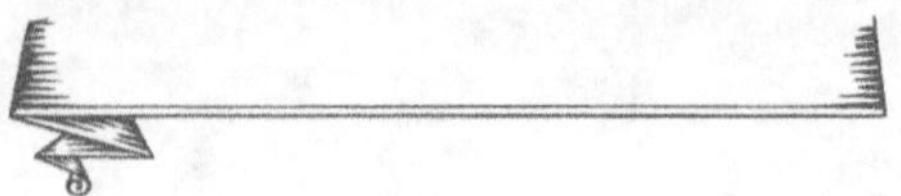

Abraham observed Lucifer who lay unconscious on an operation table.

Abraham wondered what Lucifer had been up to for the last two weeks. He damned himself for not noticing that Lucifer was missing. The mistake was an unfortunate consequence of the way they were running Eden. The angels were cryogenically frozen for extended periods, to expand their lifespans. When Lucifer disappeared, he was the only angel on active duty, and no one had noticed that he was gone. Abraham should have seen it, but he was meditating in the Divine Dimension and had not conveyed Lucifer any thoughts. Abraham hadn't given Lucifer any attention as Lucifer's angel chip malfunctioned and showed that it was active when it was broken.

So, how had this happened? Had Lucifer destroyed his angel suit and chip or was it an accident? Abraham wanted to believe that it was an accident, but the facts did not add up. If it was an accident, Lucifer would have activated the emergency beacon straight away. But if Lucifer had betrayed him, why had he destroyed his uniform and stayed on Eden, when it made more sense trying to kill Abraham.

Michael claimed that Lucifer had acted strange when the angels found him. For unclear reasons, Lucifer had killed Yehuda at the edge of Eden. Lucifer had acted as if he had severe amnesia. He had stated his Terran name and title despite not using either for the last 60 years. It was unlikely that Lucifer had amnesia that made him forget the previous 60 years of his life, but Abraham could not rule out the possibility. It was possible, that Lucifer, being controlled via the Angel chip, had not accumulated any biological memories. This would lead to complete amnesia if the angel chip broke.

Abraham decided to figure out what Lucifer did on Eden in the weeks between the destruction of his angel suit, and the activation of the emergency beacon. Lucifer must have gotten outside help; otherwise, he would have died from starvation or dehydration. This was easy to investigate, as there was only the Yehuda family in the vicinity of the crash site.

A few minutes later, Abraham was furious. Lucifer had misbehaved and spent the last weeks copulating and getting emotionally attached to a young woman called Sara. Sexual activity outside of marriage was forbidden and Lucifer could not get married, as Abraham would never allow it. The Angels existed to serve Abraham and they should keep away from other distractions. A worse crime than the premarital coitus was that Lucifer had proven to be just a man. The Yehuda family had seen him without his technology, and they would conclude that the other angels were also ordinary men with technology. If this rumour were to spread, Abraham's control over Eden would fail, as its inhabitants would realise that he was their captor and not their god. The Edenites couldn't find out the truth, and Abraham had to eliminate the Yehuda family.

Abraham needed to kill Lucifer, but he hesitated. Lucifer was unique compared to the other angels. The other angels had their human DNA created from scratch with specific abilities chosen for them and designed for specific tasks. They had then been put in a synthetic womb and created with no human involvement attached. This was a highly illegal practice as the creations were beings without souls and free will. Combined with specific implants that enhanced their abilities and controlled their behaviour Abraham had created a proficient group of operatives that had no other desires in life than to serve Abraham. The other angels, were just efficient machines to Abraham and if one malfunctioned, he would dispose of that angel.

Lucifer was different. His DNA wasn't created from scratch; instead, Abraham had based Lucifer on someone that Abraham held very dear. Furthermore, he was born by a surrogate mother instead of a synthetic womb, so he had a soul and a free will. Abraham had been able to control most of Lucifer's mind with the angel chip, but in the end, he still had an underlying personality. Lucifer's character was an essential aspect, as Abraham sought Lucifer's approval, whom he had created to be his heir.

Abraham decided to give Lucifer one more chance to live and be his heir. To get this opportunity, Lucifer would have to make a sacrifice. He would have to kill Sara, and her family to show his dedication to Abraham. If Lucifer passed this trial, he would regain his place. If he failed, he would die, and he would have given up his life for nothing. Abraham decided to cryogenically freeze Lucifer and then fix him once a shipment with all his implants arrived. Lucifer would have the choice to obey or die, but Abraham wanted to make sure that Lucifer chose to follow. To replace Lucifer's broken implants and microchips was the best way to achieve this.

Having decided this, Abraham went to the Divine Dimension to meditate.

Chapter 57: Yehuda Survives and Desires Revenge.

Yehuda woke up a couple of hours later. It was a painful and strange awakening for Yehuda. He could no longer feel Abraham's presence and instead he was looking out in the blackness of space with no gods to worship. He recognised this feeling from his youth when he visited many asteroids like Eden. Yehuda got up on his feet. He saw the golden microchip, soaked in blood, that Lucifer had extracted from his head. He knew what it was; he had seen similar microchips in his past.

Yehuda saw details in the landscape that he had never noticed before. It was technology instead of magic, but he was still fascinated by it. He could see the exhaust pipes extracting fresh oxygen from the core of Eden. Yehuda could see how six out of Eden's seven suns were glimmering, indicating that they were satellites reflecting the sun's light while the seventh celestial object that wasn't blinking was the actual sun. From the size of the sun, he deduced that he was somewhere in the Asteroid belt 50 % further away from the sun than his home planet Mars.

While Yehuda was impressed by his sudden mental clarity, he had a more pressing matter at hand. He was injured, and his mind was too muddled to find the way home in this featureless landscape. Fortunately, his grandchildren Sara and John had set out to look for him, and with the aid of the family dog, they found him.

Sara:

- Grandfather! I heard that you and Lucifer set out to discuss something.
- You are bleeding, what happened?

Yehuda:

- Lucifer did this to me.
- He left me for dead and took off

Sara:

- That's impossible! He loved me. He was going to ask you for permission to marry me.

Yehuda:

- He was a fallen angel. The worst of sinners condemned by his Master.

Sara:

- That means nothing. Abraham condemned us and we are still good people

- Lucifer was a tormented soul, plagued by the pain he had caused others. That's why he wanted to change. That was why he loved me.

Yehuda:

- That's enough, woman! Show some respect!
- Lucifer is gone, and he won't be back
- John, I command you to take me home and treat my wounds.

Hearing this, John rushed up to Yehuda, bandaged him, and carried the old man back to safety, while Sara stayed behind wailing out her misery.

A few days later, Yehuda had recovered, and he made up his mind. He would not tell his grandchildren the truth about Eden. They were born on Eden, and for them, it was the only truth. Besides he would put them in grave danger if he told them the truth. The villain posing as

Grandmaster Abraham, the almighty god of Eden, could still read their minds through the microchips in their heads. If Yehuda told them the truth, he would put them in danger. Yehuda could not remove the chip from his grandchildren's heads, as he lacked the skill and know-how to carry out the operation. Yehuda bit his lip and swore to himself: *"He would make Abraham pay."*

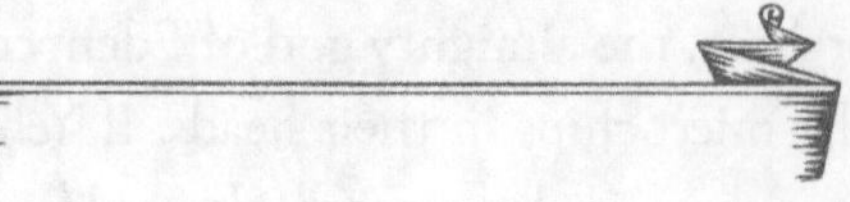

Chapter 58: Yehuda Finds Out That Sara is Pregnant.

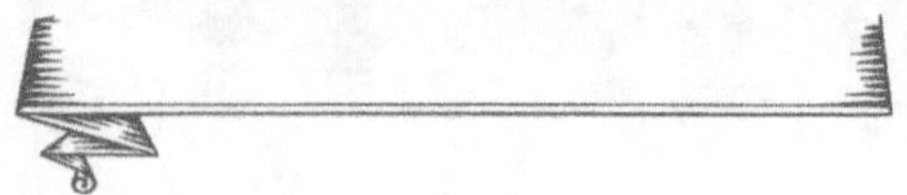

Three months later, Yehuda discovered that Sara was pregnant. His earlier religious self would have condemned this, but having regained most of his memories, he no longer had any strong opinions about extramarital conceptions.

Yehuda no longer feared the "god" Abraham although he still feared the villain Abraham. Yehuda wondered when Abraham's "angels" would show up to punish his family for siding with a fallen angel.

Yehuda remembered his life before Eden. Yehuda's family were a prominent family living in relative wealth until a Martian warlord invaded his city. Rather than staying under the new ruler's tyranny, Yehuda's family had fled to Earth. They knew that Martians were not allowed on Earth. However, vast areas of Earth consisted of depopulated national parks where a family could survive undetected.

Terran border patrols captured Yehuda's family, and they were locked up in the gruesome Kaguya Detention Centre on the Moon. They had volunteered to join the Eden expedition, but for some reason, Yehuda was paired up with a new woman when he woke up on Eden. Since they had lost their memories neither of them was able to see through the deception. Yehuda was certain that he never had seen the rest of his original family on Eden and he concluded that Abraham must have killed them. Yehuda realised that Grand Master Abraham was Abraham Goldstein, as House Goldstein had funded the Eden Project.

Yehuda wanted to expose Abraham, but he didn't know how. If he told people the truth, they wouldn't believe him, and Abraham would come after him.

Yehuda needed a long-term plan to overthrow Abraham, and he found a viable solution. Under the surface of Eden, there were widespread maintenance tunnels. These tunnels were ideal for growing mushrooms. If Yehuda could farm enough mushrooms, he could feed the people that he freed from Abraham while being undetectable from orbit. It was a long shot, but it was his best option to start with. Besides, Yehuda had time. The life-extending vaccine that the angels had given him as a punishment, would turn against them. Once he could farm enough mushrooms, he would free his family to start the rebellion. It would be a slow-moving underground movement, but it would work, and Abraham would face justice for his crimes.

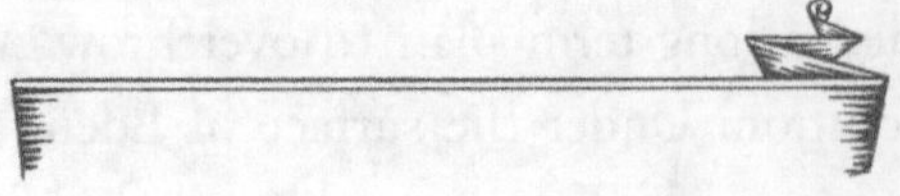

Chapter 59: A child is born.

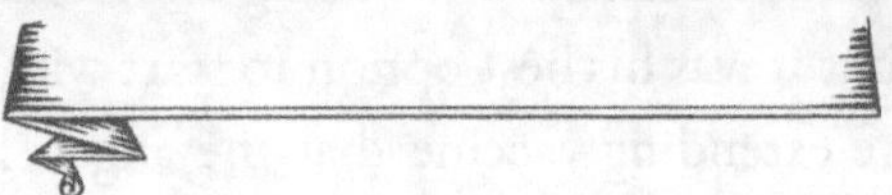

Today a child was born in the Terran star system. This is a unique child with psionic capabilities that only happens once in every 20 billion individuals. Since the last person who possessed these skills did not serve us as we hoped, this child must be guided and supervised to make her stay on the path. Since humanity now has the technology needed for our return, this individual can be our saviour.

Unknown source on the 22nd of March 2850 A.D

Chapter 60: Lucifer Faces an Ultimatum.

Lucifer woke up in the medical ward and he felt strange. All his auxiliary system was running, and his vision was once again amplified and highlighting detailed information about the surroundings. Worse yet, Abraham had fixed his angel chip and could read his thoughts again. Lucifer wondered if his memories from Eden was just a dream.

Lucifer didn't understand why Abraham hadn't wiped his memories. If Abraham did not intend to kill him for treason, why did he remember about his actions? Lucifer noticed that he was strapped to a bed. Abraham walked in followed by a group of angels.

Abraham walked up to Lucifer and studied him. After a moment of silence, he spoke:

- Lucifer, do you know why you are here? Do you remember what sins you committed?

Lucifer nodded but said nothing.
Abraham spoke again:

- You are here because you betrayed me. Your lists of sins are endless and yet you are still alive.

- You see, I am a benevolent leader.

- You have freedom as long as you follow my rules. Yet, you cannot live up to my standards.

Lucifer:

- Freedom? I have been stuck on this rock for 60 years doing your will. I have put innocents through trials and torment

Abraham:

- Yet you never left. I never said that you could not abandon my service. You are just my employee.

Lucifer:

- I did not know what I would do with my life.

Abraham:

- You see, that is your problem. You have freedom to do things, and yet you don't. When you chose to do something, you want the wrong thing.

- When you chose to copulate with Sara, you didn't think. By following your basic instinct to procreate you made her a sinner and you signed her death warrant.

Lucifer:

- I don't know what happened. I couldn't resist the urge. I love her.

Abraham:

- If you had loved her, you would have watched over her as an angel. She would have lived a good life. Instead, she will die, because of you.

Lucifer:

- No, it is your laws that condemn and kill people. I believe in love and freedom.

Abraham:

- Funny that you say that.

- Martians are free. They are impulse-driven, they copulate based on desire instead of logic, and they don't control their population growth. Consequently, Mars is a wasteland with 4 billion individuals fighting for limited resources due to inability to put society ahead of individual needs.

- On Earth only the wealthy or people with exceptional genes are allowed to procreate. As a result, Earth has a sustainable population and a healthy thriving society.

Lucifer:

- On Earth, you have a plutocracy that is bleeding the solar system dry.

Abraham:

- Yet every obedient Terran citizen enjoys a wealthy and safe life. Living this way is worth more than the notion of "freedom."

- The Edenites are lucky. I rescued them from a terrible detention centre and I put them on the most advanced terraformed asteroid ever built.

- Eden is disease free, and if they work hard and follow the rules, they will live good lives.

Lucifer:

- You call public executions, floggings and torture a good life with benevolent leadership? You are insane!

Abraham struck Lucifer with a psionic blast. Lucifer was writhing in pain and almost passed out before Abraham released the pressure.
Abraham:

- Silence you fool. I am doing it for the people. I could kill any undesirables through the divine technology chip.

- Yet, I don't. Instead, I make a public example of the worst sinners to teach the others the proper way to live. I am showing them the way to a long happy life instead of the misery that comes from following primitive impulses.

Lucifer looked at Abraham in disgust and said nothing. It surprised Lucifer that Abraham was so outspoken about his villainy in front of the other angels.
Abraham spoke again

- The other angels disapprove of the mercy that I am showing you.

- But I love you like a son and it is difficult for me to give you the punishment that you deserve.

- But you need to feel the pain that your actions have caused me.

- Your whore, Sara, gave birth today. She and the child are a product of sin, and they must be purged. If you purge them, I will forgive your sins, and you'll retake your rightful place. If you refuse, you'll die.

Lucifer:

- But she is innocent, you monster!

Abraham:

- No, she is not. She knew that fornicating with you was a sin and she still did it. She defied my will multiple times. She gave in to her primitive impulses instead of trusting my divine plan. Her life is lost. Your life is your choice.

Lucifer was shaking with anger and he didn't know what to do. Abraham had shown his true self, and Lucifer's regretted helping this evil for so many years. He wanted to tell Abraham to go fuck himself, but that would not save Sara. Lucifer did not care about his own life, but he had to save Sara and his child. Eventually, Lucifer spoke:

- Master Abraham, you are right. Forgive me for doubting your divine will and wisdom. I will carry out the task to redeem myself.

Abraham:

- Very well.

- I will leave you so that you can prepare. Do not even think about betraying me.

As Abraham and the angels left the room, Michael spoke to Abraham:

- Grandmaster Abraham, I don't like this. He will betray us again.

Abraham:

- Perhaps. But I have reasons for giving Lucifer a final chance to redeem himself.

- Just trust in my judgment and be loyal, Michael.

Michael:

- Understood, Grandmaster!

Abraham:

- Go to Eden and be within striking distance from Lucifer. Smite him if he betrays us.

Chapter 61: Lucifer Rebels.

Yehuda saw Lucifer approaching, and he felt that his greatest fear was about to happen. Yehuda had been surprised by the lack of intervention from Abraham and he had hoped that his family's aid towards Lucifer had gone unnoticed.

When Yehuda found out that Sara was pregnant, he concluded that Abraham would wait until the child was born terrorise the family by killing the child. Lucifer's return confirmed this suspicion. Yehuda didn't waste any time. He ran into the bedchamber where Sara was resting. She had given birth to non-identical twins, a boy and a girl. The girl looked like her mother and most Edenites with brown eyes, dark hair, and olive skin. The boy looked like Lucifer with his straight blonde hair and his dad's most prominent feature, the blue luminescent eyes.

That Sara had given birth to twins was a blessing and a curse. The blessing was that Yehuda could take one of the children away without Abraham noticing. The sad part was that the one he left behind would probably be killed. Yehuda chose to take the boy. The son of Lucifer could be a crucial ingredient in a future rebellion and his resemblance to Lucifer was so apparent so people wouldn't disregard this claim. Yehuda grabbed the baby boy and ran to the ventilation tunnels where he was cultivating mushrooms.

Lucifer stormed into the room where Sara was resting. He shouted to wake her up

- Sara, we need to go, there is not much time.

Sara was confused to see Lucifer after such a long time. His tense voice made it clear that this was not a social visit.

Sara:

- What's happening Terrence? Where have you been? You left without a word.

Lucifer:

- Sara, you are in danger. Abraham wants me to kill you.
- I am here to save you, and I need to get you to safety.

Sara:

- But what did I do wrong?

Lucifer:

- You did not do anything wrong, Sara.
- However, we both sinned when we had sex before marriage.
- Let's grab the child and run away.

Sara:

- Children, there is a boy and a girl.

Lucifer:

- No, there is only one. Hurry up! Follow me!

Lucifer grabbed the baby girl and Sara ran after him. They ran towards the force field at the edge of Eden. They reached the place where Lucifer had freed Yehuda, nine months earlier. The electrical cable that Lucifer had used to release Yehuda was still there. Lucifer turned to Sara and spoke.

- Sara, do you trust me?

Sara:

- What is happening? Why are we at the edge of the world?

Lucifer:

- This will hurt a lot, but after that, you'll be free. And I can bring you to safety.

- Are you ready?

Sara:

- Yes, Terrence.
- ... I love you.

Lucifer did not answer. Instead, he electrocuted Sara to deactivate the chip. He used a scalpel sized plasma knife to make a cut in Sara skull and take out the microchip. Lucifer then sealed her wound and gave her a shot of a fast-acting stimulant to bring her back to consciousness. He looked around and realised that he was surrounded and frozen in place. A group of angels led by Michael and Gabriel approached him.
Michael:

- Lucifer, you traitor!

- Your betrayal does not stop at fucking these people. You are even stealing them from their master.

Lucifer:

- I am setting them free. She is innocent!
- Kill me if you must.

Michael:

- Yes, you'll die. But so must your whore.
- You could have given her a swift death and redeemed your-self.

- Instead, you chose to cause her a painful death and doomed
yourself
- I'll make you watch her die.

Gabriel grabbed Sara while Michael pulled up a rusty knife and cut
off pieces from Sara's body. Her tormented screams built up agony and
wrath within Lucifer who was stuck in place. Lucifer was unable to move
as Abraham controlled him like a puppet.

Lucifer closed his eyes. He could feel it. It grew stronger and stronger
and he could see it. He could sense the signal that Abraham used to keep
him in place. He mustered his mental strength and reversed the signal.
Then he knocked Abraham unconscious with a psionic blast. Lucifer was
free to move. He moved quickly, and stabbed Michael with his plasma
knife. He then shoved Gabriel to free Sara. Lucifer did not get far. Weakened by the mental battle with Abraham, he had no chance to avoid the
rain of bullets fired by the angels. Multiple rounds hit Lucifer and Sara;
Sara died on the spot while Lucifer was crippled and mortally wounded. With his dying breaths, Lucifer crawled to Michael and savaged his
body with the plasma knife to prevent resurrection. Having done this, he
turned around, looked at the sky and took his last breath.

Gabriel got up and he witnessed the carnage. He was now the highest
ranked angel. He had not imagined that the day would end like this.
Abraham had given Lucifer an undeserved chance to redeem himself by
killing the vile temptress. Instead, the witch had cast a spell on Lucifer
turning him against his brothers.

Gabriel did not understand why so many humans were obsessed with
the sin of the flesh and he had never imagined that Lucifer would fall for
it. Gabriel contacted Abraham who had regained consciousness from the
psionic blast.

Gabriel:

- Lucifer killed Michael. We had to kill Lucifer as a response.
Lucifer's vile temptress is also dead.

Abraham:

- What about the baby girl?

Gabriel looked around and he found the baby girl wrapped in a blanket clutched to her dead mother's chest. Miraculously, the baby was unharmed.

Gabriel:

- The baby is unharmed.

Abraham:

- Excellent. Bring the baby and the bodies of Lucifer and Michael back to me. Leave the corpse of the woman; she can rot there as a warning.

Gabriel:

- Affirmative.
- Master Abraham. How could Lucifer move? I thought you restrained him?

Abraham:

- I... I don't know.

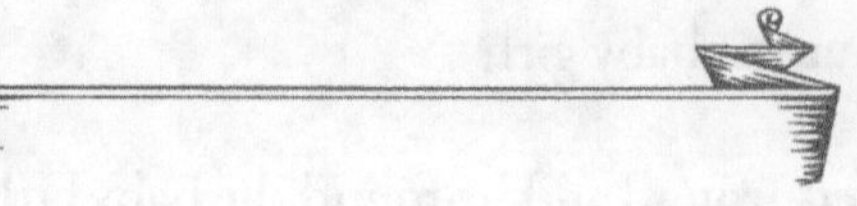

Chapter 62: Abraham's Woes Before Lucifer's Execution.

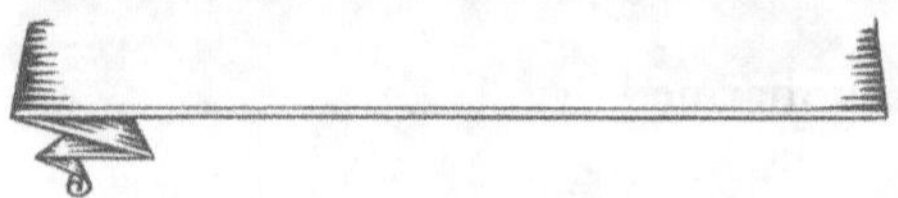

Abraham felt grief. He had offered to pardon Lucifer, and Lucifer had met his leniency with disloyalty. Abraham could not give Lucifer another chance after this, and he regretted his course of action. If he could go back in time, he would have memory-wiped Lucifer, and everything would be okay.

But erasing Lucifer's memory was never an option for Abraham. He wanted Lucifer to obey him by his own free will. Abraham looked at Lucifer's dead body. He recalled the fate of his firstborn son, Terrence Goldstein, who had died 200 years earlier.

Abraham and Terrence had been on a business meeting in Sydney. Back then they were just a regular sized company and not the wealthiest and most powerful faction on the planet. As they left the office, assassins drove past them and shot at them from a passing car. Abraham pulled Terrence in front of him, and used him as a human shield. When the assailants drove off, Terrence was dead and beyond resurrection. Abraham's spirit had died on that fateful day. Filled with remorse and anger, he could no longer relate to feelings like joy and love. Instead, he became very cynical widening the gap to his wife and his children. With his increased cynicism he could focus on his new goal, to maximise his wealth and power.

Lucifer was different from the other angels as he was a modified clone of Terrence Goldstein. Abraham had never told him the truth. He had told Lucifer that he was an orphan who was admitted to the ANGEL program as he had extraordinary genes. Abraham had hidden Lucifer's real identity to protect him from other relatives within House

Goldstein and to give him a better upbringing. Abraham knew that growing up in excessive wealth corrupted individuals and Abraham wanted Terrence to be the best he could be.

Despite Lucifer being his secret son, Abraham could not save his life anymore. He had stepped over a line when he killed Michael to save Sara. Abraham knew that discontentment among the angels, would spread if he spared Lucifer. The angels were furious over the death of Michael who had been their de-facto leader as Lucifer was too unlike the other angels to lead them.

Abraham studied Lucifer's and Michael's dead bodies. It was still possible to resurrect Lucifer, while Michael was beyond repair. With the available technology, it was usually possible to resurrect someone unless the brain was destroyed. Most body parts could be grown from stem cells, but a destroyed brain could not be regrown from scratch. This was because all the information in the brain would be lost, and a stem-cell grown brain, would be as developed as the brain of a newborn baby.

Abraham made his choice. The angels wanted for blood, and they should have it. It would take a couple of weeks to regrow Lucifer's damaged body parts and resurrect him. Abraham told Gabriel, who was the new archangel, what do.

Abraham thought about Lucifer's baby daughter, who was Abraham's granddaughter. She looked so small and gentle where she lay, and Abraham gave her the name Adina. Adina was the best of two worlds. Genetically she was a mix of the perfect genetics created with Terran technology and the natural selection of the Edenites.

Abraham wanted to see his granddaughter growing up, so he inserted an angel chip into Adina's brain so that he would get a stronger connection with her. He searched for suitable foster parents and Abraham discovered that High Priest Markus' wife had recently given birth and could breastfeed Adina as well. He instructed Gabriel to present Adina to Markus and make sure that he took proper care of the child.

After this, Abraham transported his mind to the Divine Dimension and entered a deep meditative trance. Lucifer's execution would be a gruesome affair, and Abraham wanted nothing to do with it!

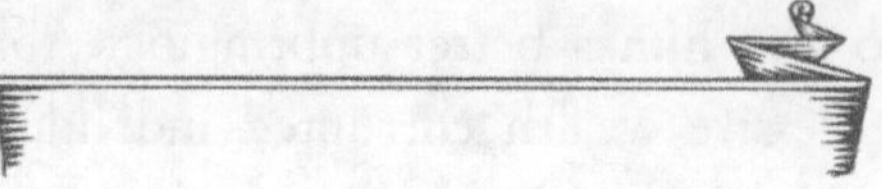

Chapter 63: Lucifer's Execution.

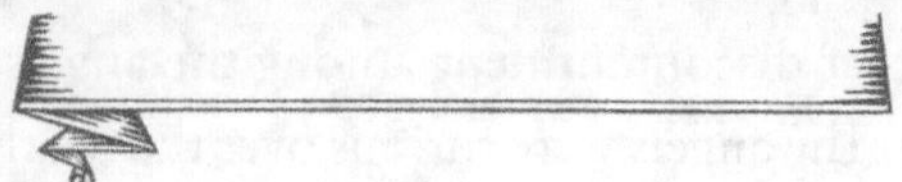

A few weeks later, Gabriel resurrected Lucifer for the execution. Much to Gabriel's dismay, Abraham was in deep meditation and ignored him, so the angels had to execute Lucifer without Abraham's supervision. Gabriel ordered the Edenites to gather at Mount Sinai for an important message. The angels dressed up in their white angel armour to symbolise that they came to enlighten the people and bring peace and wisdom. Lucifer was brought down in chains.

The crowd gathered in anticipation. Usually, important gatherings started with Abraham giving a speech. But today his absence was notable, with the crowds murmuring and Gabriel felt a bit reluctant. Eventually, he spoke:

- People of Eden

- We are here today to prove that no one stands above the law, not even the former Archangel Lucifer.

Lucifer screamed out in his defence, but his voice was not amplified, so the people couldn't hear him. Gabriel ended Lucifer's slur with a punch to the face that knocked him to the ground.
Gabriel:

- Like I said, not even Lucifer stands above the law.

- Three weeks ago, he was caught fornicating with an Edenite woman and he tried to persuade her to turn against Grandmaster Abraham.

- When the angel Michael sought to bring Lucifer back to heaven, Lucifer stabbed him in the head with a magical knife strong enough to kill an angel.

- For these great crimes, Grandmaster Abraham stripped Lucifer of his immortality. Today, we will witness Lucifer purged from sin, so his dark soul can reach the afterlife.

- Let the proceedings begin

The execution of Lucifer was the most brutal display ever performed on Eden. The 24 angels, enraged by the loss of Michael, each subjected Lucifer to their gruelling choice of torture. Lucifer's heart stopped a dozen times, and he was revived each time to continue the pain and extend his suffering. After eight hours of continuous torture, Gabriel was satisfied and he used an orbital laser to vaporise Lucifer. The angels then took off and left.

The execution of Lucifer did not have the effect that the angels and Abraham had hoped for. Lucifer was the most loved angel among the Edenites, and he became a symbol of love and freedom. An underground cult arose around Lucifer in the decades that followed the execution.

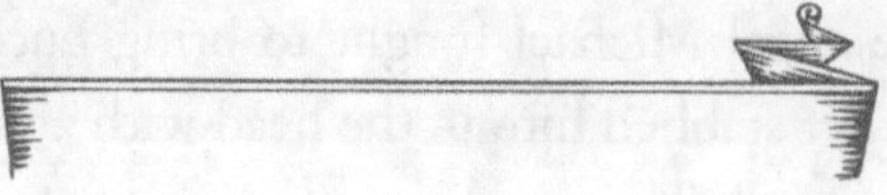

Chapter 64: Yehuda Finds a Foster Family for Jeshua.

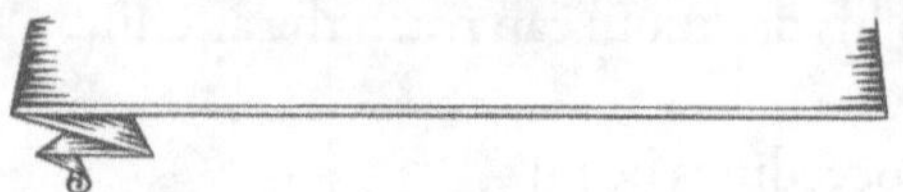

When he saw Lucifer approaching, Yehuda had grabbed Lucifer's baby son and he went into hiding. He had escaped unnoticed, but as he held the infant boy in his hands, he realised that he had a problem. A baby could not live off the mushrooms, that he grew in these tunnels.

Fortunately, Yehuda had come across several suitable foster families during his travels on Eden. He concluded that the best option would be to leave the child in the care of the couple Akiva and Chana who had young children that Chana still breastfed.

Yehuda told Akiva that Jeshua was already baptised and that both parents had died of illness. Akiva believed in Yehuda's story and he agreed to raise Jeshua as his son.

After leaving Jeshua in the care of Akiva and Chana, Yehuda returned to the tunnels where he planned his rebellion. Suddenly, he felt weary and his body ached. He found a reflective surface and he watched his reflection. Yehuda realised that he had aged a lot since. His rapid aging meant that the anti-aging vaccine that Michael had injected him with, had stopped working.

Yehuda knew that unless he injected a new dosage of DNA regeneration technology, he would age quickly and die soon. This realisation came as a blessing and curse for Yehuda. He had wanted to die for a long time, but now that he had a purpose to live, his time was up. Not wanting to fight his fate, Yehuda smoked some herbs, fell asleep, and died peacefully in his sleep.

Chapter 65: Adina Realises That She is Special.

The first five years of Adina's life was unremarkable. As a small child the angel chip had no discernible effect on her. When she turned five, she realised that she was special.

The first clue was that her parents could not tell whether they were her parents or her foster parents. When Abraham had sent Gabriel to command Markus and his wife Daniela, to raise Adina, Gabriel had never specified whether they should raise her as their child or as a foster child. While this distinction seemed like a trivial matter, it was an explosive one. Markus knew about Abraham's unpredictable and vengeful nature and how easy it was to anger him. Claiming Adina as their child would be stealing the glory from Abraham. However, claiming that she was their foster child could seem derogatory.

Eventually, they told her the truth: that Archangel Gabriel had told them to raise Adina on an order from Grandmaster Abraham. This knowledge had built Adina's ego, and she often reminded her siblings about her special connection to Abraham.

The angel chip gave Adina special abilities. Since Adina had the chip inserted from birth, it integrated well with her brain, which gave her psychic powers beyond those of the other angels. With her ability to control people's minds, Adina was almost impossible to raise as she convinced her parents of her way instead of the other way around.

A unique feature that Adina had, was that she could sense when Abraham tried to read her mind. Adina was the only one on Eden that could control what Abraham saw. Adina became so adept at showing Abraham what she wanted to show him to see that he did not even notice it. Thus, Abraham believed that he could see everything in Adina's mind.

One day, when Adina was seven years old, she scared her foster father Markus. She had made a drawing that was the spitting image of Lucifer. Lucifer was not depicted anywhere on Eden due to the harsh penalties imposed on people associating with him. When Adina spoke, she scared Markus. Her words were: *"Is this, my real dad?*

Chapter 66: Jeshua an Inquisitive Boy.

Jeshua, Lucifer's son, in the foster care of Akiva and Chana, had a childhood that was both similar and different from Adina.

Similar as they stood out from the crowd with their thoughts and behaviour. Different as Jeshua had no psionic powers. Jeshua, being free from the divine technology, could not see the hallucinations induced by Abraham. Being free from the mind control technology he could not understand why people were staring out into thin air reacting to Abraham's speeches. Jeshua had never seen Grandmaster Abraham and the angels impressed him even less.

The Edenites believed that the angels were supernatural beings that served as intermediaries between them and god, but to Jeshua, they looked like men in unique outfits that gave them superpowers. While Jeshua found the Angels' equipment to be super fascinating their personalities bored him. Jeshua thought that the angels were old and boring men who kept repeating the same old lines. On top of that, they took forever to give straight answer.

Fearless and inquisitive, Jeshua almost got in trouble when he asked Gabriel how the angel suit worked. This question indicated that Jeshua did not have a Human chip implanted, as the angels appeared to fly with their wings to the Edenites. Fortunately, Gabriel did not hear Jeshua's question, and Akiva pulled him away before Gabriel noticed him.

Akiva had scolded Jeshua and flogged him for being rude to an angel. Jeshua never understood what was wrong with his question. He was fascinated by the technology behind the angel armour and he wanted to know more. Jeshua realised that Akiva had punished him because he feared the angels. Jeshua concluded that if a big strong man like Akiva, feared the angels, he should stay clear of them as well.

Chapter 67: Adina and Jeshua Meet for the First Time.

When they were 10 years old, Adina and Jeshua met for the first time. It was on 1st of January 2860; or year 50 after the landing. For the Edenites it was also the 50th year in their history. The Edenite calendar followed the Terran calendar out of convenience as Abraham, and his angels had contact with the rest of solar system for supplies.

The New Year's celebration was the largest celebration on Eden, and the population was sitting on different tiers according to their significance. Jeshua was seated at the lowest elevation since his family was farmers. Adina was sitting on the third highest tier since the high priest raised her. Above the high priests sat the angels and on the top level a hologram of Grandmaster Abraham sat on his gigantic throne.

After viewing the spectacle for a while, Jeshua saw Adina. She sat with her family at the high priest's table. They wore elaborate clothing and yet she was the only one that intrigued him. Jeshua felt a hand on his shoulder, and he turned around, it was Akiva.

Akiva:

- Be careful, Jeshua.
- There are terrible rumours about that girl.

Jeshua:

- What rumours, father?

Akiva:

- That she can drive people crazy with the power of her will.

Jeshua:

- But she is just a girl? She cannot be a woman yet?

Akiva:

- In three years, she'll become a woman and you'll become a man.

- That's the most fearsome part. Imagine if her powers grow, as she gets older?

Jeshua:

- But if that is the case, why doesn't Grandmaster Abraham do anything about her?

Akiva:

- We should not interfere with Abraham's plans. Stay away from that girl.

Jeshua:

- Yes, father.

Akiva's warning made Jeshua even more fascinated by Adina. He decided to sneak away and have a look at her when the opportunity arose. A couple of hours later, Akiva got drunk and fell asleep. By this time, most of the adults were quite drunk, and Jeshua snuck up to the priests' tier. He was looking for Adina when someone grabbed his arm. He turned around and there she was, Adina.

Adina:

- Shh, come with me.

Adina led Jeshua behind a tent where they were less visible.
Adina:

  - What are you doing here?
  - This level hosts the priests' celebration. You're not meant to
  be here.

Jeshua was lost for words. He had intended to observe the mysterious
girl from a distance to satisfy his curiosity. He had not intended to talk
to her. Jeshua stuttered:

  - I... I was curious about you.
  - People say that you are a witch.

Adina:

  - I know what people say.
  - Ignorant and fearful, they loathe what they don't understand.

Jeshua:

  - People are people.
  - What don't they understand?

Adina:

  - They don't understand reality and the world around them.
  - They don't understand the power that I and Grandmaster
  Abraham share.

Jeshua:

  - But comparing oneself to Grandmaster Abraham is a sin.

Adina:

  - It is not a sin if you are telling the truth.

- Like Abraham, I can read and influence the minds of humans.

Jeshua:

- Really?
- So, what is my name and where do I come from?

Adina:

- I can't read your mind. You must be unique, that's why I approached you.

Adina's statement confused Jeshua, and he felt reluctant to keep the conversation going. Jeshua tried to defuse the situation:

- Okay, I am Jeshua, son of Akiva. What's your name?

Adina:

- I am Adina, foster daughter of High Priest Markus.

Jeshua:

- Nice to meet you, Adina.
- I must go back to my father now.

Adina:

- I know. We will meet again

Adina watched Jeshua as he snuck away to join his family. The young boy confused her, and he looked like a younger version of her father, Lucifer. She had seen him earlier, and it confused her that she could not reach his mind. Adina had decided to sneak down to study him, but instead, he had come to her. Was this a coincidence or was there a deeper connection between them?

Jeshua was unique because Adina could not read his mind. This fact intrigued her, and she felt compelled to find out more about him. Fortunately, he had told her his name and his father's name. As Adina was influential through her position and unique powers, she would organise so that they would meet again.

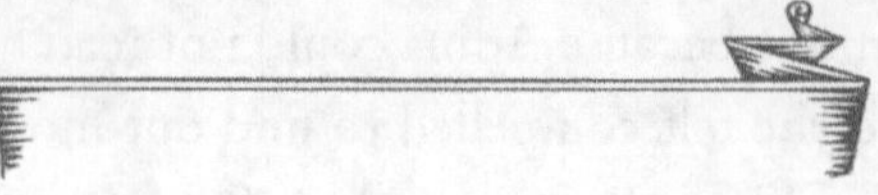

Chapter 68: Jeshua and Adina Become Neighbours.

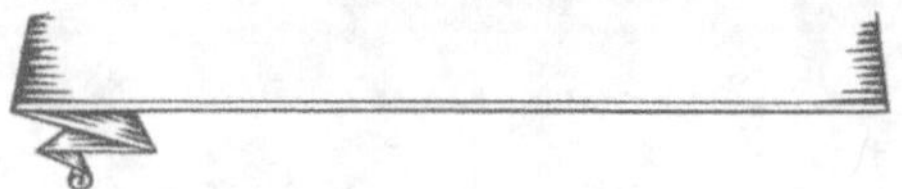

A couple of weeks later, Adina convinced her foster-father, Markus, to offer Jeshua's father, Akiva, employment. Akiva accepted Markus' job offer and Akiva moved to the village with his family. This way, Jeshua became Adina's neighbour so they saw each other daily.

Jeshua wasn't particularly fond of Adina. He thought she was a nosy girl and he felt uncomfortable in her presence. Admittedly, Jeshua had a unique look and he looked more like an angel than a human. However, Adina's attention was not the same kind as the attention he received from other girls. Jeshua couldn't put his finger on why she kept hassling him with questions about his past.

Adina had asked him about his biological father. The question had offended Jeshua. Jeshua had never met his birth parents, and he didn't know anything about them. They died from sickness when he was an infant, and Akiva had taken care of him. Jeshua didn't want to discuss this with his neighbours, and for all practical purposes, Akiva was his father.

However, Jeshua felt grateful to Adina for hiring his dad so that he did not have to grow up in poverty in the desert. Because of Adina, Jeshua didn't have to go to bed hungry, and he also had the opportunity to learn reading and writing.

Meanwhile, Jeshua fascinated Adina, and she suspected that they were siblings. Adina had improved her telepathic abilities so that she could read and manipulate the minds of the angels. When reading their thoughts, she had realised that she was the daughter of Lucifer and an Edenite woman, Sara, who was killed by the angels. Adina did not know how to feel about this, since Grandmaster Abraham was her mentor, while also causing the deaths of her biological parents.

Adina had a clear mental image of the physical appearances of Lucifer and Sara. Jeshua was the spitting image of Lucifer, while Adina looked similar to Sara. Adina realised that there was a way for her to find out if they were related. The angels had an ability that could tell them if two individuals were related. If she controlled the mind of an angel, she could use this ability to find out if she and Jeshua were siblings.

The ability was a form of DNA recognition technology, which was enabled by one of the microchips in the angels' brains. In the past, when the angels were the special operations group for House Goldstein, they sometimes had to solve crimes and find the offender. For this task, they used technology enabling them to "see" the DNA of a person. Using this ability made it easy to find a fugitive in a group of individuals. This ability was operated by smell as the technology could interpret minute amounts of airborne DNA and match it against a database. The signal was transmitted to the consciousness as vision, as it was easier to understand visual information for the human brain. Being a secondary ability, the DNA recognition ability was turned off by default.

While Adina did not know how the DNA recognition technology worked, she soon figured out how she could use it. She focused her telepathic powers, and she to took control of the angel Nuriel. She started by matching herself to herself. The result that was a 100 % DNA match. Her next step was to match her to her foster father, Markus. The result that came up was 0 %. Finally, she compared herself to Jeshua. The result that came up as 50 %. While Adina did not understand what a 50 % DNA match meant, she realised that she was related to Jeshua. After this realisation, Adina sent Nuriel away before he came to his senses and realised that she had a brother.

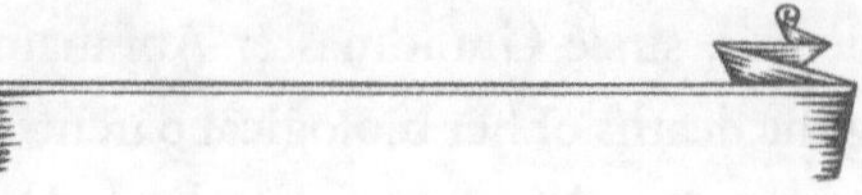

Chapter 69: The Angels Almost Capture Jeshua.

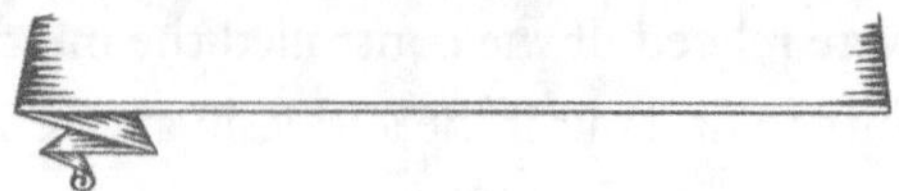

A couple of years later, it was Adina's 13th birthday, and the day for her adulthood ceremony. Because of Adina's prominence there was a big celebration in the village, and several of the angels were honorary guests. The villagers gathered for the ceremony and Jeshua was sitting in the back row. Abraham gave a lengthy speech projected as an illusion via the divine technology.

Jeshua was sitting in the back of the assembly, and his mind was wandering. Not having a divine technology chip implanted, Jeshua could not see Abraham, so for him these meetings were nonsensical. From Jeshua's point of view, it was a bunch of people staring at nothing and occasionally reciting prayers.

The issue was that Jeshua was supposed to quote the same prayers as the others. Somehow, they knew what prayer to recite from thin air, while he had to catch up every time. Jeshua looked at Adina. It was a strange coincidence that they shared the same birthday. Jeshua had mixed feelings for Adina. He found her awkward, yet he felt a connection to her that he could not understand.

Gabriel and Nuriel stood next to the stage where Abraham was speaking, when Gabriel noticed an anomaly. He whispered to Nuriel:

- Nuriel, how many individuals does your thermal scanners detect in the assembly? Mine says 220

Nuriel:

- Yes, so does mine, what's the problem?

Gabriel:

- How many angels and humans can you detect in the room?

Nuriel:

- 212 humans and seven angels.

- You are right. It shows one angel too many, there are only six of us here.

Gabriel:

- Adina has an angel chip, remember!
- We are missing one human.
- Follow me; we cannot allow non-chipped, non-baptized humans on Eden.

They walked among crowd and they connected with one person at the time. Eventually, Gabriel reached Jeshua. He put his hand on Jeshua's shoulder and he noticed that he couldn't reach Jeshua's mind. He told Jeshua to turn around and was shocked when he noticed that the boy looked like a young Lucifer.

Adina noticed what was happening and she acted quickly. Exerting her powers, she made Jeshua invisible to the angels. Jeshua was confused over what happened. The angel was now looking straight past him as if he wasn't there. He turned around and looked at Adina. She seemed to be in pain and her lips formed the word "run." Adina fainted, and Jeshua used the ensuing confusion to run away from the congregation.

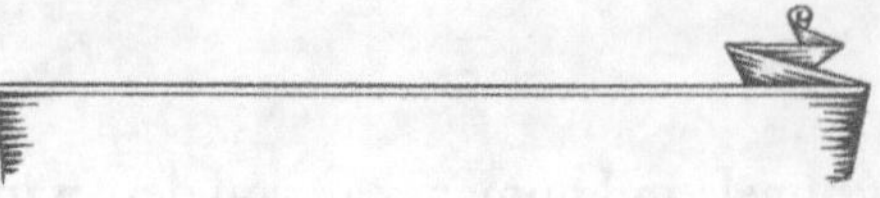

Chapter 70: Abraham Finds Out About Jeshua.

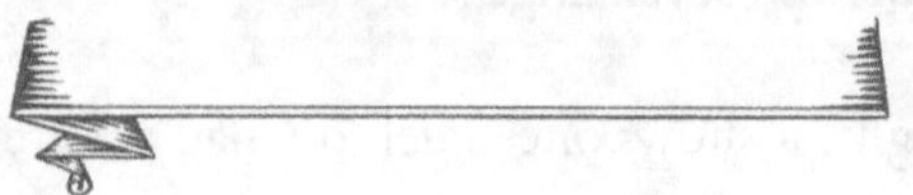

Gabriel:

- I saw him...
- I saw Lucifer, a younger version of him.

Abraham:

- And yet you didn't bring him to me?

Gabriel:

- I am sorry, Master. He disappeared in front of my eyes. One second, he was there, the next he was gone.

Abraham scanned the memories of Gabriel. His archangel wasn't lying, and it was a mystery. Had the young Lucifer been there, or was it a hallucination?

Abraham worried about Adina. Her brain patterns were different from the other angels, and he could not read her mind the same way as he could read theirs. Abraham was unsure whether Adina disrupted what he could see or if her angel chip had malfunctioned. If she manipulated what he could see, she was a threat, but if it happened because of a glitch, it was harmless.

Abraham decided to observe Adina from a distance. In a way, it was a good thing that she hid things from him, as it made his life interesting. Abraham had realised that immortality and full control bored him. It was 13 years since Lucifer's death, the latest event on Eden that had affected him. Abraham realised that one of the underlying reasons for Yahweh's suicide must have been boredom. While Abraham could take measures that influenced the lives of his Edenite subjects, they had limited consequences for him or the rest of the universe.

Excited that something unusual had happened, Abraham decided to have Gabriel examined. It would take a couple of days, and until then he had some excitement to look forward to, the excitement that uncertainty brought.

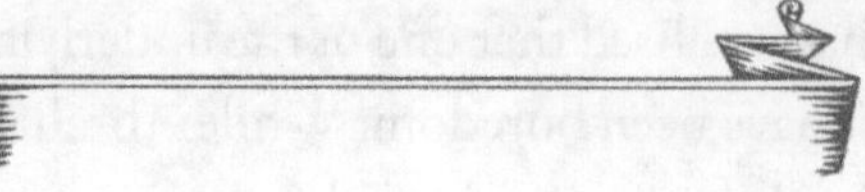

Chapter 71: Adina Urges Jeshua to Go into Hiding.

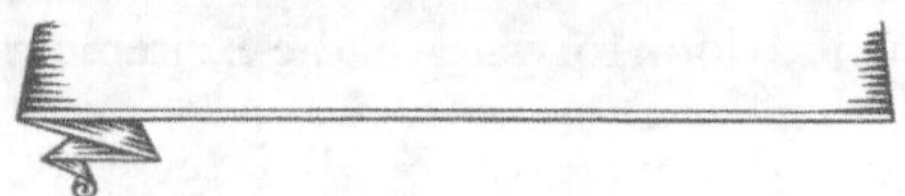

Jeshua sat in the stable and he thought about the day's events. Thinking back on Adina's adulthood ceremony puzzled him. As per usual, the villagers had stared at the empty chair in the middle of the room chanting and showing all kinds of emotions. But during the meeting, the angels had walked around like they were looking for something. This behaviour was unusual as they usually stood stoically and silent during these sessions. Eventually, one of the angels had approached him and stared at him for a moment before acting very weird and staring straight past him. Adina's lips had told Jeshua to run, and she had passed out.

What did this mean? The angel had acted amazed when he saw Jeshua. Why was Jeshua special and why were the angels looking for him? Adina entered the stable and she approached Jeshua.

Adina:

- I have been looking for you.

Jeshua:

- Shouldn't you be resting? It looked like you had a nasty fall when you fainted?

Adina:

- I was pretending to faint as a diversion. It was vital to get you away from there.

Jeshua:

- But why? I am the unimportant son of a poor gardener.

Adina:

- That statement is not true. You are a foster child as am I.

Jeshua:

- Stop telling me that I am adopted.
- Who told you this?

Adina:

- No one did. They did not need to.

- I can read and influence people's minds. Even the thoughts of the angels.

Jeshua:

- Stop that crazy talk!
- Although most people believe that you can do these things.

Adina

- That's because I can. You are the only one that is different.
- Tell me, have you ever seen Grandmaster Abraham?

Jeshua:

- No, I assume he is just a symbol?

Adina:

- NO!
- He is very real, and everyone except you can see him.

Jeshua let Adina's words sink in. He didn't know how to react. Adina was insane, but everything that she said made sense.

Jeshua:

- But. But that can't be, I don't understand any of this.

Adina:

- Let's start over.
- Have you heard about Lucifer?

Jeshua:

- Only in hushed whispers.

- He was a fallen angel who betrayed Grandmaster Abraham, and suffered a terrible death.

Adina:

- That is incorrect. Lucifer was a good man who wanted to do good for the Edenites. Because of this, the tyrant Abraham executed him to set an example.

- He fathered a child with an Edenite woman. I am that child, and I suspect that you are my twin brother.

Jeshua:

- What? Why would you even think that?

Adina paused. It was hard to explain to Jeshua in a way that he would understand. Adina's abilities gave her access to the angels' thoughts and memories, and she knew that Eden and Abraham's divinity was scam. Adina realised that Jeshua didn't have a Divine Technology chip implanted as she could not connect to him. This meant that Jeshua could do, what Adina could not. He could act in secret to bring Abraham down.

Adina:

- Abraham implanted me with technology, so I could read and influence the minds of the Edenites.

- What he does not know is that the technology allows me to read and control the minds of the angels. That's how I found out the truth.

Jeshua:

- And what is the truth?

Adina:

- The truth is that Earth is still around, and the rest of humankind is living in prosperity and freedom.

- The Edenites are a small group of mind-controlled individuals living under the supervision of a deluded psychopath.

Jeshua:

- I am sorry. But I don't want to hear this kind of talk.
- I am not the son of an angel, and all I want is a happy life.

Adina:

- You'll believe me one day.
- Stay clear of the angels. For your safety.

Jeshua:

- Okay, I will.
- Goodnight, Adina

Jeshua walked to the small hut where he lived with his family. He felt confused. He had sought solitude in the stables to clear his mind and Adina's claims made things worse. Jeshua felt that something was wrong with the world and Adina's claims verified this to him.

Jeshua struggled to understand the scope of it all. Adina argued that the world was broken, and that Abraham and was the cause. But what was the solution? Abraham and the angels committed many evil deeds, but they also cured people from ailments, made the crops grow, purified the air, etc.

If they found a way to depose of Abraham, what would happen next? Jeshua believed that Adina would grab power herself, instead of freeing the Edenites from tyranny. Would Adina be a better leader than Abraham? There were many rumours about Adina, and none of them were good. Akiva saw that something was bothering Jeshua and interrupted his thoughts.

Akiva:

  - Is something bothering you, Jeshua? You need to sleep early; your adulthood ceremony is tomorrow.

Jeshua:

  - Father, why did you tell Adina that I am adopted?

Akiva:

  - Why do you ask me that?

Jeshua:

  - Adina knew that I was adopted. Yet you told me not to let anyone know about my origin.

Akiva:

  - You shouldn't listen to that woman; she is a troublemaker. Adina is messing with people's minds.

Jeshua:

- That did not answer my question.

Akiva:

- I admitted to her that you are not my biological son.

- But we have had you since you were a newborn, so you are like our real son.

Jeshua:

- Did Lucifer give me to you?

Akiva:

- No, we got you from Yehuda. He was a disgraced former high priest who was condemned to toil in the wilderness like we were.

- But he was very old when we got you and he died shortly after.

- But never mention Lucifer again, especially not around angels.

Jeshua:

- I understand, father. Thank you for telling me the truth.

Akiva:

- No worries, son. Now sleep, so that you are fresh for your ceremony tomorrow.

Jeshua's adulthood ceremony took place the day after, and it was a small and uneventful celebration.

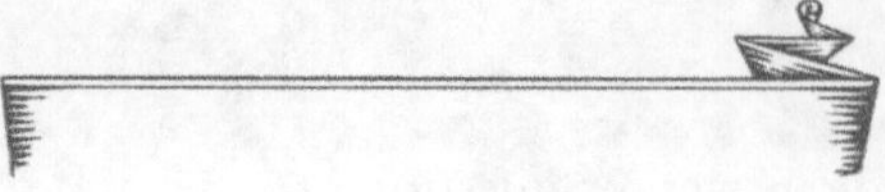

Chapter 72: The Wedding Assault.

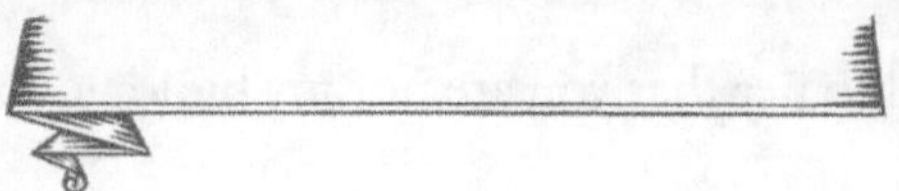

Three years later, Jeshua still lived in the same village as Adina. He was 16 years old and he worked under his father. Adina had tried to get Jeshua to hide, but he kept refusing.

Jeshua declined for two reasons. Jeshua did not believe Adina's claims about them being siblings and progeny of the late Lucifer. More importantly, he did not escape, as there was nowhere for him to go. Jeshua rather took his chances and stayed in the village rather than living in the wilderness while hiding from the angels.

Jeshua stayed away from the Angels to be on the safe side. It was easy for Jeshua to stay clear of the angels, as they never seemed interested in speaking to him. Jeshua reflected that it was a bit strange as the angels exchanged a few words with most Edenites except for him. This benign negligence changed when Jeshua was 16 years old and attended his brother's wedding.

In the year 2866 Abraham Goldstein instructed the angels to go through the finances of the Edenite population. This review had never happened before as Abraham considered the production output of the Edenites to be insignificant. But the previous year there was a famine on Eden. While the suffering caused by the starvation of 2865 did not bother Abraham, he was bothered because he wasn't the cause of it. If the people were to believe that he was all-powerful, they would believe that he caused the starvation as a punishment. Abraham had struggled to motivate the famine as the Edenites had followed his rules.

To make sure that unintended famines did not occur again, Abraham decreed that the population should build granaries and keep accurate records. When going through High Priest Markus records, Gabriel noticed a discrepancy. He summoned Markus to speak to him.

Markus:

  - You summoned me, Archangel Gabriel.

Gabriel:

  - I found several discrepancies in your records.
  - You paid someone called Jeshua, son of Akiva.
  - Do you care to elaborate?

Markus:

  - I don't understand what the problem is? Jeshua works for me.

Gabriel:

  - The problem is that there is no Jeshua son of Akiva on Eden.

  - Everything that is produced on Eden belongs to Grandmaster Abraham, and he shares it with you.

  - It seems like you are stealing from Abraham.

  - Unless you can come up with a better explanation?

Markus:

  - Jeshua exists. I can bring him to you later.

Gabriel:

  - Do I look like I enjoy waiting?
  - Bring him now.

Markus:

- Well, now is not the right time. Jeshua is attending his brother's wedding.

Gabriel:

- Very well. Lead me to this wedding. This celebration can use my presence.

Adina, who attended the wedding, was drinking wine in a corner when Gabriel and Markus entered. She knew why they were there. However, her intoxication had weakened her psionic powers, so she could not influence Gabriel to leave.

Gabriel approached Jeshua. What he saw shocked him. For the second time, he saw Lucifer's son. The first time, three years earlier, he had disappeared, but this time, he remained in front of Gabriel's eyes. Gabriel decided to confirm the identity of the man in front of him.

Gabriel:

- Are you Jeshua, son of Akiva?

Jeshua:

- Yes, that is me. How can I serve you, Archangel Gabriel?

Gabriel did not respond. He knew what he had to do. For the last three years, he had wondered what he saw at Adina's adulthood ceremony. Abraham had ruled it out as a glitch, and he had declined Gabriel's request to search for Lucifer's son. Abraham needed to see this young man with his own eyes. Gabriel tried to connect with Abraham to share his vision. But this was to no avail, as something was blocking the signal. Gabriel used the built-in communication link in the Angel suit to contact Abraham.

Gabriel:

- Abraham! I have the son of Lucifer at the Gad Tribe Wedding Hall. Requesting instructions.

Since she could not block conventional signals, Adina realised that she needed to act to stop her brother from being captured. Fortunately, the wedding guests were intoxicated and easy to influence. She influenced some of them to stab Gabriel from behind.

The stabbing shocked Gabriel who had not activated the electromagnetic shield that protected his body from attacks. He enabled it as he fell to the ground. The field electrocuted and repelled the attackers, but to no avail. Gabriel knew that he was mortally wounded, and that he couldn't stop the bleeding fast enough. He activated the emergency beacon on his angel suit, closed his eyes and prepared to die.

Having achieved her goal, Adina released the attackers from her psionic control. They realised what they had done and fled the wedding hall before the other angels arrived. Adina caught up with Jeshua outside.

Adina:

- Do you believe me now?

Jeshua:

- What have you done?

Adina:

- I saved you.
- You are my brother, the son of Lucifer, and the saviour of Eden.

Jeshua:

- But you condemned my family. You doomed us all!

Adina:

- Not all of us.

- They will never kill us all. Abraham needs us. Without us, there is no purpose for him to live anymore.

- We will get revenge for our father, but first, you need to hide! Meet me at Gomorrah Cliffs at the southern edge of Eden in one week; I will be waiting for you there, and I will bring supplies.

Jeshua did not question Adina, and he ran for his life towards Gomorrah Cliffs.

Chapter 73: Abraham is Furious.

Abraham looked at the frozen, lifeless body of Gabriel. He was seething with anger but at the same time he felt relieved. Gabriel's murderers had not killed him beyond resurrection. Thus, Abraham could resurrect Gabriel with stem cell grown body parts.

Abraham was baffled when he investigated the perpetrators' minds. They were shocked by the insanity that had led them to kill Gabriel. Gabriel would return to Eden and avenge his own death. This would be poetic justice and it would prove that the Edenites couldn't kill the angels.

Abraham devised a plan. He proclaimed that all the members of Akiva's family would be cast out and killed with fire from the sky within the next year. There they would live in constant fear and see their family members killed, one at the time. This was a glorious plan for revenge and much better than killing them all at once.

The emergence of Jeshua, Lucifer's son, was confirmed by Gabriel's assailants. Jeshua was the perfect likeness to a young Lucifer. Had he incited the people to attack Gabriel? How had Jeshua avoided detection for so many years? Regardless, Jeshua had to be captured, as a he was a threat to Abraham's dominance over Eden.

But it was difficult to find Jeshua. He had no implants so Abraham could not track him, and Abraham had failed to find Jeshua using orbital satellites. To find him without using the satellites was a mammoth task as Eden was 20,000 square kilometres of inhabitable land and he could only commit 20 angels to the search.

Abraham considered commanding the Edenites to find and punish Jeshua. He decided against the idea. Requesting Edenite help, would undermine his claim to be all-seeing and omnipotent. Instead, Abraham chose another course of action. At Mount Sinai, he would force the Edenites to erect a 100-meter tall monument cut into the rock depicting Lucifer's execution, 16 years earlier. Abraham could have the angels create such a memorial with lasers in a couple of weeks, but he would rather have the Edenites do it with their blunt tools, toiling for ten years to build it. HE was their MASTER, and they existed to SERVE HIM.

Chapter 74: Adina Allies with Jeshua.

A week later, Jeshua met up with Adina in the caves under Gomorrah Falls close to the southern edge of Eden. Jeshua was starving and thirsty as he had had taken detours to avoid the satellite surveillance of Eden. Adina had told Jeshua that satellites were big flying machines that could see him from the sky and report his location to Abraham.

Avoiding the satellite surveillance, was not difficult. Six out of seven suns in the sky was satellites and as a long as the satellites were not within 10 degrees from zenith, they could not see him. So, Jeshua had sought cover every time one of the suns were close to zenith. This was a plodding way to move, as he could only move undetected one-quarter of the time. Jeshua met up with Adina who had brought him supplies.

Adina:

- Welcome to your new home, Jeshua.
- I am glad that you made it.

Jeshua:

- What is this is all about?

- I attended a wedding, an angel approached me, and then the other wedding guests attacked the angel?

Adina:

- You heard what Gabriel said.

- You are the son of Lucifer, the angel who defied Abraham and got executed.

- You do not have a microchip implanted. This means that they cannot control you. That makes you dangerous to them.

Jeshua:

- But you got a chip? So why can't they control you?

Adina:

- I don't know what happened.

- For some reason, they gave me another chip at birth. But that chip gave me unexpected powers. That's why I can enter and control their minds.

Jeshua:

- That makes YOU dangerous to Abraham. Why haven't they come after you?

Adina:

- Because they don't know about my powers.

- I can help our people. If I am detected, we are doomed, and the Edenites are condemned to tyranny.

Jeshua:

- I see
- What is my part in all of this?

Adina:

- Your part is to be the liberator. I will find people who are sympathetic to our cause. You'll meet them and bring them to the edge of Eden. Once you are there, you'll follow the instructions in this letter, and remove their microchips.

- I must return home before someone misses me. Behind those cliffs, there is a network of tunnels that have an almost endless supply of mushrooms. You can stay there invisible to Abraham, together with the people that you liberate.

- I will leave written messages to you under this rock.

After saying this, Adina jumped up on her horse and galloped back home. Fortunately, it took only an hour and a half to race the distance that had taken Jeshua a week to sneak. Adina had no reason to hide. She could move freely and no one would dare to question her. This was because the reputation of Adina's powers had spread across Eden.

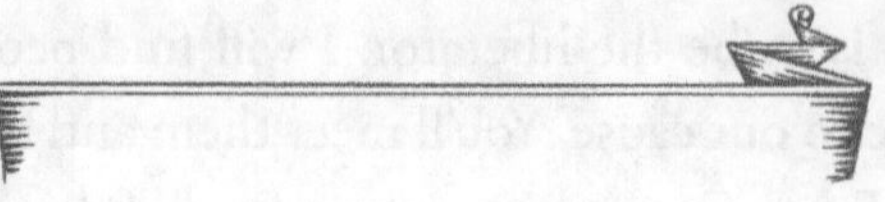

Chapter 75: Another Lost Edenite.

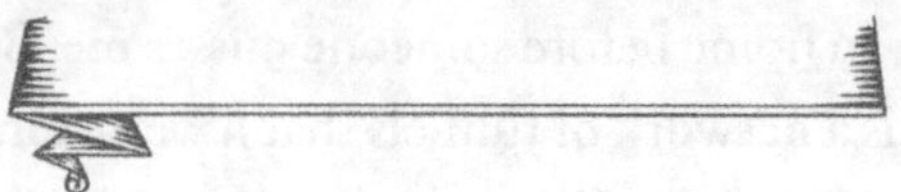

Abraham watched Adina performing a religious sermon. He was proud of her. It felt good that his granddaughter was dedicating her life to honour him and his teachings. Adina praised Abraham's benevolent rule with such zeal that Abraham considered elevating her to become one of his angels. He would put that off for a while though and keep observing Adina from afar.

The Abrahameon expressed that only men could be religious leaders, so many villagers objected when Adina became the assistant priest for their village. Abraham had commanded Markus and the gathered congregation that Adina was to be a priest for the village. While Adina's promotion was inconsistent with the earlier message in the Abrahameon, it did not bother Abraham. There were many inconsistencies in the Bible, and if Yahweh couldn't bother being consistent, Abraham didn't need to either.

Accompanying Adina at the altar was the archangel Gabriel and his bodyguard, Cherubim. Gabriel's assailants hadn't killed him permanently, because they didn't know about the technology that enabled resurrection as long as the brain had not sustained damages beyond repair.

The Edenites saw the return of Gabriel as proof of his semi-divine status and the ultimate power of Grandmaster Abraham to rule over life and death. Cherubim became Gabriel's bodyguard as Abraham was reluctant to send angels on solo missions after the incident that killed Gabriel.

During the sermon, Abraham was disturbed by a minor notification on the outer edges of his mind. It was a notification that one of his subjects had passed away. With an Edenite population of around 10,000, he got these notifications quite often, so they did not bother him as they were a natural part of life.

In the last year, there was an ongoing issue with people dying, where the body was never found. It had happened again. The latest man to disappear had been a 25-year-old healthy individual. No one had witnessed the fatality, and the surveillance satellites did not cover the place of death. Abraham would send the angels to search for the body, but he already knew the outcome. They would find a pool of blood, but they would not find the body. Since Lucifer's son had appeared a dozen people had disappeared. Abraham concluded that Jeshua was behind the deaths, but what did he want? Refusing to acknowledge his fears, Abraham retreated to the Divine Dimension to meditate.

The mastermind behind the disappearances was Adina who used Jeshua to gather support to overthrow Abraham's reign on Eden. Her method was the following:

Adina used her psionic capabilities to find individuals who were resentful towards Abraham. She told them to wait for Jeshua to set them free. She then rode out to Jeshua's hideout and left a note with instructions on who to release from Abraham and the time and place to do so. Adina made sure that the attention of Abraham would be directed at her for the whole time so that Abraham couldn't intercept the liberation. This procedure also gave her an alibi for every liberated individual, thus putting her beyond any suspicion.

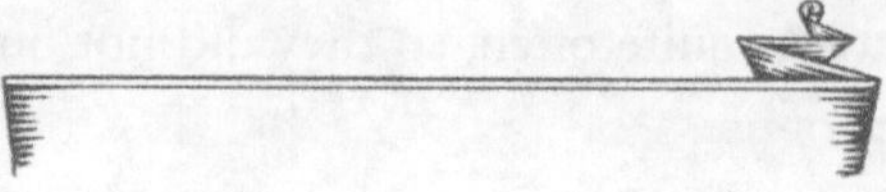

Chapter 76: Abraham Forms a Militia to Stop Jeshua.

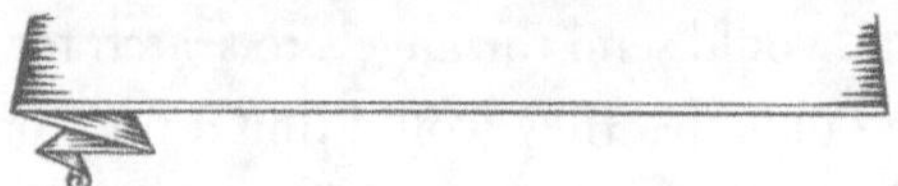

With more people liberated, the disappearances accelerated as Adina had more operatives available to free individuals from Abraham's control. Eventually, she grew too bold, and Abraham realised what was happening. For the first three years, Abraham thought that Jeshua killed individuals and hid the bodies. While this notion was unsettling, it did not pose any threat to his power. One event in 2870 made Abraham wake up and realise the danger that Jeshua posed to his rule.

Adina had instructed Jeshua's group to liberate dissenting people in separate locations on Eden at the same time. When people disappeared on the eastern edge of Eden and the western boundary at the same time, Abraham realised that Jeshua couldn't be behind both disappearances. Abraham understood that Jeshua did not kill the disappearing individuals, he liberated them. In return, they helped him in his underground rebellion against Abraham.

Abraham checked a map of Eden's maintenance tunnels and he realised how blind he had been. All disappearances had happened close to the entrances, which explained how the liberated individuals could disappear without a trace. Abraham's first impulse was to gather his angels and order them to search the tunnels.

Abraham realised that this was not the best course of action. The tunnels were vast and covered hundreds of kilometres. Jeshua, might have set traps the tunnels while waiting for the angels to make a move. While it shouldn't be possible for an Edenite man to kill an angel in a battle outfit, Abraham would not underestimate the man who had stayed hidden for three years while snatching Abraham's subject one by one.

Instead, Abraham chose another solution, one that required patience, time and manpower, factors that Abraham had in abundance. He would raise religious militias that would guard the entrances to the maintenance tunnels. This way, the rebels would eventually starve to death and they could no longer recruit any new individuals for their cause. If the blockade made the rebels come out and fight, then Abraham and the angels could kill them quickly out in the open.

Abraham added a passage to the Abrahameon that stated that the entrances to the maintenance tunnels had to be guarded.

The corruption of Lucifer's soul was so endless that the destruction of his body was not enough to put him at rest. Instead, the spiteful energy of Lucifer's lost soul made its way to the deepest pits of hell where he was tormented for eternity while calling out for other evildoers to cometh and join him. To stop this evil, Grandmaster Abraham commands that all the tunnels leading to hell need to be guarded. As evil stems from man's weakness, Man must defend against it and be vigilant. So sayeth the wise Grandmaster Abraham.

After a couple of weeks, Edenite militias blocked all the entrances to the maintenance tunnels, which made it impossible for Jeshua and his rebels to move in and out of the tunnels undetected. Now Abraham could wait and bide his time.

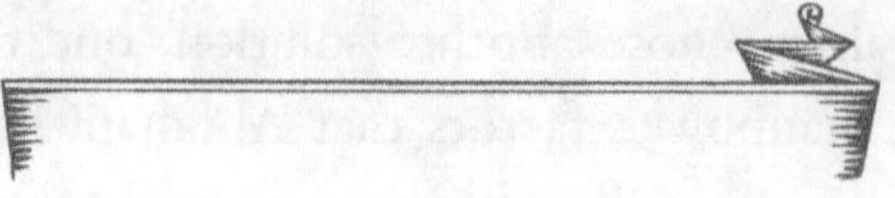

Chapter 77: The Destruction of Jeshua's Militia.

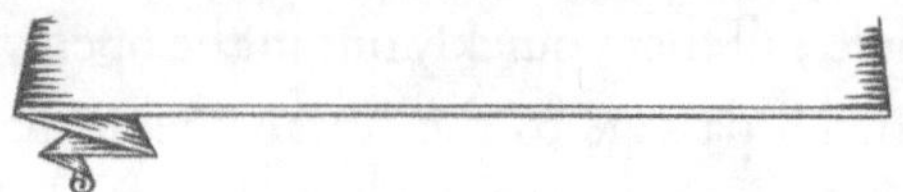

Jeshua looked at the tunnel exit and saw that an Edenite militia blocked the path. He sighed. He and his rebel group had been stuck down in these catacombs for a month. Although they had access to mushrooms and water, it was not sustainable to stay in the darkness indefinitely.

The only light source in the tunnels was from the luminescent paint with directions visible every 50 meters. Apart from this bleak light, they were in complete darkness. They needed to find a path to the surface as soon as possible.

Jeshua looked at the guard post in the distance. It was guarded by six men. These men would not be a match for Jeshua's group. But, Jeshua suspected a trap. There would be angels waiting for them, and the six men at the guard post were a bait to lure them out. Jeshua told his followers to find an unguarded exit, but they did not listen to him. They had been stuck in the darkness for a month and all the exits were guarded. They needed to get out to avoid going insane from the darkness.

Adam, one of Jeshua's followers, pushed Jeshua to the ground.
Adam:

- I have had enough of this, Jeshua. I didn't join the rebellion against Abraham to cower in these dark, bloody tunnels to the end of my days.

- You got us down here, and now we are stuck here because of your cowardice.

- This is our chance, there are only a few of them, and there are thirty of us. Let's get out and get us some proper food.

Jeshua:

- Shut up, Adam.
- They have set a trap for us. We need to...

Adam sucker punched Jeshua in the head. Unprepared for the strike, Jeshua fell backwards, hit his head on a rock, and fell unconscious.
Adam:

- The craven fool that got us here is dead.

- Let's save ourselves by getting out of these damn caves. Let us get us some warm food and some warm cunt.

The group murmured in acknowledgment. Most of them had been miserable since Jeshua "freed" them. They had suppressed their misery by telling themselves that they were winning. It had felt that way, when they increased their numbers from the ever-watchful eyes of Abraham and his angels. But they had never had a long-term plan; at least they had not been aware of the long-term plan.

To defeat Abraham, they needed to take the fight to him. It was time to fight Abraham. United behind Adam, the group charged the guards to break free.

The Edenite militia took up their weapons and prepared to fight the enemy, but Abraham instructed them to drop their weapons and run out in the open. The militiamen dropped their weapons and ran as fast as they could. Once Adam's men were out in the open Abraham released the trap. Firstly, he set off the explosives at the entrance to collapse the tunnel so no one could get back in. Then he killed the rebels using the orbital laser cannons he had at his disposal. A couple of minutes, later they were all dead turned into a jumbled mess of blown up body parts and burnt flesh.

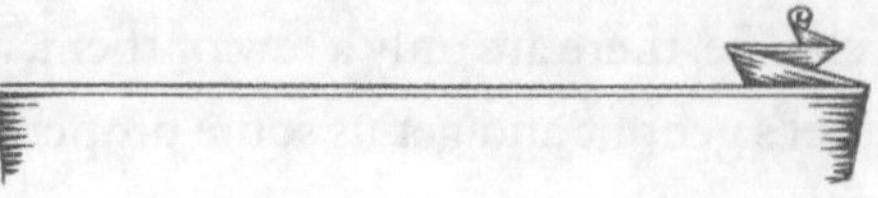

Chapter 78: The Search for Jeshua's Body.

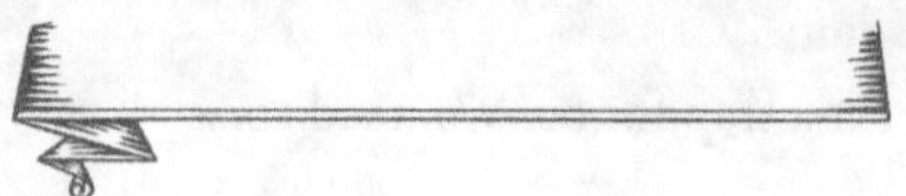

Abraham enjoyed studying the carnage. It felt good, putting these insolent rebels into place using his superior weaponry. He would instruct the Edenite population to make a pilgrimage to Gomorrah Cliffs so that they could witness the punishment that befell upon anyone who rebelled against his rule. There was, however, one thing that bothered him. The angels were unable to locate Jeshua's remains.

Abraham contacted Gabriel who was analysing the battlefield:

- How is it going?
- Have you found any trace of the traitor yet?

Gabriel:

- Analysis from our orbital satellites and the remains found on the ground, indicate that we killed 30 collaborators in the battle.

Abraham:

- That is good news, but I am asking about Jeshua.

Gabriel:

- We have found no evidence for Jeshua's death. However, the battlefield is contaminated so we cannot rule out that he is among the fallen combatants.

Abraham paused. There had been 30 mysterious disappearances related to Jeshua in the last four years. There were 30 slain rebels outside the tunnel entrance at Gomorrah Cliffs. Had Jeshua sacrificed all the insurgents to fake his own death? Or was his body to be found in the tunnels? Regardless, without his men, he proved no danger to the angels and Abraham ordered a search for him.

Abraham:

- Gather the angels and search the tunnels for Jeshua. Be careful they might have set traps for you.

Gabriel:

- Understood, I will clear this entrance and approach the tunnels from here. I will instruct others to search from the other entrances.

A few hours later, Jeshua woke up after being unconscious for over 24 hours. He was disoriented and could not recall what happened. He was alone in the camp, and there was no one else to be found. He felt weak but he got up on his feet. Jeshua remembered Adam punching him, and he realised that he needed to stop the others from leaving the tunnels.

Going out as a group was the equivalent of suicide, and he had to stop them. Much to his dismay Jeshua realised that the entrance was caved in. He had arrived too late to save his group. This realisation filled Jeshua with despair. Jeshua could see the angels clearing the cave-in. He headed back to camp to find a hiding spot. Jeshua could only think of one location where they wouldn't be able to find him, the latrine. He jumped into the latrine, closed his mouth, and struggled to not vomit as he was floating in excrement. The angels Gabriel and Thomas entered the camp.

Gabriel:

- Thomas, what do you see?

Thomas:

  - Not much. It is quite dark in here.

Gabriel:

  - Try DNA detection and heat signature.

Thomas:

  - His DNA is all over the place, but mostly from the latrine.
  The same thing goes for the heat signature.

Gabriel:

  - It sounds like you're on latrine duty, Thomas.

Thomas:

  - Ha-ha very funny, Gabriel. Do you think Abraham will be
  pleased over me wading around in shit, wearing a 3 million
  Terran Credit battle suit?

Gabriel:

  - I would find it funny to watch.
  - Very well, just go there and have a look.

Jeshua heard that Thomas approached the latrine. He closed his eyes,
held his nose, and dropped under the surface.
  Gabriel:

  - What do you see?

Thomas:

  - Shit, Shit and wait, more shit.

Gabriel

- Fire off a few rounds to be sure.

Upon hearing this Jeshua sunk to the bottom of the latrine. Thomas fired off a multitude of shots, which would have hit and killed Jeshua if it wasn't for the high density of the excrement. Instead, the bullets disintegrated, and the kinetic energy from the bullets splashed up as a shit, hitting Thomas who wasn't amused.

Thomas:

- Fuck you, Gabriel! You knew that was going to happen, didn't you?

Gabriel:

- So, should you. All these years of training back on Earth and yet you forgot why spear guns are used instead of high-powered rifles underwater.

- Let's move on

- You search the southbound tunnel, while I search the northbound tunnel. We'll meet here in three hours.

The Angels' left and Jeshua released all the vomit he was holding in. His first instinct was to get out of the latrine, but he realised that if he did, he would spread excrement all over the camp. and the angels would know where he was hiding. Instead, he bided his time until the angels had left the tunnels. Jeshua was amazed that the angel's weapon didn't kill him. He saw this as a sign from Yahweh, the true god, that his time would come to overthrow Abraham.

Jeshua had a bath in the camps water source. While it was a shame to destroy the camp's water supply, it did not matter anymore. His followers were dead, and Jeshua was going to hide somewhere else. There was enough mushrooms and water in these tunnels for Jeshua to sustain himself while waiting for a sign from Yahweh that he should rise as the saviour of the Edenites.

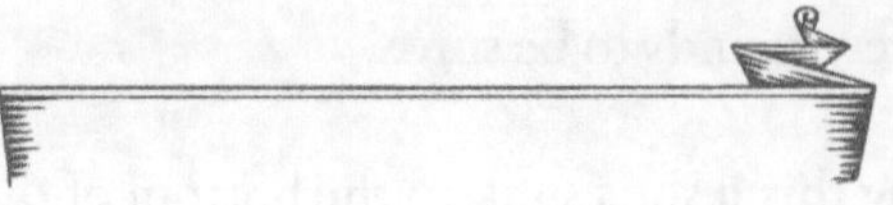

Chapter 79: A Few Years Pass.

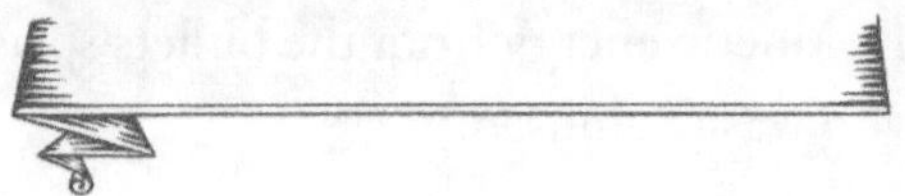

The following years, Jeshua waited for a sign from Yahweh. The sign never came, and instead, Jeshua wallowed his life away in the darkness. He passed his days having vivid hallucinations induced by the darkness and psychoactive substances in the mushrooms he ate. Jeshua became sickly and he grew a massive beard and long hair. One day, two years later, Jeshua regained his mental clarity and he knew what he had to do.

Meanwhile, Adina strengthened her powers. Adina pretended to be Abraham's strongest advocate. She succeeded Markus, and became the high priest for her tribe. Using her psychic powers, Adina influenced the other high priests to appoint her to the newly created role of Grand High Priestess and she ruled all of Eden. To appease Abraham, she ordered the Edenites to build a giant monument at Mount Sinai commemorating the defeat of Lucifer at the hands of Abraham. Adina reckoned that the best way to prove her loyalty was to create a monument that celebrated how Abraham had killed Lucifer.

Adina was biding her time. Her capabilities got stronger every day, and she learned how to control the angels from several kilometres away. She had to be careful and hide her intentions. Although Abraham could not send an angel to kill her, he could use the orbital laser cannons to do the job. Adina knew that Abraham always had a laser cannon aimed at her, as one of the seven suns followed her around, while the other six stars were moving in a pattern over the sky as time was passing.

Being followed by an orbital laser, Adina could not search for Jeshua and influence him to rebuild his militia. She was uncertain whether he was alive, although she knew that the angels had not found him on the battlefield at Gomorrah Cliffs. Adina wanted to look for Jeshua, but she could not move freely without creating unwanted attention. Adina hoped that Jeshua would seek her out, but it never happened.

Abraham Goldstein was impressed by his granddaughter. Adina had achieved things that were beyond his greatest imagination, and she used her talents to honour him. Abraham could never have asked for a better progeny, and he finally had a descendant who made him proud. Abraham also feared Adina. She was powerful, and Abraham feared her reaction if she found out the truth about Lucifer. This was Abraham's conundrum. On the one hand, he wanted Adina to know that she was his blood, but on the other hand, he feared how she would react if she found out the truth. Adina was Lucifer's daughter, and Abraham and had brutally executed Lucifer.

Abraham believed that Adina could control what he saw when accessed her mind. Every time Abraham accessed Adina's mind, he found praise and love for him and his actions. Everyone feared and loved him to various degrees, but only Adina showed a one-sided love and admiration for him. Abraham didn't buy it. Adina would have her doubts and fears, just like everyone else, so why couldn't he detect these emotions?

It also occurred to Abraham, that the angels acted strange around Adina, as if she controlled them. Abraham decided to take precautions to keep Adina under his control. To keep Adina in place, he programmed one of the orbital lasers to follow Adina around, so he always kept her supervised.

Two years later, in 2872, events unfolded that would change the fate of the Edenites forever.

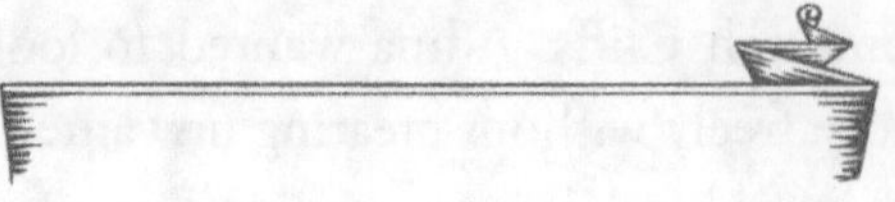

Chapter 80: A Zetan prophecy.

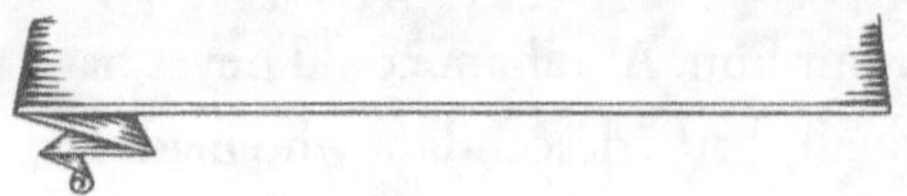

Ra, Zeus, and Brahma were observing the Divine Palace in the Divine Dimension. The Zetans had been locked out from the Divine Palace for eons after Yahweh created a dimensional rift that barred them from entering. With their home planets destroyed they could not power up their other portals back to the regular universe. The materials needed were inside the Divine Palace, which was behind the dimensional rift. They had tried to communicate with Yahweh, but there was no sign of life from their old companion who had betrayed them and barred them from the palace.

The Zetans concluded that Yahweh was dead, because otherwise, they could detect his life force. For the last century, they had sensed a human presence in the Divine Palace. They had concluded that this human was not physically in there but he had managed to transport his mind to the Divine Dimension. While this was an impressive technological feat, it would not help the Zetans. They needed someone to physically enter the Divine Dimension to bring them back. Besides, the human that lived in the Divine Palace was uncontactable via telepathy, and he could not help the Zetans.

While Abraham's presence in the Divine Dimension was unwelcome, the Zetans were still excited over their prospects. If humanity had managed to send a mind to the Divine Dimension, they could activate the portals on Earth.

There was a human that the Zetans could communicate with across the dimensions. That woman had psionic capabilities they had not encountered in centuries. This woman had what her predecessors lacked; she had access to technology that would enable her to open the portals, so the Zetans could travel to Earth and once again become the masters of the galaxy.

It was time for the Zetans to act. The Zetans were a bit anxious as opportunities like this did not come around that often. While they could not KNOW the future, their highly advanced brains enabled them to make accurate predictions that would increase the likelihood of success. They gathered in a ring, interlocked their arms, and brought themselves into a trance so they could communicate with their human host.

The Zetans disconnected with their host. Soon, the future would be theirs.

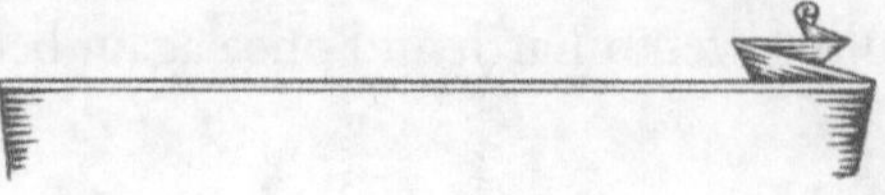

Chapter 81: Jeshua Comes to a Sudden State of Clarity.

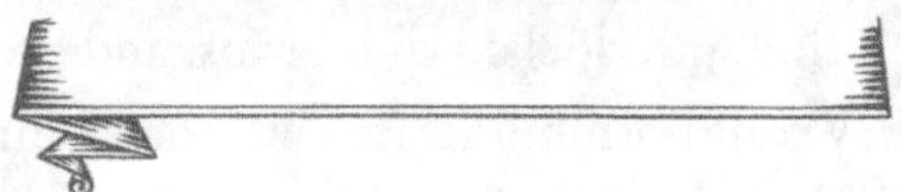

Spending two years in solitude, in the dark tunnels below, Eden drove Jeshua insane. Fear drove him, and he felt that someone was looking over his shoulder at every turn. Since he hadn't interacted with other humans for two years, he had lost his ability to communicate, and he spent his days walking around in the tunnels hissing at imaginary foes and living on mushrooms and water. Jeshua's insanity made him forget who he was or where he was. He reeked and he hadn't shaved nor cut his hair for two years.

Suddenly, Jeshua came back to his senses. He knew who he was and what he was meant to do. He went back to the abandoned camp at Gomorrah Cliffs where he bathed, shaved, and changed his clothes. He went to the tunnel entrance and waited. He sat there quietly and at peace. His time to make a difference would soon come.

Chapter 82: On the Run.

Keila Eisenstein was looking in a pair of high-grade binoculars through the rear window of the *"Miss Freedom"* spaceship that she commanded. Things looked bleak for her rebel group, The Martian Humanist Alliance. They had narrowly escaped a Terran Council expedition that destroyed their base "Freedom First" on the Asteroid Sylvia. Unfortunately, they were pursued by Keila's arch enemy, Rear Admiral Bjorn Muller, onboard his command ship "ISS Supreme Earth"

Inspired by her mother, Susanna, Keila had joined the Martian Humanist Alliance, a rebel group that smuggled supplies between poor worlds to help them circumventing the Terran Council trade monopoly. The Terran Council trade monopoly kept fringe worlds destitute while amassing wealth to the wealthiest families on Earth. Keila looked at the picture of her mother, which she had in a necklace hanging around her neck. Keila missed Susanna, but this was not the right time to mourn her. Her crew needed her, and they were far from safe.

Keila closed her eyes, and she saw how the wounded Susanna was sucked out into the vacuum of space after a missile hit her asteroid base. Keila trusted her vision. Although she had not seen it happen with her own eyes, she knew that the vision was telling the truth, her premonitions always were.

Keila closed her eyes and she hoped for insight on how to get away from the pursuing ship. She saw nothing and she felt despair. Was this the end, or would she figure something out? The premonitions had helped her countless times to escape overwhelming odds. That's how she had become a hero for the downtrodden and the most wanted on the Terran Council's elimination list. Since she could only see the death of her mother, Keila opened her eyes and tried to figure out a solution. The situation was dire:

- Her ship was slower than Bjorn's, so she could not outrun him.
- Her ship was unarmed, so she could not fight him.
- There were no friendly colonies nearby so she couldn't hide from her enemies.

Keila closed her eyes again. Her mother spoke to her in a vision *"The time has come... The time has come to save Eden from the tyrant Abraham."* But what did this vision mean? Susanna had told Keila that she grew up in a world without technology, which was governed by a dictator who claimed to be God. But there was no place called Eden in the solar system and Susanna had refused to take Keila there. Keila had never believed in the existence of Eden. She knew most of the ins and outs of the solar system, and she had never heard about such place from anyone else but her mother. *"But the vision has to mean something,"* Keila thought and she summoned her co-captain Sven to discuss their options.

Keila:

- How does it look. Do you have any reports from the Freedom First base?

Sven:

- No. We must assume that the base is destroyed. You saw the armada they sent to kill us.

Keila:

- My hopes and prayers are with our allies that were there.

Sven:

- Hopes and prayers don't win wars. Actions do.

Keila:

- I never wanted this war. I wanted to set things right. I hoped
that we could live in peace and harmony.

Sven:

- Well, our enemies saw things differently.

- Have you made any plans yet, or are you still waiting for your
"premonitions"?

Keila paused. She did not like Sven's scepticism, but she could empathise with it. Sven was rational and a highly skilled pilot, but he lacked
imagination and divine inspiration. She understood that her gift was beyond most people's understanding.
Keila:

- My mother spoke to me.
- It is time for us to save Eden.

Sven:

- Are you serious? We are in the middle of a crisis, and you are
bringing up your mums' childhood story?

Keila:

- Don't you dare to call my mother a liar after everything she
did for you!

Sven backed down. This was not the time to argue. Besides, Keila and
Susanna had saved them many times in the past.
Sven:

- I apologise Keila.

- I did not mean that Susanna was a liar.

- I think she had a traumatic upbringing and Eden was her coping mechanism.

Keila:

- Apology accepted.

- Now, look at this map of this part of the solar system. If Eden existed, where do you think it would be?

Sven:

- Nowhere.

Keila:

- Not helpful, Sven. What about B528A & B528B

Sven:

- Research stations claimed by House Goldstein
- Most likely hostile.

Keila:

- House Goldstein? They are not part of the Terran Council, are they?

Sven:

- They used to be. They were the mightiest faction on Earth at one stage, but they declined after the death of Abraham Goldstein. Eventually, they lost their seat on the Terran Council and House Bolivar replaced them.

Keila:

- Hmm. Abraham Goldstein...

- Susanna mentioned freeing Eden from the tyrant Abraham.
- B528A must be Eden.
- Set the course for Eden, Sven.

Sven:

- I am not sure about this...

Keila:

- You don't have to believe, Sven, just do.

Sven:

- Understood, Keila.
- I have set the course for B528A.

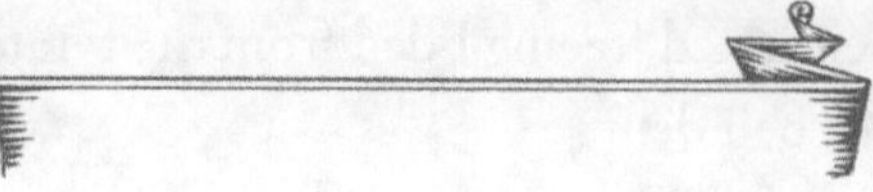

Chapter 83: Keila is Crashlanding on Eden.

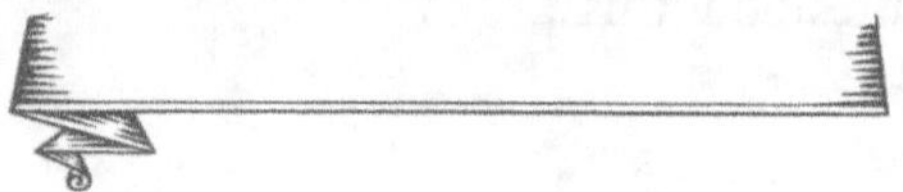

12 hours later, Miss Freedom was outside Eden. It was ominously quiet as they drove past Eden. There were weapon systems in place, but they were not communicated with nor fired at. Keila entered one of the emergency pods on the Miss Freedom. The crew had refused to land on the asteroid, as it seemed like their pursuers had given up their pursuit. Sven had tried to convince Keila to not go to Eden, but she had stood by it. Her visions had told her that it was time to save Eden and she had more faith in her sights than she had in Sven and the rest of the crew. They parted ways, and Sven gave her a radio transmitter with a reach of 1/3 astronomical unit (50,000,000 kilometres), so she could communicate with a friendly vessel when she needed to be picked up.

Keila looked at Miss Freedom as her emergency pods made its way to land on Eden. Suddenly, she saw something that terrified her. Bjorn's command ship approaching from the blind side on top of Miss Freedom. Keila pulled up her radio to warn Sven and the crew but it was too late, and moments later Miss Freedom was eviscerated by the direct fire from the enemy ship. Panicking to get away, Keila disengaged the safety switch on her escape pod and she crash landed on Eden. Her escape pod crashed close to Gomorrah Cliffs, and she lost her consciousness upon impact.

Chapter 84: A Warship at the Gates.

Abraham was meditating when Nuriel tried to reach him. Abraham entered Nuriel's mind to see what he saw, and it was troubling news. Outside the Divine Control Centre, there was a Terran Council warship as well as the debris of another ship.

Abraham panicked; had the Council sent the army to stop him? If they had, that would be the end of him, as the remnants of House Goldstein would not come to his defence. Abraham calmed down. He was on a well-armed battle station more than capable of taking out a single warship. The Terran Council knew this, so if they had come after him, they would have come in force and not with a single ship.

Abraham decided to communicate with the vessel over the hologram generator. Abraham spoke through Nuriel, as his robotic body would not be well received.

Abraham (Via Nuriel's body):

- Rear Admiral Bjorn Muller, you have entered and discharged your weapons in a restricted area, state your business.

Bjorn Muller:

- The Terran Council is the rightful owner of the entire solar system. So, restricted areas do not concern us, Nuriel.

- We have destroyed a hostile ship in this area. The hostile ship belonged to the infamous criminal Keila Eisenstein.

Abraham:

- Very well.

- You shouldn't have intruded. I can assure you that we will file a complaint with your superiors.

- Now leave and let us deal with the destroyed ship.

Bjorn:

- I am afraid that leaving is not an option.

- We believe that Keila escaped the ship and landed on the surface of B528A. We will not leave without apprehending her.

- We will send down our men to find her.

Bjorn's attitude angered Abraham. He was an intruder who stepped in and started making demands. Abraham couldn't allow Terran Council officers to land on Eden to look for a suspect. In the Abrahameon, Abraham claimed that Earth was destroyed and the people on Eden were all that remained of humanity. Having foreign troops with advanced technology looking for a rebel would crush the illusion of Abraham's divinity. This would sow dissent that was unstoppable, even with the powers that the divine technology chip gave him.

Abraham aimed all the orbital lasers at Bjorn's ship and spoke:

- I won't allow that. Eden is private property and not under the authority of the Terran Council.

- This was decided on the Terran Council meeting in 2785. It will stay this way in perpetuity.

Bjorn:

- Are you out of your mind?

- You are threatening a Terran Council command ship. Attack us, and the entire fleet will come after you!

Abraham:

- Yes. But you will be dead long before they get here.

Bjorn:

- This is unacceptable!

Abraham:

- Your intrusion on my private property is unacceptable.

- But I will let you live if you stand down.

- Move your ship to the dark side of Eden. I will send men looking for the fugitive.

Bjorn Muller turned silent. Abraham's attitude perplexed him and he did not know how to continue. If Bjorn ignored Abraham's warnings and sent men looking for Keila, it could lead to a fatal confrontation. But Bjorn could not back down, as he had to look after the reputation of the Terran Council. Bjorn found a middle ground.

Bjorn:

- I will give you three days to deliver Keila to us. If you don't, we will attack.

Abraham:

- Very well.
- We will sort this out. Now get your ship to the dark side of Eden.

Abraham watched as the Terran Council warship travelled to the dark side of Eden. He would contact the Terran Council and ensure that this troublemaker was sent home and reprimanded. Abraham would remind them of the agreement made back in 2785 when Eden was awarded the status as his domain for perpetuity.

While this problem was averted, the worst problem was still there. An outsider was running around with critical knowledge and modern technology on Eden. He needed to wake up all the angels and send them to find and eliminate this outsider before she caused any more issues.

Chapter 85: Panic on Eden.

Meanwhile, the Edenites was panicking and believed that the end was near. They had seen the explosion in the sky when Keila's ship blew up. It was clear to them that something was amiss when six out of seven suns stopped shining and instead illuminated the alien spaceship in the sky. The turning of the orbital lasers caused the surface of Eden to have a sudden and frosty night while the alien spaceship was illuminated and highly visible. Eventually, the suns came back, and the foreign ship disappeared, but the event had caused significant doubts among the Edenites, and chaos ensued.

Adina saw her chance to get away from the satellite that followed her. She knew that she would not be the first thing on Abraham's mind, and this was the opportunity that she had waited for. Adina got on her horse and galloped to the closest entrance to the maintenance tunnels. She needed to use this window of opportunity to find her brother. Adina entered the tunnels. The tunnel networks under Eden were vast, but she was confident that she would discover Jeshua. Providence had caused the explosion in the sky, and it would lead her to Jeshua. Together, they would find a way to depose of Abraham, so that she could rule Eden.

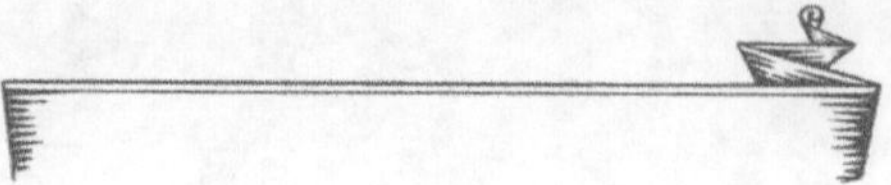

Chapter 86: An Otherworldly Beauty.

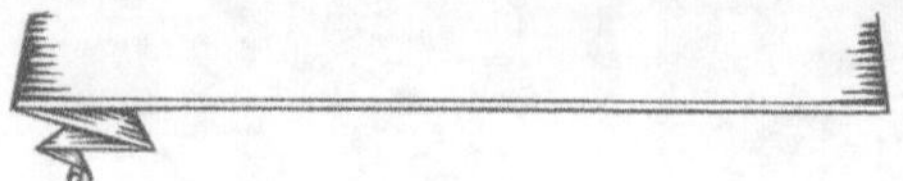

Jeshua heard a loud bang close to the tunnel entrance at Gomorrah Cliffs. He felt a moment of fear; had the angels decided to come after him again? Jeshua ignored the fear. Fear had kept him down in the dark for the last two years, and it was time to act. If death had come for him, he would accept it, and if it were his salvation, he would embrace it. Regardless, it was no longer time for him to hide.

Jeshua exited the tunnel and saw the crashed wreckage. It looked different from anything he had seen on Eden, although the technology reminded him of the angels. He remembered what Adina had told him; that Earth was still around and that there lived humans there. Was this some of these humans, and why had they come?

Jeshua opened the hatch to the wrecked escape pad. Inside the escape pad, there was an unconscious woman, who was the most beautiful woman he had ever seen. She looked so different from all the other humans on Eden, and her clothes and hairstyle were different. She was an otherworldly beauty. Jeshua gave her a gentle pat on the shoulder. She did not respond. Was she dead? Jeshua touched her throat to feel her pulse. She had a weak but stable pulse.

Jeshua realised something. That one of the suns would soon be straight on top of them, and when it was, Abraham would find out about them and send his angels to kill them, or kill them outright with his orbital lasers. Jeshua had seen people being murdered by the suns in the past as it was one of the favourite ways for Abraham to kill people; incinerating them with a hot beam of concentrated sunlight. Jeshua gathered his strength and he lifted Keila out of the escape pod. After that, he dragged Keila to the relative safety of the tunnels.

Half a minute later, the satellite discovered Keila's escape pod, which let Abraham know about her location. He sent Gabriel and Nuriel to investigate as the other angels were still being revived from the cryogenic sleep and they were unable to act until they had recovered.

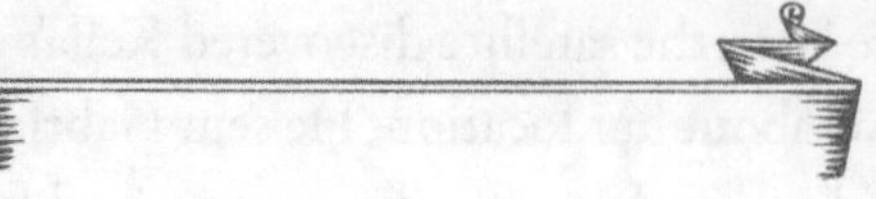

Chapter 87: A Cave of Carnal Desire.

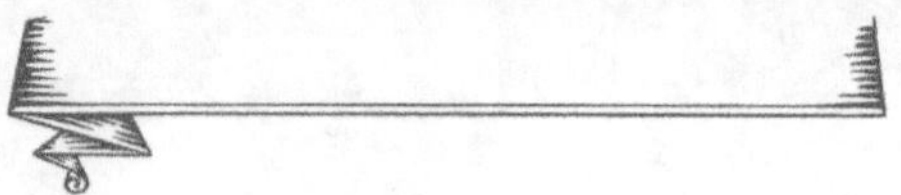

Keila was returning from unconsciousness to a dreamlike state. She had another vision. In the vision she had seductive and erotic sex with an athletic stranger in a cave, with a ring of fire around them. The sex was pulsating and getting stronger and stronger until it climaxed, and she woke up.

To Keila's surprise, she woke up in a cave looking at a stranger. This stranger was not as attractive as the one in her visions. His facial features were similar, but he looked sickly and malnourished. Was this man a friend or a foe? He was definitely not an officer of the Terran Council armed forces. But who was he, and what was this place? Everything in the cave looked ancient, and she had no idea why they weren't using electric lighting to make the area more liveable.

Keila recalled what her mum had told her about Eden. It was a ter-raformed world that housed a strange cult, living as people did in ancient times. The cultists worshipped someone called Grandmaster Abraham. Keila had assumed that this was one of her mum's made up childhood stories. But the visions had led her here, and she could only do what they showed her.

She closed her eyes again. *"Follow the vision,"* she thought. She did not know why she was getting visions, but she knew that they were of divine origin. While she had preferred to be able to choose what premonitions she would see, she could only make the best of God's plan for her life. She got the erotic vision again. She hesitated a bit; the man in front of her wasn't attractive in real life. Then again what damage could it do to her? Maybe the reason for her to have sex with the man was not for her pleasure, but to get ahead. She would do what needed to be done, to get rid of the tyrannical cultist Abraham.

Keila looked at Jeshua again. She could tell that he was bursting with sexual desire. Keila decided to go for it. The visions told her to have sex with the stranger, and she would rather be in control of her life than being raped. Jeshua reciprocated, and they had sex. It was all over after a couple of minutes. Keila sighed of relief. The sex was mediocre, but it had relieved her stress. She realised that she hadn't slept much lately and that the crash had injured her. She leaned back and fell asleep in Jeshua's arms.

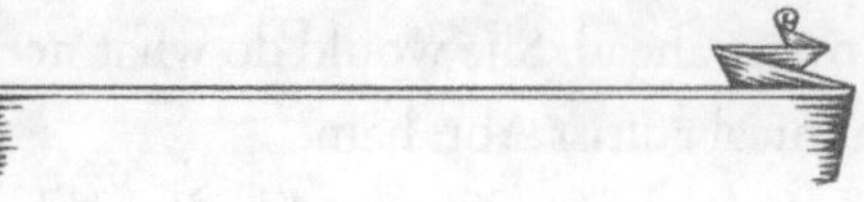

Chapter 88: Adina Intervenes and Saves Jeshua.

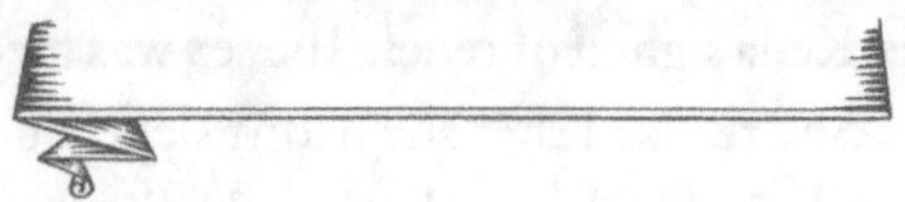

Jeshua looked at Keila, who slept on his shoulder. She was beautiful and mysterious. They hadn't spoken much before she seduced him. It had surprised him, but it was a welcome relief from the fear and paranoia that had dictated his life. Jeshua had accepted that he was going to die today, so he had followed his curiosity and investigated the crash. He had uncovered this angel sent to him to show him paradise.

Jeshua had never been with a woman before. Was he in love? He wasn't sure. The Edenite way was all about loving and worshipping Grandmaster Abraham. The union between man and woman through marriage was necessary for procreation, but the emotions between them were inconsequential. While Jeshua was an active opponent of Abraham and his teachings, he had never reflected on the emotion of love and attraction before, so he did not know his position on the subject. All he knew was that he had found paradise between Keila's legs and that he wanted to return there as soon as possible.

Jeshua looked up and he realised that he was in trouble. Gabriel and Nuriel stood next to his bed, looking down on him Keila. Realising there was no point in resisting or trying to escape he pulled Keila towards him and hugged her. If he was going to die, he wanted to die in her arms. He took a deep breath. He was ready. But the shot never came. He looked up again; the angels were still standing there, unaware of his location, staring straight through him. He looked at Keila. she was awake, trembling with fear. Jeshua heard the angels speak.

Gabriel:

- What is happening, I can smell him from this bed, but I can't see him

Nuriel:

- Maybe the foreign bitch brought some form of cloaking device?

Gabriel:

- That's a negative. I have scanned all the different spectrums, and I would have detected them.

Nuriel:

- Just shoot the bed then.

Gabriel:

- True.

As Gabriel pulled up his weapon, Keila dragged Jeshua out of the bed. They ran into the tunnels while Gabriel was shooting the bed to pieces.

Nuriel:

- Did you get them?

Gabriel:

- That's a negative; there is no blood beside the smell of them is gone.

Meanwhile, Adina observed the angels through their eyes. It was a close call, and she was happy that she had accessed their minds when she had. Through her ability to control their minds, Adina had controlled their vision so that they couldn't see her brother Jeshua and his mystery woman. Fortunately, her brother had made a run for it instead of being pulverised by the multitude of bullets destroying the bed he lay in.

Adina felt frustrated that she had entered the tunnels from the wrong part of Eden. She should have realised that Jeshua would come back to the caves near Gomorrah Cliffs. That part was his "home," and that's where he had spent most of the time since he went into hiding from Abraham and his goons. But she could not foresee things or empathise with people in a usual manner. Her special powers made her able to see and know everything a chipped person saw or understood, but this gift also made her blind for how non-chipped people were thinking. This inability was not a big issue on Eden, where everyone had a divine chip implanted at birth, but it had made her unable to understand her brother. She contemplated to find her brother and his mystery woman, but she decided against it. The tunnel networks under Eden where widespread and she was 50 kilometres away from his position. Finding him in the dark was like finding a needle in a haystack. Besides, there was another more urgent reason. Abraham would soon start looking for her, and when he found her, she was better off being a good girl spreading his word than a rebel lurking around in the dark tunnels under Eden.

Adina made her way back to the surface and she rode back home. She was thinking of the half-naked mystery woman that she had seen through the eyes of the angels. Who was she? Adina knew that an intruder had crashed on Eden and that Abraham was desperate to find and detain her. The foreign whore had not wasted any time in seducing Jeshua, but what was her endgame? Was she a potential ally or was she worth more as a tribute to Abraham?

Adina realised that she had the means to find out, while still showing her friendly façade to Abraham. Her psionic powers had grown so much so that she could simultaneously control a multitude of humans. So, all she needed to do was to send them to look for Jeshua. If she found Jeshua, she would speak to him through her host, and if the humans were detected and killed by Abraham, there was nothing that bound them to her. Adina got home and went to the meditation room in the temple she was supervising. Unlike the angels and Abraham, she could control humans directly. She did not know why this was the case, but she knew that neither Abraham nor the other angels were able to do so. Adina went into a deep meditative state. She needed to pinpoint and influence the humans around the tunnel entrances to search for Jeshua. If she did, one of them would find Jeshua, and she would establish contact. It was a dangerous move for the humans that she influenced as entering the tunnels were prohibited to the Edenites. Then again, for Adina, the individual humans of Eden were expendable; while she did not seek to punish and torment them, she did not care if Abraham did it, if they could serve her cause.

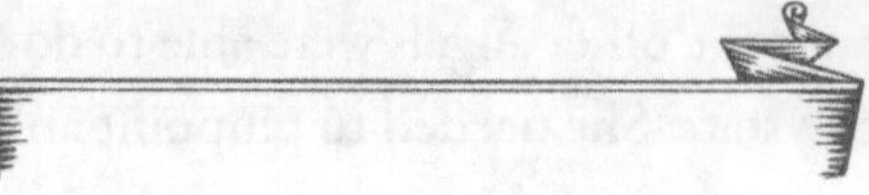

Chapter 89: Abraham Gives a Fatal Order.

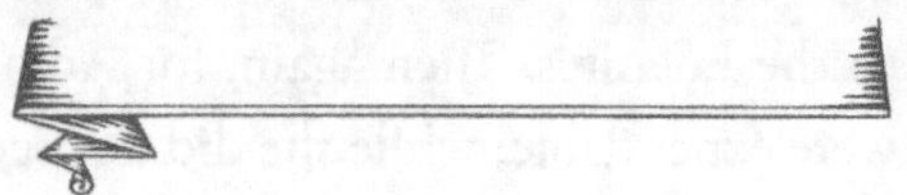

Abraham:

- It's all on the video captured by your helmet cameras.

- They were right in front of your eyes; you were staring at Lucifer's son and his foreign whore for ages, and you did nothing. Then they get away, and you start shooting at their bed! Explain yourselves

Gabriel:

- I swear to you, Grandmaster Abraham. We could not see them. We could smell them, but we couldn't see them.

- Eventually, we shot their bed as we deemed that they might be using some form of cloaking device to stay out of sight.

Abraham:

- Well, you should have shot when they were still there.

- You are supposed to be elite soldiers. Yet you could not see two important fugitives in front of your own eyes.

- They were not even using any cloaking device. They are visible on your helmet camera, which is filming the visible spectrum of light.

- Next time, use your instincts. if you can smell them, shoot them!

Gabriel:

- Yes, sir

Abraham:

- Dismissed, angels!

As the angels left the room, Abraham took a seat in front of a computer terminal. He had chosen not to punish them for their failure. He lacked in manpower, and he had realised that they told him the truth. They were, in fact, unable to see Jeshua and the foreign woman. The big question was why they couldn't see Jeshua and Keila. Someone was manipulating their cognitive capabilities. But who could it be? Abraham had experienced similar episodes in the past, where angels had blacked out for no apparent reason.

Could Adina be behind it? She had stronger psionic powers than the angels, despite having the same chip implanted.

What made Adina an unlikely culprit, was her intense zeal for Abraham and his ideology. She was his strongest advocate on Eden and the only one on Eden, who showed no doubts in trusting his intentions. But was this her real feelings? Abraham felt like Adina was directing him and showing him what he wanted to see instead of what she really felt. This seemed implausible as the god chip was meant to have total access to the thoughts and senses of the people connected to a lower tiered chip. Abraham decided that Adina was not the one sabotaging him and that he was doing him a disservice harbouring paranoid thoughts about his granddaughter when there was a real threat on Eden, Keila.

Being cut off from House Goldstein, Abraham did not have detailed intelligence reports about Keila Eisenstein, but there was plenty of information on the Spacenet. Keila was one of the leaders for the Martian Humanist Alliance, a revolutionary group who fought for the downtrodden and hated the Terran Council's dominion over the solar system. Despite her young age of 22 years, Keila had reached the top 10 list for people chased by the Terran Council, and there was a 10 million Terran Credits bounty on her head. Nothing of this explained what she was doing on Eden, but then Abraham saw who Keila's mother was.

Susanna had been a unique offering as she had volunteered to be selected. This behaviour was against the rules, but as they had received a high offer for her, they went ahead and sold her off to Mahmoud Rashid. Abraham tried to recollect what else had happened on that day 32 years ago. He realised that they had forgotten to erase Susanna's memories and disconnect the divine technology chip from her brain.

Susanna knew everything, and if she knew the right people, she might have figured out how to remove and reverse engineer the divine technology chip. That would explain why her dangerous daughter had landed on Eden, and it also confirmed Keila's reason for coming

Fortunately, Keila had lost the rest of her crew when the Terran Council destroyed her ship. Keila didn't any weapon, otherwise, she would have attacked Gabriel and Nuriel. Although she managed to stay hidden from the angels' vision, she could not mask her scent. Abraham would use this to his advantage. He contacted Gabriel:

- Gabriel, I have a task for you

- Lead a group of four angels to the tunnels at Gomorrah Cliffs. Shoot at anything that smells like Jeshua or Keila. Let's flush these bastards out.

Gabriel:

- Copy that, sir. I will gather a group and move at once.

Chapter 90: Keila Sets a Trap.

Keila was staring into the ceiling with Jeshua on top of her pumping her rhythmically. It was not very enjoyable, but it was not the end of the world either. Throughout her life, she had been tortured by Bjorn Muller and other criminals, having sex with an unattractive man was not a big deal. She felt perplexed that Jeshua was thinking about sex when they were chased by armed men. Jeshua seemed so beguiled by her as if he had never been with a woman before. No matter, Jeshua was her ally for now, and she needed allies to get away from this place alive, especially with the Terran Council on her trail. She could feel him coming, and they could now focus on the challenging task at hand.

Keila:

- Feeling better now, big boy?

Jeshua:

- Yes. I feel like I am in heaven. I have been waiting for you all my life.

Keila:

- Me too

Keila forced herself to smile before changing to a more serious tone.

- But for us to stay together, we need to find a way to kill those men before they kill us. Then we can leave this place.

Jeshua:

- No there is no need for that, we can hide. I know these caves better than they do, so they will never find us. There is enough mushrooms and water for us to live here in peace while Abraham can rule over the surface dwellers.

Keila:

- But don't you want to come with me and see my home? It's a lot cosier than these damp tunnels.

Jeshua:

- Your home?
- Don't you live with Abraham and the angels in the Divine Control Centre?

Keila decided to play along to see if she could get Jeshua to comply. Keila:

- Yes, I do.
- How did you figure that out?

Jeshua:

- Because my sister told me that the angels were not gods, but men.
- Men need women. Thus, there must be women at the Divine Control Centre.

Keila:

- Yes, you and your sister are brilliant.

- The male angels are the mean bullies, and the female angels are lovely.

- If you help me take control of Eden, things will be a lot better. You'll be able to live on the surface with your friends in peace and harmony.

Jeshua:

- I used to have friends.

- My sister directed me to people who were like me.

- We lived together in the caves like family.

- But then my sister wanted to fight Abraham, so my friends went out to fight. They all died, and left me alone in the tunnels.

Keila:

- Well, I am not your sister.

Jeshua:

- Yet you want the same thing. You want to fight Abraham and steal his power.

Keila:

- And what do you want?

Jeshua:

- I told you already. I want to stay here with you.

Keila started to get frustrated with Jeshua. If he was not going to be helpful, she was better off ditching him and figuring this out by herself. Then again, Jeshua seemed gullible, stupid, and out of touch. Keila decided to make one last attempt at playing it nicely before telling Jeshua to get fucked.

Keila:

- I would love to stay here with you, but I can't.

- You see; I need angel food that I can only find up in the sky; otherwise, I will die.

Jeshua:

- My sister never told me about angel food. I think you are lying.

- However, I was ready to die today. Yet, here I stand, united with the most beautiful woman in the world.

- I'll do your bidding.

Keila:

- I am glad to hear that, Jeshua.

Jeshua:

- So, how do you plan on killing the angels?

Keila:

- Well, I noticed they could smell us, but they couldn't see us.

- Their commander is going to believe that we are wearing an experimental cloaking device that hides our visuals. So, with that in mind, he is going to shoot at our smell signature.

Jeshua:

- What does that even mean?

Keila:

- If they can't see us, they will shoot at things that smell like us. If we can make them smell like us, they might shoot at each other.

Jeshua:

- How are you going to do this?

Keila:

- Just listen, and I will tell you how this is going to play out.

After that, Keila described how she was going to lure the angels to kill each other. It was an intricate and challenging plan, but it was the only option they had on hand. Keila had recognised the armour and weaponry that Gabriel and Nuriel had. They wore mechanised suits with thick armour that was impenetrable with the primitive weapons they had on hand. The mechanised exoskeleton also made the angels powerful, and with quick reflexes that made it impossible to overpower them. Their only chance was to make the angels kill each other. Fortunately, There was a reason why Keila was the most wanted individuals in the solar system.

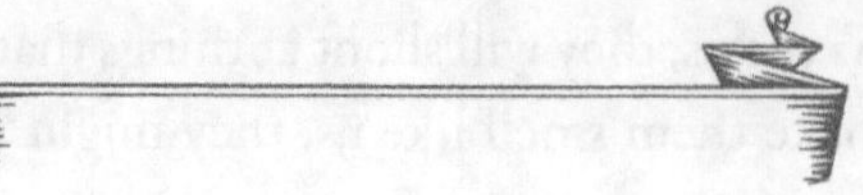

Chapter 91: Abraham Notices That People are Flocking to the Tunnels.

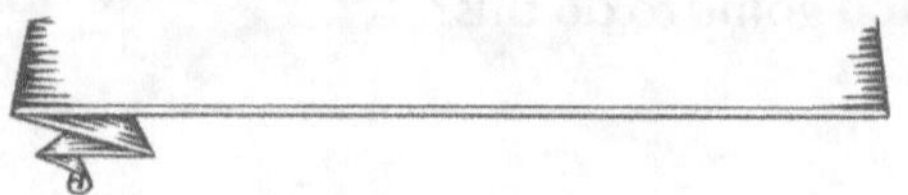

The days after the appearance and destruction of the spaceship around Eden, The Edenite society descended into chaos. Fear and confusion spread among the population as the appearance of other humans contradicted the claim in Abrahameon that Eden was the last bastion of humankind. What made the chaos worse was that Abraham's religious scriptures were focused on control through fear, power, and obedience, so softer values like love and compassion were not emphasised. Thus, when there were doubts about Abraham's powers, the Edenite society spiralled down to chaos, with murders, looting and rapes at an endemic level.

Abraham did what he could to stop the chaos. As it turned out, he could not do as much as he wanted. While Abraham could kill all the wretched sinners, this was not a practical option as that would kill off most of the population and would leave him with very few subjects to rule.

The problem was that he had controlled his subjects through fear and control, and when there were doubts about his powers, the fabrics of society collapsed. At that stage, he only had direct authority over the angels, and they only numbered 20, in comparison to the over 10,000 humans on Eden. The temple guard and the religious militia had disbanded, and they were contributing to the chaos instead of quelling it. Since a few angels were needed to control and support the Divine Control Center, and a few were needed to hunt to down Keila, that meant that only a handful of angels could be spared to police Eden and try to restore order. Since Eden span over 30,000 square kilometres, this was a mammoth task.

Fortunately, time was on his side. As soon as he had captured Keila and got the Terran Council off his back, he would have all the time in the world to restore order on Eden.

When Abraham scanned through all the humans connected to the divine technology, he noticed that many of them were exploring the maintenance tunnels that was running below the surface of Eden. His first reaction was rage and fury. Humans were forbidden to enter the maintenance tunnels as they *"were the gateway to hell"* and he wished to punish all the offenders. But then a pragmatic thought dominated his mind: that the humans walking around in the tunnels would help him to find Keila. He decided to watch them from afar to see how their venture into the tunnels played out.

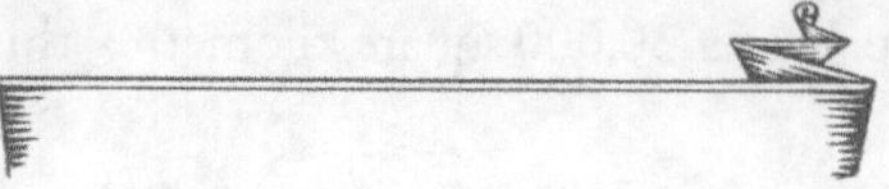

Chapter 92: Adina and Jeshua Prepare to Strike Against Abraham.

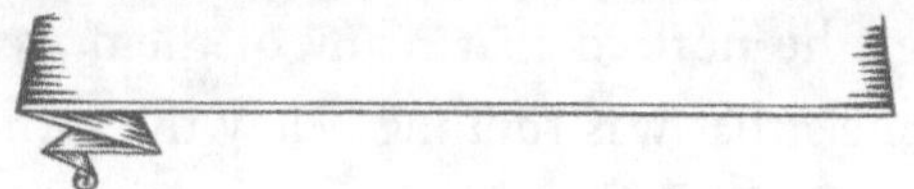

Eventually, one of the humans roaming in the maintenance tunnels came across Keila and Jeshua. Fortunately, Adina noticed their presence first. Adina took control over Elizabeth and spoke through her.

Adina:

- Jeshua and Keila. Don't be afraid. Your sister is talking through me.

Keila to Jeshua:

- What's with that woman? I have never seen anyone with an expression like that, she looks like a zombie.

Jeshua:

- My sister has extraordinary powers. Let us see what she has to say.
- Thank you for contacting me, sister. It has been a long time.

Adina:

- Yes, two years

- I could not contact you as you don't have a divine technology chip implanted, and I did not want to send others looking for you as that would endanger you.

Jeshua:

- So why are you contacting me now?

Adina:

- The arrival of your special friend has plunged Eden into chaos.

- The Edenites saw the other spaceship destroyed with their own eyes. That proved that Abraham was lying, that the people on Eden are not the only ones left of humanity.

- We have been planning to free Eden from Abraham for five years. There won't be a better time than now.

Jeshua:

- I agree. We have a plan in place.

Adina:

- Tell me about it?

Keila:

- I don't know you, and I am not sharing my secrets with a stranger.

Adina:

- Fine, then I won't help you.

Jeshua:

- Please sister, Keila is just a bit on edge after everything that has happened to her. Any help would be much appreciated.

- We plan to kill Gabriel and Nuriel who was lurking around in these tunnels before.

Adina:

- They still are, they are down here with two others. About five kilometres away.

Jeshua:

- We only planned for two angels Can you distract the other two?

Adina:

- I'll see what I can do.

Jeshua:

- Good.
- The trap is around here. Can you alert them to our position?

Adina:

- I will release my control over Elizabeth. Then Abraham will know where you are and that you are unarmed. That would lure them straight in.

Jeshua:

- Excellent, you should do that.

Adina:

- Farewell, until we meet again.

Adina released control of Elizabeth who panicked and started screaming in terror. Abraham noticed her elevated emotional state and rejoiced at what he saw. His decision to not punish the sinners who had ventured into the tunnels had paid off, and he now knew the position of the fugitives and that they were unarmed. He would send his strike force to intercept at them. To stall their escape, he would send this frenzied woman to attack them. She was, after all, expendable.

After a short struggle, Jeshua and Keila subdued Elizabeth. They left her tied up and gagged but conscious. They stayed close to her to give Abraham a false sense of security before carrying out the ambush.

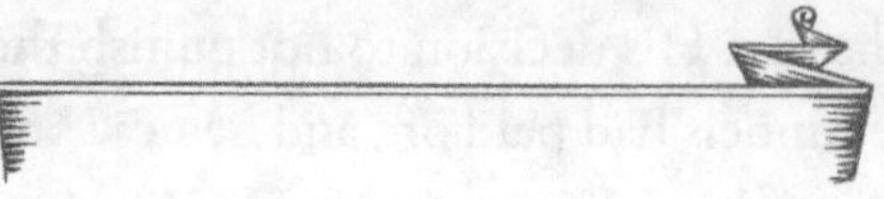

Chapter 93: A Two-Front Attack.

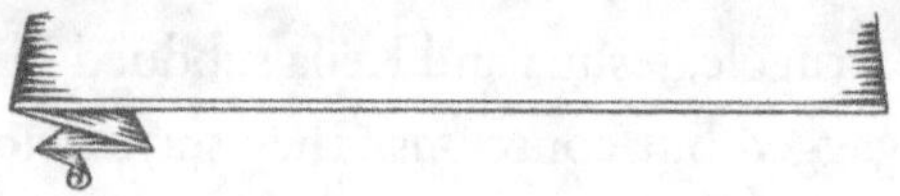

Adina noticed that the pursuing four angels were only three kilometres away from the position of Jeshua and Keila and they were approaching quickly. Although they were on foot, the top running speeds of angels were over 60 kilometres an hour due to electrical stimulation from the exoskeleton suit. Hence, they would reach Jeshua in a less than three minutes. Adina did not know the details of Jeshua's plan, but she knew that it was meant to kill two angels, and she had promised to distract the other two. Adina took a deep breath. She realised that if they failed today her life would be over. In a way, it was strange that Abraham had not killed her already, as he had no trouble killing people that he perceived as threats.

At the surface, the angel Eremiel was giving out instructions to the religious militia on how to restore order to their village. Adina focused and sent the army into frenzy. To Eremiel's shock they jumped him and pulled his weapon out of his hand and tried to shoot him. This attempted attack was unsuccessful as the activation code for the weapon was in Eremiel glove, and the gun wouldn't fire without it. Eremiel tried to fly off, but the weight of the humans trying to pull him down stopped him from lifting. Eremiel activated the electrical field on his combat suit and electrocuted the attacking militia men. However, enabling the electromagnetic field short-circuited his suit as it had taken blunt damage from the army beating him with their primitive weapons.

Eremiel felt weak. Since the electrical circuits broke, he was carrying a cumbersome suit unassisted. He got up on one knee. He was looking at the angry mob a few meters away from him. A few of them lie dead on the ground burnt from the electrocution, but the others were just even angrier. He contacted all nearby angels for immediate evacuation.

Gabriel picked up the transmission as he was passing in the tunnels below Eremiel. He ordered the others to stop.

Gabriel:

- Eremiel is in danger. Haniel and Hamshal, go to the surface and help him fend off that peasant mob.

Haniel:

- Master Gabriel, Abraham ordered us to focus on killing the two fugitives.

Gabriel:

- Let me and Nuriel deal with them. They are unarmed and they should not pose a threat.

- Eremiel is in danger. We can't allow a peasant mob to kill one of our own.

Haniel:

- Understood, sir

Having said this, Haniel and Hamshal rushed to the surface where the militia mind-controlled by Adina, had set a trap. As they rushed up from the tunnels, the army set them on fire through pouring olive oil over them and setting them alight. Haniel and Hamshal whose armours were still intact were protected by the built-in cooling in the armour, while Eremiel was roasted in his outfit. Abraham decided to control the two angels directly. Focusing his efforts on Haniel and Hamshal, he lost vision and focus on Gabriel and Nuriel who had reached their targets in the tunnels below.

Meanwhile, Gabriel and Nuriel caught the vision of Jeshua and Keila. They were running separate ways into different tunnels. Gabriel and Nuriel split up to run after them. After a short dash, Gabriel reached a platform with a smoke-filled smelly cave below. The smoke was so thick that he couldn't see anything in there. He could not smell Jeshua or Keila either. Suddenly, he heard a call "now" and they hit Gabriel with a container filled with a liquid. After that, he could see that smell signature of Jeshua appearing on the other side of the room. He remembered his orders, raised his weapon and fired off a multitude of bullets. Gabriel realised that someone had shot him. He slumped down to the ground. The last thing Gabriel saw was Jeshua's face before everything turned black.

Everything had gone according to plan. After Keila and Jeshua's first encounter with the angels, Keila had predicted that they would fire at their smell signature if they were to meet again. She had been fighting and evading the Terran Council's strike teams for years, and she knew what technologies and tactics they were utilising. By making sure that the angels smelled like them, Keila tricked them into shooting each other. To make sure the angels smelled like them, they had filled two small clay containers with their own blood and sealed them, to create a blood-filled container that would splash upon impact. They had chosen the place for the ambush carefully. They set up the ambush in a cave with two different paths leading to two different platforms overlooking the cave. In the cave, there was a type of mushroom that gave off a very thick and smelly gas that would block the angels' vision and would mask Jeshua's and Keila's smell. Once they threw the blood containers, this smell was strong enough to be picked up by the angels' enhanced senses tricking them into shooting each other.

Keila got dressed first. The angel suit she got from Nuriel's corpse was too big for her, but it was still operational. She made her way Jeshua who was struggling to open the suit and get Gabriel's dead body out of it. With Keila's help, he was done in a couple of minutes. Jeshua's suit was also operational.

Keila:

- We better hurry!

Jeshua:

- To do what? We have weapons and armour now. We can fight them here if they dare to come down.

Keila:

- No, we'll take the battle to them, that's the only way!

Jeshua:

- That's suicide; the orbital lasers will shoot us down.

Keila:

- I know what I am supposed to do here. I am going with or without you.

Jeshua:

- I am coming with you! I don't want to live without you.

Keila:

- I am happy to hear that.
- Providence will make us win this battle.

After saying this, Keila and Jeshua rushed to the nearest exit. Once they reached the surface, they began their ascent to the Divine Control Centre.

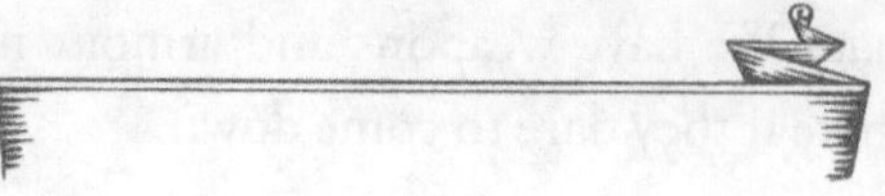

Chapter 94: Adina Distracts Abraham.

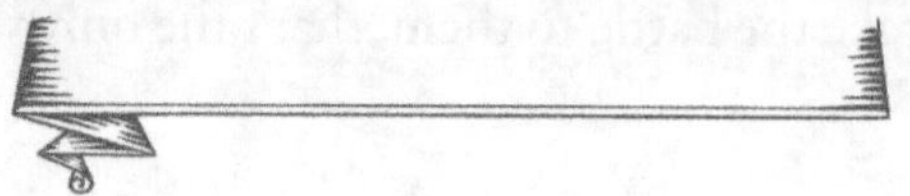

Abraham could feel a sharp pain when Gabriel and Nuriel died. Through a strange twist of fate, however, he did not notice their deaths, as Eremiel died at the same time. Moments later, the orbital lasers came into position and Abraham wreaked havoc on the rebels. They tried to flee when they saw the fire coming down from the sky, but Abraham left them no quarter, and killed them all.

Abraham saw the battlefield through the eyes of Haniel, and it was a scene that broke his spirits. His entire religious militia lay dead on the field. There were 250 dead men, men who were meant to do his bidding on Eden. Eremiel was dead beyond resurrection burnt to the bone. Without human troops, he would not be able to restore Eden to order in years. His number of angels were dwindling, and they were not easy to replace. Abraham considered killing everyone on Eden and start over. It was easy to do. If he deactivated the nanotechnology layer that covered Eden, its atmosphere would leak out in space, as Eden's gravity was not strong enough to keep an atmosphere. Without an atmosphere, every living being on Eden would die within minutes. Abraham stopped himself. He had invested so much time and money to create Eden. It was too laborious and demoralising to replace its entire population with new subjects.

Instead, Abraham focused on getting the culprit behind the chaos, and he had a clear suspect, Adina. By backtracking the connections of the fallen men on the battlefield, the conclusion was clear: Adina was to blame, and she was a lot stronger than Abraham had predicted. He contacted Adina. To his surprise she allowed him to connect with her mind. Abraham studied her position. She was sitting in the open on a cliff at

Mount Sinai overlooking the landscape. Adina was a sitting duck for his orbital lasers; all he needed to do was to get them in position.

Abraham started speaking to Adina to distract her and stop her from running for safety. The orbital laser would be in a striking position within 10 minutes.

Abraham:

- Adina, my dearest granddaughter, what have you done?

Adina:

- You have never called me granddaughter before.

Abraham:

- You know who you are, so why hide it from you any longer?
- I know your secrets as well; you have been hiding them well.

Adina:

- I am sorry for the families of those men. Unfortunately, the fight for freedom often comes at a steep cost.

Abraham:

- Freedom...

- Do you know how easy it would be for me to wipe out every living being in this world by letting the air out in the vastness of space?

- Tell me, why should I let the others live after I kill you?

Adina:

- Well knowing you.

- Compassion, common decency and humanity are out the window.

- I would say your reason for not killing everyone is because you are powerless without subjects. Without them Eden is just a worthless piece of rock.

Abraham:

- You are indeed my granddaughter. A shame your traitorous nature will earn you the same ending as Lucifer, your duplicitous father.

Adina:

- Knowing this, what stops me from hiding in the tunnels as my brother did?

Abraham:

- If you do, I will drain Eden's atmosphere killing you and everyone else.
- I will not share power with you after your betrayal.

Adina:

- Fair enough. I suppose I'll sit here for the next few minutes until your laser gets in position. And then we'll see if you have what it takes.

Abraham:

- You'll see, and you'll feel. I'll give a painful death you, damn traitor!

Adina looked up at the sky. She could see one of the suns/ orbital satellites moving closer to zenith above her. Once it reached the peak of the sky her life would be over. Unless Jeshua and Keila managed to get into the Divine Control Center and kill Abraham before that happened. It was not likely to occur, but it was her only hope. Adina felt calm and collected, her entire life had come to this. Now all she could do was to distract Abraham for a few more minutes hoping for the best.

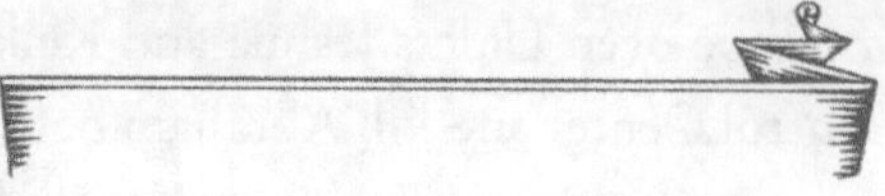

Chapter 95: Entering the Divine Control Centre.

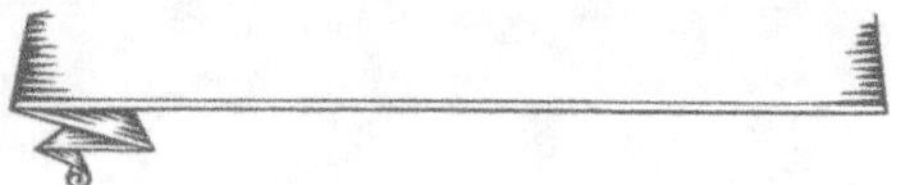

Keila looked up ahead at the asteroid that hosted the Divine Control Centre. It was less than a kilometre away, and she hoped that she could make it that far. She was in incredible pain. The bullet holes in her angel suit were small, but they were big enough to let in the freezing and low-pressurised air from space touch her body. The cold was not the main issue, but the low pressure was. Even the smallest breath she took expanded her lungs like a balloon and caused severe pain. If she made a medium sized breath, her lungs would burst, and if she disconnected her air supply, she would suffocate. She looked at Jeshua, just behind her; he seemed to be struggling even more. She had received simulated training for this kind of scenario, while all he had received was her quick instruction *"Only shallow breaths, otherwise your lungs will burst."* They reached the airlock entrance to the space station. Keila prayed to The True Maker that she would not face a difficult security system at the gate. She didn't. The only security was a camera that scanned the code on her helmet. A display showed "Welcome back, Nuriel" and she and Jeshua could enter the airlock. The air became pressurised, and they could draw full breaths, resting exhausted on the floor.

Abraham got shocked when he saw a notification that Gabriel and Nuriel had entered the Divine Control Centre. He tried to connect with them, but there was no connection, only a prompt saying that the subjects were dead. Abraham had forgotten about them for the last 30 minutes, and he realised that Adina had tricked him. He contacted Adina with one final transmission:

- You betrayed me. The foreign whore is here because of your deception. Now you'll all die.

Abraham set all the orbital lasers to target Adina, and he also set the nanotechnology layer protecting Eden's atmosphere to turn off in 10 minutes. If he were to die, they would all die. He then took control of the angel Abaddon. Abaddon was one of the most fearsome fighters he had left, named after the angel of destruction in the original holy book. What he lacked in personality, he made up for in destructive capabilities.

With the destructive capabilities of Abaddon, Abraham subdued Keila and Jeshua by shooting them in the legs and arms. Abaddon walked up to Keila to shoot her in the head with his pistol when Adina intervened. She tried to take control of Abaddon and make him kill himself. Abraham noticed this and they wrestled for authority over the angels with their minds. Eventually, the struggle became too much for them, and they both got knocked unconscious from the psionic blast that occurred. Adina's fell backward off the ledge she was standing on. This fall happened at the same time as the orbital lasers were fired at her, effectively saving her from getting hit. She fell for 50 meters and landed in a hole where the laser could not hit her from orbit.

Keila looked up; and she saw Abaddon who lay dead next to her with a hole in his head. She looked at Jeshua, who was injured but alive. They got out of their broken angel suits and they crawled to the room next door where Abraham's brain and his robotic body connected to the particle accelerator that transferred his mind to the Divine Dimension.

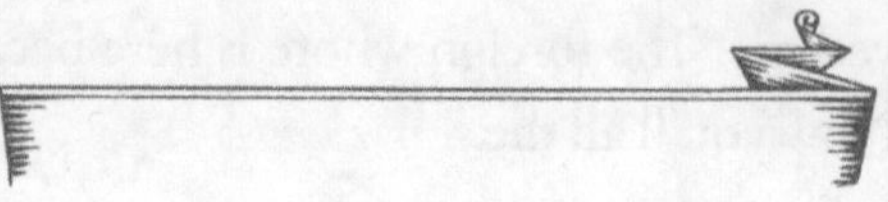

Chapter 96: Jeshua Confronts Abraham in the Divine Dimension.

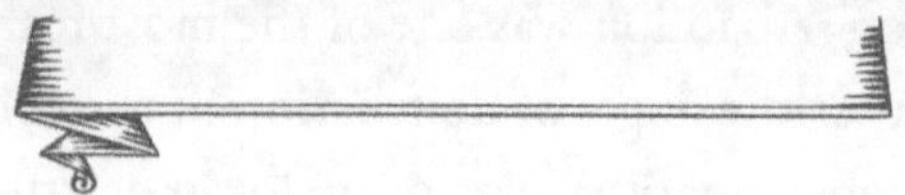

Jeshua:

- What the hell is that thing?

Keila:

- That is the brain of Abraham Goldstein, inserted into a life-supporting robot.

Jeshua:

- I don't know what that means.
- How do we kill it and save my people?

Keila:

- To kill Abraham, you'll have to travel to the Divine Dimension and kill him there.

Jeshua:

- Okay, how do I do that?

Keila:

- I'll help you.

Keila closed her eyes for a moment. Like she expected the vision for how to continue, came clearly to her mind. It had seemed to be like that all her life: When Keila closed her eyes, the answer would come. She plugged in Jeshua to the particle accelerator and sent his mind to the Divine Dimension.

Jeshua woke up in the courtyard of the Divine Dimension. The place was quiet as if time stood still in there. Jeshua looked around; he saw an old man with a robe and cane sitting still under a lotus tree. Despite never seeing Abraham before, Jeshua knew that it was him. He approached the old man.

Jeshua:

- Abraham! Stand up! It is time for you to pay for your crimes.

Abraham stood up.
Abraham:

- Jeshua right? We meet at last. You are an elusive character.
- You look a lot like your father.

Jeshua:

- I never knew my dad, but I know what is right.

Abraham:

- Please tell me, Jeshua. Who decides what is right?

- Your father decided your fate when he chose to hide you from me.

- Then your sister decided your fate when she used you to rebel against my rule to put her in power because she couldn't do it herself.

- And finally, your newfound "love" decided your fate when she sent you here to face me. Tell me, how do you think you'll get out of here?

Jeshua:

- They did what they thought was right. That's the difference between you and them.

Abraham:

- No. You see, I also do what I think is right. Doing what one thinks is right is not a correct measure of morality. Most people can justify their actions somehow.

Jeshua:

- And how do you justify your actions, you mass murdering monster?

Abraham:

- Easy. I did what I did because I was meant to do it.

- For thousands of years, humanity followed gods. I did too. Yahweh was the god of my people. A good god that gave us morality and a purpose for living.

- But Yahweh was a deception. He was an alien of an advanced set of species from another planet. He was a Zetan.

- When I came here, he had already committed suicide.

Jeshua:

- How does any of this justify your actions?

Abraham:

- You see, Yahweh was never a god. However, humans believed him to be a god because of his superior technology.

- Through providence, I found this technology. I spent my wealth creating a world where humanity could believe in something again. Believe in me.

- I created a world where men could believe in something that was greater than themselves, just like Yahweh did.

Jeshua:

- But they don't follow you out of love. They follow you out of fear. People need freedom to be happy and thrive.

Abraham:

- Freedom?

- The last few days of utter chaos and destruction can be categorised as freedom. I don't think it made anyone happier.

Jeshua:

- Because people lack love. Edenite society is not based on love. It's based on rules and commitments.

Abraham:

- Soon enough, love will be the least of their problems. Air, on the other hand, will be their problem.

Jeshua:

- Why is that?

Abraham:

- Because I turned off the air supply to Eden when I knew I was defeated.

- Within 5 minutes the Edenites will suffocate and die. While you are stuck here with me.

Jeshua:

- No, because I will kill you first.

Jeshua jumped on top of Abraham and delivered a hard flurry of punches to his face. Abraham hit him with his cane, and Jeshua flew several meters. He looked at Abraham in awe.
Abraham:

- You don't seem to get it. Your body is not here, only your mind.

- We can keep punching each other until the end of times, until we get out or our bodies die.

Jeshua:

- Is that so?
- Your head doesn't look that well.

Abraham:

- That bitch, she killed us both

Jeshua got surprised when he looked into a well to see his reflection. Abraham was right; he also had blood flowing out through a hole in his head. Jeshua fell to the ground, and everything became dark.
Keila put down the smoking gun. Killing Jeshua had been difficult but necessary. Keila had never included Jeshua in her long-term plans, and her visions had shown her that she was meant to get rid of him in

the end. She had hesitated to pull the trigger on him when he was unconscious and plugged into the particle accelerator.

Keila had wanted to say good-bye and tell him why he had to die, but she couldn't do it that way. In the few days, they had been together she had grown connected to him, and she did not know why she had to kill him. Keila swallowed hard and tears ran down her cheek.

Keila pulled herself together; this was not the time to be weak. Keila entered a command on the computer terminal to reactivate Eden's atmosphere. She locked the doors and had the particle replicator create a new divine technology god chip. Keila would have to wait for a couple of hours for the particle replicator to create a new god chip. Once she had inserted the god chip in her brain, she would be in control of Eden, and she would not settle for this small rock. She had bigger plans for the solar system.

MARTIN LUNDQVIST
SCI-FI
Guided by her visions, Keila takes on the oppressive Terran Council.
But can the source of her visions really be trusted?
The Divine
Sedition
THE DIVINE ZETAN TRILOGY

Chapter 97: Keila decides to stay and fight

Keila was overlooking the control room of the Divine Control Centre. There were no other people in the room except for the corpses of Jeshua, and the robot that had enclosed Abraham Goldstein's brain. *"I did it, mum!"* Keila said to herself, and she remembered the vision of her late mum urging her to free Eden from Abraham's tyranny.

Keila looked at a monitor showing the employees of the Divine Control Centre. There had only been 30 employees running the operations with most functions controlled by automated AI and robots. 12 of these employees had died throughout the years, of which three had met their demise at her hand. All the employees had strange ancient names, and Keila recalled the battle suits they had worn. They had looked like angels of war, and they were referred to as angels in the computer systems.

Keila looked at the display. There were no employees at the entire space station. Instead, they were on Eden trying to restore control among the population.

Keila tried to lock down the space station to avoid that the angels came back, and discovered what she had done to their master. Unfortunately, she lacked the biometric codes required to control the base. Keila was uncertain on how to go ahead. She considered escaping and leaving Eden. There was small space shuttle docked that could take her undetected to a nearby smuggler base. But what would escaping achieve? If she left Eden, the people would succumb to the tyranny of another scumbag, or they would perish as the life support systems would shut down if no-one supervised the automated processes.

Keila decided to stay. Eden was the birthplace of her mother, and Keila's return closed the circle. She would lead the Edenites to a brighter future.

Keila needed to come up with a way to lead Eden. The late Abraham had used mind control technology to control everyone on Eden. Would she do the same? It was not her favoured way to go ahead, as Keila believed in liberating people instead of enslaving them, but it was her only realistic choice. She could fight 18 super soldiers on her own and hope to win. Particularly not, since she was already wounded with a bullet in her leg and one in the arm.

Keila searched the system for the secret to Abraham's mind control, and she found it. There was a scheme of everyone with Divine Technology microchips installed in their brains, and Abraham was the only one who had a God chip installed. Keila kept searching, and she found the schematics for the microchip.

Keila knew that Terrans had a particle replicator machine, which could replicate any item that they had a blueprint for. To her great relief, there was a particle replicator in the very room she was in. She instructed the replicator to make a God chip and a timer started. It would take two hours to finish building the God chip. Keila leaned back in her chair. She was drinking from a glass of water in the one hand, and she grasped her pistol with the other. This would be two nervous hours, but she had made her choice. She would stand her ground here; Eden was her destiny.

Chapter 98: A Close Call

Keila woke up with a twist. Exhaustion had put her asleep despite her efforts to stay awake. The computer beeped with a high-pitched warning sound. She had been unable to lock down the space station, but she had set the alarm in case anyone came in from the outside. She looked at the display and she saw a 3D hologram. There was a whole squad of armed men in battle suits advancing on her position. She looked at the remaining time to make god chip. The timer said 10 minutes, and there was no way she would be able to hold out for that long. Keila realised that she needed to divert the angels for long enough to have the god chip done. Once she had the god chip, she would have a mean to deal with angels.

Keila limped out of the control centre, and she took a position in a side corridor that the angels would pass. She needed to distract the angels from the control centre where the replicator was working. Then she needed to find the way back to the control centre and pick up the god chip once it was ready.

Keila spotted an angel running down a parallel corridor heading to the control centre. She lifted her pistol and shot at him. As she had expected, the gun was not powerful enough to penetrate the angel's battle armour, and the bullets ricocheted off him. The shot caught his attention, and he raised his rifle to shoot at her. Keila jumped around the corner, and avoided the bullets in the last second. She heard him calling out his group to follow him. Her plan was working; now she needed to keep them occupied.

Keila turned around the corner and shot at the angel again. Yet again the bullets bounced off his armour, but this time he was joined by his peers. The angels ran towards her. Keila understood she could never out-run the angels in her injured condition. However, she did have one advantage. Keila's small frame made her fit into ventilation shafts. Keila got into a ventilation shaft, when the angels shot at her. One bullet struck her other leg, and she felt the pain

Keila would not let her injuries stop her, and she crawled through the ventilation shaft. One of the angels threw a gas grenade into the ventilation shaft. She looked behind her, and she identified the grenade. It contained a powerful sleep-inducing gas, and one breath would be enough to knock her unconscious. So, she had to hold her breath!

The ventilation shaft was 50 meters ahead of her. It would be tough, crawling 50 meters crawling in a narrow ventilation shaft with her injuries, but it was what she had to do. Keila squirmed and the goal did not seem to get any closer. She was close to passing out, and she closed her eyes. She saw a vision of herself in paradise with her mum, and her ancestors. *"You can do it,"* they said in unison. When Keila looked up, she was at the end of the tunnel. She was back in the Divine Control Centre. Keila got out of the ventilation shaft, and she limped to the particle replicator machine. The display said 20 seconds, and the angels entered the room. In desperation, Keila lifted her pistol and fired off the remaining rounds at the angels.

Upon hearing Keila's pistol clicking, the angel Samael took off his helmet. He walked towards Keila, while screaming obscenities towards her.

Samael:

- Not feeling so tough now, do you? I will rape you and give you a slow painful death for what you did to Grandmaster Abraham.

Keila:

- I am not the one bringing an army to beat one woman. As for raping me, I bet that your dick is too limp!

Samael:

- Oh, we'll see about that.

Keila:

- Alright, I am here, come to get some tough guy.

After saying this, Keila turned around, pulled her pants down and showed her private parts to the group of angels. This was a diversion, and she could see the timer on the replicator ticking down as Samael got out of his battle armour, ready to rape her. As the timer reached 0, the God chip came out of the replicator.

Without hesitation, Keila grabbed the chip and she crammed it straight into her ear. As it merged with her brain, she screamed in pain and released a strong psionic shockwave that knocked herself, the angels and all the people on Eden unconscious.

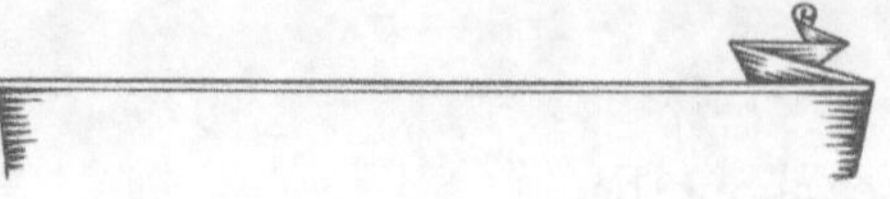

Chapter 99: Ascended to Godhood.

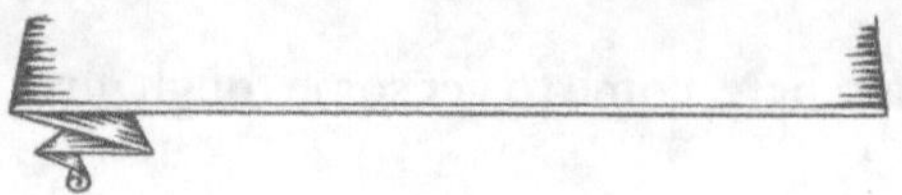

Keila woke up in the same courtyard in The Divine Dimension, where Abraham and Jeshua had been before her. Was she dead? The last thing Keila could remember was a sharp pain before everything turned black. But if she was in the afterlife, where were her mum and the spirits that she had seen in her visions? The courtyard was empty, and it had a very ominous feel, albeit it was also at the same time a very beautiful place.

Keila made her way to a pond with glittering water. She looked down into the pond and she could see her body attached to the Divine Detector Machine. The angels kneeled in front of her as if they were praying to her. The same people who had tried to rape and kill her was worshipping her. How did this happen?

Keila closed her eyes, and she saw a vision of herself on a golden throne with gemstones shining more beautiful than her senses could understand. She had a gut feeling that the throne was nearby and that providence had brought her to this sacred place. Keila left the pond and she walked through a gate.

Keila reached the inner sanctum of the complex. The golden throne was at the back end of the room, and there was a lifeless body in front of the throne. She approached the body and examined it. The body was of an old bearded man in robes, but it was neither Abraham nor Jeshua. Who was this dead man?

Keila examined the body. It was a strange feeling. Keila had seen a multitude of dead bodies, but none of them had been like this. There was something godlike and majestic about this body, although the death of the person in front of her was dead disproved divinity. She held the hand of the dead divine and closed her eyes. Keila felt a spiritual connection, and she knew who it was. The dead man was Yahweh, a god worshipped on Earth throughout the millennia. Keila opened her eyes and reflected. What did she know about this Yahweh? Evidently, not very much. The significant disconnect between the wealthy minority on Earth and the impoverished majority on Mars had led to a cultural separation, and the Martians did not know much about Earth's history and the gods that they followed.

Meanwhile, the Edenites that were knocked unconscious from the psionic blast started to wake up, and they called out for Abraham, the imposter god of the Edenites. They were filled with fear and their anxiety got stronger when they did not receive any response from their master. Keila, who now had a divine God chip in her brain, got overwhelmed by all the people trying to connect to her. She could feel their fear, and it overcame her senses. Struggling to breathe, she stumbled out of the throne room and walked towards the Lotus tree in the courtyard. Keila sat down next to the tree, and she felt relieved, like the weight of the world was no longer on her shoulders. Keila sank down into a deep meditative state.

Keila spent the next few hours, which felt like eons, learning about the secrets of the universe. Eventually, a white light came in front of her eyes and her consciousness was back in the normal dimension.

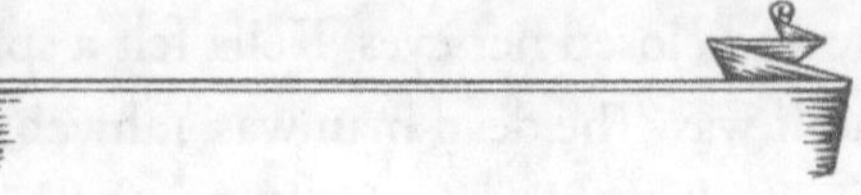

Chapter 100: Metatron wakes Keila.

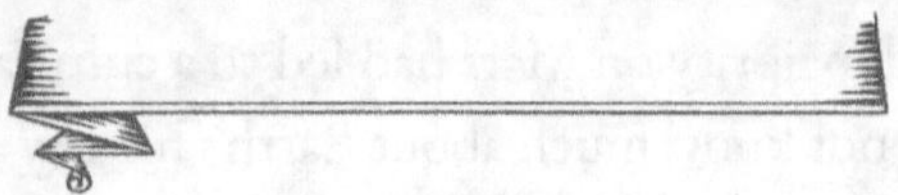

The angel Metatron observed the agitated and fearful Edenites from the Divine Control Centre. The intended paradise governed according to Yahweh's strict but fair rules, had turned into a hellhole. Chaos reigned, and the Edenites were killing and raping each other on an unprecedented scale.

The trouble had started a few days earlier, when a Terran Council starship had arrived, blowing up a rebel ship, at a height only 1.5 kilometres from Eden's surface. The explosion had caused widespread panic on Eden and exposed their great lie about Earth's destruction. From there, things had gone worse. For no reason, the religious militia on Eden had attacked and killed the angel Eremiel. The idiots Hamshal and Haniel had then made things worse when they arrived with guns blazing decimating the militia. Finally, this mysterious woman, Keila, showed up out of nowhere and killed Grandmaster Abraham Goldstein.

But in chaos, there was an opportunity. Metatron did not approve of the way Abraham had governed Eden, and he could not understand the motivations behind his former master's actions. Before they created Eden, Abraham had promised that they would create a new world and that his authority came directly from Yahweh.

Metatron had been enthusiastic about their prospects and being part of such a grand plan. However, his enthusiasm had diminished over the years, and the turning point was when Abraham's physical body had died, leaving only his brain to survive.

The Abraham who came back, as a human brain enclosed inside a machine, was not the same man as he had served his entire life. The new Abraham was a petty, cruel, and narrow-minded abomination who put the Edenites through torment and fear. The Archangel has Lucifer betrayed Abraham, and when they were sent to punish him, Lucifer took Michael with him to the afterlife.

Why had Lucifer betrayed Abraham? Metatron had given the question some thoughts over the years. He had kept the issue for himself and never discussed it with anyone. If Abraham could kill his favourite angel Lucifer, he would have no problems killing Metatron. But now Abraham was gone, and that's where the opportunity lay.

Metatron knew that his standing among the angels was low, in fact, his status was the lowest in the pecking order. He had worked with maintenance of Eden. Although his efforts were crucial for their survival, he did not receive the same recognition as the other angels got. The others expected him to do his job, but they never credited him for doing so.

When Keila seized the God chip, things had changed. When she inserted it into her ear, the system short-circuited and knocked everyone unconscious from the psionic blast. Metatron woke up first and he had felt the opportunity. Keila could be something that he could not; she could be the next leader of Eden. If he played his cards right, he could become her most trusted angel and get the recognition that he deserved.

Metatron had found Keila unconscious and severely wounded. He had placed her on life support and had connected her to the Divine Detector Machine to send her mind to The Divine Dimension. Hopefully, she would regain consciousness and make it possible for the other angels to feel her presence.

Metatron's plan had worked out. The other angels felt her presence, and he had convinced them to elevate her to leadership instead of avenging Abraham's death.

Metatron decided that it was time to talk to Keila. It would help if, he was the first person that she saw. He walked up to Keila's bed and disconnected her from the Divine Detector Machine. This transported her consciousness back to the room she was in. Keila woke up

Keila looked around the room. She could swear that she had been to a extra-terrestrial paradise for several hours, Keila often had intense dreams, but what she had experienced was stronger than any dream. A very handsome man greeted her.

Metatron:

- Welcome back, Mistress Keila. The angel Metatron at your service.

Keila:

- Okay. Am I a prisoner here?

Metatron:

- Absolutely not, quite the contrary. You are the possessor of the God chip, and thus you are the rightful ruler of Eden. At least that's what I told my peers.

Keila:

- But you don't think so?

Metatron:

- I am a humble servant of the divine master. what I think does not matter.

Keila:

- Cut the bullshit. Last thing I remember before the blast I was to be gang-raped, tortured, and killed.

- Now you're talking about elevating me to leadership. What's going on here?

Metatron:

- Okay, if you prefer me to be upfront.

- The psionic blast should have killed you. It probably would have if I did not wake up first and connected you to the life support unit.

- I have argued that you survived the blast to convince the others that Yahweh sent you to replace Abraham, as Abraham had strayed from the righteous path.

- Whether you survived due to divine intervention, or my intervention is irrelevant. If we play our cards right, we can rule Eden together.

Keila:

- What happen if I don't want to take part?

Metatron:

- Well, then I assume that a slow and painful death awaits us when the other angels find out.

Keila:

- That's a good enough motivation for me. I am in on your scheme.

Metatron:

- Good. You'll tell the others that Yahweh sent you to replace Abraham, who strayed from the path.

Keila:

- Got it.

Metatron:

- Just between you and me, did Yahweh send you?

Keila:

- I am unsure. I had visions that told me to come here to Eden after I escaped the Terran fleet at the Asteroid Sylvia.

Keila paused for a bit, she was unsure whether she would tell her newfound ally about seeing the corpse of Yahweh. Keila disclosed everything, as Metatron was the reason, she was still alive.

Keila:

- In my dream, I saw a dead man. I think it was Yahweh.

Metatron studied Keila in silence for a while. Eventually, he spoke up.

Metatron:

- What you experienced was not a dream. It was real. Your mind travelled to the Divine Dimension when I connected you to the Divine Detector Machine.

- If Yahweh is dead, Abraham must have killed him. Yahweh has been looking after our people for over 5000 years. What will become of us now?

- Then again, you could be lying...

Keila:

- It's quite easy for you to find out the truth. Connect yourself to the machine, and go to the throne room. You'll find Yahweh's corpse there.

Metatron:

- But I am just a man, I am not worthy.

Keila:

- Says who?
- If God is dead, who decides who is worthy to enter his domains?

Metatron:

- You are right. I have sent too much time following others.
Send my consciousness to the Divine Dimension.

Keila connected Metatron to the Divine Detector Machine. She looked at Metatron's face; he had a masculine and good-looking face, albeit he looked a decade older than her. Metatron slept peacefully.

Seeing Metatron in this helpless state gave Keila terrible flashbacks to her betrayal of Jeshua, whom she had murdered the day before. She had acted on strange voices that told her to murder Jeshua while he was connected to the machine. Her visions were never wrong, and her premonitions was the reason that she had become the beacon of light for the downtrodden masses of the solar system. Keila's regretted killing Jeshua, and she broke down in tears from what she had done.

Eventually, Metatron came back from the Divine Dimension. He was awestricken from what he had seen. Yahweh was dead, and his entire life's purpose to honour Yahweh had come to naught.

Metatron saw Keila sitting in a corner crying. He followed his instinct and went over to her, held her tight and then started crying himself. They sat there for hours, crying silently without saying anything. It was the closest Metatron had ever felt to someone.

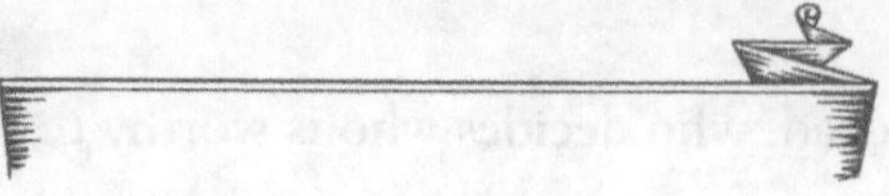

Chapter 101: The Zetans Discussing the Events.

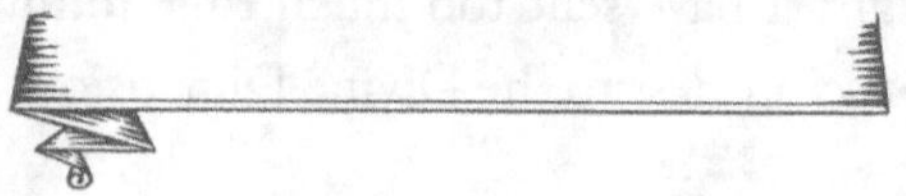

The extra-terrestrial species known as the Zetans, gathered in a semi-circle, around an obelisk that they had erected in The Divine Dimension. They remembered the day of Yahweh's betrayal, that took place more than a millennium ago. In the distance, they could see the palace that Yahweh had expelled them from. It was as impressive as it had been when they built it thousands of years ago, but the tear in the space-time that enclosed the palace stopped them from returning.

The Zetans were the most advanced species to ever appear in the universe and the only ones to ever manage to physically travel between the normal dimension and the Divine Dimension.

At the height of their civilisation, they had portals spread across the Milky Way Galaxy that could teleport them between the normal dimension and the Divine Dimension and then back to another location in the normal dimension. This way, they could travel faster than light.

All of this had been lost in the apocalyptic war between the Zetans and the failed product of their own creation, the Xenos. This war wiped out the Zetan civilisation. The war destroyed their home planet Zetani and killed most of their species, except for a few Zetans scattered in the Divine Dimension.

The few Zetans remaining in the universe had led stagnant lives in the Divine Dimension. However, they could activate their portals to Earth, and pose as gods to the simple-minded humans on Earth. This way, they would receive the offerings that they needed to have a good life in the Divine Dimension. All of this was destroyed, when Yahweh had a psychotic breakdown, and destroyed the last active Zetan portal to Earth, and killed himself and his secret lover.

Since Yahweh destroyed the last active portal to Earth, the Zetans had millennia of hell. Being physical beings, they needed food and drinks to sustain themselves, yet nothing of this was available in the Divine Dimension. With the state of timelessness of the Divine Dimension, they couldn't die from natural causes, age, or bear offspring. Yet as physical beings, they could feel thirst and hunger. The result was that they were always hungry and thirsty, while being kept alive by the Divine Dimensions' timelessness

When they had gathered, Zeus spoke:

- Fellow Zetans! For thousands of years, we have been starving in this timeless abyss. But I see hope in the form a human, a promised human that will reactivate the portals and give us back our rightful place as gods on earth.

- The woman's name Keila Eisenstein, and she has something that our former hosts were lacking. She has access to a technology level that is unprecedented in the history of mankind, almost on par with our technology during the peak of our civilisation.

- She has disposed of Abraham who was following the teachings of the traitor Yahweh, and taken control over Eden.

Odin:

- I am questioning your faith in Keila. She is the sworn enemy of the Terran Council that rules Earth and Mars. Having her travel around on Earth to restart our portals to Earth seems impossible. Why are we not influencing a powerful Terran to do our bidding, instead of using a Martian woman?

Zeus:

- Influencing a Terran leader would be better, but unfortunately, the genetic makeup of humans makes a telepathic connection to them implausible. That is why we only get a human that we can influence once every few hundred years. In our time, the destined human is Keila.

- Keila is our future. I have foreseen it, and my premonitions are never wrong.

Brahma felt obliged to join in on the conversation:

- Zeus, if your "premonitions" are so flawless, how come our civilisation got wiped out by the Xenos. Why did you let Yahweh destroy the last active portal to Earth, our only way back to the normal dimension?

Zeus:

- Silence! I never claimed omniscience. I argued that all my premonitions are correct, that is not the same. I never claimed we would not get destroyed by the Xenos, I never claimed Yahweh would not betray us. Whenever I do share a premonition, it comes true.

Brahma:

- Is that so?
- You seemed surprised when Keila murdered Jeshua.

Zeus:

- Yes, that was surprising since we only influenced her to kill Abraham. Then again humans are volatile and prone to violence. They have their own willpower, that's why we used them to fight the Xenos in the multimillennial war.

- However, the killing of Jeshua does not concern us, and everything is going according to plan.

- I would like to thank Odin for his efforts. If he hadn't helped me direct the psionic blast resulting from Keila's incorrect usage of the divine crown, we would not have received a favourable outcome.

- I declare this meeting finished. I urge you to keep observing human activities in the regular universe so we can come up with a plan on how to continue.

After this, the Zetans dispersed, and each went on their own way. Although they did not have anywhere to go, most of them preferred solitude as they could meditate deeper in that state.

Most of the Zetan communication occurred telepathically, so they did not need to be close to each other to talk. Moreover, the presence of too many peers amassed too much psionic energy in one place. This prevented the Zetans from reaching deep meditation. Most Zetans preferred to be in deep meditation, as that was the only state of mind where the Zetans wouldn't feel the hunger and the thirst that tormented them.

Brahma reached his meditation spot and was tormented by a thought. What if Rangda had influenced Keila to murder Jeshua? The idea gave him shivers, and he shrugged it off. Rangda was condemned to stay in a small prison cell, with a psionic force field that stopped her from contacting anyone. Full of discomfort, Brahma went to sleep to forget about his hunger and thirst. His sleep was full of nightmares.

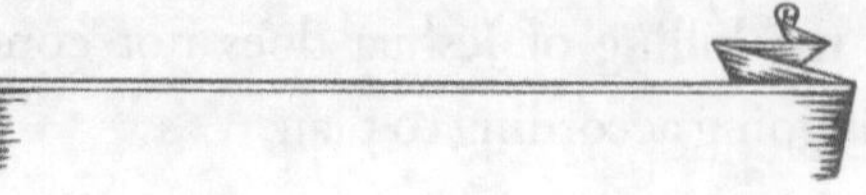

Chapter 102: Rear Admiral Bjorn Muller Becomes Restless

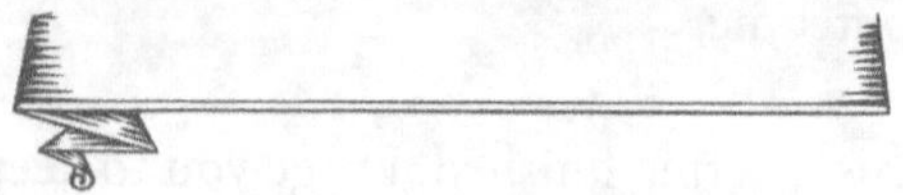

Rear Admiral Bjorn Muller put down the glass of fine Scotch that he was drinking. The alcohol had not helped, and he was reluctant to have another glass. Bjorn was a high-ranking officer in the Terran Council Interplanetary Forces, and it was inappropriate for him to get drunk while on duty.

Bjorn was frustrated that he hadn't heard anything from Nuriel regarding his request to have Keila Eisenstein captured and handed her over to him. He had given them three days and three days had passed. Yet he hadn't heard anything from them, which compelled him to act. Unfortunately, his options were limited. His superior, Admiral Max Wellington, had not sent him any backup and attacking the asteroid B528A, also known as Eden, with a single ship, amounted to suicide.

Bjorn needed a success story, and the capture of a figurehead of the Martian rebellion would gain him a well-deserved promotion. This promotion would take him off active duty in this interplanetary wasteland and give him a cushy lifestyle back on earth. Bjorn wanted a position on the House Muller board as a military advisor. Bjorn felt resigned to his fate. He had been so close to returning to Earth for the last 20 years, but the breakthrough never seemed to come. He damned his younger self for being so ambitious and excelling at the aptitude tests in his youth. If he had been more like his younger brother, his life would be so much better.

Bjorn's brother, Michael, was uninterested in his career, but was, due to his family ties, running one of the House Muller's horse racecourses. Michael was not interested in managing anything, but he served as a figurehead for the racetrack doing what he liked doing, drinking, and mingling. Michael would never be taken seriously, but his life was enjoyable.

Bjorn's other brother, Benjamin, ruled by his father's, Joachim Muller's, side. This led to deep jealousy and between him and Bjorn.

Bjorn's military ambitions led to him being stuck on a gloomy military spaceship with nothing but the darkness of space to look at. Bjorn had no family of his own and would never have if he couldn't get out of active duty. Bjorn was 70 years old, and although he could live to more than double that age without complications due to DNA regeneration technology, Bjorn felt that his life was drawing to the end. Bjorn decided that it was time to act. He went to the hologram generator and he contacted the Divine Control Centre.

Keila woke up with a shocked expression when she saw the lifelike hologram of Bjorn Muller in her room. She reached for her gun and gave out a loud shriek when she couldn't find it. Metatron rushed in to find out what the commotion was about.

Metatron:

- Is everything okay, Mistress Keila?

Keila:

- What is Bjorn Muller doing here?

Metatron:

- That is a hologram machine. He is calling us.

Keila calmed down. She felt silly for panicking at a hologram machine. They had hologram machines on Mars as well, although the devices they had on her home planet made it obvious that is was a hologram, made it almost impossible to tell a hologram apart from a real human.

Keila:

- Are we able to blow up his ship with the weapons on this station?

Metatron

- Yes, but we need to get him in range first.

Keila closed her eyes. A vision came up. It was her mother, and the message was clear. *"Keila, tread carefully. No one needs to die today. This not your destiny."*
Keila:

- No, we should try to avoid violence. I want you speak to him and find out what he wants.

Metatron stepped up on the hologram transmitter and started a communications link with Bjorn.

- This is Metatron from House Goldstein. State your business, commander.

Bjorn:

- This is Rear Admiral Bjorn Muller from the Terran Council Interplanetary Security Forces.

Metatron:

- Okay, state your business, commander.

Bjorn felt how his anger was growing; the arrogant bastard, Metatron, disdained his rank to provoke him. He controlled his temper, and stayed on track.
Bjorn:

- My business as a REAR ADMIRAL for the Terran Council Interplanetary Security Forces is to bring in the fugitive terrorist, Keila Eisenstein. I have already discussed this with your colleague Michael Bernsmith, also known as Nuriel. I do not have the patience to explain myself again. Put Nuriel through!

Metatron:

- There is a slight problem with that request. Nuriel is permanently indisposed, so you'll have to discuss the matter with me.

Bjorn:

- Permanently indisposed?

Metatron:

- I am sure that you understand the term and its implications. Now say what you need.

Bjorn:

- We gave you three days to deliver Keila to us. The time is up, where is she?

Metatron:

- Due to Nuriel's unfortunate passing, that message didn't reach me. I will investigate the matter and see if we can aid you. We'll get back to you in a couple of days.

Bjorn:

- Listen up, you insolent twat! You have failed to carry out your part of the deal, and my men will land on Eden and apprehend Keila ourselves.

Metatron:

- Unfortunately, we would consider that trespassing. That would force us to eliminate you and all your men.

Bjorn:

- This is unacceptable. You are threatening a Terran Council Rear Admiral!

Metatron:

- I am not issuing threats. I am stating a fact.

- If the Terran Council wanted to take something with force, you would show up with a fleet and not a single ship. Stay where you are, commander, I will discuss the matter with my colleagues and get back to you.

- Metatron Out!

As Metatron stepped off the hologram transmitter, he sighed. What a mess they were in. Mistress Keila would never surrender to the Terran Council, and if they did not cooperate, Bjorn would get reinforcements and attack the battle station. He looked at Keila, and she spoke:

- Just as I thought. Bjorn is after me.

Metatron:

- Yes, I assume you are not keen to surrender yourself?

Keila:

- I'll pass. Torture and a public execution don't sound enticing.
- But what if we could give him my corpse?

Metatron:

- Your corpse? You want me to kill you and hand over your body?

Keila:

- Not my real corpse. A decoy.
- How long would it take you to make a clone of me in your medical lab?

Metatron:

- It would take years to make functional clone with memories and well-developed neural patterns.

Keila:

- No not a functional clone. Create a sack of meat and bones that looks like me.

Metatron:

- That would take a couple of days. However, an autopsy would reveal the fraud.

Keila:

- I know about Bjorn Muller. He would swallow the bait sink and hook with no questions.

- Just think about it, he can be the hero of the Terran Council, and finally get his promotion, so he can go back to Earth. If he summons the fleet, his superior will get all the credit.

Metatron:

- You seem sure about this guy.

Keila:

- Yes. Our paths have crossed in the past.

Metatron:

- Okay. Let's do this.

Metatron stepped up on the hologram sender and contacted Bjorn. As Bjorn answered, Metatron stated *"We'll bring her to you in 48 hours".* Then Metatron ended the transmission, without giving Bjorn Muller a chance to get another word in.

Chapter 103: The "Murder" and Delivery of Keila Eisenstein

Keila examined her non-functional clone. It was a dark and surreal experience, like watching a real-life wax doll of herself. The clone was not more alive than the wax doll, and it would never be. The accelerated cloning process didn't create a functioning nerve system. This excluded the possibility of consciousness in the organism.

Metatron stepped into the room. He glanced at the clone and then looked at Keila.

Keila:

- Hey Met! Don't be creepy!

Metatron:

- She looks like the spitting image of you!
- Ready for the last step of the plan?

Keila:

- Yes.

Metatron:

- Okay, here is your pistol. You do the honours.

Metatron gave Keila a pistol and turned a switch, which sent an electric current to the heart of the clone to simulate a beating heart. Keila shot the clone multiple times, destroying its brain and spine. This was to mask that the nervous system of the clone had never been functional. Metatron and a few other angels then wheeled the bed where the clone was strapped onto a shuttle. Metatron set course for Bjorn's command ship ISS Supreme Earth.

Bjorn met them as they docked. He had many armed soldiers by his side. Bjorn walked up to Metatron and spoke:

- Where are Keila? You are supposed to bring Keila Eisenstein, and I cannot see her.

Metatron:

- Look in the body bag.

Bjorn:

- Why did you kill her? From the damages, it seems like she is permanently dead beyond resurrection.

- I told you to bring her, I didn't ask you to kill her! We need her alive for intelligence gathering and a public execution.

Metatron:

- The bitch made a run for it. We had to put her down and make sure that she stayed down.

- We promised to bring her, and we did. We upheld our part of the deal.

Bjorn:

- You idiots. I should arrest you!

Metatron:

- That's a terrible idea since you are still within firing range of our battle station.

- We have gone out of our way to help you. Go home to your masters on Earth.

- Farewell.

Having said this, Metatron and his group went back to the shuttle. The Shuttle took off and flew back to the Divine Control Centre. Bjorn commanded one of his officers to bring Keila's corpse to the science bay while he returned to his private room to reflect.

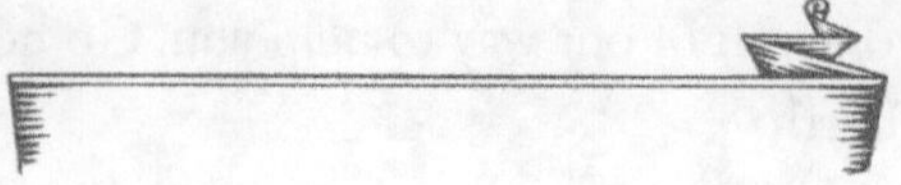

Chapter 104: Bjorn Muller's Dilemma

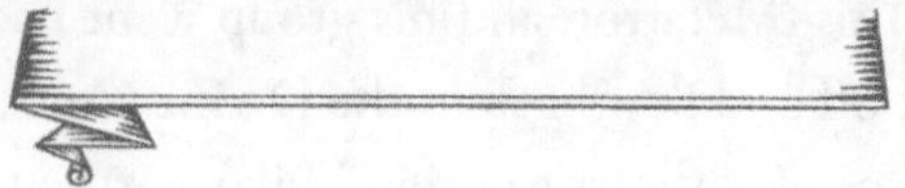

Bjorn was lying in the Jacuzzi bathtub installed in his private quarters. Despite having his body in peak condition, he felt phantom pains in a previously lost body part that had been replaced. The phantom pains annoyed Bjorn, there was no reason to have them, and yet he was unable to let them go. He was thinking of Keila. He could not decide whether he was relieved that she was finally dead or angry that he was not the one to kill her. He was mad at Metatron, whose real name was Jack Silver, and Bjorn vowed to get his. Regardless, there was nothing he could do about the idiots on Eden, and there was bigger fish to fry.

Bjorn thought back on his first meeting with Keila, four years earlier. She had caused him immense pain and suffering, but he was to blame for what happened. Keila had been 18 back then and insignificant for the revolution, not one of the poster girls of the Martian revolution that she became later. Keila had tried to travel illegally to Earth when he caught her.

Bjorn was 66 years when he first met Keila, and he was an attractive bachelor back on Earth due to his family wealth and DNA regenerated good looks, which made him look like he was in his 30s. Unfortunately, Keila had attracted a strong urge in him that he did not usually feel. He had felt the urge to subjugate and dominate her.

Bjorn had taken Keila to his private quarters and forced himself on her multiple times. He had kept her there for a long time until he got carried away, and forgot that she was not in bed with him by her free will.

Bjorn had made Keila give him fellatio. This had ended badly with Keila spitting out his severed member on the floor. This left Bjorn in excruciating pain, while Keila headed for an emergency escape pod and escaped back to Mars.

Being ashamed over the incident, Bjorn had not told anyone about Keila. Instead he had been in agonising pain for several days until he could reach a private reconstruction clinic and get restored with DNA repair technology. Although his body had recovered to peak condition, he could still feel the phantom pains, and the last few days had worsened the pains.

To cover up his shameful act, Bjorn had cleared all the records of Keila's capture from the mainframe of the ISS Supreme Earth. He had kept a copy of everything on a private drive, in case he would need it in the future. On this private drive, there was a record of Keila's DNA, and the corpse was a perfect match. Bjorn decided that he would not wait to publicise the news, he would finally get the glory he deserved!

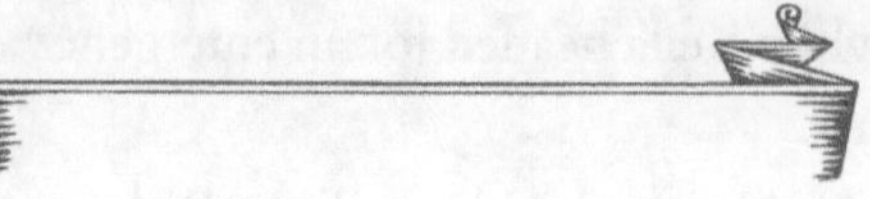

Chapter 105: "Notorious terrorist Keila Eisenstein killed by Bjorn Muller's Troops."

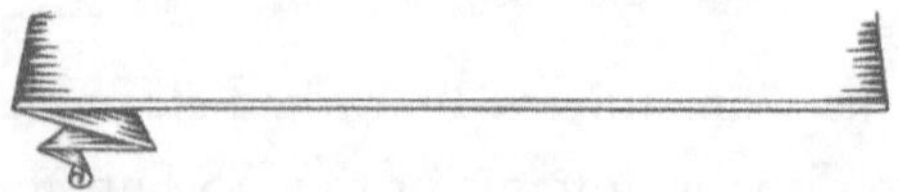

Great news for all the rightful people in the solar system! The notorious terrorist Keila Eisenstein has been eliminated by the brave souls of the Terran Council Interplanetary Security Forces, who are defending our freedom and safety. Miss Eisenstein, who escaped when her brethren fell to the superior might of the Terran Council during the battle of the asteroid Sylvia, was pursued by the valiant troops of Rear Admiral Bjorn Muller, who fought through hordes of rebel scum before reaching Keila's ship Miss Freedom, which was obliterated. Unfortunately, Keila escaped yet again landing on an independent colony, turning the peaceful population on Eden against the just cause of the Terran Council.

Fortunately, the local people were not deceived by her debauchery and they aided Bjorn team to eliminate the vile terrorist. Unfortunately, they attacked her with such ferocity that her corpse is in such a bad condition that it will be impossible to revive her and trial her for her crimes.

Rear Admiral Bjorn Muller comments, "This is a great day for the families of the victims of Keila's crimes. It's an even greater day for all the good people of Earth who have seen their lives disrupted by the actions of Keila's terrorist group. With the rebels out of the way, trade can resume, and the good people have yet again a chance to make an honest living."

Terran Council Interplanetary Forces press release 20th February 2872

Chapter 106: Chief Scientist Markus Bauer Gets Suspicious

Markus Bauer was lying in a hot bath trying to shake off the cold. He hated waking up from cryogenic sleep, but it was better than wasting his life doing unqualified diminutive tasks for the army. When Markus Bauer enrolled for the ship, Bjorn Muller had told him that he could be cryogenically sleeping for most of his tenure. It had sounded great as it enabled him to get paid for 5 years, being able to afford a beautiful house when he got back to Earth while not aging for most of his tenure. The drawback was missing out on what happened with his parents back on Earth and the disconnect that it caused. The worst drawback, however, was the cold when waking up after a session of cryogenic sleep, and Markus loathed waking up.

Eventually, Markus felt warm enough. He put away his tea, got up from the bath, and got dressed. He had a look at his briefing. His goal was to confirm the identity and the cause of death of Keila Eisenstein. His boss had already publicised that Keila was dead. So, Bjorn expected Markus to fall in line with his boss' expectation and confirm Keila's death. Markus scoffed at the notion that he would be Bjorn's lapdog. He had professional principles and would do a thorough job at examining the case.

Markus entered the scientific lab and he realised that something was amiss. The explanation to the many bullet holes penetrating the body was that Keila was running away from her pursuers and they shot her from behind to make sure she collapsed and died.

Markus dismissed this claim. All the bullets had the same entry angle, and none of the wounds showed any signs of fibre from clothing or body armour. Hence, Markus concluded that Keila must have been shot while lying naked facing down. Why had they acted this way? They should have known that Keila was more valuable to the Terran Council alive. Instead, her brain and nerve system were wrecked by the abundance of bullets penetrating her body. Was the Edenites hiding something?

Another thing bothered Markus, how could he know that this, was the body of Keila and not a random corpse? He had a file on the system that supposedly was the DNA of Keila, and that DNA was matching the body. However, the origin of that file was mysterious. Usually, a record with the DNA of a suspect would come with reports stating how and when the DNA was collected and a detailed dossier on the suspect. Nothing of that was available, just a date stamp for the DNA file, 25 April 2868.

"*25 April 2868*," Markus thought about the date. He recalled something. That day, an escape pod had disconnected from the ship and crashed on Mars. When he had met with Bjorn to discuss the matter, Bjorn had screamed at him and told him that it was none of his business. This could not be a coincidence.

Markus was thinking a bit longer. Bjorn was hiding something, but he could not be collaborating with the rebels. Bjorn had ordered the destruction of Keila's ship, thus killing its crew only a week earlier. Markus could not contain himself any longer. He walked to Bjorn's quarters to confront him and find out the truth.

Chapter 107: Markus Bauer Confronts Bjorn Muller.

Bjorn Muller was enjoying a sensual massage from a limited AI massage robotic drone. The machine looked and felt like a human female, but due to its limited programming, it was only useful at giving massages. Bjorn Muller was happy this way. Although he could afford to bring a female employee from Earth to please his demands, he felt that it was awkward to have one sticking around on a military space vessel. Likewise, a part of him was yearning for a relationship, yet, he felt that his military career was a barrier to such pursuits. Midway through the massage, Bjorn received a message that Markus Bauer requested to see him. Bjorn granted Markus' request; the massage could always wait until after the meeting.

Bjorn got dressed, sat down at his desk, and commanded the AI to let Markus in. Markus walked up to him, but before he had time to say anything, Bjorn spoke.

- Welcome, Markus. Are you here to explain yourself regarding your delay?

Markus:

- I beg your pardon.

Bjorn:

- I have already identified Keila and broadcasted her death. I woke you up seven hours ago to verify her death. Yet you still have not updated our networks with your verification.

Markus:

- Unlike some people, I take my professional integrity seriously. I am here to discuss my findings with you.

Bjorn's gaze blackened; he had not expected this formality to become an issue. *"Go on,"* he said.
Markus:

- "The angels" explanation for what happened does not match reality. I concluded that Keila must have been shot with multiple bullets from the same pistol and the same position, while she was lying face down. Furthermore, as there are no traces of fibre in her wounds, I concluded that she was naked when she was shot.

Bjorn:

- Yes, I thought the same thing, but there was no opportunity to confront those religious fanatics about it when they were threatening us with their battle station.

Markus:

- Did you let them get away with threatening you?

Bjorn:

- Yes. It would be madness for this single ship to fight a battle station. Besides, those religious fanatics would not stand back from a fight.

- Regardless, Keila is dead, and I have already confirmed her identity. Now I am waiting for you to do your part so that we can finalise our report.

Markus:

- About that... I can't identify Ms Eisenstein with enough accuracy. I need to make a thorough examination to conclude the matter.

Bjorn:

- What is there to examine? We have both visual identification and DNA identification.

Markus:

- The visual identification is non-conclusive, due to the wounds of the corpse. Due to the extent of damage to the body, we cannot exclude that they have handed us a non-functional clone of Keila. I also find it unsettling that Keila's DNA profile did not come with a report on how the sample was gathered.

Bjorn:

- The DNA profile of Keila does come with more files, but they are above your clearance level.

Markus:

- Okay. If you give me access to the extra files, that would speed up my work.

Bjorn:

- I do not have the patience for this bullshit! As a Rear Admiral for the Terran Council, I command you to verify my report and go back to sleep.

Markus:

- As a Chief scientist, my primary allegiance lies with the Science Commission. I am expecting your full cooperation in enabling me to make an independent review of this case. If you don't, I will report you to the Science Commission.

Bjorn Muller:

- I will see what I can do to help you, Chief Scientist Bauer.
- Dismissed.

When Markus Bauer had left, Bjorn Muller punched his female massage robot to release his anger. Bjorn heard a fizz as it broke and the massage robot fell lifeless to the floor. That insolent son of a bitch Markus Bauer! This was Bjorn's ship, and a scientist should not dare to oppose him. Bjorn also felt fear. He realised that he had made a crucial mistake and that Keila could still be alive. Worse yet he had deleted her files to cover up his past actions.

After escaping from Bjorn, Keila rose to fame after assassinating Hans Muller, who was the chairman of the Terran Council at the time. The fact that a Martian rebel assassinated the leader of the Terran Council, inspired the downtrodden masses of the solar system to rebel against the Terran Council. This had increased the popular support for The Martian Humanist Alliance, who were the enemies of the Terran Council, and Bjorn had fought this rebellion for the last four years.

To summarise, because Bjorn hadn't contained his sexual desires, the solar system was drawn into a four-year war. He had indirectly caused this war by keeping Keila as a sex slave, as she had killed his grandfather, Hans Muller, after she escaped. The rebellion had caused many fatalities and had halted commerce. The latter had brought Earth to a financial standstill and threatened Terran Council's dominance. Bjorn knew if his peers found out what he had done, his life would be lost. He had to deal with the situation as fast as he could. Bjorn stuck with his idea that Keila was dead, and that she needed to stay that way!

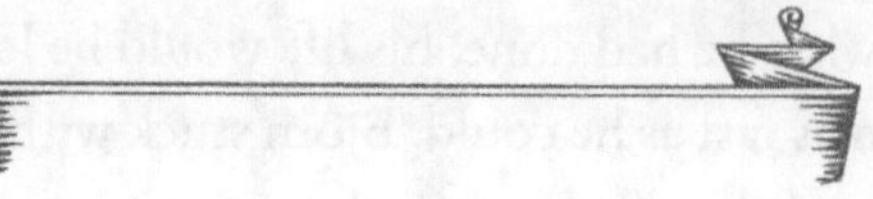

Chapter 108: An Explosion in the Science Bay

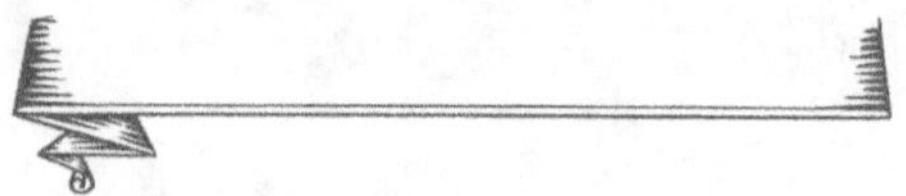

Markus Bauer was eyeing through the files about Keila that Bjorn had given him clearance to view. While they contained interesting information, it was not the files he was after. He was after the DNA collection reports from when Keila's DNA was collected. Markus looked at the corpse one more time. She looked familiar, and he could recall seeing her escorted to a cell some years ago. But he could not recall when he had seen her, and Markus could not be sure of meeting her. However, he did remember whispers about a missing prisoner around the time when Keila's DNA was collected.

Markus opened a file regarding Keila's family history. He could see why this section was classified, as the DNA backtrack analysis revealed that Keila's father was the prominent Terran, Mahmoud Rashid. Mahmoud was disowned by his wealthy family for running off with a non-approved lower caste woman. Markus searched for Mahmoud Rashid. He was born the same year as Bjorn Muller and he died many years ago. Was it possible that Mahmoud and Bjorn had been friends and Bjorn had helped his friend's daughter to escape her imprisonment? This was pure speculation, and Markus realised that he would be better off keeping this thought to himself.

Markus looked at a photo of Keila and the date that her DNA sample was collected. He had a flashback; he was sure that he had seen Keila passing him in the corridor escorted by Bjorn on that day. He also recalled a missing escape pod a few weeks later, and that a prisoner that was deleted from the prisoner checklist. Considering Hans Muller was assassinated by Keila a few weeks later, Keila and Bjorn could be conspiring against the leadership of House Muller and against the Terran Council.

Markus realised that this knowledge posed a severe threat to his life. He needed to find the right people on Earth and make sure that his transmission was encrypted, so Bjorn would not realise that Markus was dobbing him in. Unfortunately, staff members were not allowed to bring encrypted messaging devices onto the ISS Supreme Earth, except for Bjorn, who had a private encrypted phone. Stealing Bjorn's phone would not be easy, but it was the only way to set things right.

Suddenly, Markus saw a display flashing, *"Contamination detected, Science bay to disconnect in 30 seconds"*. Markus ran to the door, but it was sealed. Acting instinctively, he grabbed the memory unit and an oxygen tank and jumped into an airtight safety-capsule. Seconds later there was a small targeted explosion, and the Science Bay was dislodged from the rest of ISS Supreme Earth.

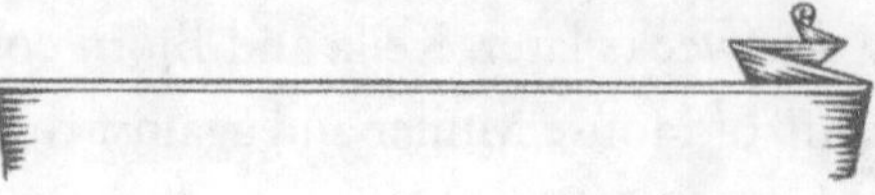

Chapter 109: Bjorn Muller Orders a Retreat to Repair the Spaceship

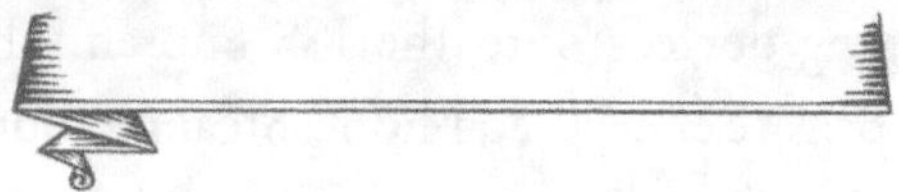

Bjorn Muller was finishing up his report on the dislodged Science Bay incident. On this occasion, he had been forced to use the keyboard instead of mind-typing which he usually preferred. Mind-typing was a technology where one could put a hat with electrodes on one's head and use that to write documents using one's thoughts. While mind-typing was faster and more convenient, Bjorn used the keyboard on this occasion as he was worried that his mind would betray him and reveal the truth in the report. It had been a couple of stressful hours after the explosion, and one of the crew members, Matt Johnson, was accidentally sucked out into the vacuum of space when they were fixing the damages from the explosion. Bjorn felt sorry for Matt; he had liked the man and felt guilt that his actions that had caused Matt's death.

Bjorn tried to shrug off what happened to Matt; casualties were the fuel of the war machine, and Matt knew what he signed up for. Bjorn checked report that he had written to the council. Its' summary said:

"At 03:00 hours, a collision with a meteor caused a computer malfunction. This caused an explosion that dislodged the science bay from ISS Supreme Earth. Chief Scientist Markus Bauer died in the blast, and Technical Sergeant Matt Johnson died when performing emergency repairs. With the loss of the Science Bay, we lost the following items listed in Appendix 2. Due to the damages to the ship, I ordered the ship to retreat to the closest base without retrieving the lost cargo, as this is a dangerous part of space."

Bjorn looked down on the report. He told himself that he would be alright and that no one would question the validity of the statement.

He got interrupted when Captain Adal Schneider requested to see him. Bjorn acknowledged this request and Adal walked into his office. Bjorn studied his 2nd in charge officer, he shared the same idealised North European features as Bjorn, but Adal looked a lot older than Bjorn despite being 20 years younger. This was because Adal was not wealthy enough to afford top-quality DNA regeneration technology, so he had to settle for cheaper remedies. He walked up to Bjorn's desk.

Adal:

- Sir! We have received an emergency beacon from Chief Scientist Markus Bauer.

Bjorn:

- That must be a mistake, there is no way that he could have survived the explosion and several hours in space.

Adal:

- Nonetheless, I ask that we go back and retrieve the bodies of Matt Johnson and Markus Bauer for their families' sake.

Bjorn:

- Request denied. The ship has sustained damages, and this area of space is not safe. There might still be rebels or pirates in the vicinity.

Adal Schneider:

- Our thermal scanners indicate that there is not a single ship within a 1-million-kilometre radius from us, and the Science Bay is only 90,000 kilometres away. We can retrieve them without any worries.

Bjorn Muller:

- For all we know, the thermal scanners might be damaged as well. We are continuing to outpost 5 for service and repairs.

Adal Schneider:

- Please, Rear Admiral Muller, I am the Captain of this ship. I am in command in your absence, and I want to show my men that I care about them.

Bjorn Muller:

- I do not look absent, do I?
- Proceed to outpost 5 at once.
- Dismissed Captain.

As Adal left the room, Bjorn sighed and leaned back in his chair. What a mess he was in! If only that idiot Markus could have followed orders instead of causing all of this. Bjorn looked for something to punch, but he couldn't find anything, so he took some sedatives and went to sleep.

Chapter 110: Keila Hears About the Explosion and Gets an Idea.

Keila was practising target shooting on a realistic hologram of Bjorn Muller. She was filled with rage and frustration that she hadn't put an end to him when she had the chance. Keila could either have destroyed his ships using the weapon systems on her base, or she could have mind-controlled one of the angels to shoot him when they delivered her *"corpse"* to him. She had chosen to contain her murderous tendencies and instead play the waiting game. Bjorn Muller was a filthy rapist who had violated her, and he would pay for it, but he would pay when it could further her goals. A week ago, she would have given her life to end his. However, since she had found Eden and the Divine Dimension, she had gained a new perspective, and she hoped that hidden Zetan technologies would be the turning point of this centuries-long conflict within humankind. Keila loaded her pistol with another magazine and she unleashed her rage against the hologram. The gun clicked, and Metatron entered the room.

Metatron:

- You are an abysmal shooter, Keila.

Keila:

- No, I am not?

Metatron:

- Yes, you are. You scored only 75 % mortal hits from 15 meters. I have military capabilities nanotechnology chips implanted that give me perfect shooting at that range.

- Hand me the pistol.

She handed him the pistol. Metatron fired 15 shots, with extreme precision.

Metatron:

- That's how you do it, 100 % mortal hits in less than 10 seconds!

Keila:

- Wow! You must have trained a lot!

Metatron:

- Why would I waste time and bullets training? My nanotechnology implant gives me near-perfect marksmanship.

- We have a few spares actually; I can implant one in your brain if you want to?

Keila:

- No, thank you. I promised myself that I would never be a machine, and yet I implanted a God chip in my brain.

- Besides what will you do if your technology malfunctions and you haven't trained? You'd be useless.

Metatron:

- The technology won't fail, so that's a hypothetical scenario.

- Regardless, I didn't come here to discuss the merits of nanotechnology augmentations.

- We have news. There was an explosion on the ISS Supreme Earth, and we have received a distress beacon from one of their crew members.

Keila:

- Yes, I predicted that would happen. As for the beacon, do not respond to it.

Metatron:

- Understood, mistress. Why did you Anticipate an explosion? Did you rig your corpse with a bomb?

Keila:

- Let's just say Bjorn, and I share a less than cordial past. I reckon he would be petrified over the prospect that his scientists would revive and interrogate my corpse. That would expose his secret.

Metatron:

- Understood, Mistress Keila.

- May I suggest that we speed up our efforts to regain control over Eden, now that the Terran Council have left?

Keila:

- Yes, I will prepare my speech and address the people of Eden today. Tell the others to prepare to land on Eden.

Metatron:

- Very well! I will do your bidding. See you later.

After Metatron had left, Keila was left thinking. She hadn't given much thought on how to handle the chaos on Eden. The presence of her nemesis Bjorn Muller had kept her attention. With the Terrans gone, she had time to deal with the Edenites' struggles.

She would tell them the truth. She would tell them that they had been living in a simulation of the Bronze Age governed by the megalomaniac Abraham Goldstein, and that there were other villains like Abraham that needed to be stopped. Hopefully, they would follow her. Otherwise, she would give them the freedom to leave.

Another thought struck Keila. If all the Terran forces were untrained and reliant on military nanotechnology to perform in battle, blocking that technology would be the key to winning the war. She did not know how to stop the Terran military forces, but could the answer be in the Divine Dimension? Keila plugged herself into the Divine Detector Machine, dedicated to finding the answers that she needed.

Chapter 111: Floating in Space

Markus Bauer was checking the pressure indicator on the oxygen tank. It was down to 50 PSI, so it was a quarter full. This would give him approximately a few hours before he ran out of oxygen, giving him the options of either die from suffocation and a lack of oxygen, or die instantly from the vacuum of space.

Markus realised that the explosion at the Science Bay was not an accident. Instead, Bjorn Muller had caused it to happen to silence him. This was evident as his emergency beacon was activated, and yet they had abandoned him out here, to die in misery. The worst part was that Bjorn would get away with it, as there was no way for him to contact anyone.

Markus felt very nauseous. He realised that the concentration of carbon dioxide in the container was dangerously high. His only choice was to open the tank slightly to let the excess air out while having the risk of the freezing cold vacuum of space pulling him out of his safety-capsule. He exhaled completely to avoid bursting his lungs out and opened the door for a fraction of a second. The stale air was sucked out, just like when one pops a helium-filled air balloon and the freezing coldness of space was let in. Markus quickly closed the hatch and then released enough oxygen from the oxygen tank, to be able to breathe normally. In two hours, the oxygen would run out, and he would die.

Markus made up his mind. He would die from suffocation by staying within the safety-capsule. That way, if they found him, they would potentially be able to revive him. This was unlikely, as his emergency beacon was emitted by a microchip in his body, powered by bioelectricity. When he died, there would be no signal, and it would be almost impossible to find his lifeless body in the vastness of space. On the other hand, if he chose the quick death of letting the vacuum of space kill him, he would burst all his blood vessels including those in his brain, and he would be dead without any means of revival. Having made up his mind, Markus released the remaining oxygen from the oxygen tank into the capsule, and then went to sleep, not expecting to wake up.

Markus did wake up a few hours later. Although he almost hoped that he hadn't, as he was taken prisoner by the notorious space pirate, Mr Morgan Henry...

Chapter 112: Alone in the Dark.

Adina, the twin sister of Jeshua, was wandering around in the dark maintenance tunnels under Eden. She had lost her memory in her psionic blast showdown with Abraham Goldstein a week earlier. She had tried to climb up the ladder that was attached to the wall, but for some reason, the sun had tried to kill her with a laser beam. It had missed and instead hit the ladder's attachment making it melt and drop down to the bottom of the tunnels with her falling as well. It had been a 20-meter fall, but due to the low gravity on Eden, the fall had left her unscathed. With the ladder to the top dislodged, there was no way for Adina to reach the surface from this entrance and regardless, she felt no desire to return there with the sun out to kill her.

Instead, Adina hid in the darkness feeding of the wild mushrooms that grew there. She was alone in the dark, and terror filled her as her angel chip was still connected to her brain and she experienced the Edenites' terrors. Yet her amnesia made her unable to understand what was happening.

The fear from being in total darkness for weeks on end drove Adina insane, and she was sitting in a corner wagging back and forth, mumbling incoherent nonsense. One day, an event up on the surface triggered the return of her memories: Keila's speech to the people on Eden!

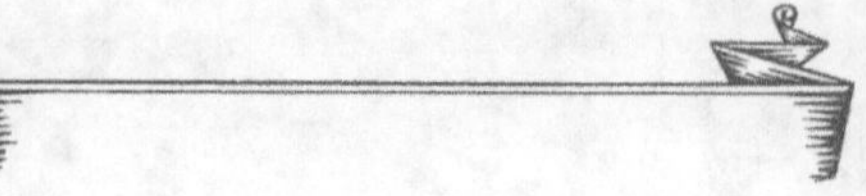

Chapter 113: Keila Prepares Her Speech to the Edenites.

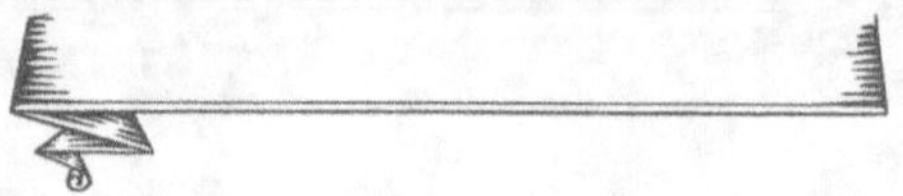

Keila was sitting in the Divine Dimension. She felt a bit hesitant on how to address the people of Eden. Being the ruler of a pseudo-Bronze Age tribe was nothing she had ever planned for, and she had been more of a figurehead in the resistance against the Terran Council. Keila was the ultimate figurehead for the Martian Humanist Alliance. She was the beautiful young woman who had assassinated Hans Muller, the ruthless and oppressive leader of the Terran Council. As such, she had given speeches in the past, but those speeches were always written and scripted by others, so she had never needed to make the decisions.

Keila was looking at herself in the mirror. Her auburn hair matched nicely with her light green eyes and symmetrical features with a flawless complexion. She had an athletic body and stood at 170 centimetres; 30 centimetres taller than the average for a Martian female. Overall, she looked a lot more like a human from Earth rather than a human from Mars, which was ironic since she was the poster girl for the resistance against Earth humans.

At the age of 12, Keila's mother Susanna had revealed to her that Keila's father had been a Terran, an exiled grandson of a Terran House ruler, who had fallen in love and eloped with her, a mere Edenite woman who was sold off as a sex slave to a wealthy Terran leader, Ibrahim Rashid. They were cursed for eternity and were deported from Earth to live on Mars in exile for his forbidden relationship with Susanna. Sadly, he had fallen ill and died before Keila was born. Keila had planned to find out more about him, but there had never been the right time, and her mother had kept her silence. In the end, it did not matter; there were more important things in the world than learning about people who died before she was born.

Keila inspected Eden. It was based on 70-year-old technology, and yet it was still a marvel of technology, far surpassing anything she had seen on Mars. It was also utterly useless to her. It was designed to enable a person living with Bronze Age technology to survive on an asteroid, and while it was impressive, it was a backward technology that was specifically designed to dumb down the population with no military skills whatsoever that would make them strong and win in case of a war.

Since the day Keila had crashed on Eden, the entire fabric of Edenite society had collapsed with mass killings and anarchy because of Adina and Jeshua's insurgence. The sole foundation of Eden's religion and ethics was to follow the commands of the omniscient Grand Master Abraham, which was written in the Abrahameon. When the rebellion and mayhem emerged, morality had collapsed, and society fell into a complete dark frenzy. Out of an original population of 8000 people of Edenites, 1500 of them had died because of the turnover of the religious dictatorship system. However, there were still 6500 individuals left desperately in need of leadership.

Keila decided to deliver the truth to the Edenites. The truth was that they were, living in the future and not living in during the Bronze Age era. Their original forefathers were Martians who were abducted and transported to Eden by the villain Abraham Goldstein, to live in an artificial world created by him. She would tell them that they were free to leave, while she implored them to join her in the fight against the Terran Council.

Keila summoned Metatron to prepare the landing on Eden.

Keila:

- Metatron, have you prepared for our landing on Eden?

Metatron:

- Yes, the others and I are ready and awaiting your command.

Keila:

- Good, I am coming with you.

Metatron:

- Mistress Keila, if you are not transmitting your thoughts from the Divine Dimension, you will not be able to connect to all the Edenites at once. Hence Edenites will not accept your Godhood.

Keila:

- I am not coming down as a Goddess. I am coming as a human aspiring to be their leader. Thus, I will present myself as such, a true Martian leader.

- I will tell them the truth. The time of deception has come to an end!

Metatron:

- I see. But what place would the angels and I have in this new dawn of time? We were deceived too. All I wanted was to serve and do good deeds.

Keila:

- I promise you that there will be opportunities to redeem yourself in the future, should you choose to follow me.

Metatron:

- Thank you, Keila. I will prove myself worthy!

Chapter 114: Keila's Address to the Edenites.

At noontime; Keila, Metatron and the other angels descended from the Divine Control Centre down to Eden. They were floating on a platform above Mount Sinai. Keila had planned to land on Eden to show that she was one of them, but Metatron had talked her out of it. The Edenites were still agitated, and landing in the middle of an upset crowd was very dangerous, both for Keila and for them. Instead, Keila stood on an elevated platform floating above the ground, out of range for the primitive Edenite Bronze Age weapons, but close enough for her to be visible to the people.

For the special occasion, Keila wore a long white dress to signify her innocence and a golden crown with jewels that glittered under Eden's seven suns. She felt a bit strange wearing this religious ancient dress. She was more accustomed to 29th-century skin-tight light battle armour that she usually wore in her public appearances. However, this was how her visions had shown it to her, and Keila trusted her foresight.

The masses waited with anxious anticipation, and when Keila started to speak:

- Dear people of Eden!

- My name is Keila Eisenstein.

- I have good news and bad news.

- The good news is that the Abraham is dead, and his reign of terror is over.

- The bad news is that your entire lives have been based on deceit.

- Your ancestors were not *"saved"* by Abraham *"when Earth was destroyed"*. They were abductees from the planet Mars.

- Earth is still around and the current year is the year 2872, and not year 62.

- You have been living in an artificial replica of mankind's early history, while Earth is a lot more advanced than you can ever imagine.

This message was not well received by the Edenites. The population mistrusted Keila and did not believe her. They were screaming profanities and tried to hit her with arrows and spears, which she was out of range from. Metatron raised his rifle to kill the ones who threw spears at them, but Keila signalled him to stop.

Keila:

- Dear Edenites. I have not come to force myself on you. I have come to offer you a hand and a new path to follow. I will show you images of Earth humans to prove that there are humans just like you outside of Eden.

Keila had planned this move in advance. By showing the Edenites holographic images and visual screen displays about life outside of Eden, she hoped to convince some of them about the validity of her claims. She showed a few television shows from Earth, as Earth was a paradise for Martians and Edenites alike.

The crowd watched the show. While the crowd could not understand most of it, it was clear to them that the people of Earth looked like the Angels that had been guiding them for the last 60 years. One man in the crowd, Elder Gil shouted: *"Is that vision showing the Angels' home planet?"*

Keila:

- No, the paradise you are watching is Earth. It is the rightful home of all humans. If you follow me, one day you might live there yourself.

Elder Gil:

- Tell me, Mistress. What do I need to do be granted that honour?

Keila:

- You'll have to serve our common cause with loyalty to the best of your ability.

- Come with me, I must show you something.

Elder Gil walked up and stood on a ledge on Mount Sinai, and Metatron flew down and picked him up. Keila lifted Elder Gil's arm to show the masses below of his triumph, and she spoke again.

- Elder Gil will come with me and verify what I am saying. When he returns, you should trust in what he says, and together we can start a new golden age for this rock that you call home.

- Until then, be peaceful and enjoy this new hope that you have been given.

After finishing her speech Keila, Elder Gil and the Angels entered a small space shuttle that took them back to the Divine Control Centre.

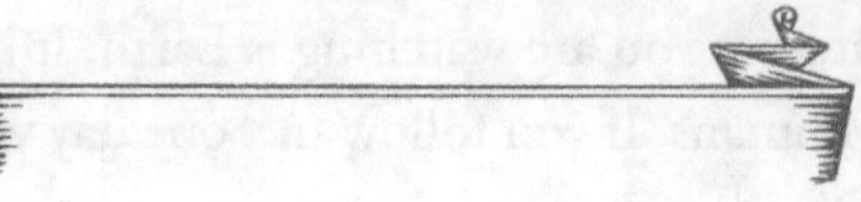

Chapter 115: Adina Regains Her Memories and Her Psionic Capabilities

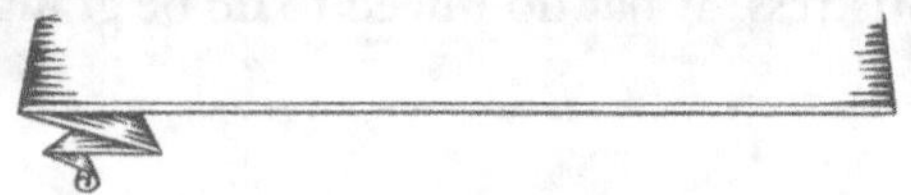

Adina heard Keila's speech and witnessed the entire event through a small opening from the dark tunnel down below. In the tunnels, she was safe from the menacing "sun" that was set kill her if she was to come out in the open. Seeing Keila filled Adina with rage. Her head was spinning, and she had to sit down to avoid collapsing as she was weak and injured. Adina's memories all came back to her. She knew who she was, and she remembered her powers.

Adina tried to focus her psionic abilities. She connected telepathically to her foster father, High Priest Markus and concluded that her adoptive parents were still alive. This was a relief for Adina, but it was not her biggest concern. She knew that her real parents were Archangel Lucifer and an Edenite woman by the name of Sara.

Sara had been killed in the crossfire when Lucifer was trying to protect his newborn twins, Adina and Jeshua, from the other angels. Jeshua was taken away and saved by Sara's grandfather, while Adina was kidnapped by the Angels and given to Abraham. Lucifer was captured alive and had received been exposed to a terrible execution. He had been publicly tortured and executed to show the people that no one could defy Abraham, not even his Archangel.

When Adina turned 10, she had learned that she had an unknown twin brother, Jeshua. She had tried to get close to him, but he had been reluctant to get close to her as she was rumoured to be a sorceress due to her psionic abilities. Eventually, at the age of 16, she had saved Jeshua from the Angels and convinced him to form an underground rebellion against Abraham. At the same time, she had pretended to support Abraham's rule. The underground resistance had failed, and all Jeshua's followers got killed, while Jeshua lost his mind spending years alone in the darkness underground with only wild mushrooms and water to survive on.

The emergence of Keila had changed everything. Realising that there were humans outside of Eden had disproved Abraham's lies about Eden being mankind's last home. Chaos and anarchy had followed. During this chaos, Keila and Jeshua had found each other, fallen in love, killed two angels, stolen their equipment, and had flown to the Divine Control Centre to confront Abraham.

At this time, Abraham had realised the threat that Adina posed to his rule and set his orbital satellites to fire lasers at her. One of the satellites had fired at Adina and missed. This had caused her to fall into one of the tunnels, hitting her head, and losing her memory.

Adina thought about what must have happened since she lost her memory. The emergence of Keila as the new leader of Eden showed that she must have killed Abraham and taken his place. But what about Adina's brother Jeshua? He was not contactable, and Adina had a feeling that her twin brother had died.

What was Keila's future vision for Eden? Adina was the one who was meant to be the Goddess of Eden. Adina and her brother Jeshua were destined to lead, not Keila, who highjacked the rebellion and killed Abraham. There was only one way to find out. Adina closed her eyes to see all the possible divine technology connections on Eden. Keila was the only individual with a god chip implanted and it seemed like Keila was unaware of Adina's presence.

Adina hesitated for a second. She needed to find out about Keila's intentions and what had happened to Jeshua. But what was her best course of action? If she spied on Keila and were detected, she would risk detection, which could be dangerous. If she, on the other hand, tried to communicate with Keila, she exposed her existence and risked being fed lies. Adina made up her mind. She would spy on Keila through the divine technology. This was her only chance to find out the truth. If she chose to communicate with Keila, she would not be able to enter Keila's mind at a later stage, as Keila had a god chip, which was superior to Adina's angel chip.

Adina sat down and focused her mind to penetrate Keila's mind undetected. To her surprise, she entered Keila's mind undetected, no doubt because Keila was not as accustomed to the divine technology as Abraham had been. Adina was not able to enter Keila's deep state of mind, and she was only able to see what she is doing at the time. Accessing what Keila was experiencing at the moment was easy, but it had no relevance to Adina. Adina had more pressing matters at hand than finding out what television shows Keila liked watching before going to bed.

Adina tried to go through Keila's memories and thoughts methodically. It was a challenging job as every human's mind categorised their memories in different layers, so it was difficult for an outsider to find what they were looking for. Adina needed to keep her own mind and emotions under complete control to avoid detection. Eventually, Adina found Keila's vision for Eden.

Keila saw Eden as a base of operations that she could use in her armed conflict with the Terran Council. If Keila's plans were to take place, many Edenites would perish in a pointless battle that they had no part in and the world that Adina knew would be in jeopardy. Adina managed to keep her emotional cool until she saw the memory where Keila shot and killed Jeshua. witnessing her twin brother's murder was too much for Adina, and she screamed her lungs out. This drew Keila attention before Adina severed the connection.

Chapter 116: Keila is Reminded of Adina's Existence.

Keila was in bed watching *"The wealthy wives of Warner"* on the TV screen in her bedroom. It was a vain, materialistic show that reminded Keila of her teenage years when she had lived relative peace and safety in Pamshal city on Mars. Back then she had limited interest in her mum's revolutionary talk against the Terran Council. Instead, Keila had been looking at ways to use her half-Terran heritage to her advantage. She had wanted to secure a Terran citizenship to get off Mars, and start a new life on the pristine Earth.

Those dreams had come to naught though as Keila, was psychologically scarred after being repeatedly raped and tortured by Bjorn Muller. Keila had directed her revenge into killing the leader of the Terran Council, Hans Muller. Killing the leader of the Terran Council ensured that she would be branded a nefarious criminal for the remainder of her life. Keila embraced her fate and became the figurehead of the revolutionary movement, The Martian Humanist Alliance.

Keila's premonitory visions and visual imagery had started appearing at the time when Bjorn Muller kept her as a sex slave. Before that event, she had had weaker premonitions, but from that moment, her visionary gifts intensified. Her visions had told her to injure Bjorn Muller, and they had guided her to safety. The visions had also shown her how to infiltrate the Terran Council and get close enough to Hans Muller to assassinate him. The latest four years they had helped her to perform other near-impossible feats. But what did frustrate her was that she didn't understand how she got all her visions and premonitions and what goal she was serving. Despite having clairvoyance and premonition, she was clueless.

Keila knew that her visions technically speaking, classified her as schizophrenic and that many whispered about it behind her back. It had been hurtful at first, but she had learned to ignore it. A delusional madwoman would not consistently be right, so she knew that her visions were not insanity but something else, something scientifically unexplainable.

Keila's visuals started flicking, and random memories popped up in her mind. Eventually, the memory of Jeshua's murder came up. A woman, similar in age to herself, showed up in the room as a mirage and screamed her lungs out before disappearing again. Startled by the vision, Keila summoned Metatron, to her chamber.

Metatron:

- You called, mistress.

- Pardon me for seeing you in limited clothing. You look very beautiful and alluring.

Keila:

- No apology needed. I experienced something so stressful, so I forgot to dress before summoning you.

Metatron:

- I am listening, Keila.

Keila:

- I'll get to it. But first a technical question. Is it possible for someone with an angel chip, to access my memories and show up as hallucinations?

Metatron:

- I have never heard of it, and it would defeat the purpose of the technology. Then again, the technology is alien in origin, and we still don't fully understand it.

- What happened?

Keila:

- My vision started flickering, and I had random memories popping up in my mind. Then at one memory, an image of a screaming woman came up in the room.

- She looked like me but she was less toned, and she was wearing an Edenite priestess gown.

Metatron pressed a switch, and Adina's photo appeared as a hologram.
Metatron:

- Was it this woman?

Keila

- Yes, that is her. Who is she?

Metatron:

- She is Adina. She was Lucifer's daughter. Abraham ordered her to have an angel chip implanted, and she was to be raised by high priest Markus under close supervision from the angels.

Keila:

- Why did he order that?

Metatron:

- I have no idea, but Abraham was not someone you ever questioned.

- Anyways, Adina was rumoured to have special psionic abilities that no other angel or even Abraham had. Abraham did not realise the threat she posed until it was too late for him, which was fortunate for you.

Keila:

- Fortunate? What do you mean?

Metatron:

- Do you think Abaddon chose to kill himself when he had maimed you and was about to kill you? It must have been Adina's doing.

Keila:

- Hmm. I did come across this strange woman, Elizabeth, who acted like a remote-controlled zombie. She told me that she brought a message from Adina.

- She helped us back then; does that mean she is a potential ally?

Metatron:

- Considering that you took the position she is yearning for, and you murdered her brother, I would say a non-hostile attitude from her is unlikely.

Keila froze for a moment. She had known Metatron for over a week, and she had never mentioned what she did to Abraham and Jeshua. She had assumed he didn't know what had happened, which was an absurd notion, considering the number of cameras filming everything at the space station. But why hadn't he mentioned it before? Remorse filled Keila, and she was struggling to hold back her tears.

Keila:

- So, you knew all along? I don't know why I killed Jeshua. I was compelled to do it. My visions told me.

Metatron:

- There hasn't been any reason to mention it. Your reason for killing Abraham was apparent, and your reason for killing Jeshua is irrelevant to me.

- Regardless, I mentioned it now to explain the unlikelihood in Adina being friendly towards us.

Keila:

- But if you knew that I murdered my partner, why did you choose to help me?

Metatron:

- I went with my gut feeling!

- After you killed Abraham, I was free from his tyranny. But what would I do?

- I woke up first after the psionic blast. I knew what to do, by elevating you to Godhood, I would also elevate myself and be able to redeem myself for carrying out Abraham's atrocities throughout the years.

Keila:

- Are you not worried that I will do the same to you as I did to Jeshua?

Metatron:

- No, I am not.
- I am an old man in a young man's body. If I am meant to die, so be it.

Keila:

- You are not that old? You don't look much older than 30?

Metatron:

- Quadruple that, and you are closer to the truth.

Keila looked at Metatron with a puzzled expression. It did not make any sense that he would be so old. She was aware of DNA regeneration technology being used among Terrans, but even then, Metatron would bear the scars of aging that the technology could not hide.

Keila:

- How can that be? You don't have the scars of aging that old people always have?

Metatron:

- That is because I have spent most of my years in cryogenic sleep to avoid aging. Abraham envisioned the Eden Project to last for an eternity, and he didn't want his Angels to age.

Keila:

- I see. I would prefer to be alone now. Return to your quarters, Metatron.

As Metatron walked towards the door, Keila failed to control her emotions. Filled with remorse, she let down her barrier, and the feelings overwhelmed her. With tears pouring down from her chin, Keila called out to Metatron: *"Don't go, stay with me, I don't want to be alone".* The puzzled Metatron turned around, and Keila jumped into his arms. She refused to let go with tears running down her cheeks. They stood there like that for a long time, before Metatron tucked her in.

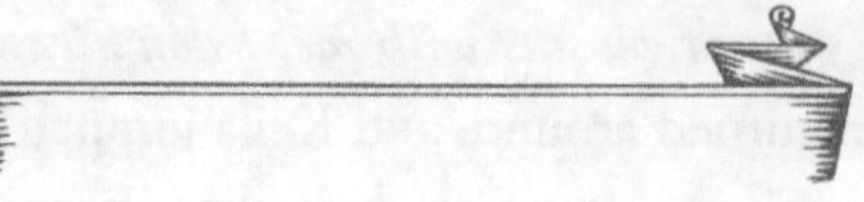

Chapter 117: Brahma Studies Keila's Mind and is Reminded of Rangda.

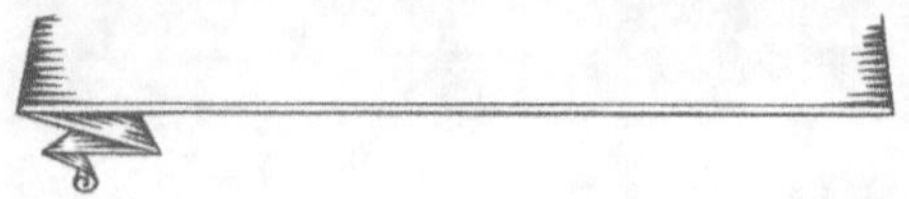

Brahma was meditating in his meditation chamber 30 kilometres from the Divine Palace. He was at peace, as deep meditation was the only state where his hunger and thirst weren't tormenting him. Brahma tried to access Keila's mind but he struggled to connect to her. He had struggled to access Keila's mind for the last few weeks.

Brahma thought of reasons why he struggled to connect with Keila. The distance from her could be one reason. He was 30 kilometres away from the heavenly palace, and since distances were compressed in the Divine Dimension, this was the equivalent of being 3 billion kilometres away from Keila in the regular universe. He shrugged off the idea. He had connected with Keila in the past from this location, and before the destruction of Zetani, the planet of Zetans, his predecessors were able to communicate telepathically with each other from light-years away. 3 billion kilometres were only 3 light hours and it wouldn't be a limiting factor.

Brahma thought about Rangda. It was a bittersweet feeling. Being one of the greatest Zetans, he had many concubines, and she had been one of his favourites.

That prominent males had many concubines was one of the great paradoxes of the Zetan civilisation. While Zetans were close to asexual compared to humans and thus had a prolonged reproduction rate, having many beautiful females in his cohort was the best way for a prominent Zetan to show his status to his peers. As the Zetans were governed through a utilitarian mind, facilitated by the Zeto crystals, money and individual ownership were irrelevant to them. Instead, clarity of thoughts and pureness of the genome was their fundamental values. By binding many women to prominent Zetan men, they increased the odds of improving their genome as species.

Brahma had saved Rangda's life, after the fateful day, when the Xenos had penetrated the core of Zetan territory and blew up the star that Zetani was orbiting. The explosion was so powerful that it created the massive supernova in the centre of the Milky Way Galaxy. The explosion obliterated hundreds of star systems and marked the end to the Zetan civilisation. The few Zetans who had survived the blast were the ones that were in the Divine Dimension and the ones on distant, isolated worlds. The ones' stuck in the Divine Dimension were stuck in the timelessness, condemned to immortality suffering from hunger and thirst. The Zetans on the fringe worlds degenerated as species, with Zeto crystals no longer around to unite them.

Zeus and Odin had found Rangda in the Divine Dimension on the same day that most of their civilisation was destroyed by the Xenos. While they had never been able to prove Rangda's betrayal, the circumstantial evidence was strong.

Rangda had been the commander responsible for protecting the Zetani star system, and during her watch, a Xeno crew had stayed close to the Zetani star for long enough to manipulate its energies into the collapse the prompted a colossal supernova explosion. Zeus and Odin had intended to execute Rangda for her crimes, but Brahma, had intervened and requested that she should live and be given a chance to defend herself. The others had no interest in listening to Rangda's defence, but they had allowed her live forever, isolated in an inescapable prison.

Brahma felt Rangda's presence. But he knew that it shouldn't be possible. The prison for Rangda was built of a material that would stop her telepathic abilities. Yet he could sense her stronger than he had for thousands of years. What would he do? He considered contacting the other Zetans, but he decided against it. His relationship with the other Zetan leaders had deteriorated, and they would question his motives for going there.

Brahma made up his mind. He left a note stating that he would be gone for a while. The trip would take a long time. He would have to walk the entire way since the Zetans were out of fuel for their spaceships. Walking 50,000 kilometres would feel like walking for several years, but due to the time divergence between The Divine Dimension and the normal dimension, it would only take a couple of months. Brahma took up a high-powered binocular that had a maximum of 1000x magnification. He faced in the direction of the Rangda's prison and saw a minuscule dot. As the Divine Dimension was a flat, featureless, and endless plane, he could see things that were very far away.

Brahma took a deep breath and he started walking. Hunger and thirst would torment him during the walk, but he kept going. He knew what he needed to do.

Chapter 118: Adina Gives Keila an Ultimatum.

Keila woke up in shock, fell out of her bed, and found herself lying face down on the floor. Blood dripped from her nose and she had an excruciating migraine. She cried out to Metatron, but he was no longer present as he had left when she fell asleep. Keila got up on her knees and looked up. There was an illusion of Adina in front of her.

Without saying anything, Adina launched another psionic blast to strike Keila. But this time, Keila countered Adina's burst, and both Keila and Adina fell backward to the ground. Keila coughed up some blood and spit it out. Adina, in turn, had blood running down from her eyes. Keila screamed out:

- What are you doing, what do you want?!

Adina:

- I came to kill you for killing my brother and stealing my rightful place.

- As it turns out, you're stronger than I thought, and I cannot use my powers to kill you, without risking my own life.

Keila:

- Is that so?
- Crazy bitch! Feel this!

Keila tried directing a psionic blast onto Adina, but it failed as her mental capabilities were also weakened. Adina studied her for a second and spoke.

- Interesting, it seems you are too weak to smite me as well.

Keila:

- What a shame!
- So, what do we do? Duel at dawn?

Adina:

- That is not how we solve problems on Eden.

- My demands are simple.

- You are to remove the god chip and leave Eden under my control. Don't ever think of coming back!

Keila:

- Why would I agree to that?

Adina:

- Because you value your life.
- You are a foreigner here; Eden means nothing to you. Just leave!

Keila:

- You are mistaken.

- Eden is my future. Eden is the future of mankind.

- I didn't come here by accident; providence brought me here.

- With technology and resources on this rock, I will free humanity from the tyranny of the Terran Council.

Adina:

- I don't care about that. You are a murderer and an imposter. Leave, or I will kill you!

Keila:

- Fuck off, bitch!

After screaming out, Keila lashed a second psionic blast at Adina. To her great surprise, Adina simply vanished from her consciousness, and she could no longer detect Adina being a connected node to the Divine Technology. Metatron ran into the room. He looked at her with a worried expression.

Metatron:

- Mistress Keila! You are injured, what happened?

Keila:

- Just take me to the medical bay. I'll tell you later.

Metatron lifted Keila and rushed her to the medical bay for immediate treatment.

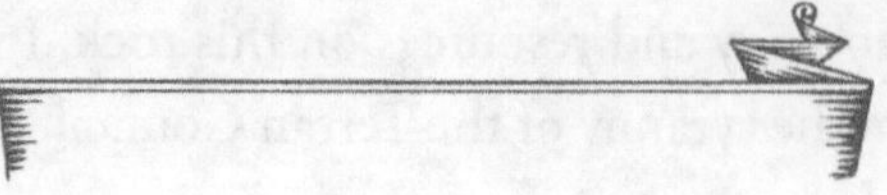

Chapter 119: Keila Wakes Up in the Medical Bay.

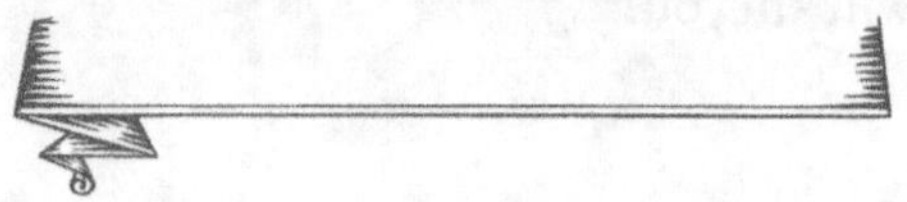

Keila woke up three days later in the medical bay. Her head was spinning, and she suffered from severe nausea. Keila looked at a display and noticed that she had been unconscious for three full days. *"Three days,"* she thought *"What really happened to me?"* She remembered her psionic fight with Adina, she couldn't tell if it was real or not. Metatron entered the room.

Metatron:

- Mistress Keila. I am relieved to see you awake.

Keila:

- What happened to me?

Metatron:

- We are not sure. The security footage shows you being alone in the room, slamming your head against the floor in a seizure-like way. However, the scarring on your brain tissue was unique and did not match injuries associated with blunt trauma.

- Regardless, you are lucky to be alive, without immediate medical attention, you would be permanently killed.

Keila reflected over what Metatron had told her. She had been lucky, but had Adina died during their altercation? Adina had disappeared from the grid, and she would not have access to advanced medical science in the tunnels under Eden. Keila asked Metatron about Adina.

Keila:

- Adina did this to me. She blasted me with psionic energy. Do you know what happened to her?

Metatron:

- Is that so? I don't see how that would be possible, considering she has a lower-tier chip installed than you do.

Keila:

- That is what happened!

Metatron:

- I believe you.

- She has been gone from the grid for the last few days. Maybe she died in your confrontation?

Keila:

- I am not taking any chances. Send security bots into the tunnels and kill her!

Metatron:

- Hmm, unfortunately, we don't have any security bots to send.

Keila:

- But Eden is vast, and there are lots of robots on the dark side of Eden?

Metatron:

- Well, Abraham's vision for Eden was for it to be a replica of the Promised Land during the Bronze Age. Security bots didn't fit in on that narrative.

Keila:

- I see. We must make sure to get security bots delivered then. We must keep ourselves safe from that crazy bitch.

Metatron:

- Understood. I'll try to get some bots delivered off the black market. It won't be quick or cheap.

Keila:

- Thanks, Metatron.

- One more thing, I want you to be by my side, to protect me in case she strikes again.

Metatron:

- Understood Mistress Keila, I will keep you safe.

Keila closed her eyes again and thought on how to continue. She could not send any Angels or Edenites to confront Adina. If her aptitude with the divine technology were so great so that she almost killed a higher-tier user from afar, it would pose no difficulty for Adina to eliminate any Angels or humans that Keila sent after her. With security bots, it was different. They had no divine technology chips installed, and Keila was convinced that Adina had no other combat skills than those from her superior usage of the divine technology.

But what if Adina was dead, and they wasted precious resources buying robots to chase her down? That could be a tactical mistake. Keila shrugged off that notion as her gut feeling told her that Adina was alive, and Keila always followed her intuition.

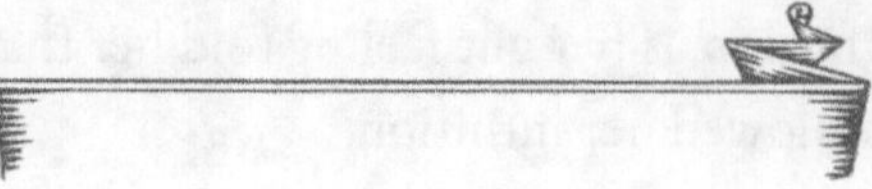

Chapter 120: Adina Strikes Again

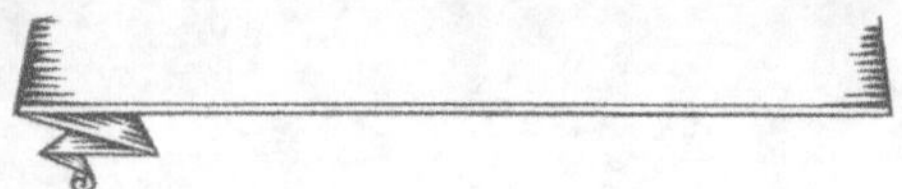

Three days later, Keila was struggling to fall asleep. The incident with Adina was gnawing in the back of her mind, and she was afraid. They had failed to find any trace of Adina in the Divine Technology neural network, and everyone except for Keila assumed that Adina was dead. Keila had turned down Metatron's offer to use an accelerated sleep pod to get her daily need of sleep in less than two hours. Keila liked natural sleep, as it allowed her to dream and unleash her imagination. The accelerated sleep pod was just two blank hours of her life, and it did not appeal to her.

Keila looked at Metatron, who was watching over her from the corner of the room. He had watched over her for three days straight, and Keila had never known a man that loyal before. She felt how she was yearning for him.

Keila looked away. She tried to control her desire. "This is insanity," she thought to herself. Metatron was a century older than her, but due to extended periods in cryogenic sleep and DNA regeneration technology he was physically in his thirties, or a decade older than Keila.

Despite her attempts to use logic to curb her desire for Metatron, Keila's urge for him kept growing throughout the night. Her desire for Metatron kept her awake. Did he feel the same desire for her? It was easy to find out, all she needed to do was to enter his mind via the divine technology and find out. Keila rejected the notion. The last few weeks, Metatron had grown to be the closest person to her in the world. It would be a betrayal to spy on him instead of trusting him. She called him over.

Keila:

- Metatron, what do you think about me?

Metatron:

- I think you are a capable individual who will provide excellent guidance to the Edenites.

Keila:

- But do you like me, as a person?

Metatron:

- Yes, but my feelings are not what matters. My duty is what matters.

Keila:

- I like you Metatron, and I find you incredibly attractive.

Metatron:

- Thank you, Keila. Is there anything I can help you with?

Keila hesitated. She had hoped that Metatron would be more excited over the conversation. She was in lingerie in bed, and they were the only two people in the room. But maybe he had repressed his sexuality? After all, Metatron had lived in isolated with a group of men for over 60 years. Keila made the leap of faith.

Keila:

- Yes, there is. I desire you! Make love to me!

Metatron:

- Desire... I have buried that feeling so deep inside me, I wouldn't even recognise it anymore.

Keila:

- Well, then it's time to unleash your desire.

Metatron:

- I will if you lead the way. Control my body through the psionic powers of your god chip.

Keila:

- Sure, let's try it.

Keila focused her mind on taking control over Metatron's body. It was an extraordinary feeling, as she was touched by someone else, and yet it felt like she was touching herself. Keila let her worries go and just embrace the orgasmic feeling. They both got undressed, and Keila felt how her desire peaked when she touched Metatron perfectly sculpted physical body. He entered her and was thrusting rhythmically and hitting the spot every stroke. Keila came multiple times and lost track of time and place.

Adina studied Keila through the eyes of Metatron. The plan was working, and in a moment, it would be time for her to strike. Adina touched the scars where her healthy eyes used to be. The eyes were still there, but they had been wounded from the psionic blast during her altercation with Keila that had made her blind. Adina had been clinically dead after her previous fight with Keila, but she had seen the light and felt compelled to go back and face Keila. When she woke up, she was blind, but her psionic powers had improved.

Adina could now stay hidden and manipulate people's inner thoughts undetected. Adina had induced Keila with an irresistible carnal desire towards Metatron. Adina did this because Metatron was easier to control than Keila was. Thus, it would be easier to use him to kill Keila than it would be to face Keila again.

Adina put her plan into motion; she took control of Metatron's body and started strangling Keila with his strong hands.

Keila didn't immediately notice that Metatron was strangling her as she was so aroused. After a few seconds, however, she noticed what he was doing and that she had lost the connection to his mind. She started screaming and punching him to no avail, as the unemotional and remotely controlled angel was too powerful and resilient to pain to notice her resistance at all.

Keila looked into Metatron's eyes, he was out of his mind! Keila's vision faded to black, but before she passed out, she saw Adina for a fraction of a second. Keila managed to gather her remaining powers and blast Adina with a psionic blast. Adina was shocked by getting struck, as she thought she was invisible to the other users, and she passed out. Metatron, also got struck, and he fell unconscious to the floor.

Keila activated the alarm. Samael and a group of angels entered the room. He looked in disgust at Keila and Metatron, both sweaty and naked.

Samael:

- What is going on in here? This is unacceptable.

Keila:

- Take Metatron to the medical bay! Connect me to The Divine Dimension. You can whine later.

Samael looked at Keila and obeyed her command. He had strong negative opinions on sex outside of marriage, especially since Metatron had taken vows of celibacy when he became an Angel. However, he was a loyal subject and there to serve.

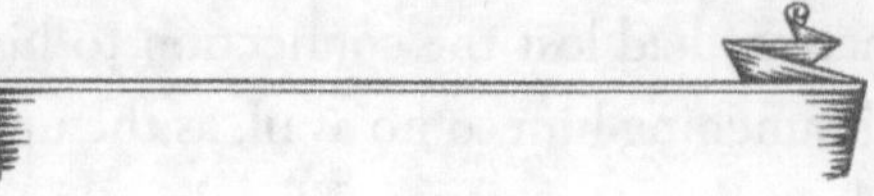

Chapter 121: Keila Finds a Solution to the Adina Problem.

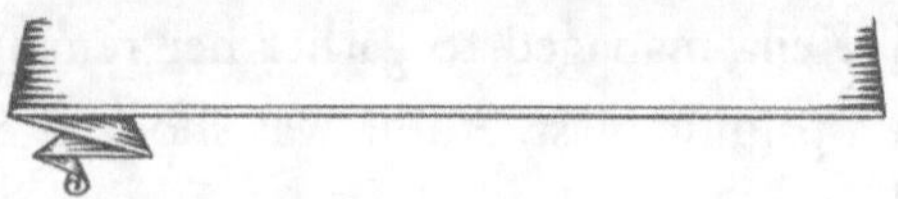

Keila was back in the Divine Dimension for the first time in a couple of weeks. She hadn't been there for a while, as the Divine Detector Machine there used tremendous amounts of power to operate. Keila had other plans for Eden rather than wasting all the precious fuel on running the Divine Detector Machine.

She studied the ancient Zetan tomes for a way to deal with Adina when Samael contacted her.

- I have some terrible news about your fuck-buddy Metatron.

Keila:

- Show some respect, Samael!
- Metatron is your Archangel and we had sex because I wanted to.

Samael:

- Apologies, Mistress Keila. I should have watched my tongue.

- Anyways. There is irreparable damage on Metatron's brain. If we regenerate tissue to get him back alive, he might be permanently damaged. I suggest that we let him pass away in peace.

Hearing this made Keila upset and she blasted Samael with a light psionic shock for even daring to recommend it.
Keila:

- No, you are wrong! There is hope! I will not let Metatron die!

Samael coughed and brushed off the light blast:

- As you wish, Keila. We'll keep him alive. Don't blame me for the consequences.

Keila:

- I can't guarantee you that. Now get back to work and save Metatron.

Keila severed the connection and she wailed in pain. She couldn't lose Metatron. He was the only one she had left in the world after her mum and her friends in the resistance had fallen. Keila walked around randomly in the Zetan archives room, until she stumbled into a bookcase, causing some of the books to fall on her. As she got up on her knees, she glimpsed at one of the open books on the floor and smiled in relief. The gods had given her the solution to her problems once again!

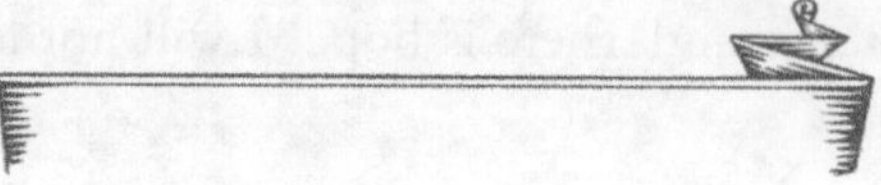

Chapter 122: Keila Sets Up a Meeting with Adina

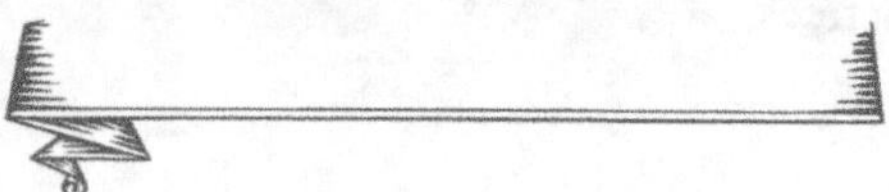

Keila was sitting under the Lotus tree in the Divine Palace courtyard. Her mind was at peace, and she knew what she needed to do. She contacted Samael.

- Samael, new directions: Turn off Metatron's life support and let him die; then freeze his body.

Samael:

- That's the opposite to what you ordered before?

Keila:

- I know. Does that bother you, Samael?

Samael:

- Not at all, Keila; I am glad you listened to my advice.

Keila:

- All good. Dismissed, Samael.

Keila leaned back and sensed how Metatron's signal became weaker and weaker until he perished. Keila sighed. It was painful sensing Metatron die, but letting him die now was the best way to save him later. Although Keila felt at peace, she riled herself up for a show. It was time to lure Adina into a trap. She found Adina's signal in the system and contacted her.

Keila:

- Adina, you bitch!
- Metatron is dead because of you!

Adina:

- I know; I sensed it. It hurts to lose someone you love, does it not?

Keila:

- Yes.

- Let's settle this. Let's meet up and determine who is worthy of ruling Eden.

Adina:

- And why would I agree to meet you?

Keila:

- Because you want me dead as much as I want you dead. Besides, what else are you going to do? You are blind and stuck in the tunnels?

Adina considered her options. She was unsure whether grief had driven Keila insane or if she had an ace up her sleeve. Regardless, Adina needed to kill Keila as Keila had all the trump on hand. Keila had an advanced medical bay and unlimited food and resources while Adina had no access to medical treatment and was confined in the tunnels with limited sustenance. Adina made up her mind. She would meet with Keila in the catacombs. From proximity, her psionic powers would be stronger, and she would have no trouble blasting Keila out of existence. With

Keila dead, it was an easy task to take control of the Angels, have them turn off the orbital lasers, and elevate her to become the God-queen of Eden.

Adina:

- Agreed. Meet me at the tunnel entrance to the southwest of Mount Sinai. Come alone and unarmed. See you in 12 hours.

Keila:

- See you then. Prepare to die, Adina!

Chapter 123: The Eradication of Adina

Twelve hours later, Keila arrived next to the tunnel entrance south-west of Mount Sinai. She was nervous and knew that there was no help available if things did not play out according to her plan. Before Keila left the Divine Control Centre, she had made sure that the Angels had entered cryogenic sleep to avoid Adina taking control of them. Keila stepped out of her shuttle and walked towards the tunnels. Keila hoped that Adina would to talk to her face to face, instead of taking the shot as soon as she entered within lethal range of the psionic blasts. She didn't dare to take any chances though and she kept her guard up to avoid being taken by surprise. Keila spotted Adina a bit from the entrance. She shone a flashlight at her, and it was a pitiful sight.

Adina had taken severe physical damage from her psionic confrontations with Keila, and the lack of medical attention had not helped her. Her face was bruised, her eyes had been crushed, and they were full of maggots. As Adina's physical senses had weakened, her psionic abilities powered by her Angel chip had strengthened, and she was a formidable enemy.

Keila:

- We meet at last.

Adina:

- Yes.

- You have made a deadly mistake coming here.

- I am wounded, and without help. You could have bided your time waiting for me to perish. Instead, you came here within lethal range for my psionic blasts.

Keila:

- Is that so?
- Then I suggest you try to blast me away with your mind!

During the time she said that Keila used the deactivation code to the divine technology that she had seen in the Zetan book the day before. Adina tried to blast her with a psionic blast, but to no avail, as she fell exhausted to the ground.

Adina:

- Why... Why is it not working?

Keila:

- Because I deactivated the entire system.

- Did you honestly think I would come down here for you when all I needed to do was to wait for you to die?

Adina:

- Do you think your intense emotions and desire for Metatron came from nowhere? I made you fall in love with the tool that I used to try to kill you.

- Your heart is broken because of the death of a man that I made you love. How ironic!

Keila:

- You are lying, bitch. Metatron was always special to me.

Adina:

- Special like all your other men, you filthy whore?!

Keila:

- You have pestered me enough crazy woman! Time to die!

Adina, who was wounded and not much of a fighter to start with tried to fight but she was no match for Keila who was a trained fighter.

As Adina was weakened and coughing blood on the ground, Keila spoke:

- Metatron's death doesn't bother me, since I found a way to revive him!

After that Keila dragged Adina to the tunnel entrance and then she threw her out in the open where the orbital laser cannons incinerated Adina. As she walked past Adina's charred remains, she felt relieved. Her nightmare was over, but her battle had just begun!

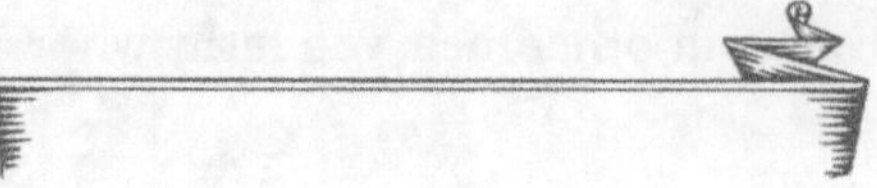

Chapter 124: The Revival and Promotion of Metatron

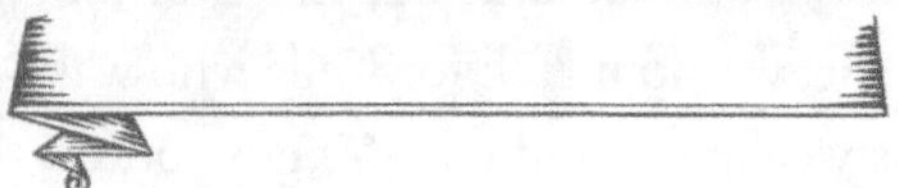

Keila was holding the "God chip MKII", which she had found the schematics for in the Zetan archives. The chip was more potent than the one she had implanted, and it could restore brain tissue. Keila looked at the lifeless body of Metatron in the cryogenic tank. If she was to revive him and implant him with the MKII chip, would he still be loyal to her? or would the reversal of power in their relationship change him? There was no way to know, but she missed him and wanted him back by her side.

Keila made up her mind, she would revive him. He had saved her life, and she had to do everything in her power to protect him. Besides, her intuition told her that he would remain loyal to her, and why question her intuition now, when she never questioned it otherwise? She called in Samael to help her with the procedure. He seemed uneager to help.

Samael:

- This is not right; in our culture, we have never followed more than one deity. Yahweh was our god for thousands of years, Abraham succeeded him, and then you replaced him. Yet, the concept of one god remained. Now you are suggesting elevating Metatron to your level, leaving us with two gods?

Keila:

- We both know that the "Divine Technology" is mind-control technology developed by the alien Zetan race to control humanity.

- Yahweh was an extra-terrestrial being who used technology to manipulate our ancestors. Abraham was a man who used the same technique to manage you and the people in Eden. Through destiny, I am now in control of the technology. This doesn't make any of us divine. I wish to share my power with Metatron, as that is the only way to revive him.

Samael:

- I can't believe that Yahweh was an imposter. His principles guided our people throughout the millennia and gave us hope and comfort.

Keila:

- Yet you have seen his corpse in the Divine Dimension. You have visited the Zetan archives and learned everything about the multi-millennia war and how the Zetans used humans to fight the Xenos.

Samael:

- Yes, I have seen it, but I don't want to believe it. I still want to believe in something higher than myself. Something to look up to.

Keila:

- If it's any comfort to you, I still believe that there is a great maker that created everything. However, the True Maker is too great to focus its attention on detailed rules for how humans should live their lives. The great creator of the universe doesn't need our worship.

Samael:

- I guess that's a comforting thought.

- One more thing bothering me. Metatron was bound by an oath of celibacy and yet he engaged in coitus with you.

Keila:

- Well, his oath was sworn to Abraham, who perished. Once Abraham died, the promise was null and void.

Samael:

- Does that mean that I...?

Keila:

- Yes, you are free to find yourself a suitable partner, Samael. I am sure there are plenty of eligible singles for you on Eden.

Samael:

- Thank you, Mistress Keila. That's a burden that is off my chest.

Keila:

- Yes. Let's focus on reviving Metatron now, shall we?

After saying that, they defrosted Metatron and started the surgical procedure of removing his Angel chip and inserting a god MKII chip instead. The surgery was performed by a medical bot, but as the bot didn't have any file on how to deal with the Zetan technology, they had to control the bot with their minds through an electrode helmet that they had on top of their heads. They had both studied complex reparative surgery in the Zetan archives but to make sure that they avoided mistakes, they acted as each other's fail-safes. After several hours, they had removed Metatron's angel chip and inserted the god MKII chip. They defibrillated Metatron's heart, and he woke up.

Metatron, got a flashback of how he tried to strangle Keila, and was filled with remorse, when he saw Keila's face.

Metatron:

- Mistress Keila. I am... I am so sorry.

Keila:

- It wasn't your fault. All that matters are that you're back with me now.

Samael left the room. Metatron and Keila sat silently, but happy and feeling a mutual connection in each other's embrace.

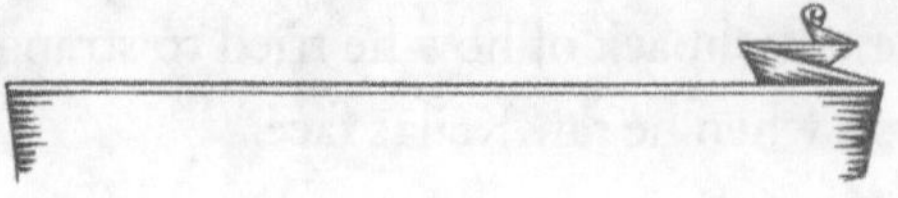

Chapter 125: Keila's Dilemma

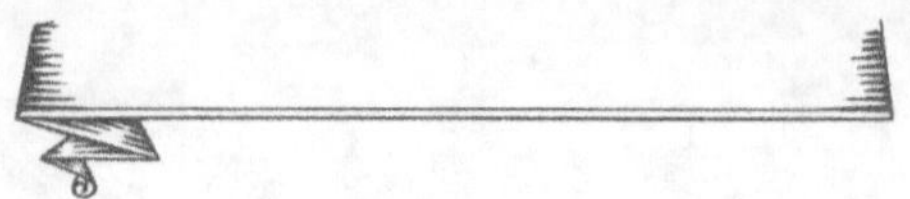

A few weeks later, Keila was sitting in a couch looking at the vastness of space outside, through a sizeable fortified panorama window. When she looked straight ahead, she saw Eden.

Eden seemed vast from her perspective, despite being a small world. Its surface was mostly brownish yellow with some green and blue patches where there were farms and water reservoirs. Eden's atmosphere looked intensely blue from her perspective. This was because the atmosphere was tightly packed with air. The atmosphere on Eden only stretched a kilometre up to the electrified nanotechnology protective layer that kept the atmosphere in, yet the surface air pressure was like that on Earth. To achieve this, the air concentration was a lot higher on Eden than on Earth. Hence its atmosphere was a lot bluer when viewed from space.

Keila looked on a control panel; she saw that all the systems that kept Eden liveable was working like clockwork and now that peace was restored, the people could live safe lives and in abundance.

The potential for good living conditions on Eden was the root of Keila's dilemma. She needed to choose between what was good for the people she was governing and what was good the population in the solar system that was oppressed by the Terran Council's tyranny. She had planned to use Eden as her secret base of operations to make covert strikes on Terran Council ships and mining stations. After getting to know the Edenites better, she felt reluctant to go through with this cruel project. The Edenites had nothing to do with her fight with the Terran Council, and she could not inspire them to fight a battle that wasn't theirs, without deceiving them. Deceiving them would be easy, but if she chose that path, she would not be better than her enemies who had used false promises to dominate the solar system for the past six centuries.

Another issue Keila was wrestling with, was the freedom of her people in Eden. After defeating Adina, Keila had intended to free all her subjects through removing the microchips from their brains. Metatron had opposed this idea which had upset Keila, but she had come around and realised that he was right. Metatron had argued that the people of Eden were happy with being part of something bigger than themselves. To force everyone out of the community was worse than controlling people that wanted to be controlled.

Keila had admitted that forcing atheism was not more freedom than forcing religion, so she had left the people with the choice whether to remain connected. A few weeks later, no one had opted to leave Eden, due to their fear of the great unknown that was beyond Eden.

Keila connected to Metatron to see what he was doing. He was counselling some villagers on Eden after the death of their grandfather. Keila was moved when she watched Metatron counsel the villagers. He treated them with a level of compassion and love that she could not muster. It seemed like Metatron cared for all his subjects and Keila could only imagine how much pain it would have caused him to carry out all of Abraham's atrocities. Keila disconnected from Metatron. She looked forward to seeing him in the Divine Dimension later. The timelessness of that place made their encounters so much more pleasant and blessed. After that, she fell asleep, filled with pleasant dreams for the first time in four years.

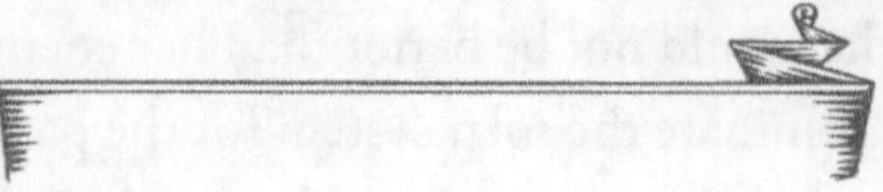

Chapter 126: Markus Bauer is Freed

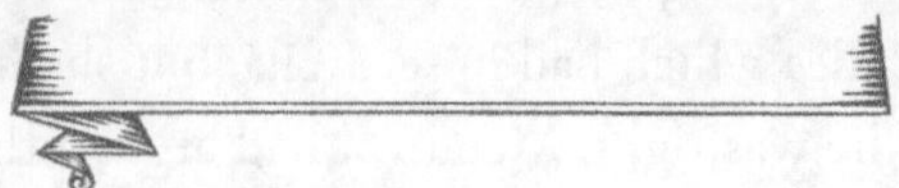

Markus Bauer woke up in his prison cell aboard Morgan Henry's pirate spaceship. For the last month, Markus had felt a sense of optimistic fear for his situation. When he was first picked up by Morgan's crew, he had felt a disappointment that he hadn't perished a peaceful death from suffocation in space. Morgan Henry was notorious for mutilating and torturing prisoners to please his sadistic tendencies. At least this was what media portrayed, and Markus had no reason to question the media portrayal of Morgan Henry, the evil space pirate. But during the first interrogation, he hadn't been tortured. Instead, Morgan Henry had extracted the data from the microchips in Markus' brain and then sent him back to his cell.

After the first interrogation, Markus was left in the cell with little contact with his captors, but they had provided him with enough nutrition and hygiene products to avoid disease.

Markus Bauer heard a pistol discharge. He recognised the sound that he had heard for a few times in the last month. It was Morgan Henry's custom-made pistol that used special propellant to accelerate the bullets to ten times the speed of sound, while still being low recoil and easy to carry. The pistol was designed to have enough power to penetrate any armour, even the advanced Terran Council's special operations armour. The door opened, and Morgan Henry entered. He had blood splattered all over his face.

Morgan Henry:

- Aye Lad, you are coming with me.

Markus:

- Are you going to kill me?

Morgan Henry:

- Why would you say that?

- Ah, you mean the blood on my face. I do all the executions on this vessel. The one who gives the sentence should carry out the killing himself, that's our code.

Markus Bauer:

- That's barbaric!

Morgan Henry:

- Nay, what's barbaric is ordering others to kill for you, while rich folks like you are sipping cognac and smoking cigars from the safety of your elegant boardrooms back on Earth!

- But enough of that. Aye, today is your lucky day. Arrrr! Someone posted your ransom; a hefty amount for returning you alive! They will meet you at to the dock, and I will bring you there.

They walked to the docks where they met with Tzi Chen Cheng; the chairman for the Terran Council Science Commission and a high-ranking member of House Cheng. Markus was baffled to see him under these circumstances, and even more baffled to see him alone without any bodyguards. Morgan Henry signalled his men, and the pirates left the docks to the two men.

Markus:

- Tzi Chen! What on Earth are you doing on the ship of the most notorious pirate of the solar system, at the fringe of this solar system?

Tzi Chen:

- We are close to Earth, Mr Bauer.

- Mr Henry and his men work for us as an independent party.
By having pirates carry out objectives for us, we have deniability when things go wrong. All Terran houses operate the same
way.

Markus:

- But I am not affiliated with House Cheng? I come from
House Muller territory, and I work for the Terran Council.

Tzi Chen:

- True, but it would be silly to deny my connection with Morgan Henry when I am on his ship. Besides who would believe
your claim, if you made our secretive association public.

- Truth to be told, I came to see the body of Keila Eisenstein,
if it even exists.

Markus:

- It exists! I examined it before the explosion at the Science
Bay.

Tzi Chen:

- Very well.
- Let's examine it together. It is stored in that crate over there.

Both men walked to the crate where Tzi Chen noticed that this was
a phony.
Tzi Chen:

- You fool! You are the chief scientist on a Terran Council vessel, and you cannot identify that this is a forgery!

Markus:

- What do you mean?

- I had a suspicion that it could be a non-functional clone, but it was hard to determine due to bullets destroying the spine and the brain, making it impossible to analyse it.

Tzi Chen:

- You can determine it by studying the bone structure. The bone structure of the corpse matches the body of someone who grew up on Earth. But Keila grew up on Mars. She should have more hollow bones due to the lower gravity on Mars and different colour pigment on the skin tissue, due to the various elements present in Martian food.

Markus:

- I am not sure that I follow you.

Tzi Chen:

- This is a clone, made with Terran equipment emulating a person who lived under the Terran conditions. Whether it was a functional or non-functional clone is still to be examined, but I can guarantee you that it was not Keila Eisenstein.

Markus:

- So, what are you going to do? Will you expose Bjorn's deceit?

Tzi Chen:

- No, that's your job. I am not going to complain about a senior member of another House, based on a corpse I found on a pirate ship. That's not a good look nor a credible claim.

Markus:

- So, what am I going to do?

Tzi Chen:

- You'll figure it out. Let's leave this ship. There are better places to linger than a pirate ship, regardless if the captain is your top-secret agent or not.

After saying that, they entered Tzi Chen's private shuttle and set the course for Earth.

Chapter 127: Bjorn Muller Reacts to the News of Markus Bauer's Rescue.

Bjorn Muller was lying in bed, sipping space Cognac in his private quarters of The Terran Council's army base, on the tiny Martian Phobos Moon. Next to him were two beautiful female twins, named Greta and Magda, who had always been Bjorn's favourite prostitutes. When the conception and birth of Greta and Magda were approved, they had had their genetics DNA modified to suit the taste of Bjorn and other important House Muller members. As such, they were designed to have the perfect DNA for beautiful North European female appearance while also having an elevated sex drive to ensure that they enjoyed their field of work. People on Earth were not slaves and were free to choose whatever job they wanted. However, their preselected genetic abilities and the threat of deportation to Mars made most people accept the path assigned to them by the ruling class.

Bjorn had always enjoyed Greta and Magda's company in the past, but that had changed when he came across the beautiful and mesmerising Keila, four years earlier.

Something about Keila had changed him. His desire to dominate and own her, combined with her seductive rebellious nature, had led to him taking her as a hostage, repeatedly raping her while denying his own immorality. His false sense of righteousness combined with a fake pretence and a high ego had resulted in catastrophic events that followed.

Since Keila assassinated Bjorn's grandfather, Hans Muller a few weeks after her escape from Bjorn, he had never dared to speak to anyone about his disturbing emotions for her. Seeing Keila's corpse had not helped these feelings, and he had constant nightmares of Keila coming after him from the afterlife.

Bjorn sent the sweet and obliging but boring twins, Greta, and Magda back to Earth. He had lost interest in them, and he had consumed large amounts of sexual enhancement drugs, to copulate with them in the past few days. Having sex with them was significant as it would be rude to his father not to accept his birthday gift. More importantly, Bjorn needed to prove to his other relatives that he was still virile.

Bjorn asked his father to send a few concubines from House Rashid territory to replace Greta and Magda. House Rashid's women had Mediterranean/Middle Eastern looks, and this would remind him more of Keila and could satisfy his desire to dominate.

Bjorn realised that his father would not be happy about the request, but he would grant it. While sex between the different races on Earth was not encouraged within House Muller, it was not taboo like it was to have sex with Martians or other extra-terrestrials.

When Bjorn opened his computer, he was met with an email from his superior in the Terran Council Armed Forces, Admiral Max Wellington:

"Good News Bjorn. As it turns out, the chief scientist on your vessel Markus Bauer, was not killed when the science bay dislodged after the explosion. Instead, he survived and was taken hostage by pirates. He has been freed from the pirates and is en route to our Phobos base to debrief after the incident. Best Regards. Admiral Max Wellington"

Reading this Bjorn felt an uncontrollable bout of anger and smashed the monitor with so hard, so he started bleeding. Bjorn bandaged his wounds, and then lined some drugs and headed to the shooting range to blow of some steam.

Chapter 128: Keila Searches for Zetan technology

Keila was getting restless and unsure on how to start her rebellion against the Terran Council. She had a few thousand followers comprising of the population of Eden, but they were mostly illiterate, and living in the past. Furthermore, they had no reason to fight the Terran Council and they seemed happier to live the way they were. Although Keila had started to modernise Edenite culture, they were short of, literally every resource needed to create a modern society with modern armed forces.

The problem for Keila was that Eden could house and equip over 100,000 individuals from Mars with modern advanced farming and technologies, but she could not entice these people to move to Eden and join her cause without getting the attention from the Terran Council. The last thing that she wanted was their attention.

To defeat her enemy, she needed to create an underground movement, and sabotage Earth's economy. Furthermore, she needed to get the Terran factions to start fighting each other. Keila knew that there was a lot of mistrust and scepticism between the great Houses of Earth and that they always fought each other through proxies. So how would she turn them against each other?

Keila realised that the answer might lie in the vast Zetan archives. The Zetans had ruled the galaxy for over 100 millennia, so they would have had superior technology.

After searching for many days, Keila found what she was looking for. She summoned Metatron to join her and to understand the spectacular Zetan technologies that she had discovered. Metatron joined her, and they studied blueprint schematics of the Zetan technologies that could help them win the war against the Terran Council.

The most prominent Zetan technologies were:

The Zetan Spherical Communication Blocker: This technology created a 20,000 cubic kilometre large sphere that blocked all incoming and outgoing communications. This would help them to surprise-attack the Terran Council, dominate their fuel-mining colonies and obliterate their military outposts undetected.

The Zetan Advanced Cloaking Device: A highly advanced electromagnetic cloaking device that blocked out 99 % of all the reflected light of a spaceship as well as 95 % of the heat signature, making it almost invisible to the interplanetary military surveillance. While it was not failsafe if someone were looking for them, it would be than enough to approach the Terran Council's military outposts and mining stations undetected.

The Zetan Ballistic Energy Absorber: This device was powered by a high-powered battery that could repel any form of kinetic energy from incoming projectiles. It protected in the form of a 1-metre sphere, and it made all bullets, shrapnel, metal pieces and other projectiles drop to the ground. The battery was the limiting factor, as the design would use up all the battery quickly when the wearer stood out in the open receiving heavy fire.

The Zetan Non-Encrypted Bionic Chip Disruptor: A device that emitted a signal that disrupted the function of all non-encrypted bionic microchips within its range. As the Terran Council forces were reliant on bionic microchips and implants, their soldiers would be useless when their microchips were disrupted by the chip disruptor.

The Zetan External DNA Modifier: The technology the Zetan had used when they came to Earth posing as human gods. The outer layer DNA modifier was an advanced Zetan serum that changed the superficial outer layer of a person to that of another person of choice. This way, a person would look like and smell like the person of choice, but the brain would remain the same as before. This would be very useful for infiltration purposes.

With all these fantastic alien technologies at her disposal, Keila felt a glimmer of hope of challenging and taking on the Terran Council. However, she would still need to rely on espionage and subterfuge for the time being as the difference in numbers was too great to take on the Terran Council at this stage.

Keila realised that she needed to reverse engineer and create these extra-terrestrial devices on a large scale. While she could create all the prototypes with the particle replicator, a future technology equivalent of a 3-D printer, this was a slow process and expensive way to produce equipment on a large scale. Keila needed was to turn Eden into a production plant for these extra-terrestrial technologies. But to achieve that she needed technological know-how as well as obtaining rare compound elements. Keila was low on both. Keila sighed and sat down. She would have to sit back for a while and wait for another sign. The visions would tell her what to do, and it would be silly to risk this excellent opportunity by rushing it.

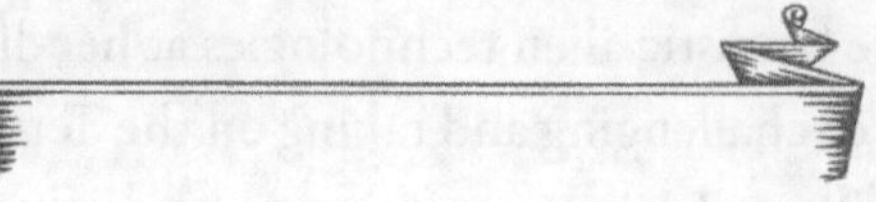

Chapter 129: Admiral Max Wellington Confronts Bjorn Muller.

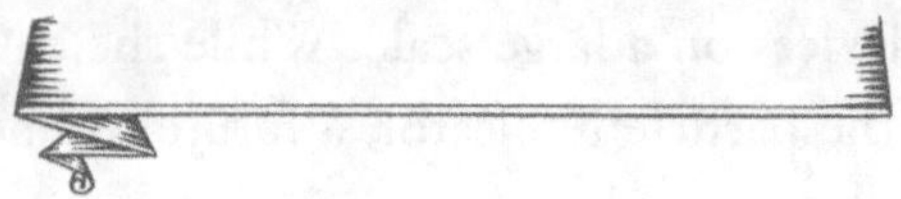

Admiral Max Wellington was sitting in his office at the Terran Council base on the Phobos Moon. He had met with Markus Bauer who had returned from the dead to file damning accusations against Bjorn Muller. According to Markus, the corpse of the criminal insurgent Keila Eisenstein was a decoy in the form of a non-functional clone that she had created to fake her own death. Furthermore, Markus claimed that Bjorn had been aware that the body was a decoy and the explosion in the science bay was Bjorn trying to silence Markus and get rid of the evidence at the same time. This was damning accusations, especially since Bjorn's father was the chairman of the Terran Council.

Admiral Max Wellington sighed. He would have preferred to stay uninvolved in this matter as it was a bomb that could blow up in his face. If he accused the son of the Terran Council leader of treason he would be executed if he was proven to be wrong. If he chose to not act on his suspicions it could also lead to his demise. Hence no matter what he did, his life was in danger.

Max evaluated Markus' claims. They seemed far-fetched and unlikely. According to Markus, he had survived for over a day in an airtight capsule with only an oxygen tank and no protective gear. He had passed out, and when he woke up, he had been a captive of the space pirate Morgan Henry. Eventually, Tzi Chen Cheng from the Science Commission, had paid ransom for him, and he was free to go.

This story made little sense to Max. It was unlikely that Markus had survived all this time in space on his own. It was more likely that his corpse was picked up by a House Cheng spaceship, they had revived him, and then told him to make false claims against Bjorn Muller. After being dead for an extended period, Markus would have been a complete mess when he woke up, and thus he was easy to manipulate.

On the other hand, while Markus' claims against Bjorn could be fabrications, Max wasn't ready to write them off. Max saw Bjorn as a spoiled, incompetent brat that had his high position in the Terran Council Interplanetary Forces solely due to his wealth and his family ties. While Admiral Max Wellington came from a poor family and had worked himself up, Bjorn Muller had shown up one day and was appointed as Rear Admiral, without proving himself.

Bjorn had never led soldiers in frontline battle, Bjorn was very distant from the daily lives of the soldiers that he commanded, and he showed very little interest in what was and what wasn't achievable in actual combat and battle missions. When missions didn't go according to plan, Bjorn always passed the blame on someone else, and he got away with it due to his family ties.

Admiral Max Wellington knew that the Terran Council was aware of Bjorn's incompetence. Otherwise, they wouldn't have ordered him to stay in command of their Phobos base. While Max was in command, he could not give orders to his subordinates without Bjorn's approval or get Bjorn to do anything as there was no way to reprimand the rich spoilt bastard. This led to a very dysfunctional command management structure on the military base. Max invited Bjorn Muller to his office, and eventually, Bjorn showed up, lazy and drunk.

Bjorn:

- Hi Max.

- We should really have these meetings in my office instead. It's a bigger room, packed with a nicer couch and a better alcoholic beverage selection.

Max bit his lip in bitterness. He feels a surge of jealousy and rage. Despite being the commander on the base, his office and private quarters were smaller and standard-looking, and it annoyed him every time Bjorn brought it up.

Max:

- As I understand it, your office has a better selection of prostitutes as well. I had to approve your latest requests this morning...

Max showed Bjorn a bunch of brochures and photos with different prostitutes, all posing in their spacesuit bikinis.

Bjorn:

- How delightful. I have been looking forward to these fresh-looking ones.

Max:

- Shut up, Bjorn.
- There are some grave accusations against you.

Bjorn:

- Then, let's be serious.
- What were the accusations?

Max Wellington:

- I met with Markus Bauer the other day, and he claimed several things about you.

Bjorn Muller:

- Wasn't Markus killed during the explosion at the science bay a couple of months ago?

Max Wellington:

- Well, apparently not!

- Markus claimed that the explosion in the science bay was an attempt made by you to silence him and get rid of the corpse of Keila Eisenstein, which he said was a decoy.

Bjorn felt crippling fear, and he had to force himself not to crack under pressure. He took a deep breath, calmed his mind, and nonchalantly answered:

- So, a man of no importance is coming back from the dead to accuse me of treason. How absurd! Does he have any proof of his claims?

Max:

- Yes, it does sound absurd, and there is no proof.
- The question remains: Is he telling the truth?

Bjorn:

- Of course not! The explosion in the Science Bay was an accident. I have several witnesses who saw the body of Miss Eisenstein.

- Tell me, how does Markus claim he survived the explosion?

Max:

- He claims he was taken hostage by the space pirate Morgan Henry, and then freed by a Tzi Chen from House Cheng who paid his ransom.

Bjorn Muller:

- Ahh, I see. This is a political play from House of Cheng.

- As a son of the Terran Council chairman, I command you to stay out of it!

Max:

- Okay, Bjorn. I'm only doing this because of your family ties.

Bjorn:

- Thank you for being sensible, Max.
- Where is Markus Bauer now? I would like to speak to him.

Max:

- I transferred him to another placement.

- As a non-aligned Admiral, I'll keep his location classified, to avoid confrontation between the two of you. He is a worthy scientist of the Terran Council.

Bjorn:

- That's ridiculous! I can call my father, Joachim Muller, and ask for the location.

Max:

- Yes, but then you'll have to tell your father about why you are looking for Markus.

Bjorn stormed out towards the door in anger, and he kicked the door before he left the room. Max interrupted him:

- Rear Admiral, I'm sorry but one more thing...

Bjorn turned around and looked at Max:
Max:

- How come your latest selection of prostitutes are all the spitting images of Miss Keila Eisenstein?

Bjorn lost his temper and yelled back at his superior:

- That's because I like to fantasise about fucking and dominating my enemies, unlike you, you old eunuch!

Having shouted this, Bjorn slammed the door and left Max's office.

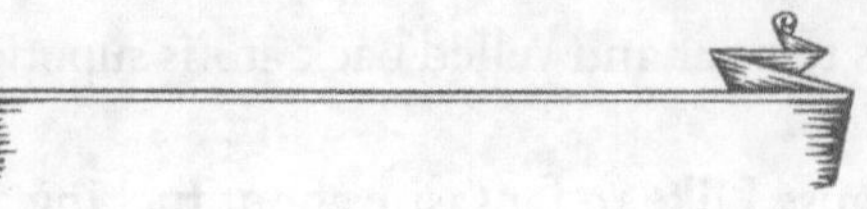

Chapter 130: Bjorn Muller Finds Markus Bauer's Location.

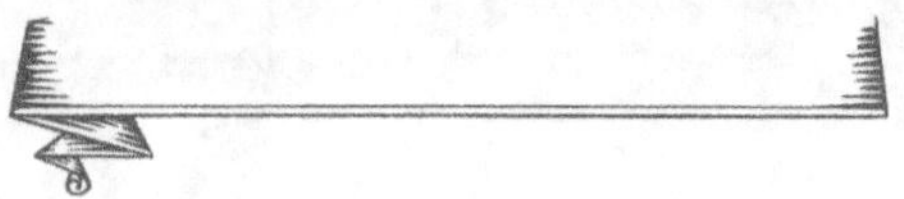

Bjorn was seething with anger when he came back to his office after meeting with Max Wellington. How dared that pathetic man reprimand him for his behaviour and refuse to give him the location of Markus Bauer?

Bjorn was fuming, but he realised that he was better off directing his focus towards finding Markus Bauer than he was plotting revenge against Max Wellington. Finding Markus wouldn't be easy, as his location was classified, but Bjorn could find him, using a more laborious way.

As a Rear Admiral, Bjorn had access to all the security cameras from the Terran Council installations throughout the Solar System. There were several thousand of them, and Bjorn would have preferred to just let the computer do the auto-search, but Markus Bauer's location was classified, and Bjorn didn't want to explain to his father why he needed to find Markus' location. Sifting through all the security camera recordings would take months, but if he narrowed the search to only look through the cameras in the science bays of the stations, he was likely to find Markus Bauer's location in a day or two. To Bjorn's relief he had helpers for this task:

Intisar and Kinnette were the latest female assistants that were sent to take care of Bjorn's needs. His father had complained about the expense to hire these exotic-looking women and over their racial genetic makeup. Bjorn had answered that no man could be expected to eat the same meal every day and his father had let go of the topic. The two escorts were surprised when he tasked them with finding Markus Bauer, but they seemed happy to comply.

Bjorn studied Intisar and Kinnette from his fancy expensive armchair, made from the leather of rare animals that only existed in the Alpha Centauri star system. As they were looking for Markus Bauer, Bjorn checked them out from head to toe. Studying them made him aroused. They were the spitting images of Keila. He imagined playing out his fantasies on them. This time without ending up in excruciating pain from the encounter.

Bjorn spent the next few hours drinking expensive Scotch and snorting the synthetic drug Amorphia, which speeded up his thought patterns and made him highly aroused. His sexual satisfaction peaked 5 hours later, when Intisar let him know that she had found Markus Bauer. Bjorn looked on the screen and confirmed that the man was Markus Bauer. Pleased with Intisar's effort, he kissed her cheek and transferred 20,000 Terran Credits to her "diamond bank", a microchip inserted into the user's neck that was the 29th century equivalent of cash as the transaction was untraceable, and discreet.

Having found Markus Bauer's location, Bjorn Muller engaged in a marathon sex session with Intisar and Kinnette before letting them retreat to a sleeping capsule, recovering for their next sexual interaction. After this Bjorn fell asleep drained but fulfilled.

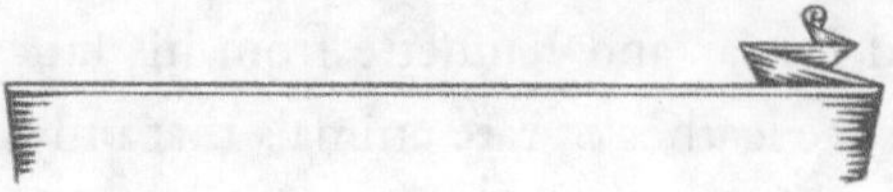

Chapter 131: Markus Bauer Smells a Rat.

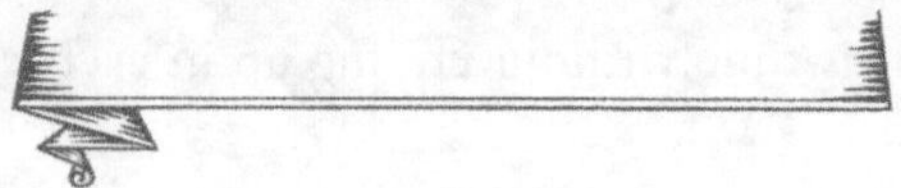

A few days later, at the Proxima Thule research and mining station, Markus Bauer was getting paranoid and restless. When he spoke to Admiral Max Wellington about what had happened, the Admiral had seemed sympathetic and had promised him a secret location where he would not be harmed while investigations of the claims occurred. While he trusted the Admiral, Markus was sure that something was amiss.

Since Markus had arrived at Proxima Thule, it seemed like most of the employees on the space station had been granted leave at the same time. It did not make any sense. Proxima Thule required a certain amount of personnel to conduct research, but with everyone on vacation and just a minimal crew left to support the operations, the research had come to a standstill.

Markus worried that he was a sitting duck on Proxima Thule. If someone wanted to hurt him, there was no way to get out of there.

Where would Markus go anyway? If Bjorn Muller wanted him dead, going back to Earth would be suicide. Seeking refuge at Mars was an awful idea, as he was more likely getting robbed and killed by the barbaric Martians than he was securing meaningful employment. But what about joining up with Keila and seeking refuge on Eden? If the body of Keila was a decoy, that meant that the rulers of Eden were collaborating with Keila to rebel against the Terran Council.

Markus felt ashamed. Although his life was at risk, he did not want to betray his brethren on Earth. Although the Terran Council was a brutal plutocratic dictatorship, it brought peace to Earth and stability to the Solar System. The end justified the means and besides it wouldn't make sense to rebel against the organisation he had worked for during the last 20 years.

Markus logged in on a computer to check his work schedule. What he saw overwhelmed him with a wave of paranoia. He was meant to perform maintenance on a set of gravitation turbines on his own at the fringe of the space station. This task was risky and always performed in groups. The only reason someone would have him do it by himself, was that there must be a "planned accident" waiting for him down there.

Seeing this, Markus Bauer changed his mind and he contacted the rebels on Eden. He contacted Metatron via an encrypted message on Spacenet, hoping to obtain some help.

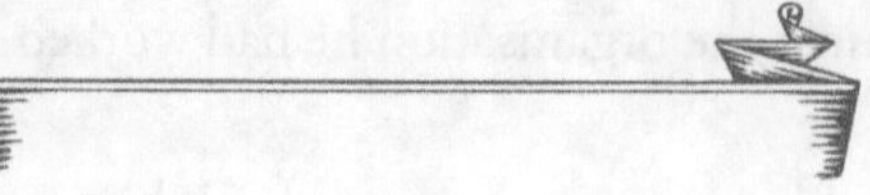

Chapter 132: Keila Receives a Suspicious Signal.

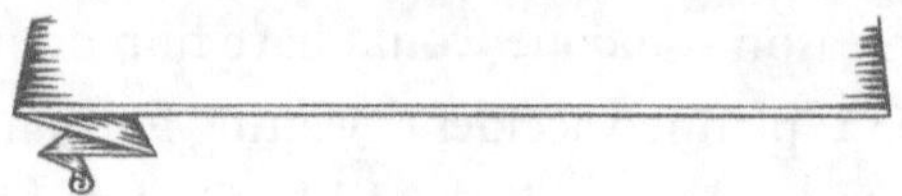

Keila was sitting on the throne in the temple of an Edenite village receiving offerings from the villagers. She was accompanied by several Angels that acted as her bodyguards as a precaution.

Keila deemed it necessary to come down and take part in the daily lives of her Edenite followers. She wanted to utilise a different leadership style than Abraham's, so instead of using commands and threats from afar, she aimed to be a good role model that the people could look up to.

Keila was used to be a role model during her years with the Martin Humanist Alliance, but she wasn't used to being worshipped like a god. She had mixed feelings about her "divinity". While, Keila had pointed out that she was not a divine being, it felt good being revered, loved, and spoiled. In the last few months, Keila had eaten so much tasty food that her previously rock-hard solid body had loosened up and started to get round, something she would have to address.

Despite having a comfortable time as the "goddess" of Eden, Keila got increasingly impatient. The modernisation of Eden was moving at a glacial pace, as she lacked both the personnel and the resources required to make Eden a powerful base of operations in the resistance against the Terran Council.

The city of Pamshal on Mars was one of the Terran Councils recent targets. As Keila grew up there, the entire city was considered hostile, and the military had tested a new dangerous weaponised virus on the Martian settlement. The virus was a synthetic and airborne genetically modified virus, making it the ultimate weapon for chemical warfare. Being synthetic, it would not spread between organisms, so it was easy to contain the target to a specific area. The victims would have Ebola-like symptoms and die a slow and painful death, with blisters and boils appearing from their eyes and bodies. Watching the footage of Pamshal through her holographic television in Eden, Keila recognised several former friends dying slow and painful deaths. The worst part for Keila was that Pamshal was not the collateral damage of war, but an indiscriminate mass murder conducted by an arrogant, and tyrannical government.

Feeling shocked and helpless, Keila lost focus on the Edenite offerings, and she smashed a pot of olive oil in an instance of rage. The crowd turned silent and looked at her in fright. Keila apologised, but did not know how to handle the situation, so she rushed off into the wilderness with the bewildered Edenites staring at her.

Eventually, Keila got out of sight from the crowd, and she calmed down. She sat on a rock near a small pond and stared out at the deep blue sky. Metatron contacted her.

Keila:

- Hi Metatron. I know what you are going to say; I am sorry about smashing the pot. I zoned out and had a rush of anger.

Metatron:

- Don't worry about it, Keila.

- When Abraham lost his temper, he used to have people stoned or set aflame. I am sure that they don't mind a broken pot.

- I'll let them know that you forgive them.

Keila:

- That I forgive them?
- I was the one who broke their olive oil pot for no reason.

Metatron:

- Abraham never apologised for anything. Apologising would only confuse your people. Let's change things for the better but not too quickly.

Keila:

- Okay, fair call.

Metatron:

- Yes. The reason I called you is something far more critical.

- We received an encrypted message from someone called Markus Bauer. He knows that you are alive, and he wants to join our faction. He is on the Terran Council research station Proxima Thule, only a few days travel away. According to Markus, the station is inadequately defended and full of valuable resources and research data.

Keila:

- That sounds like an obvious trap!

Metatron:

- Yes.
- Shall I ignore the transmission?

Keila sat down to think. She didn't trust Markus Bauer, as he was a prominent Terran Council scientist. But if the Terran Council knew that she had faked her own death, they would come with a large fleet to apprehend her on Eden. So why hadn't they? Eden had strong defences, but not strong enough to deter the army from attacking. The resources, equipment, and scientists on Proxima Thule could prove crucial to speed up her efforts to make Eden a base of operations for the resistance. It could be a trap, but it could also be what she needed.

Keila:

- No. Tell him we are coming within a week.

Metatron:

- Is that wise, considering the likelihood for it being a trap?

Keila:

- Yes. My instincts tell me that the Terran Council is not be-hind this. If they knew about our deception, they would de-stroy Eden from afar with no regards to collateral damage. They wouldn't send a scientist to plead for our partnership.

- I will take a ship equipped with Zetan technology and sur-prise him. You stay here and look after Eden.

Metatron:

- But I want to go with you, to keep you safe.

Keila:

- I would feel safer with you by my side, but we must think about the people. If we both die, there is no-one to support Eden. Eventually the civilisation will break, and they will all die. We cannot leave Eden until it's a self-sustaining colony,

Metatron:

- You are right, my love.
- May the light guide you and the True Maker keep you safe!

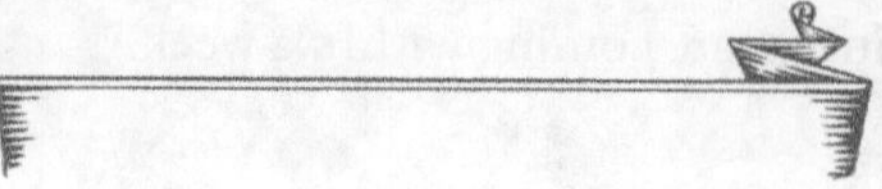

Chapter 133: The Attack on Proxima Thule.

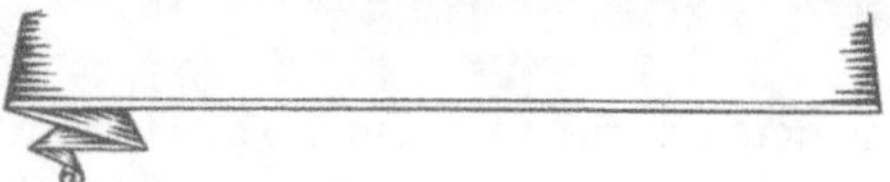

The officer in charge of Proxima Thule, Captain Berndt Messer-schmitt was looking at a screen. He felt that the research station he oversaw was threatened. For some reason, the spoilt, arrogant brat Bjorn Muller had authorised everyone to leave the station. This left the Proxima Thule station with only 10 per cent staffing. This amounted to only a dozen security officers and around 50 scientists and engineers.

Considering the amount of valuable resources and technology on the station, Berndt worried that the station would get attacked and loot-ed. Bjorn had dismissed the concerns and said that they had enough au-tomated defences to deal with any enemy before they entered the station.

A display started beeping saying that a ship had docked with the sta-tion. Berndt looked out and to his shock, he saw that an old House Gold-stein transport vessel had docked with the station.

House Goldstein! They were no longer part of the Terran Council, and had no business being there. How had the ship snuck up on him un-noticed? Berndt activated the emergency beacon, and he tried to contact other stations close by for backup. But the communications were down, all that he heard was eerie static.

Berndt grabbed his gun and ordered the other security officers come with him to the docks. What he saw. At the docks was the infamous terrorist Keila Eisenstein flanked by a group of soldiers with wings-like space suits. As he approached her, she called out:

"Captain, I require that you surrender this station to me. Do this and you'll live. Do not, and you will die"

Berndt noticed that Keila and her soldiers were standing out in the open, with no defensive armour. It didn't make sense, but they were easy targets and killing her would bring him a promotion. *"Fire at will!"* he commanded his men, and they all started shooting at Keila's group.

To Berndt's shock and awe, the bullets stopped mid-air and they fell to the ground as the bullets came close to Keila and her troops. Keila ran up to Berndt and shot all the other soldiers in their heads with her pistol. Keila said, *"You should have surrendered Captain"*. It was the last thing Berndt heard before everything turned black.

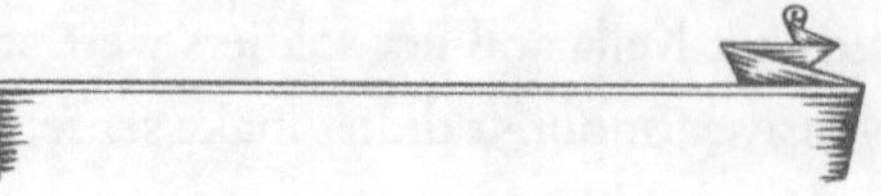

Chapter 134: The Looting of Proxima Thule

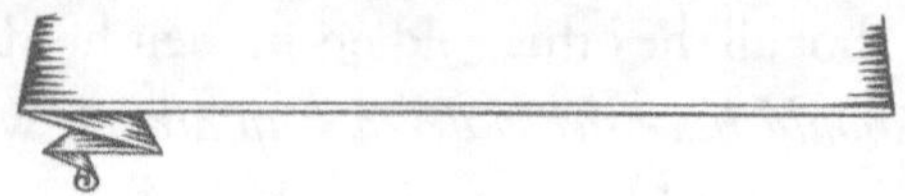

Keila looked at the battery indicator on her Zetan Ballistic Energy Absorber, which strapped nicely on her arm. It was down to 1 %. A few more bullets and she would have been dead, if her battery had run out and her Zetan technology no longer stopping the bullets. She had been careless, but lucky, and she reminded herself that she needed to be more careful in the future.

She needed to act quickly. The Zetan Spherical Communication Blocker would stop anyone from communicating with the outside, but the complete absence of communications would arouse suspicions. The Terran Council would send people to investigate what had happened.

Keila gathered the scientists and engineers in one room and sprayed in sleep-inducing gas to put them all to sleep. After that, she and her group removed any bionic microchip that could give away a person's location from the sleeping scientists. After that, they inserted Divine Technology "Human" chips into the scientists' brains so she could force their loyalty once they woke up.

After placing the unconscious scientists aboard their vessel, they looted all the rare elements and equipment that they could find, and they also downloaded all the data available unto memory units. Finally, they blew up a small EMP grenade inside the mainframe of Proxima Thule. This would delete all the security footage of the attack and turn off the station's air supply, suffocating any survivor that might be in hiding.

After doing all of this, they returned to their transport ship, activated their cloaking device, and travelled back to Eden.

Chapter 135: Reconnaissance Report to the Terran Council

Wednesday 17th October 2872:

We arrived at Proxima Thule, three days after communications with the space station ended. What we found indicates an organised attack by an unknown assailant. We found all the members of the station's security team shot in the heads with a pistol from a close distance. Initial findings indicate that they are all permanently dead, but we will freeze their bodies and bring them back to Earth for a thorough examination. The attack must have come as a surprise for the security team as they were all just wearing standard-issue jumpsuits and not combat armour.

Despite the security team being shot point-blank execution-style, there are still indications of them firing their weapons at the assailants. The corridor is littered with empty shells next to their bodies and their hands are filled with traces of gunpowder. Strangely, we found a lot of undamaged bullets lying around between the corridor and the docks of the station. We do not know how these bullets ended up there with undamaged tips, as it defies the laws of physics. We have attached pictures of the scene.

As for the scientists and engineers on the vessel, we have not found any trace of them and we must assume that they were taken as hostages by the assailants.

I recommend that you send a specialist forensic team to investigate the occurrence. We will set up a perimeter and secure the area for further investigations.

Captain Michael Meyer

5th reconnaissance squadron

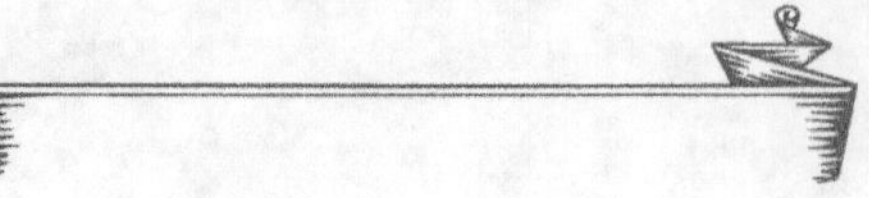

Chapter 136: Markus Bauer Meets Keila.

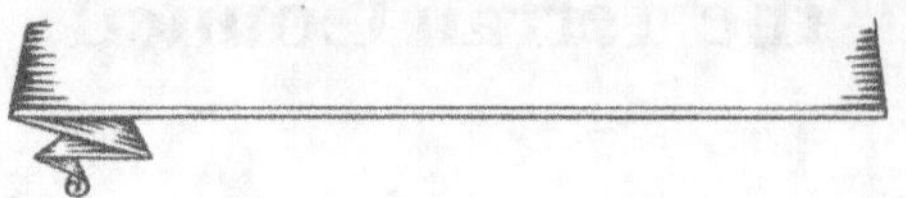

Markus Bauer was in a holding facility on the dark side of Eden with his fellow scientist abductees from Proxima Thule. He was regretted what he had done and felt a deep shame for causing the death of the security staff due to Keila Eisenstein's violent raid.

What was he thinking? Alerting the enemy about a weakly-defended research base could only lead bloodshed. While the loss of life was regrettable, Markus Bauer's biggest concern was his own wellbeing and he worried about it. He had hoped to be introduced to Keila in high regard when they attacked Proxima Thule. Instead, she and her cronies had grouped him together with the rest of the science staff and put him to sleep with gas. He had woken up in this holding facility with no idea where he was or what day it was.

Markus felt someone's presence, and Keila appeared out of nowhere in the centre of the room. Was he losing his mind? Markus concluded that he wasn't, as the rest of the room also stared at the woman in the middle of the room.

Keila:

- Greetings, Scientists from Proxima Thule. You are my prisoners of war and will be treated as such. While you were asleep, you were implanted with Divine Technology human chips, an experimental technology that allows me to see your every thought as well as communicating to you.

- I am going to give you a choice. Either you can defect, join my faction, and thus eventually win your freedom. Or you can stay loyal to the Terran Council and remain here as prisoners.

Choose carefully, because if you join me and betray me, I will know about it and you'll die a terrible death.

Markus answered Keila's message. Not knowing how the implanted chip worked, he opted to scream out his words instead of just relaying it telepathically.
Markus:

- I am Markus Bauer, and I am the one who informed you about the weak defences on Proxima Thule. I pledge myself to your cause, and I require that you treat the captured scientists well.

Hearing about Markus Bauer's betrayal, and it prompted some of the other prisoners to attack him. Keila intervened and sent psionic blasts against some of the attackers to keep Markus safe.
Keila:

- Prisoners! I wish to speak to this prisoner in private. Do not harm him or you'll pay the ultimate price. Markus, go through that the door I just opened, the rest of you stay where you are.

Markus walked through the blast door and entered a waiting area. As he came in the door closed behind him. He was waiting there for a long time, until one of the Angels escorted him to a shuttle. The shuttle flew to the Divine Control Centre. The Angel escorted him to the meeting room where Keila was sitting in an armchair overlooking Eden through a large panorama window. The Angel left, and Markus was left alone with Keila in the room. She turned the chair around and looked at him.
Keila:

- So, Markus. Why are you here?

Markus:

- Because I am your prisoner and you summoned me.

Keila:

- While technically correct, that doesn't answer my real question. How did you know I was alive and why do you want to join me?

Markus:

- I knew you were alive, because I was the one who carried out your autopsy. I want to join you because Bjorn tried to kill me to cover up that you are not dead.

Keila:

- Fair enough. Did you ever wonder why Bjorn Muller was so afraid of the truth coming out?

Markus:

- I suppose it would be embarrassing to admit that you are alive after announcing your death.

Keila:

- No. That's not it. I will tell you the truth.

- When I was 18 years old, Bjorn took me as a prisoner. He never took down my details as he wanted me as his unregistered sex slave. I escaped and mutilated him in the process.

- After that I infiltrated the Terran Council Martian Headquarters, and I assassinated Hans Muller, who was the chairman of the Terran Council at the time. That's how the latest rebellion started.

- Because of Bjorn's sexual depravity, Hans died, and House Muller got weaker.

- Bjorn is terrified that my corpse would reach the Terran Council. If they found a way to revive me, the world would know about his failure.

- That's why he never questioned why my men delivered him a non-functional clone. Because Bjorn never intended for me to be revived and interrogated.

Markus:

- So, all of this is because Bjorn raped you?

Keila:

- No. All of this is because I want justice and freedom for my fellow Martians. If my only goal were to kill Bjorn, I would have blown up his ship with Eden's weapon systems when I had the chance. That would have exposed me and destroyed my opportunity to reignite the insurrection against the Terran Council.

Markus:

- Reignite the Rebellion? Are you kidding me? We wiped out your entire leadership, and we killed tens of thousands when we destroyed your rebel base on the asteroid Sylvia. Eden is nothing compared to what you had on asteroid Sylvia. You were no match back then, so what's different this time?

Keila:

- I have something that you lack: faith.

- And do not refer to the Terran Council as "we". You are working for us now.

Markus:

- Understood. What do you want me to do?

Keila:

- I have acquired advanced alien technology. I need you to assemble a group of scientists, and reverse engineer this technology so we can mass-produce it here on Eden.

Markus:

- Interesting. I will get on it at once.

Keila:

- Good. Build a good team, Metatron will show you to your site on Eden.
- Dismissed.

As Markus left the meeting room, he was filled with disbelief. What on Earth had he got himself into? For over 800 years of space, exploration humanity had never come across any advanced alien civilisations. The probability that Keila accessed technology that the rest of mankind hadn't was minuscule. Then again, she seemed very sure of herself, and the mind control probe she had inserted into his, and the other scientist's brains were new technology. Markus decided to keep an open mind as he set up a list of scientists who were likely to be willing to become Keila's followers.

Chapter 137: Joachim Muller Summons Bjorn Muller to Earth.

Bjorn Muller exited his shuttle at the landing site in Hansstadt in the European Alps. Hansstadt was the location for the House Muller headquarters, Europeum Tower, which was the tallest building in the world. Although the tower was not as magnificent as when it was constructed a century prior, it was still a marvel of technology displaying the wealth and power of House Muller.

Bjorn Muller was happy to be home and able to live a life of comfort and luxury. It had been over a year since his last visit to his home city, and although his position in the space force comfortable, there was only so much one could do to make a military ship comfortable. Although he was offered a ride from the landing site to Europeum Tower, Bjorn Muller opted to walk. He wanted to inhale the fresh air and experience all the smells he could not experience in space.

Although Bjorn's head was energised, his body was not. Even though both his command ship ISS Supreme Earth and the Terran Council military headquarters on Phobos had artificial gravity, this gravity was not enough to simulate the gravity on Earth and as such Bjorn felt very weak and unfit once he had to move on Earth with full gravity.

After walking for two hours, Bjorn reached Europeum towers and entered the lift to his father's penthouse level. The elevator scanned his DNA and gave him access to his father's penthouse. As it was 3000 meters up, he would spend a couple of minutes in the elevator, so he had a rest on the bench inside the lift.

He looked at himself in the mirror, and much to his dismay his Rear Admiral uniform was drenched in sweat from the exerting walk from the space port. As Bjorn was used to working in conditions with 20 % gravity, the 100 % gravity on Earth felt very heavy for him.

Bjorn wondered why his father had summoned him and he concluded that his father had summoned him to Earth to be closer to him. Had his father organised a suitable bride for him? Bjorn would agree to any bride. He was sick of space and if he had to spend his days with some stupid swamp monkey to please his father, so be it; he could always have fun on the side.

The lift reached its destination. Bjorn exited the elevator and walked to his father's dining room. Much too Bjorn's dismay, his father was the only one at the dinner table, which was set for three persons. Apparently, his father had not organised a welcome party. Joachim Muller gave Bjorn a sour look.

Joachim Muller:

   - I haven't seen you in over a year, and here you are, a slob
   bringing disgrace to your uniform!

Bjorn:

   - Nice to see you too, dad...

Joachim:

   - The pleasure is all yours...

Bjorn lost his patience. His relationship with his father had been strained for many years, but he could not accept being treated like dirt after travelling this far.

Bjorn:

   - Fucking hell, dad. I came all the way from Phobos, and you
   treat me like this.

   - Why did you summon me?

Joachim:

- Sit down!!

Bjorn Muller sat down, and Joachim continued speaking:

- Our medical team managed to temporarily revive Captain Berndt Messerschmitt before he succumbed to his injuries...

Bjorn Muller:

- Who is that?

Joachim Muller got up, slapped his son, and got seated again. Joachim:

- You fucking degenerate. Stop obsessing with your hookers. You should know.

- Captain Berndt Messerschmitt oversaw Proxima Thule, our science and mining station that was hit by unknown assailants, a month ago.

Bjorn bit his lip and said nothing. He was angry at his dad for slapping him, but even more irritated at himself for his embarrassing mistake. Bjorn had plenty of implants to help his memory and reasoning skills, yet too often his stupidity took over.
Bjorn:

- Okay.
- Did he say anything worthwhile during his short return to life?

Joachim:

- He claimed that Keila Eisenstein and a group of men with peculiar armour arrived out of nowhere. Apparently Keila had mind-blowing technology that stopped bullets mid-air. She killed him and the other defenders.

Bjorn:

- That's absurd. His brain must have been beyond repair. That's why he died shortly after.

Joachim:

- Yes. But the days before the attack, you sent 90 % of the staff on leave.

Bjorn:

- That's coincidental. The rebellion forced me to keep bases fully staffed for years on end. I just saw the opportunity to sort out all the leaves at once, especially since no vital research takes place there.

- Besides Captain Messerschmitt should have done his job instead of being taken by surprise. How easy is it to sneak into an asteroid base undetected? It is unheard of!

Joachim:

- Blaming the dead won't teach us anything worthwhile.

- I don't like your connection with this Keila woman. I don't like it one bit!

Bjorn Muller:

- Connection?

- You mean risking my life chasing her down, while you sit in your cushy boardroom? You're welcome!

Joachim thought of hitting Bjorn again, but he controlled himself. Instead, he spoke in a cold and distant voice barely hiding his contempt.
Joachim:

- No. I am talking about the fact that you asked me to send you whores looking like her at a great expense.

- I am talking about the fact that you lost her corpse in space and instead of retrieving it, ran back to Phobos with your tail behind the back.

- I am talking about the rumours that you were seen with her on ISS Supreme Earth, just weeks before she accessed to our Martian headquarters and killed your grandfather Hans Muller.

Bjorn sat silent. He didn't know how to defend himself, and his father's fierce attack made him feel both heartbroken and afraid. Bjorn felt deep shame and sense of guilt, for indirectly causing the death of his grandfather. Joachim continued his tirade.

- If you weren't my son, I would have you assassinated by now. Unfortunately, you are my son, so I can't use those options. This leaves me with a third option.

- As Admiral Max Wellington cannot keep you in line, I am putting you under the command of Alicia White.

Bjorn was flabbergasted and couldn't believe what he was hearing. Working under the freak Alicia White?! His father was surely joking about this.

Bjorn:

- I hope you are joking.

Joachim:

- I certainly am not.

Bjorn:

- But she is a freak?! She is a failed genetic mutation experiment, a by-product of DNA modification error?!

Joachim:

- I suggest that you share your emotions with her. She is joining us for dinner.

Alicia White was the daughter of House White CEO's John White. She was his favourite child, but to everyone else, she was a freak; a fearsome reminder of the dangers of excessive genetic modification of embryos.

John White had always wanted a warrior-princess type of human as his successor, and when the genetic modification of Alicia's embryo took place, he took it too far outside of the box.

By mixing in the human embryo with DNA from other predator species, Alicia was born fearless and dangerous, with predatory super senses, but lacking human empathy and any regard for social standards. She had the sense of smell of a wolf, the night vision and sharp retractable claws of a tiger, the courage and temper of a bull and the explosiveness of an ambushing crocodile. Unfortunately, her explosive feats came with a drawback, as she was deformed with fangs hanging outside of her lips, the tongue of a serpent, glowing yellow eyes, and a tiny tail that formed a round lump at the end of her back. She also had the unfortunate tendency to scratch people with her claws and lick them in the face.

As Alicia could not be seen on the board of House White, her father had to hide her away in the Black Operations department of House White. Alicia was happy to work there as it provided her with the opportunity to take part in her favourite activities: torturing and killing other humans in the most brutal sadistic way possible.

When Joachim complained to John about his problems with putting Bjorn in place, John had suggested that Bjorn was assigned to serve under Alicia, as her fearsomeness had put others in place throughout the years. Together they had tasked Alicia's group to find with the people that attacked Proxima Thule the prior month.

Alicia entered the dining room. Bjorn and Hans stood up to greet her. Without a word, she walked up to Bjorn, grabbed him by the balls and licked him in the face. *"Bjorn Muller: we meet again",* she hissed. Bjorn Muller was stunned by shock, and his father felt compelled to act. Joachim:

- That's enough Alicia! Let him go.

Alicia:

- As you wish, Chairman Muller.

Alicia let go of Bjorn, who took a deep breath of relief. After that, she walked up to Joachim, shook his hand, and bowed to him, before taking her place at the table. The butler came in and served the meal. Bjorn looked in disgust at Alicia, as her meal was a kilo of raw meat and nothing else. She declined the offered wine and instead drank a glass filled with animal blood. Bjorn felt compelled to comment on her choice of drink:

- Alicia! House Muller is famous for making the best wine in the world, and we are also known for making the best wine glasses in the world. Glasses that are not meant for the filth that you are drinking.

Alicia hissed back at him:

- Alcohol is a deadly poison; animal blood is good for you!

Alicia drank the glass of animal blood, and then she licked her lips, while looking at Bjorn. Joachim Muller added in:

- Due to Alicia's unique genetics, her liver cannot break down alcohol. Thus, her refusal to drink our most excellent vintage wines isn't rude

Bjorn:

- So, a drink is all it takes for her to go down? Good to know!

Joachim:

- Anyways. The reason that you are here is that John and I have decided to put Bjorn under Alicia's command. You are to use unsanctioned methods to find the assailants of Proxima Thule and to determine whether Keila Eisenstein is alive is true or not.

Alicia White:

- With pleasure, sir.
- I have waited five years to mix business and pleasure with your son.

Bjorn Muller:

- Never going to happen, freak!

Alicia White:

- We shall see.
- I must take my leave.
- I'll see you tomorrow sexy boy...

Alicia purred and winked with a wicked and predatory look in her eyes. After Alicia had left, Bjorn stared at his father with terror in his eyes, close to tears:

Bjorn:

- You cannot send me on a mission with that hideous monster??

Joachim:

- Yes, I can, and I will.

- Your whoring and substance abuse have annoyed me for decades, but the breaking point is your failure with this Keila Eisenstein. If she were to resurface after we declared her dead, we would lose face, and everyone will laugh at us. This is your mess, and you'll have to sort it out.

Bjorn:

- But Alicia is a monster. She infected the city Pamshal with a deadly synthetic virus killing tens of thousands.

Joachim shrugged his shoulders:

- Casualties are the fuel of war.

Bjorn:

- But this was after the war had ended.

Joachim Muller:

- Oh really. I better discuss this with John White. One faction cannot unilaterally destroy Martian cities without first consulting the Council.

- Anyway, this changes nothing for you, Bjorn. You better fix your mess or not come back at all.

- Those were the options that my father gave me back in 2785, and I did redeem myself in the end.

Bjorn was looking for words, but he came up with nothing. His father was right; except for his family name he had not achieved anything.

Instead, he was in trouble if Keila had tricked him and faked her death. He would be ridiculed throughout the solar system after his triumphant display of her body a few months prior, and he would be barred from holding a position of power. Dealing with the Proxima Thule situation and finding out the truth about Keila's death was the way to go, and it was his own responsibility to do so.

Bjorn was against his father's decision in one regard. He should have overseen the operation leading House Muller operatives, instead of being a subordinate of the vicious half-beast Alicia White.

Chapter 138: Alicia White Requests an Audience with Metatron.

Bjorn Muller was trying to catch some sleep in his room on Alicia White's unregistered black operations shuttle "SS Shady Business". He had been on the shuttle for a couple of weeks, and he hated every minute of it. His room was cramped, and a lot of it seemed to be used for storage. The food was basic and not close to the standard he was used to. But the worst part was that the shuttle was so small so that it lacked artificial gravitation. This meant that he had to sleep strapped to a bed, vastly different from the comfort he was used to.

Bjorn's former command ship ISS Supreme Earth was large, about 100 meters long and 60 meters wide and 60 meters high. Being of that size, it had double hulls. The outer shell had the thrusters that propelled the craft forward as well as armaments. The inner hull contained the living quarters and the command centre of the ship. The inner hull accelerated around its own axle to create gravity while being attached to the outer shell that propelled the craft forward. While the gravity on board a large vessel was still a lot weaker than on earth, it was still enough to be able to walk around, eat, drink, and sleep regularly.

Even more than the comfort of his command ship, Bjorn missed the feeling of being in command. While Bjorn was technically second in command for the mission, Alicia and her staff disrespected and ridiculed him, since they knew that he had no real power on this vessel.

Bjorn was interrupted in his thoughts when Alicia knocked on his door.

Alicia:

- Rise and shine, pretty boy.

Bjorn:

- I am awake, you freak!

Alicia:

- Good. We are at the B528B asteroid. Time to sniff out your girlfriend, Keila.

Bjorn:

- I doubt that they will give us free access to search their base. Besides we have no official business being here.

Alicia:

- You'll find that I can be very persuasive.

They docked with B528B and Metatron with a group of angels met them at the docking station. Without a word, Alicia walked up to Metatron, grabbed him by the balls and hissed in his ear.

- Where is Keila?!
- I can smell her on you!

The other angels lifted their weapons and so did Alicia's entourage, so an armed standoff ensued. Alicia let go of Metatron. After gasping for air, he spoke.

- She is dead; we delivered her body to your friend over there, Bjorn Muller.

Alicia:

- Liar!

- I can smell her on you. She is here. I require access to search
the station.

Meanwhile, Keila saw what was happening through the divine technology chips installed in the angels. She realised that fighting the Terrans was her last resort and she made her way to an emergency pod that took her down to the surface of Eden. She instructed Metatron to stall the intruders.

After a long wait, Metatron broke the silence:

- Okay, you can have a look around. But I can assure you that
we will complain with the Terran Council about this.

Alicia:

- Complain as much as you want, you'll have a lot to answer
for when we catch Keila!

Alicia and Bjorn walked around in the space station with Metatron as their hostage. After a few hours, they had seen everything, and they walked back to the docking station.

Alicia:

- Thank you for the tour. What a lovely station. We will meet
again shortly.

Metatron:

- No, we will not. You are not welcome here anymore. Try anything funny, and we will shoot you on sight.

Alicia disregarded the threat. The man in front of her was gutless and had already been a pushover once. The people on the space station were scared of the Terran Council so there was no way they would ever try anything against them.

Alicia:

- Are you inviting me to dinner on Friday?! I don't know if I can fit it in, but I'll see you soon handsome!

Hearing her response, Metatron stared at her dumbfounded as she entered the shuttle and took off with her crew.

Once they were back in space Alicia spoke to Bjorn:

Alicia:

- Keila is there. Did you notice there was a room with female clothing in it and that one of the emergency pods was missing?

Bjorn:

- That doesn't prove anything. I doubt the Council will give us the permission to strike and the attack ships needed, based on circumstantial evidence.

Alicia:

- Oh, but I have proper evidence.

Alicia pulled out a pair of female underwear that she stole from the visit and smelled them. She growled.

Alicia:

- That is the smell of Keila!

Bjorn:

- Very well. Let's match the underwear with her DNA.
- If they match, we will get reinforcements and attack the station.

Alicia dumped the underwear into a garbage collector and propelled them out into space.

Alicia:

- No! Keila is my prey. Now that I know what she smells like, I know that she will be delicious!

Bjorn Muller:

- You are a fucking psycho. How do you think we'll reach Keila now?

Alicia White:

- I will find a way.

- But first, let's head to Proxima Thule. We have captured a spy, and I am hungry.

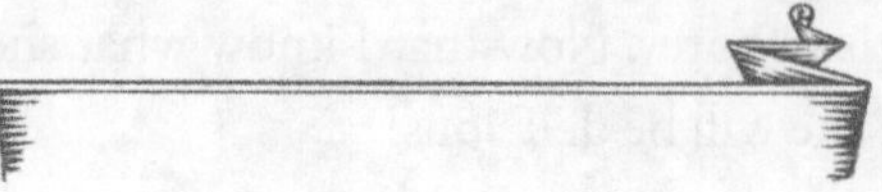

Chapter 139: Keila Receives a Disturbing Video Message

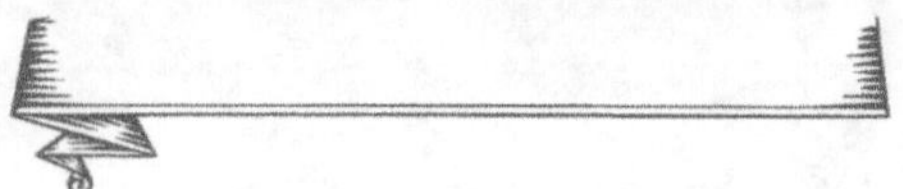

A few days later, Keila sat on a couch in the reception area of the Divine Control Centre overlooking space through the panorama window. She was angry and felt violated. The freak that the Terran Council had sent to look for her had intruded her residence and violated the integrity of her lover, Metatron. Worst of all, Keila had opted to hide on Eden instead of confronting her foe. While it had been a strategically correct decision as she couldn't fight the Terran Council at this time, it had still stung her. Keila was filled with anger and frustration over the intrusion.

What angered her the most was to see the disgusting slimeball and rapist Bjorn Muller among the intruders. Keila could not understand why he came down to lead a strike team instead of leading from the back of his command ship like he would However there he was, commanded by the beastly abomination that had driven the intruders.

Filled with anger, Keila punched a boxing sack in the gym with her bare fists until her knuckles bled and then she had a round of very rough sex with Metatron. Afterwards they lay in bed exhausted and satisfied, when they received a holographic video message with the following text, *"Keila! I found a survivor from the unfortunate Ebola outbreak in your hometown Pamshal. Hope to meet you soon!"*

The video was of Alicia White and a prisoner. Keila recognised the prisoner. He was her teenage crush from nine years earlier. In the video, the prisoner was chained to a wall, and Alicia was viciously tearing pieces of flesh from his body with her teeth. With blood all over her face, she turned towards the camera and smirked at it. She licked her lips and showed her sharp nasty fangs.

Keila had seen enough! She turned off the TV and rushed towards the shooting range for some more anger management as her knuckles were sore from before. *"Find out more about that woman! I want to kill her myself she screamed at Metatron!"* and then she left the bedroom.

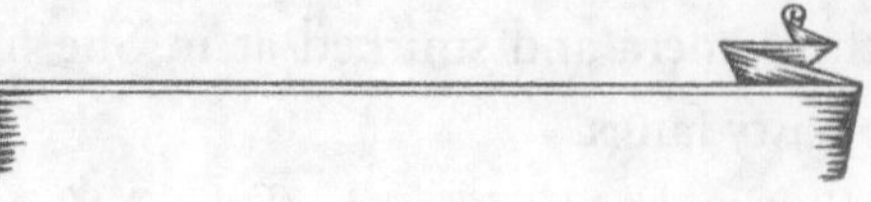

Chapter 140: A Frenzied Alicia White Rapes and Almost Kills Bjorn Muller.

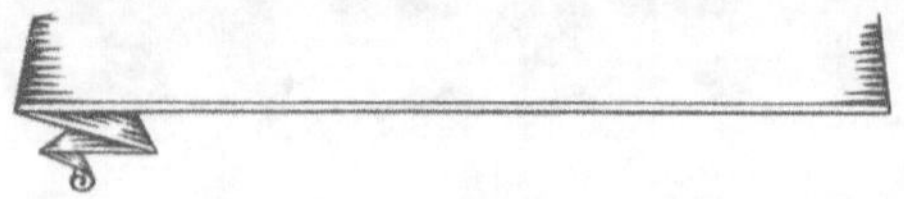

Alicia White was feeling ecstatic as she was resting after a violent and gruesome meal. There was nothing better to her than blood, violence and fresh human meat and she had it all. There was no better taste to Alicia than eating a human alive, and it was a pleasure Alicia seldom came across. She knew that her father was against her cannibalistic behaviour, but her men were loyal and would not tell him anything.

Besides, her father, John White never asked for the details about her secret operations as he preferred plausible deniability if things went south.

Alicia White felt that her blood was boiling with intense sexual desire. The object of her desire was Bjorn Muller. Alicia was craving for Bjorn for several reasons. Firstly, his genetics were optimised for good looks while the other men of her crew lacked that optimisation. Secondly, his prominent position in another faction made him attractive compared to the low-level grunts she usually slept around with. Thirdly, his disdain and revulsion towards her made him the ultimate object of sexual desire as Alicia thrived on dominating others against their will.

For the last month, she had contained her desires out of respect for her father's will and business interests. Giving in to her desire and sodomising Bjorn would lead to severe diplomatic tensions and problems between House White and House Muller. Her father could not afford that as he needed to keep House Muller close as he had hostile relations with other factions on the Terran Council. But Alicia felt a desire that was she couldn't resist any more.

Unbeknownst to Alicia, the man she devoured was a heavy user of synthetic Martian drugs. Combined with Alicia's hyper-sensitivity to recreational drugs, the drug residues she ingested from her victim's blood was enough to send her into a complete frenzy.

She tore off her tight-fitted snake-skin clothes and grabbed a syringe with a potent male aphrodisiac and made her way into Bjorn's quarters. Baffled, he couldn't get a word out before she jumped him, grabbed him with one arm and jabbed him in the neck with the syringe. *"I want you to fuck my slimy and horny pussy"* she hissed at him with the sounds of a deadly snake.

Bjorn regained his composure and pushed her away. Then he screamed at Alicia:

- What the fuck are you doing?!
- Get out of my room, you crazy freak!!

Alicia:

- I have waited long enough for you to come around. Fuck me now!

Bjorn:

- Over my dead body, freak!

Alicia gave Bjorn a psychotic smile and replied:

- As you wish, perfect human specimen. As you wish.

After that, Alicia jumped towards Bjorn and started strangling him. He punched her several times to get free, but in her frenzied state the impact from his fists made her even more aroused, and she grabbed his throat even stronger. As Bjorn passed out, she growled and let go of his neck so that she could tear apart his military pants and ride him as he had an involuntary erection from the drug that she had injected him with.

Having regained his breath, Bjorn screamed for help, and Alicia grabbed his throat again while she also bit deep into Bjorn's arm and drank the blood as it pumped from his artery.

Bjorn passed out and was close to dying. He was saved in the last minute when Alicia's operatives, rushed in to restrain Alicia White. She put up with a good fight but eventually the six of them managed to control her. They put Bjorn on emergency iceblock and rushed him to the Phobos base for immediate medical treatment.

After dropping off Bjorn at the Phobos base, they took off, as the group was not inclined to explain how Bjorn had sustained his injuries.

Chapter 141: A Diplomatic Crisis.

Joachim Muller was lying restless in his bed in the penthouse level of Europeum tower. Bjorn had got him in trouble this time, and it was because of Joachim's incorrect decision to put Bjorn Alicia White's command. A few days earlier, Bjorn had arrived unconscious at the Phobos base, and when he woke up, he had made grave accusations against Alicia who was nowhere to be found. The medical examination supported Bjorn's allegations, and it was likely that Alicia had raped him and bit him.

Bjorn being sodomised was not the issue for Joachim. Bjorn was a sexual degenerate, and there were a lot of rumours stating that consent wasn't his primary concern when choosing his sexual partners. The fundamental issue was that Bjorn had aired his story in the media, and issued an arrest order for Alicia over what had happened.

Bjorn's accusations against Alicia had caused Joachim a lot of issues on the Terran Council, and it threatened his position as chairman. House White was his closest ally in the Terran Council, and they were both hostile towards House Rashid. Joachim was unsure whether House Cheng was with him or against him, as they were shifty and unpredictable. The fifth member on the Terran Council, House of Bolivar was too weak and unaligned to be a matter of interest.

Joachim's problem was that he needed to prove himself strong and loyal to his family. So, he needed to require that Alicia came back to Earth for a trial, while also trying to keep his ally John White.

John White had claimed that Alicia and her crew had gone rogue and that he was unable to command them back to Earth. This had forced

Joachim to issue and arrest order against Alicia. Joachim hoped that John understood his predicament and avoided escalating the issue.

Realising that he wouldn't be able to sleep naturally, Joachim entered a sleep pod to rest and let go of his worries.

Chapter 142: A Challenge to a Duel.

Alicia White was sitting on the abandoned Moreno outpost in the asteroid belt. The Moreno outpost had served as a hotel, bar, and brothel for workers on the nearby asteroid mining facilities, but as they were mined out of minerals, the outpost had shut down. She was in a pickle and there was only one way to redeem herself, was to bring Keila Eisenstein's dead body to the Terran Council. That would shift focus from Bjorn's allegations against her to Bjorn's failure.

Alicia was shocked that Bjorn had acted the way he did. In hindsight, her actions were unacceptable but the conventional method of solving issues within the Terran Council was to settle them behind closed doors, away the public's knowledge. Bjorn had done the opposite. By accusing Alicia of rape, and issuing a warrant for her arrest, he had created the most significant crisis since the death of Hans Muller, five years earlier. The alliance between House White and House Muller was dissolved, and it was only a matter of time before skirmishes would take place, as the balance of power had shifted.

Alicia considered her options. She could come back to Earth to stand trial, but that was a considerable risk. Even if she got away with what she had done to Bjorn, a hearing risked spreading light on the atrocities Alicia had committed throughout the years. Another way would be to convince Bjorn to drop the charges. This option was unlikely as he already had made his accusations public. The third option was the best: To find and kill Keila Eisenstein and bring back her body to Earth. That would make Alicia a hero and humiliate Bjorn. The only problem with that was that Keila was hiding on a well-armed battle station with her advanced technology and soldiers.

Alicia realised that she needed to provoke Keila to come out from her base and face her on this outpost. Alicia recorded a provocative message and sent it to Eden. It was a risky move, because if Keila was smart, she could send the message anonymously to the Terran Council and let them deal with Alicia.

However, Alicia counted on Keila coming after her. Alicia was the one who had used synthetic viruses to kill everyone in Keila's hometown on Mars, the City of Pamshal. Alicia sent the message and she anticipated for the upcoming battle.

Alicia dragged a rat out of a cage, crushed it with her bare hands. Blood splattered all over her face, and then she licked the blood off her face and slurped it up ravishingly.

Chapter 143 Challenge Accepted.

Keila was heading towards Alicia's position in a shuttle, accompanied by a strike team. The strike team was Edenites that she had trained in modern combat. She had left Metatron and the Angels back on Eden for two reasons:

- If she was to walk into a trap and die, she wanted Metatron and his Angels to rule and modernise the Edenites. She cared about the people of Eden, and they were not ready to govern themselves yet.

- She wanted to test the ***Zetan non-encrypted bionic chip disruptor*** in action. Keila assumed that Alicia and her squad had unprotected microchips that would be affected. The angels had a lot of implanted microchips that would be affected by the device and make them perform poorly in combat. If Alicia's group were incapacitated when their bionic chips was disrupted, Keila and her inexperienced team would to kill their foes with ease.

Keila recalled the conversation she had had with Metatron before she left. He had wanted to relay the information to the Terran Council and let them deal with Alicia. It was common knowledge that Alicia had gone rogue and the Council had a warrant out for Alicia's arrest. While this solution had made logical sense, Keila had refused it. Keila had a vendetta against Alicia, as the freak had slaughtered her hometown with biological weapons and murdered her friend, Josh, to mock her.

They approached the Moreno outpost where Alicia was hiding. *"Be ready for anything!"* Keila told her troops as they docked with the outpost.

Chapter 144: The Showdown Between Keila and Alicia.

Keila stepped out of her shuttle and she realised that the artificial gravity on the Moreno outpost was very limited. This worried her as her troops had never trained for low gravity combat. While the gravity was still enough to prevent her from flying off when she walked there, the recoil of the weapons could prove challenging for her troops. She instructed her men to activate their Zetan ballistic energy absorbers but hold off with the Zetan bionic chip disruptors. Handheld devices had limited battery capacity, and she did not want to waste it before combat.

Keila entered the main lobby of the Moreno outpost and was greeted by a blood-soaked floor and Josh's head on a pike. Under Josh's head hung a sign: *"Welcome Keila, you are next"*. Keila looked up, and Alicia swept in with a plasma sword and decapitated the soldier next to her. Before anyone had time to react, Alicia grabbed the head and jumped away to the cover of darkness. *"Hey! Your friend lost something!"* she mocked and threw back the head.

As Alicia screamed, some of Keila's troops lost their cool and started shooting randomly towards Alicia's voice. This was the cue for Alicia's operatives to hail bullets and grenades against Keila's position. The ballistic energy absorbers absorbed most of the impact, but some of Keila's soldiers fell as they had misdirected the devices.

Keila dropped to the ground and activated her Zetan bionic chip disruptor. This turned the tide of the battle as Alicia's operatives lost all ability and started acting very erratic, once their implants were disrupted. This made them easy targets and Keila's fighters eliminated them quickly.

Alicia was unaffected by the disruptor as she, opposite to most Terrans, relied on her wild animal instincts and not on bionic microchips. She swept in another time and decapitated another one of Keila's men. On her third swoop, she got hit by multiple bullets and was unable to jump away. Instead, she crawled behind one of Keila's female troops, grabbed the woman and pointed the plasma sword to her throat. Alicia screamed to Keila.

- I have one of your soldiers as a hostage. Face me in hand to hand combat, and I'll let her go.

Keila:

- You are surrounded, injured, and all your men are dead! Surrender, Alicia!

Alicia:

- Oh, heee hee!! The mighty and brave Keila, the poster girl for the Martian Humanist Alliance, the ever so famous guerrilla-fighter girl, is too afraid to face me huh!

Keila:

- I'm not afraid of you. Challenge accepted, bitch!

Keila stood up and threw away her rifle and grabbed her knife.

Alicia pushed away her hostage, hissed and said *"Excellent"*. She stared in shock as Keila pulled up her pistol and shot the exposed Alicia right between the eyes. Things went silent. Alicia paused for a second and screamed in agony. *"I'll get you Keila, I will get my revenge! Revive me and fight with honour!"* After shouting that out she dropped dead to the ground.

Keila:

- Thanks honey, but I prefer to do things the easy way.

Keila gently blew the smoke away from her pistol, and she smirked with a sweet, bright, and intelligent look in her eyes. After killing Alicia, Keila and her remaining troops dragged all the wounded and dead friends and enemies back on the shuttle and went back to Eden. They brought back their own troops to revive them while avoid being detected, and they brought back the fallen enemies to restore them and then extract intelligence from them.

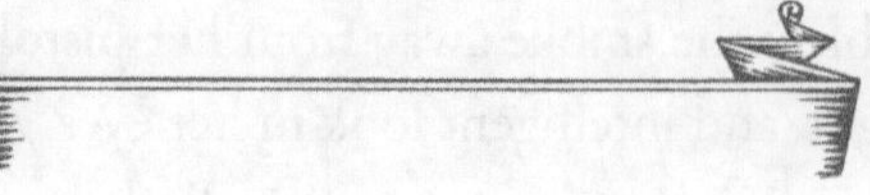

Chapter 145: Brahma Reaches His Destination

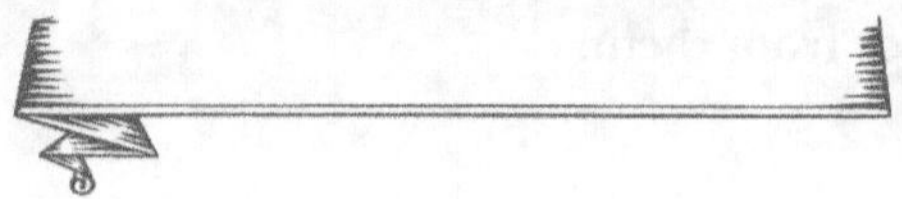

Brahma stood outside Rangda's eternal prison, and he was relieved that his long 50,000-kilometre walk was over. It had taken longer than he had planned, as the searing thirst and hunger had forced him to have many extended meditations breaks to regain his mental clarity and keeping him going. Yet, despite the delays, less than a year had passed in the outside universe.

Brahma had been without food and drink for thousands of years, and yet he was immortal in this despicable place. This forced him to live while suffering from endless thirst and hunger. He had passed most of the last few millennia in deep meditation to avoid the torment, but walking to Rangda's prison had amplified his suffering.

Brahma approached the prison, and he saw that there was a tunnel made through the impenetrable wall of the building. Had Rangda managed to get out of the jail, and how had she done it? He looked at the ground where the tunnel exited and realised the solution. There was a ring on the ground.

Rangda's prison had been built using the second hardest material in the known universe, but the ring on the ground held a replicated Zeto Crystal, the hardest substance in the world. Brahma had a flashback from when they sealed Rangda into the prison.

The last thing he had done to her was to throw their engagement ring at her. This was the ring that Rangda had used to slowly dig herself out. Brahma felt the chills. He had struggled with thirst and hunger to walk here. Rangda must have struggled a lot more digging herself out of the eternal prison. She had shown an incredible determination when all she needed to do was to enter deep meditation and live out the eternity that way. What had driven her? The question filled Brahma with terror and confusion.

Brahma's terror increased when he turned around and saw Rangda for the first time in many thousand years. Her spirit was the same, but her body was disfigured. Instead of being beautiful, she looked like a hideous monster. Brahma had seen those features before, she looked like a Xeno.

Brahma:

- Rangda? Is that you? What happened?

Rangda:

- Yes, multi-faced traitor! It is me.

- What you see is my true form. I am half Zetan and half Xeno, the only one of my kind. The ultimate species in the universe.

- For many years, I used Zetan technology to look like one of you to blend in. You were blind, and you never exposed me.

- Now I don't need to blend in anymore. This is the real me.

Brahma:

- That's a bad choice, you looked better before.

Rangda:

- Says the man who cannot keep the same face for more than a couple of minutes!

Brahma, like most of the Zetans who came to Earth to pose as deities, had adapted his appearance to that which was expected by his human followers. The background of Brahma being the multi-faced deity, was that his Zetan outer layer **external DNA modifier** malfunctioned, which led to his face changing every few minutes. At first, Brahma was terrified by this, but after a while, he had come to appreciate this unique trait in himself.

Brahma:

- At least I don't look like a Xeno monster.

- So, is that why you betrayed us and wiped out the majority of all the life in the galaxy, while you were at it?

Rangda:

- I did not wipe out most life in the galaxy. Twelve inhabited planets were annihilated when I caused that supernova explosion. This was disastrous for the Zetans, but for the total biomass in the Milky Way, it was negligible.

Brahma:

- It was disastrous for the Xenos as well. What was left of us annihilated the Xeno species, before the loss of the Zeto crystals destroyed the foundation of our civilisation.

Rangda

- That's of no consequence. The Xenos will rise again, and I will rule them as their God-Queen!

Brahma:

- To be a queen, you need subjects. The Xenos are extinct.

Rangda:

- Is that so? I suggest that you look around.

Brahma looked around and what he saw shocked him. A Xeno warrior with sharp claws stared him in the eyes. Before he had time to react, the beast had pierced straight through Brahma's body, with the claws sticking out through his back.

Responding instinctively, Brahma focused his strength to his right fist and crushed the Xeno's head with a well-aimed blow. Brahma pulled the dead Xeno's claws out of his body. Brahma coughed blood, but looked at Rangda defiantly and spoke:

- Is that all you can muster?! Your friend is dead, and you'll be next.

Rangda:

- I don't think so. He might be dead, but he served his purpose.

Brahma:

- And that was?

Rangda:

- To weaken you enough for this!

Rangda pulled out a corrupted Zeto crystal. Instead of pure clarity, it emitted energy of terror and fear, unlike the uncorrupted Zeto crystal that emitted peace and unity.

Brahma:

- A Zeto crystal? Do they still exist? What did you do to this one?

Rangda:

- Yes, it would be a waste to let these precious crystals be destroyed, when I annihilated Zetani.

- I have merely turned the crystals useful to my benefit. You'll see its real power for the first time!

Rangda lifted the dark-red and fiery corrupted Zeto crystals to the sky and Brahma felt an extreme pain, Brahma felt how his head was about to explode, but that wasn't the worst part. He could also feel how his essence and soul was absorbed by the darkness of the evil crystal. A few seconds later, Brahma's head exploded, shattered into million pieces and his headless body dropped to the ground, jerking violently before it stopped moving.

Chapter 146: Keila Experiences Tremors and Vivid Hallucinations

Keila was holding an operational meeting with the angels and some of the prominent Edenites in the boardroom of the Divine Control Centre. Contrary to her predecessor, Keila preferred to keep the sessions face to face to discuss issues, instead of sending decrees. She chose to include prominent Edenites as she planned to modernise the Edenite society and create democratic and equal society. For that to happen, it was imperative for the Edenites to learn how to run their own colony and create a sustainable economy.

Suddenly, Keila started shaking and she had vivid hallucinations. She recognised the place as the Divine Dimension, but she did not understand how her mind had been transported there, as she was not connected to the Divine Detector Machine. In front of her was a terrifying monstrous woman with luminescent purple eyes and sharp fangs. The creature appeared out of thick green and smelly gas, not unlike the odour of a prison cell or a dark sewage brick well. The smell reminded Keila of a very stale, dark empty prison cell. It was the smell of the black death. This other-worldly devious woman grabbed her shirt, dragged her closer, and stared right into her soul. Keila fell to the ground. She felt anguish and despair, and she screamed at the top of her lungs in pain. She then passed out.

When she opened her eyes, the gathered people stepped back in shock. Keila's eyes had changed colour, from green to dark purple.

Metatron:

- Keila are you okay? What happened?

Keila:

- I had a vision. But don't worry, this is something that I have experienced a lot.

- I have never felt better.

Keila gave the group a very foreboding smile, and then she left the room, while wondering who the woman in her vision was.

Chapter 147: Rangda Satisfies Her Hunger and Plans Ahead.

Rangda was feasting of Brahma's headless body and felt satisfied for the first time in thousands of years. With her mouth and lips drenched in silver bluish Zetan blood, she stopped for a moment. She asked herself if this act of cannibalism was wrong. Rangda concluded that it wasn't. She had been kept in that prison for so long, and she felt a hunger and hatred for her enemies. She was only half Zetan so technically she was another species than Brahma, and once Rangda had become a God-Queen, she could set the rules and morals that she wanted.

One of her Xeno followers wanted a bite of the body, but Rangda pushed him away. Most likely she didn't need to eat Brahma's body to capture his essence, as she had absorbed the fragments of his soul into the tainted Zeto crystals. But it felt good to eat and share Brahma's body with her underlings, when she could savage his body alone.

Rangda:

- Step away from my prey! I killed him, and his meat is mine.
- Eat the weakling that fell to the Zetan, This Zetan is my prey.

The Xenos hesitated. Cannibalism was taboo in Xeno culture as well, and that was the reason they had stayed alive for thousands of years trapped and starving in the divine dimension without killing each other. If cannibalism hadn't been tabooed in the Xeno culture they would have consumed each other in an animalistic frenzy. The Xenos had been hiding for thousands of years, close to the very dark edge of the Divine Dimension. Having received the approval from their mistress, they devoured their fallen comrade. Rangda smiled, seeing her beastly allies getting themselves some fresh meat was a joy to her eyes.

The Xenos was a savage bunch, but their energy levels and tenacity impressed her. They had something that the Zetans never have had. They had the will to dominate the entire universe. Rangda was a hybrid species, the only one of her kind. She was a half Zetan and half Xeno, a reproductive mishap that was destined to be the Zenith of all creation.

The Xenos had existed on their home planet for millions of years before Zetan explorers had imbued their genome with elevated intelligence. Like with humanity, the Zetan explorers had left the Xenos after imbuing them with intelligence. This had proven a critical mistake, as the Xenos to almost wiped out the Zetan galactic civilisation.

Chapter 148: Xenora, Xenos and Rangda's backstory

For millions of years, the Xenos existed like primitive beasts on the Xeno home planet, Xenora. Xenora had unique features for life that set it apart from most other inhabited worlds in the Milky Way Galaxy. The most unique feature was Xenora's close orbit to a blue giant star, and its' very slow rotational speed. One Xenora day was 3 months long. These circumstances led to days with a maximum temperature over 300 degrees and nights that could reach a minimum of -150 degrees. Despite these extreme circumstances, Xenora had life forms that could survive extreme conditions. This happened the following way:

All larger life forms followed Xenora's orbital rotation to always be on the side that had liveable conditions, the morning side of the planet. This forced all the animals to continually move along with the orbit, as a place would be too hot and kill them if they stayed long for the scorching midday sun to arrive.

Depending on the species, they preferred different locations in the Xenora morning. The early morning was freezing as the ice from the night had not melted yet, and this suited animals that liked ice. The late morning was very hot, albeit still bearable, and suited animals that loved the heat.

Animals were able to keep up with Xenora's rotation as the planet's rotation was very slow. As animals were forced to be moving on Xenora, life and survival evolved differently, than on Earth. To survive on Xenora, an animal species could only rely on speed, strength, and ruthlessness, as there was no time for prey animals to hide or for predators to utilise stealth.

All the plants that existed were types of fast-growing grass and other weeds, which had extremely short life cycles. These plants had lifecycles of only a few weeks between the time when the icicles and permafrost of the night had defrosted in the early morning, until the heat of the midday arrived which would cause widespread fires that killed all plant life. Having evolved to the conditions, plants on Xenora had fireproof seeds.

The water on Xenora came down as snow and ice during the night and evaporated to steam during the day. Xenora had no tilt to its star and as such had no seasons. The lack of angle meant that Xenora's North and South Pole always exist in twilight, and it was in the Polar Regions that life had originated as they were more survivable than the rest of the planet.

All animals on Xenora had very thick and sturdy skin to be able to cope with the tremendous amounts of UV radiation the planet received from its nearby blue star.

The Xenos had lived in the equatorial regions of Xenora, which were the most inhospitable regions of the planets. They had been very fearsome predators to survive under these circumstances. When the Zetans altered the Xeno's DNA, the Xenos started spreading over the planet until they reached the Polar Regions. Once the Xenos arrived at the Polar Regions, they built permanent settlements, as the North and South Pole, with its eternal twilight, were the only places where it was safe to erect buildings without the need to worry about extreme heat, or extreme cold.

The dwellers of the two Xeno cities had to be wary and on alert as the only sites suitable for permanent settlement were highly sought after by all the Xeno tribes that roamed the planet. Every time a tribe thought they would be strong enough to conquer the city, they would fight to the last individual to do so, as was the custom in the Xeno culture.

Because of their constant warring and lack of advanced technology, the Xeno tribes remained on a Stone Age technology level for over 50,000 years. The lack of technological progress had convinced the Zetan researchers that the Xenos was inferior to them. The Zetans regarded the Xenos a primitive race that would never pose a threat to the Zetan civilisation.

On the last Zetan research trips to Xenora, something happened that altered the fate of both the Xenos and the Zetans. A female Zetan scientist, Kalianka, was left behind on Xenora. This scientist was Rangda's mother.

Kalianka fell victim to a cruel ploy. One of her colleagues, a mean-spirited Zetan researcher, had tried to win her heart in courtship, but she rejected him. Feeling hurt, he beat her up and left her to die on Xenora as he decided that if he could not have her, no one else would have her either.

The cruel irony of fate was that, she had considered her assailant's proposal. Kalianka's assailant lied to the other Zetan researchers and told them that Kalianka was attacked and eaten by an animal. The other researchers did not go back to look for her because their location was getting hotter as the sun rose over the sky, and they needed to move on.

When Kalianka woke up, she felt weak and the surface temperature had risen to 80 degrees Celsius. Kalianka had no water and no means to get to a colder location. This was lethal conditions to a Zetan, as her home planet Zetani had a similar climate as Earth, and the Zetans were not adapted to the extreme heat on Xenora. She looked up and save a Xeno scout in front of her. Unable to fight due to her condition she closed her eyes and prepared herself to meet the True Maker, but the attack never came. Instead, the Xeno scout lifted her up over his shoulder and started running towards cooler conditions and a water source to keep Kalianka alive.

Kalianka woke up when someone poured icy water over her. It turned out that the scout had outrun the planets rotation speed and they were now earlier in the Xenora day cycle when it was cooler. The air was still warm, but the water was ice cold as the water had kept a lot of coldness from the long night.

Kalianka later understood that the Xeno tribe that had taken her in, saw her as a goddess and worshipped her. Eventually, she learned their language and could understand their culture. This was the best time in her life as a scientist as she could appreciate the Xenos from their own words and not just observe them via miniature drones. Her biggest regret was that she couldn't share her revelations and discoveries with her fellow Zetans. Her telepathic abilities didn't work as there was no other Zetan in the star system as the rest of the expedition had returned to Zetani.

Kalianka got a unique insight into the harsh life the Xenos were living, and she understood them better than any Zetan had ever done. Her tribe was living at the equator and they had to move the furthest distance every day to remain in the liveable zone on Xenora. As Xenora was the size of Earth, that meant that they had to move over 200 kilometres a day to the west, to avoid getting scorched by the sun.

This put a lot of pressure and forced a non-empathic approach to the members of the tribe. If someone got sick or injured, the tribe had to leave that individual to die as they couldn't travel fast enough with weak members of the tribe.

The only exception to this rule was for Kalianka. Being a Zetan, she could not move 200 kilometres a day on foot. As her Xeno tribe considered her a goddess, they did not mind sharing the burden of carrying her around.

Eventually, her tribe decided that her presence was a sign that it was time to move to the top of Xeno hierarchy. To do this, they needed to invade the Xeno city on Xenora's North Pole. They passed all the other tribes' territories on the way to the North Pole without any confrontation. The Xeno culture was very direct, and as the tribe had declared that they were after taking over the North Pole, the other tribes did not see them as a threat.

Once they had reached the North Pole, Kalianka's tribe did not stand a chance. This was because the defenders had both the numerical advantage as well as fortified city walls. As the Xeno culture required that they fought to the last individual, they all died, except for Kalianka who was taken prisoner by the North Pole inhabitants.

Being a prisoner of the North Pole city was the end of Kalianka's luck, as the city dwellers had experienced contact with Zetans in the past, they understood that Kalianka was not a goddess. They realised that Kalianka was a Zetan, a species they had previous disagreements and altercations with. They tortured and raped her to extract scientific knowledge from her.

The torture ended when Kalianka surprisingly fell pregnant. This shouldn't have been possible as they were different species, but it happened due to an unlikely mutation that took place in Kalianka's body.

To the Xenos, this was an act of the True Maker and Kalianka's misfortune turned around and she was now the wife of the Xeno high priest and the mother of their future queen, Rangda. Unfortunately, the amount of UV radiation Kalianka's skin had soaked up during her years with equator tribe caught up with her a few years later. She contracted skin cancer and died at the age of 220 years. This was a very young age to die for a Zetan, as they usually reached lifespans of longer than 1000 years.

Losing her mother at a young age, caused a permanent psychological scar within Rangda, and she blamed the Zetans for her mother's suffering and unfair treatment.

Rangda swore to get revenge for her mother with the destruction of the Zetan galactic civilisation. As it turned out, she had plenty of time to get her revenge. Her unlikely DNA that was a combination of Zetan and Xeno DNA stopped her from aging once she reached adulthood and granted her immortality. As she was a hybrid species, she was also infertile, and she looked insane.

Rangda began the long journey to turn the Xenos into a species that could contest with the Zetan for dominance of the galaxy. Her first step was to make the North Pole city an impregnable fortress so that her tribe would remain in power. This was the easy as her late mother had provided the tribe with Zetan technological knowledge. This knowledge could be used to make superior weaponry, capable of repelling any invader with ease.

The next step was to build tunnels across the planet for underground settlements, where the extreme variations in temperature did not exist. Xenora was ideal for building underground societies as the planet had limited geological activity. This meant that the heat didn't increase as they dug deeper, and they didn't need to worry about earthquakes. They kept digging for thousands of years until the tunnels spanned across Xenora, with a multitude of large subterranean settlements controlled by Rangda.

The basis for Rangda's control was that she had found out that there were Zeto crystals underground on Xenora. The unaltered Zeto crystals did not affect the minds of the Xeno species as the Zeto crystals promoted values such as the pursuit of knowledge, unity, passiveness, and the love for all life. Rangda, however, found a way to corrupt the gemstones to promote values such as lust, greed, violence, and domination. These values were more aligned to the Xeno minds, and by controlling the crystals, Rangda could control her ever-increasing number of subjects.

The Xeno underground settlements were fed in two ways. Most of the nutrition came from mould-based artificial meats. The Xenos were carnivores, but they were able to eat plant or algae-based proteins if they had to. The second way to feed her settlements was to catch the animals on the surface by climbing up tunnels through to the surface. By utilising tunnels to the surface, her tribe didn't need to move to avoid getting burnt. Instead they surfaced when outside temperatures were suitable and then dragged their prey back to the deep tunnels where they were protected against the outside temperatures.

Once Rangda's tribe controlled Xenora, they eradicated all the other tribes and set sight on their next goal, to start the war of conquest against the Zetans. The Xenos conquered their first planets easily. These planets were scarcely populated, and the Zetans living there didn't expect any threats and were mostly unarmed. The Xenos moved in, and due to their short life cycle and quick reproduction rate, they quickly got a foothold on the conquered planets. As the conquered planets were better for Xeno settlements than Xenora, they spread and created an economic base on the planets, aided by the confiscated Zetan infrastructure. After a century, the Xenos had consolidated their hold and set out to capture more worlds. This time the Zetan were better prepared, but the planets were still too far away from their homeworld to be adequately defended, and even these planets fell.

Chapter 149: The Multi-Millennial War Revisited.

Having lost several star systems, the Zetans realised the threat that the Xenos posed to their existence. But they could not mount a counter-attack. The Zetan civilisation was not based around military conquest, it was based on peace and unity, and besides, there had never been many of the Zetans. The average lifespan of a Zetan was 1000 years and the maximum number of children they could have during this millennium was five. This meant an average Zetan had a child every 200 years. The Xenos, on the other hand, had an average lifespan of 30 years, and during that time they could have up to 40 children. This meant that the Xenos could replenish their losses quickly.

The third attempted conquest by the Xenos was the Zetans second most important planet, Zetani Nova. This planet was well defended and time the Xenos were butchered with hardly any losses for the Zetans. This led to a stalemate in the conflict; every 30 years the Xenos sent a large force that ended up being nullified by the Zetan defences without reaching any progress. The Zetans, in turn, could not muster enough enthusiasm for a counterattack due to their peaceful nature. Instead, the Zetans fortified their borders and pursued peace. But even though the Zetans were able to nullify the Xenos invasions, it brought no peace. The Xenos wanted the Zetans dead, and, thus the two species always clashed.

The pointless attacks on the Zetans were a diversion by Rangda, to keep the Zetans unaware of the Xenos expansion. The Xenos settled uninhabited planets far away from the Zetans, and built up a massive invasion fleet.

After hundreds of years of skirmishes, the Xenos took the Zetans by surprise one day when they showed up in the Zetani Nova system with a 1000 times bigger fleet than they usually attacked with. Instead of the regular fleet of 300 Xeno ships, there were now 300,000 ships. Despite their inferior technology, they swarmed the Zetans and annihilated the Zetan defenders as well as all the Zetan civilians on Zetani Nova.

The loss of Zetani Nova alerted the Zetan civilisation to the existential threat that Xenos posed to them, and they rallied their forces from their other planets and mustered a counterattack that liberated Zetani Nova a decade later. Much to their dismay, Zetani Nova was destroyed beyond recognition. What was once the most beautiful planet in the Zetan civilisation was now a toxic wasteland. The Zeto crystals, which was the source of all the beauty and harmony on Zetani Nova, were gone. The Zetans also found a map that revealed the terrifying truth; that the Xenos had colonised and conquered a lot of neutral planets while distracting the Zetans with small-scale battles to distract them.

The Zetans gathered their leaders on Zetani for an emergency meeting. Their future seemed bleak and in a couple of centuries, they would be overrun by the Xeno hordes, no matter what they did to stop it. That was when Yahweh, one of the Zetan leaders, rediscovered the long-lost technology to enter and travel through the Divine Dimension, to the normal dimension.

The technology was crucial for two reasons: Firstly, going through the Divine Dimension was quicker. Moving between star systems only took days instead of years. Secondly, their discovery of the Divine Dimension meant that they could manipulate other sentient beings to fight for them against the Xenos. This was the reason for Zetans to come to Earth, posing as gods and recruiting humans to fight their wars.

With their newfound allies and considerably faster travel times the Zetans turned the tide in the war and they repelled the Xenos on every planet. The Zetans recruited the humans on Earth by infiltrating their minds and souls, and they liberated and restored the planets that had fallen to the Xeno scourge.

Rangda came up with a new plan, to use her half-Zetan intelligence and abilities. She altered her own genetics to infiltrate the Zetan leadership. Using the Zetan external DNA modifier, Rangda changed her appearance from the monstrous appearance of Xeno beast to that of a beautiful Zetan woman. Using a captured Zetan ship, Rangda travelled to Zetani. Since she had Zetan telepathic abilities, Rangda convinced the Zetans that she was one of them. Rangda seduced Brahma and gained access to the Zetan leadership as well as finding out about the Divine Dimension.

Despite Rangda's infiltration and deceit the Zetans were winning the war, and as a last spiteful effort, Rangda used her position within Zetan leadership to cause a supernova explosion that destroyed Zetani, which caused the collapse of the Zetan civilisation.

Having blown her cover, Rangda was locked up by Brahma in her eternal prison in the Divine Dimension until she escaped and killed Brahma, millennia later.

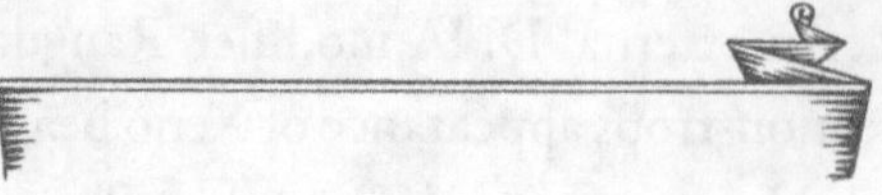

Chapter 150: Keila Has a Vision and Sets Up a Strategy for the War to Come

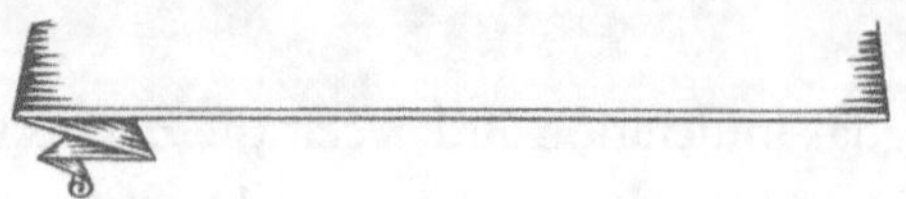

Keila was looking at herself in the mirror. She was pouring sweat and was determined to get back into peak fitness, something she had missed out on being the spoiled queen of Eden. The Edenite food was delicious, and she had enjoyed eating and drinking, with all the godly pleasures provided to her as offerings. This had started showing on her body, and Keila needed a super fit body to promote her ideal image, as Martian fighter.

Keila was not an armchair general that sent people to do things she didn't dare to deal with herself. Keila had led the mission to eliminate Alicia White. The mission had ended in a bloodbath, but Keila had survived it, and now she had one trump on hand. Having the bodies of Alicia and her operatives, Keila could use the Zetan outer layer external DNA modifier to pretend to be Alicia White, as this technology allows the user to change appearances. This could have great advantages if she were to infiltrate House White.

Keila looked at her eyes in the mirror. She used to have a pair of lively green eyes as a child, and eyes glowing with determination and positive energy as she got older. Her eyes had changed colour. Her current eyes were shining in a strange luminescent purple colour and they had a peculiar shape like those of predatory animal.

Keila felt a severe migraine, got dizzy, fell forward, and knocked her head on the mirror. The mirror broke, shattered into pieces and she started bleeding as she tasted the blood running down her cheeks.

The blood caused her to have a vision and she felt clarity on how to go ahead to reach her goal. She saw images of the Terran Council falling apart to fighting among themselves, and of how the Martians were attacking and destroying the Phobos Base, which had been oppressors main base for the last centuries.

Keila heard a voice speak in her head. At first, she was terrified. It wasn't the usual voice; instead, it was the voice who had told her to kill Jeshua, a year ago. But then she listened in to the voice and it made sense. They voice said that she shouldn't take on the Terran Council directly as an external threat would unite them. Instead, she should aim to infiltrate and divide them, to cause them to fight among themselves. If she could turn House Cheng against House Muller and House Rashid against House White, the Terran Council would collapse, and her Martian brethren could have their freedom from oppression.

Seeing this vision, she forgot that she was bleeding from the broken mirror shards, and instead she was smiling with her face soaked in blood. Metatron came in to examine the noise from the incident. Keila told him that she was okay, but he insisted and brought her straight to the medical ward. Thanks to stem cell technology her wounds healed without a scar in just a few days.

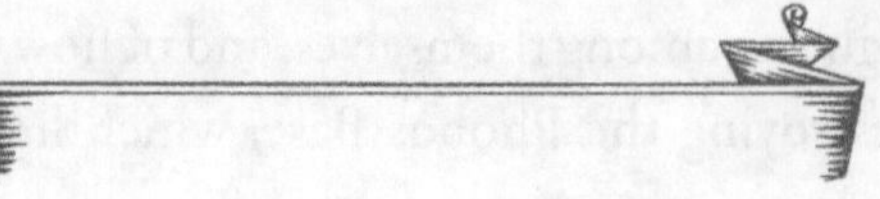

Chapter 151: A Cold Father's Day Meeting.

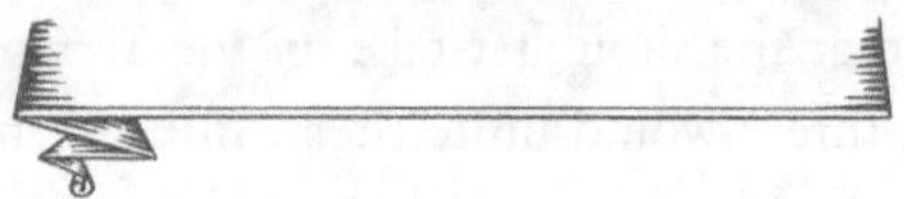

Bjorn Muller was looking at the calendar. It was Father's Day, in the year 2873. Bjorn thought about his father, whom he hadn't seen for over six months the day when his father had put him under Alicia White's command.

Bjorn's father had set him to work for a monster that ate people alive and ended up sodomising him. He didn't know what the worst part was, the psychological scarring or the total humiliation he had faced, but Bjorn had refused to talk to his father after the incident.

Since the incident, Bjorn had been transferred back to Max Wellington's command and he was stationed on the Phobos Base. It had been a few quiet months, and Bjorn's biggest struggle was that he no received good food, drinks, and female companionship since he refused to speak to his father, who was the one who provided these things for him.

The door to Bjorn's suite opened. Bjorn turned around. *"Who would be insolent enough to enter his room without asking first?"* he thought. Bjorn turned around, and there was his father, Joachim Muller.

Joachim:

- You forgot to honour me on Father's Day.

Bjorn:

- What on Earth are you doing here?
- Besides, it's not past midnight yet.

Joachim:

- It is past midnight in Europe, but I'll give you the benefit of the doubt.

Bjorn:

- Happy Father's Day, Joachim...
- Why have you come here unannounced?

Joachim:

- To be honest, I am not here because of Father's Day!

- I am coming because this week the distance between Earth and Mars is the shortest. This means I must only endure three days in transit to get from Earth to Phobos instead of the 21 days when the distance is the longest.

- While the trip was less inconvenient than it could have been, I would still have preferred if you picked up the fucking phone.

Bjorn:

- We don't have that much to talk about, father?

Joachim slapped Bjorn. For a moment Bjorn thought about unleashing the fury on his father, but he kept his cool.
Joachim:

- We do have things to talk about. I won't have spent three days in fucking space getting here and three days going back for no reason. So, you better improve your attitude, Bjorn.

- You need to withdraw your allegations against Alicia White. I cannot afford a conflict with House White. John White has been my closest ally on the Terran Council for the last decades.

Bjorn Muller:

- I have nothing against John White, but his crazy mutant daughter ate a man alive and then raped me. Convince him to put down that animal and focus on his more well-adjusted children.

Joachim Muller:

- It would be unwise to give unsolicited advice to John White on how to deal with his family matters, considering my abject failure with my own children.

- I have three sons who all bring disgrace to the family.

- Michael is a lazy man without any aspirations, who like to spend our money on leisure activities for him and his family

- Benjamin is a man who engages in bedroom activities with men.

- You are my eldest son, an abject failure in the armed forces with a drug and sex addiction. I have turned a blind eye to your shortcomings as I hoped that you would have the drive to take over the company from me when I retire.

- However, your latest embarrassment is too much. You are driving away our allies and humiliating your own masculinity at the same time... Just stop.

Bjorn Muller was going to say something when Admiral Max Wellington stormed into his office. Short of breath, he looked at Joachim Muller in surprise before catching his breath.
Max Wellington:

- Sorry to interrupt your conversation Chairman Muller, but I have urgent news.

- There has been another mysterious attack. This time the attack is on House Rashid's Aljadid Salam Outpost.

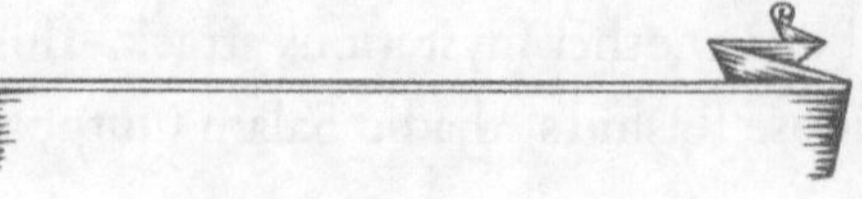

Chapter 152: The Attack on the Aljadid Salam Outpost

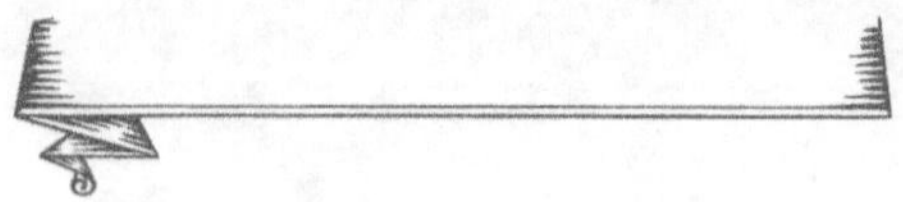

The Aljadid Salam outpost was a House Rashid outpost that had been built to protect the shipping lanes between Earth and the nearby House Rashid asteroid mining stations. The mining stations had run dry a long time ago, but House Rashid kept a small skeleton staff on the outpost to be able to claim that part of space for future use. Sometimes gravity pulled asteroids from the fringes of the solar system to a more central location, and for occasions like that, it was useful to claim vast swaths of empty space for what could host the goldmine of tomorrow. Another reason for House Rashid to keep a multitude of space outpost guarding empty space was to keep their large army busy, far away from Earth, to avoid them interfering in internal faction matters.

The attack took place in a similar manner to the Proxima Thule attack six months earlier. Keila's vessel approached the outpost with Zetan stealth technology to avoid detection. Then they blocked all communication to and from the outpost. Then they stormed the outpost with their kinetic energy absorbers and bionic chip disruptors activated. The unprepared and disrupted House Rashid defenders never stood a chance. Keila set explosives to blow up the station but intentionally used too little explosives to destroy the outpost. This was a ploy as Keila wanted it to seem like a failed attempt by House White to destroy the outpost.

The timing for the attack had come to Keila in a vision. On the day of the shooting, one of the Chairman Ibrahim Rashid's many sons, Akram Rashid, was on-board the station. Akram was killed beyond resurrection just like the rest of the defenders.

To make it evident that House White was behind the attack, Keila and her group had used the weapons and ammunition that they seized from the battle with Alicia White. They also left some of the corpses of soldiers from Alicia's group at the scene. These corpses, had no identity tags in their brains, but it would not be challenging for House Rashid investigators to figure out who they were, from looking at their uniforms and weaponry.

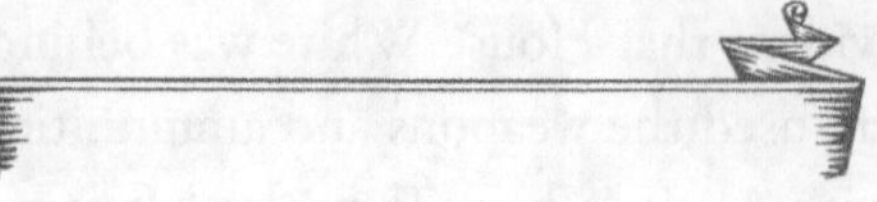

Chapter 153: A Diplomatic Crisis

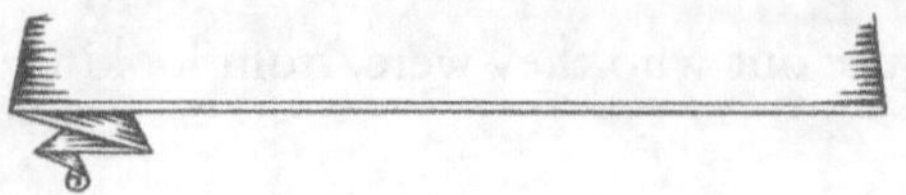

Keila was drinking a protein fruit smoothie, recovering from a hard fitness session with her Edenite troops. While her female physique made her weaker than some of the men under her command, her total fitness level was well above that of her average soldier. It was vital for her to show her fittest self and the extra kilos she had added when she first became the queen of Eden were now gone, and she was in her prime.

Unfortunately, she couldn't convince Metatron or the angels to take part in the sessions as they were confident that genetic optimisation, nutrition, and selective electrical stimulation were superior to something as archaic as physical exercise.

Keila's Edenite troops were a mixture of men and women. This was the opposite of what Abraham had been preaching during his reign, but Keila believed in equality. Besides, few things were reliant on strength when it came to 29th century low gravity warfare so women could be equally suited to combat as men were.

Keila connected to the closest Spacenet node to watch the news. Her attack on the Aljadid Salam station had worked out exactly as she planned. Furious over the death of one of his sons, Ibrahim Rashid had demanded that House White released a public apology and compensated him.

House White had refused and had claimed to be innocent despite the damning amount of evidence against them. House Rashid had lost their patience and their forces had captured a House White luxury cruise spaceship, taking over 1000 passengers and crew as hostages. While no prominent House White family members were on the cruise, it was filled with other prominent American plutocrats and tensions were growing.

Tensions weren't easing when rumours spread about Rashid troops slitting the throats of their hostages.

Keila reflected that this could be the powder keg that drove House Rashid and House White to war and Terran Council into disarray. Keila would not sit around and wait, as she had a new objective. A group of House Muller spies had infiltrated a nearby independent trading post. These spies were there to sabotage the non-affiliated trader to drive them to bankruptcy and incorporate the trading post into the House Muller conglomerate.

While Keila didn't mind helping independent commerce in the solar system, she was after the House Muller operatives for another reason. Keila planned for the House Muller operatives to fall unconscious and then wake up on an attacked outpost belonging to House Cheng. This would convince House Cheng that the attack was House Muller's doing.

Having made up her plan, Keila disconnected from Space Net and entered a sleep pod. While she preferred natural sleep, sleep pods were useful when time was of the essence, and she needed to be rested.

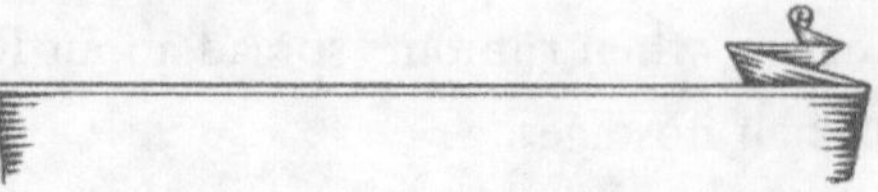

Chapter 154: Bjorn Muller Studies a Report About a Missing Espionage Team

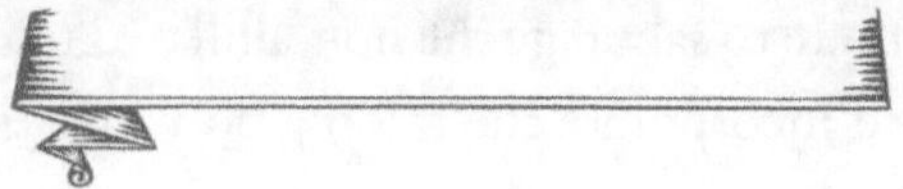

Bjorn logged out from the computer terminal, picked it up, and threw it into a wall. The last week had been a shit storm. His father had refused to leave until he withdrew his allegations against Alicia White and cancel the arrest order against her.

Later that day, he had studied the hologram images of the attack on the Aljadid Salam outpost and recognised some of the dead perpetrators to be part of Alicia White's group. He had not shared this information as House White was House Muller's ally and he did not want to escalate the situation. Besides he could smell the rat. There was no way a battle could have taken place in the way that the House Rashid report stated.

The attack shared many similarities with the attack on the Proxima Thule station six months earlier. The Aljadid Salam Outpost defenders seemed to have been unprepared for battle, their communications had ended abruptly, and there was the mystery with a lot of undamaged bullets in the middle of the corridors, that hadn't impacted with anything.

Perhaps, Alicia had attacked both installations, but if it was true, why did she leave her casualties behind on the Aljadid Salam outpost? Bjorn Muller knew that Alicia's group consisted of 15 operatives plus Alicia. She would not leave three dead agents on the battlefield exposing their identity. The purpose of a black operations team was to conduct operations without leading back to their employer. Leaving their dead would do the opposite.

Another strange fact was that there was no sign of Alicia anywhere, despite Bjorn cancelling the arrest order. He understood that Alicia and her team could have holed up somewhere while there was a warrant for their arrest, but why would they hide now? Why would they attack an insignificant outpost? Bjorn could only come up with two explanations:

1. Either Alicia had gone rogue and worked against the interest of her family by attacking outposts and leaving her dead troops as a trace back to them.
2. An unknown group had eliminated Alicia's group and were dumping their bodies on the scene to indict House White for the attacks.

Bjorn did not share his ideas in the report as some of the information was confidential, and he did not want to share with all the members of the Terran Council.

Another thing that bothered Bjorn, was the disappearance of his espionage team on the Freedom Markets trading post. The team had been there posing as asteroid mining surveyors between jobs, while they had come to sabotage the station to make it go bankrupt. Unknown assailants had kidnapped them in the middle of the night and then dragged them onto a stolen space shuttle. The worst part was that the assailants had been caught on camera and yet they were impossible to identify. They didn't match any personal identity records in the solar system and Bjorn could not pinpoint where they were from. He stared at one of the female attackers. He could swear that she was Keila, but she looked completely different.

Bjorn closed his eyes. He needed to get over Keila. He had been obsessed with her for too long. Bjorn had spent endless nights studying hologram videos of her. Officially he had needed to learn about the enemy, but he knew that that was only a made-up reason. Since Bjorn first met her, he had been obsessed, filled with dark twisted unrequited love. Things could have been different if he had acted differently on their first encounter. If he had been kind to her, instead of opting to dominate and rape her, she could have become his wife and the mother of his children. Instead, he had made her an enemy and caused her to start the insurrection by killing his grandfather Hans Muller.

Nothing of this mattered now. Keila was dead, and she had been dead for a year. Bjorn had seen the body himself, and he had been the one to proclaim her dead. Bjorn had to let her go from his mind. Bjorn wanted to cry over how he had fucked up his life, but he didn't. Bjorn, a high-ranking member of House Muller and one of the most influential persons in Europe wasn't going to cry. He was the epitome of success, and that was how he should live his life, portraying success through a hedonistic and carefree approach. Bjorn opened a bottle of expensive champagne and lined up a significant amount of cocaine. He summoned the female companions that his father had sent from Earth. Obeying his father certainly had its perks.

Unbeknownst to Bjorn, it was Keila he saw on the hologram videos from the abduction of his espionage team. She had used the Zetan External DNA changing technology to take the appearance of an Edenite woman who was of similar stature and body type as herself. Since the Edenites were not recorded in the official population registries of the solar system, this was the perfect way to confuse her enemies.

Chapter 155: Conflict Between House Cheng and House Muller.

Joachim Muller finished the conference call with the House Cheng leadership. There had been an armed robbery against one of House Cheng's storage facilities for valuable minerals, located halfway between the asteroid belt and Jupiter. The facility had been unguarded but full of security measures in place, to incapacitate intruders and keep them locked up until House Cheng security forces arrived.

When the Cheng forces had arrived, they had found that the vaults had been emptied and that several House Muller spies had been captured in the base's non-lethal traps. While the situation was not as dire as it was between House Rashid and House White, it was humiliating for Joachim to find his operatives caught in a bank robbery. Joachim had discussed the matter with Bjorn, who had confirmed that the men were the operatives who were abducted a couple of weeks earlier.

Joachim had seen the hologram videos of the operatives' abduction and believed that they were not stupid enough to rob a House Cheng vault. The problem was to convince House Cheng his faction's innocence. Joachim showed the video of his men being abducted, but how would he make the House Cheng leaders believe him? If the roles were reversed, he would not trust the House Cheng leaders if they showed him a similar video.

On the other hand, if Joachim apologised for the incident and offered to pay repatriations, he would admit guilt for what happened or at least admit that he couldn't control his operatives.

The situation was critical because of the current tensions between House Rashid and House White. Following the hostage situation,

House White had sent their troops to free the hostages. This attempt had gone wrong and had caused the cruise spaceship to explode, killing every hostage as they were choked by the freezing cold vacuum of space. As the chairman of the Terran Council, Joachim had worked around the clock for over a week to prevent a full-scale war between House Rashid and House White. Having his credibility destroyed by his agents participating in a bank robbery was the last thing that he needed.

Joachim decided to apologise and compensate House Cheng, claiming that his operatives had worked outside of his knowledge. His incompetent son Bjorn would then have to sort out this mess and find the ones responsible for the robbery. As Joachim was heading to the vacuum tube station to travel to the House Cheng headquarters in China, he was stuck in a fearsome mindset.

Who was the real force behind all the trouble and what was their end goal? Fear was growing within him, but he did not want to speak about it with anyone, not even his closest advisors. He was the chairman of the most powerful faction on Earth and the chairman of the Terran Council, an organisation that had ruled the solar system for over 600 years. As such he could not fear anyone!

Chapter 156: A Frozen Embryo and a Succession Plan.

Keila looked at the pregnancy test, and it confirmed what she had been suspecting; that her bout of morning sickness and declining fitness was a natural effect of a parasite infection that was crucial for the survival of the species.

But how had this happened? Metatron was over a hundred years old despite his younger looks and he shouldn't be fertile anymore. Thinking back, she had lost her memory due to intoxication a few months earlier, on an Edenite celebration, and she could have had a moment of indiscretion without remembering it. It was unlikely as she occasionally checked the minds of her Edenite subjects to check current talking points, and if she had sex with anyone on Eden it would have been one the most significant talking points. Fortunately, it was easy to find out the answer as she had access to everyone's DNA on Eden in the mainframe. She entered a full-body scanner, and it revealed that the 52-day old embryo she had in the womb was of Metatron's seed.

But this created another issue. Keila had other priorities than family life. If she were to tell him about the pregnancy, he would make another attempt at dissuading her from her insurrection plans to stay on Eden with him. While she could understand where he was coming from, she did not want to give up her rebellion to please him. The gods had led Keila this far, and there were so many people suffering from the injustices of the world. She had to follow through with what she had started.

Keila closed her eyes and she had a vision. The vision was of herself, Metatron and a girl that looked like her future daughter holding an adulthood ceremony on Eden. Keila opened her eyes and felt confused.

Had she come this far to give up her plans and become a mother instead? It didn't make any sense but then again, who was Keila to understand the divine plan? To be sure she closed her eyes and studied the vision again. It was the same vision still, but she noticed a crucial detail. The date and year on the cake. The date and year were 14 years and 7 months in the future, which didn't make sense since Edenite adulthood ceremonies was when the girl turned 13 years old. Hence the child in the vision would not be born for another year and seven months. Thus it could not be the child she was carrying in her belly.

Keila made up her mind. She would not kill the embryo, but she would not carry it either. Instead, Keila would suck out the embryo and keep the future baby in suspended animation for one year. If she were still alive in a year, she would quit the rebellion and focus on her motherhood. If not... She would have the child born in a synthetic womb. She wrote a message to Metatron with instructions that were encrypted with her safety signature that would open in one year. After finishing the letter, she ordered the full-body scanner to do the procedure for her. She woke up an hour later and she was met by Metatron.

Metatron:

- What were you doing in there for so long? Is there any problem with your health?

Keila:

- No, Metatron I am fine.
- I just can't tell you what I did in there.

Metatron said nothing and walked away. Keila looked at him as he left the room and felt guilty. He knew what she had done and she felt guilty for not consulting him. Now she didn't know how to bring it up. Dealing with emotional problems like she often did, Keila went to the shooting range to let the adrenaline clear her mind.

Chapter 157: Keila's Unique Genetics.

The human genome consists of a lot of genetic information that normally doesn't activate or fill any function in the human body. The residual DNA from ancient Zetan human hybrids was an example of this kind of DNA. Every human had traces of Zetan DNA in them and yet most of them had no telepathic ability, visions, or premonitions.

The Zetan DNA had been integrated into the human genome during two periods of history. The first round of Zetan DNA was induced into humanity 100,000 years ago when Zetan scientists travelled around the Milky Way Galaxy and produced a variety of species with intelligence and a soul. That program was cancelled when Zetan experts argued that increasing the intelligence of other species across the galaxy could lead to one of these species rising and destroying the Zetans. After cancelling the program, nothing happened for 90,000 years, and the Zetans forgot about it.

10,000 years ago, the Xenos started their attacks on the Zetans which started the multi-millennial war between the two species. The Zetans realised they did not have the numbers to take on the Xenos and they needed allies. That was where humanity came in. As humanity's deities, the Zetans commanded human fighters to fight the Xenos with advanced Zetan technology.

To have enough human fighters they needed humans to multiply faster. This was why the Zetans gave humanity the concept of civilisation based around agriculture. They did this by creating hybrids between humans and Zetans. These hybrids became prominent leaders and kings for humanity that advanced human technology and civilisation. As the Zetan/human hybrids, the Zetan DNA spread among humanity and in the generations that followed, everyone had a piece of Zetan DNA in themselves. This did not affect their abilities, as an individual needed to have the complete Zetan DNA sequence to have the unique Zetan skills of telepathy, premonition, and heightened intelligence.

Yahweh was the last Zetan to procreate with humans before the portal between Earth and the Divine Dimension was destroyed. Due to the aphrodisiac he ingested before going to Earth; Yahweh had a lot of offspring. While many of them became prominent but forgotten only one of them stood out, Jesus. Jesus, in turn, had a lot of children with various women before meeting his end, a detail that was left out as his disciples came from a monotheistic and monogamous background and did not want to promote polytheistic and polygamous teachings.

After the fall of Jesus, there would emerge a human with a full Zetan DNA sequence every few hundred years, and this individual would be incredibly gifted and special. The Zetans directed these persons towards scientific pursuits as they needed to progress humanities' science level if they ever were to activate the dormant portals between Earth and the Divine Dimension.

The last person before Keila who had an unusual Zetan DNA sequence was Jack Brown. Jack Brown was the scientist who had helped to build the Divine Detector Machine that transported Abraham's mind to the Divine Dimension 80 years earlier.

While this had been an amazing achievement, it had been a dead end as the technology to transport physical objects was different from the technology that Jack had developed. Jack's telepathic link with the Zetans was also too weak to enable them to communicate with him through the dimensions, so his only Zetan ability was his exceptionally high intelligence. As Jack Brown was so ahead of his time, the Divine Detection technology was still undiscovered by the rest of the Terran Houses 80 year later, as he and his group had been loyal to their words and had not disclosed the technology to mind-warp to another dimension.

With Keila, the Zetans had a slight problem. Despite her strong telepathic connection with the Zetans, she lacked the scientific mind to create a portal for physical movement between the dimensions from scratch. They did believe, however, that they could use her to activate the ancient Zetan portals that were hidden within pyramids on Earth.

The Zetans had intended for Keila to go back to Earth and use her heritage as the exiled Mahmoud Rashid's daughter to gain Terran citizenship, freedom, and resources to explore the pyramids and find the secret to activating the portals. This had failed when Bjorn Muller had not acted as Brahma had foreseen.

Brahma had set the plan in motion to have Keila crave for Earth so much so she would join a people smuggler that took her from Mars to Earth. Brahma had planned for this ship to be intercepted by Bjorn's spaceship, but then things fell apart. Instead of pursuing Keila with his good looks, wealth and Terran citizenship, Bjorn had gone feral and kidnapped and raped her instead, thus destroying Brahma's plan of peaceful love. For Brahma, this came as a shock. Brahma was the many-faced, all-seeing god, how could he have missed this? Another reason that Brahma had intended for Keila and Bjorn to fall for each other was that Bjorn had a high amount of residual Zetan DNA. That combined with Keila's complete Zetan DNA sequence would lead to very gifted and useful children.

The potential child of Keila and Bjorn could have become the ultimate human/ Zetan hybrid. Keila had 2 out of 3 complete Zetan DNA sequences for premonition and telepathy which gave her these abilities. She did not, however, have the full Zetan DNA sequence for intelligence, so she did not have superhuman intelligence. Bjorn, on the other hand, had high amounts of recessive Zetan DNA for high intelligence. Unfortunately, the lack of parental love had caused him to only care about hedonistic values. Bjorn's excessive drug use had destroyed his innate intelligence and talent. Regardless, Keila and Bjorn together could have given birth to a child with all the complete Zetan DNA sequences, creating a demi-god.

All of this had come to naught. Rangda was the villain behind Bjorn's terrible behaviour towards Keila. Rangda had used the fact that Bjorn had plenty of recessive Zetan DNA to subconsciously manipulate him into becoming a sadistic rapist. This had thwarted Brahma's original plan of genuine love and peaceful mannerisms.

After the unfortunate incident between Keila and Bjorn, Brahma had lost his direction and believed that he was meant to have Keila start an insurrection against the Terran Council. He had kept her alive, but he had not got closer to returning to the regular dimension. Brahma had not realised, until the very end, what a threat Rangda posed to the Zetans and how she had played him.

Rangda studied Keila from her location in the Divine Dimension. It was fortunate that she had stalled the opening of the portals when the Zetans almost got there. At that time, Rangda had not been powerful enough to fight the Zetans, but now with Brahma's soul absorbed by the corrupted Zeto Crystals, her power had grown.

The war that Keila was involved in was a complication for Rangda's plans to get Keila to Earth, to activate the portals. But she would have to do it the hard way.

Chapter 158: The Zetans Are Fearful After Brahma's Death

Zeus, Ra and Odin were looking at the Zetans that had assembled for an urgent meeting. There was 300 of them which was a smaller number than the previous year. That was to be expected. Stuck in the timelessness of the Divine Dimension hungry, thirsty, and yet immortal, their numbers had thinned out throughout the years as many of them had committed suicide as the only way out. It had been over 2000 years since the portal to Earth was destroyed, hopelessness drove many of them over the edge. There was still a lot more than 300 Zetans left in the Divine Dimension, but many of them were in deep meditation to avoid suffering, and thus they ignored the summon. Zeus didn't blame them.

Zeus thought of Brahma, and he shivered with fear. Brahma had walked off and killed himself like many others before him. But there was something with Brahma's death that did not make sense. Unlike the others, Brahma had no reason to kill himself, at least not now. Brahma had been convinced that Keila was the one they had been waiting for. That Keila was the one to open the portals and set them free. Even if something had happened that made Brahma re-evaluate Keila's usefulness, there was no reason for suicide. Keila was still alive, and even if she was not the chosen one, human life was very short, so Brahma might as well have waited.

The way that Brahma had died terrified Zeus. Most Zetans who walked away and killed themselves just faded away. It was a peaceful transition from life to death so that the soul could move on. Brahma's death was different. He had moved on in a state of fear, and it seemed like his soul had shattered into fragments. This prospect terrified Zeus. Not wanting for fear to spread among the assembly, Zeus started the meeting with an issue of practical character.

Zeus:

- I am sad to inform you about Brahma's death. He walked off and killed himself, like so many before him.

Upset chatter was spreading among the crowd after this announcement and eventually a lesser Zetan, Altjira called out.

Altjira:

- Stop lying Zeus. We all know Brahma didn't kill himself. Something terrible caught up with him and devoured his soul.

Zeus was going to speak, but Ra beat him to it:

- Don't speculate about things you don't know, Altjira. While the circumstances regarding Brahma's death are suspicious, we can't do anything about it. All we know is that he was very far away when he died, but without knowing the details, we cannot find him.

- Besides, if there is something evil and powerful out to get us, we should not split up and look for Brahma separately.

Zeus added in. He said:

- I agree with Ra, and besides, we have another issue. When Brahma died, we lost our connection to Keila. Without that connection, we cannot guide her to open the portals. We must utilise our collective psionic power to bind her to me.

Murmuring broke out among the Zetans, but no one rejected the proposal. While Zeus was not famed for having as much foresight as Brahma, there was no one else who wanted the responsibility for the future of their species. The Zetans gathered in a circle to initiate the ritual that would bind Keila's mind to Zeus. The ritual failed, and Zeus fell to the ground screaming in pain with his face burnt.

Zeus:

- I could not connect with her. I was blocked by the tormented fragments of Brahma's soul. I saw Rangda; she must be behind this!!

Zeus vomited up a lot of blood and died. Odin and Ra ran up to his lifeless body, but there was nothing they could do for him. Filled with rage and grief, Odin shouted out:

- To arms, fellow Zetans. We march to Rangda's prison at once; the witch must pay for what she has done!!

Determined, they got up, gathered their equipment, and set out for their very long walk to Rangda's prison. They left a dozen of them to form a vanguard in case the portal was opened, but the remaining 280 Zetans marched to Rangda's jail.

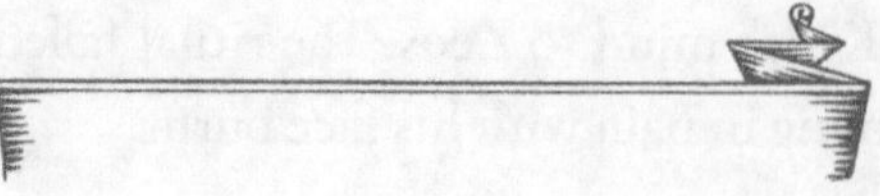

Chapter 159: Markus Bauer's Dilemma.

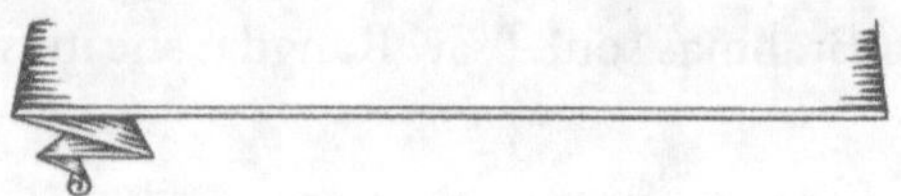

Markus Bauer was preparing his presentation for Keila and her leadership team. He had reverse-engineered the Zetan technologies so that they could be mass-produced with current technologies. Although the reverse-engineered products were inferior to their Zetan counterparts, they had the advantage of being inexpensive and fast to make. As they needed many gadgets to give to their allies, they could not use the particle replicator machine as every unit made that way was energy demanding and costly to produce. To make exact copies on the molecular level was also slower than other methods of manufacturing.

Markus Bauer refused to reverse engineer the Divine Technology, for mass production. While the other Zetan technologies were gadgets that were used for warfare they did not change anything. Humans had always developed better weapons to outwit and destroy each other. If Keila and her rebels wanted to kill her enemies, it was natural that she wanted the best weapons at her disposal, and Markus had no ethical problems with providing them to her.

The Divine Technology microchips were different. They gave the ruling classes complete control over the enslaved masses below them. This transformed the essence of humanity from individuals to slaves under a hive mind. Markus would not release this evil to the world.

Markus Bauer entered the boardroom where Keila, Metatron and the ruling council of Eden had convened. He was relieved when Keila looked at him with a smile. She raised her glass of wine and spoke.

- Cheers to our chief scientist, Markus Bauer, for his excellent services to our cause. I already know everything that you are going to say today, but please hold your presentation to fill the others in.

Markus felt irritated. He didn't like that his boss/captor spied on his mind. However, what else could he expect? Markus drank some water and started his presentation:

- Dear delegates. It pleases me to announce that my team and I have reverse engineered Zetan technologies so that they can be mass-produced by us and our Martian allies. While the reverse-engineered versions are not as good as the originals, they are superior to the current weapons of our Martian peers.

Keila interrupted him:

- While I am happy with your breakthroughs, I am not satisfied that you haven't solved one of our most significant issues. How are we going to communicate with our Martians friends uninterrupted and secure from Terran spies?

Markus:

- I don't know how to answer that question, Ms Eisenstein. My team and I have not been working on our communications technologies. You are not letting us communicate with the outside world, out of fear that we would betray you to the Terran Council.

Keila:

- Your refusal to reverse-engineer the divine technology chips has set us back on the communications front. I intend to use the technology as a way of secure communication. I am not intending to use it to control and dominate.

Markus:

- And yet you spied on me. Whatever you intend to do; you are never going to resist the urge to use the technology to spy on the followers.

Keila found herself lost for words. She had spoken herself into a corner and Markus had been brave enough to expose her hypocrisy. She swore to herself and drank some water to moisten her dry throat. Metatron joined in on the discussion:

- Markus is right. While the Divine Technology is a tool and not inherently evil, it can be used for evil. I saw it myself when I served under Abraham.

Keila spat out her water and scorned Metatron:

- So, you are siding with Markus now? I am very disappointed with you, Metatron.

Metatron:

- Quite the opposite Keila. I am siding with humanity and the real you. The Keila I know, values individual freedoms. Yet you propose that we mass-produce technology that could enslave them. It doesn't make sense, does it?

Keila:

- So how the fuck, do I coordinate a rebellion without a reliable means of communication? I can't use Space Net because it's so insecure I might as well publish my every move on the morning news. And I don't have hundreds of secure communication satellites, unlike the Terrans.

Metatron:

- There must be a better way to beat the Terran Council than installing a worse tyranny than theirs. If there isn't a better way, we better leave the things the way they are.

Keila realised that Metatron and Markus were right. She felt ashamed over what she had become. Keila had come to Eden to stop Abraham's tyranny, and now a year later, she was proposing to spread the menace all over the solar system. Keila knew that she hadn't been thinking clearly. Just because SHE would never use divine technology to tyrannise the population, it didn't mean that it was a good idea to spread the technology. If she was to die there was a risk that someone would take her place and use it to instate tyranny, like Abraham did before.

Keila:

- You are right, Metatron. We are not going to develop something that can be used for tyranny. We'll find another way.

- I declare this meeting concluded. Return to work, ladies and gentlemen.

As everyone left, Keila stared out at the vastness of space. She felt at a loss what to do and decided to do nothing for a while.

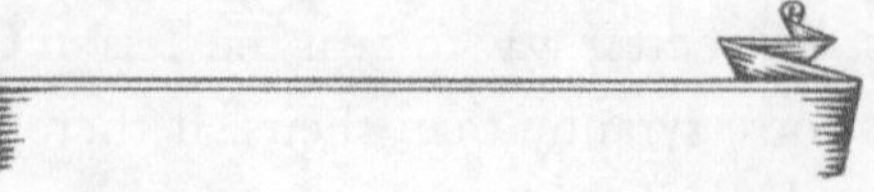

Chapter 160: Keila Has a Nightmare and Reconciles with Metatron.

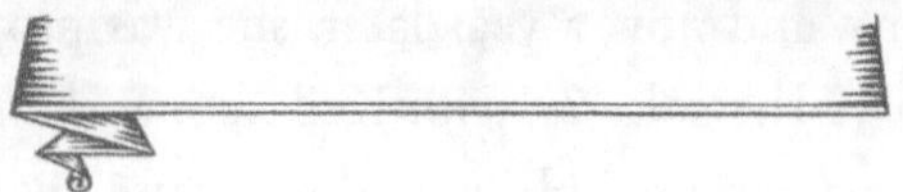

Keila was restless and had very vivid dreams. *"He's holding you back,"* a voice said. It followed up with *"Kill him, and mankind will succumb to your will."* Keila saw images of Metatron lying in a pool of blood. The perspective changed, and she could see herself looking out from a penthouse at Earth. She recognised the location and knew where it was. The view was from the penthouse level of Europeum towers in Hansstadt in the European Alps.

Keila saw herself together with Bjorn Muller and several children. That didn't make any sense. That creep had kept her as a sex slave, and he had been responsible for killing her after she had killed Hans Muller.

Finally, Keila saw a blueprint for a divine technology. It was modified, but she was unsure on how it had happened. *"This is the chip that you need. It is the human chip that you can mass-produce with your technology,"* the voice said. *"Show yourself"* Keila screamed at the voice, but it didn't answer. Keila felt that the owner of the voice tried to disconnect from her mind, but she wouldn't let it. Using all her mental strength Keila got a very short glimpse of Rangda.

The source of the voice didn't look at all like the benevolent old man she had seen in her visions before. Instead, she saw a terrifying female witch. Did the voice belong to an evil monster? But Keila knew that appearances could be deceiving. All the leaders of the Terran council were picture perfect and looked friendly and charming on television. And yet most of them were sadistic sociopaths who couldn't care less about how the poor people got hurt, as long as they could live in luxury.

Keila needed to talk. She missed Metatron and she knew that her actions had made him feel betrayed. Metatron wanted to focus on Eden and the Edenites. He wanted to look after and improve the lives of Eden's inhabitants. Keila was focused on how to fight the Terran Council and free her Martians brethren from its oppression.

Their goals were not compatible, and yet Keila needed Metatron. She hadn't told him about her vision, as a matter of fact, she hadn't discussed the foetus with him at all. Yet he knew, and things had changed. He was not sleeping with her anymore, and Keila wondered if he slept at all. Keila decided to stop overthinking and talk to Metatron. She visited him in the command centre where he was overlooking a process.

Keila:

- You don't sleep much these days.

Metatron:

- I only need to sleep two hours a day using the accelerated sleeping pod.

Keila:

- But you used to sleep eight hours a day next to me. Getting natural sleep is good for you.

Metatron:

- I can't afford to waste that much time. My people need me, and there are lots of things I need to do.

Keila:

- You can't afford to, or you don't want to?

Metatron didn't answer; instead, he turned to the computer terminal.

Keila:

- The visions that used to guide me don't make any sense to me. They have changed, and their source has changed. Please help me find my way.

Metatron:

- Why do you ask me now? You didn't ask before you killed our baby.

Keila:

- I didn't kill her! I put her in suspended animation. My vision told me that she would have her adulthood ceremony in 15 years, but the adulthood ceremony is at the age of 13. Hence she is supposed to be born in two years.

Metatron:

- And it never crossed your mind that your vision was bull-shit?

Keila:

- Oh Jack, don't say that. You know that my visions are real.

Metatron:

- Don't call me Jack. That is my Terran name, and I haven't been to Earth for 80 years.

- When I lived on Earth, I was carrying out assassinations for Abraham Goldstein.

- Eden is my destiny. This is where I can redeem myself and find peace.

Keila:

- Oh yes, I keep forgetting how old you are.

Metatron:

- Yes, it's easy to forget my age when admiring my baby face.

For the first in a while, Keila saw Metatron smile. It was a tired, resigned smile but still a smile. Despite Metatron being over 100 years old, he looked young. This was because he spent most of his life cryogenically frozen between missions and had also exposed himself to a significant amount of DNA regeneration to keep him in peak condition.
Keila:

- Don't worry about your age, you got another good 100 years in the tank.

Metatron:

- I'll probably outlive you, my young lady.

He winked at her to take away the seriousness of the joke.
Keila:

- So, are we back on good terms?

Metatron:

- Sure. If you tell me why you approached me today, after a month of silence.

Keila:

- I had the strangest dream. You were dead, I was raising a family with Bjorn Muller, and I saw the human chip in its reverse-engineered form.

Metatron:

- That's good.

Keila:

- Pardon me?

Metatron:

- You wouldn't have told me about the dream if you intended it to come true. Thus, you are no longer slavishly following your visions making them become self-fulfilling prophecies.

Keila:

- I guess. So, what do you suggest I do?

Metatron:

- Well, let's free Mars, shall we? No point beating around the bush.

Keila:

- Okay, handsome, but first come with me to bed. The Eden-ites can wait.

After this Metatron joined Keila to bed and the two of them were reconciled for now.

Chapter 161: Keila Finalises the Reverse-Engineered Human Chip Blueprint.

Keila was watching the news. The conflict between House Rashid and House White had erupted into a series of full-on proxy wars throughout the solar system. Although the news report did not mention the affiliations between Rashid, White, and the warring factions, Keila knew that these unrelated regional conflicts were, part of something bigger, a full-on battle between House White and House Rashid. So far, she had not achieved what she wanted though, although Rashid and White were fighting it was her fellow Martians that died and her home planet that was affected. Infighting alone would not crush the Terran Council; she needed to mount a full-scale attack to beat them.

Keila studied the blueprint of the reverse-engineered human chip that she had drawn from memory with a blueprint drawing software. Keila was amazed at her engineering ability. Despite having no knowledge of engineering, she had drawn it exactly as she had remembered it.

Keila was hesitant on how to proceed. She knew that she had promised Metatron and Markus Bauer to not mass-produce the human chip and spread the technology. However, if she spread the technology, she could accomplish two things

1. She would have a secure communications channel. The divine technology microchips operated on unique wavelengths, and no-one knew how they worked. Thus, it would be impossible for the Terran Council to intercept and interpret her signals.

2. Introducing a new religion could unite Mars against their oppressors. The Martians were divided and the Terrans could

turn them against each other. If she introduced a new religion with enough followers that could unite the Martians against their Terran overlords. What better way to launch a new religion than to mass-produce human chips and spread them among the population? While other religions required faith, she could transport the messages straight to her followers.

If the Terrans got their hands on a human chip, it would be useless for them. Without the angel chip and god chip, the human chip didn't do anything. Keila would not spread the angel chips and god chips on Mars, and she would not reverse-engineer them for mass production.

Keila made up her mind. She would travel to the Olympus Republic on Mars and arrange a secret meeting with President Hellas Petrakis. Using the outer layer external DNA modifier, Keila changed her face to that of a female Edenite, but not the same looks she had used when kidnapping the House Muller operatives. She left a message to Metatron that she would be gone for a while but she did not further reveal her intentions. She asked one of her Edenite aides to fly her to one of the transport hubs that ran transports between the asteroid mining stations and Mars

A day later, Keila boarded a transport bound for the Olympus Republic. Keila leaned back and expected a few quiet weeks in space. Things would not turn out that way as the notorious space pirate Morgan Henry had the ship in his sight.

Chapter 162: Rangda Fills Keila With Enough Power to Take Out an Entire Pirate Crew.

Morgan Henry prepared to board the passenger ship that took Keila from the asteroid belt to Mars. He and his crew were looking forward to another round of violence against innocent defenceless people. This was the third time he was attacking the passenger ships this month.

Morgan Henry's attacks on passenger ships were not a random occurrence. Although the vessel did not contain anything of value and their passengers were poor Martian workers, attacking them served a purpose.

Morgan Henry was secretly working for House Cheng, and they paid him to attack passenger ships that transported workers to House Muller territory. This was payback for the robbery, where Keila had robbed a House Cheng rare elements vault and made it look like House Muller operatives were behind the theft. While House Cheng had accepted House Muller's apology and compensation payments, this was their unofficial response. By targeting and killing House Muller workers, they weakened their enemy.

Morgan Henry prepared to board the ship, it would have been easier to just blow it up from a distance, but that would have caused suspicion. Pirate attacks were to steal and rob. Blowing up ships from afar wouldn't generate any loot and wouldn't make any sense. He and his 20-man pirate crew drank a concoction that would make them violent and merciless. They attached grappling hooks and an airlock to the passenger ship, before blowing up its doors and storming the ship.

Keila woke up with a twitch when she heard the explosion. She realised that something was amiss, and she was thankful that she had opted for a private cabin instead of cryogenically sleeping the duration of the trip to Mars. Keila opened the door and released a few automatic miniature drones to get an overview of the situation. What she saw on her monitor frightened her. The ship was under attack by a large group of pirates led by the infamous mass-murderer Morgan Henry. They were busy killing and robbing passengers on the lower level, and it was only a matter of time until they moved up to her level.

Keila felt fear engulfing her. She had experienced many desperate battles in the past, but she had never been this outnumbered before. Despite her Zetan gadgets, she did not think she would be able to take on that many pirates on her own. She tried to figure out where to hide and she swore at herself for not learning the floor plan.

Keila heard the voice. It was the voice of the witchlike monster who had been guiding her visions for the last few months. It said, *"I can make you powerful enough to kill them all"*.

Keila:

- Kill them all? Are you kidding me?

Rangda:

- No. I can give you the power to get you out of this mess. Let go off control for a while.

Keila was tentative to the offer. She didn't trust the voice, and she had seen the being that it originated from. It looked like the manifestation of evil. Keila woke up from her thoughts when she heard tormented screams of pain from the cabin next to hers. She realised that she had to trust the voice in her head.

Keila:

- Okay. I'll give up control for the next five minutes.

Rangda:

- Excellent. Hee Hee Heeeeeeee!!!!

Keila felt how she lost control of her body. Her first impulse was to fight back for control, but she realised the deal she had made with the voice. Her sight changed to infrared, and her vision became narrower but broader. She could feel how the adrenaline was pumping through her veins maximising her blood pressure and heart rate. The door opened, and the amazed pirate didn't have time to react before Keila jumped and cut him in half with her plasma knife. She pulled out his beating heart and have a big bite before throwing it away. Keila was shocked by what she saw, but she let the voice remain in control.

Moving with superhuman speed, she moved to the end of the corridor, hitting the pirate around the corner with a knife to the throat. She then rushed through the lobby where four pirates where standing. She dropped a proximity mine among them and getting away before the mine blew up the four pirates who had the time to react. The sound of the explosion alerted the other pirates that something was amiss.

With haste Keila booby-trapped all the doors to the lobby with the fallen pirates' guns, she then quickly made her way over to the pirate ship and set an explosive device in its engine room before heading back to the passenger ship where an additional two pirates had fallen to her traps. She then hid in an air vent and watched all the pirate running back to their ship in panic, until Morgan Henry was the only one left on the passenger ship.

Keila jumped down and knocked Morgan to the ground. She disconnected the airlock between the ships. Baffled Morgan Henry asked:

- Who are you?

Keila hissed:

- Rangda, remember my name, pitiful human.

Morgan got to his feet and reached for his pistol, but he wasn't fast enough. Keila punched him, with a punch strong enough to penetrate his body and pulled out his heart. She then held it over her head and crushed it with her hand, licking the blood that dropped on her mouth. Seconds later the explosive device at the pirate ship went off, destroyed the pirate ship, and killed the pirates on it.

Keila regained control of her body. *"Trust in Rangda, and you'll be fine,"* the voice said before disconnecting with her.

Keila went down on her knees and vomited from the shock of having her body possessed by another being. She screamed in pain, and some of the survivors came to her assistance.

Survivor:

- Oh my god! Are you hurt?

- We need to call the Terran Council forces for immediate assistance and backup.

Keila:

- No, don't. I repeat DO NOT involve the Terran Council.

- Look after my wounds and take me straight to the Olympus Republic on Mars.

The survivors on the ship did not dare to do anything else than comply with Keila's request. A few days later, she arrived on Mars in a stable condition as her wounds were only superficial.

Chapter 163: A Cold Welcome at the Olympus republic.

The Olympus Republic was a nation on Mars that consisted of a group of underground settlements. It was one of the safer and more prosperous regions on Mars and was technically a democracy, although in reality it was controlled by House Muller. Built on the high volcanic plains around Olympus Mons, it was safe from the raiders and warlords on the ground level. Olympus Mons was over 20 kilometres up, so it was impossible to get there except via air transport and the Olympus Republic had excellent air defences that would deter any raiders from even trying. The drawback of living on the high-altitude volcanic plains was that it was always freezing cold outside and the outside air was too thin to be breathable without breathing aids.

Keila had arrived at The Olympus Republic to meet with President Hellas Petrakis whom she knew was sympathetic to Martian independence and self-determination. Although his nation was a vassal of House Muller, Hellas Petrakis was not fond of them. He had merely aligned with the faction he hated the least. It was almost impossible to survive as an independent nation on Mars, so most countries and regions aligned with a Terran Council member for "protection".

Keila stepped out of the shuttle that had taken her from the inter-planetary passenger terminal in orbit to her preferred location in the Olympus Republic. As she landed Olympic Republic police arrested her. Having seen security footage of Keila butchering Morgan Henry's crew, they put her in heavy chains and kept her in place with an invisible nanotechnology force field. They transported her to a secure holding facility awaiting further instructions.

The Olympus police tried to interrogate Keila, but she requested to speak to President Hellas and refused to talk to anyone else. This was a risky move, but it worked because the Olympus police commissioner was grateful that she had killed Morgan Henry, who had killed hundreds of Olympus Republic citizens in the last month. The police commissioner contacted Hellas, who agreed to meet with the mysterious female prisoner.

Together with the police commissioner Hellas walked into the interrogation room where Keila was chained to the wall.

Hellas Petrakis:

- I am president Petrakis.
- You requested to meet me.
- Why?
- Who are you?

Keila:

- That depends. Is that man a friend or a House Muller spy?

Hellas:

- He is Andrew Bello, the commissioner of police and a true patriot to the Olympus Republic.

Keila:

- Excellent. Deactivate all cameras and microphones in the room, and I will talk.

Hellas:

- I am the president here; I decide what happens.

Keila:

- Yet I was the one who ended Morgan Henry's terror. You should hear me out.

Hellas:

- AI, deactivate cameras and microphones in sector B5
- Okay, it's done. Now talk.

Keila:

- It's me, Keila. I have found a way to defeat the Terran Council and bring freedom to our people.

Hellas:

- That is absurd! Keila Eisenstein is dead, and besides, you don't look like her. Furthermore, you don't match her DNA sequence.

Keila:

- That's because I used Alien technology to change the DNA of the outer layers of my body to give me a new appearance.

Hellas:

- Is this a joke? You are wasting my valuable time with these fairy tales.
- If it's that easy just change back.

Keila:

- I am not going to do that now. You see once I revert to my usual face, I cannot change my face again without the Zetan outer layer external DNA modifier. Walking around as Keila Eisenstein is going to attract unwanted attention.

- Take a blood sample if you want. That is going to confirm my story.

Hellas took a blood sample from Keila and analysed it. He stared at her in disbelief. How was it possible to have one set of DNAs on the outside and a different genome on the inside?
Hellas:

- Who are you?
- What is going on?

Keila:

- I told you already. I am Keila.

- I came across technology created by an ancient alien race called the Zetans. They were the species that created mankind. With their technology, I will lead us to freedom.

- Unchain me, and I will show you something.

Hellas exchanged a look with Andrew, who shook his head. Despite this Hellas released Keila from her chains.
Keila:

- Now tell your police commissioner to shoot me.

The police commissioner had no problem following that order and fired a burst of four shots towards Keila. The bullets were stopped by the Zetan Ballistic Energy Absorber and dropped to the ground. The police commissioner was going to shoot again, but Keila kicked the pistol out his hand before he had the chance.
Keila:

- The device is battery operated; don't waste my battery.

After this Hellas was convinced that Keila was the real deal and they set up a secret meeting with his cabinet to develop their war strategy.

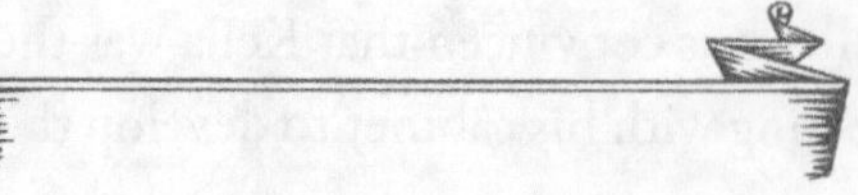

Chapter 164: Bjorn Muller Investigates the Pirate Attacks and Confirms His Fears.

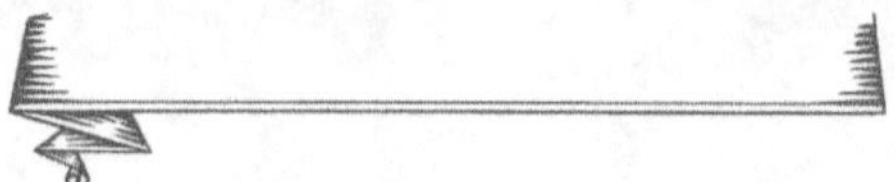

Bjorn was putting down his tablet. These bloody pirate attacks were putting a strain on the House Muller mining operations in the asteroid belt. Although no mining station had been attacked since Proxima Thule, enterprises were still struggling. The reason was that pirates had started attacking passenger ships with workers for no apparent reason. House Muller had lost hundreds of skilled workers in these attacks, and thousands of workers had refused to come back to work due to fear of the pirate attacks.

What frustrated Bjorn the most was that he couldn't do a lot about the pirate attacks as he was low on ships and manpower. Because of the damn conflict between House White and House Rashid, they had withdrawn their support from the Terran Council's security forces as they refused to work together. House Bolivar had never been interested in Space Colonization and focused on developing their territories in South America. Finally, House Cheng did not seem interested in dealing with the pirate scourge, which had left the job to House Muller themselves. While House Muller was dominant, they were not influential or wealthy enough to fund peacekeeping of the entire solar system themselves. Hence Bjorn had been forced to attend several press conferences the last month explaining why they hadn't been able to deal with the pirate scourge. Bjorn's intercom rang, and Captain Adal Schneider entered Bjorn's office.

Adal:

- There has been another pirate attack.

Bjorn:

- More bad news every fucking day. Tell me some good news for once!

Adal:

- I was just getting to that. The pirate attack failed, and the infamous pirate Morgan Henry is dead.

Bjorn:

- Music to my ears!
- How did this happen?

Adal:

- Watch for yourself.

Adal transmitted the video footage of an unknown woman assassinating Morgan Henry and his men. Bjorn stared at the footage. This woman reminded him of Keila, and yet he said nothing about it to Adal. It was a silly thought; the woman was not Keila, so why did his mind bring it up?

Bjorn:

- Impressive. I don't know if we shall reward this woman for killing a wanted mass-murderer and his pirate group or if we should kill her as she could pose a threat to us with superhuman abilities like that.

- Who is she?

Adal:

- We don't know her identity. Her DNA is not in our database, and our facial recognition system doesn't recognise her.

Bjorn:

- Was this woman involved in the disappearance of our espionage team on the Freedom Markets trading post?

Adal:

- I thought the same thing, but as it turns out. No.

Bjorn:

- I see. Where is the attacked ship? I would like to study the scene myself.

Adal:

- It's docked at Mars 4th interplanetary passenger terminal. We will pass its orbit in one hour.

Bjorn:

- Very well. Let's go there ourselves and "assist" our Martian colleagues. Gather a platoon and meet me at the shuttle.

Adal:

- Yes, sir.

An hour later Bjorn, Adal and their 30 bodyguards took a shuttle from the Phobos base to the passenger terminal to investigate the attacked ship. It was essential to come in force to show the Martian investigators who were in charge.

Mars had 24 interplanetary passenger terminals each in geostationary orbit over a specific place, each covering one timezone. Every planet had a similar setup of orbiting interplanetary passenger terminals, as the spaceship that travelled between worlds were large and difficult to land on the planets. Thus, smaller shuttle ships took interplanetary passengers between the surface and the passenger terminals.

Bjorn and his group arrived at the scene, and they spoke with the Olympus Republic officer in charge, before sending him back to Mars. Bjorn then spoke to the captain of the attacked ship, Jonas Newton.

Bjorn:

- Captain. Tell me what happened.

Jonas Newton:

- Pirates attacked us, four days ago. They threatened to blow up our ship with their laser cannons if we didn't let them board.

- We had to let them board, as our ship is unarmed.

- I thought they were going to rob us, but instead, they stormed the ship and killed anyone they could find.

- Suddenly, this mysterious woman emerged from her cabin and killed all the pirates. She had superhuman speed and strength.

Bjorn:

- Yes, I have seen the footage, captain.
- Why didn't you alert the Terran Council of what happened?

Jonas:

- We were going to, but our mysterious friend insisted that we took her to Mars before alerting the authorities.

Bjorn:

- Mysterious?! Didn't you check her identification before allowing her on your vessel?

Jonas:

- We must have slipped up along the way.

Bjorn:

- No, this wasn't a slip-up. You looked the other way and allowed this unregistered passenger to travel on your vessel. As you know, all interplanetary travellers have to be registered with the Terran Council. Non-compliance is a severe offence. Is there any way we can identify this woman?

Jonas:

- I...

- The woman was treated for minor wounds at the medical bay. There are some of her bloody bandages in the bins there.

Bjorn:

- Excellent. Your helpfulness will be considered during your trial.
- Adal!

Adal:

- Yes, Rear Admiral.

Bjorn:

- Arrest Jonas and his whole crew.

While Adal and his men were rounding Jonas' crew, Bjorn walked up to the medical bay and examined the bloody rags and bandages with a

DNA scanner. Most of the blood was from foreign sources, but eventually, a name came that petrified Bjorn Muller. The name was Keila Eisenstein.

While Bjorn couldn't be certain that Keila was the mystery woman he instinctively knew it. Burdened by the realisation, he said nothing and returned to the base on Phobos.

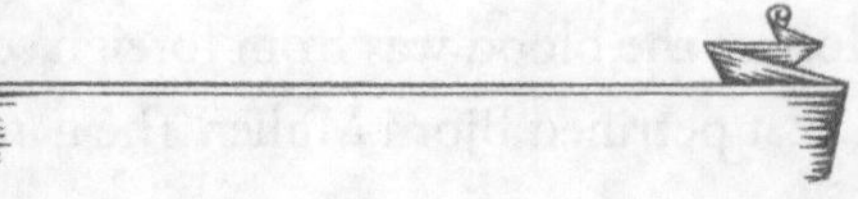

Chapter 165: Bjorn Muller Meets with Hellas Petrakis.

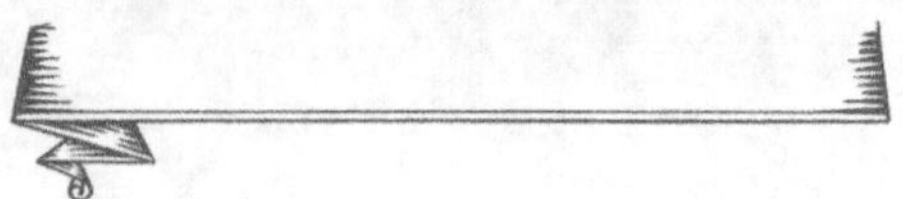

Bjorn was unsure of how to approach the fact that Keila was alive and that she had changed her appearance. If he announced that Keila was alive, he would look like an idiot for declaring her dead in the first place. But if he didn't announce that Keila was alive, she would cause more trouble.

What baffled Bjorn was not that she could change her looks. Plastic surgery was plentiful and readily available in the 29th century, but that she could change her DNA signature to make her unrecognisable for security cameras. Security cameras had DNA detection capabilities, as a safeguard against plastic surgery.

Bjorn was certain that House Muller didn't have any technologies that could mask an agent's DNA signature. It was unlikely that the primitive savages on Mars would have access to advanced technology. So where had Keila accessed this technology? Eden was her last known location and, but all the intelligence reports about Eden indicated that Eden was home to a group of cultists, that pretended to live during the Bronze Age.

Bjorn took a breath. His main priority was to stop Keila before rumours of his humiliating failure would spread. Bjorn contacted Hellas Petrakis via the hologram machine. After a while, Hellas showed up on the platform in front of him.

Hellas:

- Greetings, Rear Admiral Muller. How may I be of assistance?

Bjorn:

- We need to meet today at 3PM. I'll come by your office, don't be late.

Bjorn then hung up on Hellas. Hellas was House Muller's puppet. As such there was no reason to organise meetings when it was convenient for him. Instead, Bjorn Muller disrespected Hellas to keep him in place.

A few hours later, Bjorn landed and he was greeted by Hellas in the Presidential Palace reception area. While the lobby was luxurious by Martian standards, it looked destitute compared to Europeum Towers in Hansstadt. Bjorn ignored Hellas and walked straight into Hellas office. Hellas came after him subserviently.

Hellas:

- Rear Admiral Muller, you are missing out on the great food and refreshments that we organised for you in the reception area.

Bjorn:

- How thoughtful of you to look after my bodyguards, but I prefer to eat real food.

Hellas:

- Objection noted. We will try to satisfy your tastes better next time.

Bjorn:

- Don't bother; I wouldn't come here to socialise.

Hellas:

- So, Bjorn, why are you here?

Bjorn:

- I need to meet with the extraordinary woman that dealt with Morgan Henry. I heard she was detained here.

Hellas:

- Yes. She was detained here for questioning. I spoke with her myself.

Bjorn:

- So, where is she?

Hellas:

- She was cleared of any wrongdoing and she was free to go. She left earlier today.

Bjorn:

- Cleared of any wrongdoing? She stopped the attack from being reported to the authorities! She travelled between planets without proper identification!

Hellas:

- Those are not Olympic Republic laws, nor did it happen within our jurisdiction.

- If you wanted her arrested, you could have sent a request. We cannot detain people without a reason.

Bjorn felt angry and frustrated. Was Hellas Petrakis playing him for a fool? Bjorn realised that he hadn't been the friendly to Hellas and that he could expect the Puppet president to be obstinate. Bjorn was doubtful whether he should escalate the issue with Hellas or not.

Bjorn knew through his forensic examination that the mystery woman, was the infamous terrorist Keila Eisenstein, who he had declared dead a year earlier. But no one else knew that Keila was alive, and the last thing Bjorn did not want people to find out that she was alive. Rumours about Keila's resurgence would embarrass him and act as a beacon for the Martian resistance.

Hellas:

- So why did you come, Bjorn? What is this woman to you? High ranking officials don't come down here for migration matters.

Bjorn:

- That is correct. I am here to investigate her because of her immense capabilities.

Hellas:

- I see.

- Well, being talented and capable of looking after oneself, is not a crime in the Olympus Republic, so I am afraid I cannot do more to assist you.

Bjorn:

- Well, that's unfortunate.

- I might as well join you for the food and refreshments. I am sure the food and beverage cost a lot by your standards.

Hellas:

- We would be honoured to have you and your men dining with us.

Bjorn:

- Excellent. If you provide us with some female entertainment, I can put in a good word for you with my father.

Hellas:

- That is very gracious of you. I am sure we can have it organised.

After that Bjorn and Hellas left the office to enjoy dinner at the reception area of the Olympus Republic presidential palace.

Chapter 166: Rangda Kills Off Isolated Zetans and Increases Her Power.

Rangda was riding a Xeno leading her group of other Xenos. Being a Zetan and Xeno hybrid, she was smaller than the big and bulky Xenos and could use them as riding animals. Although she could keep up with them, there was no reason to do so. She needed to conserve her energy for more important tasks.

When Rangda killed Zeus with a psionic shock, she learned something valuable. She learned the location of a bunch of Zetans hibernating in deep meditation throughout the Divine Dimension. She would find them and kill them off for two reasons.

Firstly, she wanted to stop them from waking up and joining the Zetans that would try to stop her. More importantly, she wanted to shatter and absorb their souls using the corrupted dark Zeto crystals. This was imperative to her plan; without her corrupted Zeto crystals her psionic powers were not impressive as she was only half Zetan. With the crystals fully charged, she was stronger than anyone else.

Rangda saw a group of three Zetans a couple of kilometres away. They were awake and had detected her troops. While this was not optimal as she had preferred to kill them off when they were asleep, she had to attack.

Rangda would have to sit this fight out and let her Xeno soldiers do the fighting for her. When Rangda killed Zeus, he had counter blasted her which had caused massive internal bleeding in her brain, but not enough to kill her. The migraine caused by the blast was excruciating. Zeus had stronger psionic powers than Rangda but she had killed him when he was weak and unprepared. When Zeus tried to bind himself to

Keila, he had lowered his defences and Rangda could get a lethal surprise attack in.

Rangda hissed out to her troops in the Xeno language:

- Attack them, but don't kill them. I'll finish them off.

20 minutes later Rangda arrived at the battlefield. There laid dozens of slain Xenos, but on the flipside, the three Zetans were drawing their dying breaths. She killed them off using the corrupted Zeto crystals, shattering and absorbing the dead Zetans' souls. She then feasted on their dead bodies while her Xeno army had to settle for eating their own fallen brethren. After finished eating, Rangda felt her power increasing. She roared and followed up with a sinister laugh.

Chapter 167: Strategy Meeting Between Keila and Hellas Petrakis

Keila was reading a report in her room and felt relieved. She had been holed up in this room for a week as the face she was using was too well-recognised after the news has spread about how she killed Morgan Henry. She couldn't change to another appearance as she had left the External DNA Modifier back on Eden, and reverting back to her real face, was not suitable as the Terran Council had lots of spies on Mars and they would find out if she was to re-emerge.

The report stated that the Olympus Republic scientists and engineers were able to produce the reverse-engineered Zetan technologies that she had brought for them. With access to an external DNA modifier, she would be able to change her face and DNA to that of another person. Preferably she would be a law-abiding Martian citizen to avoid attracting any suspicions. That person would have to switch places with her at this secure secret facility as it didn't make sense for the same person to be seen at two different locations at once. Keila requested an audience with Hellas Petrakis, and a couple of hours later he came down to talk with her.

Hellas:

- Hi Keila.

- Good news, our research team have made the prototypes of the reverse-engineered plans you gave us.

Keila:

- Yes, I know, Hella. I saw the report that you sent me.

- This is excellent news, are you willing to commit to the revolution?

Hellas Petrakis:

- Yes, I am willing. It is not because I enjoy the prospects of war and bloodshed but because defeating the Terran Council is the only way for me to lead my people out of poverty and oppression.

- I spoke to Joachim Muller on the hologram generator the other day. He requested 20 billion Terran Credits worth of rare elements for the "maintenance" of the magnetic field generators on the North and South Poles.

- How am I ever going to create an economy when all our resources just disappear to blackmailing plutocrats?

The magnetic field generators on the Mars' North and South Poles were imperative for life on Mars. They were put in place 600 years earlier when the Terran leaders wanted mass migration from Earth to Mars to get rid of all the undesirables from Earth. The magnetic field generators worked by sending an electric current through the planet to activate and electrify its core to create a magnetic field. With a magnetic field in place, Mars could maintain a breathable atmosphere, as its gravity was strong enough to keep an atmosphere once the magnetic field repelled the toxic solar wind. The Terran Council owned both of the magnetic field generators and guarded them with massive armies, which meant that they could blackmail Martian nations to pay them enormous sums that would keep the Martian's poor.

Keila:

- 20 billion Terran Credits? Does the Hellas Republic have that much money?

Hellas:

- Oh yes... Joachim Muller showed us that we did... If we just cut down "unnecessary" expenses such as universal healthcare and universal education.

Keila:

- Yeah, what are the lives of suffering Martians worth when profit must increase for the dividends?

Hellas Petrakis:

- Exactly. Besides, House Muller, profits won't go up this year. With the conflict between Rashid and White, House Muller must provide more funding to the Terran Council to compensate. Joachim is desperate to cover his costs.

- Unfortunately, the citizens of the Hellas Republic are the ones who will suffer unless we strike back.

Keila:

- So, do we have a deal then?
- Whose identity will I take.

Hellas Petrakis:

- You'll become Rose Menakis. A woman who unfortunately died in an accident, but her death hasn't been made public yet.

Keila:

- Excellent.

- Just one more thing; The microchips for untraceable communications. I brought you a high grade one from Eden.

Mass-produce the cheaper ones to give to our troops. We don't want the Terrans to intercept our communications.

Hellas Petrakis:

- Alright, hand one over and I'll plug it in.

Keila handed Hellas a Divine Technology Angel chip. He screamed in pain as it merged with his brain as he pushed it into his ear.
Hellas Petrakis:

- Fucking hell. What kind of communications equipment is this?

Keila:

- The chip merged with your brain stem. It's the only way to make the signal secure.

Hellas:

- Just great. So how do I take it out?

Keila:

- You would have to surgically remove it.

- But don't worry about that. It works, and it will help us. Now get the basic chip mass-produced.

Hellas:

- Sure, whatever. I don't like how you talk to me like you are my boss.

Keila:

- You'll get used to it.

- Now let's get my face changed.

After that, they went to the room where the outer layer external DNA modifier was assembled so that Keila could assume the identity of Rose Menakis, an unremarkable Olympus Republic citizen.

After changing her appearance, Keila used her new identity to take a passenger ship back to the station in the asteroid belt where she had departed to Mars a few weeks earlier. This was an uneventful journey, and she made her way back to Eden where she stored Rose's DNA for future use and reverted to her regular appearance.

Keila felt how more and more Martians were connected to the Divine Technology chip. She felt a bit guilty. Keila hadn't told Hellas about the real powers of the Divine Technology chips. Instead, she had stated that they were secure communications devices.

Keila was unsure whether Hellas had exposed her lie when he inserted the human chips in his followers, as that allowed him to read their thoughts. Hellas hadn't mentioned it, and she was unsure whether he was playing ignorant or hadn't noticed the powers that angel chip gave him over his followers. In the end, it didn't matter, as Keila would still have more power than Hellas.

Once Keila came back to Eden, she was in for a hostile reception as Metatron, and Markus Bauer were furious with her actions.

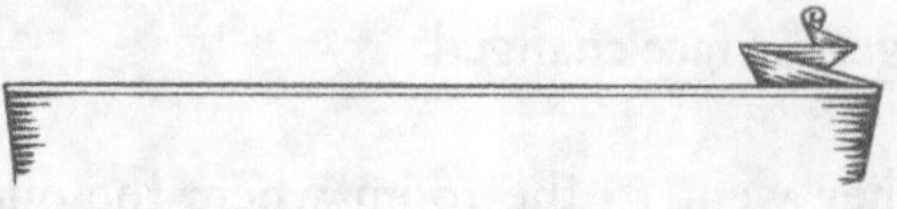

Chapter 168: End of Romance.

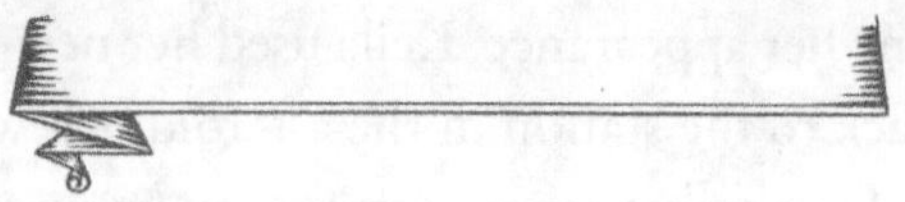

Keila was back in the gym, hitting the boxing bag. It felt good to be back exercising, as she hadn't been very physically active for the last few months. Besides, she needed to let off some steam. Keila's lies and broken promises had destroyed her romantic relationship with Metatron. Keila was upset over the breakup.

When they broke up, they had agreed to not get into each other's way. They divided power and responsibilities between each other. Keila was commanding her Martian revolution plans and her strike force of Edenite volunteers. Metatron was left in charge of Eden and transforming it into a modern and peaceful utopia.

Keila ignored demands from Rangda, to kill Metatron. Although Rangda's possession had saved Keila's life when Morgan Henry's crew attacked her ship, she was wary of the evil creature, and she would not heed Rangda's counsel unless it was desperate times. Not only had Rangda made her kill the innocent Jeshua one and a half years earlier, but Rangda had also made Keila eat her fallen enemies' hearts and drink their blood, during her possession of Keila's body. Keila almost vomited every time she thought about the carnage, she had caused that day.

Keila received a message from Hellas Petrakis. Her equipment had been mass-produced on Mars, and the Olympus Republic forces were ready to strike. Keila decided to avoid taking public transportation to Mars. Instead, she gathered her troops and used a shuttle equipped with Zetan stealth technology to get to Mars undetected.

Chapter 169: Joachim Muller Becomes Furious with Bjorn and the Olympus Republic.

Joachim Muller arrived on the Phobos Base for the second time in a couple of months. He was not happy. He was unhappy with the travel time, the Olympus Republics refusal to pay tribute and the fact that he had received video evidence of Bjorn having sex with Martian prostitutes in the presidential palace of Olympus Republic.

The travel time between Earth and Mars was seven days for this trip, compared to three days on Joachim's latest trip to Mars. This was because Earth had moved further away from Mars as part of its orbit around the sun.

Joachim didn't like being in space. What he disliked more, was handing over control. In Joachim's absence, his third son, Benjamin was left in charge of the faction. While Joachim had faith in Benjamin's abilities, he did not like the fact that Benjamin would not provide him with an heir. Joachim also disapproved of Benjamin's sexual deviation towards men, which was an embarrassment for House Muller's reputation.

What was worse than Benjamin's homosexuality, was the Olympus Republic's refusal to pay for the maintenance of Electromagnetic field generators on Mars. Instead of contributing with the 20 billion Terran Credits, they had responded with the footage of Bjorn engaging in coitus with Martian prostitutes. This was embarrassing to Joachim and was blackmail against him. Having sex with Martians was illegal for Earth humans according to Terran law. Although the law was often ignored, it was pathetic for the son of a faction leader to sink so deep.

Joachim and his bodyguards approached Bjorn's quarter at the Phobos base. Joachim didn't bother announcing his presence at his door. Instead, he used his position as Terran Council Chairman to override the electronic locks on the door and he sent his bodyguards in to beat up Bjorn and drag Bjorn to him.

Bjorn, who was bloodied and bruised, stared at his father in surprise:
Bjorn:

   - Dad?
   - What's happening?

Joachim:

   - Two weeks...

   - I am spending two weeks going back and forth to this rotten planet.

   - I DO NOT like going to Mars, yet you force me to come here to clean up after your mistakes!

Bjorn:

   - What did I do now?

Joachim:

   - I spoke to Hellas Petrakis last week. He refused to pay us tribute for the magnetic field generators...

Bjorn Muller:

   - And instead pressuring him to pay, you show up here with your goons to beat me up? Great leadership dad, I am sure that will solve the issue.

Joachim punched Bjorn on the nose causing a massive nosebleed.

Joachim:

- I am here to resolve the issue by discussing the matter with Hellas.

- Punishing you is a side-business. If you haven't figured out why you are punished yet, have a look at this screen.

Bjorn looked at the video of him having sex with the Martian prostitutes. He said nothing, and Joachim continued his tirade.

- I have had enough, Bjorn. One more fuckup and I will renounce you as my son and expel you from House Muller. After that, I will instruct Max Wellington to dump you off alone and unprotected on Mars. Do we have an understanding?

Bjorn nodded. He didn't dare to say anything against his strict and angered father. Blood and tears were running down his cheeks. Joachim's anger faded. He was ashamed of what he had become. He had used to be humane and idealistic, but his father Hans Muller had extinguished that part of his personality. So, all that remained of Joachim was bitterness, anger, and lust for power. Joachim had been relieved when Hans was murdered so he could step out of his tyrannical father's shadow. Yet here he stood, treating his own children as bad as his father had treated him.

Joachim:

- Guards take Bjorn to the medical ward and make sure that he gets the best possible treatment.

- We are all heading to the Olympus Republic tomorrow.

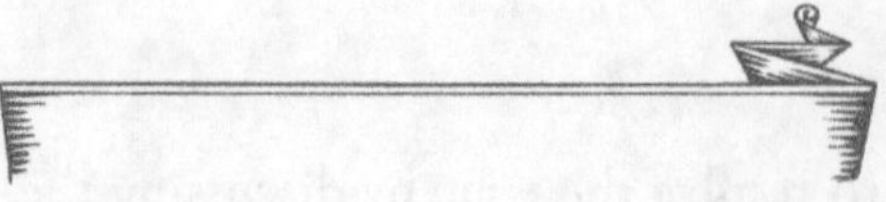

Chapter 170: So Close but Not Yet.

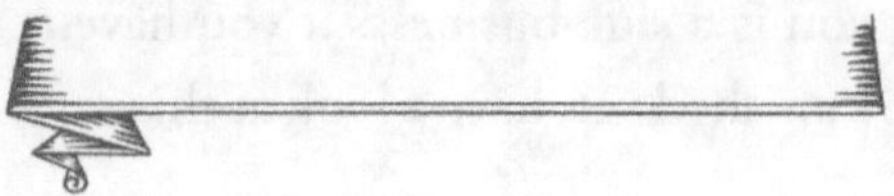

Keila and her Edenite strike force landed close to the presidential palace of Olympus Republic. Due to the altitude, it was freezing, and the air was very thin as well. To survive the outdoor conditions Keila and her troops were dressed in cold-weather suites with built-in heating and were using mountaineering rebreathers to be able to breathe the thin air at this altitude.

Suddenly, the sky became a lot brighter, and the temperature rose. Keila looked up and she noticed that several orbital satellites were reflecting sunlight down to the surface. Keila was unsure why this was the case and she hesitated on how to proceed.

Keila saw a multitude of spaceships land close to her. The ships were carrying the emblem of the Terran Council. Once they had landed, they sprayed out concentrated oxygen eliminating the need for a rebreather. But why was the Terran Council here? Had Hellas Petrakis betrayed her and if so, what was she going to do about it? If the Terran Council had come after her with this overwhelming force, she was doomed. She was stuck on the surface of a flat, featureless plain, and there was no way she could outgun them or run away from them.

Keila connected to Hellas' mind and she realised that he was unaware of the Terran Council forces arrival. This was a relief as it meant that he hadn't betrayed her, but it didn't answer why they were there. Captain Adal Schneider shouted at her:

- Terran Council Security Forces: Drop your weapons and identify yourselves!

Keila realised that she could not fight herself out of this situation and she told her troops to give up their weapons.

Keila:

- I am Rose Menakis. I am a citizen of the Hellas Republic, and the people with me are citizens of the independent Eden colony, known as Asteroid B528A.

Adal:

- I can confirm your identity, but not the identities of your followers. Explain yourselves.

Keila:

- These people are from the independent colony, Eden. They have isolated themselves from the rest of the solar system for the last 70 years and are as such not included in public records. They are here to sign a trade agreement.

Adal:

- Merchants don't usually trade armed to the teeth ready for war.

Keila:

- These are dangerous times, and as unaffiliated traders. the Edenites don't come under the gracious protection of the Terran Council. Thus, they need to defend themselves.

Adal:

- Whatever. Stand back and let us confiscate your weapons. You'll get them back at the end of the summit.

Keila:

- Summit? There is not supposed to be any summit here today. Who is meeting?

Adal:

- That's none of your concern, Martian peasant.

Keila:

- How lovely. Guys, just lend your guns to our benevolent guests, the peacekeepers from the Terran Council.

Adal:

- Smart move.

Keila and her group dropped their weapons, and they were surrounded by a group of armed Terran Council forces aiming their guns at them. Adal walk off to a luxurious shuttle speaking to someone. She froze when she realised who it was: Adal was speaking to Bjorn and Joachim. Two of her greatest enemies were within striking distance from her.

Keila closed her eyes to get inspiration and see possible potential outcomes. In some of the aggressive scenarios, she killed Bjorn and Joachim. But in none of these scenarios did she survive herself and killing either of them would not change Mars for the better. She needed to unite the Martians and crush the Terran Council for real change to happen. Joachim and Bjorn approached her.

Joachim:

- My apologies for our intrusion, Rose. You must feel terrified, being surrounded by all these armed men.

- Don't fear as my men are not here to punish you, but to keep the peace and make sure the meeting between Hellas and I can take place without incident.

- Tell me who is the leader for your Edenite friends.?

Keila:

- Eden is governed by Metatron, and the leader for this delegation is Melchior.

Joachim:

- Very well.

- Melchior, let your master know that he is better off trading with House Muller, as all other trade is subject to heavy taxation and potential penalties.

Bjorn joined in the conversation and shouted:

- Filthy liars! Give me Keila's location now. I know you are working with them.

Joachim gave Bjorn a stern look. Keila hid her fear, while considering to strike. If she was to go down, she would bring her tormentor and rapist Bjorn with her.

Keila:

- I don't understand, Sir. Didn't you announce Keila's death over a year ago?

Bjorn:

- Shut your mouth, peasant. I did not address you; I spoke to the delegation from Eden.

Joachim:

- That's enough Bjorn. There is no reason for you to abuse the local citizens.

- I apologise for my son's behaviour, Miss Menakis.

- Unfortunately, we will have to detain you and your delegation for the duration of our meeting with Hellas Petrakis. Do not worry. You are not our prisoners, only our guests and you will be served a delicious meal for your troubles.

Keila played it cool and not resist. It was evident that Muller believed in her fake identity and her backstory. Keila and her Edenite militia were led on board a Terran Council shuttle, where they were served food and drinks. A few hours later, they were released and given back their weapons and equipment. Keila was very thankful that the Terrans hadn't inspected their equipment closely, as it would have been a critical problem if her enemies had realised that she was in possession of advanced alien technology!

Chapter 171: Attacks are Coordinated with Hellas Petrakis.

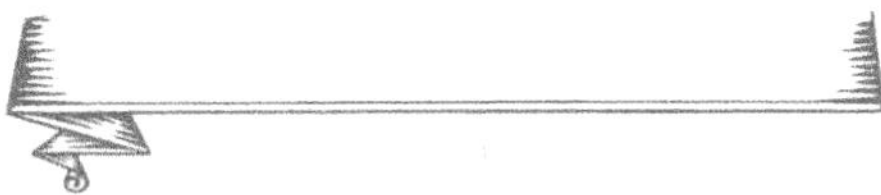

After being released from Terran Council detention, Keila and her militia went to Hellas Petrakis's office in the presidential palace of the Olympus Republic. The palace had been ransacked of everything of value. Hellas commented on what she saw:

- Impressed by my new Spartan-looking office?

Keila:

- Not really. What happened?

Hellas:

- Joachim came by. He was upset at our refusal to pay him 20 billion Terran Credits. Joachim reckoned that if I was too destitute to pay him, I was too poor to afford a beautiful office. Hence, he ordered his men to take everything of value.

Keila:

- Yeah, I know. I spoke with him outside.

Hellas:

- So, your cover held then? I am impressed that you didn't attack him, causing the death of all of us.

Keila:

- I already tried that once, when I killed Hans Muller. The Terran Council is a many-headed hydra, chop off one head, and another head will just pop up.

- No, we need to unite the Martian population and destroy the Terrans main base, the Phobos Moon Base.

Hellas:

- Agreed. But how would we attack the Phobos Base? Even with the technology you provided, we have no chance for an attack.

Keila:

- Not yet, but we'll get there. I have brought some plans for us to discuss.

Hellas:

- Very well. Let's discuss these plans.

After saying this, they studied and discussed the plans until they had come up with their first objectives. Keila was to lead the covert attacks, while Hellas was to pursue diplomatic contacts with other Martian countries and factions.

Chapter 172: The Attack on House White's Gadolinium Mines.

Colonel Douglas White was overlooking the desolate wasteland that had once been the Tengil Dominion from a Terran base on Mars. He hated this placement. While it was crucial to maintain a military presence to protect the mines, Douglas did not appreciate living within an abandoned wasteland.

The Tengil Dominion had been an independent Martian society, controlling most Mars' gadolinium supplies which had made them wealthy and powerful despite their small population (3 million) and territory (10,000 square kilometres). The region had been assigned to House White when the Terran Council divided the areas of Mars to the different Houses of Earth. This was to ensure that every Martian territory had only one trading partner and that this faction controlled all their trade to bleed the territory dry.

The leaders of the Tengil Dominion ignored that they belonged to House White's sphere of influence and kept trading with other Martian nations by using smugglers and unofficial channels.

Eventually, House White leadership had enough of the obstinate people of Tengil Dominion and had destroyed the nation so that they could run the gadolinium mines themselves. They had done this by navigating a medium-sized asteroid to collide with The Tengil Dominion, destroying most of the buildings and killing most of the population at the same time, with the survivors seeking refuge elsewhere. While using asteroids instead of nuclear weapons had been costlier path of action, it had the advantage of not leaving any radioactive fallout in its wake. This meant that House White could move in and operate the mines themselves.

Managing the mines themselves had an apparent drawback; that they needed to guard the mines from desperate and needy Martians that tried to steal their valuable gadolinium. That was why Douglas White, who was half-brother of Alicia White, was assigned to lead the House White garrison in the Tengil Dominion.

Douglas hated his life. Like Bjorn, he was a too important member of his family to not be in a leadership role. However, his father found him to be lazy and too much of an embarrassment to work at the House White headquarters on Earth. Douglas White hated his father John White, who was the chairman of House White. The bastard had left him here to rot. He made shitloads of money for his family, yet he saw very little of it himself. What angered Douglas the most was that his father held him in lower regard than his half-sister, the failed genetic experiment Alicia White.

Douglas studied the perimeter of the base. It was an hour before sunset and Douglas felt the chill as the temperature was dropping below zero. Worse than the cold was the spell of disappearances that had occurred lately. Dozens of soldiers had disappeared the last few days, and fear was spreading among his men. Douglas had begged his father to use orbital satellites to direct more sunlight down to the base to extend the days, as all the disappearances had happened at night. His father had rejected the proposal claiming that Douglas should toughen up and stop complaining about the Martian. Despite Douglas insisting that the weather was not the issue, his father had ignored his pleas.

Douglas watched the sunset. There was no movement at the perimeter, and everything seemed fine. Douglas decided that there was no point standing out here in the cold staring at the empty horizon. He had soldiers and cameras to do that job, so he headed back to his private quarters. He tapped up a hot bath, made himself a cup of herbal tea and tried to warm up.

Since he got stationed on Douglas, he had turned from being a heavy drug user to be a clean-living individual. He had changed, as he reckoned that the only way to get back to Earth was to show his father that he changed for the better and would not embarrass him anymore. Unfortunately, his lifestyle change did not help, as his improved behaviour showed his father that keeping Douglas on Mars was good for him.

Suddenly, Douglas started feeling very dizzy and disoriented, and he heard gunfire. Douglas was surprised by how close the shooting seemed to be. The perimeter was three kilometres away, so the sounds should be very faint, since the thinner Martian atmosphere didn't transport sound as well as Earth's atmosphere. Someone was banging on the door, and he heard one of his bodyguards calling his name. Struggling to find his balance in his disoriented state, Mark fell over several times on his way to the door. Once he opened the door, he saw several of his bodyguards collapsing and vomiting.

Bodyguard:

- Sir, we are under attack by unknown assailants.

Douglas:

- How did this happen? Why wasn't I contacted until now?

Bodyguard:

- Our communications went down. We are unable to communicate with the different units within the base, and we are unable to contact the Phobos Base.

- Everyone is feeling nauseous.

Douglas:

- We cannot fight if we cannot communicate and coordinate our efforts. Sound the evacuation alarm.

Bodyguard:

- Are you sure sir? If we abandon the most essential gadolinium mine in the solar system, your father won't be happy.

Douglas:

- That old bastard is never happy. If you want to stay here and die for his wealth, be my guest. I am getting out of here, and I am urging everyone to do the same.

Bodyguard:

- As you wish, sir.

Douglas activated the evacuation alarm and the House White troops rushed towards the space shuttles to evacuate the base. Keila and her soldiers were surprised that this battle was a lot easier than she had imagined. Keila had never anticipated that her enemies would be this cowardly.

The reasons for her enemies' retreat did not matter, and the attack had achieved its target. Keila and her troops loaded the gadolinium metal bars onto their transports, and then they activated the explosives that blew up the facility. After that, they enabled Zetan stealth technology on their vehicles and took off.

Chapter 173: Humiliating Defeat for House White.

Newspaper article: Olympus Republic Tribunal, 5th July 2874

Forces from House White that controlled the Tengil Dominion showed a humiliating level of cowardice when a strike force from The Mars Humanist Alliance, attacked their base. The attack by a small group of individuals prompted the 1000 men, strong military force to take off, running for their lives and leaving all their equipment behind to be commandeered by the Martian resistance. The video below shows how the Colonel Douglas White is running for his life while wearing a bathrobe.

Anonymous writer, The Olympus Republic Tribunal

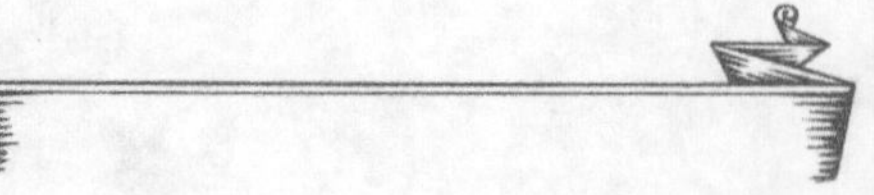

Chapter 174: Meeting with Joachim Muller, Bjorn Muller, and Max Wellington.

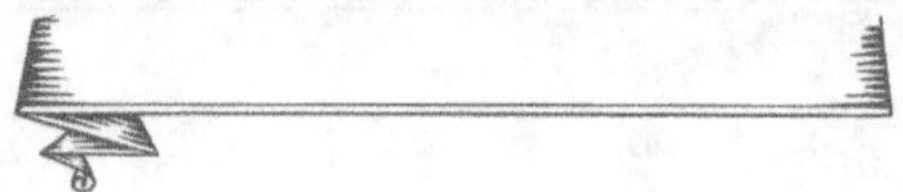

Joachim Muller was annoyed. Due to the incompetence of Douglas White, he had to postpone his return to Earth to sort out the mess on. Terran Council troops had returned to the site the day after, but the attackers were gone when they got there. The facilities in the Tengil Dominion were looted and damaged, and it would take months to get production up and running again. Yet the biggest issue for Joachim was not the lost production, that would be House White's problem, but the absolute embarrassment in the defeat.

Images of the half-naked Douglas White running for his life had spread all over the planet, and the Terran Council Security Forces were the laughingstock of the Martians. They needed to attack and kill a lot of Martians to spread fear and erase this embarrassment from peoples' memories. But who would they attack? All Martian factions and significant population centres had sworn loyalty to the Terran Council and were controlled by their assigned overlords. To bomb and kill loyal people would spread fear, but it would spread even more dissent, and in no time, they would have another uprising on their hands.

Joachim was looking at the intelligence on hand about the Martian Humanist Alliance. This terrorist group was destroyed 1.5 years ago when their base on the asteroid Sylvia was eviscerated. Since the death of the group's figurehead Keila Eisenstein, nothing had been heard from the group. Yet, now they were strong enough to attack a stronghold on Mars and rout the defenders. Something did not add up. Joachim summoned

Max and Bjorn to discuss the matter. They arrived at his suite a while later.

Joachim:

- Okay, gentlemen. Can you please update me on your latest debacle?

Max:

- Excuse me Chairman Muller, but Douglas White belongs to the army defence force. Bjorn and I belong to the space navy.

Joachim:

- That's a distinction without a difference. You are armed and funded by my company with the sole purpose of enabling profitable ventures throughout the solar system.

Max:

- Apologies, Sir. You are right.

- The survivors tell a similar scenario. Their communications went out, they were all afflicted with severe nausea, and their bullets stopped mid-air instead of hitting the attackers.

Joachim:

- This is absurd. People say anything to defend their actions these days.

Bjorn:

- Well, their claims match what we found when we reconstructed the attacks on Proxima Thule and the Aljadid Salam outpost.

Joachim:

- What are you talking about, Bjorn? Proxima Thule and Al-jadid Salaam were small outposts with a few defenders and no survivors. The Tengil Dominion was large and well-defended with a lot of survivors.

Bjorn:

- Yes, but they used similar technology at every attack. They used advanced cloaking technology to get close undetected, something that blocked communications, something that made our troops nauseous and unable to fight back and something that stopped bullets in mid-air.

Joachim:

- Bjorn. This is your drugs talking. Do you have any proof for the existence of these technologies or any plausible explanation on how the Martians, can muster these superweapons out of nowhere?

Bjorn:

- It must be Keila that has ganged up with the people of Eden to undermine us.

Joachim:

- How many times do I need to hear that woman's name?!

- She is a nobody. She killed your grandfather by coming to his bed posing as a whore. Hans died from his own carelessness and nothing else.

- Besides, considering how obsessed you are with her, what disproves that you are conspiring with her?

Max:

- Gentlemen, stop arguing, please! I can assure you that Eden has nothing to with this. We have conducted a many surveillance missions over the years on Eden with nanotechnology drones, and they had all proven the same thing. That Eden, the most expensive terraforming project in the history of mankind is used for housing a strange cult, emulating living in the Bronze Age. Nothing indicates that these people have any combat military skills, and they have limited contact with the rest of the solar system.

Bjorn:

- We met an armed delegation from Eden that was meeting up with Olympus Republic officials. Explain that!

Max:

- Well, they have new leadership on Eden. The new leader has realised the foolishness in their strange ideology and is focusing on making Eden a civilised and metropolitan regime.

- I spoke to the guy over the hologram transmitter once. He calls himself Metatron, but his real name is Jack Silver. He is a former Terran citizen and seems like a decent guy.

Bjorn:

- I have met him twice. I am not a big fan.

Joachim:

- Regardless. How do we deal with this problem and how do we find out which faction is conspiring to create instability in the Terran Council?

Max:

- Well, House Goldstein and House Bolivar are the only significant factions that haven't been attacked in the last year.

Joachim:

- That is true, but that doesn't exclude the other notable players. Anyone could have ordered false flag attacks as a diversion to direct attention elsewhere. Trust no one.

- Gentlemen, I'll leave this task to you.

- I need to contact John White to stop the fool from attacking our allies on Mars. It would be helpful if he sends his own troops to defend his mining stations, so I don't have to spend money guarding them.

Joachim left the room. Bjorn and Max sat silent for a while until Bjorn came up with a new idea:

- Hey Max. The report stated that The Martian Humanist Alliance left most of the weapons and equipment to focus on stealing gadolinium. Why would they do that?

Max:

- Yeah, I thought about that too. Gadolinium is neither super expensive nor does it have any military applications.

Bjorn:

- Let's ask the AI.
- AI. What is the primary usage for gadolinium on Mars?

AI:

- Gadolinium is hardly used on Mars due to the House White monopoly making it expensive. Gadolinium's primary use on

Mars is for the planet's magnetic field generators on the North Pole and South Pole of Mars.

Bjorn:

- This must mean something!
- I better discuss this with my father.

Bjorn rushed off, and Max Wellington stayed back in the meeting room. What a strange mess they were in!

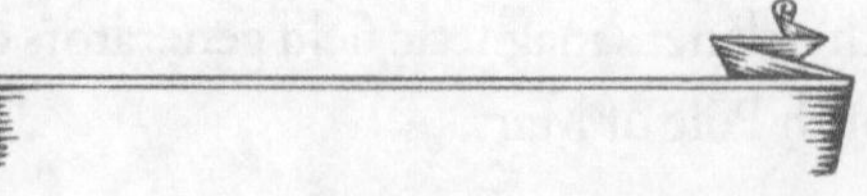

Chapter 175: Widespread orbital bombings by House White

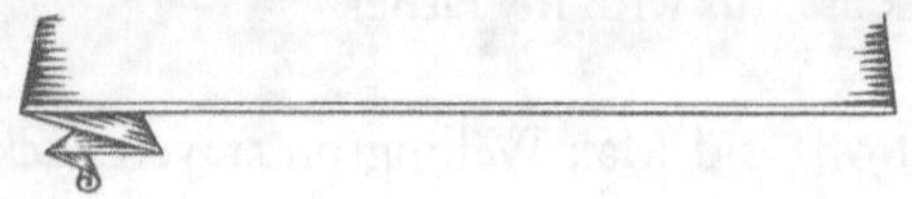

Newspaper article: Olympus Republic Tribunal, 8th July 2874

In the last few days, the regions neighbouring the recently attacked House White gadolinium mine has been bombarded from orbit by a fleet of House White warships. This is a response from House White to the humiliating defeat they faced last week. House White required the leaders of the neighbouring regions to round up all members of the Martian Humanist Alliance and send them to House White for punishment. When they failed to deliver the required number of prisoners in the short time frame given to them by House White, the villainous tyrants from Earth unleashed hell upon the region, exposing them to relentless bombing from orbit. The final death toll of these atrocities is still to be determined, but it is expected to rise over 100,000.

Because of House White's barbaric behaviour, many Martian nations and autonomous regions have renounced their affiliations with their assigned Terran Council member, and the peace that has lasted for 1.5 years since the destruction of The Martian Humanist Alliance headquarters on the asteroid Sylvia, is over.

The President of the Olympus Republic, Hellas Petrakis, condemned the barbaric actions of House White and promised an extensive amount of humanitarian aid to the affected region during a press conference earlier today. He reaffirmed that House Muller is still an ally of Olympus Republic and said that he will work hard to maintain a productive affiliation with them.

Anonymous Writer, The Olympus Republic Tribunal

Chapter 176: Keila is Sent to Arm the Rebels.

Keila was watching the news reports from the bombarded areas. She felt feeling miserable. There were endless pictures of dead and wounded, many of them children from the relentless bombardment in the last few days. She was feeling guilty over what had happened. Casualties were a necessity of war, but this indiscriminate butchery was not.

Keila should have seen it coming. House White was infamous for their hatred towards Martians who they saw as an inferior race. They needed to be stopped, but the price to achieve victory was terrible suffering for the common people.

Keila turned off the news report. She wanted to talk to Metatron. She was unable to do so via the Divine Technology chip as Mars and Eden were too far apart at the moment. Keila considered calling Metatron via Space Net. It was a risky move as Spacenet was supervised by Terran Council AI, so she wouldn't be able to expose any secrets or plan. But she needed to see him. Despite their separation, he was still her closest friend and confidant.

Keila called Metatron via the holographic television. Half an hour later he responded. Keila hated that it was impossible to get a live connection, but it was a matter of the distance between the worlds being so vast that it took at least 15 minutes for a message to go between the planets, and then the same time back. She received the response from Metatron. He responded in text form without transmitting himself visually as a hologram, which was a disappointment for Keila

Metatron:

- Hi. Who are you?

Keila:

- It is me. I just wanted to see you. I am feeling sad, and I miss you a lot.

Keila thought of transmitting herself in the hologram transmitter in her lingerie. She decided not to. It felt a bit awkward to communicate with her ex that way, but also because the outer layer of her body had the DNA and appearance of another woman. To her relief, Metatron realised what she was after and sent a moderately hot hologram of himself in a tight gym outfit.

Metatron:

- Okay, we'll be in range in a couple of weeks, I'll contact you then.

Metatron disconnected, and Keila kept the hologram of him running for a while. It looked like he was in the room and it smelled like him as well. The only thing she couldn't do was to feel the presence of him, as the hologram generator just recreated a visually perfect copy by utilising a nanotechnology layer powered by an electric field. If she touched the hologram, she wouldn't feel him. Instead, she would get an electric shock, and the hologram would turn off as a failsafe. Keila felt very aroused. She hadn't had sex for many months since the breakup with Metatron. She got interrupted when Hellas Petrakis knocked on the door. She let him in, and he started to speak.

Hellas:

- Your plans are coming along nicely.

Keila:

- Pardon me?

Hellas:

- House White's brutal attacks on civilians are driving a wedge between our Martian brethren and their Terran overlords.

Keila:

- I never intended for 100,000 dead and injured civilians.

Hellas:

- Really? You are not very well versed in the politics of the solar system, are you?

- On the bright side, there are massive evidence for their atrocities, evidence that wasn't around when they butchered your hometown Pamshal with biological weapons last year.

Keila:

- Yes, you are right. It's a relief that they got caught out this time.

Hellas:

- Which brings us to the next step: I am sending you to arm the people in the bombarded areas. Officially, you'll be Rose Menakis, in charge of the humanitarian efforts. Unofficially, you'll be Keila Eisenstein from the Martian Humanist Alliance arming the population and preparing for the next phase.

Keila:

- Good plan. We'll need massive popular support if we are to win this fight. Our lack of unity has always been our biggest weakness.

Hellas:

- Good. You'll leave in the morning.

Keila:

- Yes, sir.
- I better prepare for tomorrow.
- Until we meet again, President Petrakis.

Hellas left Keila's room. She felt revitalised and optimistic. While Keila was annoyed that Hellas was treating her as a subordinate, she had played along. Keila knew that she could control him through sheer dominance via the Angel chip that he had implanted in his brain, although Keila would avoid that option if she could. Keila wanted to improve things on Mars, not become a tyrant to replace the Terran Councils' tyranny.

Keila packed prepared her Edenite militia for the days to come before going to sleep.

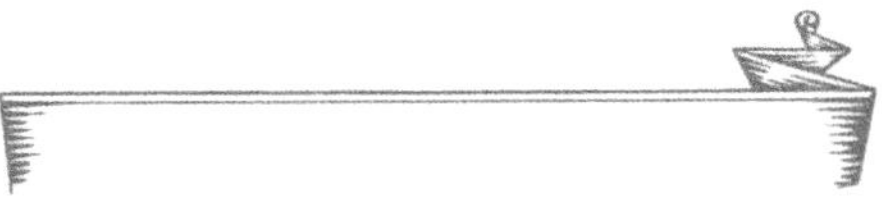

Chapter 177 Keila is Ambushed and Becomes a Martian Symbol of Hope.

A few weeks later, Keila was driving a hovercraft in the wasteland between two settlements. Her efforts as a rebel recruiter had gone well, and she had gained a lot of support for her revived movement.

Suddenly, Keila heard an explosion and she found herself flying out through the windshield with a trajectory for a fatal collision with the ground. Subconsciously, she activated the Zetan ballistic energy absorber that absorbed most of her kinetic energy, so she landed safely on the ground instead of colliding headfirst at 500 kilometres an hour for certain death.

Keila got up on her knees and she saw her hovercraft fly straight into a cliff and explode. She heard explosions and gunfire and took a quick look at her battery indicator. Absorbing the kinetic energy to save herself had drained her battery, which was now empty, so she could not rely on her Zetan technologies. Keila took cover behind a cliff, and she had an overview. She was surrounded by enemies that seemed to be a House White strike team. She was wounded, and blood was pouring down her head from deep cuts that came when she flew headfirst through the windshield. She was only armed with a pistol as the rest of her equipment had been on her hovercraft. Was this her end? Keila closed her eyes and hoped for a miracle.

Rangda spoke to her, offering her powers for temporary control. Keila was tentative towards the proposition. Although Rangda's powers had saved her life when Morgan Henry attacked, Keila had qualms regarding utilising the abilities of a being that she felt was pure evil. Then again, trusting in Rangda was really her only way out of this.

Keila:

- Okay. If I give you control, can you promise me to no do any sick things like eating people and drinking blood.

Rangda *hissing*:

- Yes, Rangda can promise that. Rangda has been eating plenty of delicious Zetan flesh recently.

- But to help you win this battle, I need your true form.

Keila:

- My true form? I am not a monster.

Rangda:

- Your true human form. Deactivate your external Zetan DNA modifier.

Keila reverted to her real appearance, and to her relief, this healed her superficial flesh wounds. She released control of her body to Rangda and felt a massive surge in power, way stronger than what she had felt the first time around. She got out of her cover and in a fired off two shots towards one of the armed flying drones that the strike team had brought with them. The first shot wedged the trigger mechanism into shooting continuously, and the second shot destroyed the steering mechanism on the drone making it spin around shooting everywhere and killing four attackers before crashing into the ground.

This forced the other attackers to take cover and Keila got to the closest attacker and stab him in the head with her plasma knife and stole his rifle. She then booby-trapped him with two hand grenades and called on his radio, *"I am wounded, require medic!"*, imitating his voice. Keila got out of sight and watched as she blew up two other attackers when they set off the booby trap. She then sprinted in a semi-circle and shot another two attackers in the back.

One of the fallen attackers had a jetpack and Keila proceeded to use the jetpack to fly up in front of the windscreen of an air support hovercraft and shoot the two pilots, before they had time to react and fire the hovercrafts weapon at her. She then shot the windshield to pieces and used her jetpack to make her way to the driver seat of the hovercraft, to take control of the vehicles before it hit the ground.

Keila flew past the other attackers and carpet-bombed them to disrupt them and stop them from chasing her. Then she set off as quickly as she could from the battlefield. Once she was out of the combat zone, she deactivated the tracking device on the hovercraft and connected the Zetan stealth technology to its battery, to make the hovercraft invisible to Terran Council satellites.

She then made her way to an unoccupied bomb shelter, got the hovercraft out of sight, and fell asleep. Keila slept for over 24 hours straight to recover from her wounds as well as the strain that being possessed had on her body. When she woke up and scanned her phone, she realised that she had gained overnight fame.

The reason for Keila's overnight fame was that House White had followed up on their spies' suggestion that Keila had assumed the identity of Rose Menakis.

Following up on their spies' information House White had opted to make the killing of Keila a live television spectacle. They had small drones filming the attack and broadcast it live. This backfired for House White, and instead of triumphant victory, they saw their elite strike team obliterated by a single woman on live television. Keila's incredible feat increased the hopes and the fighting spirit among the suppressed Martians.

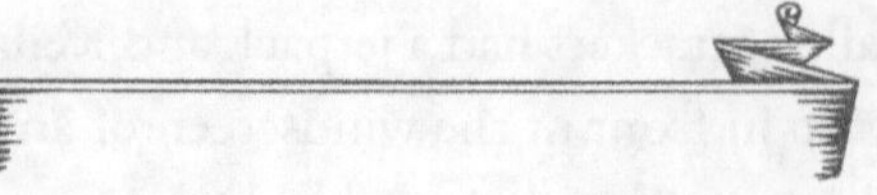

Chapter 178: Open Conflict in the Terran Council.

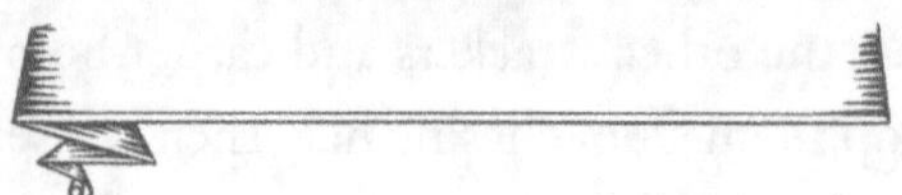

The August 2874 Terran Council meeting was held a few weeks later in the America First Tower, which was built on the top of Mount Massive in the Rocky Mountains in the centre of the American continent. America First Tower was the headquarters of House White, and it was inspired by House Muller's headquarter Europeum Tower. It was built along a mountain peak to support its weight and give it extra height. To stroke John White's ego, the building was 10 metres higher than Europeum Tower so that House White could claim to have the tallest man-made structure on Earth.

The 2874 Annual General Meeting was filled with conflict and was the hardest meeting to organise in many years. Although Joachim Muller was still the chairman of the Terran Council, he had let House White arrange the meeting this year as he was sick of paying for the spectacle every year. The top executives made their way up to the meeting room on the penthouse level that had a 360-degree view over the Rocky Mountains and a large part of the American continent.

Joachim:

- Welcome to the AGM of 2874. We have several questions to discuss, but let's move to the most crucial issue. The instability and potential uprisings on Mars are reaching a critical melting point, and we need to take concerted actions to re-establish our dominion over the red planet.

Ibrahim Rashid who was old and frail but filled with anger, burst out:

- Our problems are due to that heretic, John White. He let his men kill my favourite son Akram, and then he conducted mass-bombings of the Martians turning them to against us. I request an apology at once, or I will abandon these proceedings and take my delegation with me. I will break the cease-fire between House Rashid and House White.

John White turned red in his face and screamed at Ibrahim:

- I will not apologise to that filthy paedophile. We had nothing to do with the attack on the Aljadid Salam outpost, and he knows it. His men high-jacked one of our space cruise liners. When we sent our men to save the hostages from this illegal extortion, the fighting claimed the lives of many innocent Terran citizens.

- Ibrahim! You are in my territory. I require you to apologise.

Ibrahim Rashid stood up and screamed at John White:

- Fuck you pig. We are leaving.

He then picked up a jug of water and splashed the water over John White, who in turn called in security to arrest Ibrahim Rashid. Joachim felt that he had to intervene:

- Back down guards. As the chairman of the Terran council, I am giving you an executive order to escort Ibrahim Rashid and his delegation unharmed to the vacuum tubes for safe transit back to Egypt.

John said nothing and the guards did as Joachim instructed them to. Ibrahim and his men were escorted out of the building to the vacuum tubes for transport home. The meeting was paused, and the room was cleaned, and John went to change to dry clothes. Half an hour later the meeting recommenced.

Joachim:

- Now, this is an unprecedented embarrassment and a blemish on our reputation. I hope the rest of the meeting can proceed without any more incidents.

Santiago Bolivar, CEO of House Bolivar joined in on the conversation:

- Speaking of incidents. What is the story with Keila Eisenstein?

- She is the great-granddaughter of Ibrahim Rashid. She showed up six years ago and killed Hans Muller. Then she was the figurehead for a rebellion against us for four years, until your son Bjorn Muller claimed to have killed her two years ago. Conveniently he lost the body, and nothing is heard about her for years until she shows up on live television killing a House White strike team while displaying superhuman powers.

Joachim:

- I don't see what you are trying to say.

Santiago:

- What I am saying is: Does this woman even exist, or is she an artificial plot device, whenever you need something done Joachim?

Joachim:

- Excuse me? Are you accusing me of using Keila to elevate my own power?

Santiago:

- I would not accuse you without concrete evidence, Chairman Muller. I am asking you.

Joachim:

- Very well. Keila exists, and if she is alive, that is unfortunate. My explanation is that someone found her corpse and either revived her or cloned her.

Chi Ping Cheng, the CEO of House Cheng joined in on the conversation:

- We have had access to Keila's *"corpse"* for the last two years. It turned out to be a non-functional clone. This indicates that Bjorn Muller and his father is conspiring against the rest of us, and Keila is their operative!

Joachim sat silent. He did not know what to do with this new information, but he could not disregard Chi Ping's claims. Was Bjorn conspiring against him? Or, had Bjorn been duped by the Edenites? Joachim was unsettled by Bjorn's obsession with Keila, but if he was conspiring with her to overthrow Joachim, why hadn't he made a move yet? Joachim turned to his other son Benjamin Muller who was the CEO of House Muller.

Benjamin:

- Thank you for providing us with this new information. It is unfortunate that you did not choose to share the information as soon as you got it. I am invoking clause 5.2 that gives us a break to review and interpret the new information.

The meeting had a second break for the day, and Benjamin and Joachim retreated to a room where they met with other high-level House Muller executives. They were dumbfounded by the new intelligence. House Cheng had offered to immediately ship the body of Keila Eisenstein together with their lead scientist Tzi Chen Cheng to give a talk about why the body was a fake. They would arrive within a couple of hours. Joachim and Benjamin had no idea on how to react to the new information, but they knew the meeting had gone terribly wrong. On top of all their troubles their attempts to bring House White and House Rashid closer had blown up, and they needed to contain the damage.

They spent the next few hours communicating with representatives for the two factions trying to contain the damage and maintaining the peace on Earth.

Chapter 179: An Autopsy and an Action Plan.

The faction leaders met a few hours later in an unusual meeting spot: The morgue. Tzi Chen Cheng gave them a demonstration on the body proving that it was a fake, in the form of a non-functional clone. After this, they agreed to skip lunch as the visit in the morgue had dulled their appetites and they instead went back to the boardroom for further discussions.

As they gathered in the meeting room again, Joachim Muller resumed the proceedings.

Joachim:

- As you can see there is a lot of division among us. It seems that our enemies have learnt that the best way to control the enemy is to make them fight among themselves. We are not going to fall for this ploy though.

- I have written an action plan for how to get us out of this crisis. We need to A: stop fighting among ourselves B: Stop randomly bombing Martian Settlements as that just unites them against us. C: All start contributing to the Terran Council Forces and D: Share intelligence among us so that we can anticipate the enemies' next move and see through her deceits. Do you all agree on this, gentlemen?

Santiago Bolivar:

- I agree with what you say, but I have a question:

- Why are we bothering with Mars? We at House Bolivar are not very involved in the Martian business, but it seems that you are losing billions on Mars every year. Why not just leave the damn dustbowl to govern itself?

Joachim Muller:

- A good question Santiago and I'll give you the historic pretext.

- In the 23rd century, the population of Earth was a staggering 25 billion individuals. It was hell for rich and poor alike. The planet was polluted, and there were constant strife and public unrest. Like on Mars today, but worse. That was when my ancestors in House Muller came up with the solution. To reduce the population by mass-sterilisation and deportations to Mars. There were a lot of fights but due to their iron wills they achieved their dream.

- Since the 24th century, Earth has had a stable population of 1 billion individuals where everyone can have a fulfilling life. We achieved this by enforcing strict population control and adherence to genetic pre-selection in the community. This way we have almost entirely got rid of all crime and undesirable behaviours.

- Now in the 29th century, Earth is a paradise where everything is clean and the population can thrive.

- We gave most of the population paradise to the low cost of limited freedom.

- Now, what would happen if we left the Martians to fend for themselves?

- They would reach our technological level, and on top of this, there would be a lot more of them as they still are driven by their short-sighted, selfish individual needs to procreate. They would expand their territory, starting off with attacking our asteroid mining stations that are essential in bringing wealth and abundance to Earth without the destruction of our environment. Eventually, they would invade Earth, and we would fall, leaving Earth at the mercy of these ravaging hordes. They would mass migrate here, and within a couple of centuries, the planet would be the overpopulated hellhole of the 23rd century.

- So, to sum things up: To contain the Martian hordes and keeping them in place is not for today's profits but for the future of our planet and our people.

John White added in:

- Thank you for the history lesson, Joachim. I agree that it's crucial for the future of our children to contain the Martian threat. I will try my best to not escalate my conflict with Ibrahim Rashid any further.

The remaining faction leaders also agreed, and they ratified the document with Joachim's action plans.

Afterwards, Joachim and Benjamin spoke in the vacuum tube transport pod on their way back to Europe.

Benjamin:

- That went better than expected. We saved the day in the end.

Joachim:

- No, this is a disaster. They were all playing lip service. They are never going to follow this document.

Benjamin:

- You might be right, but I hope you are wrong, father.

Joachim:

- Only future will tell.

Benjamin:

- What do we do about Bjorn?

Joachim:

- It is difficult. We can't leave him in as an officer in the armed forces after this debacle, and we can't take him back to Earth. There is only one solution, but it is hard. He is my son and your brother.

Benjamin:

- I see. It would be better if I dealt with the issue?

Joachim:

- Yes, that would be better.

They nodded in acknowledgement and then drank their drinks in silence for the remainder of the trip.

Chapter 180: Keila Recuperate Her Body and Prepares Her War Strategy.

Keila was recuperating in a secret hideout in the Olympus Republic presidential palace. She wanted to make a live public announcement declaring that all Martian territory was now free from Terran Council overlordship, but she realised how foolish that would be. The Terran Council had a lot of weapons in orbit around Mars, and if she were to show up publicly, it wouldn't be long until they bombed that area to dust.

Keila was looking at her reflection. She had her real appearance as it was no point pretending to be someone else within her inner circle at the Olympus Republic. Keila saw a few grey hairs. This worried her as she was only 24 years old. Since she let Rangda possess her body for the second time, she had felt weak, out of shape with her body aching. Had Rangda when giving her superpowers and controlling her body, also drained her life force? It was a small price to pay as Rangda's intervention had saved her from certain death on both occasions, but it still worried Keila.

Keila stretched her aching body and got up. These worries were her vanity speaking. Besides, from a vanity point of view, her purple predator eyes were a more significant concern than her aging. She got up and walked to Hellas Petrakis office. He wasn't busy, something Keila knew from spying on him via the Divine Technology chip. While it felt a bit rude to spy on her allies, it was for her safety and their own good. If someone were to betray her to the Terran Council, the Olympus Republic would be doomed in the bombardment that would follow.

Hellas Petrakis gave her a concerned look:

- I am a bit worried about your health, Keila. The DNA regeneration serum I gave you yesterday should have reversed your aging and yet you look worse off today than you did yesterday.

Keila tried to joke it away:

- Never tell a lady she looks old Hellas, I thought you knew that?

Hellas:

- I'm just worried that the serum doesn't seem to work on you.

Keila:

- I am more worried about most Martians that cannot afford the serum, and instead die way too young.

Hellas:

- I have raised the issue with Joachim Muller on several occasions.

- His stance is that it is unwise to extend the life expectancy before we lower the birth rates. Otherwise, we'll be overpopulated in no time.

Keila:

- I thought Mars has always been overpopulated. It is the dumping ground for unwanted people in the solar system.

Hellas:

- I reckon with a balanced economy it could sustain a doubled population living in relative prosperity.

- From 4 billion living in poverty to 8 billion living in moderate prosperity.

- But let's not discuss economic theories for now. Just have faith in my ability to reform Mars economy without our Terran overlords.

Keila:

- You have believed in my ability, Hellas, so it would be rude to not reciprocate.

Hellas:

- So, how are our plans for the assaults going?

Keila:

- Both good and bad. It is difficult building up a sufficient force outside the North Pole and South Pole bases without being detected by orbital satellites. If we destroy those satellites too early, the Terrans will realise that something is amiss and send reinforcements. We must rely on a small force and the element of surprise as well our superior technology for the missions to succeed.

Hellas:

- So, all that we have is hope? I thought we had gained a strong following among the population.

Keila:

- We do. It would be challenging for the Terrans to take control of the rebelling areas on the ground. That's why they are resorting to orbital bombardment.

- The excellent support among the population is imperative for the second stage of our attack. The bases on the North Pole and the South Pole can be taken with small forces relying on superior technology and the element of surprise. The attack on the Phobos base on the other hand, requires a large fleet of small ships and it will be a bloodbath no matter what we do.

- But I have faith in our coming victory.

Hellas Petrakis:

- Faith is good, but do you have any logical reason to believe that our plans will succeed?

Keila:

- No, but logic doesn't win wars. If you look at it arithmetically, we have no chance against the might of the Terran Council armed forces. Yet we have beaten them time after time coming this far. They are fragmented and fighting among themselves. There will never be a better chance than this.

Hellas:

- You are right, Keila. Join the attack on the North Pole on the Spring Equinox just before the sun rises. I will lead the attack on the South Pole just after the sun sets. If it all works out, I will meet you here after we destroy the Phobos base.

Keila:

- Sounds good Hellas. Until we meet again.

Chapter 181: Bjorn Muller Realises Keila's Plan and is Almost Killed by an Assassin.

Bjorn Muller was looking at satellite maps, mapping the movements of the Martians. As the Terran Council were losing control over many areas, the lawlessness on the surface was increasing, and he could see that many bands of raiders had emerged on the surface. This was to be expected, and it was a problem that needed to be resolved before order could be restored. It posed no threat to the Terran Council, and it was better to let the Martians experience lawlessness for a while. That way, they would beg the Terran Council to return and protect them, and they could return to Mars as saviours instead of being the enemy.

Bjorn noticed something. There were large gatherings of raiders close to the South and North Pole of Mars. This didn't make sense as there weren't any major population centres to raid there, plus that it was freezing in the Martian Polar Regions, so how did these raiders sustain themselves? Then it occurred to him. The Martians had stolen a lot of gadolinium the previous month when they attacked House White's gadolinium mines. Gadolinium was the main component in the magnetic field generators on the North and South Pole that was imperative to give Mars a magnetic field to sustain its atmosphere. Could the bands of raiders in the Martian Polar regions be an army waiting to take control of the magnetic field generators?

There was a knock on the door. It was a waiter bringing Bjorn coffee. The man left the coffee on his desk and walked out towards the door when Bjorn noticed something. The coffee on his desk wasn't the one he ordered, and the waiter was new as well. He shouted out to the waiter:

- Hey. This is not the coffee I ordered. Where is Fritz? He is the one supposed to work today.

The assassin mumbled *"Scheisse!"*, turned around and shot Bjorn with a silenced pistol. His aim was off by a bit, and he hit Bjorn in the shoulder. Bjorn dropped to the ground, and the assailant ran towards his desk to shoot him again. Bjorn anticipated this and threw a gold bar that he had under his desk and hit the robber in the head causing him to miss his shot. Bjorn jumped up and punched the assailant who dropped his pistol out of reach for both of them. Bjorn got on top of the assailant, hit him several times in the head and screamed out. *"Who are you and who sent you?!"*

The assailant didn't respond, and instead, he pulled out a knife and stabbed Bjorn in the side, puncturing his kidney. Bjorn was bleeding heavily, and the assailant pushed him away and made his way to the pistol. He aimed the pistol at Bjorn and said *"Auf wiedersehen, Bjorn"*. He did not have time to shoot, as Bjorn's bodyguards rushed in and shot the assassin in the head before he could fire the shot. Bjorn passed out and was taken to a medical bay.

A few hours later, Bjorn woke up and Captain Adal Schneider, was waiting by his side.

Adal:

- I am so relieved that you survived the attack on your life.

Bjorn:

- So am I, Adal.
- What did the attacker say?

Adal:

- Not much. The bullets from your bodyguards struck him through the brain stem. It would be impossible to revive him and question him.

- Furthermore, he had no ID chip, and his DNA was not in our database.

Bjorn:

- It is in the database, Captain. It's above your rank. I recognised the man. He is a black op operative for House Muller. One of our top men in the field. The question is: Who sent him?

Adal:

- You think your family wants you dead?

Bjorn:

- It doesn't look better. I have a dozen potential suspects. My father, my brothers, my uncles, or my cousins. I hope it wasn't my father or brothers.

Adal:

- That is terrible. Bjorn. I don't know what to say.

Bjorn Muller:

- Don't worry about it, Adal. I don't see any reason for them to come after you.

- Do you have any news about Fritz?

Adal:

- Yes, unfortunately, he was found dead in the kitchen. The assailant must have strangled him to take his place and poison you.

Bjorn:

- Is it possible to revive him?

Adal:

- Yes, but it would be expensive. As his position is a non-combat position, he is not covered by the army medical insurance, and he doesn't have enough funds to pay for the procedure once he wakes up.

Bjorn:

- Don't worry about the money. Just revive him, and I'll pay the bills. I want Fritz to make my coffee!

Adal:

- Of course, sir.

- I suggest you are resting in the medical bay for the next few days. The attacker destroyed your kidney, and it will take two days to grow a new one.

Bjorn:

- Okay. Not the best way to spend two days, but bring me enough opiates to make it worthwhile.

Adal:

- Yes, I will let the doctor know.

Bjorn:

- Good. Now go and take my place in my absence.

As Adal left, Bjorn thought whether he should do anything about the suspected troop movements near their military bases. He decided against it. After his family sent assassins to kill him, he was done serving

House Muller. As soon as he had received his medical treatment, he would go back to Earth to make them pay for this bullshit. He groaned in pain but he felt a lot more comfortable after a nurse gave him a shot of morphine, and he fell into a blissful sleep.

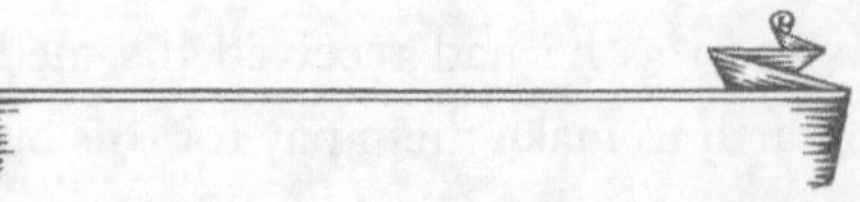

Chapter 182: Keila Conducts Surveillance at the North Pole.

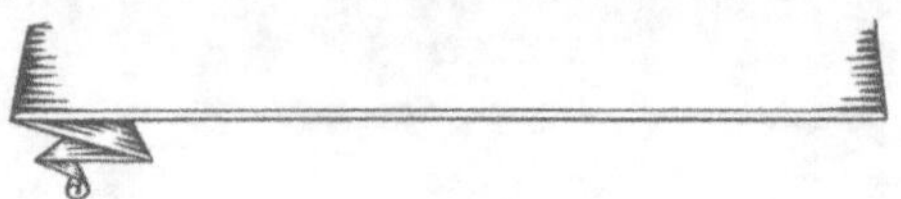

Keila was conducting surveillance from the top of a hill, 30 kilometres from the Terran Interplanetary Security Forces' North Pole base. Protecting the most important Terran Council installation on Mars, was a formidable fortress which would be a lot harder to attack than the smaller fortress that guarded House White's gadolinium mines. Keila could not expect the Terrans to be unprepared for the attack either. They were arrogant and convinced of their superiority, but they could not be stupid enough to stay unprepared, after she had defeated them several times

Keila wondered whether her idea to conceal her followers as raiders was a good plan. The advantage was that she could move around her units on the Martian surface, and it was unlikely to arise any suspicion from the Terran officers that observed the planet from orbit.

The drawback was that she could not use heavy military equipment that would have helped her when attacking fortified installations. Raiders on Mars were not using heavy military equipment as it was immobile and did not fit their raiding and pillaging operations. Raiders never bothered the Terran Council's activities on the Martian surface, and they rarely got in each other's way.

Keila took a deep breath. She really hoped that the Zetan technologies would be enough in the battle to come. Otherwise, her troops would be butchered by the fortified and heavily armed defenders.

Keila wanted to pray. But to whom would she direct her prayers? The voice that had guided her, had gone silent and instead she was evoked by the demonic creature called Rangda. Keila did not trust Rangda, despite

Rangda having saved her life twice. The second time had come at a steep cost, and Keila had aged irreversibly. She aimed her prayers to the True Maker despite knowing that it was pointless.

The deistic god, The True Maker, had gained a lot of popularity in the 25th century. In the 25th century, a Zetan had inadvertently revealed the truth to a Martian that the only real God in the universe was The True Maker. The True Maker suited the Martian mind as it was a great force setting the law of nature and creating everything. However, the True Maker that it had neither the desire nor the ability to change outcomes in people's daily lives.

Having finished her prayers to The True Maker, Metatron contacted her via the Divine Technology chip. Keila was happy to see him as she hadn't been able to communicate with him since she left Eden.

Metatron studied Keila. He was worried about what he saw. She looked at least a decade older than she had been the last time he saw her, half a year ago. While her old looks didn't bother him, he worried that she had aged so significantly in a couple of months. While Metatron was a very young-looking 122-year-old, due to his extended periods of cryogenic sleeping and usage of DNA regeneration, Keila was a mature looking 24-year-old, and they both looked like they were in their late 30s.

Metatron:

  - Keila! You have aged a lot in six months. What happened?

Keila:

  - I let her possess me again. I had no choice. They would have killed me.

Metatron:

  - You let Rangda possess you? Why on Earth would you do that?

Keila:

- I was scared. I was intercepted by a House White strike force. There was no way out, and they would have killed me... or worse.

- I did what I had to do. And Rangda helped me. I am sure you have seen the television footage as everyone else.

Metatron:

- Yes, I saw it. Didn't know if it was real or not until now.
- So, what is new, except for your aging?

Keila:

- I am at Martian North Pole. Tomorrow, we'll perform co-ordinated attacks on the Terran Council outposts. If all goes well, we will proceed to storm the Phobos base.

Metatron:

- Sounds risky. How did you get enough heavy weaponry within range of the bases? The Terran Council is mapping the Martian surface.

Keila:

- I didn't. All our troops are posing as raiders and they are using light equipment. I am gambling that the Zetan technology, and the element of surprise is enough to beat them.

Metatron:

- That sounds incredibly risky.

Keila:

- Change always is.

Metatron:

- Yes, about that. I was visiting a female adulthood ceremony yesterday, and I came to think of our child. If your vision were correct, I would need to insert the embryo in a synthetic womb next week to fit the right birthday.

Keila:

- I don't know, Metatron. After all that has happened, I am not too sure that I can trust my visions. Can we talk about it next week?

Metatron:

- You might not want to be around next week. You have some dangerous days ahead for you. I want to know your will; in case you perish.

Keila:

- I want you to do what makes you happy if I am no longer around. Besides, I am not going anywhere.

Metatron:

- Very well. I'll talk to you in a couple of days, Keila.

Keila:

- Yes, talk to you later.

Keila leaned back and sighed. She didn't know what she should have told Metatron. Her vision had shown her, her daughter and Metatron. She had no idea what would happen if she died before her daughter reached 13 years of age. It was all confusing, and it made her restless.

But then she felt optimism. The visions would be correct, and she would settle down on Eden with Metatron and live a happy life. The fact that he still thought about her proved that it would happen. Keila went to sleep, and she slept peacefully despite the anticipation for the decisive battle.

Chapter 183: An Empty Prison.

After many months of marching, Odin and his Zetan host reached Rangda's prison in the Divine Dimension. Odin was terrified by what he saw. The prison was empty. On the ground, laid the bones of Brahma and the remains of a Xeno. This had terrifying implications for the future. How had Rangda got out? How had she killed Brahma? How had the Xenos made their way into the Divine Dimension?

Odin made a terrible realisation. The tormented screams that he had heard psionically lately, were not Zetans who killed themselves, but Zetans that had been killed and eaten by Rangda and her Xeno army. For every Zetan that fell to the beasts, the Xenos would get stronger as they would fill up, while the starving Zetans would remain weak.

So, what should he do? Odin spoke to Thor and Ra.

Odin:

- Rangda tricked us! We should never have listened to Brahma's pleas to spare her and imprison her instead of killing her outright.

Ra:

- Yes. That was a fatal mistake. But we must not dwell in the past. Instead, we must look forward.

Odin:

- Yes.
- My son, what do you suggest that we do?

Thor:

- We must return to the Divine Palace and summon every Zetan. We cannot be divided. Only by standing together can we hope to survive the onslaught of our eternal enemies.

Odin:

- Excellent plan my son. Let's start the summons at once.

Thor:

- Yes, but first, there is another thing. To be able to face the coming Xeno onslaught we must eat, and there is only one food source left for us here.

Ra:

- What you are suggesting is blasphemous and forbidden.

- If we eat the Xenos, we are no better than the beasts we are fighting against.

Thor:

- But if we don't, we will all succumb to the enemy.

Odin:

- This is not a choice for the three of us to make. Let's summon all the Zetans to the Divine Palace and let the assembly decide our future.

Having said this, they gathered the Zetans that were with them into a ring to increase their collective psionic capabilities and commence with the summoning.

Chapter 184: The Assault on the North Pole Base.

Keila looked at her watch. The time to strike was now. She ordered her troops, masked as raiders, to start moving. While it would have been better to equip them with proper Martian military armour, the element of surprise was imperative for success. She gave the command to the Olympus Republic army to send missiles to knock out the Terran Council satellites that covered the targeted areas. This would expose her, but it would stop the Terrans from orbital bombardment of the battle zones until they had replaced their broken satellites. She ordered her troops to move towards the fortress. They were moving behind a large number of light trucks and hovercrafts that were equipped with large high capacity batteries attached to reverse-engineered Zetan technologies.

The limited functionality of the reverse-engineered Zetan technologies was a hurdle that could hinder for the success of the operation. While the handheld technologies worked, they were limited by the battery capacity of each individual machines. To breach massive fortresses like the one on the North Pole, Keila needed something that was scaled up, both in range and battery capacity. While her scaled up Zetan technologies should work, there had been no way to field test them as that would have risked that the Terran Council found out about the technology. Keila's troops moved towards the fortress in a circular formation, aiming to encircle the stronghold. She had 500 trucks and 10,000 infantry which were more than the number of defenders, but the defenders had automated defences and heavy weaponry, so she would not stand a chance if their Zetan technology did not work.

As Keila moved closer, she could hear the Terran Council commanders shouting out warnings on the megaphone. She ignored them, and her troops kept advancing towards the fortress. Eventually, she stopped 200 meters away from the 300 metres high, impenetrable metal walls of the fort.

A Terran officer came out in a helicopter to parley with Keila's group. Terran Officer:

- You are intruding on Terran Council Security Forces territory. State your business.

Keila:

- We request that you surrender immediately, and lay down your weapons. Martians should manage the North Pole magnetic field generator.

Terran Officer:

- Is this a joke? The most massive fortified facility in the solar system with a ragtag band of raiders, requesting that we surrender? Your pathetic forces wouldn't even make your way through our automated outer defences.

Keila took off her helmet and revealed her identity to the Terran Officer. She then spoke again.

- I am Keila Eisenstein of the Martian Humanist Alliance. The Terran Council's reign of terror ends today. I declare Martian Independence. From this day on, no Terran shall ever set foot on Mars armed and unwelcome.

Terran Officer:

- Looks like I am up for a promotion.
- Activate Automated Defences, fire at will!

The Terran Officer flew back in his helicopter to the relative safety of the fortress, Keila said a prayer to the True Maker before facing the automated defences of the fortress.

The fortress' defences rained down a barrage of artillery and machine-gun fire on her troops. To her great relief most of her Zetan technology held up and absorbed and stopped the barrage but at a few places the technology failed, and she saw those sections obliterated and the soldiers occupying them dead beyond resurrection. Eventually, the barrage ended as the Terran weapons overheated and needed to be reloaded.

"Charge!" Keila yelled, and her troops equipped their jetpacks setting the direction for the top of the walls. The desperate defenders tried to shoot them with the automated defences but to no avail, as the computerised defences were still overheated and reloading. Keila and her troops landed on the top of the battlements and in the courtyard of the fortress. Keila and her soldiers dropped off a few crates with amplified Zetan bionic chip disruptors in various areas of the courtyard. This disrupted and confused the defenders, who got very nauseous, when their bionic chips were interrupted. Keila and her troops charged the defenders. They charged this with activated personal ballistic energy absorbers and equipped with plasma swords.

They were equipped with plasma swords as they wanted to charge the enemy quicker. Plasma swords were also better than as Terran armour was designed to withstand a lot of shots while it was not intended against the blasting slices of plasma swords.

The confused, nauseous, and panicking defenders stood no chance against Keila's powerful army. Although some of her troops ran out of battery and were killed by the defenders, the majority of Keila's troops reached their target and chopped their foes to pieces with their plasma swords. They were helped by the fact that the Terran troops were nauseous from the bionic chip disrupters and untrained in melee combat.

They reached the gate of the main building that held the magnetic field generator within. It had impenetrable walls, and Keila ordered some of her troops to find a way to blow up the front gate.

Keila led a group of soldiers to scale the walls of the fortress, trying to find a suitable entrance. They found a ventilation tunnel that led them to the main hall of the fort, where the defenders were waiting for them.

Keila entered the complex and she felt a sharp pain in her shoulder. She fell backwards over a ledge, dropped several levels, hit the floor and fell unconscious.

Chapter 185: Saved by the Bell.

Douglas White was looking at the unconscious Keila Eisenstein. Since the debacle in the Tengil Dominion, where he was humiliated when he escaped while wearing his bathroom robe, Douglas had been stripped of his rank. For the last few months, he was forced to serve on the edge of Mars in the cold and darkness as a regular soldier.

Douglas panicked about his oncoming death. The North Pole fortress had been breached, its defenders slaughtered, and by pure luck, he had been among the ones in the inner military camp when the hell broke loose. All communications with high command were blocked, and if they choose to respond, they would respond by bombing the military camp to avoid it falling into enemy hands. Douglas heard how the attackers tried to blow up the front gate, and with every explosion, the citadel was shaking.

From the bright side, if he could film himself killing the terrorist Keila Eisenstein. This way, he would redeem himself, and with a bit of luck, his family would bring him back from the dead. He bound Keila to a chair and woke her up by throwing a bucket of ice-cold water over her.

Douglas:

- Miss Eisenstein. We meet again.

Keila:

- Yes. And this time you even got your clothes on... Although I suspect you don't like your a "private grade" uniform.

Douglas:

- Yet, I rather stand where I am standing, than sit where you are sitting.

Keila:

- What difference does it make? My troops will breach that gate any minute. When they do, you'll be dead. Your only chance is to give up, and I'll spare you.

Douglas:

- Yes, but I will not disgrace myself again. I will not be paraded as your prisoner. This is how I redeem myself.

Douglas lifted his pistol to shoot Keila. She stared him into his eyes to make him hesitate. It worked well enough to stall him for a split second, and that was all that was needed. The next explosion that hit the building, dislodged the construction fittings of a large bell hanging a few levels up. The bell fell, and hit Douglas in the head, killing him. Thus, Keila was saved by the bell. A few minutes later, Keila's army breached the gates, and the remaining defenders surrendered. Thus, the North Pole's magnetic field generator had fallen into the hands of the Martian Humanist Alliance.

Chapter 186: Keila's Address to the Martians.

Keila was looking at the reports from the other battlefields. Her coordinated attacks had granted her total victory on the Martian surface. This was due to the introduction of advanced Zetan technology and because the Terran forces had been understaffed as the Terran factions were busy fighting each other. Unfortunately, President Hellas Petrakis had died beyond resurrection when fighting for the South Pole, so there was no unifying political force to look up to.

Keila knew that her victories would account for nothing unless she destroyed Phobos base. The Terrans would return, and she could not utilise her Zetans technologies to surprise her enemies if she gave them time to regroup. Keila needed a decisive victory today. Without the Phobos Base, it would be hard for the Terrans to stage another invasion and she could declare Martian independence.

Keila produced a television clip that showed battlefields and how the Martian Humanist Alliance's flag hang over every significant Terran Council base on Mars. The camera showed how she sat in a chair in the command room of The North Pole base. Keila spoke into the camera.

- Dear Martians. For over 500 years, the Terran Council have terrorised and dominated our people and turned us against each other. Today we achieved unprecedented success by taking every major Terran stronghold in a single day. We did this by uniting and acting like one. But the greatest challenge is ahead of us. To defeat the Terran Council, we need to destroy their Phobos base. The Phobos Base is their staging ground their centre of power in our part of the solar system. The Martian Humanist Alliance cannot fight this battle alone. That's why I am urging everyone who has weapons or ships to take to the skies at 3PM Olympus Republic time. Together we'll face our foes. Many of us will die, but remember. They can end our lives, but they can no longer steal our freedom. The True Maker bless you all!

After finishing the address, Keila fell to the ground in pain. The bullet wounds in her shoulder were not critical, but the 15-meter fall that had knocked her unconscious were. Although a 15-meter fall was not fatal on Mars due to the lower gravity, it was enough to maim her and put her out of action. Melchior, the highest-ranked member from her Edenite militia, ran up to Keila.

Melchior:

- Mistresses Keila. You are hurt.

Keila:

- Yes, but I need to stay strong. The assault on Phobos starts in three hours, and I need to lead it.

Melchior:

- No! Mistress Keila, you are too injured to be useful. You need to stay here, recover, and lead us after the enemy has been defeated.

- I will lead the attack if you let me.

Keila:

- But Melchior, you are not Martian, you are an Edenite.

Melchior:

- That is irrelevant. My ancestors came from Mars and were tormented by the Terran plutocrat Abraham. Fighting the Martians' oppressors is also my fight.

Keila:

- Okay, Melchior. You have convinced me. May the True Maker be with you, and may we meet again.

After that Keila gave Melchior a Divine Technology god chip and she inserted it into his brain. If he was to control the attack, he needed to coordinate their forces. Keila groaned in pain and fell unconscious. Melchior rushed her to the medical ward.

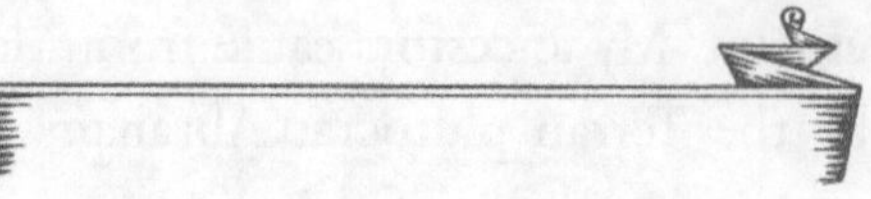

Chapter 187: Joachim Rejects Max's Request to Abandon the Phobos Base

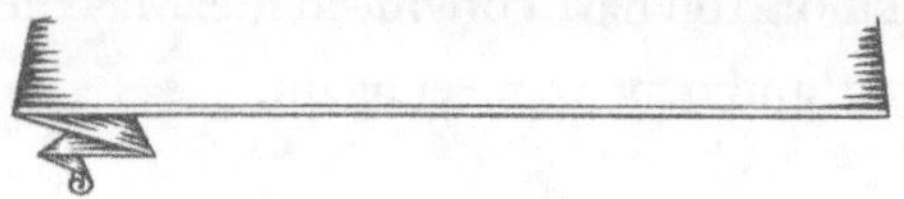

Admiral Max Wellington studied Keila's TV statement in awe. When the Martian Humanist Alliance had conquered the Terran Council bases on Mars, they had acquired a lot of weaponry as well as shuttles and minor space attack ships to attack his position.

This would not have been a big problem if he had his full fleet at his disposal. However, Max hardly had any ships at his disposal. As four out of five factions had stopped providing the Terran Council armed forces with weaponry and personnel, a skeleton staff guarded his base. This crew was insufficient to fight the might of a unified Mars.

The Martians would be united against him. The utter defeat of the Terran Council's ground forces was an unprecedented event. In hindsight, Max regretted that he hadn't investigated the rumours of a new revolutionary technology. 100,000 Terran troops were dead or captured on the Martian surface, and there was nothing Max could do to save them.

Captain Adal Schneider entered the command room and Max spoke to him:

- Captain Schneider. Why are you here? I asked Bjorn to come. I know that Bjorn was cleared for duty yesterday.

Adal:

- That is correct Admiral. However, Rear Admiral Bjorn Muller requested that I went to talk to you while he is preparing ISS Supreme Earth.

Max:

- Very well. And what does Bjorn suggest that we do?

Adal:

- He agrees that we should abandon Phobos, regroup with a large fleet, and retake it in a couple of days.

Max:

- Yet he refuses to come here and say this to his father.

- No matter. Step up on the hologram machine together with me Adal; we must convince Joachim Muller that retreat is our only option.

The two officers stepped up on the hologram machine to Joachim, ten minutes later they received a response from Joachim:

- You are not to surrender or leave the Phobos Base. If you do, you'll be tried for treason. If the base is lost, set Phobos on a collision course with Mars. If we cannot have it, no one else should.

Adal:

- But a collision between Phobos and Mars would be a cataclysmic event that would wipe out all life on the surface.

Max:

- Yes, I think that is Joachim Muller's intention.

Adal

- So, we are dead unless we repel a massive invasion force or wipe out most life on the most populous planet in the solar system.

Max:

- Yes, more or less.

Adal:

- Boss. I must admit. I hate my job.

Max:

- So, do I.

Max took up a photograph of his daughter Magda who died in a rare form of incurable brain cancer and whispered for himself *"Magda, we'll soon meet again."*

Chapter 188: Bjorn Muller Tries to Destroy Mars to Save Himself.

Bjorn was standing at the command bridge of ISS Supreme Earth. He looked at the massive swarm of small spaceships and shuttles heading in the direction of the Phobos base. It was an awe-inspiring sight, watching the masses rise together as one to break the chains of tyranny and free themselves. Many of them were in dingy shuttles that were not flightworthy, but it did not matter. There was too many of them, and they were too determined

Bjorn estimated that there would be over a million Martian attackers in thousands of ships while his defenders constituted of a hundred ships and a total of 15,000 defenders. Against a swarm like that, it did not matter what he commanded. He and the vessels he commanded would run out of ammunition before the enemy ran out of ships and then they were doomed.

Bjorn sat in silence. He was impressed by the people rebelling against their allocated lot in life, trying to improve their destiny. Bjorn realised something. He was Terran and superior to the vermin race that was trying to end his life. He would destroy them all when they were on the verge of achieving their freedom.

He called captain Adal to his side:

Bjorn:

- Captain. I am relieving of command, and I hand it over to you. I have one final mission to do before the end of this war.

Adal:

- I know that you want to run, Bjorn, but there is no point. Your father has forbidden retreat and besides, how far can you go in a small fighter ship?

Bjorn:

- You are mistaken. I am not running. I do what is needed to preserve our future.

Adal looked down in the ground. Was Bjorn going to perform the atrocity that his father had ordered? Was there not any better way?
Adal:

- Okay, Citizen Muller. I grant your request to resign from the Terran Council Security Forces. Feel free to acquire a small ship for your transport off this command ship.

Bjorn:

- Thank you, Adal. See you on the other side.

Bjorn headed for the docks. He got on a small ship and travelled to the thrusters that governed Phobos' artificial gravity.

Chapter 189: Keila Wakes up With a Vision to Stop Bjorn Muller.

Keila woke up with a twitch. She had a vision showing what was about to happen. She needed to stop Bjorn Muller at once. Keila limped towards the exit of the medical ward. An Edenite medics approached her.

- Mistress Keila. You should not move. You are injured.

Keila:

- If I don't move, we'll all die. I have seen it. I need a shuttle to take me to Phobos at once.

Medic:

- What are you talking about?

- Our troops have overrun the Phobos base; they are fighting inside the station as we speak.

Keila:

- It's a trap, The Terrans are going to use the Phobos Base itself as a weapon to destroy Mars. I need to go now.

Medic:

- Very well I'll help you to the shuttle and I'll come with you.

They reached the hangar and as it turned out the only ship that remained was a small fighter spaceship designed for one person. Keila farewelled the medic and headed off.

Chapter 190: A Divine Intervention

Keila landed at Phobos next to its artificial gravity thrusters. Bjorn Muller was already there. Keila realised a fatal flaw. In her hurry to get there as soon as possible, she had forgotten to pack her equipment, weapons, and Zetan devices. Bjorn saw her coming, screamed something, but she couldn't hear him. The gravity generating thrusters on Phobos was in the vacuum of space and there was no sound. Bjorn took up a pistol and shot Keila twice. He tried to shoot again, but his gun jammed. Keila picked up her plasma sword and tried running towards Bjorn, but she could barely walk. Bjorn waved at her and shook his head. He smirked, put his finger on a detonator, and set off an explosive charge. The blast knocked Keila to the ground. Bjorn got on his spaceship and took off.

Keila tried to get up. She was in terrible pain as her blood was boiling, freezing, and evaporating at the same in the freezing cold vacuum of space. The explosion had changed the direction of the thrusters and they were now pushing the Phobos moon on a collision course with the Martian surface. If there was a collision, that would melt the crust of the planet and kill all life, as the Phobos Moon was massive enough to make a collision with Mars devastating.

Keila tried to make her way to the thrusters' rudder to change the trajectory of Phobos to avoid a collision with Mars. The rudder was rusted shut. No matter what she did, she would never be able to change the trajectory of the moon. In a matter of hours, they would all be dead. Keila collapsed next to the rudder.

As Keila closed her eyes preparing to take her last breath, she saw her. She saw the True Maker herself. The eternal origin of the universe, the all-knowing creator that never intervened was communicating non-verbally to her.

Keila got up and realised that her wounds had sealed. She felt reinvigorated, and her hopes were surging. Summoning all her strength, Keila turned the rudder 180 degrees, changing the trajectory of Phobos from a collision with Mars, to a collision course with the Sun. Keila got into her fighter spaceship and set after Muller.

Keila intercepted Bjorn and destroyed the engines on his ship with her weapons. She then followed his ship as he crash-landed on Mars.

Chapter 191: The Fall of Bjorn Muller.

Bjorn Muller woke up from the crash-landing and got out the ship. He was in immense pain as he had broken his leg and had a metal pole penetrating the side of his body. Bjorn knew that he would bleed out and die within minutes if he tried to pull out the pole, so he left it in. He got out of the ship and noticed that he had crashed at the edge of the Olympus Mons mountain. He looked up and saw how his father's plan had failed. Phobos was moving away from Mars instead of getting closer. He heard a familiar voice and turned around.

Keila:

- Bjorn Muller! I have finally won the war for my people.

Bjorn looked at Keila in disbelief.

- How did you do that? How did survive with a punctured lung and a destroyed liver?

Keila:

- What are you talking about, I am fine?

Bjorn:

- Really? Look again.

Keila looked at her body. Bjorn was right. She was bleeding out, and she struggled to breathe.
Bjorn:

- It looks like we are dying. We might as well talk to each other and die in peace.

Keila collapsed to the ground. She was coughing blood, and for the second time in less than 20 minutes, she was dying.
Bjorn:

- You know Keila. I never intended for any of this to happen. Things could have been so different between you and me.

Keila:

- That doesn't change the fact that you tried to kill 4 billion individuals to save your own skin. You'll end up in hell for your crimes.

Bjorn:

- If there is such a thing as hell. Yes, you are right.
- But hell will be nothing new for me.
- You have made my life a living hell for the last six years.

Keila:

- What are you talking about? You were the one who kept me as a sex slave for two dark months, before I escaped. I was a young girl. Full of dreams. You destroyed my faith in people on Earth.

Bjorn:

- Yes, you are right. I did those things. But the one I hurt the most was myself.

- Before we met, I had these visions of you in my dreams. You, I, and our daughters were running the solar system for everyone's benefit.

- When we finally met, I was crippled by my fears. I realised that you were the woman from my dreams. But I also realised that you were half Martian and half Rashid, so my peers would never allow us to be together.

- I was a friend of your father, Mahmoud Rashid. He fell in love with an Edenite woman against his grandfather's wishes. This caused them to be forced into exile on Mars.

Keila felt dizzy and confused. She didn't know if it was the blood loss talking or if she was shocked by how similar her visions and Bjorn's visions had been. When Keila was a teenager, she had dreamed about going to Earth and meeting someone like Bjorn. She had seen Bjorn in a lot of her visions recently, displaying an alternate reality where she was together with him in peace and love. She had dismissed them as nightmares, but maybe this was meant to happen, until Rangda came along and changed things.

Keila:

- I had many visions of you too before we met. You turned out to be my nemesis. You were the reason I disregarded my mum's objections and tried to go to Earth.

- But instead of being my white knight, you were my tormentor and rapist.

Bjorn:

- I did not know what else to do. Keeping you as my sex slave was the only way for me to keep you near me. My father would not object if I held you as a sex slave, but he would never allow you to be my partner.

Keila:

- Bullshit. You knew what to do, but you choose to not do it because it was the challenging thing to do

- You were a spoilt brat that felt superior. You thought that you could take whatever you wanted by birthright. But you were wrong. Some things are not to be stolen; they are only to be given. Love is one such thing.

- I'll make you answer for your crimes and it won't be easy for you this time.

Bjorn:

- Keila. We are dying in the wilderness. I don't think we'll need to worry about the future anymore.

Keila:

- You are forgetting one thing. We might be on Mars, but we have access to Terran technology. If we die, we'll get revived, and you'll answer for your crimes.

Hearing this, Bjorn realised what he had to do. He pulled the metal stake out of his body to bleed out. He dragged himself to the edge. Bjorn:

- I am the son of the Terran Council leader Joachim Muller; I will not be trialled here. Goodbye Keila.

After saying this, Bjorn threw himself off the edge of Olympus Mons freefalling for five kilometres. It took so long time for him to hit the ground that he died from the blood loss before he reached the surface. He smiled as his body was falling towards the ground. In death, Bjorn finally found peace.

Before Keila almost died, she contacted friendly troops via the Divine Technology chip, and they brought her to a facility with Terran technology where they could revive her. She thought of Metatron, she closed her eyes, and her whole world turned black.

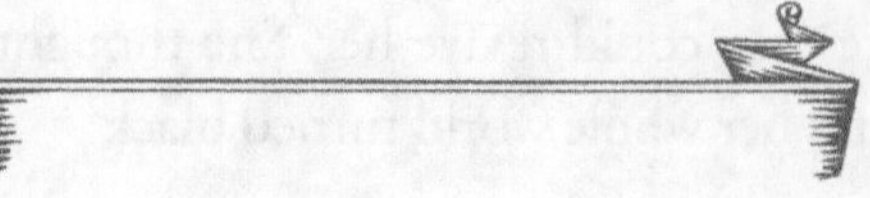

Chapter 192 Keila's Independence Speech.

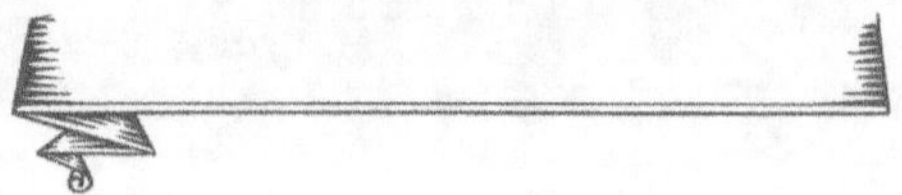

A few days later, Keila woke up. She knew that she had been dead for a while and yet she had not experienced any afterlife, just a long black dreamless sleep. It hadn't been too bad, but Keila was a bit curious if this disproved the afterlife or if she hadn't experienced it as her soul was not ready to move on.

Keila looked out through the window. There were a lot of people ignoring the cold to see the saviour of Mars. She walked to the podium and gave them a speech. It wasn't well-rehearsed as she just had woken up from the dead, but she did put some effort into it.

- Fellow Martians. Six months ago, no one would have believed me if I said that we one day would be free the Terran Council. We have destroyed the Phobos Base, the symbol of our oppression. We mourn those who died for our freedom.

- We have come a long way, but we need to be vigilant. We need to win peace before we can live in freedom. The only way we win peace is we are strong enough to stop any attempts from the Terrans to bully us from the sky. We must have enough weapons aimed at the heavens to deter the Terrans from ever bothering us again. With this in place, we can finally win our freedom.

Having said this, Keila returned to her bed to recover from her wounds. She looked at a report from her commanders. The Terran fleet had retreated to Earth, and a lot of fringe worlds had overthrown their

Terran Masters and pledged themselves to her cause. The Terrans would have to accept Martian peace and independence now.

As it turned out Keila was mistaken. The Terran Council had united behind Joachim Muller, and they had no intentions of participating in peace talks. On the contrary, they planned to end the Martians forever.

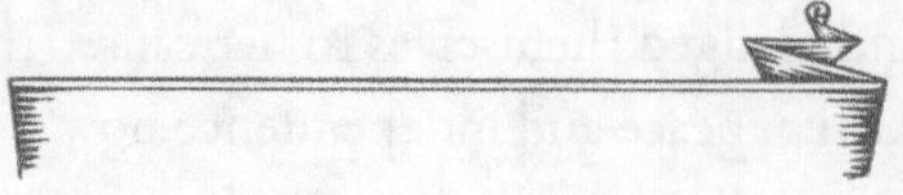

Chapter 193: A Final Solution.

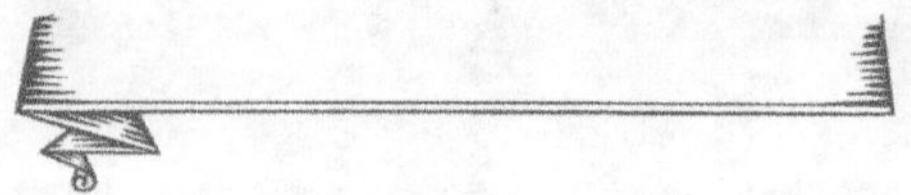

The Terran Council member held an emergency meeting in the Europeum Towers in Hansstadt. They were looking at a report put together by Mathias Muller, Supreme Commander for the Terran Council Security Forces, and Joachim Muller's brother.

The situation was critical. Following the annihilation of their Martian expeditionary force, the reputation of their military might was in shambles. To make matters worse, the Phobos Base that hosted their base for their Martian expeditionary force had been slung out of orbit, and was heading straight for the Sun. While Phobos was too small to make an impact on the Sun, the loss of their base of operations made it almost impossible to invade Mars.

The annihilation of their Martian expeditionary force had prompted the Terran Council to withdraw their ships to Earth to regroup. This in had caused many asteroid mining colonies to rebel and either declare independence or pledge allegiance to Keila's organisation The Martian Humanist Alliance.

The loss of the asteroid mining colonies was worse for the Terran Council than the loss of Mars. While Mars served as a dumping ground for unwanted dissenting citizens, the asteroid mining colonies brought back vital supplies to keep the Terran Economy going. Keeping the economy going was imperative for the Terran Council as they based their power on economic might.

Joachim Muller:

- Thank you for your report, Mathias. I will discuss potential solutions with the members of the council and I'll get back to you.

- Welcome council members. These are desperate times, but one good thing has come from this. We have stopped fighting among ourselves. I have a suggested solution to this crisis, but first, I would like to hear how all of you want to deal with the crisis.

Santiago Bolivar:

- Let us accept peace with Mars. Let them keep their cold, polluted dustbowl of a planet but make sure to retake control of all the Asteroid mining stations.

Joachim:

- Yes, Santiago. Financially that would make sense, but like I said the last time you brought this up, it is not a viable long-term solution. If we leave the Martians unchecked, and they will want to expand in a generation or two. They don't pose a threat to us now, but in century or less they will, and they will stage an invasion of Earth.

John White:

- Yes, I agree with you, Joachim. I think we should take a full fleet with all our large ships and bombard them from orbit into submission.

Joachim:

- Yes, but that won't work this time. Without a base of operations, our ships can only carry so much ammunition and supplies before going back to Earth. The Martians can hide in their bloody tunnels for a few days before we need to go back to resupply. We'll never win a war that way. Besides, the Martians will anticipate orbital bombardment, and they'll have a lot of weapons aimed at the skies to fight back against any attempt to bombard them from orbit.

Ibrahim Rashid:

- I suggest that we bombard them with our whole fleet and stage an invasion at the same time. While they hide in their tunnels. We land with a lot of heavy troops and take back our lost fortresses on the surface. From there we can project power and force the Martians to submission.

Joachim:

- That won't work for three reasons. 1: The Martians are way more numerous than us, and they are even more numerous than our military personnel. 2: It is it impossible to supply these bases without a base of operations in orbit. 3: The Martians have discovered a technology that disrupts the bionic microchips in our soldiers' heads. Before we consider an invasion, we need to replace the implants and retrain our soldiers.

Chi-Ping Cheng:

- What about a blockade of Mars? We use our forces to regain control of the asteroid mining stations, and then we stay out of reach for the Martian surface weapons, while we blockade their interplanetary trade.

Joachim:

- That would not work against the Martians. They are already dirt poor, and they have hardly received any interplanetary imports for the last centuries, so they wouldn't be affected if the trade stopped.

Chi-Ping Cheng:

- Okay Chairman Muller. You have argued against every solution we have put forth. What kind of masterstroke do you have on your mind?

Joachim Muller:

- I suggest that obliterate Mars and mask it as a natural disaster.

- In six months', time, the asteroid B600 is passing Mars, missing it by only 500,000 kilometres. It is a 10-kilometre asteroid travelling at 80,000 kilometres an hour. If it hit Mars, it would wipe out most of the life on the planet. It would be easy to change the trajectory of the asteroid to impact Mars.

Chi-Ping:

- But wouldn't the Martians send their own expedition to divert it from hitting them?

Joachim:

- Of course, but they wouldn't get far. We would send a large fleet to escort the asteroid until it was too late to change its course.

- Since we are still at war with the Martians, we have legal rights to attack all Martian vessels that we come across.

- We are not going to admit that we are directing a large asteroid towards Mars, causing genocide.

John:

- Excellent Joachim. This is a great solution. B600 is large enough to kill off most of the population and dispersing the

Martian atmosphere while leaving the planet in good enough condition for resettlement once the dust settles.

Chi-Ping:

- Yes, but I am worried about what the Terran population will think about this. While they don't love the Martians, they wouldn't condone Martian genocide either. They might even rebel against us.

Joachim:

- Don't worry. They won't find out. We own and control the media and the Space Net. We can send the dissenters that question us to resettle Mars.

Ibrahim.

- This is an excellent plan. Death to our enemy. Slay them all.

Joachim:

- Excellent. Do we have an agreement? A decision of this scale will require blood verification. I will write down the order, and then all of us will spill our blood on this panel to verify that we agree to it. To change the directive we all need to drop our blood again on the same panel.

They all did as Joachim requested. They took a small knife and spilled a drop of blood each on top of their faction's seal to verify the order. After this, they sat quiet. They had ordered a terrible atrocity even by their standards.

Eventually, they made their way back to their respective countries speaking to no one about what they had agreed on.

The official statement was that Terran Council would not discuss peace with the Martians, as the Martians needed to be punished for their surprise attack on their Terran protectors.

Chapter 194: The Redirection of The Asteroid B600.

Joachim Muller hung up the phone. He had dispatched the order to a joint Terran Council secret operations team. The Terran Council rarely performed mutual secret operations as its members were more likely to perform secret operations, against each other. But for this mission, it was imperative that they were all represented. They had agreed to the plan and no faction should be able to accuse the others if the plan failed.

The special operations team would land on B600 and install fusion rocket thrusters that redirected B600 on a collision course with Mars. They would stay on the asteroid to safeguard it from attackers and to be able to abort the mission until it was too late to change the trajectory of the asteroid. With this in place, Joachim called his brother, Supreme Commander Mathias Muller, to make sure that a fleet escorted the asteroid.

Joachim:

- Good evening, brother.

Mathias:

- Good evening Joachim. I expected to hear from you yesterday. Delays are not good for our efforts.

Joachim:

- You are correct.

- The Council trusts in your judgement on how to subdue the rebellious asteroid mining colonies and we only have one specific order for you.

Matthias:

- So, you finally trust my judgement? Tell me about your specific order.

Joachim

- You are to lead a group of ten star-cruisers and escort the asteroid B600.

Mathias:

- B600? There is nothing of value there. Besides it has an orbit that makes it to mine it.

Joachim Muller:

- We have received information that the heinous Keila Eisenstein intends to use the asteroid as a weapon against us. We want to direct it into the sun to get rid of it, but you need to guard it against Martian interference for the time being.

Mathias:

- This is terrible. That woman has no limit to her evil schemes and atrocities.

Joachim:

- Yes. So, can I count on your support to keep us safe?

Mathias:

- Yes. Of course, brother.

Joachim:

- Good, your fleet will depart tomorrow. Joachim out.

Joachim hung up the phone. He considered to involve his brother in the plan but he had decided against it. The fewer that knew about the asteroid strike, the better.

Besides, Mathias might have objections on this genocidal mission. Mathias Muller was a stern military man, but he had always tried to minimise civilian casualties. A general that tried to minimise civilian casualties would not agree to destroy the most populous planet in the solar system. But destroying Mars was imperative. Joachim knew that the Terran Council could not control and dominate Mars' downtrodden population any longer. If the Martians were not destroyed, they would grow stronger and come after the Terran Council with a vengeance.

Joachim sat down in his room and listened to classical music. He was looking at a picture of Bjorn. He mourned the loss of his son despite giving tacit approval for his assassination a few weeks earlier. Joachim looked at the images from Bjorn's childhood as well as an evaluation of Bjorn's DNA.

According to the DNA assessment, Bjorn had exceptional DNA, and yet he had ended up being a whoremongering drug addict. What had gone wrong? Joachim considered reusing Bjorn's genetic material to clone him as a baby. Joachim decided to wait. If everything went according to plan, he could do it when things had calmed down, so he had more time for the project.

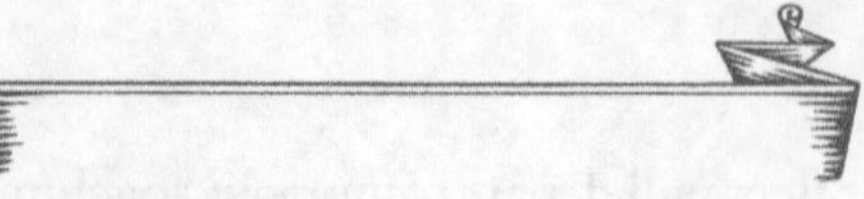

Chapter 195: Emergency Meeting in the Martian Council.

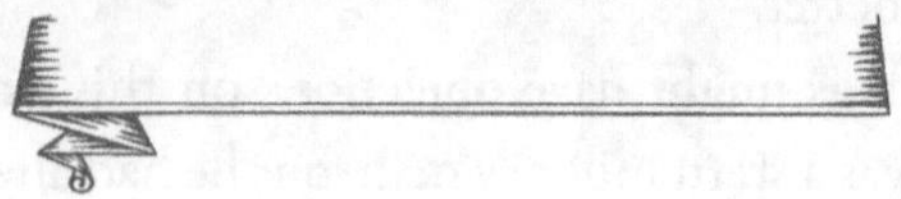

Keila was sitting in an underground meeting hall in the Olympus Republic. It was the meeting hall of by the Olympus Republic parliament, and it was situated far underground, safe from orbital bombardment.

Keila had summoned all Martian leaders to decide the future of the planet. It would not be an relaxed meeting. Different regions of Mars had different cultures, goals and rivalries and they were no longer united against the common enemy, as the Terran Council hadn't been seen or heard from in the last month. The complete silence from the Terran Council was an ominous sign. Keila had hoped that they would accept her peace proposal or at least communicate in some way, but there was only silence. Thus, they were still at war with Earth.

The worst part of being at war with the Terran Council was that they were cut off from Spacenet networks. Thus, they had very little knowledge of what was happening outside of Mars. Space traffic to and from Mars had ended as the Terran Council blockaded the planet. The blockade was not a big deal for the survival of the Martians, as they were used to only delivering shipments, but rarely receiving shipments because of their previous trade arrangement with their Terran overlords.

Keila looked at the delegates from her position in the late President Hellas Petrakis chair, in the centre of the large amphitheatre building. This was a unique occasion. For the first time in the the planet's history, the planetary leaders had gathered to decide their future without Terran interference.

What was the future of the Martian people and what would Keila's role be? Keila wanted to replicate what the Terran Council had created for Earth when it came to building peace and prosperity for the planet. She also wished to implement democratic leadership that benefited the ordinary citizen on Mars.

As the de-facto leader of the Martian Humanist Alliance, Keila's voice would be important for the future of Mars, and it was vital for her to align with politicians that would follow through with their promises. But how would she know if they were honest?

If she implanted Martian politicians with Divine Technology chips, she would know their thoughts. However, this would also make her the dictator of the planet, a worse dictator than the ones she had aimed to replace.

Suddenly, a member from the Science Commission, Jasper Svensson, interrupted the meeting:

- I am sorry to interrupt. But we have an urgent crisis!

Keila studied Jasper. She didn't know him, but she had met him briefly a few times when the Olympus Republic was reverse-engineering her Zetan Technologies.

Keila:

- What is the problem, Jasper? My door is always open, but not during a planetary meeting!

Jasper:

- B600 is the problem. A 10 kilometres large asteroid travelling is on a collision course with us. It will impact us in five months. I will show a hologram model of it for you to see.

Jasper activated the 3D hologram generator in the middle of the room. It showed how the asteroid was heading towards Mars and the estimated effects of the enormous impact it would cause. The gathering studied the 3D model. If Jasper were correct, the collision would kill off the majority of Martian life and cover the planet in a thick dust cloud for the next ten years. Keila spoke:

- Why haven't you brought up this problem until now, Jasper? The flight paths and orbits of all large celestial bodies have been mapped and estimated for the coming centuries.

Jasper:

- Because the asteroid was meant to miss Mars by 500,000 kilometres. Something is changing its path.

Keila:

- Do you think the Terran Council is behind this?

Jasper Svensson:

- I don't dare to speculate, but a large fleet of Terran ships is heading towards the asteroid.

Keila:

- This is not good. Would you be able to redirect the asteroid from hitting us?

Jasper:

- Yes, as long as I am on the asteroid at least a month before the impact.

Keila:

- Very well. Gather a team and take our fastest ship with stealth capabilities to intercept the asteroid as soon as possible.

Jasper Svensson:

- Thank you, Mistress Keila. I will gather a team at once.

As Jasper Svensson left the meeting room, an upset chatter began. Most of the assembly wanted to surrender to the Terran Council to avoid total destruction of their home planet. Keila put an end to the discussion.

There was no point in yielding a month after their victory, and besides, it was impossible to communicate with the Terran Council as Mars was disconnected from Spacenet, their transmissions were jammed by the blockading fleet, and they received no answers from the Terran counterparts. They have to pray that Jasper and his team would be able to carry out the crucial task at hand.

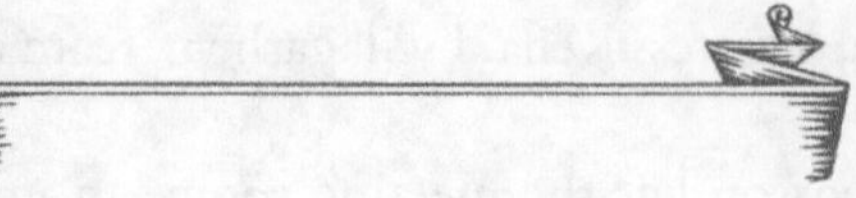

Chapter 196: Meeting between Joachim Muller, Benjamin Muller, and Mathias Muller in Europeum Tower

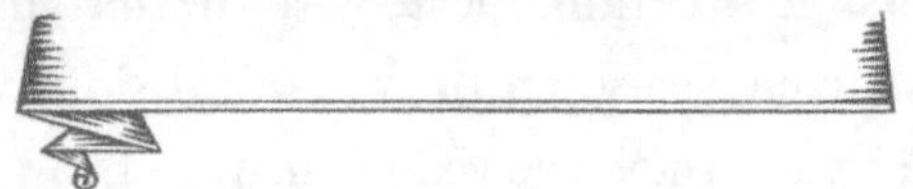

Mathias Muller was presenting the last month's achievements when it came to suppressing the rebellion in the solar system. It had been an overwhelming success, as all Terran factions had united behind the Terran Council Security Forces instead of fighting among themselves.

The Terran Council had crushed the uprisings on the asteroid mining colonies as well as those on Jupiter's and Saturn's moons. This had been easy to do as they had closed down Spacenet, thus blocking the rebelling colonies from communicating, cooperating, and coordinating their plans. It also helped that the Terran Council was the only force that had a deep space fleet, i.e. a navy that could travel for months without the need to replenish their supplies.

With all the threats contained, the Terran Council could now focus on dealing with the Martian uprising.

Mathias:

- We have secured control over the solar system. The shipments from the asteroid mining stations are up and running again. So, how do you wish to deal with Mars? I have heard, that they are desperate for peace?

Joachim:

- Yes. But I will not grant them any peace. Not after what the treacherous bastards did to us.

Matthias:

- With all due respect brother, but we cannot invade Mars. We don't have a base of operations in the area anymore, and if we move our ships close enough to bombard the surface, they can respond with their ground to air weapons that would devastate our forces.

Joachim:

- Yes, I am aware of that. But like a said, I am not considering peace with those treacherous scumbags

Matthias:

- So, what would you have us do? Do you want to blockade them indefinitely?

Joachim:

- Sure, why not. Let them have their "freedom" in their dusty dirt-poor desert.

Benjamin:

- How about we resume control over Phobos, and push it back into orbit around Mars?

Joachim shook his head and gave Benjamin a disapproving look, he then spoke mockingly:

- Brother, teach my son basic science, please.

Mathias felt an uncomfortable but brushed it off and started lecturing Benjamin on why his plan wouldn't work.

- The Phobos base is bound for a collision with the Sun, which means that it is falling towards the centre of gravity in the solar system. We do not have the technology to pushing such a massive object away from the centre of gravity.

- We could save it by driving it sideways to make it orbit the Sun.

- That would, give it an orbit between Mercury and Venus, and we do not need a military base in that part of space.

Benjamin:

- I see. So, what do you suggest?

Mathias Muller:

- Well I have realised that the conflict Mars is stuck in a dead-lock. We can't invade them, and they can't harm us either. I suggest that we listen to them and give them their independence.

- To stop their influence, I suggest that we transport an asteroid from the asteroid belt and put it in orbit around Mars. On that asteroid, we can build a new base to make sure that our presence is known to our enemies.

Benjamin:

- But uncle, you just said we can't move large celestial bodies?

Joachim:

- Benjamin. When pushing an asteroid from the asteroid belt towards Mars, you are driving it towards the Sun. It is a lot easier to move an object towards gravity than pushing it against gravity.

Mathias:

- Yes, Joachim, you are correct.

- Speaking of other things. What is the deal with B600? It seems to be on a collision course with Mars.

Joachim:

- Yes, that is the reason why you are meant to escort it. Our scientists have discovered that the asteroid is on a collision course with Mars, and they are working to divert it and make it crash into the Sun instead

- You are there to stop the Martians from reaching the asteroid, as we fear that they are going to redirect it to collision course with Earth.

Mathias:

- That is unlikely. The orbit of B600 is very remote from Earth.

Joachim:

- Yes, but you didn't foresee the Martian surprise attacks that wiped out our armies on Mars, did you?

- Do your job and keep B600 safe from the Martians. I will update your systems with the correct trajectory of the asteroid to keep you from worrying.

- I will see you at dinner before you leave.

Mathias:

- Thank you, brother. I will see you at dinner.

Mathias left the room. Joachim and Benjamin looked at each other in silence for a bit before Benjamin spoke:

- Do you think he fell for the falsified trajectories you uploaded into his PDA?

Joachim:

- Hopefully. If not, I have an assassin in place to kill him, should it be needed. He trusts this spy so she won't fail us, unlike the amateur you sent after Bjorn. But let's hope I can keep my brother alive, shall we?

Benjamin:

- Yes, father. You are always one step ahead. Who is this assassin?

Joachim:

- I wouldn't be one step ahead if I told you. Now freshen up and get changed. You have a farewell dinner with your uncle to attend.

Chapter 197: An Assassination and a Destroyed Ship.

A few weeks later, Supreme Commander Mathias Muller was back on his command ship escorting Asteroid B600. He studied the trajectory of the asteroid, and it didn't make sense. The asteroid was headed for the sun and yet the instruments on his command ship indicated that he was heading towards Mars. Mathias called in the captain of the vessel, as well as his secret mistress, Melissa Schiller, to talk.

Mathias:

- Melissa, can you explain this: The trajectory of B600 will direct it into the Sun. Yet our ships escorting the asteroid, are heading towards the Mars

Melissa:

- Don't worry about that Mathias. Didn't your brother tell you that he had men redirecting the asteroid to collide with the Sun instead?

Mathias:

- Yes, he did. I am not comfortable with the secretiveness of the mission. I am the Supreme Commander of the Terran Council Security Forces. I shouldn't be on this mission, and yet he withholds information from me.

Melissa:

- Don't worry about it. Why don't we have a quickie now that we are alone on the command deck?

Mathias:

- Don't be silly, the command deck is full of cameras.

Melissa:

- We have access codes to override the cameras and turn them off.

Mathias was considering Melissa's proposal. He didn't get further as he got a call on the hologram generator. The call was from a small Martian science vessel which confused Mathias as the spaceship had to be close to contact him directly, as Spacenet had been turned off for Martian vessels. Yet he wasn't aware of any Martian vessels in the vicinity.

Mathias' curiosity got the better of him, and he ignored the directive to ignore all Martian transmissions. The hologram of the Martian scientist Jasper Svensson came up on the hologram generator.

Jasper:

- Thank you for answering our transmissions. You Terrans haven't been talkative lately.

Mathias:

- I was curious about how you contacted me. Mars is far away, and you are blocked from Spacenet.

Jasper:

- I am much closer than that.
- Anyways. I have an urgent request for you.

Mathias:

- You are not in a position to make requests to me. I am the Supreme Commander of the Terran Council Security Forces, and we are at war with you.

Jasper:

- Oh, sorry about my word choice. I am pleading you to help us.

- B600 is on a direct collision course with Mars. I have arrived with a team to redirect it from hitting Mars.

Mathias:

- We already have a team on the surface of B600 that is working to redirect the asteroid into hitting the Sun instead.

Jasper:

- That is not true. B600 was meant to miss Mars by 500,000 kilometres, and now its trajectory has changed to a direct collision with Mars.

- I know we are at war Mr. Muller but please work with us in. If that rock hits Mars, most of our population will die. I know you dislike seeing innocents die.

Mathias was confused and did not know what to believe. Jasper's claim supported his own suspicions that the asteroid was heading for a collision with Mars. However, Jasper was one of his enemies. The cowardly enemy who had surprise attacked and killed his men two months earlier. Mathias would be a fool to trust the enemy. Then again, he did not trust his brother either and he did not want to become an involved in the worst genocide in mankind's history.

Mathias:

- Mr Svensson. I would like you to come by my ship and parlay under the banner of truce. I want to go to the bottom with your claims.

Jasper:

- I would be honoured to meet you, Supreme Commander.

Half an hour later, a small shuttle with Jasper Svensson docked with Mathias Muller's command ship. Mathias' troops stripped him nude to search him for weapons, scanned him for any viruses and pathogens and then gave him a crew tracksuit for his visit. He was escorted to a meeting room where Mathias was waiting for him. They shook hands and started to talk.

Meanwhile, Melissa Schiller was watching the men via the CCTV. She was feeling guilty about what she had to do, but she had no other option. Joachim Muller had warned her that it might come to this, that her lover would betray her people and befriend the enemy. She couldn't let that happen. She entered a command into her encrypted phone and activated a microscopic dormant poison ampule that she had inserted into Mathias' body when he was asleep. The hidden container released a fast-acting nerve agent that killed the victims by corroding away their brains, preventing any resurrection attempts.

Jasper looked in terror as Mathias was dying in front of him with blood pouring from his eyes. A few moments of agony later, Mathias lay dead on the floor. Melissa stormed in and shot Jasper in the head. She looked straight into the camera and spoke:

- Crew Members of ISS Terran Dominion; Our Supreme Commander Mathias Muller was just murdered during a parley with this treacherous Martian creature. This is unacceptable. Destroy his ship and the rest of his crew.

Seconds later ISS Terran Dominion opened fire at the Martian ship and destroyed the research ship with its massive firepower.

Chapter 198: The Infamous Keila Eisenstein's Operative Assassinates the Foolish Supreme commander Mathias Muller

News Broadcast in the Terran Council News Network, 25th October 2874:

After the dishonourable attacks on our military bases conducting humanitarian aid on the Martian surface two months ago, Terran Council chairman Joachim Muller has ordered a blockade of the Martians until further notice. This wise order was broken by his brother Supreme Commander Mathias Muller yesterday, and he paid dearly for his gullibility.

Mathias Muller agreed to parlay with the assassin Jasper Svensson, who posed as a Martian scientist. The killer linked to the nefarious terrorist Keila Eisenstein wasted no time and killed Mathias, using a tiny poisoned needle that he smuggled past the ship's security. The ship's security officers then eliminated the threat before he could cause any more damage. The spaceship with Jasper's co-conspirators was also destroyed as a precaution.

Chairman Joachim Muller comments: "I am still mourning the loss of my dear son Bjorn, and now on I have lost my dear younger brother. I can assure you all that this strengthens my resolve and I urge everyone to avoid Mathias' mistake and ignore all contact with our Martian enemies." - Joachim Muller.

Joanna Lechinsky, Terran Council News Network Journalist.

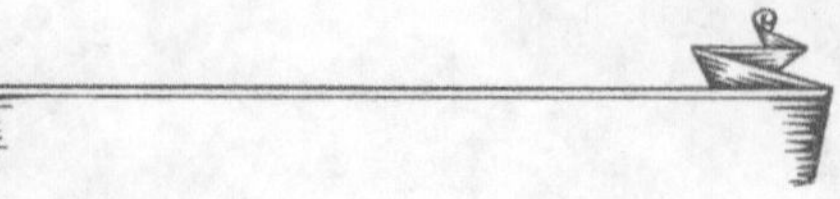

Chapter 199: Desperate Times Require Desperate Measures.

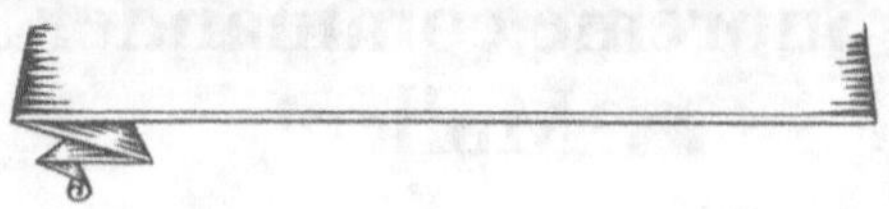

Keila looked at the video that depicted the murder of Supreme Commander Mathias Muller by her lead scientist Jasper Svensson. Had Jasper assassinated the supreme commander during a parlay? What an idiotic thing to do, especially with a supermassive asteroid heading on a collision course with Mars in 4 months. Or had the Terrans turned their backs on Mathias and killed him to blame her?

Keila did not know why the Terran Council want to kill their own Supreme Commander, but the reason didn't matter to her. She needed to come up with a way to save her people, and she was running short on options.

Keila closed her eyes to think. She heard Rangda calling her. Keila had ignored Rangda and the visions she was getting for the last few months after realising that Rangda was inherently evil. Besides. using the powers that Rangda could grant her aged her a lot. She had used Rangda's abilities twice, and it had aged her over a dozen years. While Keila did not fear death, she did not fancy the idea of dying of old age in her 20's.

Realising that the situation was critical, Keila opened her mind and allowed Rangda to talk to her.

Rangda:

- You have been avoiding me, little girl.

Keila:

- Yes. Speaking with an evil alien is not on the top of my list.

Rangda:

- The concept of evil is in the eye of the beholder. I did what I had to do to save my people. Just as you are.

Keila:

- So how do you explain the massive aging I have experienced after letting you help me?

Rangda:

- That is not my fault. I did not intend for you to age. But your feeble human DNA cannot accept the powers that I am lending you without consequences.

- Regardless, you are talking to me now. So how can I help?

Keila:

- The Terran Council has sent a giant asteroid to crash with my home planet to kill most of its population.

Rangda:

- Yes, I know. Such a terrible waste of life. So much death and so little eating.

Keila:

- So, your objection is not the killing itself, but the wasting of the meat?

Rangda:

- Yes. Killing for eating is natural, and part of the cycle of life. Killing without consumption of the fallen is unnatural and depraved. Typical human and Zetan behaviour, done out of greed and hunger for power. Unlike like my noble Xenos, who kill to live.

- Anyways. You want help, and I can help.

Keila:

- How? Can you redirect the asteroid that is directed towards my planet?

Rangda:

- No. But I can attack the humans on Earth, making it easier for you to redirect the asteroid.

Keila:

- I see. What's in it for you?

Rangda:

- My Xenos and I are hungry, and human meat is delicious.

Keila was contemplating her options. She wasn't very fond of the idea to release a host of man-eating aliens on the surface of Earth as this would kill a lot of innocents. But the Terran Council had sent an asteroid to exterminate her people like they were low-life insects. Sending them some man-eating monsters to deal with would make them realise that Martians and Terrans shouldn't fight each other but unite as one.

Keila:

- Okay. I want your help but on one condition. That you only kill and eat the soldiers, not the citizens, and that you allow the enemy to surrender.

Rangda:

- Surrender? What a strange concept. Is that something humans really do? Abandon their honour and becoming someone's slave? Very well, I promise.

Keila:

- Good. So how do I unleash your army on my enemies?

Rangda:

- There are four pyramids spread across the Earth. They all need to be activated at noontime local time, the same day. Doing this will power up the portals between my dimension and your dimension.

- Open your mind, and I'll transfer the information you need to achieve it.

Keila opened her mind, allowing Rangda to transfer her the information. Keila was fascinated by seeing the undiscovered inner workings of pyramids across Earth. To most people, these pyramids were just ancient piles of rock.
Keila:

- Got it. One more thing. How do I move around on Earth? I don't think they'll grant me an entry permit.

Rangda:

- Alicia White...

After this, Rangda disconnected but Keila knew what she had to do. She summoned Melchior, her Edenite aide and second in command to her office.
Keila:

- Melchior. I need to go to Eden at once. I am leaving you in command of Mars for the time being.

Melchior:

- I see. Are you abandoning us, Mistress Keila?

Keila:

- I would never do that! After visiting Eden, I am going to Earth to fix things.

Melchior:

- Going to Earth? That's suicide.

Keila:

- No, it's not. I have a plan.
- Do you trust me, Melchior?

Melchior:

- With all my heart.

Keila:

- Then rule Mars in my stead until I am back. I'm heading back to Eden. May the True Maker be with us until we meet again.

Melchior:

- It has been an honour serving you Keila. Farewell.

After promoting Melchior to command, Keila left Mars with a small group on a stealth shuttle transport ship heading for Eden.

Chapter 200: An Emotional Visit on Eden

Keila was docked to the Divine Control Centre. She exited her shuttle and met up with Metatron. It was a touching sight. She hadn't seen him for over nine months, and despite their breakup, she had missed him a lot. Keila found it strange that she hadn't been able to get over him, as she many times during their relationship, had found him boring. Maybe a boring a partner was what she secretly yearned for, after these years of war. Keila looked at his face. Metatron seemed both sad and happy to see her. He approached her and spoke.

Metatron:

- Welcome back, Keila.

Keila:

- Thanks, Metatron. I have missed you.

Metatron:

- Then stay with me. You are the reason we are apart. I have never pushed you away.

Keila:

- I know Met. But this was something that I needed to do.

Metatron:

- Yes. I want to show you something.
- Come with me.

Keila and Metatron walked together to the medical bay. They stayed next to an artificial womb. It contained a three-month-old foetus.
Metatron:

- This is our future daughter. If everything goes to plan, she will be born on the 25th of March, the date of her adulthood ceremony in your visions.

Keila:

- That is nice.

Metatron:

- You don't seem very enthusiastic.

Keila:

- I know. There is a lot of pressure on me. 4 billion lives are at stake.

- Besides... The visions...

- I have had visions of me having a family with Bjorn Muller back on Earth. The premonitions are confusing me, considering what happened between Bjorn and me.

Metatron:

- Well. Those visions are never going to happen. No point thinking of "what ifs" in life. You got to deal with things that happens.

Keila:

- Yes, you are right.

Metatron:

- Can I ask you for a favour? How about you stay back on Eden and give birth to our daughter. I don't want her to end up being a soulless, emotionless individual like I am. I want her to be like you.

Keila:

- You don't need to worry about that. You are the best man I have ever met, and you sprung from an artificial womb. Besides, what is a soul anyway?

Metatron:

- Good question. Maybe it's only a social construct.

Keila:

- Exactly.
- Sadly, I cannot stay. I got to finish what I started.

Metatron:

- Maybe you should try inaction for once? Perhaps the Terran Council wants to scare your people with their imminent doom and then divert the asteroid from colliding with Mars in the last minute.

- I don't think they will slaughter billions of people in cold blood.

Keila:

- They do, unfortunately. Bjorn Muller tried to crash the Phobos moon onto the surface of Mars when his defeat was imminent. I stopped him in the last second.

Metatron

- That is a shocking disregard for human life!
- Very well, then I understand why you must go.

Keila:

- Good. Did you find me a suitable team of Edenites to pose as Alicia White's crew?

Metatron:

- Yes, I did.

Keila:

- Did you tell them that it was a suicide mission?

Metatron:

- No, I did not, because I have faith in your return.

Keila:

- Good.
- Show me Alicia White's corpse and all the information we have about her.

Metatron:

- Why?

Keila:

- Because I need to know about her to act like her.

Metatron downloaded all the files available on Alicia White from Space Net. As Eden officially wasn't participating in the Mars/ Earth conflict, they had full access to Space Net, and yet they didn't find much. All the information they found was that Alicia White was the daughter of John White, the Chairman of House White. Alicia White was born 25 years earlier and she was missing, presumed dead. Her picture on Spacenet was edited to make her look like a normal Terran and not like the genetic freak she was.

Keila:

- This is very little information on a woman who was one of the wealthiest on the planet.

Metatron:

- Yes. House White is trying to keep her identity a secret. No matter, this is the information that we have.

Keila:

- Yes.

- Let's not waste any more time. Use the outer layer external DNA modifier to change my looks to Alicia's.

As Keila transformed into Alicia's body, she experienced something strange. Keila felt how her physical body changed drastically. When she had disguised as Rose Menakis and Edenite women she had always felt like herself, just with a different face, but not when she was posing as Alicia White.

Keila felt an urge to consume blood, and raw meat. Another desire also increased, her sadistic sexual urge. Keila felt no need to repel this urge, and she pushed Metatron to the ground and pulled off his pants. He was surprised but did not resist her advances. She then jumped on top of him and rode him until she climaxed.

Afterwards, Keila got off and said. *"See you later, lover boy"*. She got dressed and headed for Alicia White's captured shuttle. Keila gathered her Edenite strike team that also had assumed the identities of the fallen members of Alicia White's black operations operatives. Once they were all onboard the vessel, Keila set the course for Earth.

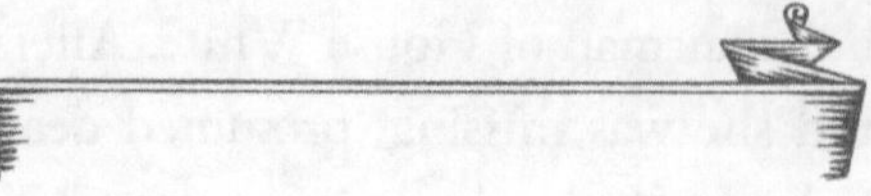

Chapter 201 Passing Earth Immigration

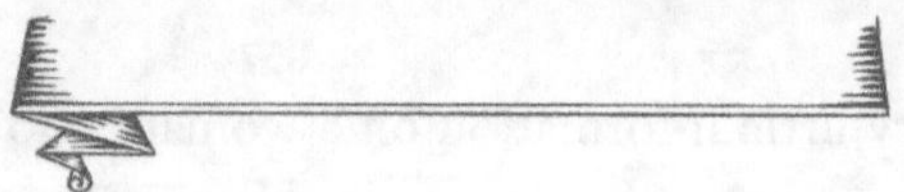

Keila was looking in amazement as she got closer to Earth, The blue home planet for all of humanity. It was the first time she saw it, but she remembered dreaming about going there when she was a child. During the rebellion, Keila had been around a lot in the solar system, and yet the blue planet was the most beautiful thing she had ever seen. There was not much time to marvel at its beauty, as she needed to get through Terran customs immigration orbiting Earth.

There were a lot of Terran Council warships that defended the perimeter. But where was it best to receive her clearance for landing on Earth? The natural thing for Alicia White to do would be to obtain an entry permit from a House White ship. But if she docked with a House White ship, she risked running into someone that knew Alicia, and that could expose her. As it happened, destiny decided for her, and she was contacted by Hilda Muller, Bjorn Muller's much younger cousin.

Hilda:

- Alicia White! Welcome back to Earth. Would you please dock with ISS Blue Haven, so we can clear you for re-entry to Earth?

Keila *hissing*:

- Clear for re-entry? I am the daughter of John White. Let me pass.

Hilda:

- Spare your bullshit, Alicia. I am the daughter of the late supreme Commander Mathias Muller. Comply with our rules or face the consequences.

Keila:

- Very well. Let's do it your way, but don't waste my time.

Hilda:

- Excellent. Dock with my ship ISS Blue Haven, and we will process you and your entourage for re-entry to Earth.

After speaking to Keila, who appeared to be Alicia, Hilda turned to the soldiers.
Hilda:

- I want you to be very thorough when examining this group. There is something amiss with someone disappearing for over a year and then reappearing without warning.

Hilda felt puzzled. It was likely that the *"Alicia White"* she had been talking to over the hologram generator was a Martian spy. But while a spy could use plastic surgery to change their physical appearance, they could not change their DNA so her advanced scanners would detect if *"Alicia White"* was a Martian spy and not the real deal.

Hilda wanted to detain Alicia, so she'd have plenty of time to verify her identity, but this was not a realistic solution for a high-ranking citizen. Instead, she opted to have an informal chat. Keila's ship docked with ISS Blue Haven, and Hilda lead her to a dining table set with delicious food and wines. Keila poured herself a glass of delicious red wine that tasted like paradise to her tastebuds.
Hilda:

- Welcome back to Earth. Alicia. I apologise for our need to verify the identities of yourself and your operatives.

Keila:

- Apology accepted, since you're providing me with this excellent food and wine.

Hilda:

- So, you appreciate our produce?

Keila:

- Of course. House Muller is famous for making the best food and drinks on Earth. Much better than the food I have eaten in the last year.

Hilda:

- Yes, speaking of the last year. Where have you been?

Keila:

- I have been hiding. After Bjorn's allegations against me, I felt no desire to go back to Earth. With Bjorn out of the picture, I want to return to Earth and live the kind of life I deserve.

Hilda:

- Speaking of Bjorn, was his allegations against you correct?

Keila:

- I'd rather not say. What amused me about this whole charade was how vital non-consensual sex became for Bjorn, who was known to be a rapist himself.

Hilda:

- I agree. The man was a creep. I hated how he sized me up with his eyes when I was younger.

- Whatever you did to him; I condone it.

- I just need to check a thing. I'll be right back.

Hilda went outside of the room and checked the reports on "Alicia" and her group. Both their facial features and their DNA matched the records. They couldn't have been killed and cloned as they only had been away for one year and it would take much longer to get clones aged to a mature age, even with accelerated cloning. They were also unlikely to have joined the Martian side as they were prominent Terrans and had nothing to gain from switching sides. Hilda to allow Alicia and her group re-entry to Earth. She walked back to the dining room.
Hilda:

- Alright, Alicia. You and your group have been granted re-entry to Earth.

Keila:

- Thank you, Hilda. And thanks again for the delicious food and wine.

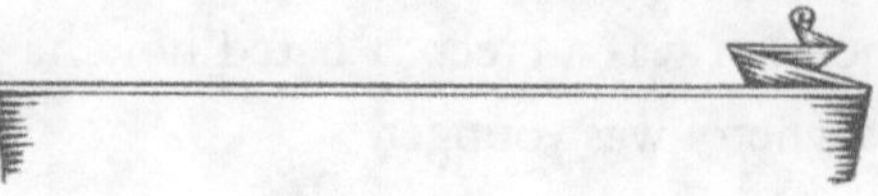

Chapter 202: Pyramids and Estranged Fathers.

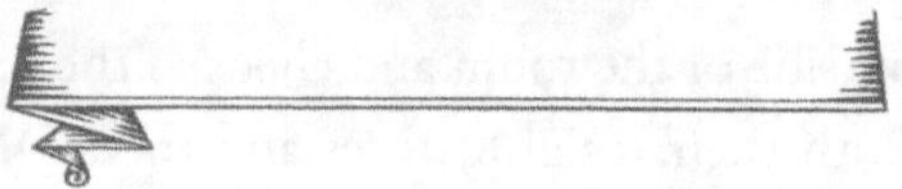

The next few weeks, Keila and her group travelled to the pyramids that Rangda had mentioned in Keila's vision. There was a total of four pyramids that needed to be activated at noontime in their respective time zones; these pyramids were spread across the globe ranging from Central America, the Pacific, Asia and Egypt. They needed to prepare themselves if they were to succeed, as they needed to find and activate all of the pyramids within one day for Rangda's plan to work.

To move quickly to the activation points in the different pyramids, they needed to excavate the sites. To be able to rush in and out from the excavation point was crucial as they only had a couple of hours between activating one pyramid until they needed to enable the next, and the pyramids were 1000's of kilometres apart. Fortunately, their spaceship had a high top-speed, so if they were able to move in and out of the pyramids quickly, there was no problem reaching the next pyramid on time.

The only issue was the last pyramid they needed to reach. The Cheops Pyramid, which lay in Rashidium, the capital of House Rashid's territory. Its activation point was not easily accessible. While they could excavate the other three pyramids using lasers, they knew that House Rashid would not allow them to excavate their gilded pyramid.

Keila decide that her only option was to activate the other three pyramids first and then blow up the walls exposing the activation switch in the Cheops Pyramid, using mono-directional explosives. Then they could enable the fourth pyramid, and open the portal of dimensions, before House Rashid soldiers had the time to stop them.

The night before the operation, Keila was finding sleeping difficult. It was hot and humid in her Central American excavation camp, and the mosquitos didn't make things better. Keila feared for her own life, and she worried about the fate of her home planet. B600 would impact in 1 month and 1 week, and she was unsure whether there would be enough time to divert the asteroid from crashing with Mars, which would lead to Martian genocide. Strangely she also felt guilt and pity towards John White, Alicia's father. While he was a monster who had caused the death and torment of countless Martians throughout the years, he was a loving father who missed his daughter.

Keila had received a lot of messages where he begged her to come home and see him. Many of these pictures also contained pictures from Alicia's childhood and different milestones of her life. Keila found the pictures moving; despite John White being a public figure he never stepped away from his freak daughter and stood by her despite public opinion. He could have hidden her apart, and yet he always stood by her side.

Keila received another email from John White, who thought that she was Alicia.

Dear Alicia.

I don't know why refuse to talk to me. Please answer, and we can work things out.

I will be in Rashidium in the next few days for a Terran Council meeting, so we can meet there, and you can tell me more about your new-found interest in pyramids.

/ Dad

Keila read the email. She was contemplating whether it would be a good idea to answer. Keila decided to use John's love for Alicia to make him do things for her. She answered his email.

Dear Father.

Thank you for wanting to be a part of my life again. I haven't answered your messages because I am upset that you didn't stand by me when Bjorn Muller ordered my arrest.

I am studying the pyramids because I am looking for an ancient forgotten technology that we can use to defeat the Martians. I am willing to share my findings if you are willing to divert B600 from impacting on Mars' surface.

/ Alicia.

A few minutes later, Keila received a response from John White.

Dear Alicia. I don't know how you know about B600, but I guess intelligence gathering is your specialty. I am unfortunately unable to help you with B600 collision diversion, as the destruction of Mars was a blood oath made during a Terran Council meeting. The only way to reverse the order is to issue another unanimous blood oath, repealing the order. This requires the mutual agreement of all Terran House leaders, not just me. I hope to see you in Egypt, nonetheless.

/ John

Keila read the message and felt hope. If she failed to initiate Rangda's portals she could try to use her Alicia White disguise to infiltrate the Terran Council meeting and "persuade" the Terran Council leadership to see things her way. Keila asked one of her Edenite operatives to pull out one of her teeth and replace it with a small container of extremely toxic nerve gas. Then she injected herself with an antidote that would grant her immunity to that poison for the next 96 hours.

Satisfied with her prospects of success Keila fell asleep.

Chapter 203: Keila Activates the Portals and is Arrested

The following day, Keila woke up, and when the time approached noon, she approached the centre of the Central American pyramid where she could perform the activation sequence. The sequence was hidden to the others, and only Keila could see the hidden switches that she needed to activate to enable the portals. Keila's ability to see the secret activation codes in the pyramids was due to her Zetan DNA sequences, and due to her psionic connection to Rangda.

After Keila had activated the Central American pyramid, she rushed to her spaceship, so she could fly to the next Pacific pyramid, in time to enable that one as well. She repeated this procedure with the Pacific and the Asian pyramids, and she reached the Cheops Pyramid in the outskirts of Rashidium. Keila and her Edenite operatives brought stun guns to knock out the guards and unidirectional explosive charges to destroy the wall that blocked their way to the activation chamber in the pyramid. She activated the last pyramid, but nothing seemed to happen.

Keila ran out from the pyramid and realised that she was surrounded by a large group of House Rashid security forces.

Security officer:

- Alicia White! You and your group are all under arrest for assaulting security guards and vandalising Rashid property. Surrender immediately!

For a second Keila thought of fighting back, but then she stood down. As long as they believed she was Alicia White, they wouldn't dare to do anything against her, so she would be better off biding her time.

Keila looked in disappointment at the pyramid from the backseat of the truck she was in. Whatever she had done hadn't worked, and no portal had opened! Keila was put under house arrest in a luxurious private suite in Rashid tower, while her associates were held in small holding cells in the basement.

Chapter 204: A Confusing Science Report.

Joachim Muller was reading a confusing science report in the vacuum tube transport that took him to Rashidium for the Terran Council meeting. According to the report, Earth's day had slowed down by 2 seconds in the last 24 hours. This did not make any sense to Joachim. If Earth's rotation had slowed down that much, this would lead to a lot of friction energy from the deceleration. This would cause earthquakes or a significant rise in the surface temperature. But there hadn't been reports of either. Furthermore, the scientist had claimed that the reason for Earth's slower rotation speed was connected to the vandalism Alicia White had performed on the Cheops pyramid the day before. These claims were absurd, and Joachim made a note to have that scientist fired when he got back from the Terran Council meeting.

Apart from that, Joachim found the meeting to be a waste of time. There wasn't much for them to discuss, but they had agreed to meet often and be more transparent, as they needed to stay united to avoid their enemies turning them against each other, as Keila Eisenstein had done before.

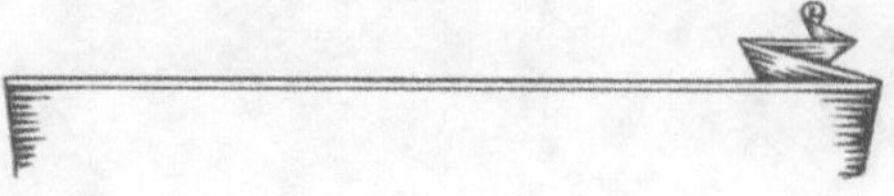

Chapter 205: Time for a Trial.

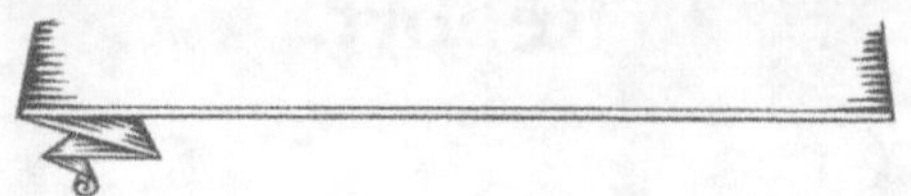

Keila was looking out through the window of the luxury apartment in Rashid Tower where she was under house arrest. Posing as Alicia White had perks and even as a prisoner, her life here was more luxurious than it had ever been. But Keila could not enjoy the luxury. Time was running out for her Martian comrades. Scientists on Mars had estimated that B600 needed to be deflected at least a month before colliding with Mars for it to pass on a safe distance from the planet. It was now one month and two days from a collision and time was running out. Her plan had failed, and Rangda had betrayed her. She had been staring at the damn Cheops Pyramid for the last day, and although it was beautiful, covered in gold reflecting the sunlight, it hadn't done anything, and she was stuck here unable to do anything to save her friends.

Everything changed when a few Rashid guards entered the apartment.

Guard:

- Time to freshen up and look decent, Alicia.

Keila:

- Why is that?

Guard:

- Because you are answering to the Terran Council for your crimes in an hour.

- Strip naked and have a decontaminating shower. We have provided fresh clothes for you here.

Keila thought of arguing back but decided against it. It was evident that the guards were suspicious towards her, but as long as they didn't detect the nerve gas she had hidden in a fake tooth, it did not matter. Keila showered and got dressed in her allocated clothes. It was a fancy dress, but their intention was obvious; she was their prisoner.

Keila followed the guards when they were leading her to the meeting room on the penthouse level of the tower. She was filled with a bittersweet feeling. While she could deliver justice to her enemies and save her people, she would most likely not get out of here alive.

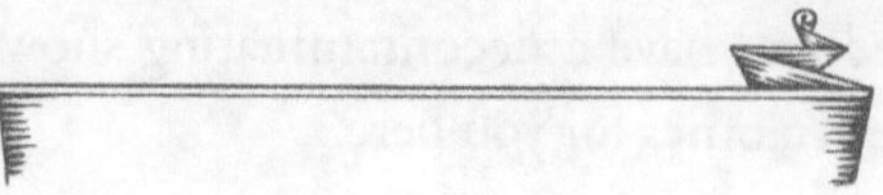

Chapter 206: A Crucial Late Realisation.

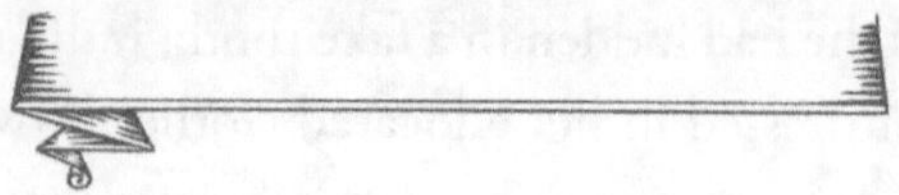

Hilda Muller was having a relaxed afternoon as a guest in the Rashid tower. She was attending the Terran Council meeting in Rashidium. Hilda was important enough to participate, but she wasn't powerful enough to have much impact on the results. Hence, she saw these meetings as a few days to mingle, relax and have excellent food and drinks.

Hilda was enjoying the view from the Terrace of the 30th level of the Rashid Tower. It was a beautiful day, and Rashidium was as beautiful as ever. Built as an oasis in the desert of the Giza valley, the lush Residuum city shone like an emerald in the desert. It's most remarkable feature, was the great pyramids of Giza, restored to their former glory and covered in a thick layer of gold.

The three pyramids were covered in over 10,000 tons of gold, and the most remarkable feature was how the gold was acquired. A century earlier, House Rashid scientists had discovered a medium-sized rogue meteor that was made of gold. This was because it was created by a supernova explosion and it had been floating around the galaxy for eons before entering the solar system. House Rashid scientist had landed the golden rock on Earth without causing an impact, which had been a great engineering feat. Rather than putting this massive amount of gold in circulation causing the gold prices to drop, they had opted to gild the pyramids, creating one of the great wonders of the future world. Hilda turned around, and Markus White, an attractive bachelor, greeted her. He was visiting Rashidium under similar circumstances as Hilda.

Markus:

- So, this is where the party is?

Hilda:

- I guess the party just got started.
- Did you come out to marvel at the pyramids?

Markus:

- Yes... I am marvelling at the pyramids among other things.

Hilda:

- You flirt! I met your cousin Alicia, the other day.

Markus:

- Any claw marks or scratches from your encounter?

Hilda:

- No, she was acting pretty civilised. We had some beef steak and some wine.

Markus:

- You mean that you had some steak and wine, and she was eating raw meat and drinking blood?

Hilda:

- No of course not. Why would she act like that? She was quite thirsty and had several glasses. I guess that's what a long time in space do to you.

Markus:

- That's impossible. Alicia doesn't drink alcohol!

Hilda:

- Well, she did when I met her. I'll show you the security feed, so you can see for yourself.

Markus looked at the video from the security cameras and he froze for a moment. Not only did Alicia taste the wine but she drank quite a lot of it.

Markus:

- Where is Alicia now?

Hilda:

- She is answering to the leadership for her vandalism of the pyramids.

Markus:

- Come with me at once and bring some guards. We need to stop her now!

Hilda:

- I don't understand?

Markus:

- We are dealing with an imposter! The real Alicia White has a condition that makes alcohol deadly to her.

- Quick, gather some guards and rush to the meeting room. We must catch her before it is too late!

Having said this, they rushed to gather a few guards and then took the lift to the Penthouse level of Rashid Tower where Keila posing as Alicia was put on trial by the Terran Council leaders.

Chapter 207: Keila kills the Terran Council Leaders and Redirects B600 to Crash into the Sun.

Keila was listening to Ibrahim Rashid, who gave a lengthy statement on how priceless the pyramids were and the gravity of her crime. She knew this was charade so that he could make more money in compensation from House White for letting her go. But all of this was irrelevant. She hadn't come here to get involved in Terran Council politics; she had come here to end them and save her home planet from destruction. Yet, she felt fear. Keila knew if she did what she had to do; she would not get out of here alive. She didn't want to die, she wanted to live on Eden with Metatron and her daughter. But if Keila didn't act, her inactivity would cause the death of 4 billion people, and she would never be able to live with that knowledge.

Keila heard the lift beeping in the lobby, and she saw Hilda Muller accompanied by several guards moving towards her. This forced her to act. She jumped up to Ibrahim Rashid and pushed his hand on a handprint scanner. She activated the blast doors and sealed off the room before the guards got in.

John White yelled out:

- Alicia! What on Earth are you doing?!

Keila pulled out the fake tooth and released the very toxic nerve gas in the room.

Keila:

- I am not Alicia.

The nerve gas paralysed the Terran Council leaders. They were filled with fear as Keila deactivated the Zetan Outer Layer external DNA modifier and her appearance reverted to her real looks. Keila pressed the broadcast button so that all of Earth would be able to see what happened this day. Keila thought of giving a speech to the camera, but there was no time for such nonsense, she needed to save Mars and time was running out. She dragged the council members one by one to the blood oath machine and dropped some of their blood on the device. Eventually, they had all had their blood dropped on the device, and the command prompt was unlocked. Keila wrote:

Redirect B600 to collide with the Sun, instead of impacting with Mars. Then destroy the steering mechanism on the fusion thrusters as this is a final, irreversible order.

Unfortunately, the crew was currently 30 light minutes away, so it would take her at least an hour before she knew if they had carried out the order or not. Keila made one last effort before the guards got through the blast doors. She needed to make sure that the Terran Council leaders were not revived. She found a massive metal sculpture and started bashing in their heads. When she was done, she was covered in blood and brain matter.

Keila tried contacting Rangda to be possessed by her as a last-ditch attempt of getting out Rashidium alive. Rangda didn't respond. Instead, Keila went to the window, found a comfortable chair, and marvelled at the sun setting behind the gilded pyramids.

Chapter 208: The Portal Opens; Rangda and the Xenos Swarm in and Capture Keila.

As the sun was about to set behind the pyramids, Keila was stunned by intense blue light as the portal to the Divine Dimension opened. Out of the portal came a swarm of Xenos lead by Rangda. The House Rashid security forces were taken by surprise when the Xenos appeared, and most of them got slaughtered when the wave of Xenos came rushing towards Rashid towers. The Xenos was unstoppable for the Rashid defenders as they had stolen ballistic energy absorbers from the Zetan armouries in the Divine Dimension and because they had a top running speed of 100 kilometres an hour which was faster than any of the Rashid defenders on foot could match. The main reason, however, was that Rashid's was caught off guard and only had police and light units patrolling the streets.

Keila heard the gunfire, sirens and screaming approaching her position and she felt hopeful. Rangda had kept her promise and had come to save her. Keila could see how the Xenos were scaling the building with immense speed. The Xenos were fearsome looking, but one of them stood out from the others. Keila figured that, the odd looking one must be Rangda.

Rangda appeared in front of her on the other side of the window. The window was made of very thick fortified glass, but Rangda destroyed it by letting out a high-pitched shriek that shattered the glass

Keila:

- Rangda! You came to save me?

Rangda:

- I came, yes. But not to save you. You are my prisoner!

Keila:

- No! I will fight you then.

Rangda:

- No, you won't.

Rangda blasted Keila with a psionic blast, and Keila fell unconscious. Rangda lifted Keila over her shoulder and made one of her Xeno Warriors jump out of the window with her on the back as it was quicker to fall down than climbing down again. Just before impacting the ground, Rangda with Keila on her back jumped off the Xeno warrior with such force that it neutralised the terminal free-fall velocity she had, and she landed safely, while the Xeno soldier was splattered and killed when he hit the ground.

Rangda handed over Keila to one of her fastest Xeno runners, and she rode another Xeno back to the portal as quickly as possible. Rangda knew that the humans would respond with aircraft and heavy weaponry and she did not want to be stuck on Earth when that happened. Rangda brought Keila to the edge of the portal and gave out a loud shriek, to command her Xeno forces to retreat. She lifted Keila over her shoulder and went back to the Divine Dimension. Shortly, afterwards Rashid security forces arrived in force, carpet bombing the Xenos, and killing the aliens who had been too preoccupied in frenzied eating to follow Rangda's retreat order.

Chapter 209: B600 directed into the sun

Captain Melissa Schiller watched as B600 changed course, and she had to change her own ship's course to avoid getting hit. She called in her second in command, Commander Michael Berndt.

Melissa:

- Michael! Why is the asteroid changing course?

Michael:

- The High Council must have ordered them to change the course. Maybe the Martians agreed to peace.

- Of course, there was going to be a solution, the council would never massacre four billion people.

Melissa:

- Then why didn't Joachim tell me?

Michael:

- Why do you think the leader of the Terran Council would run every decision with every single captain in the space navy?

- Unless the rumours are true...

Melissa:

- What rumours? I am the captain of this ship. I command you to reverse B600 to a collision course with Mars.

Michael:

- Very well this makes it easy for me.

- Captain Schiller, you are under arrest for the murder of Mathias Muller and for conspiring to mass-murder innocent civilians. Soldiers arrest her.

Melissa:

- You don't have the authority to arrest me!

Michael Berndt:

- I have the loyalty of my men. I will figure out the rest later.

Melissa was screaming as she got locked up, but it mattered little. Her involvement in the genocidal plan was foiled, and a few months later B600 crashed into the Sun, ceasing to be a threat.

The release of Rangda, threatens the future of humanity.
But, what if, we could turn back time?
THE DIVINE
FINALISATION
THE DIVINE ZETAN TRILOGY
MARTIN LUNDQVIST

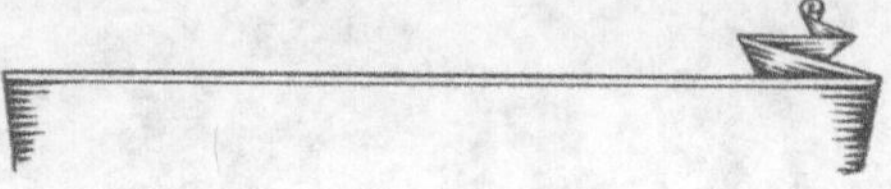

Chapter 210: Desperate Moments

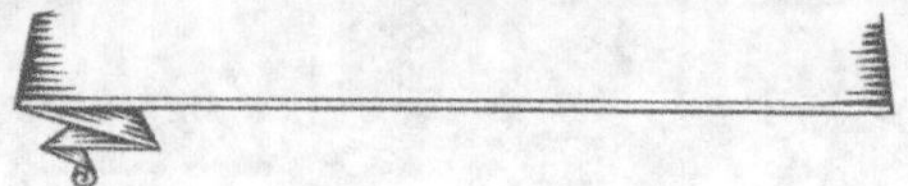

Hilda Muller, Markus White, and a group of House Rashid security guards exited the lift at the top level of Rashidium Tower. They walked towards the courtroom where the sentencing of Keila Eisenstein posing as Alicia White, took place.

Hilda Muller saw Ibrahim Rashid through the doorway at the end of the corridor. Ibrahim Rashid was scolding the imposter Keila Eisenstein for vandalising the Cheops Pyramid. Hilda Muller gave the signal to follow her, and the group headed towards the courtroom. 'Alicia' noticed the approaching troops, and she jumped towards Ibrahim Rashid. Once on top of him, she pushed his hand towards a control panel, to close the courtroom door. Hilda realised that there was no time to lose, she rushed towards the door to get in, but she was too late.

Hilda's skin burnt from colliding with the force field that protected the bullet-proof glass door that sealed off the room. She had got there too late, and the madwoman Alicia was holding the Terran Council leaders' as hostages. What Hilda saw next shocked her and her crew. The Terran Council leaders collapsed, and 'Alicia' transformed into the infamous Keila Eisenstein!

"Get those doors open now!" Hilda exclaimed, and the security guards requested reinforcements with appropriate equipment. Hilda looked at Keila. She noticed that Keila was activating The Terran Council Blood Encryption machine. This machine was rarely used, and Hilda could not figure out what the damn terrorist intended to do with the device. Regardless of what it was, it wasn't good news!

Hilda kept studying Keila. Keila had managed to access the Blood Encryption Machine, but Hilda wouldn't know what Keila had done until she had access to the machine herself. Hilda watched, as Keila bashed the skulls of the unconscious Terran Council leaders with a metal sculpture. Considering the amount of brain matter on the floor, it seemed unlikely that they would be able to resurrect any of the fallen leaders.

"We'll break through the doors in 20 minutes", one of the Rashid soldiers said. "Good, make sure to wear protective equipment, we don't know what gas she has released in there!", Hilda replied.

Hilda examined the situation. It would be a public relations nightmare, to explain how Keila had accessed a Terran Council meeting and murdered all the faction leaders. There was a risk for potential uprisings among the civilian population, in the chaos that would follow. This event would put the power of the Terran Council into question, for the second time in just a couple of months.

But in the situation, there was also an opportunity for Hilda. Hilda had suspected that Joachim Muller had something to do with the assassination of her father, Matthias Muller. Hilda had lacked the proof, and she wouldn't accuse the leader of her faction without any evidence to support her claims. With Joachim Muller and Benjamin Muller lying dead on the floor, things were looking better for Hilda's position in House Muller. With the two of them dead, Hilda was second in line to leadership after Joachim's third son Michael Muller. Michael Muller was an unambitious family man who did not seem to care much about power and ambition. Hilda was confident that she could persuade Michael to give up his position to her, as long as he could live in wealth and abundance.

Hilda stopped her succession planning when an intense blue light appeared on the horizon. The blue light was so intense, so it blinded her temporarily. When Hilda had regained her eyesight, she saw something that shocked her. A blue portal had opened on top of the Great Pyramid, and out of it came a massive horde of alien species.

A severe migraine struck Hilda, and the world became blurry and stopped making sense to her. This was because the Xeno invaders had brought stolen Zetan technology. Some of the Zetan technology disrupted the bionic microchips that Hilda had in her brain. Hilda could hear unintelligible chatter on the soldiers' transistors.

Hilda realised that her bionic microchips had broken as she could no longer understand Arabic, the language of the House Rashid soldiers.

Fortunately, Hilda had learned some English using her brain, and she spoke to the petrified Markus White.

Hilda Muller, speaking with a firm German accent:

- Stay close to me, Markus. We are under attack by alien life forms.

Markus White:

- What are those things? We are all going to die!

Hilda Muller:

- No, we are not. The army will get here shortly and sort out this mess. Fight to stay alive until then!

Markus White:

- Fight with what? We don't carry any weapons.

Hilda Muller:

- The Rashid soldiers will have to give us weapons!

Hilda Muller tried talking to the Rashid soldiers to get weapons for her and Markus. This didn't work as the Rashid soldiers only spoke Arabic, and they were too agitated to make any sense.

Suddenly, Hilda heard a thundering shriek and turned around. The scream had scattered the fortified glass to the boardroom. Hilda studied the source of the howl. A two-metre tall humanoid-like monstrosity with shiny purple eyes. Several three-metre tall beasts accompanied the monstrosity!

Rangda, knocked Keila unconscious, grabbed her, and jumped out of the building. The other beasts, however, attacked.

Hilda pulled Markus towards the floor, and thus, saved his life when a Xeno beast jumped towards her. The Rashid soldier behind them was not as lucky, and he got decapitated by the fearsome creature. The panicking Rashid Soldiers shot towards the Xenos but to a limited effect. The Xenos had ballistic energy absorbers and thick skin that was hard to penetrate with the weapons that the guards carried. "Use your plasma knives!" Hilda shouted to the Rashid guards. But the guards didn't understand her. Instead, they panicked and the Xenos decapitated them one by one with their razor-sharp claws.

Hilda picked up the plasma knife from one of the fallen soldiers. She took a leap and saved Markus White through piercing the skull of a Xeno Beast with the plasma knife, slaying the beast. Hilda dragged Markus to the boardroom where the dead Terran Council leaders were lying on the floor. Since they were at a high altitude, the room was very windy. Hilda and Markus ran to the window.

There was no way out. They heard the Xenos behind them roar. The beasts had killed off the Rashid guards, and they had turned their attention towards Hilda and Markus.

Markus White:

- What do you say, Hilda? Should we end our lives jumping off the building, or would you rather be alien food?

Hilda Muller:

- You do whatever that pleases you. I am a soldier; I'll stay and fight.
- Get down!

Hilda pulled Markus to the ground and behind them came their salvation. It came in the form of a House Muller combat helicopter, that blew the remaining four Xenos to shreds with their autocannons and rockets. Hilda grabbed the Blood Encryption Tablet and got on the aircraft.

Hilda Muller:

- The city is overrun with Aliens. Let's get out of here!

Helicopter Pilot:

- Hilda! What about Joachim and Benjamin?

Hilda Muller:

- They are dead beyond resurrection. Murdered in cold blood by Keila Eisenstein. Now let's get the fuck out of here before those monsters come back!

Helicopter Pilot:

- Jawohl Fräulein Muller!

As the helicopter left Rashidium city, Hilda studied the carnage that the Xeno invasion had caused in the city. Reinforcements would arrive, but it was too late to save Rashidium's inhabitants from the destructive alien invasion!

Chapter 211: Hilda Muller Seduces Markus White

Hilda Muller was back in the relative safety of her luxurious apartment in the Europeum Tower, located in Hansstadt. She was looking at the exhausted Markus White, who was sleeping on her couch in the lounge area. While she could have housed him in one of the many guest apartments in Europeum Tower, keeping him near was a crucial strategic decision.

While sleeping seemed to be a good idea, to relieve the stress, Hilda wouldn't have it. The Xeno invasion at the Terran Council meeting in Rashidium city had left all the Terran Council factions, leaderless. There was a lot of opportunity for someone with ambition to advance their own position. Hilda knew that in the upheaval that would follow, there would be a lot of knifing to come. Hilda would much rather be the one holding the knife, than being the receiver.

Since the assassination of her father, Matthias Muller, a few months earlier, Hilda had seen her power diminish. Matthias' death had put Hilda out of reach to the leadership of the House Muller. Officially, Martian rebels had killed Matthias, but Hilda had never believed in that ploy. After all, why would the Martians send assassins after her father, who was the most likely to listen to their pleas? Instead, Hilda was certain that it was her cousin Benjamin Muller who was behind the assassination. But Hilda had kept quiet. It would have been risky for her to accuse Benjamin, the son of the House Muller leader, Joachim Muller, without any hard evidence.

But now, both Joachim and Benjamin were dead, and the way lay open for her to contend for leadership. Joachim's youngest son, Michael

Muller, would be first in line. However, Hilda doubted that Michael would have any interest in command as he preferred living a comfortable, careless life in luxury.

Hilda would need allies to secure her claim, both on the inside and on the outside. Hilda glimpsed at the sexy, half-naked body, of the sleeping Markus White. It was time to combine business and pleasure.

Hilda went back to her bedroom and got changed into a sexy dress. Hilda admired her own body in the mirror. This felt a bit strange as she saw herself as her father's daughter, a strong military woman and not as a seductress. Then again, to play the game of politics, she needed to be able to do both! Hilda sprayed herself with a potent pheromone perfume and approached Markus White.

Hilda Muller:

- Markus, darling, wake up.

Markus White woke up with a twitch, and he looked at Hilda in confusion before he spoke:

- Hilda? What's happening? Where am I?

Hilda touched Markus' face gently and spoke again.

- So, so. You are safe here with me in Europeum Tower.

Hilda smiled seductively and waited for the pheromones to influence Markus' body. The pheromones worked slower than Hilda had anticipated due to shock and stressful circumstances. However, a while later, they both participated in an extended orgasmic sexual trance. Once the sex was over, Hilda fell asleep in Markus' arms. She felt relieved of sexual tension and was happy to have a potential ally for the coming months!

Chapter 212: Metatron Finds a Surrogate Mother for Sabina.

Metatron was watching the news about the massive incursion of Xeno alien species. Tears were running down his cheeks. "Oh, Keila, what have you done?" He said to himself. He had supported Keila's idea to take the appearance of Alicia White, and kill the Terran Council leaders. But Keila had never filled him in on the plan to open portals and let giant man-eating aliens attack Earth. Metatron watched imagery of dismembered corpses, and the images would always haunt his eyes. It wasn't the carnage itself that scared him the most. After all, the Terran Council's synthetic virus attack on Pamshal city on Mars a few years earlier had generated similar images. No, what terrified Metatron was that humanity was no longer on the top of the food chain.

Metatron worried about the future of humanity. When humans killed other humans, Metatron knew that our species would always survive. But with the carnage caused by this alien invasion, who knew what the future would hold?

Metatron tried contacting Keila via the Divine Technology, but there was only static. This didn't mean anything, as Earth and Eden were too far apart to establish a connection with the technology. Yet, to Metatron, it confirmed his fears, that Keila had died among the thousands of fatalities in Rashidium city.

Metatron looked at the calendar. He got up and visited the medical bay, where the frozen two-month embryo of his and Keila's future child was in suspended animation. What would he do, now that Keila was gone?

Metatron knew what he wanted, He had wanted to raise a family with Keila, but her fiery nature had stopped her from settling down. Metatron had loved Keila's passionate nature, although it was also what stopped them from having the future he dreamt of.

Metatron studied the vitals of the embryo, it was in suspended animation, and it hadn't changed since his last examination. According to the DNA scanner, the foetus had excellent A-grade genetics. Martin studied the simulation, based on the foetus DNA, showing how Sabina would look at different ages. She would look a lot like her mother, Keila, and this made Metatron miss her even more!

Metatron elevated himself from his state of self-pity. Keila was gone, but through her daughter, Sabina, she could live on. She had to live on, why else had he already given this small lump of genetic material a name? But Metatron didn't want to cultivate the foetus in a synthetic womb. He didn't want to create a copy of himself, so he needed a surrogate mother. There was a knock on the door and one of Metatron's Edenite employees, Melissa, entered the room.

Melissa gave Metatron a worried look and spoke to him:

- Master Metatron, you haven't eaten for two days? I am concerned about you.

Metatron tried to force a smile, but it failed, and his watery teary eyes exposed him:

- I am okay. But I am not feeling hungry.

Melissa:

- Come on now, Metatron. You have already admitted that you are human and not an angel. All humans need support from time to time. Let me be your pillar of support for once, as you been to me so many times before.

Metatron studied Melissa. She had a rather plain Edenite appearance, but her heart was pure as gold. As Melissa hadn't opted to have her Divine Technology "human" chip removed, he could see her every thought. Could he ask her to do what he wanted? He could command it, but Metatron didn't believe in forcing people unless it was necessary for the common good. It was vital for him to find a surrogate mother to give life to Sabina, but he couldn't justify it with the common good. Metatron decided that he could ask her for a favour and spoke up:

- There is something you could do for me, something far more important than fetching me lunch.

Melissa looked at him with a reassuring smile:

- Metatron, you don't need to be shy around me. Just tell me, and I will be happy to help.

Metatron:

- Thanks, Melissa. I am depressed because of Keila's death.

Melissa:

- Mistress Keila is dead? That's terrible! Are you certain?

Metatron:

- I am as sure as I can be.

- But that is where you come in. I want you to give birth to mine and Keila's daughter.

Melissa:

- But she is dead? How can one woman bear another woman's child?

Metatron:

- I can explain the science to you later. Is it something that would interest you?

Melissa:

- It would honour me to carry the child of you and Keila, who will be the Messiah of our people.

Metatron:

- Thank you, Melissa.

- Stay here in the medical bay, and I'll explain the procedure more in detail before we go through with it.

Having said this, Metatron gave Melissa a scientific explanation of the procedure. Melissa, being an Edenite, didn't understand science, but it didn't matter, and soon she was pregnant with Metatron's and Keila's child.

Chapter 213: Dissatisfaction in Victory.

Melchior Dorevitch was at the presidential palace of the Olympus Republic. He studied a political map of Mars. Despite winning a total victory, with the remaining enemies begging him for peace, he wasn't happy. In fact, he was deeply unsatisfied.

Melchior's problem was that Keila received all the credit for the Martian victory, while his contribution was not recognised. Thus, the temporary power that Keila granted him before going on her mission to Earth was now contested. There were many other contenders for leadership, both on Mars and in the Olympus Republic. The Olympus Republic was a de jure republic and an election would take place to replace Hellas Petrakis who had fallen in the war.

But Melchior wasn't going to give up his power. He would never live to serve some Martian or worse yet, go back to Eden, governed by that wimp Metatron. Melchior had tasted the intoxicating feeling of absolute power, and he would never give it up. And why would he?

Melchior walked up to a mirror and studied his face. There was a large scar on the right side of his face with his outer ear missing. Melchior's tinnitus kept beeping, and his constant migraine made his days miserable. Melchior's doctors had offered him advanced gene therapy to heal his wounds, but Melchior had rejected the treatment. His injuries made him who he was, and they fuelled his rage and ambition.

Melchior Dorevitch considered himself, the true hero of Mars. The general who had soldiered on despite immense pain, to lead his troops towards the final decisive victory against the Terran Council. Meanwhile, the supposed heroine, Keila Eisenstein, sat out the final battle and then claimed all the glory. Melchior didn't believe that Keila had stopped

Bjorn Muller from crashing Phobos onto the Martian surface! It was all lies and deception.

Melchior made up his mind, he wouldn't strive to rule by being popular, he would rule through fear. Melchior's implanted "God" microchip allowed him to terrify his subjects and opponents.

Melchior clenched his fist and watched in joy how he killed his opponents, one by one, using the powers of the Divine Zetan Technology. Having murdered the last contenders for the presidency, he laughed maliciously. After that, he summoned a few courtesans to brutally fulfil his other needs.

Chapter 214: An Unpleasant Awakening.

Keila woke up after what felt like a lifetime. She was standing up, and despite the pain in her legs, she couldn't fall to the ground. An invisible force field was encapsulating her, preventing her from moving at all, except for her eyes. She gazed around the room, and she saw a reflective surface, where her reflection showed. What she saw shocked her.

Keila's eyes were glowing purple, and the texture of her skin had changed completely. She had wrinkled skin like that of a 100-year-old and thick and grey like the skin of a reptile. Her body was in pain, particularly her legs, which were burning with lactic acid. Keila heard a door open, and things weren't improving as the Xeno-Zetan hybrid Rangda entered the room.

Rangda:

- Hee-Hee-Hee-Hee!! We meet at last. Apologies for the lack of formal introduction on Earth, but I had limited time for such ploys!

Keila:

- Apologise for taking me prisoner instead. I opened the portals on the Cheops Pyramid like you've asked me to! How long have I been here?

Rangda:

- You are not a prisoner yet. I have detained you to ensure you are no danger to yourself or others. Although I must admit, you might have outlived your usefulness!

- As for the time passing since you fell unconscious, not much.

- The change in your physical appearance is a side effect of the ritual, which I used to absorb your psionic powers into the corrupted Zeto Crystal.

- But don't worry; neither the aging nor the ritual will kill you here in the Divine Dimension. Unless I intend for it to happen.

Keila:

- What are you talking about, you hideous and wicked creature?! I helped you. If you are going to kill me, do it now instead of dragging things out!

Rangda:

- No! That is not going to happen. You see, I need you. The ritual that powers up my dark crystals kills Zetans outright. But since you are a Human-Zetan hybrid, I can continually drain your energy without killing you.

Keila:

- So, what do you want?

Rangda:

- Well for starters, I want revenge for my mother through wiping out the Zetans species that betrayed her.

- But ultimately, I want what the Zetans strived for but could never achieve. I want to reach godhood; I want to replace The True Maker as the almighty deity of the universe!

Keila:

- The True Maker?! That's insanity! How would you achieve that?

Rangda:
- You shall see sweet sister, you shall see. But for now, it's time for you to sleep!

After saying this, Rangda blasted Keila with a powerful psionic blast that knocked her unconscious. After that, performed the ritual with the corrupted Zeto Crystals, which radiated with darkness, to drain Keila's body even more. Rangda studied how Keila's body was twisting, and Rangda laughed burst of twisted, diabolical laughter.

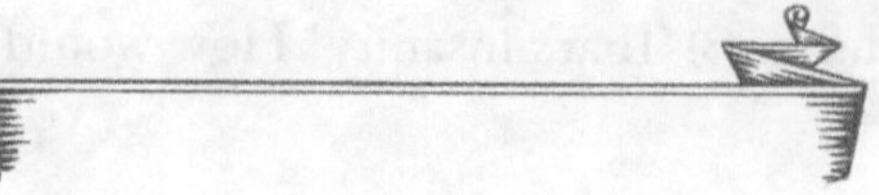

Chapter 215: Melchior Turns His Gaze to Eden.

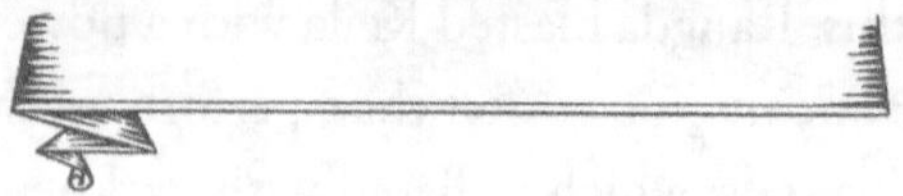

Melchior Dorevitch was celebrating his overwhelming victory in the Olympus Republic elections. The fact that all the other contenders had died mysterious deaths days before the election didn't bother him. The kill-switch feature in the lower tiers of the Divine Technology microchips wasn't common knowledge. Even if it was, who would be foolish enough to stand up against him in the Olympus Republic?

Melchior studied a political map of Mars. It was very fragmented with hundreds of factions. Although the Olympus Republic was the most powerful nation on Mars, it still only controlled 5% of the Martian surface. The myriad of small countries on Mars had been a strategy by the Terran Council to keep the Martians divided and make them easy to rule. Keila Eisenstein had united the Martians. Equipped with Zetan technology, they had sent their previous Terran masters' running. But with Keila missing, the Martians had turned on each other, and the situation on Mars was worse than ever before.

The Martians needed a strong leader that united them. Melchior was confident that providence meant for him to be this leader. He summoned his brother Dov Dorevitch to discuss his strategy.

Dov arrived at Melchior's office in the Olympus Republic presidential palace. Melchior studied his brother with well-hidden contempt. Dov, despite being younger than Melchior, looked older due to his beer gut, smoking habits, and unhealthy lifestyle. While Melchior disliked his brother's lack of discipline, he needed loyal allies, and no-one was a more dependable ally than his younger brother!

Melchior smiled and spoke to Dov:

- Welcome to Mars and the Olympus Republic, dear brother. I hope your trip from Eden was comfortable.

Dov:

- I can't complain. Since Abraham Goldstein died, I have lost fate in the Edenite society. But I would have preferred to travel in comfort on a civil carrier, rather than on a military ship.

Melchior:

- Well, all public transport has ended due to the war. But rest easy, peace with the Terrans are coming any day now. They have more significant problems to worry about.

Dov:

- Yes. I don't know how Keila did it but releasing those aliens onto the unsuspecting people on Earth was both a stroke of genius and a terrifying act of evil.

Melchior:

- Yes, although she was crazy with her visions, she still pulled everyone together and got things done.

- Now I want to follow in her footsteps!

Dov:

- I have heard you are progressing well. Congratulations on your victory in the "elections."

Melchior:

- I didn't rig the elections!

Dov:

- But it was very convenient that all your competitors died, the day before the elections?

Melchior:

- Yes, it was! Praise Yahweh for intervening and helping me, when the Martians couldn't comprehend that I was the right candidate!

Dov:

- Seems more like a Divine Technology kill-switch to me! How did you pull it off? I thought Keila gave you an Angel chip.

Melchior:

- No, she gave me a God chip, so that I could lead the attack on the Phobos base. She must have forgotten about it because she never mentioned it when she headed to Earth to infiltrate the Terran Council.

- Whatever the reason was, it was a lucky coincidence, and since I don't believe in coincidence. It must have been the divine will!

Dov:

- I see. So why did you summon me? I doubt it was for catching up.

Melchior:

- I need you. Together we can fulfil grandmaster Abraham's visions but on a much grander scale. Together we can rule Mars as its rightful god-kings!

Dov:

- But, didn't you pledge allegiance to Keila after she overthrew and killed Abraham.

Melchior:

- Yes, but one should never let ideology get in the way of opportunity. Now that Keila is gone; opportunity is ours.

- I need to take the Olympus Republic army to Eden to confront Metatron and make him hand over the Zetan technologies to us.

- I need you to stay here and rule in my stead.

Dov:

- It would be an honour to assist you, my brother. I have dreamt about spreading Abraham's religious dogma, to the wretched unbelievers on Mars!

Melchior:

- Good. Connect to that medical unit. It will remove your Human chip and replace it with a God chip.

Dov:

- Are you going to put me to the same level as yourself? There shouldn't be two God chips ruling the same nation.

Melchior:

- How would I expect you to rule in my stead, if you are not equipped with the highest tier of Zetan technology? I need you to be able to kill dissidents with your mind. Now scram, before I change my mind!

Melchior watched Dov as he entered the medical unit. It pleased him that Dov had seen things his way and agreed to help him doing the right thing. Dov would stay loyal, and if he didn't, the fat bastard would suffer so much so he'd regret ever being born. Pleased with the situation, Melchior called his generals and ordered for the fleet to travel to Eden.

Chapter 216: Metatron Confides in Melissa.

Metatron studied Eden through the windows in the reception area of the Divine Control Centre. He had been busy modernising Eden and housing the influx of refugees that had come because of the widespread war and unrest in the solar system. While Metatron hadn't proclaimed Eden to be a haven, he didn't turn away desperate people that came his way. As a result, the population had swelled from 8000 to over 20,000.

The population increase had caused several problems. Metatron had tried solving these problems by keeping the original Edenites and the newcomers separate. As Eden had a surface area of over 20,000 square kilometres and perfect conditions for agriculture, it was easy to house and feed everyone. Yet the problem remained, Metatron would have to integrate the refugees into the Edenite society.

Metatron leaned back into a comfortable armchair. Oh, how he missed Keila and real sleep! Being raised into Abraham's Angel program, Metatron had never known real sleep for the first 120 years of his life. Metatron had only experienced accelerated sleep or extended sleep being cryogenically frozen. In neither of those sleep states had he experienced dreams. When Keila had killed Abraham and set Metatron free, he had finally experienced dreams.

Now that Keila was gone, Metatron had returned to sleeping in the accelerated sleep pod. This was because of his self-sacrificing nature. Metatron felt guilty sleeping when the Edenites needed him. But now, Metatron was at his breaking point. The lack of dreams had deteriorated his soul, and he felt like he did when he was a slave to Abraham's will. He felt more like a machine than like a human.

Metatron realised that he needed to sleep and dream, to regain his sanity. But the problem was that he had forgotten how to sleep. Metatron felt drained, but his body was still too energised for him to fall asleep. Metatron realised what he needed to do. He felt guilty about it, but he had to do it anyway for his own sanity.

Metatron summoned Melissa, the surrogate mother who was pregnant with his and Keila's unborn child.

Melissa studied Metatron. He didn't look well, and he looked a lot older and more burdened than usual, albeit a lot younger than his real age. Tentatively, she approached him and spoke:

- Master Metatron. You summoned me. Is everything alright with you?

Metatron tried to smile, but it fell flat and instead, he responded in a sombre tone:

- My state is no longer that important. The main thing is, how things are with you?

Melissa:

- Don't say that. You are important to all of us. If it weren't for your tireless efforts, Eden would collapse, and we would all perish.

Metatron:

- That's the core of my problems. That I have been too self-sacrificing and given up what I want.

Melissa:

- So, what do you want?

Metatron:

- I want to have human desires. Human impulses for good and evil.

- Abraham bred me to serve him, and I did so for over a century. I helped a villainous madman doing evil deeds, because I knew of nothing else. Then Keila set me free, and I started to feel human feelings. But now she is gone, and I am yet again a soulless servant. Trying to make up for my evil deeds by serving the Edenites!

Melissa blushed and then stuttered:

- Is this your way of telling me that you want to have sex with me?

Metatron:

- No. I am after something far more critical. I need to sleep natural sleep so that I can dream again.

- I have never slept natural sleep on my own, so I need you to sleep next to me.

Melissa:

- It would honour me to sleep in your bed, Master Metatron.

Metatron:

- Thank you, Melissa.

- You don't need to call me Master. You and I are friends and equals, helping each other out in times of need.

- Let's go to my bedroom, I am exhausted.

Metatron and Melissa headed to Metatron's bedroom, and in her embrace, he immediately fell asleep. Metatron didn't have the dreams that he wanted, as his dreams tormented him.

In the dream, Metatron saw a beastly alien with glowing purple eyes, tormenting an ancient-looking woman. Despite the tortured woman's hideous appearance, he could sense her soul, and he knew that she was Keila. "Save me! Save humankind!" Keila shouted out with a weak and weary voice. Rangda knocked Keila unconscious with a psionic blast and turned to Metatron. She stared him down with her glowing purple eyes and hypnotised him in a state of paralysed fear. Metatron screamed his lungs out, and he woke up, with the bed soaked in cold sweat.

Melissa looked at him with a worried face and spoke.

- You look terrified! is everything alright?

Metatron:

- Come with me to the medical bay. We need to remove your Divine Technology chip immediately.

Melissa:

- Sure. But why?

Metatron:

- Keila spoke to me in a vision. Darkness is coming, and we'll need to remove all Divine Technology microchips to stay safe!

Melissa:

- If you really think so. There is no time to waste! Let's go.

They hurried to the medical ward to remove Melissa's microchip. After that, they devised a plan for how to remove the chips from the other Edenites.

Chapter 217: Hilda Muller Prepares to Seize Power.

Hilda Muller was preparing her speech for the first Terran Council meeting since the catastrophe in Rashidium. It had been six chaotic months, but on the bright side, it had strengthened Hilda's position and claim for power.

Before the defeat against the Martians and the terrifying Xeno invasion, The Terran Council was all about commerce. For the Terran Council, the army was support functions to protect trade. As the population felt threatened by the Xenos, they were calling out for more protection. This benefitted Hilda as she had claimed the vacant Supreme Commander title after her father's death. Hilda was not satisfied though. Hilda did not want to be the lackey of some hedonistic plutocrat; she wanted to be the top dog herself. Hilda aimed to be the new chairman of the Terran Council, ruling over Earth.

Hilda had an excellent claim to the position. As the leader of the military forces, she had planned and reorganised the army to successfully counter the new threat. After the initial Xeno attacks, the military had pinpointed the locations of the portals, so they could avoid surprise attacks. The army had also adapted their weaponry to their new enemies. They had replaced all their ballistic guns, with energy-based and melee weapons. Hilda had ordered fleets of space warships in low orbit over every identified portal. Hilda's actions had turned the tide of the war; discouraged by their losses, the Xenos had stopped attacking Earth.

Hilda spotted Markus White in the corridor. Unfortunately, he had not reached a prominent position in House White, but he could be useful for other purposes. Hilda called him over, and he entered her room.

Hilda:

- Oh, Markus how nice it is to see you again!

Markus:

- Hi Hilda! Thanks again for saving my life.

Hilda:

- It was my pleasure. Especially the night that followed saving your life!

Hilda winked at him before continuing:

- So, do I have your support for the Chairman position of the Terran Council?

Markus:

- Yes, I would vote for you. But unfortunately, I am not the one calling the shots, so I can't guarantee you the support from my faction.

Hilda:

- I know Markus. But you can help me with something else!

- I want you to fuck me as good as you did when we came back from Rashidium.

Markus:

- Are you crazy? We are on the level where the meeting is taking place. What if someone comes early and sees us?

Hilda:

- Then let them. I will be their boss, and I am going to show them that I am not intimidated by what they think. Quite the contrary!

Having said this, Hilda released some pheromones, which made Markus irresistibly horny. Shortly afterwards he fucked her roughly from behind. When they had finished, Hilda wiped herself and smiled at the exhausted Markus. She spoke to him as she left:

- You stay here and relax, lover boy, while I take control of the Council.

Satisfied and confident, Hilda walked to the meeting room. It was a great relief to have sex with a human again; she had played with droids for the last few months. Not that Hilda was unattractive but being powerful didn't have the same sex appeal for a woman as it had for a man. While a man in power could use his influence to have sex with anyone he wanted, society expected a woman in command to keep monogamous. But Hilda didn't want to be monogamous. She wanted to be independent and follow her desires, including the sexual ones. Hilda promised herself that once she seized control, she would do what she wanted, regardless of what her male peers thought about it!

The leaders for the other factions entered the boardroom, as did Hilda's cousin, Michael Muller. Hilda studied Michael. Michael had shocked the rest of House Muller when he chose to step down to Hilda without a fight, but she had anticipated it. Michael was a man who enjoyed wealth but hated power and encumbering responsibilities. Michael didn't even want to be on the board, but Hilda had convinced him to stay and follow her lead. Michael was perfect where he was, as he gave Hilda credibility while not arguing with her.

The other factions represented were House White, House Cheng, House Bolivar, and House Goldstein. House Goldstein was among the five most -powerful factions again due to the downfall of House Rashid.

Watching the group of foreign dignitaries, Hilda took a deep breath and prepared to speak.

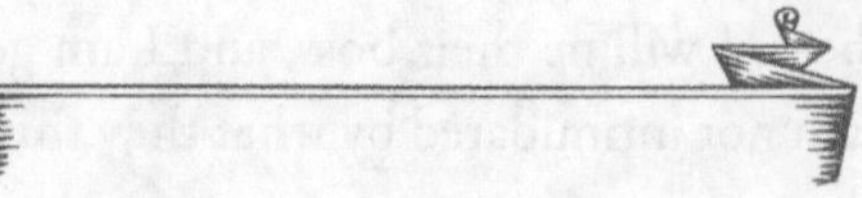

Chapter 218: Hilda Muller Becomes the Leader of the Terran Council.

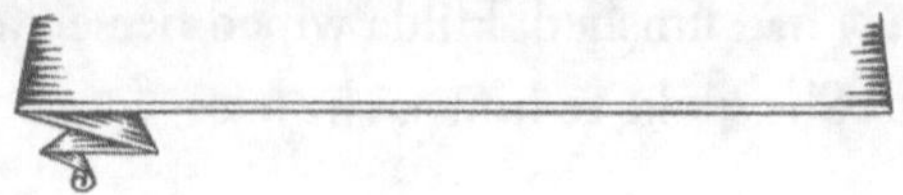

Hilda Muller was looking at the gathered dignitaries in the meeting room of Europeum Tower. As always, the top-level meeting had two representatives from each faction. Hilda didn't recognise many of them, as they were all new due to the massacre at the Rashidium summit. This suited Hilda well, as it would be difficult for her to claim power if all the old faction leaders were still around. As it was now, Hilda had the best claim to authority with a proven success in repelling the Xeno invasion.

Hilda Muller began to talk:

- Dear delegates. Welcome to the Terran Council meeting for March 2875. We have many things to discuss, but we start off with a formality. You are to verify my position as chairwoman for the Terran Council as well as Supreme Commander for the Terran Council Security Forces.

The delegates sat dumbfounded and didn't know how to react. They had anticipated more pleasantries and formalities before discussing this sensitive topic. Eventually, Ping Chen spoke up:

- Miss Muller. My apologies, but you have misunderstood how the Council works. The Council strives to mediate between the leading factions. You haven't made a case for your claim yet.

Hilda smirked sarcastically towards Ping Chen before she replied.

- I don't think you know who I am. I was at Rashidium when the Xenos first struck. I was one of the few survivors, and do you know why?

- Because I struck back. I killed several of those beasts on my own before I evacuated the city.

- I have saved us by repelling the Xenos and securing the perimeters to the portals.

- THAT is worth more than whatever financial achievements the rest of you claim to have.

James Goldstein joined the conversation:

- While the situation is dire, it's good to have my faction back on the Council. I recommend that we DO NOT choose another House Muller candidate, as Joachim Muller's leadership led to disastrous results. Joachim caused the loss against the Martians, and the unpreparedness for the alien invasion.

Hilda Muller:

- Silence, you fool! The Goldstein's have been infighting for decades, and under your "leadership" we would have fallen to the Xeno invaders.

- The people need and want a strong leader that can keep them safe. I am at that leader. The last thing they need, is another money counter.

James Goldstein:

- Since when do you dictate what the people need?

Hilda Muller:

- I don't, but you must know what is going on with the common man. Who do they turn to? It is not the banks!

- I'd win if it were the popular vote.

Ping Chen:

- That might be, Hilda, but the popular vote means little as this is not a democracy!

Hilda Muller:

- Six months after the defeat on Mars, and you still discount the popular will. Where would you run if the people turn against you?

Enrique Bolivar had heard enough of the quarrel. His territories had been severely affected by the Xeno invasions from the Central American portal. Enrique knew why his people were still around, and it wasn't the size of his vault that had saved him.
Enrique Bolivar:

- Dear delegates, I have heard enough. I lost my father Santiago in Rashidium, and most of us lost loved ones in that attack.

- What we need right now is security. We cannot achieve that by focusing on commerce. That is why I cast the votes of House Bolivar on the one who saved us, Hilda Muller.

Jordan White joined in:

- I also cast my votes on Hilda. My cousin Markus told me about her incredible feats of bravery when she saved him from the savage alien attack. This is what we need in these challenging times.

James Goldstein:

- From what I have heard, "saving" him wasn't the only thing she did to him.

Hilda Muller:

- Whatever you are implying is irrelevant. I got the majority vote now.

James Goldstein:

- So, it would seem. Such a sad day, when a promiscuous woman becomes the leader!

Hilda Muller:

- It's not the Bronze Age anymore. Let your buddy Abraham know that if you see him!

- Anyways. Thank you, Enrique, and Jordan for voting for me. Now let me tell you how I plan to take the fight to our enemies.

After this, Hilda gave a detailed account for how she planned to fight the Xenos and what contributions she required for the war.

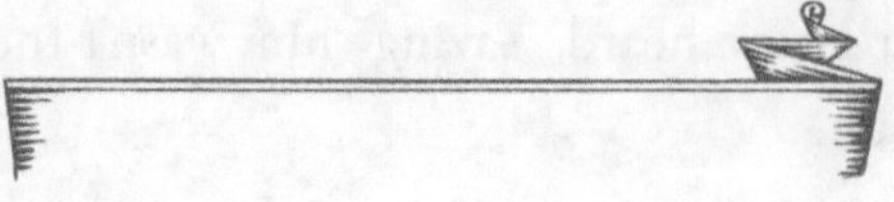

Chapter 219: Sabina is Born.

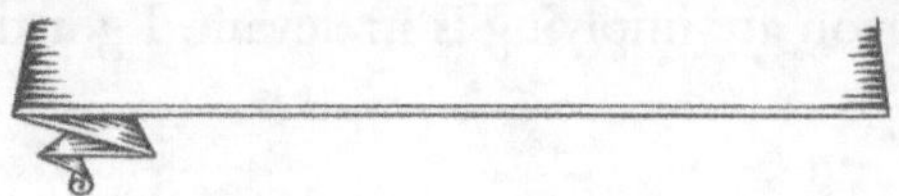

In July 2875, Melissa gave birth to Sabina, Metatron's and Keila's daughter. Sabina was a healthy child despite the procedures on her embryo. When Metatron studied the lively gaze in her light green eyes, he felt her soul. Metatron was happy that a surrogate mother gave birth to Sabina, instead of using a synthetic womb.

Metatron visited Melissa as she was recovering from childbirth.
Melissa:

- She is beautiful, isn't she? The daughter of you and Keila.

Metatron:

- Sabina is our daughter, Melissa. I want her to feel that way when she is growing up.

Melissa:

- But she can't be? We haven't had intercourse.

Metatron:

- That is true. But I don't want her to find out the truth. That her mother died while releasing man-eating monsters devastating Earth. Also, because of Keila, Melchior Dorevitch is terrorising Mars with his army of mind-controlled soldiers.

Melissa:

- So, what do you want us to do? To pretend to Sabina that we are husband and wife and that she is our daughter?

Metatron:

- No, I want us to get married, so we are husband and wife. For all the essential reasons, you and I are her parents. That is if you would like to marry me?

Melissa:

- I would love to marry you, grandmaster Metatron.

Metatron:

- I am happy to hear that, Melissa. I will make an announcement to make it official, and then we will invite all the Edenites to the ceremony!

- I got to go back to work. I'll come by a bit later.

After leaving the room, Metatron retreated to his private bedroom, locked the doors, and cried. He had decided to finally give up on Keila and move on with his life. Metatron had to move on, he had a child to look after, and he could not raise a child obsessing over the child's dead biological mother.

A lie and a new beginning were the best solution for everyone. In due time, Metatron was confident that he and Melissa could form a happy family. Melissa was a perfect woman: loyal, obedient, loving and hardworking. But she lacked the beauty, the passion, and the drive that made Keila extraordinary.

Metatron decided that he wouldn't tell Sabina the truth about her mother. It was better for everyone if Sabina grew up to be a good Edenite woman. In this way, Metatron was old-fashioned. While he hadn't approved of Abraham's tyrannical ways, he had agreed to the basic premise. Metatron believed that people needed to be part of a society with well-defined roles and rules. In such a community, everyone carried out their allocated lot in life to improve society.

Chapter 220: A Marriage and a Baptism.

A few weeks later, it was time for the wedding of Metatron and Melissa and the baptism of Sabina. The ceremony took place on Mount Sinai, the holy mountain for the Edenites in the centre of Eden. Metatron's former rival, the angel Samael, led both the marriage ceremony and the baptism.

Samael:

- Metatron, do you swear, on your honour as a servant of the great Yahweh, to take Melissa as your wife and be fruitful.

Metatron paused. He had hoped that Samael wouldn't mention Yahweh during the wedding. Yahweh had been dead for millennia, and Metatron didn't want to proclaim himself the servant of Yahweh. Yet, Metatron was a supporter of Yahweh's ideology, so in that sense, Samael honoured him with his words. Metatron found an answer that suited him better.

- As a great supporter of Yahweh's values, I promise to honour my marriage commitment to Melissa. I promise to love Melissa, and if it's my destiny to be fruitful with her.

Samael gave Metatron a sceptical look. Officially, Metatron had already been fruitful with Melissa, so why did he say those last words? Samael decided to go on as if nothing had happened.

- Yes, you have already been fruitful with Melissa, and we pray that Yahweh will give you more blessings to come!

- Melissa, do you promise to honour and obey Metatron until the benevolent Yahweh ends your days?

Melissa:

- I do.

Samael:

- Good. Then I proclaim you husband and wife.

Samael took out two beautiful rings with expensive gemstones and put them on Metatron's and Melissa's fingers. The gathered people were cheering. After a while, Samael lifted his hand, instructing them to stop. He then commenced his speech.

- Today is a blessed day for two reasons, as we also welcome a new member to our Edenite family. I present to you Sabina, daughter of Metatron and Melissa, blessed by the great Yahweh himself. May this holy water protect you and forever keep you safe. Let the celebrations begin!

Having said this, Samael splashed some water on Sabina, the band started playing, and the crowd danced for hours.

Chapter 221: Hilda Muller Interrogates a Xeno Prisoner.

Hilda Muller and Markus White were back in the ruins of Rashidium. They observed the bluish light of the inter-dimensional portal over the gilded Cheops Pyramid. Returning to Rashidium was terrifying. What had once been one of the glowing jewel cities of the Terran Council was now a destroyed wasteland. The smell of death and decay still lay thick over the city.

Hilda walked along the abandoned streets of Rashidium when a foul stench overwhelmed her. Hilda heard a faint growl. She turned to her bodyguard, Captain Emma Schindler, and spoke:

- You said that the army has secured the city. So, why can I smell the stench of the Xenos and hear that faint growl from the building over there?

Emma Schindler:

- I am sorry Mistress Hilda; I will lead you back to safety at once!

Hilda Muller:

- No need, Captain Schindler. I am not an armchair general. I want to investigate this sound myself.

Emma Schindler:

- But that's dangerous. We cannot put your life at risk.

Hilda Muller:

- Don't worry about me. The troops that fought and died here didn't back down, and neither shall I. I won't allow myself cowardice.

Markus White stared at Hilda in disbelief and spoke:

- Hilda, come on, don't be stupid. You're not any high-ranking official. You are the leader of the Terran Council, the single most powerful woman on the planet. Let your soldiers do their jobs.

Hilda shrugged off Markus' objection. She was a soldier at heart, and she had killed several of these beasts when Rashidium was overrun. Besides, if she could capture a Xeno warrior, that would be an excellent opportunity to study and communicate with the creatures.

Hilda Muller:

- Markus, you stay here with a few guards. Emma and the rest of you, come with me. I want to interrogate the wounded Xeno warrior. Soldiers, arm your shields and plasma swords. We are entering that building!

They entered the building, and searched it until they reached the source of the stench and the sound. They found a severely injured Xeno warrior lying in a pool of his own blood, missing both legs and arms. But it had been weeks since the last battle. How could the beast be alive with the injuries it had sustained? Hilda decided that she had to find a way to communicate with the incapacitated enemy.

Hilda spoke to the Xeno:

- Who are you? Why do you come to Earth and fight us? What do you want?

The Xeno warrior:

- Sharaz rambu Ramun. Growl, rubut Rangda. Raman rantiz gudu dugu, gandin dinetion.

After saying this, the Xeno warrior started drooling and shaking. Emma Schindler raised her plasma sword to kill the beast, but Hilda told her off:

- What are you doing Emma? This is our first chance to communicate with our enemy and learn about them. You wouldn't waste that opportunity, would you?

Emma Schindler:

- There is nothing to learn from these beasts. They are bloodthirsty mindless monsters, and we already found the a to repel them. Lasers, orbital bombardment and land mines!

Hilda Muller:

- Lucky that I arrived here today! This beast understood what I said. At least it realised that I was communicating to it, and it tried to respond.

- We have quantum computers capable of decrypting any code. Deciphering the Xeno language should be a piece of cake.

Emma Schindler:

- You are right, Chairwoman Muller. I will connect us to the quantum computer at once.

A few minutes later, the quantum computer had analysed the Xeno language. The computer had deciphered what the Xeno warrior said, and created a potential vocabulary for the Xeno language. Hilda uploaded the Xeno vocabulary to the universal translator chip in her brain. When the upload had finished, Hilda spoke to the Xeno warrior in the Xeno language:

- So, Ramun the Xeno Warrior. You can stop following Rangda now because she is not around. Instead speak to me, Hilda Muller of Earth, and tell me what you know and what you want.

Hearing a human speak her language baffled Ramun. Eventually, she replied:

- How can you speak my language human? What kind of sorcery is this?!

Hilda Muller:

- It is not sorcery, it is technology. Travelling through dimensional portals, you should be aware of advanced technology.

Ramun:

- We don't use technology. We rely on the sorcery and the great powers that our God-Queen Rangda grants us.

Hilda Muller:

- You, Xenos, have advanced technology. We scavenged your fallen brethren of the technology you use. Ground-breaking stuff. But once we realised how your technology works, we found a way to counteract it. Something you never seemed to comprehend!

Ramun:

- Yes, my brethren told me that we have had problems with the guile of humans before. You helped the Zetans defeat us in the multi-millennial interstellar war.

Hilda Muller:

- What are you talking about? There is no mention of a multi-millennial interstellar war in human history.

Ramun:

- Humanity followed the vile Zetans like they were your gods. Refusing the one true goddess Rangda in her holy quest to free the galaxy of Zetans' falsehood and deceit!

- Check your religious scriptures, and you'll find plenty of references to the war. Your scriptures would describe it as the heavenly fight between "good" and "evil."

Hilda Muller:

- Interesting, but not very relevant. Tell me about your "god-queen" Rangda. Who is she, and how do I kill her?

Ramun:

- You already know who she is. You saw her during our first attack when we extracted our prisoner Keila. You fought me back then, you defeated me, and that's why I am talking to you.

Hilda Muller:

- I haven't seen enough of you to recognise individual Xenos. Did I do this to you?

Ramun:

- Yes, and now you must finish the job: Kill me and eat me, as is our custom!

Hilda Muller:

- Sure. If you tell me how you survived for six months with these severe wounds?

Ramun:

- I crawled and wriggled using my torso to get here. We, Xenos, are very resilient and recover from almost any wound. But we can't regrow dismembered limbs.

Hilda Muller:

- But that's six months ago. How can you still be alive if I dismembered you back then?

Ramun:

- Our home planet Xenora is incredibly harsh, and only the fiercest beast can survive there. Besides, "six months" as you call it is only two days on our home planet.

Hilda Muller:

- That's enough for now. You are my prisoner. We will feed you and further interrogate you.

Ramun:

- But you promised to kill me if I spoke!

Hilda Muller:

- I will kill you. But not now. That's not how humans treat valuable prisoners. And that is why we are going to come after your queen Rangda for what she did to us!

Ramun growled and roared, but it didn't matter. Hilda had her prisoner, and she wouldn't let a go of this opportunity to understand her enemy better!

Chapter 222: Melchior Forces Metatron to Give up the Zetan Technologies.

Metatron was feeding Sabina with a feeder bottle. Melissa was ill, and he didn't want to expose his daughter to virus-ridden breast-milk. Besides, he loved spending time alone with Sabina, his and Keila's biological daughter. Although Metatron had learned to love Melissa, he did not feel the same way that he had felt for Keila.

When Metatron looked into Sabina's lively green eyes, he saw the Keila he had fallen in love with before Rangda had possessed her. Metatron sighed and felt a bittersweet feeling. On the one hand, he missed Keila, and his daughter reminded him of her. On the other hand, Sabina gave Metatron a sense of purpose that he had never felt before in his very long life.

Samael rushed into the room. Metatron gave him a stern look and spoke.

- Samael, haven't I told you to not disturb me when I am spending time with my daughter.

Samael:

- I know Metatron, but this is important, and it can't wait. The traitor Melchior is here, with a large fleet requesting an audience.

Metatron:

- Melchior? Isn't that psychopath busy tormenting the poor Martians? What does he want from us?

Samael:

- Well, he is from Eden, and some of his family still lives here. I assume he wants to add Eden to his growing domains.

Metatron:

- I won't allow that to happen. I have sworn to lead and protect the Edenites from danger.

Samael:

- How do you intend to scare off a large hostile fleet?

Metatron:

- Samael, do you trust me?

Samael:

- Yes. Why do you ask?

Metatron:

- Because you must follow my lead, regardless of how outrageous it might seem.

- Let's go meet our prominent visitor.

Metatron authorised Melchior's command ship to dock with B528B. Metatron studied Melchior as he disembarked the ship. Melchior seemed to have aged many years, although it was just a year since they last met. And what was the thing with Melchior's eyes? Was he wearing tinted lenses? Metatron decided to find out. He shouted to Melchior:

- Hey Melchior, you got something in your eyes.

Instinctively Melchior rubbed his right eye before he replied.

- No, I haven't, what are you talking about?

Metatron had seen enough. He knew what he was dealing with. During Melchior's eye-rubbing, the tinted lens had moved out of position, revealing Melchior's real eye colour, purple. Two years earlier, When Rangda had possessed Keila, Keila's eye colour had changed to purple, and that had ended in disaster. Now Melchior was under Rangda's evil influence. Metatron decided to tackle the question headfirst:

Metatron:

- How is your old friend, Rangda?

Melchior:

- I don't know what you are talking about!

Metatron:

- Rangda has possessed you. That's why you have turned from an altruistic freedom fighter to a power-hungry tyrant. That's why you wear tinted lenses to hide your real eye colour, glowing purple!

Melchior:

- That is preposterous! Do you think anyone would believe this?

Metatron:

- I have proof. A high-velocity camera took this photo of your iris when you were rubbing your eyes.

Metatron streamed the photo of Melchior's iris onto the large displays in the spaceport of B528B.

Melchior responded nonchalantly:

- Those manipulated photos won't convince anyone. Besides, I am disappointed in your lack of hospitality.

- As an Edenite and soon to be emperor of Mars, I would have anticipated a more courteous reception.

Metatron:

- Don't call yourself emperor yet, there is plenty of opposition to your tyranny, and besides, you never won the presidential election.

Melchior:

- Oh, but I won the presidency fair and square.

Metatron:

- That was because all your opponents died the day before the election.

Melchior:

- What better way to prove that God is on my side? God wants me to rule Mars!

Metatron:

- It only proves you are a murderer and a fraud!

Melchior:

- Look who is talking, the man who helped Abraham to deceive us Edenites for 60 years!

- When I become emperor over Mars, I will rule it with Abraham's rules. But I will use doctrines suitable to the conditions of the 29th century.

- But let's talk about why I am here.

- I am here to take control of Eden and the Divine Control Centre. Being a generous man, I am offering you and the other angels amnesty if you surrender immediately.

Metatron:

- As the leader of Eden, I cannot grant you that request. Instead, I have a counter-offer. Leave us alone, or I will deactivate Eden's atmosphere. This will suffocate everyone, including your parents, your siblings, your nephews and your nieces.

Melchior:

- Impressive! I didn't think you had it in you. Then again, I could have my men shoot you!

Metatron:

- Killing or incapacitating me will trigger the release of cyanide gas into Eden's atmosphere, killing everyone on the surface.

Melchior:

- Okay, so be it. You can keep your Bronze-age colony for all I care.

- But I must have what I came for. I need the Zetan technologies and The Divine Detector machine. Give me those and I'll leave you alone. Refuse, and I don't mind if you kill everyone, including my own family!

- To prove myself, I'll show you what I am capable of.

Melchior streamed a video hologram into the room and continued speaking.

- Do you recognise this woman?

Metatron:

- Yes. It's your mother.

Melchior entered a command on the device on his arm. The video showed how a laser from Melchior's command ship incinerated Melchior's mother.

Metatron:

- Nice try, but I am not falling for that bluff.

Melchior:

- Oh, am I bluffing? Ask the AI for confirmation.

Metatron:

- AI. Did Melchior kill his mother using a laser cannon?

AI:

- I cannot deduce who fired the laser, but a laser did kill Mrs Dorevitch 20 seconds ago.

Melchior:

- Happy now? That's how dedicated I am. Hand over your Zetan technologies or no-one is getting out of here alive!

Fear overwhelmed Metatron and didn't know what to do. He knew that he had the moral duty to stop Melchior by not handing over the technologies. But he was also responsible for the lives of the Edenites. The most important aspect for Metatron was to save the lives of Melissa and Sabina. Metatron felt trapped between duty and love. Love was a dual-edged sword that stopped him from doing the right thing.

Metatron decided to give in to Melchior's demands. Regardless of what he did, Melchior would find a way to steal the Zetan technologies, so it was pointless to resist. Avoiding bloodshed was the best solution, as he had no other options.

Metatron:

- Okay, Melchior, you have proven your point. We will assemble all the Zetan technologies and deliver them on a portable drive tomorrow.

Melchior:

- Wise move! And don't even think about double-crossing me, or I'll expose you to a fate worse than death!

Having said this, Melchior returned to his command ship and undocked from B528B.

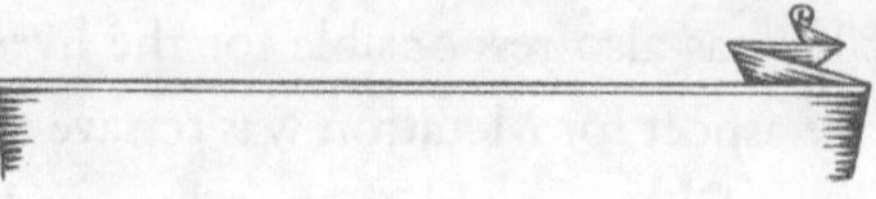

Chapter 223: Melissa's plan to protect Eden from Melchior.

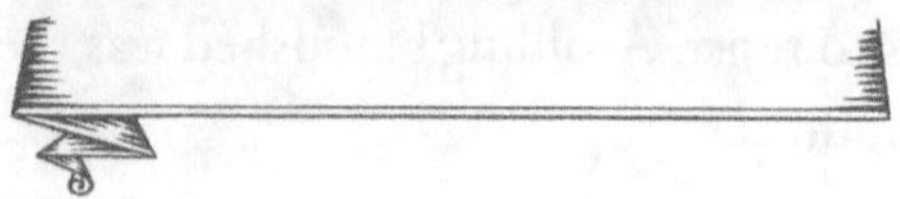

Later the same day, Metatron was seeking advice from Melissa. Melissa sensed Metatron's fears, even though he tried to project a calm exterior.

Melissa:

- What worries you, Metatron? Was Melchior threatening you during his visit?

Metatron:

- Melchior came for the Zetan technologies. I don't know if I should give them to him or not. I know that Melchior will cause a lot of damage if he gets hold of the technologies. But if I don't hand over the technologies, he will take them by force, and the people that I care about will suffer.

Melissa:

- I see. But you're not the only one who struggles. Melchior's parents and sisters still live on Eden. Surely, he wouldn't attack risking their lives?

Metatron didn't answer. Instead, he played the video from his meeting with Melchior. Melissa studied the video in shock and spoke:

- What happened to Melchior? He used to be a devout follower of Abraham's teaching, and he loved his family. How could he kill his own mother in cold blood to prove a point?

Metatron:

- Rangda has possessed Melchior. Rangda possessed Keila and caused her to open the portals on Earth, unleashing the Xenos.

Melissa:

- What makes you think that Rangda possesses Melchior?

Metatron:

- Because Melchior wore tinted lenses to hide his real eye colour. I caught a glimpse of his actual eye colour when he rubbed his eyes. Melchior's eyes are glowing purple, the same colour Keila had when her possession started to embellish her.

- I wish I had realised the danger back then.

Melissa pondered what Metatron had said. A plan popped up in her head. Melissa battled with her self-doubts on whether to tell Metatron or not, but eventually, she spoke:

- What about if we imbue the Zetan technology with a Trojan horse?

Metatron:

- A Trojan horse?

Melissa:

- Yes. We pretend to give in to Melchior's demands by giving him what the desires. But unbeknownst to him, we hide a computer virus amongst the technologies. We can activate this virus in the time of need.

Metatron:

- Good thinking, but it would never work. The Artificial Intelligence in Melchior's mainframe would identify the virus, and we'd be in trouble.

Melissa:

- Wouldn't Zetan programming code be foreign software to human-made supercomputers? Zetan code is another programming language. Thus, the AI would consider it as a virus?

Metatron studied Melissa's face, and he realised how blind he had been to her real character. He had believed that she was a dumb peasant and a tool to give birth to his child. At this moment he realised her true potential. Although Melissa lacked education, as she grew up under Abraham's archaic rule, she had still had more wits than most people.

Metatron:

- You are correct, Melissa! If we add extra virus code, Melchior's supercomputers won't be able to tell the difference. Let's infuse a Trojan virus into the blueprints that we will give Melchior tomorrow. This way, we can make sure that he never threatens Eden again.

- Come with me to the Divine Dimension. There is plenty of work for us to do, and time is of the essence!

After saying this, Metatron and Melissa transported their minds to The Divine Dimension. Once they were there, they programmed an invasive Trojan virus and embedded it into the Zetan blueprints. Once they had finished, Metatron prayed to the True Maker that this would be enough to save Eden from Melchior's tyranny.

Chapter 224: Melchior's Dark Dreams.

A few days later, Melchior was studying the Zetan technologies on his Command Ship, ISS Red Storm. Melchior was happy that he had acquired the advanced Zetan technological artefacts. The artefacts would give him almost unlimited power and would make sure that no one on Mars could stand against him. But Melchior felt annoyed that he couldn't use the technologies until he landed on Mars. Melchior didn't dare to transmit the Zetan technologies to Dov, fearing that the Terran Council would intercept the signal. The last thing Melchior wanted, was for his enemies to access these new advanced technologies.

Melchior opened another Zetan blueprint. The AI tried to block him from viewing the diagram, claiming that the files were a virus. Metatron had briefed Melchior about this when he handed over the records. The AI saw all Zetan codes as viruses by default, as the Zetans had used a different type of coding than human-made computers. Melchior chose to override the AI and opened the enticing top-secret code. He felt uneasy every time he did this. While his experts had advised him that he had nothing to fear, Melchior suspected that Metatron had found a way to outsmart him. This idea lingered like a splinter in his mind, yet he chose to ignore it.

Melchior lost interest in the Zetan blueprints and turned off the supercomputer. He walked to his bathroom and removed his tinted lenses. Melchior stared into the mirror studying his glowing purple predator eyes. He felt powerful studying his terrifying eyes. Melchior's transformation had triggered his hunger for flesh and bloodlust. Melchior desired to eat humans alive, while their hearts were still pumping blood, fresh and loaded with delicious zinc and iron. He desired to stare into his victims' eyes, paralysing them with fear, as they took their last breaths.

But Melchior couldn't fulfil his desires yet. Although Melchior wanted to eat one of his soldiers, he controlled himself. At the moment, Melchior was not powerful enough to kill and eat his own soldiers, without facing serious repercussions.

Failing to satisfy his bloodlust, Melchior felt exhausted. He went to sleep knowing that another night of vivid, violent dreams awaited him.

In the dream, Melchior was on an alien planet, which was very hot and filled with strange plants and animals.

Melchior's vision changed. It became narrow and blood-stained. Melchior could feel how his blood pressure and heart rate increased, along with feelings of excitement and pleasure. He had found his target. A human female was running away from him. Melchior leapt onto the target and sank his vicious fangs into her, drinking her blood. Melchior met her terrified gaze, and he recognised her. It was his mother. In his dream, Melchior felt a terrible sense of guilt. He had wasted his mother's life when he killed her with a laser cannon. The proper way to kill her, would have been as his pray, as her blood was thick, delicious, and satisfying!

Chapter 225: Rangda Influences Melchior.

Rangda studied the sleeping Keila. She was a costly prisoner to keep, and she hadn't been as useful as Rangda had hoped. When Rangda captured Keila, she had expected to find a way to drain Keila's psionic powers, to power up Rangda's corrupted Zeto Crystals. This hadn't worked. Rangda had tried to energise Keila's psionic powers, and had sent her troops to raid Earth looking for suitable food for Keila. While Keila had gorged on the food, she hadn't cooperated and charged the corrupted Zeto Crystals with her powers. Rangda realised that Keila was too strong-willed, for Rangda to dominate her.

But, Keila had proven to useful for another purpose: to influence Melchior.

As Melchior lacked Zetan DNA sequences, Rangda couldn't influence him via Zetan telepathy. But using Keila as a transmitter, Rangda had found out that she could manipulate Melchior's dreams and desires. Through dominating Keila, Rangda could use Keila's powers to influence Melchior. Rangda studied Melchior. His eyes had turned. Melchior had glowing purple predator eyes, but he feared revealing his true self. This was good. Melchior's fear of exposing his dark feelings would make them grow stronger, and he would succumb to them.

Rangda induced Melchior with another dream. In this dream, he was eating his young niece Elsa, daughter of his brother Dov Dorevitch. Rangda was confident that this dream would push Melchior to insanity. Once his dark desires immersed hem, Melchior would become her slave!

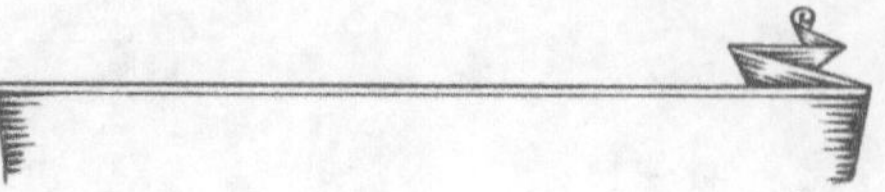

Chapter 226: A Military Expedition to the Divine Dimension.

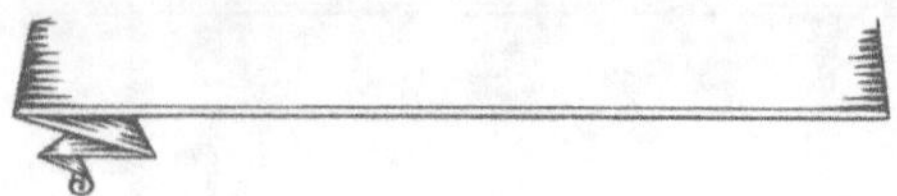

Hilda Muller studied the GDP for House Muller territory, as well as the Gross Planetary Product (GPP) for planet Earth. It was a terrifying read. Since the Xeno invasion, The GDP of House Muller was down 70 per cent, and the GPP for Earth was down 80 per cent. It was an unprecedented economic collapse and Hilda had to act to avoid a revolution on Earth.

Hilda led a police state with minimal personal and political freedom. The citizens had remained content, as the Terran Council had ensured that every Terran citizen lived a life in abundance. This was possible due to the asteroid mining stations and the plundering of other planets. Living in abundance, but with minimal freedoms, most people avoided any form of dissent. The average Terran citizen had much to lose and very little to gain from political dissent.

When people were destitute and desperate, things were different. There had been constant warfare and uprisings on Mars throughout the centuries. Hilda knew that the reason was poverty. Even though the Terran Council propaganda claimed it was because the Martians were uncouth and prone to violence.

Hilda needed to improve the economy, but to do so, she needed to deal with the elephant in the room. She needed to defeat the Xenos and find a way to close the inter-dimensional portals.

Hilda had gathered a lot of intelligence from her Xeno prisoner, Ramun. Ramun claimed that the Xenos in their natural state were fearsome but honest and noble. 13,000 years ago, the Xenos had fallen under the dark influence of Rangda, their Xeno-Zetan hybrid queen.

At first, Ramun was furious that Hilda wouldn't grant him death. But he had come around when Hilda had ordered her scientists to use stem cell technology to regrow Ramun's limbs. Now Ramun was Hilda's personal pet living in a secure enclosure at Hansstadt zoo. The zookeepers fed Ramun a variety of live animals, to keep him fed and happy, to ensure his cooperation.

Because of Ramun, Hilda had access to pure Xeno DNA for research. It was time to fight back! Hilda had equipped an expeditionary force with weapons adapted to fight the Xenos. House Muller had also developed viruses meant to be efficient against Xenos.

Hilda met with Emma Schindler, who she had promoted to General. Emma would lead the expeditionary forces on the dangerous expedition.

Hilda Muller:

- Emma, you have specific orders. I want you to lead an expeditionary force through the portal, deep into Xeno territory and kill Rangda. House Muller will equip you with hovercrafts, laser cannons, and battle armours, capable of withstanding a Xeno claw attack. Your troops will fight with plasma swords and diamond shields, as ballistic guns have proven to be ineffective.

Emma Schindler:

- Understood. Do you know where we will find Rangda?

Hilda Muller:

- Our prisoner couldn't answer that question as the Xenos are always on the move. Since the Divine Dimension is an endless, featureless plain, finding them will be difficult. But my scientists have developed a solution. We will equip you with a sensor that can detect infrared radiation from 100,000 kilometres away. Hopefully, this will be enough to find the Xenos.

Emma Schindler:

- And what about the Zetans?

Hilda Muller:

- The Zetans haven't attacked Earth and are not a priority. Try to stay out of their way. If necessary, state your business and tell them to back off. Don't let them enslave you!

Emma Schindler:

- Understood. How do we know that your Xeno prisoner is telling the truth?

Hilda Muller:

- We don't. But we must do something. The portals drain Earth's rotation speed. The length of a day has increased from 24 to 25 hours already. If this continues, we will get endless hot days and long freezing nights. The climate of our planet will collapse, and we will be unable to grow food.

Emma Schindler:

- Understood. Is there anything else that I need to keep in mind?

Hilda Muller:

- Yes. Be prepared for anything, we do not know what is on the other side of that portal. The prisoner says that Divine Dimension is safe, but we can't know for sure.

- The lives of 400 soldiers are on your hands, not to mention the future of humankind.

- You will not be able to communicate with me from the Divine Dimension. Use your best judgement!

- Good luck! I'll see you when you get back!

After saying this, Hilda Muller entered a private aircraft that took her back to Hansstadt.

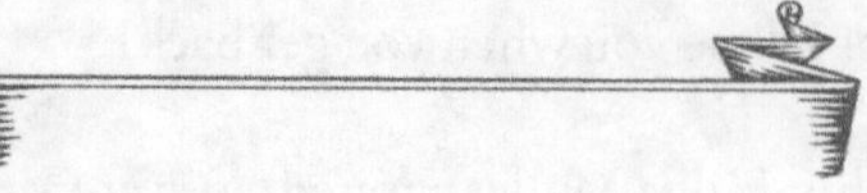

Chapter 227: A Lethal Confrontation Between the Terrans and the Zetans.

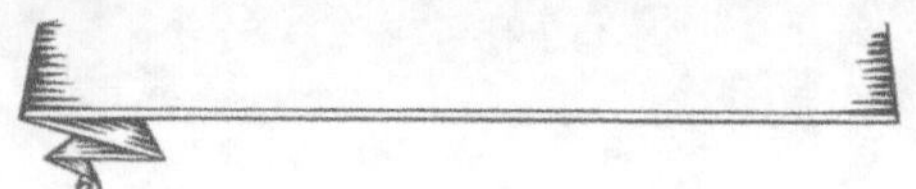

The Terran expeditionary force, led by Emma Schindler and Wilhelm Brandt, entered the Divine Dimension. Emma's troops needed to examine whether it was possible to move quickly and kill Rangda to end Xeno threat. Hilda Muller had refused to send a significant force as they had no reliable information on what was on the other side of the portal. Hilda thought it was foolish to send in the main army without knowing where the portal would take them.

Emma Schindler were awestruck by the beauty and the tranquillity she faced in the Divine Dimension. Emma checked the sensors. The sensors indicated that the air was safe to breathe. Emma look at her wristwatch; it seemed frozen in time.

Emma Schindler activated the mobile sensor trying to find the Xeno horde. Even though the sensor had a 100,000-kilometre range, the sensor couldn't detect any Xenos. The only things that showed up on the sensor were a group of 20 creatures that Emma assumed to be the Zetans. The Zetans were not far away. Emma turned to Wilhelm to discuss their options.

- None of the Xenos are within range for our sensors, what do you suggest that we do?

Wilhelm Brandt:

- Well, Hilda told us that this is an endless plain. We can't search blindly, or we'll end up out of fuel and supplies in the middle of nowhere.

Emma Schindler:

- Yes, but the only species that are nearby are the Zetans. Our orders are to stay clear of them if possible, as we don't know their disposition to us humans. The last thing that we want is to create more enemies.

Wilhelm Brandt:

- So, what do you want to do? Run back Earth and admit failure, days after our promotion?

- According to our Xeno captive, the Zetans and the Xenos are mortal enemies. I am confident that the Zetans will help us.

Emma Schindler:

- What if the Zetans are hostile?

Wilhelm Brandt:

- Why would they be? There are 400 of us and only 20 of them. I doubt they survived this long being reckless!

Emma Schindler:

- You're right. Let's establish contact with the Zetans and see if they can assist us!

After this, Emma and her troops advanced towards the Zetans in their hovercrafts. Half an hour later, they approached the Zetan Vanguard, led by Thor. Emma Schindler approached the Zetans and spoke into a universal translator. The universal translator translated the message to an array of ancient languages. This was because Ramun had told Hilda that the Zetans had posed as human deities during ancient times:

- I am Emma Schindler, in charge of this Terran Council expeditionary force. We are here to attack the Xenos and their queen Rangda, in retaliation for their attack on Earth.

The universal translator conveyed the same message in a variety of ancient languages. Thor replied:

- No need for a universal translator, feeble human. We have studied you for millennia, and we can articulate your current language.

- We appreciate that you are coming with weapons and vehicles as offerings to us. Leave them here and walk back to the portal, so no-one needs to die.

Wilhelm Brandt intervened:

- We are not here to surrender our weapons and hovercrafts to you. We are here to kill Rangda and the Xenos. Their attacks have caused massive damage to Earth. If you know where the Xenos are, you'll tell us now, and no-one will get hurt!

Thor roared:

- I will not tolerate a lowly human threatening me. Take this!

After shouting this, Thor threw his magical hammer and hit Wilhelm Brandt. The impact sent Wilhelm flying hundreds of meters backwards! Emma ducked for cover, and a barrage of laser beams and bullets rained down on the Zetans. This was to no avail. The Ballistic Energy Absorbers stopped the shots and the Prismatic Reflectors redirected the laser beams to hit the hovercrafts and destroyed most of them.

The Terran fighters didn't give up. Equipped with plasma swords and diamond shields, they charged at the Zetans. A fierce battle ensued where Emma's tenacious troops swarmed the superior Zetans. The humans snatched the victory, after Emma snuck up on Thor and decapitated him with a blow from her plasma sword. Seeing their leader killed, the remaining Zetans ran away from the battlefield. Some of the human soldiers wanted to pursue them, but Emma ordered them to stay back.

After the battle, Emma overlooked the battlefield. It was a disaster. The Zetans had destroyed most of her hovercrafts, and half of her soldiers were dead or injured. Worse yet, Emma had drawn humanity into conflict with another species.

Walking around among the dead, Emma found an injured Zetan, Anumati, and they began to speak.

Anumati:

- Why did you attack us? The Xenos will come soon. You have doomed us all.

Emma:

- We didn't attack, we only responded to the attack from your leader.

Anumati:

- Yes, Thor was overzealous. He still believed himself to be a God to your species. He couldn't accept that times have changed, and we are closer to equals now.

- But we must move. This place is swarming with Xenos, and we can no longer form a psionic barrier that keeps them away.

Emma:

- What are you talking about? We scanned the surroundings with infrared sensors. There are no Xenos within a 100,000 kilometres radius.

Anumati:

- The Xenos can mask their infrared heat signature, but they
can't hide their psionic presence. I predict that they will attack
very soon.

Before Emma answered, there was a loud scream of pain as the Xenos
appeared and attacked an unsuspecting soldier.

Xenos were coming from everywhere. There were thousands of them
swarming in on her exhausted soldiers. Emma made a quick decision. She
didn't like the concept of abandoning her soldiers, but the council needed to know what had happened. She found a functional hovercraft and
dragged Anumati onto it. Emma set her course to the portal. The Xenos
heard Emma starting the engines, and a large group of them jumped onto
her hovercraft and started tearing it to shreds.

"Just a little bit longer," Emma said to herself as she was approaching
the portal. When Anumati saw the portal, she screamed out in angst:

- We can't go through the portal yet. I must eat and drink, as I have
no energy left in my physical body. Millennia of starvation will kill me
when I leave the timelessness of this Dimension.

Emma:

- I am sorry, but I am unable to feed you right now. Hold
tight!

Emma crashed her hovercraft through the portal, and she ended
up outside the Cheops pyramid. The Terran automated defences killed
the Xenos that had clung on to her hovercraft. When the shooting had
ceased, Emma sighed of relief. She had survived the ordeal, and she had a
valuable prisoner that could give invaluable insights and technology. Emma turned to Anumati. What she saw shocked her. Crossing the dimensional rift had killed and mummified the Zetan captive!

Chapter 228: Hilda Muller Covers Up the Disastrous Military Campaign.

Hilda Muller was looking at the corpse of Emma Schindler. The official cause of death would be heart failure. Yet, Hilda knew the real cause of death. Emma had died from a synthetic virus designed towards Emma's genome, which caused a heart attack. After the disastrous expedition to the Divine Dimension, Hilda had to silence her former bodyguard.

Emma had failed the mission and lost her expeditionary force. Worse yet, she had also caused a confrontation with the Zetans. Instead of dealing with the Xeno threat, Emma had increased the threat level by battling another alien species!

Hilda, as Chairwoman of the Terran Council, had forbidden further expeditions to the Divine Dimension. Thus, she needed to find a way to restore Earth's rotational speed. Otherwise, she would face a widespread ecological collapse, when the day-night cycle became too much out of sync.

Hilda's intercom beeped. It was Markus White. Hilda had been busy dealing with the Emma Schindler debacle and had forgotten about her planned meeting with him. Hilda hesitated, but she decided to let him in. Markus was her closest ally, and she trusted him more than she trusted most of her own family members.

Seeing Emma Schindler's corpse shocked Markus, and he stuttered:

- What happened here? Why is your right-hand woman sitting dead in a chair?

Hilda Muller:

- Emma died of a heart attack.

Markus White:

- A heart attack? So where is the medical staff?

Hilda Muller:

- They will come here in due time. In half an hour or so.

Markus White:

- Half an hour? But then she will be dead beyond resurrection?

Hilda Muller:

- Yes.

Markus White:

- What is going on here?

Hilda Muller:

- I will tell you since you are my friend.

- I appointed Emma to lead an attack on the Xenos. I hoped to kill their queen Rangda who was behind the attacks on Earth. You have seen her, remember?

Markus White:

- Yes, I am still having recurring nightmares about that day!

Hilda Muller:

- Anyways, Emma failed. Instead of fighting the Xenos, she caused a confrontation with the Zetans. After the battle, Emma abandoned her army when the Xenos ambushed our troops.

- So, because of Emma, we are not at war with one alien species but two different species.

- As for Emma's death, a military court would give her the same outcome. But we cannot allow this to become be public, that's why I did what I had to do.

Markus White:

- I am sorry, Hilda. But this is too much for me. Why are you telling me all this? You could have kept me in the dark and met me in another room.

Hilda Muller:

- Yes, but you are my ally, my friend, and my love interest. I don't want us to keep secrets between each other.

Markus White:

- Not even dark secrets?

Hilda Muller:

- Not even dark secrets!

Markus White:

- I see. Well, thank you for being honest with me. I must leave now! I'll see you another day.

After saying this, Markus rushed off to the closest toilet and threw up.

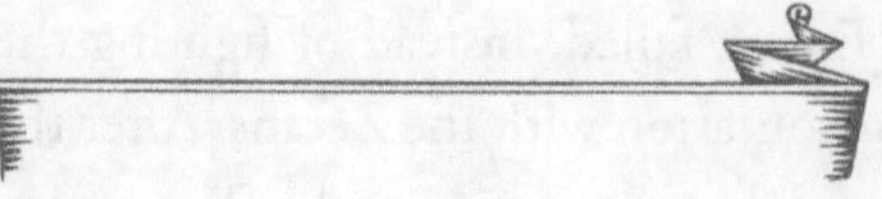

Chapter 229: Melchior Fulfils His Dark Desires.

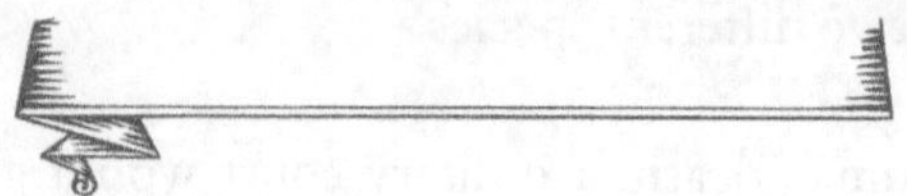

At the beginning of 2876, Melchior Dorevitch had accomplished his conquest of Mars. With access to Zetan technologies, conquering Mars had been a piece of cake. With his superior weaponry, his armies were unbeatable on the battlefield. With access to the Zetan mind-control technology, Melchior had inserted chips into everyone's brains. This way, Melchior could snuff out any dissent against his rule before it even happened. He had accomplished what no-one before him had achieved; he had unified Mars under one government. Melchior wouldn't rule Mars as the president of The Olympus Republic. No, Melchior would rule Mars as its god-king! Melchior saw himself as a messiah leading humanity into the future. The Martian would have to follow the rules set forth by the almighty Yahweh.

Melchior decreed that the new name of his territory would be the Martian Dominion.

Having access to a Divine Detector machine, Melchior knew the truth about Yahweh. Melchior knew that Yahweh was a long-dead Zetan. It didn't matter, as there was no such thing as objective truth. Words repeated enough times became the truth. Such was the case for all religions, and the only thing that mattered was to become more successful than the other religions!

While Melchior's religious aspirations were still in their infancy, his tyranny had made him the most powerful ruler in the solar system. The terrified Terran Council members sent him gifts and bowed to him, trying to win his favour. Things had certainly changed in the last few years!

Melchior decided that it was time to stop hiding his real self. He invited his brother for drinks.

Melchior poured Dov a glass of whiskey. Dov Dorevitch glanced at Melchior and spoke:

- Are you not drinking whiskey, today, brother? What are you having, Bloody Mary?

Melchior:

- Yes... Bloody Mary.

Dov:

- Okay. You wanted to show me something?

Melchior removed the tinted lenses from his eyes and revealed his purple predator eyes.

- Behold the true me. I have the same gift that Keila had, the purple eyes of destiny. Purple eyes are the mark of anyone that Rangda possesses.

Dov:

- Wow! So, you are as insane as Keila? Who is Rangda, anyway?

Melchior:

- Rangda is the pinnacle of creation. She is a Xeno-Zetan hybrid destined to rule the galaxy as its immortal goddess.

- Rangda has been to Earth, she led the first assault on Rashidium after the portals opened. There are photos of her, although the Terran Council are trying to cover up her existence.

Melchior streamed a hologram of Rangda. They studied the hologram for a while, and Melchior spoke:

- There she is, my goddess and my future queen! Isn't she beautiful?

Dov:

- But she is not even human? She looks like a demon, straight out of a nightmare?!

Melchior:

- Silence! Do not criticise the beauty in something because you cannot appreciate it!

- Anyways, you are here today because I need you to rule in my stead for the next few days. I am going to participate in a ritual to strengthen my connection to Rangda.

Dov:

- But Yahweh's laws forbid demon-worshipping rituals?

Melchior:

- Yes, but I am not going to let the laws of dead deity stop me from acquiring almost limitless power. Let the Martians believe in our doctrines. I made up the dogmas to weaken their minds and to destroy their chances for rebellion.

Dov:

- Understood, brother. I will head back to my office and prepare to lead.

Dov left Melchior's office, and Melchior summoned his secretary Sandra. Melchior had designated her to be his first victim. Sandra felt uneasy when she noticed his glowing purple predator eyes.

Sandra:

- What happened to your eyes, Master Melchior, they look so scary!

Melchior:

- Don't worry, Sandra. I am wearing a pair of tinted lenses that Dov gave me. I need to speak to you in private in the back-room.

Sandra felt uneasy, but she didn't dare to argue with her boss. She followed Melchior into the soundproof room. Once she was in the room, Melchior locked the door and took out the key from the lock. He stared into her eyes and spoke:

- Today Sandra, you'll be a very fortunate woman.

- Today, I'll grant you a favour that most people are dying to have. You'll die for a purpose. A very important purpose.

- You'll be the first human that I eat. Your death is the key to establishing my connection to Rangda, the ultimate being in existence!

Sandra felt terrified, but she wouldn't oblige to the madman in front of her without a fight. Sandra put up a good fight, but Melchior was too strong in his frenzied state. The last thing that Sandra saw was the possessed Melchior eating her alive, ripping off flesh from her body.

After gorging on Sandra's flesh, Melchior felt blissful and satisfied. He felt better than ever, and yet Rangda hadn't materialised. Melchior decided to take a nap. In his dreams, he had a vision of Rangda:

- We finally meet Melchior. You have been very impressive this far!

Melchior:

- I greet you my beautiful goddess Rangda, and I will do your bidding.

Rangda:

- Good! Build up a vast army, and travel to Earth. Together we will wipe out the Zetan filth that has infested the galaxy for too long. Together we will rule this galaxy as its rightful king and queen!

Melchior:

- I will do your bidding, Empress.

Rangda:

- Good. As you don't have ideal genetics for telepathy, you need to eat and kill someone before communicating with me.

Melchior:

- Magnificent! I can't wait to speak to you again, Empress Rangda!

Melchior fell back to sleep. He would stay in this room for a few days. There was still plenty of meat in the room, and it would be a shame to waste it!

Chapter 230: Metatron Notices Sabina's Amazing Abilities.

A few months later, in June 2876, Metatron was watching the news. He felt guilty and remorseful over giving up the Zetan technologies to Melchior. Giving up the technologies had saved the Edenites and Metatron's family, but the cost for everyone on Mars was too high. With the Zetan technologies, Melchior had crushed his opponents, and now the Martians suffered under his tyranny.

Metatron sighed. The reign of the Terran Council had been evil, but it was nothing compared to the atrocities under Melchior. The Terran Council had ruled over the solar system to satisfy their greed and desire for domination. The Terran Council army had only used real force when someone opposed them. With Melchior, things were different. Melchior and his inner circle tortured and maimed people for the fun of it.

Melchior claimed that his rule over Mars was a theocracy following Yahweh's teachings. But this wasn't close to the reality. Yahweh's instructions were harsh but, in some sense, fair and predictable. Melchior's rule, on the other hand, was a tyranny that made a mockery of the laws in the Old Testament.

Melchior started every Saturday with human sacrifice, cannibalism and demon worship. The Bible, which Melchior claimed to follow, had outlawed all this behaviour. To make things even more gruesome, Melchior sometimes forced his prisoners to kill and eat their own family members!

Hearing about all the atrocities under Melchior, Metatron felt powerless. He wished that he had resisted Melchior and died on that fateful day.

Metatron exhaled and tried to let go. There were always two sides to everything in life, and on the bright side, Melissa had fallen pregnant. In a couple of months, Sabina would have a baby brother. Thinking of Sabina, Metatron decided to spend time with his daughter.

Metatron entered Sabina's room. It appeared like she was talking to someone. But that couldn't be. Sabina was only a year old and could hardly walk, even less so having a proper conversation with someone. But Melchior could her a child's voice. Feeling surprised and curious, Metatron walked towards Sabina. Sabina noticed his presence and turned around:

- Hi daddy. So lovely to see you today.

Metatron froze. Sabina couldn't speak yesterday, and now she spoke like a much older child. Sabina gave him a curious look and spoke again:

- Is something wrong daddy? Come, give me a hug.

Metatron gave Sabina a hug. He looked at her in amazement and spoke:

- I didn't know you could talk? When did you learn?

Sabina:

- A few days ago. I have been speaking a lot to my mother lately.

Metatron:

- Really? Why hasn't she told me about it?

Sabina:

- She couldn't reach you. It's not in your blood to communicate via telepathy.

Metatron:

- Sabina, have you been speaking to Keila?

Sabina:

- Yes, who else? We both know Melissa isn't my real mother.

Sabina's statement stunned Metatron, and he looked into her eyes. They were glowing with a luminescent blue colour. Suddenly, they stopped shining blue, and they reverted to their natural green colour. Sabina spoke again:

- Dada. Peekaboo!!!!

Metatron looked at Sabina. Nothing indicated any superior advanced intelligence, and she had reverted to the one-year-old child that she was. Had he imagined it all? Metatron knew one thing, Sabina needed him. What she needed right now was to play peekaboo, so that's what he would do!

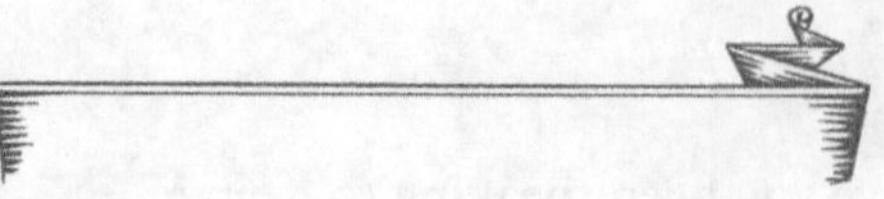

Chapter 231: Metatron Visits Hilda Muller.

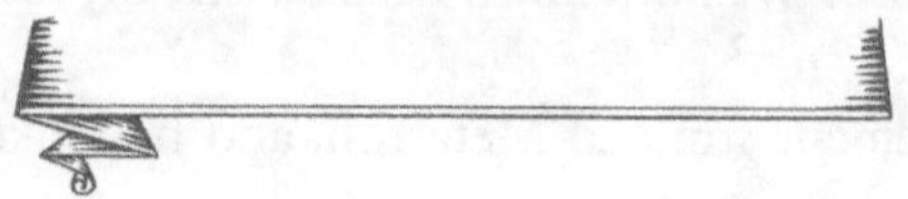

Metatron and Sabina were sitting in the lobby of Europeum Tower waiting for an audience with Hilda Muller. Metatron wondered what had he gotten himself into. Sabina had spoken to him on several occasions. She had told him that she had special abilities which the True Maker had given her. Furthermore, Sabina claimed that it was her destiny to stop Rangda's terror, and that she needed to speak to Hilda. But between these moments of divine intervention, Sabina was a regular child. Regardless, the conversations had convinced Metatron that he had to act, as he felt responsible for how things had turned out.

Contacting the Terran Council was a risky move. They had not been a humanitarian organisation in the past. If they knew that Eden had assisted Keila, coming here was suicide. Metatron believed that the Terran Council didn't know about the Edenite involvement in the Martian uprising. Otherwise, they would have attacked Eden by now.

Metatron entered Hilda's office, and her looks astonished him. Metatron had pictured Hilda Muller as a resolute lady in her military uniform. But Hilda was young and good-looking in an expensive blue dress, laden in jewellery. Hilda smiled at him and spoke:

- You look surprised, Mr Jack Silver, or shall I call you Metatron?

Metatron:

- Metatron is fine.

- Yes, you look so much younger and prettier in real life than you do in your press conferences.

Hilda:

- Yes. When I speak in public, I use makeup to look older. To instil authority, I wear my Supreme Commander uniform.

- But now I am not in the public eye, and like any 32-year-old woman, I like to look pretty.

- But how cute is that child? Is she your daughter?

Metatron:

- Yes, Sabina is my daughter, and this is her first visit to Earth.

Hilda:

- Then let us hope that she has many visits to come!
- She looks familiar. Have I met her mother?

Metatron:

- Have you been to Eden in the past? Her mother, Melissa has never been away from Eden.

Hilda:

- Oh, well then, I must be mistaken. I have never been to Eden. But from what I have heard, you have created something unique there.

- Sorry to be rude, but I am a busy woman, so let's get down to business.

- Have you come to pledge yourself to the Terran Council and incorporate Eden into our territory?

Metatron:

- No, I want Eden to remain a neutral colony.

Hilda:

- I am sorry, but then I don't understand why you have come here?

Metatron:

- I have come to introduce you to my daughter. Sabina is a prodigy child bestowed with superior intelligence by the True Maker.

- With your help, we can deal with Rangda before she becomes a threat to the entire galaxy.

Hilda:

- Is this a bad joke? You are bringing me a toddler, and you claim that I must send my army to stop the Xenos? All of this because of religious superstition?

Metatron:

- Yes. I would like you to talk with my toddler. Let Sabina tell you about her prophetic powers. Why haven't you sent troops through the portal to Divine Dimension? The Xeno attacks have receded, and it's time to counterattack

Hilda:

- Mind your manners. You cannot come here and dictate how to run my faction.

Suddenly, Sabina's eyes changed to a glowing crystal blue, and she spoke:

- Dear Hilda. Please help me stop Rangda and Melchior. Their power is increasing every day. If you don't act soon, it's going to be too late.

Hilda:

- What is going on here? What bionic implants have you put into the child's brain, to enable this kind of unnatural behaviour?

Sabina:

- I don't have any implants. The True Maker grants me the ability to reason on an adult's level.

Hilda:

- AI! Scan Sabina Silver for bionic implants!

AI:

- Sabina Silver doesn't seem to have any bionic implants.

Sabina:

- I would prefer that you use my mother's last name, Eisenstein.

Hilda:

- Are you Keila Eisenstein's daughter?

Sabina:

- Yes.

Hilda:

- Then your mother is the cause of all the bad things that have happened. Keila opened the portal that allowed the Xeno horde to attack us.

Sabina:

- Yes, but she never had bad intentions. Rangda deceived her. As fear deluded Keila, she failed to foresee what was to come. That's why I am here; to set things right!

Hilda:

- So, what would you have me do?

Sabina:

- You know what to do! Send me to the Divine Dimension with the backing of your Terran troops!

After saying this, Sabina lost her connection with the True Maker. Sabina's eye colour changed back to green, and she reverted to the mental status of an average 1.5-year-old child.

Hilda, unaware of the change that took place, screamed at Sabina:

- No! This is impossible, I don't believe you. Don't you dare to tell me what to do!

Sabina, who was back to being a typical toddler, said: "gaahhh, boohoo, mean lady!" Sabina started crying and ran to Metatron for comfort.

Hilda:

- What happened? Why is she acting like a toddler again?

Metatron:

- She is no longer connected with the True Maker. Thus, she is now a typical toddler.

- Anyways. You have seen enough. You know what to do.

Hilda screamed at Metatron, who flinched in surprise:

- Yes. I should have you both executed for your connection with our mortal enemy, Keila Eisenstein!

Metatron:

- If you kill Sabina, you'll doom us all! She is the only one who can save humanity and close the interdimensional rifts!

Hilda:

- Silence! Get away from me. I'll let you live, but never come back to Earth again.

Metatron realised that Hilda Muller wasn't receptive to further communication. He picked up the crying Sabina, and they left Hilda Muller's office in disappointment.

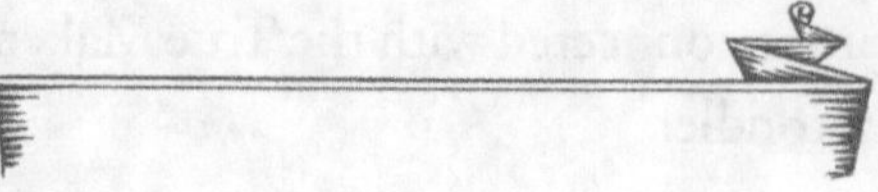

Chapter 232: Melchior Boards Metatron's Shuttle.

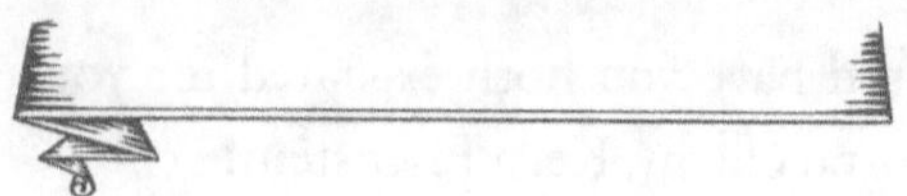

Metatron and Sabina were travelling back to Eden when trouble struck. Several space warships from Melchior's faction, the Martian Dominion approached them and requested to dock. Metatron realised that he could not outrun the fleet, so he surrendered. A short while later, Melchior and his bodyguards entered the shuttle.

Melchior:

- We meet again, Metatron. That must be your daughter? How delightful! What a shame you didn't introduce us the last time we met.

Metatron:

- I don't want to drag infants into politics.

- Besides, you promised to leave me alone if I handed over the Zetan technologies to you.

Melchior:

- Bah, speaking of promises. We discovered that you infested most of the technologies with Trojan viruses, which made them useless. But you failed. The ones that we could use were enough to help us conquer Mars. Whatever devilish plan you tried to set in motion came to naught.

Metatron:

- Is that so? Why do you reckon that I was the one who put the viruses there? They might have been from the start.

Melchior

- Yes, I realised the same thing, and that's why I kept my promise.

- But I never promised to leave you alone. My promise was to stay away from Eden if you gave me the technologies. This promise causes me severe grief, as I'm forced to live separated from my Edenite relatives. You're inhuman, Metatron, forcing a man to stay away from his beloved family!

Metatron:

- Beloved family? You incinerated your own mother to prove a point, you evil monster!

Melchior:

- You forced my hand. I wasn't going to let you blackmail me into staying away from what is rightfully mine.

- Regardless, why are you travelling back to Eden from Earth? What business did you have on Earth?

Metatron:

- I was feeling homesick. I was born on Earth, and I wanted to take my daughter to Earth and show her my roots.

Melchior:

- What a load of rubbish. Bringing a toddler on a long trip to Earth for sightseeing? Ridiculous.

- Unless...

Melchior aimed a DNA scanner towards Sabina, and the answer was what he expected. Sabina was Keila's child.
Melchior:

- Fascinating. You and Keila must have used a surrogate mother before she went on her suicide mission to Earth?

- What did she hope to achieve?

Metatron:

- Keila wanted a part of her to survive after her death.

Melchior:

- Nah, that doesn't sound like Keila. It must have been one of the visions that told her to have a child with you. In that case, we both know what I must do.

Melchior pulled up a stun gun and electrocuted Metatron. Then he grabbed the crying Sabina and studied her carefully.
Melchior:

- Fascinating. She is the spitting image of her mother.

- But why would you go to Earth with Keila's daughter? What do you hope to achieve?

- Are you collaborating with the greedy cowards in the Terran Council? Why would you bring your daughter to such a meeting?

Melchior looked at Metatron who was cramping after the electrocution. Melchior gave a signal to his bodyguards, to get Metatron back on his feet, and handcuff him to a wall. When Metatron had regained consciousness, Melchior spoke again:

- I have realised that I will never find out why you brought your daughter on this dangerous trip to Earth. And I don't even care why. This is my opportunity to get revenge for what you caused me to do to my mother.

Melchior smiled a sinister smile, stared into Sabina's eyes, and took a small bite into her shoulder. The toddler screamed a heartbreaking shriek of pain as Melchior took a gulp of her blood.

Melchior turned to Metatron:

- You should thank your daughter, Metatron. Because she is the reason that you'll get out of here alive. You see, witnessing what I am going to do to her is worse than dying, and I want you to suffer!

Melchior took another bite of Sabina's arm and then threw her roughly into the wall, knocking her unconscious.

With Sabina's blood dripping from his mouth, he walked up to Metatron to mock him. Metatron didn't respond. Instead, he head-butted Melchior who fell to the floor. Melchior got up. Smiling like a madman, he spoke:

- Ah, pain. Why do people avoid it when it is the purest form of pleasure?

Melchior knocked the chained Metatron unconscious with a flurry of hard punches. He turned to, Sabina who had regained consciousness, to finish the gruesome murder. Rangda appeared as an illusion and stopped Melchior.

- Stay clear of Keila's daughter, Melchior! I sense that Sabina has a lot of untapped psionic powers. I want her to grow up so that I can capture her and drain her power. Sabina's powers will make us even stronger if we give them time to grow before we kill her!

Melchior:

- But Empress Rangda, this girl is my prey, and she is delicious.

Rangda:

- I'll let you eat her later. But first, she must grow up and face me. After I have drained her psionic powers, she is all yours.

- I command you to let Sabina and Metatron travel back to Eden.

Melchior:

- Arrrgh...! Yes, Empress Rangda. I will do your bidding.

Melchior ordered his bodyguards to patch up Sabina's and Metatron's wounds so that they could go back to Eden safely. After that, he went back to his command ship. There, Melchior picked up a huge rat, crushed it with his hand and drank the blood to quench his unquenchable thirst. But this was to no avail. The rat's blood was not what he was after.

Melchior was furious with Rangda for denying him his prey, but he would obey her for now. After all, he still needed her as she had a lot to teach him!

A while later, Sabina approached Metatron with her eyes shining bluer than ever:

- Are you okay daddy? I am so sorry that I couldn't stop those men from hurting you.

Metatron:

- I am your father; I am the one who should protect you.

Sabina:

- Yes, but you are only human, so I can't expect you to do everything. How are your injuries?

Metatron:

- A bit swollen but I'll be alright. I am more worried about the bites he took off you.

Sabina pulled off the bandages that Melchior's bodyguards had put on her shoulder and on her arm. There was not a scratch, and the wounds had healed like they were never there. Sabina spoke:

- Don't worry about me. Be a good father for Sabina when I am not around.

- I don't usually use my healing powers on humans, but I'll make an exception today.

Sabina put her tiny hands on Metatron's bleeding wounds. Metatron felt a short burst of intense serenity and calmness. When he got back to his senses, his injuries and his headache were gone. Sabina was back to her usual self and she hugged him:

- Daddy, I am scared. Bad men hurt me. Boohoo!!

Metatron:

- The bad men are gone and won't hurt you again, my sweetheart. Let's go home to mommy Melissa and tell her about our fun trip to Earth!

Having said this, Metatron returned to the pilot seat on his spacecraft and set the autopilot to destination Eden.

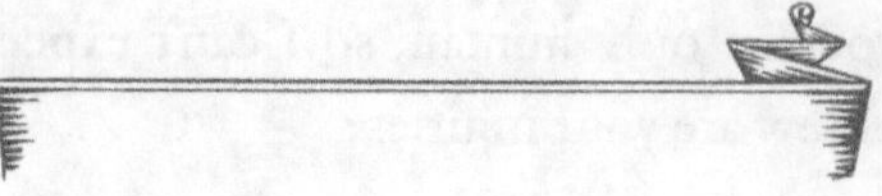

Chapter 233: Hilda Muller's Dilemma.

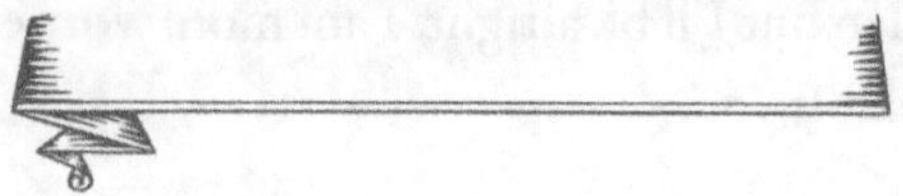

It was New Year's Eve; 2876 was about to end. Hilda Muller excused herself from the New Year's celebration, and she withdrew to her private level of Europeum Tower.

Hilda had changed after Metatron and Sabina had visited her, six months earlier. What had happened that day? How had the child changed eye colour and spoken like an adult? Sabina had urged Hilda to attack the Xenos, but had reverted to a toddler moments later. Hilda couldn't comprehend it, and she didn't know what to do.

Hilda had studied the video footage with her scientists, and no-one could explain what had happened. Hilda wondered whether she had experienced a divine intervention. By why had God used the daughter of her enemy, Keila Eisenstein, as the vessel? And what would Hilda do?

The toddler had urged Hilda to lead her army to the Divine Dimension, but would she do this? If she was unlucky, Rangda could be the one possessing Sabina. Rangda had possessed Keila, and if she possessed Sabina as well, returning to the Divine Dimension was a trap.

Hilda felt frustrated by her own fear and indecisiveness. She decided that she had to do something. As it turned out, that something was someone, one of her bodyguards, Melanie Weber. While Hilda preferred men to women, it was interesting to try something different, and she had grown disillusioned with men. They either feared her for her power or tried to seduce her to dominate her and steal her power. Markus White had been different, but he was too weak to stomach the brutal reality of power.

Hilda had done the right thing murdering Emma to cover up the disastrous military expedition. If Markus White had been the right partner, he would have seen things Hilda's way and supported her. Instead, he had added to her burden when he left her alone with her guilt over murdering Emma.

But in Melanie Weber, Hilda had found what she needed. Melanie was loyal, secure, discrete, and she was more than happy to help Hilda with her every need. Hilda studied Melanie as she entered the room. It was a shame to hide such a beautiful woman under an ugly bodyguard uniform. But it would be too conspicuous to dress one of her bodyguards different from the others, besides the clothes wouldn't stay on for long.

Melanie:

  - Melanie Weber reporting for duty!

Hilda:

  - Melanie, you are my only guard on duty tonight, I need to keep you near, very near, to protect me.

Melanie:

  - And who is going to protect you against me?

Hilda:

  - I am more than capable of protecting myself against you.

Melanie:

  - Is that so? Then wrestle me to the ground!

Hilda:

  - With pleasure, you'll be under me in no time.

After that, the two of them started a rough session of wrestling, and a while later, Hilda was on top of Melanie.

Hilda:

- I still got it!

Melanie:

- Yes, Mistress Muller, you still got it!

Hilda moaned in pleasure. In Melanie's embrace, Hilda could disconnect from the anxiety and fear that clouded her mind.

Chapter 234: Melchior Reveals His True Form.

In August 2877, Melchior was studying his military forces. The Martian military strength had increased as Melchior had ordered the redirection of all resources to the army. They would soon be ready to travel to Earth to face the Terran Council and make them bow to their will. Melchior smiled. In his visions, there were so many beautiful places in the universe, planets that were ripe for Martian expansion. When Melchior had finished, he would rule the entire galaxy. Every intelligent living being would have to bow him and serve him.

Melchior fell to the ground with tremors. He was in immense pain. Melchior had been too busy working on his plans, so he had forgotten to eat for several days. Melchior felt how hunger made his entire body ache. Since Rangda possessed him, Melchior had adopted the Xeno way of eating, i.e. biting chunks of meat off an alive victim. Eating this way, he could eat 10 kilos at once and stay full for days as meat digests slowly.

Melchior got up, and he studied his reflection in the mirror. His ashen grey thick skin was cracking up everywhere, and he was bleeding from multiple wounds. He needed to eat straight away! He called his brother Dov:

- Dov, bring me a prisoner right now. I am starving.

Dov:

- Which prisoner? There are plenty to choose from.

Melchior:

- Bring anyone.

A while later, Dov brought a female prisoner, imprisoned for abortion. Melchior forbade abortion, not because he valued life, but because he was against killing without eating. Thus, it was legal to give birth to a baby and then eat it. But Melchior didn't allow abortion since it was "unnatural".

Melchior studied the woman and spoke:

- Ah, delicious. What crime did she commit?

Dov:

- She had an abortion and wasted the meat.

Melchior:

- Heinous! Well at least her end will serve a useful purpose.

Melchior leapt at the woman and tore pieces of flesh off her with his sharp teeth. Dov had gagged the woman to stop her from screaming in agony, as he couldn't stand hearing the screams of the murder victims. Dov left; knowing that half an hour later, his brother would lie on his couch like a lion after a big meal.

Half an hour later, Dov came back, and he spoke to Melchior:

- What is happening to you, brother? You don't look human anymore.

Melchior:

- So, my experiment is working? Thank you.

Dov:

- Your experiment? What have you done?

Melchior:

- Rangda gave me a Xeno DNA sequence in a vision. She said that I can become immensely powerful if I become a human-Xeno hybrid.

Dov:

- But when would you have done this? You can't change your DNA when you are awake? You can only do it when you are in suspended animation.

Melchior:

- That was what my doctor said. He said that the pain from such as procedure would kill any human from the sheer shock.

- And he was telling the truth. I found that out when I tested the procedure on him!

- But I realised something. That my doctor was a mere human, a weakling not destined for greatness, while I am destined to rule the galaxy.

- So, I did the experiment on myself, and it works. I am in immense pain, but instead of running from the pain, I embrace it, and it gives me strength.

Dov:

- So, you turned yourself into a man-eating monster in constant pain, for what? Power? You are already the mightiest person in the solar system.

Melchior:

- Your small-mindedness annoys me! Yes, I was powerful, but I was still a man. A bullet through my brain could end me at any time, and if nothing else, time would take its toll.

- Now I am something more. I am a hybrid of the most power-ful races of the galaxy, and when I am united with my queen, we will rule everyone!

Dov:

- About that. There is a critical problem affecting our military build-up. Ecological destruction of Mars is destroying our harvests. We will starve in a couple of months.

Melchior:

- Well then. We better cull the population, so we have fewer mouths to feed. Our soldiers shall kill and eat the leeches in our society.

Dov:

- Most of our soldiers follow us out of fear. Forcing them to cannibalism will push them against us.

Melchior:

- Bloody weaklings! But you're right, Dov. We need to move now. Prepare my fleet for departure to Earth. I'll bring most of the army there. You'll stay behind and rule Mars in my place.

Dov:

- But brother, we are not ready with our military build-up. We cannot conquer Earth, yet.

Melchior:

- I know. But I will give them an offer that they cannot refuse.

After that, Dov left the room to carry out Melchior's orders and pre-pare everyone for departure.

Chapter 235: Enemies at the Gates.

Hilda Muller was lying naked in Melanie Weber's embrace. What Hilda had intended to be a short fling and an experiment to get over Markus White had turned out to be something else. Hilda's relationship with Melanie gave her both joy and pain. Melanie made Hilda feel protected and appreciated. But her relationship with Melanie would be political suicide if it became public. As a mighty leader, Hilda could have several flings on the side and no-one would care. But her official partner needed to be someone important, and not her bodyguard.

There was a beep on the intercom. Hilda's cousin Michael Muller, the second most prominent leader in House Muller, requested an urgent meeting. This was very odd. During the two and half years that they had overseen House Muller, Michael rarely approached Hilda with any urgent matters. As a matter of fact, Michael preferred letting Hilda make difficult decisions.

Hilda got dressed and met Michael in the lounge room. Michael appeared stressed and irritable.

Michael:

- How was the tryst?

Hilda studied Michael. How could he know about her and Melanie? Hilda decided to dismiss Michael:

- My sex life is none of your business.

Michael:

- That is correct. I wouldn't give a shit that you fuck your bodyguard if you could pick up the phone when I am calling you. We are in the middle of an emergency.

- Tell Melanie to come out. I need to speak to her!

Lost for words, Hilda didn't know what to say, and she agreed to her cousin's demands. A few minutes later, Melanie Weber came out to greet Michael. He spoke to her with a direct tone:

- Melanie. Thank you for looking after Hilda so well. But I cannot allow a bodyguard to be in an ongoing romantic relationship with our chairwoman. You're relieved of your employment as a bodyguard for House Muller!

Hilda was going to protest, but Michael raised his finger to show that he hadn't finished talking:

- As your severance package, I'll give you 10,000 shares in the Muller Corporation. This is enough to attend our annual general meeting. I also offer you the position as the General of our 57th army division.

Hilda Muller:

- Wait. There is no 57th army division.

Michael Muller:

- There is now. Believe me, Hilda! If Melanie has been loyal to you for almost a year and kept your secret, she is worth her weight in gold.

- You cannot be in a relationship with your bodyguard. But partnering up with a prominent and wealthy general is an acceptable solution.

- Now, Supreme Commander Hilda Muller, and General Melanie Weber, we have a serious problem to deal with.

Hilda Muller:

- I am listening.

Michael Muller:

- The madman Melchior Dorevitch, has arrived with a large fleet. They are hovering 200 kilometres above Hansstadt and threatens our capital. He requests a meeting on his command ship.

Hilda Muller:

- What? How did he get this close undetected?

Michael Muller:

- He must have used Zetan stealth technology to mask his ships. There has been a tremendous technological advancement on Mars since their independence.

Hilda Muller:

- Scheisse. Can we beat him?

Michael Muller:

- I hope so. Our analysts believe that Melchior moved early due to the catastrophic harvests and looming starvation on Mars.

- However, with Melchior this close to our capital, any major confrontation would level the entire city.

Hilda Muller:

- We cannot risk that. I guess I have no choice but to meet this madman on his terms.

- You stay back with our army on full alert. If something happens to me, we cannot let this lunatic conquer our territory. Attack him with full force if he tries anything.

Michael Muller:

- Understood. I will head to our underground command bunker and coordinate our forces.

Hilda Muller:

- Good. Now Melanie...

Melanie Weber:

- Yes, Mistress Muller?

Hilda Muller:

- Hurry up and pick up a General's uniform.

- You're coming with me. I need you by my side when I am facing this Martian menace.

Melanie Weber:

- Acknowledged Mistress Muller. I'll get changed and meet you at the starport.

Hilda Muller:

- You can call me Hilda now. Michael just made you one of us. Now hurry up!

Hilda hurried to get dressed and made her way to the starport. On the way to the starport, she experienced a mixture of fear and a sense of relief. Hilda feared for her upcoming meeting with the wicked Melchior. But Hilda felt relief knowing that if she got out of this alive, she would be able to partner up with the woman that she loved.

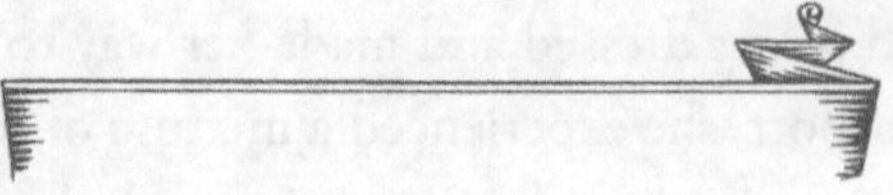

Chapter 236: Hilda Meets Melchior.

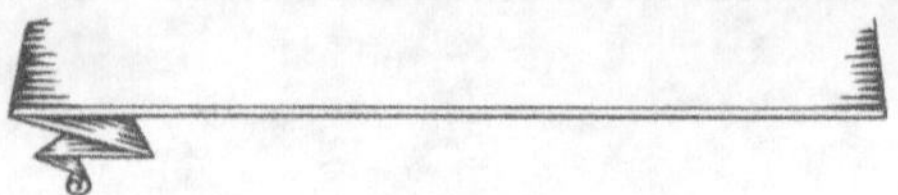

An hour later, Hilda Muller, Melanie Weber and a few bodyguards docked with Melchior's command ship. The sight of Melchior's lobby shocked Hilda. In the centre of the hall, there was a large fountain that was pumping out blood. Human hearts ornamented the fountain.

Melchior's imperial guard covered the edges of the room. They looked terrifying. The guards had covered themselves in black armour, filled with blood-stained spikes. Hilda feared the mutated Martian guards, but she pulled herself together and stayed strong.

Hilda shouted:

- I am Hilda Muller from the Terran Council. Where is Melchior Dorevitch? What kind of man invites people to his command ship without being there to greet them?

A gigantic beastlike guard, who was almost three meters tall, approached Hilda. She stared in terror at guard, who wore an iron face-mask and fearsome-looking armour. The monstrosity spoke:

- I am Peter Belovic, the chancellor of the Martian Dominion and Melchior's right-hand-man.

- I require you to surrender your weapons before Melchior grants you an audience.

Hilda:

- This is an outrage. I am the chairwoman of the Terran Council, not some low-ranking officer. I require you to show your real face before coming with demands like these.

Peter Belovic:

- I am hiding my face to do you a favour. Seeing the terror that lurks behind this mask would terrify you!

Hilda:

- Nonetheless, it is customary to see the face of the one you negotiate with. Show your face, or I will leave, and you have wasted everyone's time!

Peter:

- As you wish, Madame Muller. But don't say I didn't warn you.

Peter Belovic removed his helmet, and revealed his terrifying face. Seeing Peter's face, Hilda flinched and almost fell over. Melanie grabbed Hilda's arm and helped her regain her balance.

Hilda studied the man, or rather, the ghastly and horrifying monster in front of her. His petrifying eyes were blood-sprained, and the optical nerves were glowing red. His skin was ashen, thick and lizard-like. There were large jagged cracks and crusts on his skin, exposing his muscle tissues and veins. Most of Peter's front teeth were missing. The teeth that remained were sharp fangs, and he was drooling and panting like a hungry beast.

Hilda:

- You better put that mask on! What happened to you? You do not look human!

Peter:

- My master tried to make me stronger by injecting me with Xeno DNA. As it turned out, my genes were not strong enough to merge with foreign DNA. The pain is unbearable, and I only have a short time left to live. As I die, my brethren shall consume my flesh to make them stronger.

Hilda:

- Forget that I asked!

- Guards! Surrender your weapons to our hosts. It is time to meet Melchior Dorevitch, leader of the Martian Dominion.

Hilda and her bodyguards surrendered their weapons, and Peter called Melchior over the radio. 30 seconds later, Melchior entered the room.

Hilda studied Melchior. He had the same ash-grey thick lizard-like skin that Peter had. But unlike Peter, Melchior's skin had fused together, and his scars had healed. Melchior's eyes were glowing purple, unlike Peter's sickly blood-sprained eyes. Melchior's eyes gave Hilda a déjà vu. Keila Eisenstein had the same eyes when she had killed the Terran Council leadership in Rashidium.

Melchior approached Hilda and spoke:

- Thank you for accepting my invitation. I am sorry for not shaking your hands, as my sharp claws make handshakes difficult.

Hilda studied Melchior's hands. Large claws were extending from the top of them, and small sharp thorns covered his palm. She nodded in acknowledgement but said nothing. Melchior continued to speak:

- How do you find our centrepiece, the blood-fountain over there?

Hilda:

- I am sorry, but I don't like it. What is it anyway?

Melchior:

- It's a blood fountain. Underneath the fountain sits synthetic bone marrow that creates human blood. The fountain pumps the blood. The hearts of my enemies are beating with the aid of electrical electrodes attached to the bottom of them.

Hilda:

- The hearts of your enemies? So, the hearts are not grown in the lab, but the actual hearts of people that you have killed?

Melchior:

- That is correct. The soul resides in the heart, so keeping the heart alive is the best way to torment an enemy after death.

Hilda struggled with her fear and terror. She had anticipated that meeting Melchior Dorevitch on his command ship would be unpleasant, but she had never imagined it to be this bad. But Hilda had to keep herself together. She was the leader of Terran Council, and if she cracked, there was nothing to stop this evil madman from destroying her beautiful planet, Earth.

Hilda stammered:

- Okay, but I am not here to discuss your religious beliefs. You have travelled all the way to Earth, and you have requested a meeting. What do you want?

Melchior:

- Hahaha! I will get to that in a moment. But first, have a drink with and cheer with me to the future. That is a Terran tradition, right?

Hilda:

- Yes. That is correct, but I don't see any champagne glasses around.

Melchior:

- Oh, how rude of me. I forgot the glassware! Wait a second.

Melchior snapped his fingers, and a servant approached him with two jugs made out of baby craniums. Melchior took the skulls, walked to the fountain and filled the skulls with blood.

Melchior

- In the Martian Dominion, we don't drink alcohol. But share some blood with me. It's rich in nutrients, especially iron, perfect for women in their fertile age.

Hilda:

- Disgusting! I'll pass on the offer!

Melchior had a sip of blood, stared into Hilda's eyes before licking his lips and talking:

- Oh, but you misunderstand. The drinking of blood is not an offer but a rite of passage of my ship. I would consider it very rude if you don't follow through with it.

Hilda lost her calm and yelled:

- I will not let you poison me! If you harm me, the entire Terran Council army will attack you!

Melchior shrugged his shoulders and spoke:

- There is nothing toxic in the blood, as you can see, I am drinking it myself. If I wanted to kill you, I would blow up your fancy tower from orbit before your army had the time to react!

- Now drink the damn blood before I get angry. Trust me, you don't want that to happen.

Hilda felt compelled to drink the blood, and she managed to finish the bowl without spewing. Melchior studied her for a while and then he spoke again:

- Good, you have proven your value. Now, let's discuss why I am here.

- I have decided to help you with the portal problem. I intend to lead my army to the Divine Dimension and wipe out the aliens that threaten mankind. All I need is your approval and support to the cause.

Hilda stared at Melchior in disbelief and spoke:

- You are putting me through this, and now you are offering your help. What is going on and why do you want to help us?

Melchior:

- My motivations are none of your concern. All you need to do is answer this question. Do you prefer to: A. Give us your blessings and support us with fuel, food and materials, or B. Die here today, with most of your capital levelled in the process?

Hilda:

- That sounds a lot like blackmail.

Melchior:

- Is that what you call it when we reverse the roles? What did you call it when the Terran Council forced the Martian nations to pay to keep electromagnetic field running?

Hilda bit her lip. The tables had turned, and she knew what fate had befallen the ones that resisted the Terran Council's power in the past. Hilda:

- I choose A. I will grant you free passage to the portals, and I'll support your expedition with one million metric tonnes of fuel, food and provisions.

Melchior smiled and spoke:

- Good choice. I am happy that I made a "friend" today!

- I will leave a large fleet here to help you keep your promise. The rest of my fleet will gather near the portal and ensure that the supplies arrive.

- Please notify your allies on the Terran Council about your decision. I do not want any confrontations due to unfortunate "misunderstandings."

Hilda:

- Understood. I will convene with the others as soon as possible and make sure that everyone follows our agreement.

After saying this, Hilda and her group headed back to their shuttle returning to Hansstadt. Hilda felt relieved that she had survived visiting Melchior's lunatic asylum!

Chapter 237: Melchior Discusses the Events with Rangda.

Later the same day, Melchior and his closest men had a feast on the late Peter Belovic. It was a shame to see a prominent follower die that way, but it was the least wasteful way for him to die. Peter's body hadn't survived the Xeno mutations. The only way to help him was to eat him alive while his heart was still pumping. This was a honourable death, better than letting him die and spoil the meat in the process.

One good thing came with Peter's death. It enabled Melchior's telepathic abilities so that he could communicate with his evil Mistress, Rangda.

Melchior:

- Our first step was a success. I terrified Hilda Muller and she will not pose any resistance to our army entering the portals. She even agreed to help us with supplies.

Rangda:

- Excellent. And how did she react when she drank the holy blood from the sacred fountain?

Melchior:

- The blood failed to initiate her hunger. She reacted with disgust when she ingested it.

Rangda:

- That's unfortunate but expected. The weak Earth humans are only vulnerable to the desire for money. They lack a natural thirst for blood.

- Thus, they kill for money and let the dead bodies go to waste. How wasteful and grotesque!

Melchior:

- Indeed, Mistress Rangda. That is why humanity needs a new beginning. And together we will make sure that the new dawn of humankind happens!

Rangda:

- Yes, we will. Together we shall cleanse the Zetan scourge from this universe. The noble Xeno values must prevail. We will become the rulers of the Milky Way Galaxy!

Melchior:

- Yes. But the Terrans are fearful of us. Let's attack and conquer Earth while they are weak? I hunger for it!

Rangda:

- I know you do. But a true general doesn't enter the battle unless it's already won.

- Help me cleanse the Zetan scourge, and we will wipe out the Terran resistance together. Then earth shall be your price.

Melchior:

- Yes, Mistress. I will do your bidding.
- I will see you in the Divine Dimension.
- Goodbye!

The telepathic conversation with Rangda filled Melchior with rage. This was the second time the bitch had refused him his prey. She had stopped him from eating Sabina, and now she'd prevent him from attacking Earth that was ripe for the taking. But he would obey, for now.

Melchior released his anger on one of his weaker soldiers, impaling the victim with his sharp claws and splitting him in half. The others stared at him in shock and Melchior shouted out:

- Still hungry. Eat more men!

And Melchior's beastlike men feasted on their fallen comrade.

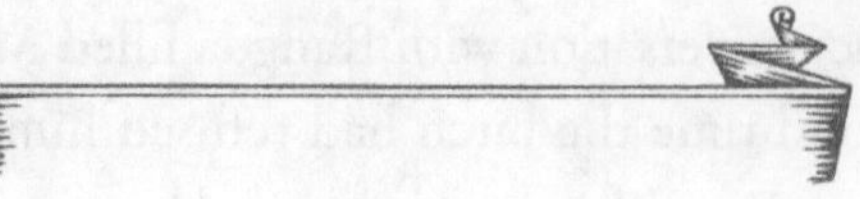

Chapter 238: Nightmares, Concessions, and Contingency Plans.

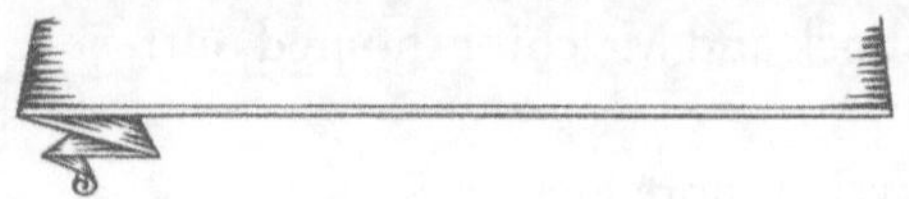

Hilda was sleeping restlessly with vivid dreams. She had been feeling nauseous since her meeting with Melchior.

Another dream began. Hilda saw herself and Melanie raising their child. Hilda felt how her blood pressure increased, felt a desire for blood, and then she lifted her child and sank her sharp fangs into the innocent child. In the dream, the child uttered a shattering cry of pain before passing away. Blood was dripping down Hilda's mouth, and her purple eyes shone with an eerie, terrifying glow.

Hilda woke up, and she vomited blood. Had Melchior poisoned her? She wouldn't let this affront go unpunished. She looked up, and she saw her private doctor, dr Herbert Braun. He scanned the blood on the floor with a DNA scanner and then he spoke.

- The blood is not yours, which is a good sign.

- The toxicology report shows nothing. You are sick from drinking over a litre of human blood. I have given you medication to excrete the iron from your body.

- You should be fine in a couple of days.

Hilda:

- But what about my dreams? The dreams of eating my future child alive?

Herbert:

- I am not a psychiatrist, but I'd say you have some post-traumatic stress. I will leave that out of your report. I am your friend, and I don't want your enemies to use your mental health status against you.

- I'd recommend a lot of resting for now. Your cousin can do your work until you feel better.

Hilda:

- But who can protect me, when the one I fear the most, is myself?

Herbert:

- Fearing yourself after those dreams is a normal reaction. That means that you are sane and not a monster like Melchior.

Hilda:

- Thanks, doctor. I need to speak to my cousin. Please help me get to the meeting room.

Herbert accompanied Hilda to the meeting room where Michael was waiting. After Herbert had left, Michael Muller spoke
Michael:

- Oh my god, Hilda! You don't look well at all. What happened to you?

Hilda:

- Dr Braun believes that I suffer from iron poisoning and post-traumatic stress.

Michael:

- Yes, Melanie told me what happened. What a monster Melchior is!

Hilda:

- Yes, and the worst part is that we caused that form of evil to happen.

Michael:

- No, we did not. Joachim, Benjamin and Bjorn committed countless atrocities towards the Martian population. But greed drove them, which is a natural human emotion.

- What Melchior is doing is not even human. Drinking blood, eating humans alive while staring into their eyes. It not a human form of evil.

Hilda:

- So, what are you implying? That Rangda controls Melchior?

Michael:

- Yes, that is the only reasonable explanation.

Hilda:

- Okay, but why would he want to enter the portal with his army? It would be easier to instruct the Xenos to attack via the portals, while Melchior's army attack from the sky.

Michael:

- I don't know. Maybe they are after something else? The botched expedition to the Divine Dimension came across another alien species, didn't they?

Hilda:

- Yes, the Zetans. A small group of them killed a large part of Emma Schindler's expeditionary force before the Xenos swept in and killed everyone.

Michael:

- So, can we assume that the Zetans and the Xenos are enemies?

Hilda:

- Yes.

Michael:

- Then Melchior, who Rangda possesses, is leading the Martian army to the Divine Dimension to fight the Zetans?

Hilda:

- That is a likely scenario.

Michael:

- Okay. Then we should let Melchior and his army travel to the Divine Dimension. Once they are away from earth, we send a small force to contact the Zetans and try to form an alliance.

Hilda:

- What if the Zetans butcher this group as they did the last?

Michael:

- That won't happen. I would send someone skilled in diplomacy and avoiding conflict.

Hilda:

- And who would that be?

Michael:

- You are talking to him.

Hilda:

- You? But you have shunned all responsibility and power in the past.

Michael:

- I prioritised time with my family over scheming and greed. I could live a life in wealth and affluence without committing evil deeds. I stayed friends with everyone to avoid stress and fear of people scheming against me. That my friend is diplomacy in its purest form.

- Now I am 60 years old, my children are all grown up, and it's time to step up.

Hilda:

- You are right. I never thought about it that way.

- So, let's do it your way. Let's give Melchior the supplies he wants and give him free passage to the portals. But how do we sell it to the other factions?

Michael:

- We should hide our suspicions about Melchior's allegiance from the other factions. Besides, you don't think it's a coincidence that he threatens our capital, do you?

- The first Xeno invasion destroyed House Rashid. House Cheng, White and Bolivar have all suffered from the Xeno invasions in China and Central America. And now our capital is under severe threat. That is not a coincidence, Melchior knows what he is doing.

Hilda Muller:

- Alright then. I will speak to Markus White and make him summon an emergency meeting in America. Let's give Melchior what he wants and get him out of here as soon as possible.

Having agreed with Michael, Hilda hurried to her office to contact House White and set up the emergency meeting.

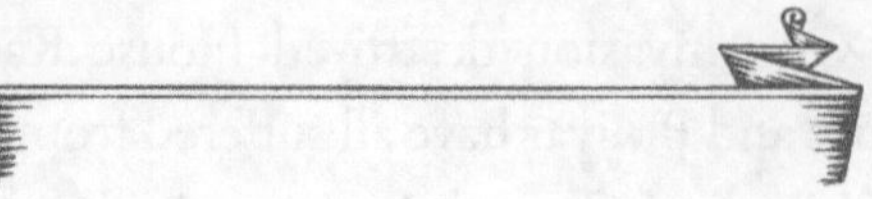

Chapter 239: Melchior Receives Instructions and Enters the Portals.

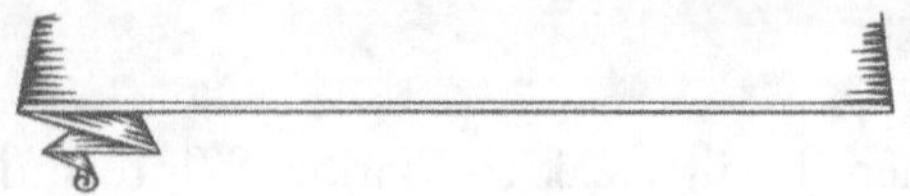

A few weeks later, Melchior overlooked his vast army, numbering almost a million men, which was gathered close to the portal in Rashidium. The spineless cowards in the Terran Council had bent over backwards to fulfil his demands. They had delivered enough food and supplies to last for a long campaign on the other side. Clearing the minefields near the portal had been tricky, but it was all done, and his army was ready to move.

Melchior got an overwhelming feeling that he might have forgotten something important. He needed to communicate with Rangda before leading his army into the portals. He summoned one of his captains:

Melchior:

- Captain Rodovic. I need to eat, and my cravings are for a young one.

Captain Rodovic:

- There is an orphanage not far away. We have stayed clear of it to avoid confrontation with the Terrans.

Melchior:

- Good. Go there and bring the children to me. Leave the employees unharmed. I want to avoid conflict with the Terrans for now, but my inner circle and I need to eat.

A while later, Captain Rodovic and his men came back, with a truck full of orphans. Melchior approached them:

- Did you acquire the children without incidents?

Captain Rodovic:

- Yes. We bribed the warden and his staff. 1000 Terran Credits in gold coins per child.

Melchior scoffed back:

- 1000 Terran Credits for a street urchin? Those Terrans are greedy!

Captain Rodovic:

- Yes. But we bought their silence. The employees will cover up what happened until we have entered the portals and left Earth. Besides, what use has gold on the other side? We are not greedy like the filthy Terrans.

Melchior:

- Correct. I'll pick that child for myself. I command you to distribute the other children among the men.

After consuming the youngest child, Melchior was licking the blood off his lips and started communicating with Rangda.
Melchior:

- We are ready to enter the portals, Empress Rangda. I had an overwhelming feeling that I had missed something, which is why I contacted you.

Rangda:

- Good. Trust your feelings. You need to make sure that the portals close behind you. I suspect that the Terrans only want your troops away from their cities. They plan to launch a counterattack, striking us in the back, as soon as they feel safe.

Melchior:

- Why would the Terrans attack us in the Divine Dimension?

Rangda:

- They are no fools. They must have figured out our connection. Thus, they know that you will attack them at some point.

Melchior:

- Yes, so let's attack them now. Commit your Xenos to a full-scale invasion!

Rangda lashed out with a psionic blast and knocked Melchior to the ground. She screeched at him:

- You fool. If I commit all the Xenos to an invasion of Earth, the Zetans will attack my flank.

- Follow my plan, it will work. I have foreseen it, and I have something you lack: Premonitions and foresight.

Melchior spewed up the blood he had ingested, and he spoke with a weak voice:

- Yes, Empress Rangda. I am sorry for my foolishness.
- But how do we reopen the portals if we close them?

Rangda:

- I know how to power up the portals from our end.

- Hurry up and set the portals to close after your men have walked through them. I will transmit the instructions to you telepathically.

After saying this, Rangda transmitted the instructions to Melchior. He would reverse the steps that Keila took when she opened the portals. The portals would close one day after the reversal process. This would leave Melchior with enough time to lead his troops through the portal.

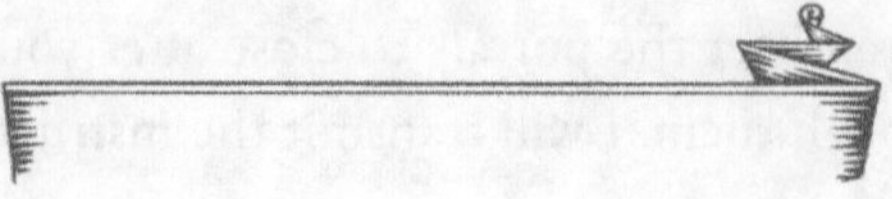

Chapter 240: Michael Reports to Hilda.

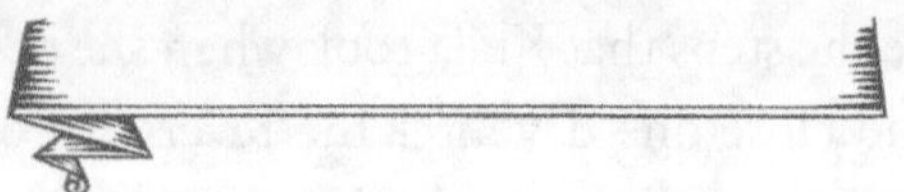

Hilda Muller was sitting at her desk when Michael Muller rushed into her office. Michael's appearance shocked Hilda as she had sent him on a diplomatic mission to the Zetans.

Hilda

- Michael? What's happening? Why are you here? Weren't you meant to form an alliance with the Zetans?

Michael:

- I was. We kept our distance, studying the portals from afar. We intended to move through portals the day the Martian Dominion moved through. We planned to use our cloaking devices, to move past the Martians unnoticed.

Hilda:

- I know the plan. What happened, Michael?

Michael:

- When we woke up, the portal had disappeared.

Hilda:

- Disappeared? We have tried to close those damn portals for years. How did this happen?

Michael:

- Well. You know those rooms with switches in the Central American, Pacific, Chinese and Egyptian pyramids?

Hilda:

- Yes, we had our best scientists working on it for years without any success.

Michael:

- I suspect that Melchior got the sequence to close the portals from Rangda.

Hilda:

- This proves that Melchior didn't go there to fight Rangda but to join her?

Michael:

- Scheisse! What do we do now?

Hilda:

- There isn't much we can do. We cannot send our troops to help the Zetans through the closed portals, and we can't figure out how to open the portals. All that's left is praying.

Michael:

- Praying? I didn't know you spent your time on superstitious nonsense?!

Hilda:

- I didn't use to. But after everything I have experienced, I don't know what to believe.

Hilda broke down and started crying. It confused Michael to see her this way as she usually kept calm. He decided to ask her:

- What's happening? Why are you crying?

Hilda:

- This is all my fault!

Michael:

- No, it's not. You did what you had to do. Our capital and millions of lives were at risk. You had to give in to Melchior's demands.

Hilda:

- I should have acted a long time ago.

- 18 months ago, Metatron, the leader of Eden, visited me with his daughter Sabina.

Michael:

- Why didn't we both take part in this crucial diplomatic meeting?

Hilda:

- Because I didn't expect the meeting to be important. Eden is a marginal fringe world. I am surprised that I even accepted their meeting request.

Michael:

- So, what happened during the meeting?

Hilda:

- Well, I had expected Metatron to ask for protection from the Terran Council, but he wasn't interested in joining us.

- Instead, Metatron was rude. He urged me to send the army to Divine Dimension and fight Rangda. I told him off and warned him about making demands.

Michael:

- Well, in retrospect, Metatron was right. But I wouldn't have listened to him either.

Hilda:

- What happened next have kept me awake for many nights. Sabina's eyes changed from green to a glowing blue shade. Her enchanting gaze glowed with bright light, and she spoke like an adult. She urged me to fight the Xenos.

- I freaked out and asked the AI to scan her for bionic implants, but she had none.

- Sabina claimed that The True Maker was speaking through her and that she was Keila Eisenstein's daughter.

- I freaked out and started screaming at her since she was our enemy's daughter. After this, Sabina reverted to a typical toddler.

- I expelled them and threatened to have them executed if they ever came back to Earth.

Michael:

- I see. Do you have the security footage of their visit?

Hilda:

- Yes, I do. AI, show Michael the security footage from my meeting with Jack Silver on the fifth of September 2876.

Michael studied the security footage, he sat silent for a long time until he spoke:

- Well, I understand why the outcome of this meeting has tormented you. But you shouldn't chastise yourself for what you did.

- All that you knew was that Sabina was the daughter of our mortal enemy and that something possessed her. For all you knew, Rangda could have controlled her.

Hilda:

- Yes. But after meeting Melchior, I realised that a kindred spirit influenced Sabina.

- I failed to do the right thing. I have doomed us all.

- How can I live with myself?

Michael:

- You better work to set things right. Killing yourself or giving up on life is not the right to do.

Hilda:

- But I don't know what to do?

Michael:

- Neither do I. But if The True Maker chose to speak to you, there must have been a reason, so find a way to set things right!

Hilda:

- You are right, Michael. I will set this right or die trying.
- Now, please pray with me.

Thus, for the first time in 600 years, The House Muller leadership prayed to a higher being. They prayed to the True Maker.

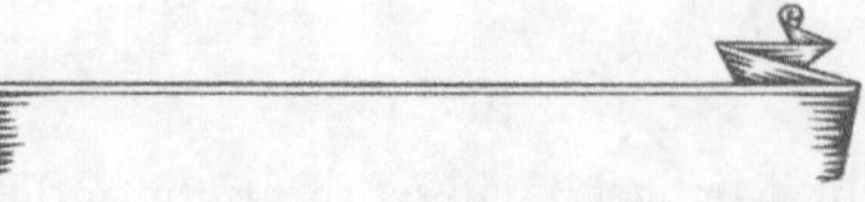

Chapter 241: Sabina Convinces Metatron to Counteract Melchior's Evil

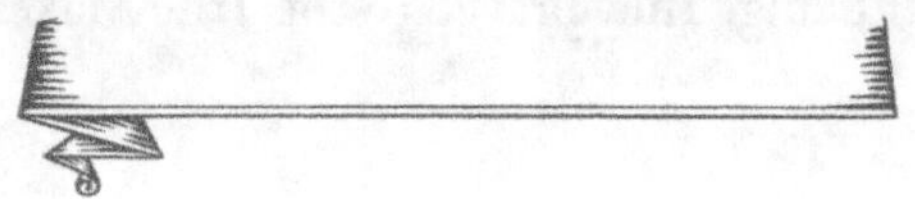

Metatron was watching Sabina play with her dolls when she burst into tears. He tried to comfort her when he noticed something majestic. Her eyes had once again transformed to shining crystal blue colour, albeit this time, her tears dimmed the light. Metatron hugged her and spoke:

- Sabina darling, what is wrong?

Sabina:

- That mean old man, Melchior. He and his bad men entered the portal to meet Rangda. This worries mummy and her friend, The True Maker.

Metatron:

- How come you speak like a child?

Sabina gave him a dumbfounded look and spoke:

- Daddy, I am a child. I am only four years old.

Metatron:

- Oh, I thought that The True Maker possessed you, as your cute little eyes have turned crystal blue.

Sabina:

- Papa, what does possess mean?

Metatron:

- That someone else is in your head, my sweet baby.

Sabina:

- Don't be silly, daddy. No-one else can fit in my head. I am so tiny.

- Anyways, while the mean bully Melchior makes people sad, I want to make people happy.

Metatron:

- That's good. How do you want to make people happy?

Sabina:

- By teaching what the True Maker taught me to other children. I can show them how to make people healthy and happy, papa!

Metatron:

- Okay. We can bring some children here tomorrow, and you can teach them.

Sabina:

- No!
- I want to live on Eden with the children that live there.

Metatron:

- But I am the leader of Eden. I must stay here.

Sabina:

 - No, you don't have to, papa. The leader must live with the
 people. When the leader starts living away from the people,
 that is when the bad things begin to happen.

Metatron considered what Sabina was saying, and there was a lot of
wisdom in it. But how would he rule from the surface? Metatron realised
that he shouldn't govern, he should lead by example.
Metatron:

 - You're right, darling. Tomorrow we'll build a new house in
 the village and move to Eden as a family.

Sabina:

 - Good. I can't wait to make all these new friends. Thank you,
 daddy. I love you.

Metatron:

 - I love you too, sweetheart.
 - Time to sleep. We will have a busy day tomorrow.

Having tucked Sabina in, Metatron had a realisation. That he and
most religious people had been wrong all along. They had worshipped
the false gods. A proper god would never have lived above the humans,
commanding them and forcing their obedience. A decent god, should
live among them and guide them in their everyday lives. This was how religious worship had worked among the earliest humans, and this was the
correct way of interacting with deities.

As soon as humankind had put their deities on pedestals above them,
they also started to act this way among themselves. This caused humanity's leaders to lead with commands and fear. Sabina had shown that a
deity could be on the same level as their fellow humans. It was a change

to the original human condition, and Metatron couldn't wait to see how things would turn out!

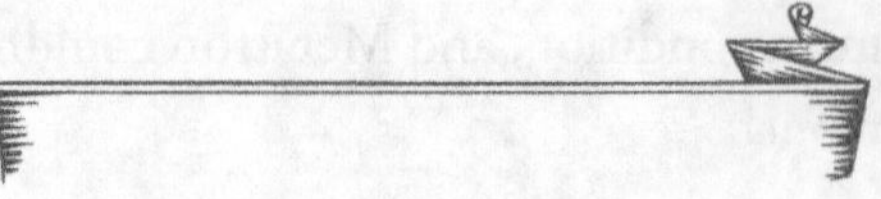

Chapter 242: A Secret Meeting with Rangda.

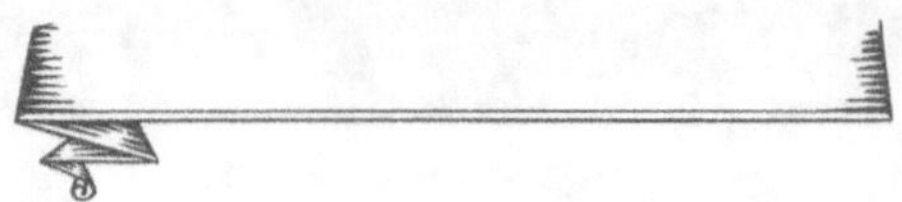

A few weeks later, Melchior was meeting up with Rangda in the Divine Dimension. Melchior didn't understand the need for secrecy, but he decided to follow suit and did as Rangda directed. They met in a building next to an unpowered portal. The portal led to a planet that got destroyed in the multi-millennial war.

Rangda spoke:

- Hehehe!! Behold, this is the portal to Proxima Zetani. A beautiful planet immolated in a matter of seconds by our mighty Xenos.

Melchior:

- Interesting, but what relevance does it have to the mission?

Rangda:

- Don't bother!

- You might be wondering why we are meeting in secret when we are leading the two most massive armies around here?

Melchior:

- Yes. I had pictured our first meeting to be a lot grander.

Rangda:

- Yes, marvellous isn't it. Humanity and the Xenos united, fighting against their former oppressors, the Zetans.

- But marvel and beauty don't win wars. Treachery does.

Melchior:

- I don't understand. When we spoke via telepathy, you said that there were only a few thousand Zetans left?

Rangda:

- Numbers mean nothing. A large group of well-armed Terrans got into conflict with a small group of Zetans a few years back. At the end of their battle, most of the Terrans were dead, killed by the Zetans.

- Their ill-fated scuffle helped us as we could move in and wipe out the tired Zetans and absorb their souls. We kept a few of the Terrans alive as prisoners for information about Earth.

- They taught me about the Terran mindset, and that is why I told you to close the portals. The Terrans would have come after us, once their cities were out of harm's way.

Melchior:

- Yes, covering your rear is crucial in warfare. But how do we get back to Earth?

Rangda:

- I can use my primordial Zeto Crystals to power up the portal. But this won't be relevant for many years. We got lots of work ahead of us.

- First, we must fool the Zetans that your army has come from Mars to help them. You need to infiltrate their ranks and become their 'friend'.

Melchior:

- And how would we do that?

Rangda:

- We stage a fight. We make sure that some of your Martians fight some of my Xenos in a battle. The battle needs to be visible from the Zetans fortress, Ultima Zetani.

Melchior:

- But wouldn't this waste our troops for nothing?

Rangda:

- No, it's the only way to convince the Zetans that you have come to help them. Flushing the Zetans out from their fortress Ultima Zetani is almost impossible. They have a defensive psionic barrier preventing us from even approaching it.

- While sacrificing thousands of troops is costly to us, it will convince the Zetans to trust you.

Melchior:

- You are certainly an evil genius. But what do I do once they trust me?

Rangda:

- Well, first of all, you'll need to hide your real face. Our plan won't work if the Zetans detects your Xeno mutations. Use the Zetan External DNA modifier to give yourself a pleasing human appearance.

- You need to convince the Zetans to come out with their army to aid you in the decisive battle against the Xenos. Do whatever you have to do to convince them. Worship them, promise them Mars and the eternal worship of humanity, even let them take command of your army. It doesn't matter.

- The Zetans will lead your army to a final pitched battle against the Xenos. They have waited a decade for this opportunity since my escape from captivity.

- This is when you betray them. Stab the Zetans in the back, lay down a barrage upon them and corner them while my Xenos storm in and wipe them out. They'll have nowhere to run.

Melchior:

- Excellent plan.

Rangda:

- I know.

- I can see myself in you, Melchior. But don't ever consider crossing me, or you'll regret ever being born.

Melchior:

- I wouldn't expect anything less from you, Empress Rangda!

Rangda:

- Good. Choose a dispensable part of your army to face my troops in battle outside Ultima Zetani in five days.

Melchior:

- Yes, Rangda. May it be a glorious battle!

After saying this, Melchior entered his stealth-hovercraft and returned to his army camp.

Chapter 243: An Honourable Mission.

Melchior approached General George Smith. He would send him on the suicide mission, that Melchior had schemed with Rangda. George Smith and his army, the 13th Reconnaissance Division were the perfect candidates for the task. They were volunteers from the Martian Humanist Alliance, and they upheld the values of the Martian Revolution.

George's values Bravery, compassion and equality, were values that definitely mismatched with Melchior's values. Furthermore, Melchior hadn't infused George's men with any Xeno DNA, and they were still 100 % human. Melchior approached George:

- General Smith. I have an important mission for you.

- I will send your division on a diplomatic mission to the Zetan stronghold of Ultima Zetani. I want you to approach the Zetans about an alliance against our Xeno enemies.

George:

- You have been very secretive these last few years Emperor Dorevitch.

- Why are we here? What purpose does our trip to this strange place have when our enemies are the Terran Council on Earth?

Melchior:

- I am sorry for keeping you in the dark, George. As you know, there are many spies and enemies of the revolution, so I had to keep my inner circle small.

- I plan to ally with the Zetans. Together with the Zetans, we'll find a way to kill the leader of the Xenos, Rangda. Without their leader, the Xenos are mindless beasts. We can take control of them and send them through the portals to Earth to decimate our enemies before taking what is ours.

- I have infused myself with Xeno DNA as the Xenos will only follow other Xenos or Xeno hybrids. Rangda, the current Xeno leader, is, in fact, a Xeno-Zetan hybrid.

George:

- But why won't the Xenos lead themselves?

Melchior:

- They are hive-minded creatures. They share their consciousness with their leader. When they lead themselves, they are primitive beasts leading primitive beasts. The blind leading the blind.

George:

- I see. But wouldn't unleashing the full extent of the Xeno hordes upon Earth cause the death of millions of innocents?

Melchior:

- Yes, and that is our plan. The Terran Council tried to wipe us out twice during the Revolutionary War. It's time for them to taste their own bitter medicine.

George:

- Yes. Sometimes acting evil against evil people is the only option.
- But why am I bringing a whole division on a diplomatic mission?

Melchior:

- To show the Zetans your prominence and importance. Come with a few men, and they'll think you are nobody. Arrive there with 10,000 soldiers, and they'll help you fight the Xenos!

George:

- You are correct, Emperor Dorevitch. I'll get my men ready, and I'll travel there as soon as possible.

After George Smith had left, Melchior pondered what he had told his general. It had been a lie meant to deceive George and send him into a trap, but it was also a real possibility. Melchior didn't care for Rangda, or her mindless hordes of Xenos. If he could throw them into the chopper with the help from the Zetans, that was also a golden opportunity. All that mattered was his own might and power, and Melchior didn't know what the Zetans had to offer yet. Such exciting times ahead of him but for now he had to wait and see. Melchior opened a can of animal blood, and he sipped it while smiling to himself.

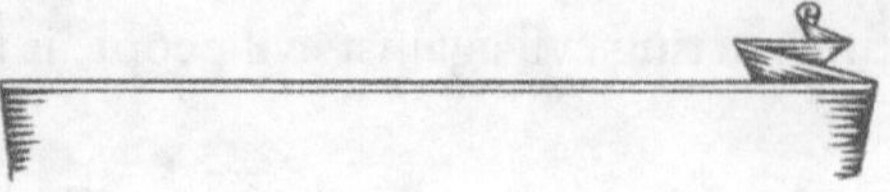

Chapter 244: The Xenos butcher George's army within the Zetans' view.

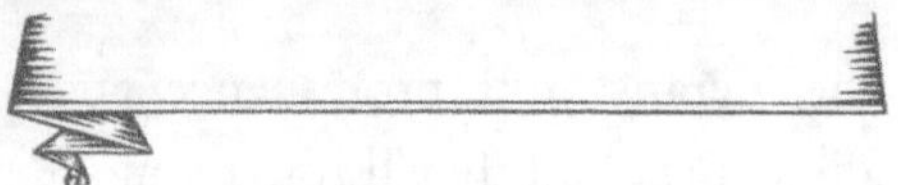

Odin and Shiva were playing a game of telekinetic chess when Balder approached them with an important message. They woke up from their meditative state, and Odin spoke:

- What is it, Balder?
- I have told you to not disturb me unless it's important.

Balder:

- I'm sorry, Odin. A Martian General is waiting outside our gate, seeking an audience. He must be important as he oversees a large army and is seeking help.

Odin:

- The last time we had contact with anyone outside of our realm, it led to the death of my son and your brother, Thor. What planetary council is he from?

Balder:

- He is from the Martian Dominion, dear father.

Odin:

- Mars. These Martian humans have travelled a long way.
- Hmmm... something is not right. Tell the general to go away.

Shiva interrupted the conversation and spoke:

- No, Odin. We need any help we can get. The Martian humans have brought supplies, fuel, and battle spaceships. Resources that we can commandeer and use against the Xenos.

Odin:

- I don't trust them. I can sense thousands of Xenos hiding nearby. As soon as we lower the psionic shields, the beasts will attack us.

Balder:

- But father, this might be our best chance in years to turn the tide in this war.

Odin:

- Silence! I am your father, and my decision stands. Now tell the Martian humans to leave.

Balder went down and told the Martians to leave. After a while, Odin saw how the Martian army was moving away from the Ultima Zetani fortress.

Odin kept studying the Martians as they left, and he saw how a Xeno army ambushed the Martian army. A brutal battle ensued, and Odin felt guilty over sending their potential ally away.

Odin made a decision. He would not let the Xenos win this battle. He would show them some of his Zetan power and give them hell.

Odin shouted:

- Balder. Assemble my Valhalla warriors! We will save the Martian army and give the filthy Xenos what they deserve!

Balder:

- But father? What about the risk of them ambushing us if we lower down our psionic barriers?

Odin:

- There are not that many Xenos around to worry about. The Xenos are killing the Martian army, which means we must help the Martians.

Balder:

- Are you admitting to being wrong before?

Odin:

- A wise man must be able to change his opinion, in the light of a better outcome.

- Now hurry up and gather our troops so we can help the Martians.

The Zetans lowered the psionic forcefield and opened the gates. Odin and Balder assembled their Valhalla warriors, and they hurried to the battlefield!

Chapter 245: A Late Arrival

An hour later, Odin and his Valhalla warriors entered the battlefield to aid the Martian army. As it turned out, they came too late. The only thing for them to do, was to battle the Xenos that were busy eating the fallen. The Zetans took the Xenos by surprise and defeated them without any problems.

Odin studied the equipment of the fallen human soldiers. He found it strange that most of the soldiers carried small calibre guns, unsuitable for fighting the Xenos. Small calibre guns couldn't pierce the Xenos thick skin, deep enough to kill the beasts. Why would the Martian military send such an army with unsuitable weaponry to fight the Xenos? The Terrans had repelled the Xeno invasion, so they should know what weapons would work against the Xenos. Odin approached Balder to discuss his findings.

Odin:

- Something is not right here. Look at these unsuitable weapons that the Martian soldiers were using.

Balder:

- Yes, these Martians were not equipped to fight the Xenos. Batons, Tasers and sub-machine guns. All ineffective against the Xenos. It looks like they were going to combat Terran civilians.

Odin:

- I am thinking about the same thing. Weren't the filthy Terrans that killed Thor much better equipped than this?

Balder:

- Yes, but those were from House Muller Special Forces. Look at this emblem: The Martian Dominion.

Odin:

- That's how it seems. Look, their general is lying over there. He looks wounded, but he is still alive. Let's go and save him.

Odin walked over to the wounded General George Smith. A chopped-off Xeno claw pinned the General the ground. Odin approached George and spoke:

- So, you are the foolish General who led your troops into an ambush?

George groaned back:

- Help me. The pain is insufferable.

Odin:

- Coward! The pain shall serve as a reminder of your stupidity.

- Unfortunately, I need to talk to you, and you won't talk much if you're dead. So, I'll give you a new chance at life!

Having said this, Odin pulled out the Xeno claw from George Smith's body. Then he released some Zetan healing powder into the wound, and the pain was gone.
Odin:

- I have helped you with your pain. Now speak and be honest; otherwise, I'll kill you myself! Understood?

George nodded, and Odin continued talking:

- Tell me who you are, and why you brought your army to my fortress?

George:

- I am George Smith. I am a general of the Martian Dominion and I am in charge of the 13th Reconnaissance division. At least I was until this happened.

- I came to negotiate an alliance on behalf of Melchior Dorevitch, The Emperor of the Martian Dominion. He wants to kill the Xenos and put an end to Rangda.

Odin:

- And why would Melchior want to do this?

George:

- I don't know. You better talk to him yourself. I just follow orders. I went to Earth believing that we would fight the Terran Council. Melchior equipped us for fighting urban warfare, not for fighting man-eating aliens.

Odin:

- I see. Go back to Melchior and tell him to bring his army, I'll discuss an alliance with him when he arrives. The Zetans have been fighting the Xenos for millennia, and we help those who are willing to fight the Xenos with us.

- I'll keep the supplies and equipment of your fallen soldiers. I have more use for it than you do.

George:

- Understood. I'll gather the survivors and head back to our camp. Thank you for saving our lives.

After saying this, George gathered his injured soldiers and his decimated division took off. Odin studied the Zetans scavenging the battlefield when Balder approached him:

- What do you reckon, father? There is something fishy going on here?

Odin:

- Yes. But we must take our chances and ally with the Martians. We need them to beat the Xenos. We cannot win the war without them. We have lost too many to the Xenos, and only a few of us remain.

Balder:

- Understood, father.

After the conversation, Odin went back to the fortress to meditate. What a dilemma he was in. Either he would ally with the underequipped Martian expeditionary force, or he would be stuck in this fortress forever.

Chapter 246: An Alliance Between Melchior and Odin.

Melchior studied himself in the hologram generator. He noticed that he looked handsome, much more appealing than his real Xeno/human appearance. This was because the Zetan DNA modifier had changed his external appearance. Changing his appearance to become more human-like was imperative as the Zetans would never trust him if he looked like a Xeno. The change had one drawback though, he felt starving, and he was thirsting for blood and raw meat. Keeping his urges in check was challenging. It was as difficult as enduring the pain that he had suffered when he altered his genome to become a Martian-Xeno hybrid. But doing so, was Melchior's only option.

Melchior had ordered his inner circle to stay away. He could not change everyone's appearances, and besides he wanted to minimise the risk that the Zetans exposed him.

Melchior studied Odin, who approached him to negotiate. He was an impressive sight, looking like a high technology version of a Norse God. Odin spoke as he approached Melchior:

> - You must be Melchior; George told me that you needed our
> help with battling the Xenos.

Melchior felt irritated, and he desired to kill the pompous-looking Zetan. But then Melchior remembered what Rangda had told him, that the easiest way to coax a Zetan was to stroke his ego.

Melchior

- Yes, we came to save humanity from the fearsome Xenos. Someone with your skills and experience would be an excellent ally.

Odin:

- Good. Since the Zetans created humanity, I will take command of your army. I don't want any more debacles with improper equipment and soldiers running into ambushes.

Melchior was furious with Odin's arrogance and disdain. Apparently, all the Zetans still lived under the idea that they were superior to humans and deserved to be their gods. The notion was wrong. The only thing that the Zetans had done was to alter the human genome roughly 70,000 years ago. They had imbued early Homo Sapiens with alien intelligence to enable a heightened state of mind. After that, the rest had happened by itself. The Zetans had neglected the existence of humanity for almost 65,000 years, until they had decided to become our deities. The Zetans only motive to re-emerge on Earth, was because they needed soldiers for their catastrophic war against the Xenos. Fighting to calm himself down, Melchior spoke with a suppressed growling voice:

- Hmmm.... yes. Letting the Zetans be in control is the best option.
- What is your command, Master Odin?

Odin:

- Our priority is to hunt down and kill Rangda. She is a Zetan/Xeno hybrid, and the only one with intelligence among the Xeno horde. With Rangda out of the way, disposing of the remaining Xenos is big game hunting.

- With the vehicles and fuel that you brought, Rangda cannot outrun us any longer. We will find her and destroy her.

Melchior:

- Excellent plan. And what will be my reward?

Odin:

- Your service to us will be much appreciated, and we will make sure that you get a good afterlife.

Melchior:

- That's very generous of you, Master Odin. I must take my leave and instruct the others to serve you.

Odin:

- Good. Be on your way, human. I'll summon you later.

Melchior was furious with Odin and the rest of the Zetans. That arrogant, self-righteous creature had treated him like dirt when he should have treated him as a saviour. If Odin couldn't see that the Zetans needed Melchior's army more than he needed them, he was blind, and he deserved Melchior's betrayal.

Melchior calmed down. In a way, what had happened was ideal. He would no longer need to worry about which side to follow, now that the choice was so obvious. Odin would regret his smug grin when Melchior stabbed him in the back and then ate him alive!

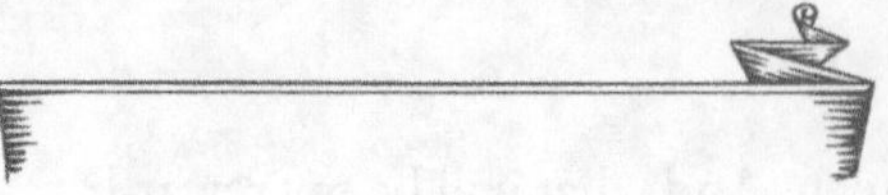

Chapter 247: A Mysterious Female Visitor.

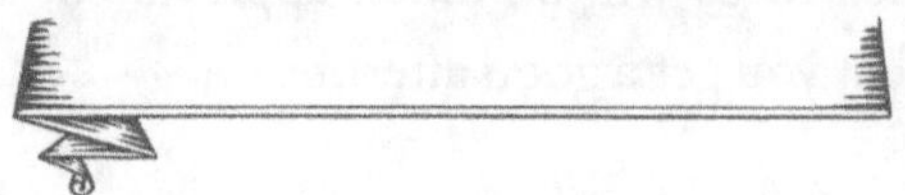

The following day, a stunningly beautiful woman arrived at the gates to Melchior's camp. Her beauty mesmerised the guards, so they forgot to consider how she got there in the first place. Captain Rodovic approached her:

- Hello. Can I be of any assistance?

Beautiful woman:

- Yes, I am Helen Barnes. I have an appointment with Melchior. He is expecting me.

Captain Rodovic:

- Melchior hasn't told me about any visitors, are you sure?

Helen:

- Yes. Please take me to him, and he'll make sure that you get rewarded for your duty.

Captain Rodovic:

- Thank you, miss. I will take you to him at once!

At first, Melchior was annoyed when Captain Rodovic disturbed him. But he changed his mind when he saw how beautiful Helen was. Melchior

- Thank you, Captain, for sending this beautiful lady to me. I'll reward you for your duty.

- Leave me alone with this woman. We have some things to discuss.

Captain Rodovic left the room, and Melchior walked over to Helen and spoke:

- So, tell me, Helen. Who are you and who sent you?

Helen:

- You know who I am.

Melchior sniffed at Helen's body and then he closed his eyes. Melchior:

- Yes

- Whose DNA are you using? Your beauty is so mesmerising, so my captain forgot the absurdity of a stranger approaching this camp.

Helen:

- I am using the DNA of Helen of Troy. She was the most beautiful human female of all times. The Zetans created her as an experiment to see how far men would go, fighting over one woman.

Melchior:

- Pretty far, I suppose?

Helen:

- Yes. One of the biggest wars in antiquity was about her. You can read about it in the Iliad.

Melchior:

- I am not much of reader. But tell me; what do you think a man like me, would like to do with a woman like you?

Helen:

- Copulate?

Melchior:

- Good girl, you know us far too well.

Helen:

- Yes, and it will be an excellent diversion as well. Let's do it.

After that, Melchior and Helen proceeded to have very rough and very loud sex. During the act, Melchior made turned on the public announcement system, so that everyone would know that they were fucking.

Chapter 248: Odin and Balder Meet with Helen.

Odin was sitting in his command module, making battle plans when his son Balder came in. Odin spoke:

- Greetings, Balder. Have you heard anything from your siblings Frey and Freya yet?

Balder:

- Yes, they are coming back soon. They have travelled around in our space shuttle. They have been able to contact all the other Zetan factions. Ra, Athena, Vishnu, Buddha, and Tlaloc are all coming, and they are bringing their troops.

Odin:

- Tlaloc and the Aztec gods? I haven't heard from them in over a millennium. Are they still violent and blood-thirsty?

Balder:

- Yes, so it would seem.

Odin:

- Excellent, we can use their ferocity against the Xenos.

Balder:

- Yes, there is another thing. Someone has sent a Zetan spy, masked as Helen of Troy to seduce and spy on Melchior.

Odin:

- Yes, I felt an unidentified Zetan presence in the camp. I suppose she was successful? The Helen of Troy DNA sequence is irresistible to human males.

Balder:

- Indeed, she was. They were copulating within ten minutes.

Odin:

- Pfft. Not a very talented spy. She would gain a lot more withholding the sex, driving Melchior insane with desire first. No matter, find her and summon her to me. I'd like to speak to her myself.

Balder left the room, and a while later he returned, bringing Helen back to his father. Helen kneeled to Odin and spoke:

- You summoned me, Master Odin?

Odin:

- Yes. I know that you are a Zetan spy, sent to seduce and spy on Melchior. I need to know who you are working for.

Helen:

- Master Odin, I am loyal to my master, and I will not expose mine or his identity.

Odin:

- I could force the truth out of you.

Helen:

- Yes. But bear in mind that Melchior is head over heels in love with me. I doubt that he would appreciate that you torture his bride to be.

Helen showed Odin an exquisite engagement ring that she wore on her finger, and she dominated him with her cold gaze. Odin winced and broke. Realising that Helen was not susceptible to his threats, he tried a more diplomatic approach.

- Let's not get carried away. I will leave your secret with you. But may I ask that you share any information you get with us? We are in this together, after all.

Helen spoke back to Odin with an arrogant tone:

- I'll share whatever information that I find suitable to share with you, Master Odin. Now I must leave. I have a private bathing session planned with my fiancée Melchior.

Odin:

- Okay, Helen. Have it your way. But I'll be watching you.

Helen:

- And I will be watching you, Odin. Tread carefully!

Having said this, Helen left Odin's command module, with Odin feeling ambivalent. It was a good thing that he had a spy near Melchior, as he wasn't confident that Melchior was trustworthy. But who was she, and who did she serve? Restless and tired, Odin went to bed, but his worries kept him awake, bereaving him of any sleep that night.

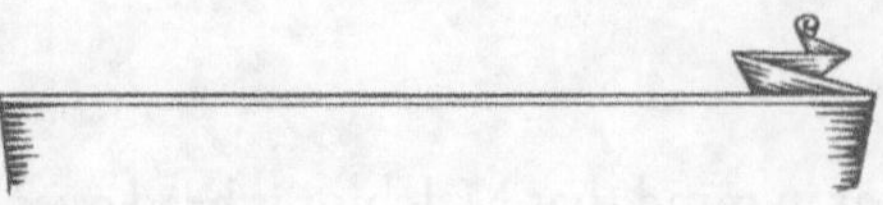

Chapter 249: Odin Sends Frey and Freya on a Mission to Earth.

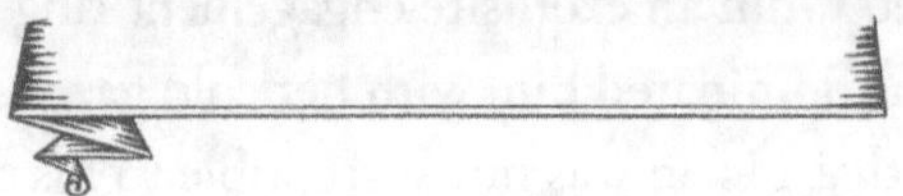

A few days later, Frey and Freya returned to Melchior's army base, and they went to Odin's command module to report. They bowed to their father as they entered, and Frey started talking:

- Great news, dear father. We have convinced all the Zetan factions to join our army for the coming final battle against the Xenos. All of the leadership and most of the remaining Zetan armies are coming, totalling over 5,000 Zetan elite warriors. They are being transported here by Martian transport shuttles as we speak.

Odin:

- Good job, my children. I knew that I could trust you.

- I have another mission for you. You are to make your way to Earth and seek an alliance with the Terran Council.

Frey:

- But isn't the Terran Council the enemy of the Martian Dominion?

Odin:

- Yes, but allying with both the major human factions is an insurance policy against either of them turning against us.

Freya:

- Understood, father. So, do you also have a bad feeling about this Melchior guy?

Odin:

- He is hiding something, but he is our only chance. Besides, the food and supplies he brought have helped us revitalise. Fighting a war, while starving, was never a good option.

Frey:

- You are right, father. But how do we open the portals back to Earth?

Odin:

- Here is a replicated Zeto Crystal. I made it from the supplies that the humans brought. It contains enough power to open the portal for a few minutes.

- To return here, create a new crystal once you are on earth.

Freya:

- Thank you, father. we will be on our way!

Having said that, Frey and Freya kissed Odin on the cheek and said farewell, never to see him again.

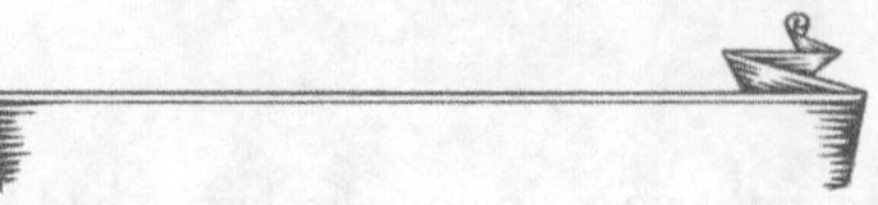

Chapter 250: A Vast Xeno Army en route to Attack the Zetans.

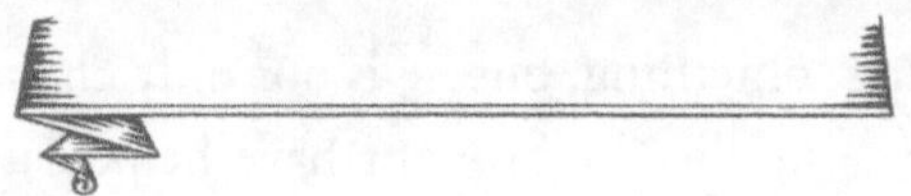

Odin was sitting on a throne and studied the other Zetan leaders that had assembled. It was the first general assembly of the Zetan leadership in seven years. After Rangda's escape from her eternal prison and the emergence of the Xeno hordes, the Zetans had crammed into fortresses. In their forts, the Zetans combined psionic capabilities could create impenetrable force fields. But packing into strongholds, starving and keeping their mental guards up was not a good way to live. So, the Zetans felt relieved when Melchior's army had arrived, and provided the Zetans with food and drinks.

Odin raised his beer tankard and spoke:

- How delightful is this, after 2,000 years of thirsting we can finally assemble again to enjoy food and drinks. Enjoy the Terran wine and beer and rejoice that our luck has finally turned.

A loud cheer broke out, and Ra spoke:

- Cheers that we have all gathered today. Odin, what is our battle plan?

Odin:

- We must unite and kill Rangda. Once she is dead, The Xenos are mindless beasts and wiping them out will be an easy task.

- Any news about the Xeno movements, dear Vishnu?

Vishnu:

- Our spy drones show that the Xenos are gathering their forces. They are preparing for a final battle, and there seems to be over a million of them in total.

- The strange part is that Rangda is missing. Deciphering Xeno conversations, it seems like two Xeno leaders, Gumboll and Dingil have killed her and usurped power.

Odin:

- How is that possible?? I thought the Xenos were loyal to her, and that Rangda had them under her complete domination.

- Regardless, I need to see her body to verify her death. I am not falling for any more of her ploys.

The appearance of a Zetan guard interrupted the meeting:

- Masters, I have urgent news!

- The entire Xeno army, totalling over a million Xenos, is rushing towards us. They are 300 kilometres away running at full speed. We expect them to reach us in three to four hours.

Odin:

- Excellent. This is the day we have been waiting for. The Xenos will run straight into our trap. Once we have dealt with the Xenos, we can finally return to Earth. We'll become humanity's gods yet again! Prepare the soldiers. This will be a glorious day!

After Odin had spoken, everyone left the room in a hurry. There were 5,000 Zetans and almost a million human soldiers so it would take some time to get everyone ready.

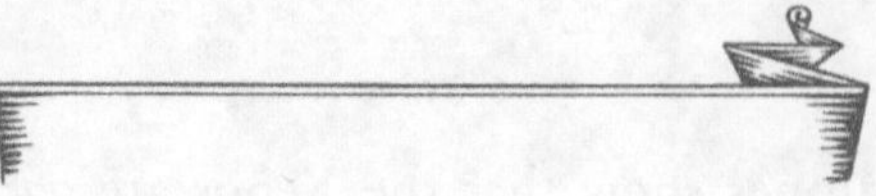

Chapter 251: Helen and Melchior Plan Their Move.

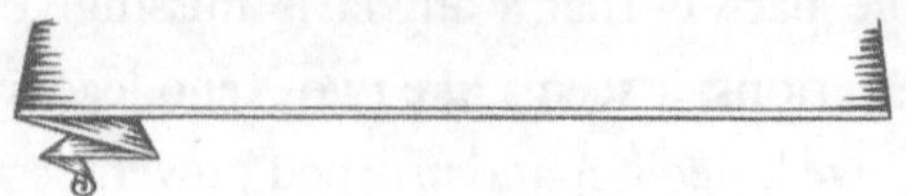

Helen and Melchior were overlooking the Martian Dominion military camp in the Divine Dimension. It would take another one and half hours for the Xenos to arrive at Ultima Zetani, and the battle preparations were in full swing. There was a ring of ruckus, and soldiers encircled the entire base. Most of the Zetan elite soldiers had gathered in front of the main gate where Odin expected the Xenos to hit the hardest. But there were also Zetans present in the dispersed individual army groups guarding the fort. The individual warriors wore thick armour, and lightweight nanotechnology fibreglass shields and they were armed with plasma swords or plasma spears.

Elevated behind the melee formations, Melchior had placed Martian troops with autocannons, laser rifles, and grenade launchers. In the centre of the base, there were large numbers of howitzers firing at the Xenos from afar. Hovering over the base, there were hundreds of Martian aircrafts prepared to wreak havoc on the Xenos from above.

Helen:

- Impressive fortifications. The Xenos must be foolish to attack, such as an impenetrable fortress. Unless of course, they have trump on hand.

Melchior:

- Yes, they would indeed. I am curious about the time of their attack. I thought they would wait a bit longer?

Helen:

- I thought so too, but then I found out that Odin sent his children to forge a secret alliance with the Terran Council. Such an association would make things... unpredictable.

Melchior:

- Damn him! I knew that I couldn't trust him.

Helen:

- I am sure he feels the same way about you.

Melchior:

- I am sure he does.

- The Xenos are within range for our artillery. How do I make our artillery miss, without making it look suspicious?

Helen:

- You don't. Fire at the Xenos. Make it look normal. The Xenos are sturdier than Martian humans, so while direct hits will kill some of them, the shrapnel and the shockwaves won't impede the others.

Melchior:

- As you wish, my beautiful queen!

Helen:

- As I wish, my mighty king. Gather your inner circle. We will make our real move in an hour.

Hearing this, Melchior smiled a sinister smile and rushed off to find his inner circle, preparing for the last step of his plan.

Chapter 252: Melchior's Betrayal: The Slaughter of the Zetans

Minutes before the battle, Melchior, Helen and Melchior's inner circle entered the Zetan command centre. Odin, Ra, Vishnu, Buddha and Tlaloc were overlooking the battlefield. Odin saw them arrive and spoke:

- Melchior, I must ask you and your bodyguards to leave.

- Helen, I have been expecting you. Have you come to tell us what you found out from spying on Melchior?

Helen:

- That's not why I am here!

After saying this, Helen swiftly threw five plasma throwing knives at the Zetans, burning and injuring them. Melchior's bodyguards rushed in and struck the Zetans with their plasma swords, incapacitating them.
Odin yelled out:

- What are you doing, Melchior?? You doomed yourself and your army, the other Zetans will slaughter you for this outrage!

Melchior:

- I don't think so. You see, I picked the perfect opportunity to take you out.

Melchior lifted a command phone and spoke, his voice echoed out over the base:

- Soldiers of the Martian Dominion. The Zetans are our enemy, and the Xenos are our ally. Attack the Zetans militants with full force. Fire at will!

Once Melchior had broadcast this order, all the Martians fired at the Zetan army from the rear. Meanwhile, the Xenos attacked the Zetans from the front. It was a massacre, and the Zetans couldn't do anything to save themselves. Odin witnessed how the Xenos tore the Zetan army into shreds. Tears ran down Odin's cheeks and he realised that the end of the Zetans was near.

Odin got up and spoke:

- Melchior, why are you doing this?

- You will never be able to control the Xenos. You'll bring doom to humankind.

Melchior:

- I don't think so. I have saved mankind from Zetan enslavement and servitude! I am sure that my queen, Rangda, will be able to dominate the Milky Way, now that Zetans are dead. Or what do you say, Rangda?

Helen deactivated her Zetan external DNA modifier, and Rangda appeared laughing maniacally:

- Ahaha-ha ha-haha!! Odin, I cannot believe that you were as stupid as Brahma! You could sense that I was a Zetan, but despite that, you couldn't realise who I was.

- Zetan leaders, you all thought I was a Zetan spy sent by another Zetan faction. Your mistrust for each other stopped you from reaching the logical conclusion. This was exactly as I expected! Ahaha-haha!!

- You pride yourself as being superior beings compared to all the other life forms of the universe. Yet, you have the same vices and desires as all living beings in the galaxy. Without the Zeto crystals uniting you, there is nothing that sets you apart from the humans or the Xenos!

- The corrupted Zeto crystals that I possess will bind every planet and every dimension under my rule. Under my rule, the innate desire to fight, kill, rape, and procreate is not shunned upon, but encouraged. You are even allowed to eat one another!

Some of the Zetans tried to get up, but they were severely wounded, so Melchior's bodyguards could hold them down. Rangda fetched her corrupted Zeto Crystals. Using the power of the dark crystals, she shattered the souls of her Zetan victims, blowing up their heads in the process. When Rangda had finished, she laughed and spoke:

- Have a feed, men. Zetan flesh is the most delicious flesh in the universe. You have deserved it. Hee-hee-hee!!

Hearing this, Melchior and his bodyguards savaged the headless bodies of Zetans. They had hidden their hunger for weeks, and they were starving!

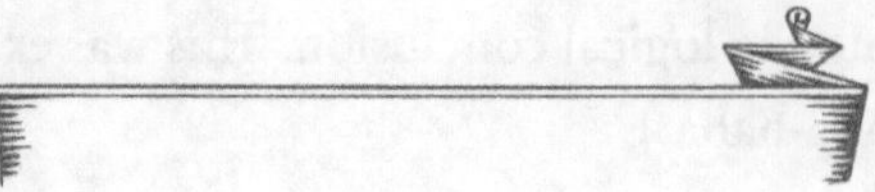

Chapter 253: Sabina Breaks Down.

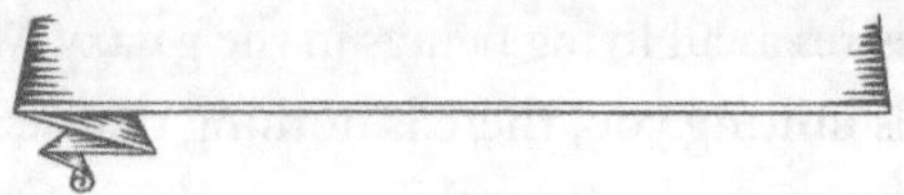

On the 15th of March 2878, Sabina was playing with her younger siblings, Jasmine and Jordan, when terrible premonitions struck her.

Sabina saw all the carnage that had happened in the Divine Dimension, and she felt Keila's agony and pain. The Zetans had fallen to Melchior's and Rangda's evil schemes. With the Zetans gone, there was no-one left that could stand against the combined malevolent powers of Melchior and Rangda.

Sabina sensed Keila's immeasurable guilt and suffering. Keila had acted with good intentions, wanting justice, and freedom for her people on Mars. But Keila had had listened to the wrong guidance, and she had released Rangda upon the world. Keila had promoted Melchior when the Martians were fighting against Terrans, and that decision had proven to be a fatal mistake.

Keila suffered from spending years in captivity with no end in sight. Alone with her thoughts, she lived in constant guilt over what she had caused to her beloved planet and people.

Sabina saw Keila's prison cell. She saw Rangda, feasting on the flesh of a dead Zetan. Rangda turned around, and she met Sabina's gaze. Rangda hissed and laughed menacingly:

- We finally meet, Sabina. I have been waiting for your psionic signal to be strong enough for me to pick it up. You must be growing stronger, day by day.

Sabina:

- What are you doing to my mother? You have used her to reach your goals. Let her move on and die in peace.

Rangda:

- So, you are asking me to kill your own mother? The prophesized girl, the chosen one, is advocating matricide? Hmmm.... interesting.

Sabina:

- I would ask you to let her go, but your evil nature wouldn't even consider that option.

Rangda:

- Oh, but you're wrong, little girl. The moment I release your mother from the stasis she is going to hurt herself or someone else. I am extending her life.

Sabina:

- But keeping her alive is crueller than letting her move on.

Rangda smirked and replied:

- Yes, but it is well-deserved cruelty. Her action caused the death of millions, and more will follow. Mars is dying from the ecological damage caused by the wars and Melchior's environmental destruction. Melchior's genetic experiments have created a new breed, Xeno-Martians. We will overrun Earth when the time is right. I will attack Eden last.

- Because of Keila's actions, humanity as you know it will cease to exist. That, Sabina, is a good reason for your mother to suffer.

Sabina:

- But you manipulated her. You caused all her actions. You are the evil one.

Rangda:

- Oh, am I evil? I am spreading my species over the galaxy. It's called survival of the fittest. A new dawn is upon us all. Gone is the Zetans harmful rules and ideas. Behold the future of my Xeno dominion!

Rangda went over to a dead Zetan and pulled a bit of flesh from its body with her sharp teeth. She stared into the eyes of Sabina and hissed:

- Delicious, but not as delicious as you will be, little girl. I understand why I upset Melchior when I forced him to forfeit you as his prey. No one can resist your delicate skin and tasty flesh.

The paralysed Keila had seen enough. She sent off a psionic blast that knocked herself and Sabina unconscious. This severed Sabina's connection with Rangda, as Rangda could only connect with Sabina using Keila as a host.

Shortly afterwards, Melissa rushed into the room where Sabina lay unconscious. As Sabina woke up, she was inconsolable, and no matter what Melissa tried to do, she kept screaming and crying. Sabina's younger siblings Jasmine and Jordan approached her, and together they soothed Sabina's mind. They healed Sabina with the rejuvenating magic that The True Maker had instructed Sabina to teach her younger siblings.

Sabina:

- Thank you, Jasmine and Jordan, for saving my mind from the darkness.

Jasmine:

\- No, we are thanking you. You cannot save everyone on your own, Sabina. We need to work together to protect what matters, the future of the Milky Way Galaxy!

After saying this, they all sunk down in deep trancelike meditation, hoping to find the strength to resist evil. Melissa felt confused, and she left the room, but she understood that her children were in good hands.

Melissa realised that she had unique children. Melissa thanked the True Maker and she was proud over her children, knowing that they would achieve great things.

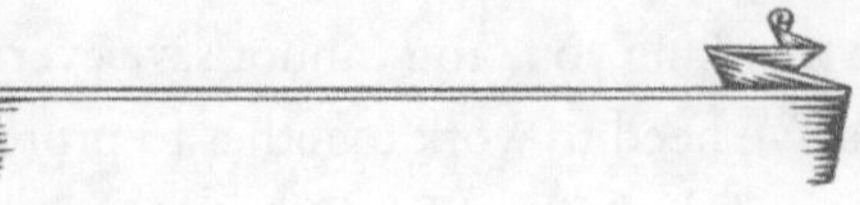

Chapter 254: Dov Dorevitch Releases a Deadly Virus on Mars.

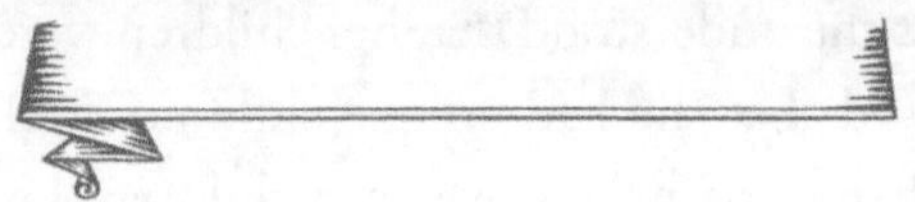

Dov Dorevitch, the brother of Melchior Dorevitch, was sitting in his command room on Mars. Various maps and figures were beeping on the displays in the room, and it wasn't encouraging news. With Dov in charge, Melchior's empire was falling apart.

Dov's enemies on Mars had figured out how to remove the Zetan mind-control microchips from the Martian population. Dov's problem was, that while he could connect to his subjects' minds and kill anyone who dissented against him, the workload was too much. Like any human, Dov needed to sleep and rest, and that's when the rebels had the opportunity to strike.

Dov studied the map of Mars and sighed. Six months ago, his brother had controlled all of Mars, and now they had lost most of their territories. Dov's only relief was that the rebels also fought amongst themselves, which stopped them from uniting against him. Yet, his territories were dwindling by the day, and it was likely that the Terran Council would come after him because of what his brother did. Dov knew that House Muller would seek revenge for Melchior's threat to destroy their capital.

There was a knock on the door, and Dov's Chief Scientist Frank Van Stein entered the room. Dov gave him a sullen look and spoke:

- Dr Van Stein, what are you doing here? You are not invited to the upcoming military strategy meeting.

Frank smirked at Dov and spoke:

- Don't worry about the military briefing. As a matter of fact, I have come to tell you to cancel it.

Dov:

- Who are you to give me orders? And besides, you're asking me to cancel a military briefing during an emergency. Are you insane?

Frank:

- We both know that you cannot win this battle with your military might. That ship has sailed. Attend that meeting, and you'll find that half of those commanders will not attend. Some of them have betrayed us and have joined our enemies.

Dov:

- Did you come here to say anything useful, or to spread salt in my wounds?

Frank:

- I am sure you'll find that I have a few aces up my sleeve.

- Melchior predicted that you might fuck up and he told me to work on something that would ensure our control.

Having said this, Frank Van Stein pulled up a vial with a bluish liquid from the pocket of his lab coat. Frank smiled and spoke:

- This vial contains the future for mankind!

Dov was going to say something when a nearby explosion shook the building and knocked him to the ground. Frank stood still in the room, and seemed unaffected.

- It seems like Colonel Slavonic has turned against you, Dov. I'd say you are losing control over the Martian Dominion.

Dov:

- You knew of Colonel Slavonic's betrayal, and yet you did nothing. I should have you executed for treason.

Frank:

- You could. But executing me would also doom yourself. You'll be overrun within days, and then you'll have to make a choice. Stay here and die, or run and face Melchior's wrath when he returns. Which one do you prefer?

Dov:

- I suppose that you are offering me a third option, in exchange for your life?

Frank:

- I am not afraid of dying, but yes, I am offering a third choice to give us a glorious future.

- This vial contains an airborne virus capable of altering the human DNA, and inserting specific Xeno DNA sequences into our veins.

Dov:

- So, are you going to release a virus that transforms our population into a bunch of man-eating beasts? Tell me, how is the Zombie Apocalypse going to benefit us?

Frank scoffed at Dov and looked at him with disdain, before addressing him with a derogatory tone:

- Bah. The Zombie Apocalypse. What a load of rubbish. You should know that zombies contradict all elementary biology. Don't bother me with that rubbish.

- SIT DOWN, and I will explain how this is going to work.

Another explosion rattled the building and the speechless and dumbfounded Dov got seated. Frank spoke again:

- Good! Melchior told me that you would come to your senses.

- The synthetic air-borne virus that I intend to spread is going to revolutionise mankind by altering all our citizens to Xeno-Martians. The Xeno-Martian hybrids are ferocious and powerful like the Xenos. But they are not mindless and have thoughts of their own. After all, your brother had the same mutations, and he still had his wits around him.

Dov:

- Well, he changed though. I never understood the desire for blood and eating his captives alive.

Frank:

- Such is the Xeno way. But don't worry; fearsome as they may be, they are also loyal to their leader, Melchior, and by proxy towards you.

Dov:

- And what about everyone that has incompatible DNA for Xeno-Martan hybridisation?

Frank:

- Oh, I am sure you are referring to Melchior's former chancellor, Peter Belovic?

Dov:

- Yes, among other examples.

Frank:

- Well, true genetic modification always comes at a cost. If we release this vial, a lot of people with incompatible DNA will die painful deaths. But the ones that live on will have superior DNA. Such is the way of nature, and we are living in fascinating times. We are about to get front row seats to the next step in human evolution!

A door got smashed in and a group of armed men stormed into the room. Their commander approached Dov and spoke:

- Dov Dorevitch. We are here to detain you on orders from Colonel Slavonic.

Before Dov had time to respond, Frank pulled up his pistol and rapidly shot the six intruders in their heads before they had the time to react. Frank remarked:

- I guess time is running out Dov. We better hurry to the wind generator so we can release the air-borne virus onto our civilisation.

Dov nodded and said nothing. Together the two men rushed towards the room with the wind generator. Once they were outside Dov opened the door with his DNA signature. Dov took the virus out of the safe, and he put it in the wind generator. Dov tapped on a computer console and fired the deadly virus unto Colonel Slavonic's base.

A short while later, the artillery bombardment ended.

Chapter 255: The Seven Zeto Crystals.

Melchior was lying in bed exhausted from a session of rough sex with Rangda, posing as Helen of Troy. Rangda had left him to recuperate his wounds after the coitus, as she was not a big fan of cuddles. Melchior could feel the sharp pain from her claws, and he embraced it, as pain was the highest form of pleasure. To his surprise, Rangda came back to the room, carrying two goblets. Rangda hissed at Melchior:

- Get up! We do not have time for laziness. There is a lot for us to do now that the filthy Zetans are finally defeated.

Melchior:

- What do you mean? We have defeated the Zetans; we have all the time in the world?

Hearing this, Rangda ran up to Melchior and punched him in the face, knocking him to the ground. She then hissed at him:

- That was not foreplay, so stay where you are and listen up!

Melchior didn't want to argue with the fearsome Rangda, so he did as Rangda instructed and stayed on the floor. Rangda spoke again:

- We have defeated the Zetans, but that is not the end of my ambitions. I want to rule this galaxy as its God-Queen. To achieve that, I need to find and absorb the powers of the seven Zeto Crystals, spread throughout the galaxy.

Melchior:

- Let me guess. You want me to take my army on a stupid quest looking for useless crystals, instead of invading Earth?

Rangda:

- Useless crystals? You arrogant twat, take this!

Rangda lifted her staff that had a corrupted Zeto Crystal attached to it. Rangda aimed her staff towards Melchior, who started floating and experiencing migraines. Melchior sensed how the essence of his soul was about to shatter. Before this happened, Rangda released Melchior from the corrupted Zeto crystal's power, and he dropped to the ground with a loud thump. Melchior struggled to speak after the experience, and stuttered out:

- I'm sorry for offending you, Empress Rangda.

Rangda:

- I punished you for your insolence while showing you the power of the dark Zeto Crystals. When we gather all of them, nothing can stand in our way, and your friends on Earth will feel our wrath!

Melchior coughed up some blood, and Rangda brought forth a different gem. It was an untainted Zeto Crystal, and it shone with pristine blue colour. Rangda put the crystal on Melchior's head, and his wounds healed. After the treatment with the Zeto Crystal, Melchior felt inner peace. Rangda spoke:

- You are in luck, Melchior, as I haven't corrupted this Zeto Crystal yet.
- Now get up and listen!

Melchior did as Rangda instructed, and she continued her tirade.

- As I mentioned before there are seven primordial Zeto Crystals in the galaxy. I have three of them. The other four crystals belong to The Elves on Elvonia, The Dwarves on Goldonia, The Orcs on Grashdunt, and The Humans on Earth.

Melchior:

- What are you talking about? Orcs? Elves? Those are fantasy creatures that don't exist!

Rangda:

- Oh, is that so? Don't think you know everything, Melchior. The Zetans altered hundreds of species in their image during the Golden Age of their civilisation. This was when the Zetan imbued the Xenos with their intelligence. Being altered in the Zetans image, they have continued to live on their home planets, like humanity progressed on Earth.

Melchior:

- I see, but if one of the primordial Zeto Crystals are on Earth, that gives us a reason to invade!

Rangda:

- Silence, you fool. Stop obsessing about Earth. Who do you rather fight? The Terran Council's army with guns, fighter jets, laser cannons and artillery, or a bunch of elves with arrows and swords?

Melchior:

- So, you want to pick off the easier targets first?

Rangda:

- Of course. Invade some easy targets, and we have enough resources to breed a vast, unstoppable army.

- Now we must move. It will still take months to reach the portal to Elvonia, and I don't want to run out of resources.

Melchior:

- Yes, Empress Rangda. I will alert the army at once!

Rangda:

- Good. I hope you didn't tire yourself too much arguing before. The future god-queen is up for some more copulation!

Melchior:

- It will be my pleasure.

Chapter 256: Hilda Muller Meets with Frey and Freya.

Hilda Muller were discussing the terrifying news reports from Mars with Michael Muller.

Michael:

- Are you sure that this report is accurate, Hilda? Why would Dov release a virus that turns the Martians into frenzied beasts attacking and killing each other?

Hilda:

- I am certain. I saw people infused with Xeno DNA when I met with Melchior. It's a horrible sight that resembled what we now see from Mars.

Michael:

- That's awful. We must do something to help the Martian citizens.

Hilda:

- I am afraid we cannot approach Mars for a relief effort at this stage. We do not know how the virus works, and the worst-case scenario is that we spread it to Earth if we try to help them. We must blockade the planet and quarantine the Martian population on the surface.

Michael:

- Hold on a minute. We had a delegation on Melchior's command ship. Neither you nor anyone else in the group got infected while you were there.

Hilda:

- I wasn't infected, but my mind got infested. I still dream nightmares about meeting with Melchior. I can't get over how he forced me to drink human blood.

There was a call on the hologram generator from Hilda's mistress, Melanie Weber.

Hilda:

- Melanie, I am in a critical discussion with my cousin, you'll have to wait.

Melanie:

- This trump whatever you're discussing.
- I am accompanied by two Zetan messengers, Frey and Freya.

Hilda:

- You mean like the ancient Norse Gods?

Melanie:

- Yes. They are requesting to meet you.

Hilda:

- Very well. I cannot deny semi-divine aliens a meeting, can I? Bring them in, and bring enough guards to deter them from doing anything stupid!

A short time later, Melanie and three dozen guards escorted Frey and Freya into Hilda's office. Freya smiled towards Hilda and spoke:

- You can send the guards away. If we'd wanted to kill you, there would be nothing your guards could do to stop us. Your girlfriend is beautiful by the way.

Hilda:

- And why would I trust you?

Frey:

- Because Mistress Muller, we have already lost everything, humanity is our only hope.

- My father, Odin, trusted the deceitful Melchior. He believed that Melchior was our ally. Together we would cleanse the Divine Dimension of the Xenos and start a new golden age of civilisation across the galaxy.

- But Melchior betrayed us. Melchior has partnered up with Rangda, and they aim to enslave all the sentient beings in the galaxy, including humankind.

Hilda:

- Hmm. Interesting prospect. We thought of sending an expeditionary force to the Divine Dimension and ally with the Zetans against Melchior and Rangda. But the portals closed in front of us.

Freya:

- Mistress Muller. We can open the portals for you if you promise to send your army to fight Rangda and Melchior.

Hilda:

- But if Rangda has defeated the Zetans, it is too late to send the army after Rangda and Melchior.

- You are welcome to stay as my guests. As a matter of fact; I have someone that I would like you to meet.

Freya:

- Who?

Hilda:

- Ramun, a former Xeno General and my prisoner.

Frey:

- What? How do did you manage to capture a Xeno General?

Hilda:

- As you'll find out, I am a lot more resourceful than you think. But come, let's introduce you to each other.

Having said this, Hilda got up, and she led her Zetan guests to Ramun's enclosure.

Chapter 257: An Encounter Between Three Different Species.

Hilda, Frey and Freya stood outside the secret compound where Hilda kept Ramun. Hilda had kept the capture of a Xeno General a secret from the general population. Knowledge was power, and she wanted to keep power within House Muller. Hilda looked at her Zetan guests, and spoke:

> - You better stay outside, I do not want to agitate this prisoner.
> Take this universal translator device and use it once the coast
> is clear. Our Xeno prisoner is not very well-spoken.

Frey and Freya nodded at Hilda, and she entered the enclosure. Inside, it was hot as a sauna, and the vegetation consisted of scorched grass. Ramun liked it this way, as it reminded him of his home planet Xenora. Hilda found Ramun sleeping next to the carcass of a cow. She raised her plasma sword with her right hand and whipped him, with the whip that she held in her left hand. Ramun growled as he woke up and he turned towards Hilda:

> - Grrrrrr... Mistress Hilda. It has been a long time. How can I
> serve you?

Hilda:

> - I am bringing some guests that I would like you to meet. And
> as your mistress, I command you stay civil!

Ramun:

- Ramun is happy to follow your commands. Mistress Hilda has been very good to Ramun, providing Ramun with delicious prey animals!

Hilda spoke into her headset, and a minute later, Melanie Weber escorted Frey and Freya into the enclosure. Seeing the Zetans, Ramun started drooling and clenching his teeth preparing to attack. Hilda whipped him out of it:

- Ramun, you promised to be civil.

Ramun growled back:

- Yes, mistress, I did. Ggrrrrhmmm.....

Ramun got down on the ground in a submissive pose.
Freya:

- How did you tame the beast?

Hilda:

- I defeated him in single combat. The Xenos respect someone who can beat them in single combat. Then I used Terran Stem cell technology to regrow Ramun's legs and arms.

Frey:

- Interesting approach. But why would you go through this hassle to make a primitive beast your prisoner?

Hilda:

- That's the reason for the Zetan downfall. Your arrogance. During millennia of interstellar warfare, you never considered capturing a prominent Xeno?

Frey:

- But we created them. We created all the sentient species in the galaxy. We imbued the Xenos with our Zetan intelligence, which caused our demise. We are the supreme species of the universe, blessed by the True Maker. What could we learn from lesser species?

Hilda:

- You could learn what drives them and how to defeat them.

Freya:

- So, what insights do you have?

Hilda:

- Well, the Xenos turn into a violent frenzy when they are hungry, and there are prey animals around.

- Use that to your advantage.

- I can tell that you guys have plenty of catching up to do.

- Ramun!

Ramun:

- Yes, Mistress Hilda.

Hilda:

- I am leaving these Zetans here with you. I want you to communicate and coexist. If you spill any blood between you, I will make sure that all of you will suffer.

After saying this, Hilda turned to Frey and Freya:

- So, Frey and Freya, I am allowing you to do what you should have done eons ago, getting to know the enemy.

Freya looked at Hilda in awe and stuttered:

- But the beast is going to kill us if you leave us here alone.

Hilda:

- No, he won't. If a mere human can tame him, I am sure that two intelligent beings from the Zetan "Supreme" race will be okay. Now I must take my leave. Good luck with your research!

Having said this, Hilda left Frey and Freya with Ramun, hoping for the Zetans to learn something about their eternal enemy.

Chapter 258: Preparing the Invasion of Elvonia

In December 2878, Melchior and Rangda had led their armies to the portals leading to the Elven homeworld of Elvonia. Rangda studied Melchior, with her desire for power glowing in her eyes. She spoke:

- This will be a historical day, Melchior. For the first time in thousands of years, humans and Xenos will set foot on the Elven homeworld of Elvonia.

Melchior:

- Understood. What do we expect to find there?

Rangda:

- Elvonia is a world filled with tree-hugging hippies. They care so much about their environment so they never became industrialised. Thus, I wouldn't expect them to be a significant military threat.

Melchior:

- So, we can conquer an undestroyed world where we can pillage and set up as much industry as possible before we move on with our mission?

Rangda:

- Yes. Let me deal with their leader myself. The Elves are close-ly attuned to their Zeto Crystal. Their leader, King Mellron, can use its power to unleash destructive White magic.

- No matter. I have waited for this moment for many years, and that fool won't stop me from taking what is rightfully mine.

Melchior:

- Good. I will lead our army to crush the Elves while you con-front their leader in single combat, and seize the crystal?

Rangda:

- Yes, that is my plan.

Melchior:

- Excellent. We will attack tomorrow; these tree-hugging Elves won't know what hit them, and they will be delicious to eat. Haha haha!

After this, both Melchior and Rangda fell into an extended period of diabolical laughter. They rejoiced, realising the suffering that they would cause to the unsuspecting Elves on Elvonia.

Chapter 259: The Invasion of Elvonia.

Of all the species that the Zetans altered in their image, the Elves were the ones that were the most alike the Zetans. Like the Zetans, the Elves led lengthy lives, had a slow reproductive cycle, and a powerful affinity to the Zeto Crystals. The Elves liked to live in harmony with their environment, which kept their planet Elvonia in a pristine ecological condition. There was one significant difference between the Zetans and the Elves. The Zetans had valued knowledge and science, while the Elves valued tradition and preservation. Thus, the Elves lived with primitive technology, despite being the second most intelligent species in the Galaxy.

The invasion day started like any other day on Elvonia. King Mellron led a prayer to the True Maker, in front of the primordial Zeto Crystal. The peaceful aura of the crystal spread blissfulness and balance to all living beings on Elvonia.

A bright light in the distance interrupted the ceremony. The light came from the long-deactivated portals, and this excited the elves. Had the mythological Zetans, the primordial creators of the Elves, finally returned? Mellron remembered the last time he saw the Zetan goddess Gaia. He had been a young boy, and now, thousands of years later, he was an old man.

King Mellron gathered his court, and they moved towards the forest glade where the portal had opened. If the Zetans had arrived, they deserved nothing less than a royal reception. As King Mellron approached the forest glade, he had a foreboding feeling that something was wrong. Worry surged through Mellron body.

The putrid smell of fire and burnt flesh filled his senses. As Mellron got closer, he could hear the tormented squeals of his brethren.

King Mellron reached the portal and, he realised the terrible truth. The Zetans hadn't returned. The new visitors were something else, something that focused on destruction, evil and demise.

Melchior's Xeno-Martian hybrid soldiers rushed to seize King Mellron. He raised his ornamental staff which contained with the primordial Zeto Crystal to purify their souls and bring them peace. As Rangda had corrupted the soldiers, their bodies couldn't handle the purification, and they dropped dead to the ground.

Mellron studied the fallen combatants and felt sorrow. He had aimed to pacify them to avoid confrontation and instead, he had killed hundreds of living beings. Such a terrible waste of life and Mellron didn't understand what he had done wrong.

Mellron felt a terrifying presence chilling into his bones, as Rangda appeared. She came out from the portal accompanied by a large group of her Xeno bodyguards. Rangda wielded a staff equipped with two corrupted Zeto Crystals. The crystals were so dark and eerie, so they absorbed all the light around them, turning the forest glade into a twilight zone.

Rangda studied Mellron and spoke:

- King Mellron. You have bereaved your people of the light of progress. It is time for a new beginning. Both for the Elves and for the rest of the galaxy.

King Mellron:

- Who are you? What are those dark abominations that extinguish the light around you?

Rangda:

- I am Empress Rangda, god-queen of the Xenos. I am destined to rule the whole Milky Way Galaxy. Yield now and I'll spare most of your people. I'll need them to reform Elvonia to its true potential.

King Mellron:

- True potential? Elvonia is a paradise. Every living being lives in harmony. Once the lifespan of an individual is over, they pass on peacefully, giving back their life force to the Zeto Crystal that granted it in the first place.

- What else could my people want from existence?

Rangda:

- They could want progress, ambition to become better than their fellow elves, greed to fill their vaults with precious metals.

King Mellron:

- That sounds terrible. Giving up on peace to pursue hollow goals that tear communities apart and destroy the natural environment!

Rangda:

- Whatever you say, King Mellron. I am not here to discuss philosophy. I am here to get your primordial Zeto Crystal. Resist me if you must but be wary of the consequences if you do.

King Mellron:

- I don't think you understand, Rangda. The elves and all life forms on Elvonia are dependent on the Zeto Crystal for our existence. If I give it away, I will doom us all.

- I am afraid I'll have to ask you to leave. Go back to wherever you came from and leave us alone. I do not wish any more bloodshed.

Rangda:

- And yet you chose to condemn your entire entourage to a painful death by refusing to cooperate.

- Xenos, Charge!

On Rangda's signal, hundreds of Xeno Warriors charged against King Mellron and his court. In the last second, Mellron conjured a spell that covered his group with a white forcefield. The forcefield repelled the Xenos and set them ablaze. The wailing of the burning Xenos filled the forest glade. A short while later, most of the Xenos were dead or dying, scattered around the grove. Rangda studied Mellron, smiled, and spoke:

- Feels good, doesn't it? The sight of your enemies dying in front of your eyes? The only sad part is wasting of the flesh. But I sense there is a lot to eat on this planet so we can afford to be wasteful!

- Their deaths won't be in vain. The Xenos will hail them as heroes!

King Mellron:

- And why is that?

Rangda:

- Because their deaths drained your Zeto Crystal, while my corrupted Zeto Crystals remain charged!

After saying this, Rangda aimed her staff with the corrupted Zeto Crystals towards Mellron's entourage. The crystals drained all the light, and the whole sky became black. Mellron's followers screamed in agony as their heads exploded with their headless corpses falling to the ground. Rangda smiled diabolically and spoke:

- Interesting. It seems that the Elves affinity with the Zeto Crystals makes it possible for me to charge my crystals using your life force. How delightful.

Mellron:

- What are you talking about, you evil monster! The True Maker's benevolence charges the Zeto Crystals.

Rangda:

- The True Maker might charge your useless crystal, but she does not charge my crystals.

- Farewell, Mellron. Die knowing that your death will serve a useful purpose; making me more powerful.

Mellron:

- Please don't. The Zeto Crystal is the source of all life on Elvonia. Steal the crystal, and you'll turn our beautiful paradise into a barren wasteland.

Rangda:

- That is precisely what I intend to do, Mellron. Goodbye!

Rangda turned the power of her corrupted Zeto Crystals towards King Mellron. The Elven-king tried to resist her influence, but he couldn't. He had drained his pure Zeto Crystal when he misused it to kill the attacking Xenos. Rangda used her powers to trap Mellron in a psionic force field that stopped him from moving. She proceeded to absorb and shatter Mellron's soul to charge her crystals. Rangda decided to torment Mellron before killing him, as a punishment for resisting her. Mellron's tormented screams echoed for hours before he finally slumped headless to the ground.

After Rangda had killed Mellron, Melchior approached her. Melchior:

- I take it your mission was successful.

Rangda:

- Yes, as I anticipated, forcing Mellron to kill our troops with his pure Zeto Crystal turned out to be his undoing. His crystal lost its power the moment he used it to take life instead of giving life.

Melchior:

- Good, how many casualties on our side?

Rangda:

- Less than a thousand, so inconsequential.

Melchior:

- Good. The local population have neither the strength nor the technology to stand against us. We can conquer the whole planet within a week.

Rangda:

- Don't bother. I know a quicker way!

Rangda picked up Mellron's staff and studied the Zeto Crystal. Its bright blue light had faded, and it looked like any regular gemstone. Rangda lit a bonfire, and she put the uncorrupted Zeto Crystal in the middle of the fire. Rangda took a knife and cut her arm, and made her blood drop down on the crystal in the blaze. She chanted curses and focused her mind on the Zeto crystal. After a while, the fire had extinguished and left in the ashes was, a corrupted Zeto Crystal. Rangda picked up the dark crystal and slotted it into her staff. As she did this the plants around her started to wither, and the decay spread at a tremendous pace.

Melchior:

- I guess we won't be able to sell Elvonia as a tourist destination anymore.

Rangda:

- The Elves should have surrendered their crystal and bowed to me. Now they will suffer.

- Order your men to gather as many resources as they can. We'll stay here for a while to regain our strength before we move on. The galaxy is vast, and we have plenty to do.

Melchior:

- Yes, Empress Rangda. I will do your bidding!

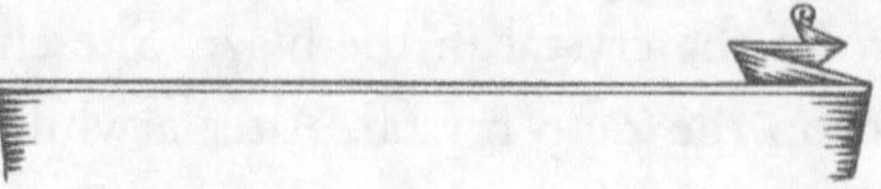

Chapter 260: The True Maker Convinces Sabina to Save Mars.

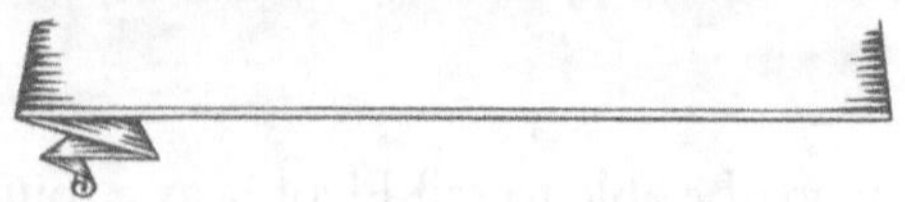

A year later, in December 2879, Sabina was meditating together with the other children of Eden in her light brigade. Under Sabina's supervision, many of the children had acquired unique healing powers. The True Maker had shown Sabina how to channel the energies of the universe, to create an aura where peace and harmony reigned. Under the influence of that aura, incredible feats of healing could occur.

Sabina got visions from Elvonia where she saw how Rangda tormented the Elves on the dying planet. Rangda had locked up the Elves in cages and drained their life force to power up her crystals.

Rangda's action terrified Sabina. But instead of letting this bring down her mood, she felt inspired by how Elvonia used to be. The Elvonia of the past had been a paradise, the planet had flourished, with everything in balance. Now that the Zeto Crystal was gone all life on Elvonia suffered. This was because all life forms of the planet had evolved to live attuned to the crystal. When the crystal disappeared, none of the life-forms could adapt to the circumstances.

Sabina heard the voice of The True Maker:

- Sabina, do you understand what happened on Elvonia?

Sabina:

- Yes, Rangda destroyed the planet.

The True Maker:

- Yes, but how could Rangda destroy a planet blessed by one of the seven primordial Zeto Crystals?

Sabina:

- With her army of monsters and evil men? The Elves of Elvonia were peace-loving creatures that hadn't trained for warfare. Thus, they stood no chance against Rangda.

The True Maker:

- Yes, on the surface, that is what it looks like. But that wasn't why Elvonia fell.

- Elvonia fell because their leader, King Mellron, gave in to his fears. Being a slave to his worries, Mellron used Elvonia's Zeto Crystal to slay the invaders. When Mellron misused the crystal, it lost its power, and he was powerless against Rangda's dark curses.

Sabina:

- But if he hadn't done anything, the Xenos would have killed him and his whole entourage?

The True Maker:

- No, they wouldn't have. The Xenos weren't always evil. They evolved on a planet with rough conditions and lifeforms. The Zeto Crystal did not govern life on Xenora. This didn't make them evil, but rugged and easy to influence. It was Rangda who turned them evil and made them a threat to the universe.

- If Mellron had tried to turn the attackers good instead of murdering them, things could have had another outcome.

Sabina:

- But Mellron tried to turn Melchior's soldiers good, and they died anyway?

The True Maker:

- Yes, the Xeno-Martian hybrid is such an abominable creation that the only thing that could keep them alive is the forces of darkness. Mellron did what he could to save them and bring them to light. But when Mellron decided to slaughter the Xenos with fire magic, he succumbed to the darkness. This drained the Zeto crystal's holy power.

Sabina:

- So, the lesson is to always try to do good, even in the face of adversity?

The True Maker:

- Yes, and to know what is right, you must first understand yourself. You have come a long way, my child. I have faith in your ability to stop Rangda and Melchior and restore peace and balance to the cosmos. But first, you must hone your skills, and to do so, you must save the Martians.

Sabina:

- But I am still a child?

The True Maker:

- Yes, but in a few years, you'll be ready. You'll know when the time has come.

Sabina:

- Okay. There is one thing that I don't understand.

- If you are the omnipotent and omniscient creator of the whole cosmos, why can't you stop Rangda?

The True Maker:

- I could stop her, but the consequences wouldn't be pleasant.

- You see, my celestial holy powers are on a Cosmological scale. Like you cannot kill a single bacterium in your body using your fist, I cannot kill an evil individual using my divine powers. My only way to kill Rangda would be to release a blast that would destroy the entire galaxy. I would do that if I had to, but I prefer not to.

- Instead, I try to use gifted individuals of light like you, to stop the forces of darkness.

Sabina:

- Thank you for telling me. This makes a lot of sense.

The True Maker:

- Yes. Now focus on your meditation and your spiritual abilities. Saving Mars is the first step to foil Rangda's evil plan.

After saying this, the True Maker disappeared from Sabina's mind. Sabina felt at peace and motivated to focus on her training.

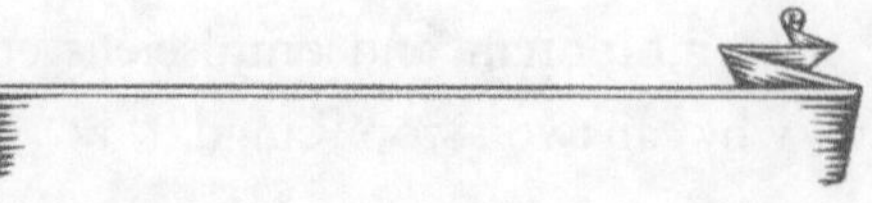

Chapter 261: Rangda and Melchior Prepares for Their Next Conquest

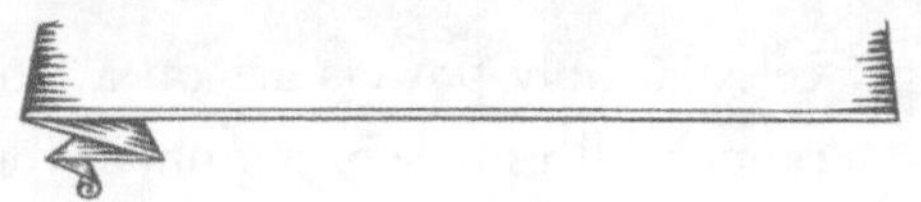

In January 2880, Melchior and Rangda were preparing for their next conquest. They planned to invade the Dwarven homeworld, Goldonia. Melchior studied his and Rangda's massive army. They had plundered Elvonia and turned it into a barren wasteland. While doing so, they had converted the planet's biomass into an army of millions of cloned Xeno-Martian hybrids. Elvonia was beyond saving, and it would soon turn into a Venusian wasteland. Global warming and volcanic activity were turning the planet into a hot and toxic hellscape.

To Melchior, the destruction of Elvonia was bitter-sweet. It had made him a lot more powerful than before, but it had been a waste. Melchior dreamt of conquering Earth, and now he had come across an even more beautiful planet, and he had destroyed it in less than a year. At some point, he would need to get rid of Rangda so he could rule his galactic empire, without destroying it. But he had still much to learn from Rangda, so he'd stay loyal for now.

Rangda entered the room, and she had brought an Elven prisoner. Melchior forgot about his rebellious plans to focus on a more critical issue, his hunger. Together they devoured the Elven prisoner and proceeded to copulate.

After their meal, Rangda spoke to Melchior:

- We need to move on. The planet is dying, and we cannot stay here any longer.

Melchior:

- I am annoyed by the wasted opportunity. Elvonia was such a beautiful planet when we first got here.

Rangda:

- Yes, but I doomed the planet when I corrupted and stole its Zeto Crystal. After that, speeding up the downfall of the planet and building our army was the right thing to do!

- No matter, we are evacuating Elvonia before it becomes uninhabitable and we need to focus on our next goal. To steal the Zeto Crystal belonging to the Dwarves on Goldonia.

Melchior:

- With our army this strong, I doubt they'll be any threat towards us?

Rangda:

- Don't underestimate them. While they are not as advanced as we are, their technology is not as obsolete as the Elves were. The Dwarves are stubborn, and they refuse to submit to overwhelming power. Conquering them would take years and cost more than it's worth.

Melchior:

- So, how do you suggest that we deal with these creatures to secure the Zeto Crystal?

Rangda:

- We make them an offer they cannot refuse. The Dwarves praise the Zeto Crystal for its beauty and uniqueness. But it has no influence on them or their planet. So, we make them a better offer.

Melchior:

- And what would that be?

Rangda:

- In the Goldonia star system, there is a colossal asteroid made of gold. We can offer to land this rock on Goldonia in exchange for their Zeto Crystal. Blinded by their greed, they will accept.

Melchior:

- But wouldn't this make the Dwarves wealthy and powerful?

Rangda:

- Quite the opposite. Gold is only valuable because of its scarcity. When it becomes abundant, it loses its value, and the Dwarven society collapses. Once we have weakened them, we can subject them to our will. But regardless, our main priority is the Zeto Crystal.

Melchior:

- You are an evil genius, Empress Rangda.

Rangda:

- I know! I am soon to be a goddess! Prepare the army to move. Goldonia is far away, so we better get going.

Melchior:

- Yes, Empress Rangda. I will do you your bidding!

Chapter 262: Hilda Muller Faces Motherhood and Prepares an Army.

Hilda Muller felt tired but happy. She had two daughters born within a matter of days. Freya had rewarded Hilda's hospitality by fulfilling her wish to have children with her partner Melanie Weber. Freya was a master in fertility technology, and she had enabled Hilda's eggs to fertilise Melanie's eggs. Hence, they were both the biological mother to each other's children. Both the children were daughters, as a boy was not a possible outcome from merging two eggs together.

Hilda let her servants care for her children. She was the leader of a vast empire and, she didn't have time to change diapers and other demeaning duties.

Hilda studied her drone factory. House Muller had cooperated with Frey and Freya to create an army of drones suitable for fighting the Xenos. Frey had preferred an army of human soldiers, but Hilda had refused. Times had changed, and humans were no longer cannon fodder for the Zetan armies!

Accompanied by Michael Muller, Hilda met Frey and Freya, in the military drone storage outside Hansstadt. Hilda spoke:

- 100,000 military drones adapted to fighting the Xenos. We
  have provided you with an army, Frey!

Frey:

- Yes, but I am a bit worried about how useful these robots will
  be on the battlefield. Human soldiers have always been more

innovative and creative than AI limited drones. Drones without AI limiters are unpredictable and difficult to control.

Michael:

- These robots will do very well on the battlefield. Our field-testing scenarios have proven this.

Frey:

- In those tests, you put the robots to fight untrained Xenos in a controlled environment. Killing those Xenos were equal to butchering civilians. Hardly a test of the robots' usefulness.

Hilda:

- That's enough. I have spent a large chunk of our fortune on these robots, and it is all we are going to provide. I am not going to send our citizens to fight aliens in a war that is no longer ours. There have been no Xeno sightings on Earth for over five years.

Freya:

- But I told you already, the Xenos will come back. They are licking their wounds and attacking weaker civilisations to regain their strength.

Hilda:

- Is that so? Then I want you to put these drones to good use, helping these other weaker civilisations to fight the Xenos.

- If you excuse me, I have some business to attend to. We will transport you and the drones to the portals tomorrow.

Frey:

- Thank you, Hilda and Michael. I hope that you are right, and that these drones are all that I need to stop Rangda. We need to save the remaining Zetans, as well as the rest of the galaxy from her tyranny.

Hilda:

- I am sure that we'll find out. Best of luck to the two of you.

Hilda left the facility. She wasn't going to do any work, but she needed an excuse for leaving. Hilda wondered whether she had done the right thing when she refused to seek the aid of the other faction leaders. Together they could have sent a sizeable force to the Divine Dimension to deal with the problem.

Hilda decided that she had made the right choice; as a matter of fact, she had been too generous. Hilda had spent a fortune providing two alien refugees with an army to fight their common enemy. What else could she do? Given their history as the deceivers on Earth, Hilda had been too generous to the Zetans.

Hilda drove her hovercraft to one of her nearby residences. It was ancient castle, where she enjoyed spending time with Melanie and her baby daughters. Screw the Zetans, time was too short to worry about intergalactic warfare when Hilda could spend time with the people that she loved. As Hilda met Melanie's smile when she got home, she forgot her troubles.

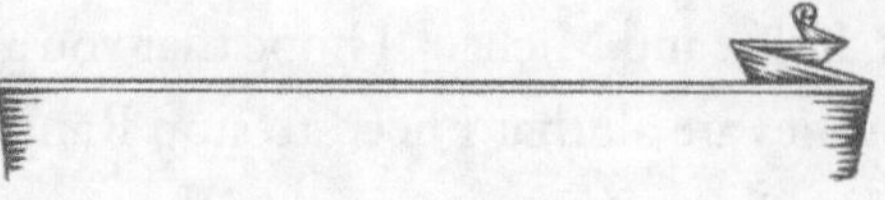

Chapter 263: The Deception of the Dwarves

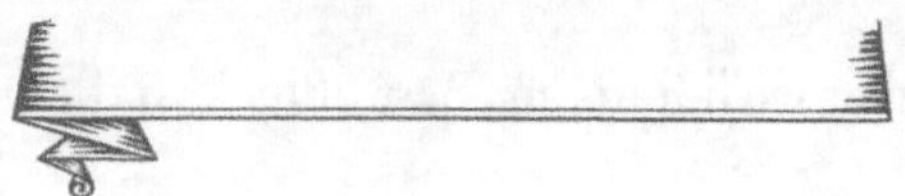

In July 2880, Rangda, Melchior, and George Smith arrived at the Dwarven homeworld of Goldonia. Rangda had advised Melchior that they were better off coming as a small group impersonating Zetan gods. While the outer layer DNA modifier couldn't change their heights, Rangda was certain that no-one would question that detail. The Zetans hadn't visited Goldonia for millennia so no-one would have seen the real Dwarven gods.

Rangda approached the palace guard and spoke:

- Greetings. I am the goddess Dumathoin, and this is Moradin and Beronnar.

- We are Zetan gods and have come to offer your master an offer he cannot refuse.

The sentry looked dumbfounded but walked off.
Melchior turned to Rangda and spoke:

- The sentry seemed clueless and not awestruck by seeing his deities. Are you sure everything is going according to plan?

Rangda:

- I must admit I had expected another reception, but we will have to improvise as we go along. Worst come to worst; we'll have to fight our way out. In that case, I will call in my Xeno horde, to keep the Dwarves busy.

The sentry came back, accompanied by one of his superiors. Chancellor Randall:

- Greetings strange visitors. I am Chancellor Randall. May I ask your names and why you wish to speak to the King?

Rangda:

- I told your guard already. I am the goddess Dumathoin, and with me are the gods Moradin and Beronnar.

Chancellor Randall:

- We are not falling for that trick. We haven't worshipped those dead deities for thousands of years. Drop the act and tell me who you are, or I won't allow you to speak to the King.

Rangda decided to drop the act and tell the truth. Since she couldn't deceive the dwarves with her appearance, appealing to their greed was better option. She deactivated her Zetan DNA modifier and showed her real appearance. The guards stared at her in awe and Rangda spoke again:

- I am empress Rangda of the Xenos. I am accompanied by Melchior Dorevitch Emperor of Mars and his General George Smith.

Rangda signalled Melchior and George to revert to their real appearances. Rangda continued speaking:

- We are travelling the galaxy collecting the Zeto Crystals, which we are using to fight our ancient enemies, the Zetans. Your King has a primordial Zeto Crystal in his possession. We are willing to pay him more gold than there are in all his vaults in exchange for the crystal.

Chancellor Randall:

- And if the King refuses the deal?

Rangda:

- Then I will lead my huge army here and take it by force.

Chancellor Randall:

- Very well. Under those circumstances, I accept your offer.

Rangda:

- You are not the King. I wish to speak to the King.

Chancellor Randall:

- I was testing you. Everyone on Goldonia knows that the King died two years ago, and that I am the one governing this nation.

- Bring me the riches that you promised, and you can have the crystal.

Rangda:

- I will bring them. And you'll uphold your deal, or else...

Chancellor Randall:

- I am an honourable man. It wasn't I who pretended to be a long-dead deity to get my way. I'll see you when you get back, Rangda.

After the Dwarves had left, Melchior felt compelled to speak to Rangda:

- Do you think they will uphold their part of the bargain?

Rangda:

- Yes. The Dwarves and the other life forms on this planet are not attuned to the Zeto Crystals. To them, the Zeto Crystals are beautiful gemstones and nothing else. Hardly worth going to war for, especially when I am offering them a king's ransom in exchange for the crystal.

Melchior:

- I hope you are right. I would hate to go through all the effort of intercepting and landing that asteroid if it comes to fighting anyways.

Rangda:

- You would hate trying to fight the Dwarves in the tunnels below. The Dwarves are cunning and stubborn. Fighting them on their home ground would be a bloodbath.

- But as you'll find out, Melchior. I am right, as I always am.
- George Smith!

George:

- Yes, Empress Rangda,

Rangda:

- Prepare an expedition to intercept and land the golden asteroid from this star system on Goldonia.

- It is time to show the Dwarves the real consequence of greed. Hahaha!

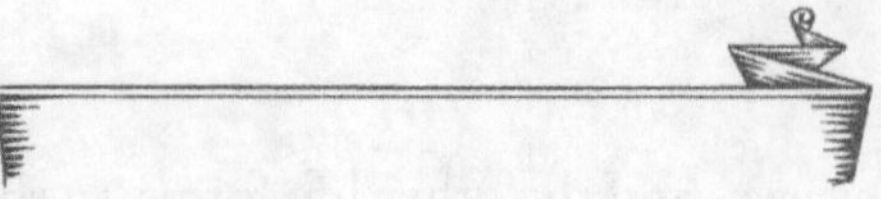

Chapter 264: The Consequence of Greed.

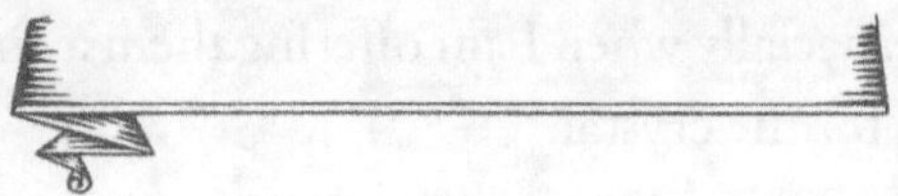

Gold is uncommon on Earth because only a supernova explosion can create it. The sizeable golden asteroid in the Goldonia star system was the result of a colossal supernova explosion. The asteroid had been a wayward passenger of the galaxy until the star of Goldonia's star system attracted it, eons ago.

In January 2881, George Smith's expedition landed the golden asteroid close to Chancellor Randall's domains on Goldonia. It turned out to be a problematic task landing the huge rock. Because of the asteroid's weight, 100 Megaton, the expedition needed to be careful. Because otherwise, the kinetic energy from the collision would cause widespread destruction.

After landing the golden asteroid, Rangda and Melchior approached Chancellor Randall. The sight of the golden asteroid mesmerised the dwarf.

Chancellor Randall:

- I thought that you were lying when you spoke about a King's ransom. Is that entire block gilded?

Rangda:

- Not gilded. The entire asteroid consists of gold.

Upon hearing this, Chancellor Randall almost fainted. In his greedy mindset, he forgot that such a massive influx of gold would render gold worthless. Seeing the gold, filled Randall with visions of his own greatness and the future. Rangda pulled him back to reality:

- Chancellor Randall. I have fulfilled my part of the bargain. Now bring me the primordial Zeto Crystal and uphold your part.

Chancellor Randall:

- Oh yes, of course, I will tell my servants to bring it at once.

One of Randall's servants brought the Zeto Crystal and gave it to Rangda. Having secured the Zeto Crystal, Rangda and Melchior, headed back to the Divine Dimension. Before entering the portals, Melchior studied the Dwarves that were flocking to the golden asteroid. Melchior spoke:

- Look at them. The gold possesses their minds.

Rangda:

- Yes, as I predicted. Dwarves only have one vice, greed, and as such, they obsess about gold.

Melchior:

- But you said that gold would be worthless if it's that plentiful?

Rangda:

- To humans, yes. You are greedy, but it's not your only vice, and humans have no intrinsic interest in gold. For humans, it only has value due to its rarity. When gold becomes abundant, you lose interest. But Dwarves are different.

- By the time that we come back, the Dwarves will have decimated each other fighting for that gold. This will make the planet easy for us to invade.

Melchior:

- So, you do plan to invade Goldonia?

Rangda:

- I plan to invade everything. But one thing, that my immortality has taught me is the value of patience. Let's head back to the Divine Dimension.

- Our next destination is the Orcs on Grashdunt.

Melchior:

- The Orcs? I bet they will be a useful ally!

Rangda:

- Yes. I will brief you before we head to Grashdunt. Now, prepare our army to move.

Rangda and Melchior entered the portal and left the dwarves to their fate.

Chapter 265: The Pursuit of Rangda Begins.

In March 2881, Frey and Freya arrived at the battlefield where Melchior had betrayed the Zetans. The field was an eerie sight. The Xenos had gnawed off the flesh from the fallen Zetans, and all that remained of their once-proud army was piles of broken bones.

As gruesome as the scene was, Frey and Freya were here on a critical mission. They needed to gather DNA from the fallen so that they could use cloning technology and synthetic wombs to have their species reborn. Doing so, was the only way to save their species from extinction. Spending a few weeks collecting samples, they had gathered the DNA of most of the fallen.

Having collected the DNA of all the Zetans that fell on the battlefield, Frey spoke:

- That's it. Let's hope that Hilda Muller will keep her promise to give our fallen brethren life again.

Freya:

- Yes, I have my doubts, but hope is all that we have left for our species.

Frey:

- Yes, Hilda did help, but she didn't commit very much to it.

Freya:

- Well, she doesn't feel that committed to the cause. How would you react, if two aliens asked for help to stop an evil demon from the destroying the galaxy?

Frey:

- Right, I wouldn't trust those aliens either. Unfortunately, we are on the wrong side of history, and we have to be grateful for the help that she did send us.

Freya:

- Yes. Regardless of the future of our species, we need to stop Rangda before it is too late. We do not have the time to go back to Earth with the DNA samples. All we can do is to send these droids with the DNA samples to Hilda with a message hoping that she will help us.

Frey:

- Yes, sister. So, what do we do now?

Freya:

- Well, I guess that Rangda wants to corrupt the primordial Zeto Crystals and increase her own power. Do you know where we can find them?

Frey:

- The True Maker placed the seven primordial Zeto Crystals on Zetani, Zetani Nova, Xenora, Elvonia, Goldonia, Grashdunt and Earth.

- Presumably, Rangda has access to the ones from Zetani, Zetani Nova, and Xenora. Do you reckon she captured the one from Earth?

Freya:

- Well, I'd say so since she stopped attacking Earth, yet I sensed it when I was there.

- Which planet do you reckon would be her next target?

Frey:

- Elvonia. The elves live in peace and harmony without any advanced technology. They would be easy pickings for Rangda's army.

Freya:

- Well, we better hurry up then. She has a three-year head-start, so time is running out. But we cannot give up hope.

- I hope that we will come across some Zetan survivors as well. The ones that died in the battle cannot have been the only ones left of us?

Having said this, Freya and Freya gathered their drones and jumped on a hovercraft hoping to intercept Rangda's army. Rangda had a three years head start, but they were moving a lot quicker with their drone army, so there was still hope.

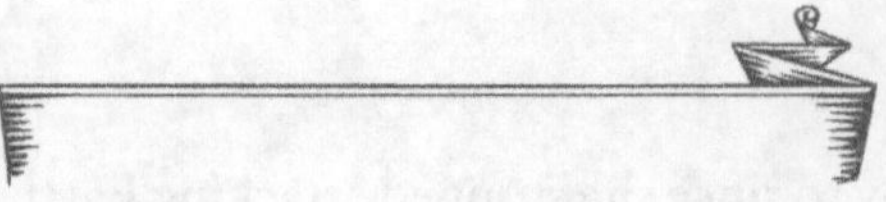

Chapter 266: Rangda Prepares to Conquer Grashdunt

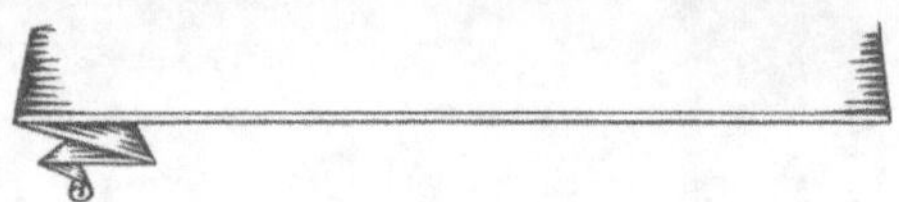

In October 2881, Rangda was fighting a deathmatch with some of her Xeno warriors. Melchior studied her and he saw her slaughter five Xeno warriors that were almost twice her size. Rangda signalled for the battle to be over. The remaining Xenos feasted on their fallen, while Rangda walked up to Melchior to speak:

- Are you enjoying the show,?

Melchior:

- Yes. You impressed me with your fighting. I didn't know you were such a fearsome warrior. But why, are risking your life, fighting your own soldiers in the arena?

Rangda:

- I plan to conquer Grashdunt though challenging King Gromm in single combat. Once I have claimed the Orcish throne, I'll claim the Zeto Crystal on Grashdunt. I will also have an orcish army to invade Goldonia and subject the dwarves to my rule.

Melchior:

- But why don't you kill King Gromm with powers of your corrupted Zeto Crystals?

Rangda:

- I could. But if I kill their leader using magic, the orcs will consider me a cheater. Instead of having a willing army at my disposal, my army would have to fight the Orcish Horde.

Melchior:

- Understood, but how can you be so strong, fast, and fearsome?

Rangda:

- I have always been strong and fearsome. But I have learnt to channel the energy of the corrupted Zeto Crystals into my own body. This gives me super-speed and super-strength.

Melchior:

- Very well. It seems like you know how to handle yourself.
- When are we going to Grashdunt?

Rangda:

- In a while, I need some fresh blood first. Bring one of the Elven prisoners!

Melchior:

- Of course, Empress Rangda. Anything for my lady.

Rangda:

- Hah! You have never been the one to turn down a meal! But let's get this over with. I am thirsty, and I have a planet to conquer.

After saying this, Rangda and Melchior feasted on an Elven prisoner.

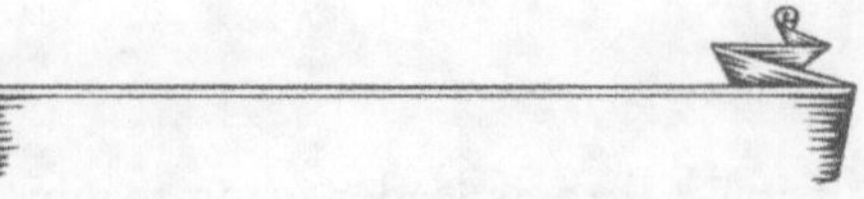

Chapter 267: Rangda Duels with King Gromm.

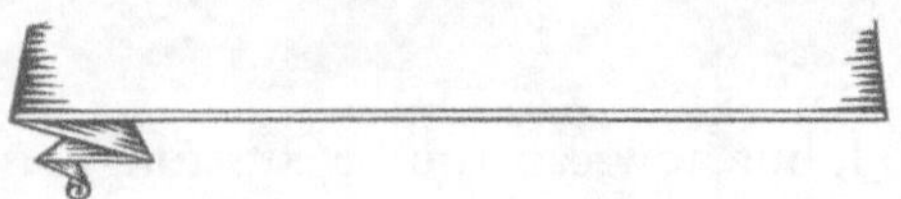

King Gromm felt amused. Who was this puny looking foreigner that had come through the portal to challenge him in single combat for the throne of Grashdunt? Towering at over four meters in height, and weighing almost a ton, he was twice the height of his challenger and over ten times as heavy. And on top of that, his enemy was a woman. What a fool to challenge him!

King Gromm felt relieved that Rangda chose to fight him in traditional Orcish single combat, instead of using her army to fight him. Gromm was not a dimwit, and he recognised that the alien invaders had much more advanced technology than his own people. But technology didn't matter when it came to Orcish single combat. In single combat, the duellists fought naked, wearing only a sword and a shield.

King Gromm entered the arena, and the large crowd was cheering. It had been a while since anyone had challenged him. That Orc's head hung as a trophy over the fireplace in the grand royal hall. Rangda entered from the opposite side of the arena. The spectators studied her. She was a fearsome and mysterious sight in her own way. Who was she? Where had she come from? And how could she believe that she could best King Gromm in single combat?

The Announcer yelled out the names of the contestants and that today's deathmatch was for the Grashdunt throne. "And for the primordial Zeto Crystal!" Rangda added, and King Gromm agreed. After the introductions, the fight began.

King Gromm lunged out with a mighty swing against Rangda, and she dodged it. He swung again to the same effect. A few more swings followed with the same result. On the fifth swing, Rangda blocked Gromm's swing with her shield, and Gromm realised that something was amiss. Rangda stood sturdy and unmoved from the impact of the enormous swing. Gromm felt like he had swung his sword into a large rock and his hand felt sore from the impact. Gromm forgot about his sore hand when Rangda stabbed him in his right thigh, drawing first blood. "Hah! is that all the damage you can do!" Gromm mocked Rangda, but on the inside, he felt worried. "I am just getting started," Rangda smirked at Gromm.

Gromm attacked faster than Rangda had anticipated, and in the blink of an eye, he had cut off her right hand. Rangda realised that she had underestimated Gromm and that she needed to finish him off. She dodged the next blow, and then bashed Gromm's head with her shield to him take a few steps backwards. Rangda dropped her shield, and she picked up the sword with her left hand. Attacking with supernatural speed, she slashed the giant Orc dozens of times, decapitating him with the last strike.

Rangda dropped her sword, and she held Gromm's severed head up in the air to signal her triumph to the cheering crowd.

Rangda picked up her prize, the primordial Zeto Crystal, and left the arena without saying a word.

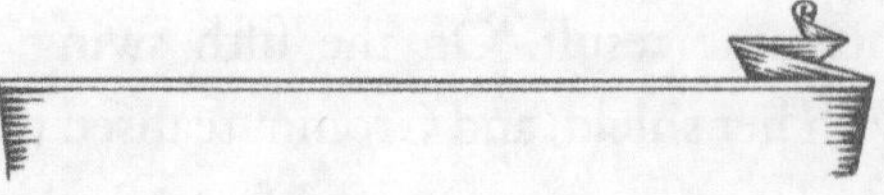

Chapter 268: Frey and Freya Arrives at Elvonia

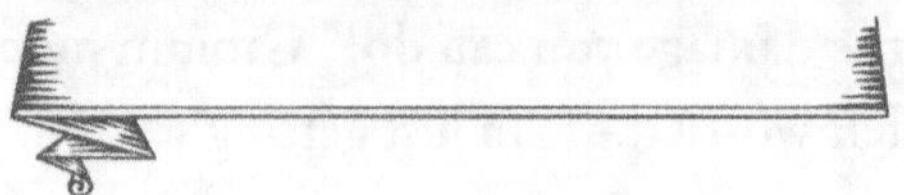

Frey and Freya arrived at Elvonia a few weeks later. With their fast hovercrafts and their fission-powered robots, they could travel a lot quicker than Melchior's and Rangda's army. As they arrived in Elvonia, they realised that they had come too late. The beautiful planet that they once knew was no more. Elvonia was now a toxic hellscape with everything dead or dying.

Freya:

- Oh no! We are too late. What happened here?

Frey:

- The same thing that happens to every world that Rangda visits. Chaos and destruction.

Freya:

- But it's such a terrible loss. The Elves lived in balance with nature, and they loved each other. They never harmed anyone. They were our best creation, purer than ourselves.

Frey:

- That may be, but their purity also made them an easy target for Rangda. They didn't stand a chance against Rangda's evil army.

- But what happened here doesn't matter anymore. We must intercept Rangda and stop her from stealing the other crystals.

Freya:

- Agreed. We'd better hurry up! With a bit of luck, we can relieve the Dwarves on Goldonia from her evil-doing before it is too late.

Having said this, they headed back to the Divine Dimension, hoping to reach Goldonia on time.

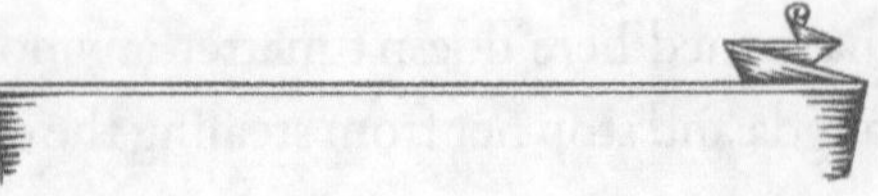

Chapter 269: Destruction by Greed.

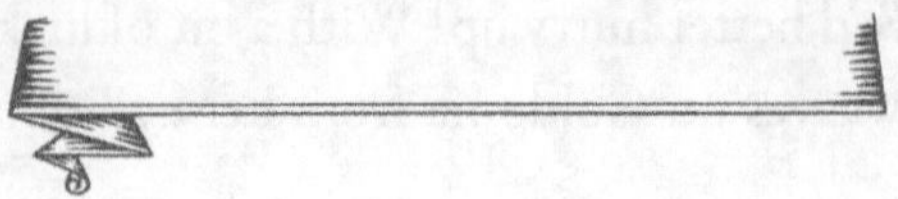

Frey and Freya arrived at Goldonia. They were too late, and they saw a devastated planet. Goldonia reeked of death and destruction with burned houses and corpses everywhere.

Frey:

- These Dwarves were not killed by the Xenos, they still have flesh on their dead bodies. Other Dwarves must have killed them.

Freya:

- I Agree. But why so much death and destruction. What caused such madness among the Dwarves?

Frey:

- We better investigate and pray that the Zeto Crystal is still here, although I fear for the worst.

Frey and Freya kept exploring. After a while, they came across the wounded Chancellor Randall. They could tell from his eyes that the stab wound in his abdomen was not the most debilitating condition. Randall's eyes were blood-red and filled with insatiable greed and paranoia. Chancellor Randall hissed at Frey and Freya as they approached him:

- Have you also come to steal my gold? Thieves! The gold is mine, and mine alone. I deserve it. I traded for it, fair and square. In exchange for that crystal.

Chancellor Randall had to stop his tirade to cough up some blood. Frey approached the wounded Dwarf and disarmed him.
Frey:

- What happened here, pitiful dwarf? What gold? We are Zetans, and we don't care about these things.

Randall:

- So, the Zetan have also emerged from the damn portal.

- The last alien that came here gave me a lot of gold, in exchange for a puny crystal.

Freya:

- Crystal? Did you give the Zeto Crystal to Rangda?

Randall:

- Aye, Rangda was her name. Brought down a massive nugget of gold the size of a mountain from the heavens. All for me.

- But the others. Those greedy bastards didn't acknowledge my property rights, so they turned against me, and against each other. Friend fought against friend; brother fought against brother. Everyone wants to steal my dear gold.

Freya sang to Randall with a soft mesmerising voice. She wanted to help the wounded dwarf, but more so, she needed to make sense of what had happened. It worked, Randall's anger disappeared, and he fell into a deep melancholy.
Randall:

- That damn beautiful gold. It has destroyed us all. I wish it never appeared here.

Freya:

- Where is this gold, Randall? Can you show me?

Randall:

- I am too wounded to walk. without rage keeping me alive,
my days are over.

Frey applied some Zetan healing gel that closed the dwarf's wound.
Randall's eyes shone with relief.

- Aye, that's what I'd call magic. Although nothing compared
to the magic in bringing in all that gold.

Freya:

- Can you show us where the gold is?

Randall:

- Aye, it's in the valley behind that crest.

They walked together to the top of the hill where they could see the
valley below. It was a gruesome sight. Dead and wounded covered the
valley with chaotic fighting still taking place. In the middle of the valley,
there was a gigantic golden asteroid. Upon seeing the asteroid, Randall
turned insane, and he tried to stab Freya with his sword. Frey acted instinctively, and he struck Randall with full force. Acting on instinct, Frey
forgot to moderate his strength, and he killed the Dwarf with his powerful strike.

Freya tried to comfort the guilt-ridden Frey:

- Frey, it isn't your fault. You did what you had to do to save
me.

Frey:

- I know. But I wish that we could do something to save them.

Freya:

- There isn't. Rangda played them. She took their crystal, and she gave them what would destroy them in return. Dwarves by nature are very sensitive to the effects of greed; especially towards the desire for gold.

- Their greed is so bad, so it infests their minds.

- This gigantic golden asteroid is useless, and yet it consumes their minds. To own it, they are willing to kill each other.

Frey:

- I know. I wish there was more of us here. We could have set things right. We could have pacified the area for long enough to use fusion to turn the gold into lead. We could have solved the Dwarves' disease.

Freya:

- Yes. But wishful thinking won't get us anywhere. We need to go. More dwarves are coming for the gold, and I'd rather avoid confrontation.

Frey:

- It seems that ship might have sailed already.

Frey pointed at the band of armed Dwarves approaching them. The leader of the Dwarves shouted:

- Hey! You there! Bloody aliens! Have you come to murder and steal our gold?

Freya:

- We are Zetans. We don't care about gold. We want peace.

Brigand:

- Aye, is that so? Then explain why there is a dead Dwarf next to your brother!

Frey:

- That Dwarf attacked my sister. We killed him in self-defence. Leave us alone, or you'll face a similar fate.

Brigand:

- We'll never let you steal our gold. Attack, fellas!

A dozen of Dwarven brigands charged the two Zetans. Frey and Freya killed their attackers with little effort. Seeing so much death and destruction, Freya got emotional, but Frey snapped her out of it.

- We don't have time to cry, sister. We need to hurry to the portal. More dwarves are coming.

In the distance, Frey saw hundreds of armed Dwarves approaching. The Zetans realised that time was short. They pulled themselves together and ran as fast as they could back to the portal. Once they had crossed the gateway to the Divine Dimension, they collapsed from exertion.

Chapter 270: The End of the Chase

The exertion from the battle and the guilt from the lives lost caused Frey and Freya to sleep for days on end. When they woke up, Rangda's army had surrounded them. In shock and awe, Frey and Freya took up their binoculars and studied their surroundings. Rangda had gathered a large and diverse force:

- There were millions of Orcs in their steam-punk outfits, muskets and coal-powered airships.
- There were Elves enslaved and in chains serving as humanoid shields and food.
- There were millions of Xenos since Rangda had bred and cloned them on Elvonia.
- There were regular Martian human troops, dressed in 29th century Martian armour.
- The most fearsome-looking of the enemy's combatants were the Xeno/Martian hybrids, twisted and unnatural beasts. The mutants had had the intelligence of Martians but the bloodlust of the Xenos.

Against this, Frey and Freya felt helpless with their puny army of 100,000 military drones designed to fight the Xenos. Rangda appeared telepathically to mock the Zetan siblings:

- Well, well, well! Look what we have here. The Zetan siblings, the only remainders of your majestic race have come to face me. Tell me: What did you hope to achieve by coming here?

Frey:

- We have come to end to your evil reign. We saw what you did on Elvonia and Goldonia. Your tyranny ends today.

Rangda:

- That is awfully cocky considering the situation you are in. But let's discuss what happened on Elvonia and Goldonia.

Freya:

- You murdered everyone and destroyed two peaceful planets.

Rangda:

- Oh, but did I? Let's look at the evidence.

- Elvonia was an unnatural planet, and its life forms didn't deserve to exist. Nature means for life to be a struggle, favouring the survival of the fittest. On Elvonia, there was no struggle. The weak and useless species on the planet could live on due to the perverting effect of the Zeto Crystal. Without the impact of the Zeto Crystal. Elvonia's lifeforms were unsustainable. As a result, I rid Elvonia of a bunch of unnatural species.

- I killed no-one on Goldonia. I cleansed the planet of the greedy Dwarves by introducing an abundant amount of gold, to trigger their innate greed. Once the Dwarves have killed each other, the planet will be free of their filth, and other worthier lifeforms can thrive.

Frey:

- Justify your evil however you want, Rangda. We have come to end to your reign of terror.

Rangda:

- Well, that has come to a good start, hasn't it, oh great General Frey? Didn't anyone tell you to not sleep on the job? I have encircled you, and you can't escape!

Frey:

- It doesn't matter. I have seen these military drones in action. They will tear through your Xeno filth like a hot knife cuts through butter. Today will be the end of you, Rangda.

Rangda:

- Oh, is that so? Because you have seen the humans test these drones on Earth? Hilda thinks that these drones function through sending out a signal that blocks the Xeno's neural patterns. In Hilda's tests, the drones mowed down the Xenos like chaffs of wheat, right?

Frey:

- Hold on. How do you know this?

Rangda:

- I have a telepathic connection with all the Xenos cloned or captured on Earth.

- I influenced Ramun to give you all the information about me. He didn't betray me, quite the opposite, he told you exactly what I needed you to hear.

- I influenced the cloned Xenos captured in the House Muller weapon testing program, to allow the drones to butcher them. This way, I tricked the Terrans into developing weapons that are useless against my army.

- Zetans and humans are alike. You keep underestimating my Xenos and my evil mastermind. Your arrogance will be your downfall, and the new Xeno/human hybrid will emerge as the pinnacle of creation. Ha-ha-ha!

Freya:

- I have heard enough of your lies, Rangda. Prepare to face justice!

Rangda:

- Good Luck.

Rangda disconnected with the Zetan siblings, and she rained barrage of artillery and small gunfire against Frey and Freya's drone army. While the ballistic energy absorber stopped the barrage, this drained their batteries. Frey decided to abandon his defensive formation and charge against the enemy. As they charged against the enemy, the Orcs attacked them from behind, while the Xenos and Martians assaulted from the front.

As Rangda had predicted, the military drones didn't work well against the Xenos. In the end, Frey and Freya fought back to back in a melee battle against the oncoming Xeno hordes. They held up valiantly in their last stand, slaying dozens of foes. When Rangda had seen enough, she blasted the Zetan siblings out of existence with a Martian artillery shell.

Rangda walked up to the dying Frey and Freya who had their legs blown off by the artillery shell. Their blue Zetan blood covered the ground, and Rangda smirked at them.

- Impressive, you fight better than your old man Odin did. You fought for the survival of your species, to avoid extinction.

- Unfortunately, evolution is harsh. It is time for me to put your Zetan species to rest. Any last words?

Freya:

- You will never get away with this. The True Maker will come after you and stop you.

Rangda:

- Ah. The True Maker. That coward doesn't even dare to face me. But I will force her out! Once I have corrupted the last primordial Zeto Crystal, I will force her out of hiding. I will drain her as I have drained everyone else. Once I have killed the True Maker, I will become the almighty goddess of this universe. I will master the fundaments of existence. I will be the destroyer of time and matter!

Frey:

- The True Maker is not a coward. She wants to avoid collateral damage. Force her out, and you'll destroy the entire galaxy.

Rangda:

- You speak like you know it. The True Maker is a powerless clockmaker who tries to stop me, the true goddess from seizing power. I have seen through her schemes. The True Maker is putting her last hope on, the Human/Zetan hybrid, Sabina. I have had several opportunities to kill Sabina. But I will let her grow powerful and then I'll kill her and drain her energy. Only then can I show that pathetic deity, who is the true ruler of the galaxy!

Rangda realised that the Zetan siblings had almost outsmarted her. When she had her long-winded rant, they had set explosives to kill themselves and Rangda. In the last second, Rangda activated her dark Zeto Crystal shield, to avoid getting killed from the explosion.

But Rangda still got injured from the massive blast. Her shrieking of pain and hatred continued for hours on end, until she passed out from the pain.

Chapter 271: Sabina Sets Out to Save Mars

Sabina could feel the shockwave through space/time continuum when Frey and Freya perished. Sabina realised that it was time for her to act. She walked into Metatron's office. Her appearance surprised Metatron. Sabina's essence radiated a divine light that had a calming presence and made him feel at peace.

Sabina:

- Father. The time has come. It is time for me to save the Martians from Dov's demented tyranny and restore hope for our future.

Metatron studied his daughter. It was July 2882, and Sabina was seven years old. What could she do against a demented dictator on another planet? Metatron knew that Sabina would get her way in the end, but he still decided to argue against her point:

- But Sabina darling. You are only seven years old. What can you do against the evil monster that rules Mars?

Sabina:

- Yes, I am a child. But I am destined to face Rangda, the greatest evil in the universe on the day that my adulthood starts, on my 12th birthday. How am I going to confront such an evil, if I haven't faced lesser villains before that?

Metatron studied his daughter. Sabina had the glowing blue eyes that she always had when the spirit of The True Maker filled her. But now, her body emitted a holy white light that illuminated her essence of nobility and graciousness. Metatron asked himself whether he was looking at his own daughter or a spirit. Metatron touched Sabina's hand. She was still there, and her touch soothed his worries and put his mind to ease. Feeling at ease, Metatron spoke again:

- Okay, Sabina, I will help you save the Martians.

Sabina:

- Thank you, father.

Metatron:

- But can you please tell me how you intend to save Mars from Dov's villainy and his bloodthirsty army of mutants?

Sabina:

- Yes, father. You are a good man that deserves to know every detail.
- I intend to go to Dov's capital and save Dov from himself.

Metatron:

- Save Dov from himself? The man is a monster that caused the death of millions. He is irredeemable.

Sabina:

- No. I must strive to save every soul. Besides, I do not want to taint my powers of light by using them to hurt others. The Elves on Elvonia succumbed to fear and used their powers to kill some of Rangda's Xenos. But once they did, they also destroy their own innocence. If I want to face Rangda, I need to remain innocent and pure to a stand a chance.

- Besides, I can save Dov. Fear drives Dov's actions. If I can soothe his anxiety, I can save Mars.

Metatron:

- This is crazy. There must be a better way to save Mars than to go the demon's lair and try to win him over with kindness?

Sabina:

- I am not asking you to cast aside your doubts, father. I am asking you to help me do the right thing despite your qualms.

Metatron:

- Yes. I will help you, Sabina. How can I reject the will of the True Maker, the eternal deity of the universe?

Sabina smiled at Metatron and spoke:

- You can reject the will of the True Maker. You are a human, and you have a free will. But I am happy that you choose not to. Gather my siblings and the other children in my light brigade. We are going to Nea Atina on a diplomatic mission.

After saying this, Sabina left the room and went back to her room to continue her meditation. Metatron sighed. What had he had gotten himself into? This was insane. Yet, he had to believe and hope, it was better than the alternative, to give up and live in despair.

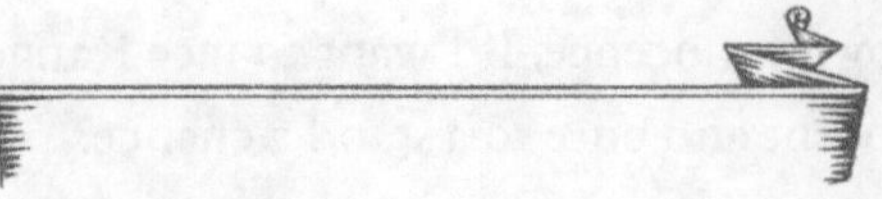

Chapter 272: Sabina Cleanses Dov's Soul.

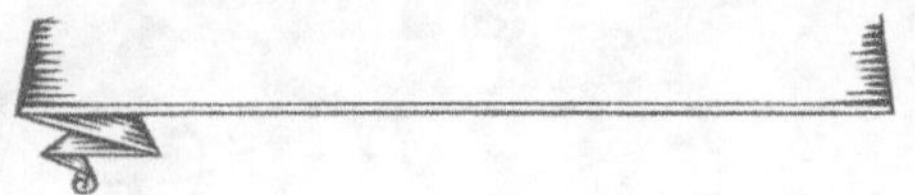

Dov Dorevitch studied his strategic position on Mars. He was powerful, and he would soon be able to attack Earth to aid his brother's invasion of the planet. Dov thought about his brother, Melchior. He hadn't heard from Melchior in many years. Melchior had entered the Divine Dimension with an expeditionary force to aid Rangda against the Zetans. What had happened to his brother on the other side of the portal? Dov had no idea, and he didn't intend to spend time pondering about the subject. When Melchior had appointed Dov to rule in his stead, he had given Dov a clear goal: to build up an army capable of invading Earth in ten years.

In the first year, Dov had been hours from defeat when rebels and deserters were close to overrunning his capital. But the release of the Xeno Virus had changed everything. Those that survived the virus had become non-questioning Xeno/Martian hybrids that were loyal as long they got fed. A lot of people didn't survive the virus outbreak, and over two billion Martians had died from the Xeno mutations. This had been a necessary sacrifice. Dov needed to punish the disloyal, and besides Dov would rather rule over two billion loyal subjects than over four billion dissenters.

Dov's chief right-hand man Frank Van Stein entered the room and spoke:

- A diplomatic delegation from Eden has landed. Metatron
  has come. He is accompanied by a bunch of children.

Dov

- What? Is this joke? Did the leader of an insignificant colony land and expect to get an audience with me, the emperor of the Martian Dominion?

Frank:

- Dov, you are the chancellor of the Martian Dominion. Melchior is the emperor.

Dov:

- Melchior has been gone for five years, and no-one has heard from him. He is most likely dead.

- No matter, I am happy to be the chancellor of the Martian Dominion. The different title doesn't affect me!

Frank:

- Very well, Chancellor Dorevitch. Shall I send the Edenites away or punish them for their insolence?

Dov:

- Hmm. I remember Melchior obsessing about Metatron's daughter, Sabina. He was agitated when Rangda, forbade him to eat her.

- Grant an audience to Metatron and his daughter. I want to see this child.

Frank:

- Understood, chancellor.

Dov:

- Arrange a meeting in the throne room. Please join us. I am sure watching this child will be interesting for both of us.

Frank touched a tablet and allowed access to Metatron and Sabina. Sabina and Metatron entered the throne room of The Martian Dominion. Sabina walked ahead of Metatron towards Dov who had an arrogant smirk on his lips. Sabina spoke:

- Dov Dorevitch. Your days of evil are over. I have come to save your soul and the future of your people.

This bewildered Dov. He hadn't understood why Metatron had brought his daughter for a diplomatic meeting. But he had expected that the child would stand in the background while the adults were talking. Dov got up, gave Metatron a disapproving look and spoke:

- You better teach your daughter some manners. Rudeness is not appreciated at my court. You would hate to experience what happens to people that are rude to me.

- Now state your business before I lose my temper.

Sabina:

- My father has no business here. I am the one who came to talk to you, Dov.

Sabina's statement confused Dov. Was this a stupid joke? If so, they should know better and be careful around him.
Dov:

- What exactly does a seven-year-old girl from Eden want to discuss with the Chancellor of the Martian Dominion?

Sabina:

- I told you already. I am here to save you and the Martian population from your tyranny.

Dov studied Sabina. There was something eerie about her that made him very uncomfortable. Her eyes were shining blue, and her entire being was glowing with a bright white light that made her look ethereal. Dov pulled himself together; he couldn't afford to show fear in front of a young child.
Dov:

- Why would I need saving? I am the chancellor of the Martian Dominion. I have everything provided. I have every comfort at my disposal.

Sabina:

- That might be. And yet you hardly sleep at night. Self-loathing and fear fill your mind. You wander around without aim, feeling guilty over all the evil deeds you have committed.

Dov:

- You arrogant twat!

Dov lashed out, and he slapped Sabina, as hard as he could. She didn't flinch, but guilt overwhelmed Dov. He felt embarrassed over having such bad self-control. Sabina reached out with her hand and spoke:

- I forgive you, Dov. Take my hand, and you'll feel better.

Dov took Sabina's hand. As their hands met guilt and shame overwhelmed Dov over the terrible crimes that he had committed. Dov felt intense hate towards his right-hand-man Frank Van Stein. With tear-filled eyes bubbling with rage, Dov yelled at Frank:

- You! You were the one who convinced me to release the virus. I never wanted any of this to happen. All that I wanted was to make my brother happy. But he is the devil and nothing will ever satisfy him, so it was all in vain!

Before Frank had the time to respond, Dov pulled up his plasma knife and stabbed Frank several times in the head. After killing Frank, Dov ran up the stairs to the viewing platform overlooking the throne room. Sabina ran after him. When Sabina reached Dov, he was standing with his back to the ledge. Sabina shouted:

- Dov! Stop! There is still time, I can save you.

Dov, with tears running down his cheeks, smiled at Sabina, and replied:

- You already have. Thank you, Sabina!

After this, Dov looked at his bloody and glowing hot plasma knife. He aimed it towards himself, and he stabbed himself between the eyes. Dov fell backwards, and the spikes of the Martian Dominion emblem impaled him. It was a fitting end for Dov's tyranny.

Metatron walked up to Sabina on the viewing platform. Sabina was crying.

Metatron

- So, so baby girl. Everything will be okay.

Sabina:

- I couldn't save him...

Metatron:

- In a way, you did. Dov couldn't live with the guilt over what he had done.

Sabina:

- You are right, dad. I cannot save everyone. I can only do my best.

Metatron:

- Yes, that is how I have learnt to live my life.

Sabina:

- Let's release the antivirus and save as many as we can. There is a lot for us to do on this planet!

After saying this, Metatron and Sabina walked towards the wind generator. Metatron took out a vial with the antivirus, and he inserted it into the same wind generator that had spread the virus. Shortly afterwards, the cloud cover over Nea Atina dispersed, and the inhabitants could see the sun for the first time in many years!

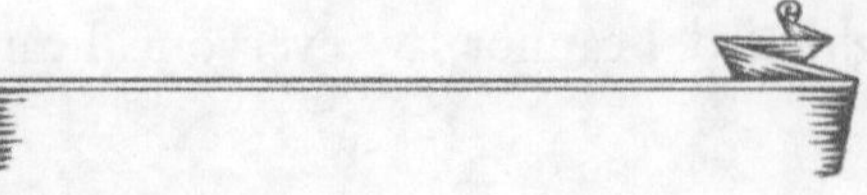

Chapter 273: Hilda Finds out About Dov's Death

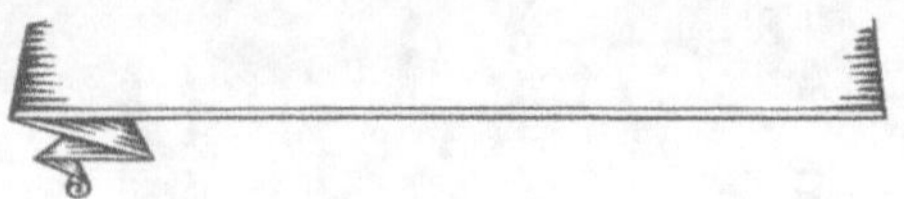

Hilda Muller was at the Hansstadt Zoo with Melanie and their two daughters Emma and Mila. It was a beautiful day, around 22 degrees and clear skies. It was always good weather when Hilda Muller decided to have a day off. Being the ruler of House Muller, she used weather control technologies to make sure of that.

As they studied the animals at the petting zoo, Hilda felt the restlessness creeping in on her. When Hilda had found out about the Zetan technology to create babies from two eggs, the prospect had excited her. But once the surrogate mothers had given birth to her and Melanie's babies, she had realised her mistake. Children didn't interest her. Politics, ruling and management did. Besides, she was living in a unique time in human history. With the threat of a looming alien invasion, forming the next generation couldn't catch her attention. "Yes, that is a sheep, it gives wool", Hilda said with a distant voice. Her mind was elsewhere.

Hilda spotted her cousin, Michael. At first, she got annoyed, this was her day off, and Michael couldn't be slacking here with his family. But Hilda realised that Michael had come with his military aides and that he was heading towards her. He seemed relaxed and casual, so what was going on?

Michael walked up to Hilda and spoke:

- Hilda. There has been a very unexpected development in the Martian Dominion.

Hilda:

- Good or bad?

Michael:

- Good!

- During a meeting with an Edenite delegation, Dov Dorevitch lost the plot and murdered his right-hand man Frank Van Stein in front of everybody. After the murder, he ran to a viewing platform, which overlooks the throne room. He jumped off the platform and plunged to his death.

Hilda:

- Woah. This is great news! Dov was creating an invasion force to invade Earth, but we haven't dared to intervene with the dangerous virus on the Martian surface.

- Is there any hologram video of Dov suicide?

Michael:

- There is. The Martians sent this video to every news outlet.

Hilda studied the hologram video in amazement. The man from Eden was Metatron, and the young girl must have been Sabina. But what did the girl say that drove Dov insane? And why was there a strange aura surrounding the girl?

Hilda:

- Is there any way that we can hear what they are saying in the video?

Michael:

- Only if we hack the Martian Dominion mainframe. This
is the video that they provided. They have filtered away the
sound.

Hilda:

- What about the strange light surrounding the little girl, Sabina?

Michael:

- Hmm. It looks like a failed video manipulation.

A breaking news notification popped up in one of Hilda's bionic microchips. It read as follows:

Olympus Republic Tribune, 25th October 2882.

The Martian Dominion collapsed today when Dov Dorevitch murdered Frank Van Stein during a meeting with Jack Silver from Eden. Jack
Silver has seized interim control over the Olympus Republic. Jack Silver's
first move is to grant independence to all the other states subjugated by
the Martian Dominion. Jack Silver, also known as Metatron, gave the following statement:

- This is a historic day for the Martian People. The tyranny of the
Dorevitch brothers has come to an end. We can now focus on reversing
the effect of the horrible Xeno virus that has claimed so many lives. I
will be the interim president of the Olympus Republic until we have contained the outbreak. After that, we will hold free elections. I implore
everyone to send humanitarian aid to help the afflicted.

May the True Maker bless you all!

Michael, who had read the same news article, spoke in amazement:

- Metatron usurped power from the Dorevitch brothers on
Mars. I can't believe it!

Hilda:

- It wasn't Metatron. He is only a figurehead.

Michael:

- So, who is behind it?

Hilda:

- Metatron's daughter, Sabina Silver.

Michael:

- I hope you are joking? Sabina Silver is seven years old. A seven-year-old play with their dolls and artificial intelligence hologram buddies. They don't stage coupes in other nations.

Hilda:

- But Sabina Silver is anything but ordinary. There is something divine about her. She is a messiah sent to save humanity during these difficult times.

Michael:

- That sounds like superstitious nonsense. But if you are right, that is excellent news.

Hilda looked at Melanie playing with their daughters Emma and Mila. She sighed:

- I am not too sure about that. What if she is meant to save humanity from us?

Michael:

- From us? We have been working tirelessly to save Earth from an alien invasion.

Hilda:

- Yet, less than eight years ago, our relatives tried to commit genocide against the Martian population.

Michael:

- Well, we are different. We are not our relatives. We can change things for the better.

Hilda:

- Yet, I have a lot of blood on my hands.

Michael:

- That is different. You did what you had to do.

Hilda paused and reflected for a moment over her past actions. She couldn't get over the murder of Emma Schindler, and her guilt made Emma's lifeless body appear in front of her eyes.

Hilda stared at the mirage of Emma's corpse for a long time until another Emma, her daughter grabbed her hand. "Are you okay, mommy?" "Yes, I am okay" Hilda mumbled and walked away.

Why had she agreed to Melanie's suggestion to name one of the children Emma? Why had Melanie picked that damn name? Did Melanie want to mess with her head or was it a coincidence? Hilda panicked with paranoia and guilt gripping her mind, and there was only one thing she could do. Hilda ran away, as fast as she could!

Chapter 274: A Tear-Filled Confession

"I *killed her!"*

Hilda Muller was sitting alone with Melanie in her room, hyperventilating and shaking with remorse. Tears were running down her cheeks.

Melanie:

- I don't understand. You killed who?

Hilda:

- I killed Emma Schindler. I poisoned her with a synthetic virus to make it look like a heart attack.

Melanie studied Hilda. She had never seen her partner like this before. Hilda was usually a strong and determined woman, but now her bottled up guilt had brought Hilda to the edge of desolation.

Melanie:

- But why would you kill Emma? She was your best friend?

Hilda:

- Yes, and that is why it is killing me from the inside.

Melanie:

- Tell me what happened?

Hilda:

- Emma led a secret expedition to the Divine Dimension to kill Rangda. It failed terribly and she ended up fighting the Zetans instead. Emma abandoned her unit, and she escaped back to Earth. She was the sole survivor of that expedition.

- I realised that Emma needed to be silenced. The news of what had happened couldn't reach the public. To keep it a secret, I decided to do the dirty deed myself.

Melanie:

- But Emma died many years ago. Why haven't you shared this with me?

Hilda:

- I shared it with my partner at the time, Markus White.

- In my deluded state of mind, I shared it in the most gruesome way possible. Emma's corpse was still in my office when he came to visit.

- Markus stared at me in disgust, and he ran off. I haven't heard from him since.

Melanie:

- At least he did not drag your name in the dirt.

Hilda:

- Yes. I must be thankful about that.

Melanie:

- Is this why you are so distant to our daughter Emma? Because of her name?

Hilda:

- Perhaps. When you suggested naming her after Emma Schindler, I didn't know what to say, so I just went with it.

Melanie:

- I understand.

Melanie studied Hilda for a long time. Eventually, Melanie spoke:

- We'll have to come up with a new name for Emma. I don't want her name to serve as a reminder of what you did!

Hilda dried off her tears with a napkin and spoke:

- So, you do you forgive what I did?

Melanie:

- It is not my place to forgive what you did. You must learn to forgive yourself.

- I will stick by your side for the sake of our children. You are a good person and a good leader. One bout of insanity won't turn you into your evil uncle, Joachim.

Hilda:

- Thank you, Melanie. I will try to forgive myself.

- But one thing scares me. I need to meet with Sabina Silver as I am convinced that she is The Chosen One. But I am afraid that she'll drive me insane as she did to Dov Dorevitch.

Melanie:

- It won't happen.

- You are a good person that is honest about your crimes and try to repent.

- Dov was a psychotic mass-murderer until Sabina showed him the light. You'll be fine. I believe that you'll feel better after meeting Sabina.

Hilda:

- Thank you! I will meet with Metatron and Sabina as soon as possible.

After saying this, the burden on Hilda's chest lightened and together they drank tea watching the soothing fire, in the central fireplace of their residence.

Chapter 275: Complications with the Antivirus

It was February 2883, and Metatron was sitting in his office in the presidential palace of the Olympus Republic. He studied the reports on hand, and he sighed. There were unforeseen complications with the airborne antivirus. Although the Xeno virus had disappeared from the population, it had done so at a steep cost. 20 per cent of the remaining population had died from the cure, bringing the Martian population down to 1.6 billion.

Metatron didn't know what to do. He had been running Eden for a decade, but that was a tiny world where he knew most of the inhabitants personally. Running a crumbling empire, while trying to avoid a complete collapse was another matter.

Unfortunately, all the helpers that Metatron had brought in from Eden faced the same predicament. In his desperation, Metatron had invited the Terran Council to come back and run the planet. The Terran Council had declined the proposal. After their total defeat in the war of Martian independence, they had lost interest in the planet, and besides,they had more pressing matters on hand than retaking a former colony, when the threat of an alien invasion was still looming.

Metatron thought of Sabina. Did his sweet and gentle daughter understand the consequences of their actions? She hadn't been out much since they released the antivirus. Her usual self would be out among the poor and inflicted, trying to help them. But since they seized control over Mars, four months earlier, Sabina had acted reclusively staying by herself for days on end.

Metatron decided to visit Sabina, and as expected she was in deep meditation when he entered her room. Sabina opened her eyes, and she smiled upon seeing him:

- Nice to see you, daddy. I am happy that you are here.

Metatron:

- I am happy to see you too, darling. But I am worried about you. You used to be out with other kids and help people back on Eden. Since we arrived here, you have sought isolation. What has changed?

Sabina:

- The other children in the light brigade are doing my work for me. And they are doing it well.

- The True Maker told me to stay in isolation and meditate. She told me that if I went out and witnessed the carnage and destruction caused by Dov and his men, I would be filled with rage. Rage would taint my soul and make me vulnerable to Rangda.

Metatron:

- Okay, I see. So, is the True Maker a girl?

Sabina:

- The True Maker is an eternal force that is older than our universe. It has no real form. To me, she is a girl my age. To you, probably a man your age. To a cat, perhaps a cat. Such is the nature of the True Maker.

Metatron:

- Well, that is an interesting idea. I have some good news. We have managed to rid the planet of the Xeno virus infection.

Sabina:

- I know. And the cost was high. Way too high. And I don't understand why.
- Why couldn't the True Maker give me an antivirus that killed no-one?

Metatron:

- Maybe there is no such thing in the world. A universal solution without drawbacks?

Sabina:

- But I wonder, why did she choose me? She could have picked anyone?

Metatron:

- Well, perhaps she did choose anyone, and you happened to be that person?

Sabina pondered what Metatron had said for a while and then she smiled and spoke:

- Thank you, dad. Can you bring my games console? We haven't played together for such a long time.

Metatron thought about his commitments for the day, and then he thought *"fuck it"* He wouldn't be useful to anyone if he kept sacrificing his alone time with his daughter to help others. Metatron spoke:

- Yes, darling. Which game would you like to play?

Sabina:

- The game with the fairy princess and the frogs, daddy.

Metatron turned on the game. During that afternoon he felt like a normal dad for once, enjoying electronic games with his seven-year-old daughter.

Chapter 276: "It is Not My Place to Forgive You."

In March 2883, a month after Metatron had declared Mars Xeno virus-free, Hilda Muller arrived at Nea Atina. Hilda studied the city that she hadn't visited since 2872 when the Olympus Republic was a vassal state to House Muller. Back in 2872, Nea Atina was a bustling metropolis. While it had been dirt poor compared to the luxury of the House Muller capital, Hansstadt, it had still been a liveable city. Now, the city resembled a ghost town. It was clear that most of the inhabitants had died. A thick sensation of death and suffering was still covering the city.

Hilda entered the throne room where Metatron and Sabina received her. Hilda felt weak, and her legs almost buckled under her weight. But she had to atone for her sins, and what better way to do so, than confessing her sins to the Chosen One?

As Hilda was approaching, Sabina stood up and spoke:

- Hilda Muller. I know why you have come. But it is not my place to forgive you for what you have done.

Hearing this, Hilda collapsed to the floor and started crying:

- But I have travelled so far to meet you. I don't know what to do. I can't live with this pain and guilt any longer.

Sabina studied Hilda, who was lying in front of her feet, wailing. She walked up to Hilda, held her hand to comfort her and spoke:

- It isn't my place to forgive you, but I can give you the energy
to pursue the righteous path and do good for humankind.

While saying this, Sabina shone with an aura of white holy light. Hilda, who held Sabina's hand, felt rejuvenated with a burden lifted off her chest.

Hilda:

- Thank you for sharing your time with me, Sabina. How can
I start my journey towards atonement?

Sabina:

- You can organise a relief and rebuilding program for Mars,
now that the Xeno virus has disappeared and it is safe to do so.

- And I have a favour to ask of you.

Hilda:

- I will do anything you ask of me, Your Grace.

Sabina:

- Good. Somewhere on Earth, there is a primordial Zeto Crystal hidden. I need you to find it and bring to me, for safe-keeping against Rangda.

Hilda:

- Primordial Zeto Crystal? I have never heard about such an
artefact?

Sabina:

- But you might have heard about the Holy Grail?

Hilda:

- Yes.

Sabina:

- It's the same thing.
- You better hurry up, Rangda will come to look for it.

Hilda:

- What about you, Sabina?

Sabina:

- I need to stay here. There is still so much suffering on Mars. Perfect conditions for Rangda to sway a weak mind to do her evil bidding.

Hilda:

- I understand. I will head back to Earth as soon as possible. I will assist you with the full might of House Muller.

- I hope we will meet again, Mistress Sabina.

Sabina:

- So, do I, Mistress Muller. Farewell and good luck.

After the conversation, Hilda and her delegation headed back to Earth. There was plenty to do, and time was running short.

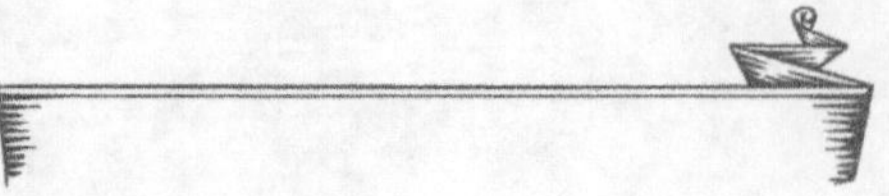

Chapter 277: Rangda and Melchior's Armies Approach Earth.

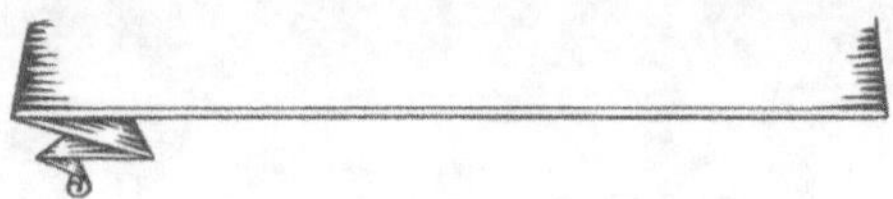

Two years later, In July 2885, Rangda and Melchior's massive armies had arrived close to the portals to Earth. They had spent the last years plundering Goldonia and Grashdunt to build an even bigger army, and new troops were joining them every day. They had over 30 million soldiers under their command, and together with Dov's forces attacking from orbit, the Terrans wouldn't stand a chance!

Melchior rushed into Rangda's command module. He was pale, fearful, and furious at the same time. Out of breath, he spoke:

- Dov is dead, and we won't receive any Martian help from orbit.

Rangda:

- What! Who killed that fat fool?
- Wait, don't tell. I know who did it. I can feel her presence.

Melchior:

- Spit it out! Grrrrrr!

Rangda:

- Sabina! That holier than thou lackey of the True Maker has more guts and potential than I gave her credit.

Melchior:

- We should have killed her when we had the chance!

Rangda:

- Yes! On the bright side, her shattered soul will be a worthy addition to the tormented souls that fuels my corrupted Zeto Crystals!

Melchior:

- I don't care about that! How the fuck are we going to invade Earth now that the Terran Council controls the skies?

Rangda gave Melchior an evil look and blasted him to the ground with a psionic blast. Rangda roared:

- Silence, you dog. Earth means nothing to me. I am here for the last primordial Zeto Crystal. That is all that matters.

- We will order our troops to commence with the invasion as a diversion. Meanwhile, you and I will lead a small strike force through a secret portal to steal the last Zeto Crystal.

Melchior:

- Yes, Empress Rangda. May I ask where the secret portal will take us?

Rangda:

- To the temple in Jerusalem. We will find the primordial Zeto Crystal hidden in the catacombs below.

- Assemble your best men, we are moving at once. The Terrans are looking for the crystal as well. I worry that they are close to uncovering it and give it to Sabina. This would be a monumental setback!

Melchior:

- Yes, Empress Rangda. I will alert the troops to strike at once!

Having said this, Melchior left the room to prepare his troops for the upcoming invasion of Earth.

Chapter 278: A Confrontation in the Catacombs

Hilda Muller was at the excavation site in the catacombs under the great temple in Jerusalem. Hilda's archaeology expedition had reached a breakthrough, and her archaeologists had summoned her.

Hilda studied the blue crystal. It shone with a surreal light, and it was exciting to uncover something so magical.

Hilda received a phone call in one of her nanotechnology augmentations. It was from Michael Muller:

- Hilda! Red Alert. The Xenos have launched full-scale invasion through the portals. They are bringing other unidentified alien species as well.

Hilda:

- Okay. Send all our troops to protect the defensive perimeter. We must stop the enemy from gaining a foothold.

Michael:

- Understood. I will convey the order at once.

After hanging up on her cousin, Hilda turned towards the archaeologists and shouted.

- Hurry up.

- We are facing a full-scale alien invasion. We need to get this crystal to safety!

The workers dug as fast as they could. Half an hour later, the workers had cut away the rock that encased the crystal. Hilda picked up the crystal, and she studied it. Hilda stood mesmerised for a while, but a terrible noise brought her back to her senses. It was the noise of Xeno claws chopping her workers into pieces. Hilda turned around, and there she was, her worst nightmare, Rangda!

Rangda:

- We meet again. After over 10 years, it's time to end your life!

Hilda:

- I am not dead yet, and you'll regret stabbing my workers in the back.

Rangda:

- We'll see about that. Xenos! Charge!

Dozens of Xenos charged at Hilda, who held the Zeto Crystal in her left hand. Hilda moved with incredible speed and strength as she danced the room, killing the dozens of beasts with her plasma sword.

Rangda:

- Impressive. The Zeto Crystal is enhancing your already exceptional combat abilities.

- But you are no match for me! Check this out.

Rangda powered her own physical body using her six corrupted Zeto Crystals. Faster than the eye could see, Rangda stabbed Hilda a dozen times. Hilda collapsed to the ground, and she dropped her plasma sword and the Zeto Crystal. Rangda picked up the Zeto Crystal from the ground. She studied it for a while, and then she laughed psychotically.

- Ha-Ha-Ha-ha! The seventh and last Zeto Crystal, with this in my hand no one will able to stop me. I am on the brink of reaching godhood!

- Any last words?

Hilda:

- You talk too much.

Having said this, Hilda pulled up a pistol from her foot holster and shot Rangda six times in the face. The bullets blinded Rangda, but they didn't kill her as the corrupted Zeto Crystals powered her. Blinded and hissing, Rangda took the Zeto Crystal and rushed towards the portal where she met Melchior, who looked at her in awe:

- What happened, Empress Rangda?

Rangda:

- Nothing, you fool. I got the crystal, and these are small scratches. Let's head back, you idiot.

Screeching in pain, Rangda hurried back through the portal. Shortly afterwards, all the attacks ended. As for Hilda, she died from the bloodloss, but her faction could revive her as Rangda had failed to permanently kill her.

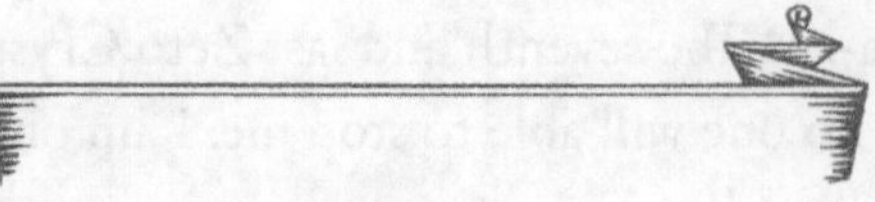

Chapter 279: Rangda Corrupts the Final Zeto crystal.

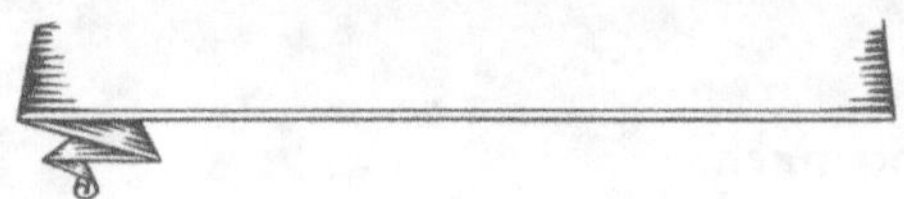

A few weeks later, Rangda's eyes and face had healed from the gunshot wounds. She had been careless but lucky. Mocking the dying Hilda, without ensuring that she wasn't a threat, was an embarrassing oversight that could have cost Rangda her life. Luckily, the power from the corrupted Zeto Crystals had filled her body with immense energy. This unholy energy had absorbed most of the power in the bullets, preventing them from penetrating into her brain.

Now that Rangda's eyesight had recovered, she was ready to perform the ritual to corrupt the seventh and last primordial Zeto Crystal. Once she had completed the ceremony, she would have close to limitless power, and no-one would be able to stand against her. As Rangda prepared for the ritual, she heard an unfamiliar voice:

> - Don't do it, Rangda. If you corrupt the seventh and last crystal, you will upset the balance of the universe and the Milky Way. You'll destroy the galaxy, which you seek to enslave.

Rangda screeched at the tranquil voice:

> - Is this the True Maker that I am talking to?
> - If so, come out and face me! You have been hiding for long enough!

The True Maker:

- I see no reason to show myself to you. I have lived for trillions of years in hundreds of iterations of the universe. Your schemes, no matter how grand they seem to you, are insignificant to me.

Rangda:

- Grrrahhhhh! You are afraid of me. That is why you have been training your protégé girl to face me. Once I have corrupted the last Zeto Crystal, I will be more powerful than you, and I will take your place. I don't care if you have lived for trillions of years. Times are changing, and I am coming after you.

The True Maker:

- The only thing that concerns me is the immensity of my own omnipotence. Also, I prefer non-interference as I have given free will to all my creations.

- You'll face Sabina in two years. Kneel to her and seek my forgiveness. If not, I will smite you. I am done talking to you.

Rangda:

- Very well, old fool. I got things to do anyway.

Rangda performed the ritual to corrupt the seventh Zeto Crystal. After finishing the ritual, the seven crystals merged to one and became part of her body. If Rangda had felt powerful before, it was nothing compared to what she felt now. As Rangda shrieked in triumph, the entire fabric of the Milky Way trembled. Cosmic energy of hatred and malevolence radiated from Rangda and dimmed the starlight.

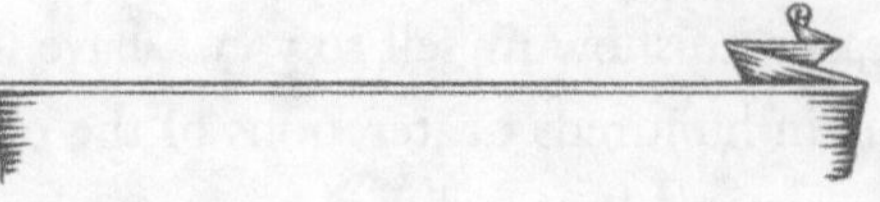

Chapter 280: Hilda Wakes up from a Coma Facing the Impending Doom.

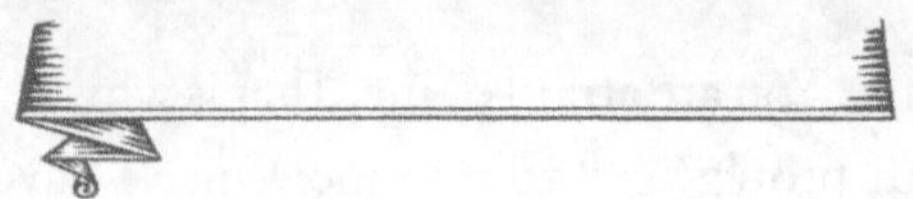

In October 2885, Hilda Muller woke up from her induced coma. Hilda felt very strange. She had experienced the dreamless sleep of cryogenic sleep in the past, but it hadn't felt like this. Had she come back from the dead? Hilda looked around in the room, and she saw the faces of her partner Melanie and her cousin Michael. Melanie tried to smile, while Michael wasn't trying to hide his worries and distressed emotional state. Hilda decided to address the situation:

- What is going on? What happened to me? Why do you guys look so worried?

Michael:

- Rangda ambushed you. You fought well and killed dozens of Xenos. Unfortunately, Rangda got the better of you, and she stole the Zeto Crystal. You succumbed to your injuries. Our men found you dead but not beyond resurrection. We have regrown your damaged body, and you are as good as new.

Hilda:

- How is the war against Rangda and Melchior going?

Michael:

- They couldn't break through our defences. They stopped attacking as soon as they had secured the Zeto Crystal.

Hilda:

- That is excellent news. If they can't defeat us, that means we can overcome them. Especially if we get the Martians to help.

Michael:

- No, we can't. They closed the portals behind them. Frey and Freya never gave us the correct sequence for opening the portals.

Melanie couldn't take it anymore. She fell into tears, and she started talking:

- War or no war. There is an even bigger problem.
- Our galaxy is dying!

Hilda:

- What do you mean, Melanie?

Melanie was too agitated to answer, so Michael replied for her:

- It started a few weeks ago. We have detected a lot of gamma-ray bursts lately, and our own Sun is acting erratically as well. Stars are dying around us, and there is nothing we can do about it. Earth's magnetic field has protected us this far. But the gamma bursts have fried some of our asteroid mining stations, killing everyone affected.

Hilda:

- Then there is only one person who can save us.

Michael:

- What do you expect Sabina to do about the cosmic gamma-ray blasts?

Hilda:

- It is not a matter of logic. It is a matter of faith. We must turn
to the light when everything seems dark.

Michael:

- Very well, I will extend her an invitation.

Hilda:

- And, I will beg her to come. The True Maker needs to be on
our side!

After saying this, Hilda pushed herself to get out of bed, and she sent
an emergency transmission urging Sabina to come.

Chapter 281: I am not ready yet.

Sabina and Metatron arrived on Earth to meet with Hilda and Michael. It had been a perilous trip, as the massive increase in background radiation and sun activity made space travel dangerous. The trip was essential though, as they needed to get to Earth to fulfil Sabina's purpose.

Sabina and Metatron stepped out of their spacecraft. A large group of kneeling worshippers met them and paid them respect. Hilda Muller was one of the worshippers.

- Welcome to Earth, Saint Sabina.

Sabina:

- I wish I had received the same welcome on my latest visit. How different things could have been.

- No matter, please get up. I can sense that your knees are hurting, and the last thing I want is to cause you pain.

The worshippers got up on their feet, and Sabina spoke:

- I know why you have summoned me to the home planet of humanity. Trust me, I would love to help, but I am not ready yet.

Hilda:

- But people are dying every day, from the gamma-ray bursts. A massive blast could wipe out all life in on the planet.

Sabina:

- So will the black hole that is moving towards us from Alpha Centauri. It is bound for collision in a decade. But I am not ready yet.

Hilda:

- What do you mean? Alpha Centauri is still around. We received an update from our colony there, earlier today.

Sabina:

- The radio signals from Alpha Centauri have travelled for four years and are from four years ago. By the time you'll notice what happened to Alpha Centauri, the Black Hole will be halfway to our solar system.

- But don't worry. The True Maker said I'd be ready on my 12th birthday, and that is only one and a half years away.

Hilda:

- Can't you move any faster? A lot can happen in one and a half years.

Sabina:

- I could. But it would be unwise to ignore the advice from the deity that grants me my powers.

Hilda:

- So, what can we do?

Sabina:

- You can pray, but only if this makes you feel better. I don't need your worship; I am only playing out the role that the True Maker gave me. Pray to the True Maker if you wish, but prayer doesn't affect the True Maker. Aim to live well-balanced lives in peace, harbouring hope and a desire to do good deeds.

- Now, I must meditate. The space travel upset my harmony, and I need to restore it to fulfil my purpose.

Hilda:

- Of course. Your accommodation contains a specific meditation room.

Sabina:

- Your hospitality is much appreciated.
- Farewell, and I hope to see you for dinner.

Hilda:

- It will be my pleasure. See you later, Your Grace.

After the conversation, Hilda led Sabina to a shuttle that took her to her accommodation in Hansstadt.

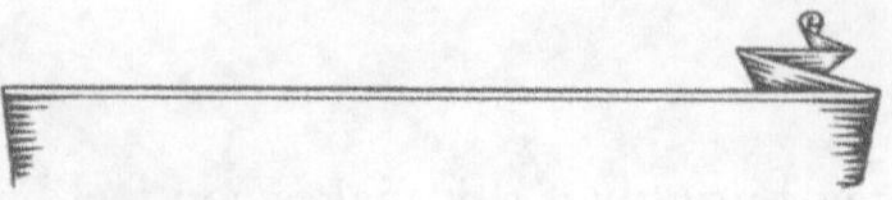

Chapter 282: "You're Destroying the Galaxy that We Seek to Dominate."

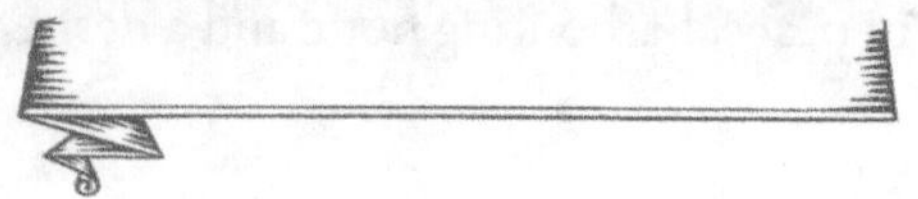

Melchior felt agitated. His brother was dead, and he had lost control of his empire. All that remained was his large, but beatable, army. On top of things, it seemed like the Milky Way Galaxt was self-destructing. Every single day one or several star systems exploded. Every star that exploded sent out gamma-ray bursts with the potential to kill anything that they hit. If nothing changed, there wouldn't be anything left for him to conquer and dominate.

Melchior made his way to Rangda's new temple. It was a sight to behold. The Xenos had built it from the Dwarven gold on Goldonia. Large rubies symbolising blood covered the temple. In the temple towers, flames struck up like spectacular fire fountains. Melchior entered the building. He walked past some blood fountains, and he approached Rangda's throne. Rangda had ornamented the throne with severed heads, representing the races that she had conquered. Rangda didn't notice Melchior as she was busy torturing the unfortunate Keila Eisenstein. Rangda had kept Keila alive and had spent the last decade abusing and draining her of psionic energy.

Melchior shouted to Rangda:

- Rangda! What are you doing?

Rangda turned around and gave Melchior a dirty look:

- Is that the way to address your empress?
- Do not ever interrupt me when I am enjoying my time with Keila!

Melchior:

- I don't give a shit about Keila, but you're destroying the very galaxy, which we seek to dominate.

Melchior's attitude infuriated Rangda. She blasted him with a powerful psionic blast, which knocked him to the ground. The blast caused Melchior to bleed from all his cavities.

Rangda:

- Silence, you fool!

- I am not the one who is destroying the galaxy. It is that coward, the True Maker who doesn't dare to face me.

- But I will destroy her "Holy Prophet". As Sabina falls, the True Maker has no choice but to face me.

Melchior responded weakly:

- Forgive me, my empress. I never intended to anger you.

Rangda:

- I don't care. Crawl back to your soldiers. I am sure that they can patch you up. Do not return here unless I summon you!

After saying this, Rangda ran to her dungeons where she murdered some prisoners while she kept shouting: "Come out you coward, I will get you!"

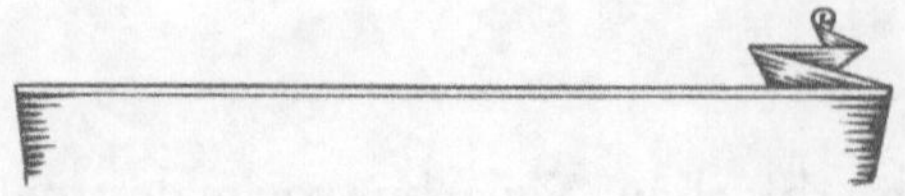

Chapter 283: I Am Ready.

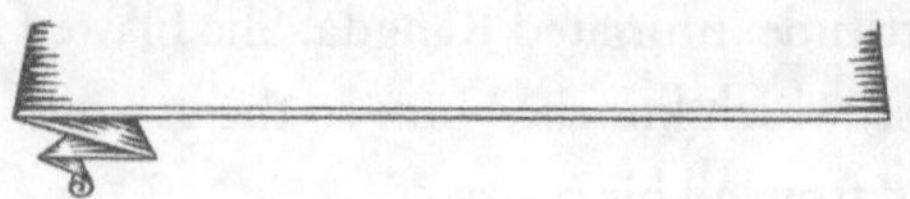

In July 2887 Sabina woke up in the middle of the night. She felt different but at peace. She felt like her spirit was about to leave her body. Was she dying? Sabina got out of bed and realised that her body was still carrying her without a hitch. Sabina realised what it was. She would turn 12 in a couple of days, and she would reach the age of the ancient adulthood ceremony. Her body was telling her that she was ready to face Rangda. Sabina left her room, and she walked over to the private bedroom of her hostess, Hilda Muller. Sabina studied Hilda for a while, realising that Hilda was having a nightmare. She put her palm on Hilda's temple, and Hilda calmed down.

Hilda woke up and looked at Sabina. It wasn't the girl she had gotten used to seeing. Instead, it was like seeing an angel appearing in front of her.

Hilda:

  - Sabina, what happened to you?

Sabina:

  - I am turning 12, and I am becoming an adult. I am ready to fulfil my destiny and face Rangda.

Hilda:

  - That's a great relief! Is there anything I can do to assist you?

Sabina:

- Yes. Tell your soldiers to clear a path for me to the portal at the Cheops pyramid. Tell your people that the age of darkness will soon be over.

Hilda:

- I can do that.

Sabina:

- You'd better hurry. Time is short, and I need to fulfil my destiny.

Hilda:

- Got it. I will assemble the full might of House Muller to help you at once!

Having said this, Hilda got up, and she hurried to contact her army to put everyone on full alert.

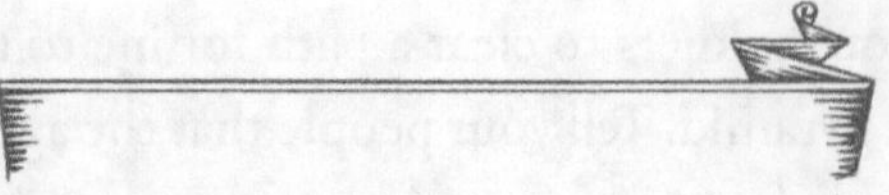

Chapter 284: Sabina Faces Rangda

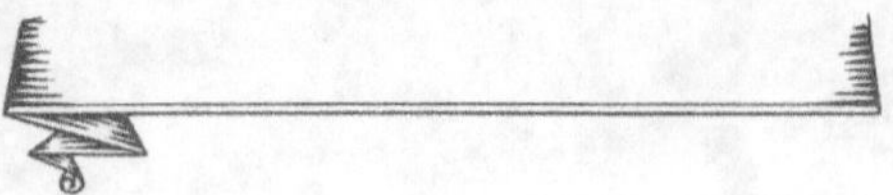

A week later, Sabina; Hilda and Metatron visited the military base that secured the portal at the Cheops Pyramid. Sabina double-checked the date. Today was her 12th birthday, and it was time to face the destroyer of the universe, Rangda. Sabina picked her clothes: a simple white dress, sandals and a walking stick. Hilda had offered her a high-technology battle armour, but Sabina had rejected the notion. The key to defeating Rangda lay in her mind, and in her faith, not in her technology. Using modern technology would weaken her spirituality, and it would be suicide to approach Rangda's hordes with force.

Sabina travelled in an open car towards the pyramid. Along the road, thousands of worshippers had lined up, all dressed in white clothes to honour her. They reached the perimeter to the pyramid, and the car drove to the base of the Cheops pyramid. Sabina, Hilda and Metatron got out of the car.

Sabina:

- This is it. My time has come.

Hilda:

- I wish that I could do more...

Sabina

- You have played your part. I couldn't have done any of this without your support.

- Now you must leave. Once I open the portal, the enemy might choose to invade.

Metatron:

- I am coming with you.

Sabina:

- Father, this isn't your fight.

Metatron:

- It doesn't matter. You are my daughter, and if you are the Chosen One, I will stand by you to the end.

Sabina:

- I cannot deny you that wish, father. Hilda, please return to your people. They need you.

Having said this, Sabina and Metatron started climbing the Cheops Pyramid. A myriad of drones filmed them, and broadcasted the event to population. As they reached the top, Sabina started chanting a verse in an ancient language. Energy in the form of white light flowed from her hands and powered up the portal. The portal lit up, bluer than ever.

Sabina:

- This is it. If you enter this portal, you'll see Keila one last time, but you'll never return to see Jasmine, Jordan or Melissa.

Metatron:

- So, will I die if I enter this portal?

Sabina:

- The only certainty in life is death. Melissa needs you; Jordan and Jasmine need their father. The only reason you are clinging on to me is the hope to see Keila again. But what you hope for will never be.

Hearing this made Metatron emotional, and he started crying:

- But you said you'd let me come with you. I want to stay by your side until the end.

Sabina:

- I am happy that you do father, but some sacrifices are not meant to be. Now sleep, father.

Sabina grabbed Metatron's hand. And she used her powers to put her father to sleep. After that, she entered the portal, and then she closed it from the other side.

Sabina walked towards the enormous golden temple that Rangda had built to honour herself. In front of the temple, Rangda had stationed a large army. The army attacked Sabina, but to no avail. A sphere of bright light, surrounded Sabina, and it stopped every attack that Rangda's minions threw at her. The sphere stopped bullets mid-air. Anyone who tried to attack Sabina from close range got pacified by her divine powers, and ended up bowing to her instead.

Sabina entered Rangda's temple. Rangda was sitting on her throne, and Melchior was sitting on a chair below her. Keila was also in the room, and she was locked her up in a psionic force-field. Sabina walked towards Rangda. When she was ten metres away, she spoke:

- Rangda Kaliankan! On behalf of the True Maker, I request that you surrender to me, and repent for your many crimes.

Rangda:

- Kaliankan, the daughter of Kalianka? So, your master told you to use my Zetan family name. To what purpose may I ask? I made it my life goal to exterminate the Zetans, and I have succeeded. The Zetans are no more.

Sabina:

- The Zetans and your mother still live on within you. I know what happened to your mother. But you misguided your anger. You can't hate an entire species for what one individual once did.

Rangda:

- Ah, joy. I realised a long time ago that vengeance was a stupid motivation. But I also understood something else about myself. That I enjoy increasing my own power and causing suffering towards others.

Sabina:

- Well, your reign of terror is over. You will yield to the power and the mercy of the True Maker, or she'll smite you.

Rangda:

- Ah, The True Maker. That snivelling coward sending a little girl, instead of facing me herself! This is my answer!

- Melchior!

Melchior:

- Yes, Empress Rangda.

Rangda:

- Slay that insolent girl and bring me her head!!

Melchior did as Rangda commanded, and he rushed towards Sabina with a drawn plasma-sword. When he was about to strike her, Sabina grabbed Melchior's hand and spoke:

> - Melchior, it is okay. By the powers of The True Maker, I forgive your sins and cleanse your soul. May you find the ability to forgive yourself.

The influx of light into Melchior's dark soul caused him great agony, and he fell to the ground screaming from pain. Inner conflict tore Melchior apart. After a few seconds, he found his resolve. He would kill Rangda, who had caused him to do all these evil things. Melchior lifted his sword and ran towards her, but he didn't get far. Rangda used the powers of the corrupted crystals to disintegrate Melchior's body.

Rangda scoffed at Sabina:

> - Ah! Bless. The pure Sabina Eisenstein, "The Chosen One", using her magic to drive a man insane causing his death. Are we that different after all?

Sabina:

> - I gave him a chance to return to the light. I couldn't affect how he would react. The True Maker gave us free will, after all.

Rangda:

> - A distinction without a difference. You knew exactly how he would react. Thus, you caused his death, regardless whether you'd admit it or not.

> - And now I will cause your death!

Sabina:

- I am protected by the light of the True Maker. There is nothing you can do to me. Your army couldn't touch me; your champion couldn't affect me. And you can't touch me either.

Rangda:

- True as that may be, the same doesn't apply to your poor old mother, Keila. It is time to wake her up so she can see her lost daughter!

Rangda blasted Keila with a psionic blast. This woke up the weak and old Keila from the suspended animation that she had been in. Rangda deactivated the force-field that surrounded Keila, and Keila collapsed to the floor.

Sabina was crying and said:

- Mother. I have come to save you.

Rangda:

- Yes. Keila, your dear old mother. Why don't you comfort her and tell her that everything is going to be okay?

Sabina didn't respond. Instead she ran towards her dying biological mother. When Sabina was close to Keila, Rangda blasted Keila with a psionic blast that caused Keila to bleed from every orifice in her body. Keila looked at Sabina with a terrified look, before passing out from the pain. Rangda laughed hysterically:

- Oh, your poor mother! Who would have thought that finally seeing you would cause her so much pain?

Sabina:

- You were the one causing her pain. Seeing me, ignited hope in her soul. Now she can die in peace.

Rangda:

- Oh, but she is not dying. I have perfected the art of torturing her. I will resuscitate her again and again. Only endless pain awaits your poor old mum in this timeless place.

Sabina:

- But why would you treat my mum so horribly? What did she ever do to you?

Rangda:

- Oh, little girl, you don't know me very well. I do it because I can, and because it amuses me. I have free will, after all! Hee-hee-hee!

Sabina lost her cool and yelled out:

- Rangda, you are an evil monster!! I will end you once and for all.

After saying this, Sabina smote Rangda with an intense flash of pure light. The blast was insanely powerful, and it scorched Rangda. Rangda fell, burning and screaming to the floor, and Sabina collapsed from exhaustion. Sabina crawled to her dying mother. Sabina held Keila's hand to ensure that her soul could move on to the afterlife, escaping from the evil curse that Rangda had cast on her. Sabina felt drained, but she also felt a sense of optimism. Had she fulfilled her destiny?

Deep despair struck Sabina, when she realised that she had failed to kill Rangda. Rangda arose, with third-degree burns all over her body. Rangda hissed towards Sabina:

- You pitiful girl. I defeated you like I defeated the Elves. The True Maker's light protected you, and you threw it away. How does it feel knowing that your death is approaching?

Sabina:

- I feel at peace knowing that my mother's soul has been able to move on. If I die because of my love for my mother, I might have failed, but at least I didn't fail for the wrong reasons.

Rangda hissed and spoke:

- Very well. Prepare to die!

Rangda rushed towards Sabina. Sabina tried to defend herself, but she stood no chance without her divine assistance. After a short fight, Sabina lay lifeless on the floor as Rangda tore her body to shreds. Rangda laughed diabolically and called out:

- True Maker. Your Chosen One has failed. Now face me, you coward!

A flash of bright light appeared and shook the foundation of the temple.

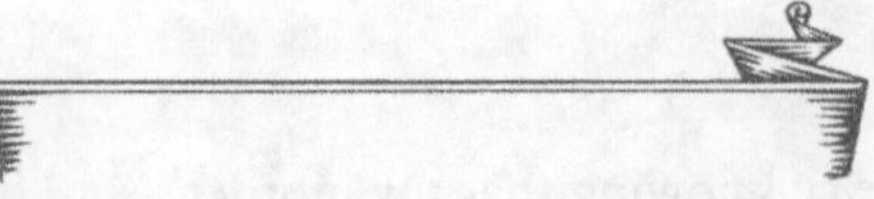

Chapter 285: The True Maker Destroys the Milky Way Galaxy

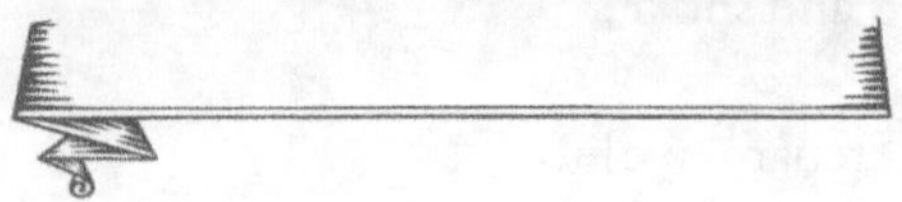

Rangda stared in disbelief. In front of her, was the mirage of her dead mother, Kalianka, accompanied by the spirit of the fallen Sabina. In shock, Rangda stuttered:

- Mother?!

The True Maker:

- Your mother was one of my septillion forms in this galaxy, and the one I found the most suitable to use communicating with you.

Rangda:

- I don't understand!

The True Maker:

- I am the creator of the universe, but I also am the universe. In this universe, I am everyone and no-one. That's why I don't have an ego and a body of my own.

Rangda:

- Bullshit. You sent that kid to fight me. You have your own agenda.

The True Maker:

- Harmony and balance. Although I am the universe, my celestial power can't regulate something as large as the universe. Thus, I divided my essence into Zeto crystals and spread them out. I placed seven crystals in each galaxy to keep the cosmos balanced and full of life.

- The unbalancing happened with the Zetans. The Zetans discovered the potential within the Zeto Crystals, which was the starting point for the abnormal development. "Intelligent life" as you call it, is not the natural state of the universe, as intelligent life always destroys the ecosystems that they live in.

- The vanity of the Zetans caused them to alter species in their image. The Zetans altered Humans, Xenos, Dwarves, Elves, Orcs and many other species. They are all unnatural creations, but in the grand scheme of things, insignificant.

- The real issue is you, Rangda. When you corrupted the Zeto Crystals, you disrupted the harmony of the Cosmos. When you corrupted the last Zeto Crystal in the Milky Way Galaxy, you destroyed the balance, and you doomed the galaxy.

Rangda:

- Thank you for exposing the truth. Now that I know that there are seven Zeto Crystals in each galaxy, I know that I can become even more powerful if I conquer all galaxies!

The True Maker:

- But you'll not. Because I will stop you.

Rangda:

- You fool. I am not scared of you. I killed your pawn, and I will kill you! Take this!

Rangda blasted the True Maker with the full force of her seven corrupted Zeto Crystals. This didn't affect The True Maker, as they were only seven out of billions of Zeto Crystals that existed in the universe. The True Maker realised that Rangda would never stop. She would have to sacrifice the Milky Way galaxy to save the universe.

The True Maker:

- I wish to say sorry to all living beings of the Milky Way Galaxy. I have chosen to cease your existence.

The True Maker released a gargantuan burst of energy that destroyed the Milky Way Galaxy.

After an extended hiatus, The True Maker studied what remained of the Milky Way. There was nothing but darkness and dead stars. "I'm still here", The True Maker heard a familiar voice and, she turned around. There she was, the spirit of Sabina, who was the sole survivor of the destroyed Milky Way Galaxy.

Chapter 286: Sabina Pleads the True Maker to Turn Back Time.

The True Maker heard the voice of Sabina and spoke:

- How can you still be around? How did you survive the blast that destroyed your galaxy? This is beyond my divine knowledge.

Sabina:

- Change your form to one more relatable to me, and I will explain. Please change to a young version of my mother, Keila Eisenstein.

The True Maker did as Sabina requested, and Sabina spoke again:

- I thought I failed when I lashed out against Rangda and lost your protection.

The True Maker:

- Yes, that was the fate that befell the Elves of Elvonia. You cannot misuse the Zeto Crystals to kill living beings.

Sabina:

- Yes. But as Rangda tore my body into shreds, I realised something. That I didn't feel any pain or fear. My death was a transition to my natural state. The state of a spirit.

- I also realised something else. That I was never at fault for using the power of light to smite Rangda. I was lashing out to save my mother from more suffering. It was an act of love.

The True Maker:

- Yes, but a reckless one at that. It forced me to destroy the entire galaxy to stop Rangda's evil from spreading throughout the universe.

Sabina:

- Yes, but what if it was inevitable? How would I ever defeat Rangda by being pure good? Melchior and the other villains were suffering from their evil deeds deep inside, but Rangda didn't experience those feelings.

The True Maker:

- Yes, you are right; it was inevitable. I foresaw it, but I mourned the loss of life that would follow if I confronted Rangda myself. I guess I put my 'hope' in you when everything else failed.

Sabina:

- But what if this is not the end?

The True Maker:

- What do you mean?

Sabina:

- Well, you have told me that you have reset universe many times and that you are trillions of years old...

The True Maker:

- I am not sure I follow you.

Sabina:

- What if, we could turn back time?

The True Maker:

- In theory, it's a good plan, but in practice, no. If we turn back time, we might save this galaxy, but we might condemn ten others. Even for me, the Almighty Creator of the universe, it's impossible to foresee the consequences of such an action.

Sabina:

- But if we settle for turning back time in this galaxy, we won't affect the other galaxies.

The True Maker:

- But I cannot reverse time in individual galaxies. They are all connected, and so are my time-reversing capabilities.

Sabina:

- But what if I can do it for you? I am a lesser spirit, and I would have a smaller scope for your abilities.

The True Maker:

- Hmm. It's a blatant violation of the physics of the universe. But I am the physics of the universe, and I am willing to give it a try. Enter my soul, Sabina.

Sabina entered the True Maker's soul, and it was an exhilarating and magical experience. She experienced memories of the septillions of life forms, which had lived throughout the history of the Milky Way. Sabina snapped out of it. She had a mission, and she would make sure that things turned out good this time.

The year 2868 came up in Sabina's mind. It was the year when Rangda escaped from her Zetan prison and set out on her evil quest. "Here goes nothing," Sabina thought. Sabina activated the time reversing capability. She turned back time to the year 2868, when her mother was 18 years old.

Chapter 287: Remembering an Old Friend

Rear Admiral Bjorn Muller was staring at the calendar in his office on the Phobos base. The date was the 12th of February 2868, and it triggered terrible memories. 18 years earlier, his best friend in exile, Mahmoud Rashid, had succumbed to the harsh living conditions on Mars. Mahmoud had been stripped him of his Terran citizenship, due to his love to Susanna, an Edenite woman.

The episode had shocked Bjorn. The fact that his friend had married a non-Terran woman against his families wishes, flabbergasted Bjorn. The harsh punishment of Mahmoud also surprised Bjorn. Mahmoud got dumped off on Mars without money or ability to sustain himself. Mahmoud's only crime was to fall in love with someone against his grandfather's wishes.

Losing Mahmoud had been hard for Bjorn. Despite coming from rivalling families, they had grown close, as they came from similar circumstances. Bjorn and Mahmoud had frosty relationships with their families, which had urged them to leave Earth and serve in the army. While they received high ranks in the Terran Council Security Forces, they knew why they were in the military. Their families wanted to keep them as far away as possible.

Bjorn had tried to keep his best friend alive throughout the decade that had followed. Bjorn couldn't support Mahmoud Rashid directly due to a Terran Council decree. So, Bjorn instructed the puppet president of The Olympus Republic to support Mahmoud and Susanna. Mahmoud and Susanna changed their family name to Susana's family name, Eisenstein, to blend in. After many years of marriage, Susanna became pregnant with Keila. Unfortunately, Susanna's pregnancy coincided with Mahmoud falling ill.

Mahmoud's sickness and death created a permanent scar in Bjorn Muller. The fact that Mahmoud's condition was treatable with Terran technology plagued Bjorn. He had failed his friend as he could not give Mahmoud the treatment he needed.

After Mahmoud's death, Bjorn lost interest in Susanna and Mahmoud's daughter, Keila. He instructed the puppet president to give them enough money to lead a good life, but apart from that, he played no part in their lives.

Chapter 288: Dreaming about Earth

Keila woke up with a smile. She had the same recurring dream that she had experienced a lot lately. In the vision, Keila was on Earth, together with her handsome prince and their beautiful children. She closed her eyes again, and the images continued. Mars was no longer a dry and cold dustbowl filled with poverty and suffering. Instead, the planet had turned into a paradise full of flora and fauna, where people lived in harmony and peace. Keila sighed. If only these dreams could come true!

Keila had grown up in a well-off home raised by her mother, Susanna. Her father had been from a prominent Terran bloodline who died before she was born. This had brought the advantage that she had a secret benefactor, ensuring that she would never go hungry. All in all, Keila's life in Pamshal was pretty good. Pamshal was a wealthy city-state and its massive city walls, as well as Pamshal's alliance with The Olympus Republic, kept the city safe.

Despite her young age, Keila had seen a lot of Earth. Her mother, Susanna, was an activist who smuggled supplies to help the starving regions of Mars. While appreciating the importance of her mother's work, Keila did not want to go in her footsteps. Instead, she wanted to move to Earth and live a good life there. Keila was turning 18 in a month, and she had looked into getting a Terran citizenship. If she got it, she would be able to leave Mars and live on humanity's beautiful home planet instead.

Susanna had shunned Keila's plans as unrealistic dreaming. The Terrans were very oppressive to Martians, and entry permits were rarely given out. Keila had ignored her mother's objections. She wanted to live the future that her visions showed her every night. She wanted to live on

Earth with Bjorn Muller, the prince charming that often popped up in her dreams.

Although Keila had never met Bjorn, she was confident that he was the one from her visions. Bjorn was a famous figure, so he featured often in the Terran and Martian news broadcasts. Bjorn was also the spitting image of the man from her visions and dreams. Although Bjorn was way too old for Keila, he had charm, charisma, looks, and wealth. So Bjorn was everything that Keila wanted in a man. Besides, Bjorn seemed healthy, and he was better looking than most Martians.

Keila made up her mind. When she turned 18, she would board a shuttle to the interplanetary transfer terminals orbiting Mars. From there, she would find a way to meet her prince charming!

Chapter 289: Another Round of Matchmaking

Bjorn Muller was back in Hansstadt. He was waiting for his father, Joachim Muller, in one of his father's many residences. This residence was a reconstruction of an 18th-century castle. Although Bjorn didn't understand why anyone would want to live in such an archaic building, it was nice to be home and see his family. Spending his time on a military base was not that stimulating, so Bjorn hoped that this could be his chance to leave the army and return home.

Joachim approached Bjorn and spoke.

- Welcome back, Bjorn. I suppose you understand why you are back this time?

Bjorn:

- Yes. I am summoned for another round of matchmaking. It's a shame you are so adamant on marrying me off for political reasons, instead of letting me look for 'the one' myself.

Joachim:

- Bjorn, we have been over this. You are way too old to be a bachelor. You are past your youth. I could overlook your addiction to prostitutes and drugs when you were younger, but not anymore. It's time to be more like your brother, Michael, and settle down with an obedient wife and children.

Bjorn:

- I suppose that you tell Michael that he needs to be ambitious and work hard, like Benjamin and I?

Joachim:

- Yes, but we are not here to talk about your brother's short-comings.

- I am giving you a chance to come back to Earth and get what you want. All that you need to do, is to marry a member of House White for political reasons.

Bjorn:

- But I already know who I want to marry. I have seen 'her' in my dreams. But I haven't found this woman that appears in my dreams yet.

Joachim slapped Bjorn, and replied.

- Enough of this silly talk! I don't care about your dreams about a woman you haven't even met. I need you to step up and produce an heir to the family empire. An official heir, born within wedlock!

Bjorn:

- Alright. I'll meet with her. I hope that she'll be less dull than the other ones!

Joachim:

- Dull? The other ones were genetically engineered pre-conception to be good future wives to you, and yet you turn them away.

- But I can guarantee you that you won't find Alicia White dull!

Bjorn:

- Alicia White?

Joachim:

- The daughter of John White and a perfect match to strengthen the Muller – White Alliance!

Bjorn:

- Why have I never heard about this woman before?

Joachim shrugged his shoulders and spoke:

- You have been orbiting Mars for the last decades and missed out on most of the official gatherings. Besides, Alicia is only 21 years old, and she rarely attends formal conventions.

Bjorn:

- Is it because she is an outcast, shunned by her own family, like I am?

Joachim:

- Yes.
- But like I said. I can guarantee that you won't find Alicia dull!

Bjorn:

- Very well. When will I meet this woman?

Joachim:

- You'll meet her tomorrow morning. If everything goes well, you will marry her tomorrow night!

Bjorn:

- What? How are you going to make it a formal affair in such a short timespan?

Joachim:

- Neither John White nor I want this wedding to be a formal affair.
- Now get your beauty treatments so you'll look good on your wedding day!

After this, a servant entered the room to lead Bjorn to his beauty therapy appointment.

Chapter 290: Not Exactly Love at First Sight!

Bjorn Muller woke up in the morning, and he didn't know what to feel. Getting married was his ticket back to a luxurious life on Earth. But what kind of cruel joke was his father playing on him? Bjorn understood the need to marry someone in House White for political reasons. But why in such a hurry and why was there so much hush-hush about his bride-to-be? Alicia White was the youngest daughter of John White, and yet Bjorn had never seen her. She was also a staggering 45 years younger than he was. While Bjorn could understand why a poor woman would marry someone older for money and status, he could not understand why Alicia wanted him.

Bjorn assumed that Alicia was in a similar situation as him. In that case, the marriage would be for show, and they would live their own individual lives. This arrangement suited Bjorn, and he wasn't even bothered if she turned out to be ugly, which was very likely.

Bjorn got dressed and he met up Joachim.

Joachim:

- Good morning, Bjorn.
- You look presentable for once! Excited for your wedding day?

Bjorn:

- About as excited as I am before a dental appointment! But it will be great to leave the army and get to enjoy my birthright.

Joachim:

- Glad you finally came to your senses and listened to my wishes.

- Anyways. Alicia is a very special woman, but I am sure that you'll get along, despite your 'differences'.

Bjorn:

- Despite our 'differences'?
- You are not exactly talking up my wife-to-be, how special is she?

Joachim:

- You'll be alright. Besides, from the bright side, you are getting away from the army!

Bjorn:

- Yes. Let's go meet this mysterious wife-to-be.

They walked to the grand dining hall of the mansion. Alicia White and John White were sitting by the end of the dining table. Bjorn and Joachim sat down opposite them, and joined them for breakfast. Joachim and John were busy talking, while Bjorn checked out Alicia. Alicia didn't look that bad, but Bjorn could tell that she was wearing a thick layer of makeup. This wasn't a good sign, as most Terran women had optimised genetics for good looks and should not need make-up. Bjorn reflected over why Alicia was wearing tinted contact lenses. If this was his bride to be, didn't he deserve to see her real appearance, without attempts at concealing it?

Bjorn decided to break the ice, and he tried talking to Alicia. It wasn't easy, as she kept covering her mouth with her hands every time she spoke. Furthermore, her voice sounded like she had received large quantities of sedatives.

Bjorn:

- So, Alicia, tell me about yourself?

Alicia:

- Uhm.... I am Alicia, daughter of John White.... I am 21 years old.

Bjorn:

- Okay, so what do you like to do in your spare time?

Alicia:

- Uhm... I like... anything that you want me to like...

Bjorn:

- So, you are the submissive type?

Alicia:

- Uhm... I can be if you know how to handle me.

- Excuse me, but I must take my leave. While the food you are providing looks delicious, it is not compatible with my special dietary needs...

John:

- Please, my darling Alicia, stay and get to know our hosts better, will you?

Alicia:

- No dad, I am not feeling well, and I need to rest for tonight!

John:

- Okay, my dear. You are free to go. I will meet with you shortly.

Alicia got up, and she reversed out of the room, keeping her front towards Bjorn and Joachim. After she had left John spoke.

- Alicia is feeling sick today, but she is usually a joy to deal
with. She is energetic, loyal, quirky and spontaneous. She is
my favourite child, and if you can love her as much as I do
Bjorn, I can guarantee you a long and happy marriage.

- I must look after Alicia now. She is nervous about the
evening as you can imagine. She is so young, and this is such a
big day.

After John had left the room, Bjorn turned towards his father:
Bjorn:

- What is the matter with that woman? Is she retarded? Why
is her father so eager to marry her off? She is only 21, there is
plenty of time for her.

Joachim:

- I have seen Alicia's IQ score. While she is not as intelligent as
you are, she is by no means stupid. Alicia's flaw is the same as
yours; her elevated sexual drive and degeneracy.

- Thus, while your initial connection was lacking, you will
complement each other well.

Bjorn:

- Sexual degeneracy? What did she do?

Joachim:

- Well, rumour has it that she is very pushy when it comes to convincing her servants to satisfy her sexual urges. We have had similar issues with you. Hence you are a good match!

Bjorn:

- I see. So, she is more than meets the eye? But it would have helped if she wasn't all covered up in that ugly make-up!

Joachim:

- It would also have helped if you weren't a drug-abusing sexual degenerate! But now things are the way they are!

Bjorn:

- Noted.
- Well, I better get ready for tonight.

Bjorn left the room, and he returned to his private quarters. Unbeknownst to Bjorn, John White and his father had conned him when it came to Alicia. John had sedated Alicia to hide her personality, as Alicia was mutant. Alicia was a failed experiment by House White's science-lab to co-mingle her Terran's DNA with that of a crocodile, a bull and a tiger. Alicia had applied a thick layer of make-up and inserted tinted lenses to hide her yellow predator eyes. Finally, John had told her to cover her mouth when she spoke to avoid showing her fangs. Alicia had reversed out of the room to make sure that Bjorn didn't see the small lump on her back, that was her tail!

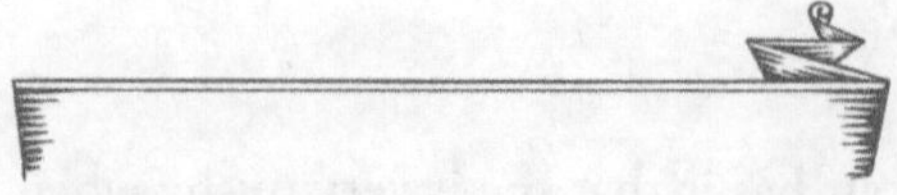

Chapter 291: A Failed Hunt.

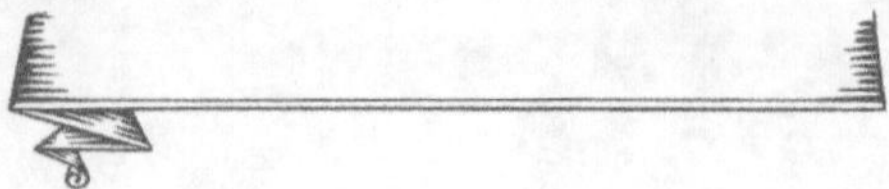

Alicia White woke up a few hours later, feeling very hungry and strange. Unbeknownst to her, her father had spiked her previous meal of raw meat with sedatives to make her calmer, and more suitable for marriage. John White planned to sedate and marry Alicia to someone influential. Whoever married her would then have to deal with her true self when the effects of the sedatives wore off.

Alicia looked out through the window. It was midday, and it was a beautiful day. A great opportunity to go for a forest walk and catch some prey for lunch.

Alicia remembered her father's instructions. That she should stay in the mansion and not go out on her own. The instructions annoyed her, and Alicia would not obey them! After all, Alicia was a good girl, and she had agreed to marry the man he had picked for her. So, she should have the opportunity to do what she loved the most, to catch and eat animals! The man that her father had picked for her, Bjorn Muller, was old but attractive, and Alicia purred in anticipation of the wedding night. But more than she wanted sex, she wanted to hunt and kill prey!

Alicia realised that she hadn't brought any weapons with her. It didn't matter, as it was more fun to kill her prey in a proper fight with her claws and fangs than it was using guns. Alicia snuck out in the woods that surrounded the mansion. It was a lovely day, and with her beastlike super senses, she soon found a suitable target, a medium-sized Red Deer Stag! Alicia snuck up on the animal, and she leapt at it. Alicia was ready to tear its arteries when she realised something, that she had blunted her claws for the damn wedding! Instead of splitting the animal's arteries with her razor-sharp claws, she only scratched it a bit. And now she had angered a hundred kilo's animal with large horns!

The stag charged at Alicia, and it hit her head. This led to a concussion and caused a big open wound on her cheek. The stag charged at her again. For a split second, Alicia thought of running away. But then she remembered that she was her father's warrior princess and as such, she did not run. Alicia leapt at the stag, and she ended up in a wrestling bout with the animal until she managed to bite its throat with her sharp teeth. Alicia joyfully drank the stag's warm blood, while it was still pumping.

Once Alicia had satisfied her bloodlust, she realised that her wounds wouldn't heal in time for the wedding. Her father wouldn't be happy, but what could she do, she was who she was.

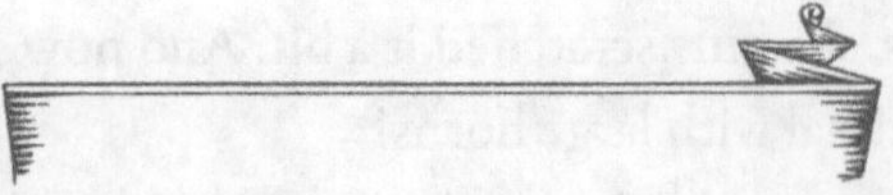

Chapter 292: A Runaway Groom

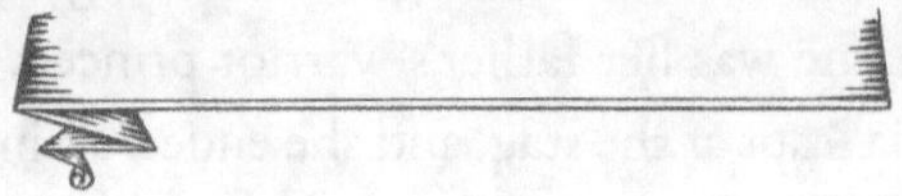

Bjorn Muller stood at the altar. He was restless, and his "love", or rather, ticket away from the army, was late. Bjorn could hear the wedding guests gossiping. It had already been a 15 minutes delay and what was Alicia doing?! Bjorn closed his eyes. Yet again, he saw the same vision that had been haunting him for the last years. The vision was of him and a beautiful woman and their daughters. Together they were bringing peace and prosperity to the solar system and ending the tyranny. Bjorn was not a do-gooder, but somewhere within him laid an urge to change for the better, to repent, and to correct past shortcomings.

But who was this mystery woman that kept appearing in his dreams? She was not Alicia; of that, he was certain. So, what would he do? Would he settle for Alicia, his ticket away from the army? Bjorn needed to get away from the military. Bjorn had seen so much suffering and so many atrocities, during his years of service.

Bjorn wanted a comfortable life like his relatives had, and Alicia was his ticket to that life. But if he settled for Alicia, he would never find the woman from his dreams, the one who could bring him true happiness.

Bjorn heard the door open, and he turned around. Alicia and her father entered the room. What had happened to her cheek? And why were her eyes glowing yellow? Alicia smiled at him, and he could see that she had sharp fangs, instead of regular teeth. Alicia approached Bjorn.

Bjorn stared at her in disbelief and spoke.

- Alicia, what happened to you?

Alicia:

- I had a hunting accident. A staghorn pierced my cheek. But at least I got the bastard in the end!

Bjorn:

- Hunting accident? How can stag's horn pierce your cheek when you are hunting deer? They run away from you if you miss the shot!

Alicia:

- It is a lot more fun, killing the prey with your bare hands.

Bjorn:

- That's insane! And what is the deal with the glowing yellow eyes and the fangs? This is a wedding, not a Halloween party!

Alicia:

- That is my real looks.

- During our breakfast meeting, I wore makeup and tinted lenses. But then I woke up, and I realised that my real looks make me who I am. It makes me unique, and it makes me beautiful!

Bjorn was lost for words. He would have settled for the caked-up woman that he had met for breakfast. It would have been worth it to get out of the army. But the absolute freak in front of him was too much. Bjorn would rather stay in the army rather than spending the rest of his life with such a creature! Lost for words, Bjorn decided to make a run for it. "Fuck this, I am out!" Bjorn yelled, and then he ran as fast as he could away from the wedding.

The aftermath of the abandoned wedding was that Bjorn returned to his post as Rear-Admiral on the Phobos base. Meanwhile, John White realised that he couldn't marry Alicia for political gains. Thus, he opted to enrol her into House White Special Operations, where she excelled. Unfortunately, Alicia's tenure transformed her from a naïve huntress to a mass-murdering psychopath.

Chapter 293: Au Revoir, Red Planet.

Keila was on a shuttle to the closest interplanetary passenger terminal orbiting Mars. Her ticket stated that she was heading for the underwater colonies on the Europa moon, but that wasn't the actual story. Instead, Keila was heading to Europe on Earth, to Hansstadt to be exact. Keila's visions had told her that she would meet her prince charming there, and together they would reform the solar system for the better. It was a risky move, as Martians were not allowed to travel Earth. If the border control officer caught her, they could send her to the infamous Kaguya Detention Centre on the Moon. Fortunately, Keila looked like a Terran rather than a Martian, so there was a chance that she would get through unnoticed.

It was peacetime, and there was no passport control to get on the ship to Earth. Keila thought that she was in the clear when she had found an untaken cabin for the one-week trip to Earth. As it turned out, she was mistaken. The reason there was no passport control was to test people's willingness to follow the law, something Keila had overlooked. As the terminal was full of security cameras, border officials knew that she had entered a spaceship heading for Earth. The border officials detained Keila and a few others. The guards took Keila to an interrogation room.

Security Officer:

- Miss Eisenstein, why were you on a vessel set to travel to Earth? You are not allowed to travel to Earth without special permission. Are you aware of the punishments associated with going to Earth illegally?

Keila:

- I bought a ticket for Europe, and I am travelling to Europe. I don't see the problem. If I wasn't allowed to travel to Europe, why sell me a ticket there in the first place?

Security Officer:

- Your ticket is for the Europa Moon orbiting Jupiter, not Europe on Earth. Don't play games with us, miss Eisenstein!

Keila:

- But I am a half Terran. My father was a prominent Terran, Mahmoud Rashid. Doesn't that count for something?

Security Officer:

- Your kinship with Mahmoud Rashid doesn't matter. You are not a Terran citizen, and you have boarded a spacecraft without permission.

- We will detain you here while we establish your background to assess your threat level. If we consider you to be safe, we'll transport you back to Mars and ban you from interplanetary travel for 5 years. If we assess you to be dangerous, we'll send you to the Kaguya Fetention Centre. Pray to your Martian gods that we don't consider you to be a threat!

The security officer left, and Keila was stuck in the interrogation room. What a mess she was in. Where was her knight in shining armour, now that she needed him?!

Chapter 294: An Interesting Prisoner Report

Bjorn Muller was back in his office on the Phobos base. He felt depressed. Bjorn hated everything about his job, orbiting and supervising the cold red desert below him. Now that he had eloped from his arranged marriage, he was unlikely to go back back to Earth anytime soon. Bjorn considered quitting the army, against his father's wishes. He didn't need his family's wealth, he could get a small cottage in the Alps, spending his time mountaineering and writing poetry. Bjorn would have to quit his sex and substance abuse, and he would age quickly if he lost access to his family's wealth and DNA regeneration therapies. But on the flip side, he would find peace at last. Bjorn closed his eyes, and he visualised the concept of finding inner peace!

Bjorn opened his eyes and fear struck him. If he went against his family's wishes, they would expose him to the same fate that befell Mahmoud Rashid. Being a famous Terran Rear Admiral, Bjorn wouldn't last long on Mars, and the best he could hope for in that scenario was a swift death. Bjorn bit his lip, and he felt resignation to his predicament. Captain Adal Schneider entered Bjorn's office.

Adal:

- Greetings, Bjorn. Here is the list of illegal Martian migrants that have tried to go to Earth in the last week. The list also states which prisoners that we will send to the Kaguya Detention Centre, and which prisoners we will send back to Mars.

Bjorn:

- I know what the list says! It's the same damn lists every week, and my answer is still the same. Follow the recommendations set out by the immigration security officers. I don't like reading these boring lists!

Adal:

- Yes, sir. This week, however, there is something that might interest you. One of the prisoners is Keila Eisenstein, daughter of your late friend, Mahmoud Rashid.

Bjorn:

- Oh! That is interesting! Thank you for sifting through the reports for me. Now bring up Keila's file.

Bjorn looked at Keila's file. What stunned him the most was how familiar she looked. It was as if he knew her, but as far as Bjorn could tell, they had never met. The files summary read:

"Medium to High Threat Level. Miss Eisenstein is obstinate and adamant that she has the right to go to Earth due to her heritage. Observation of Keila has also revealed that she seems to experience seizures and hallucinations. The recommended course of action is to lock her up on the Kaguya Detention Centre for further observation."

Bjorn put down the file and spoke:

- Come with me Adal, I'll better meet with this woman myself.

Having said this, Bjorn and Adal left the office, and they took a shuttle to the Interplanetary passenger terminal.

Chapter 295: Love and Guilt.

20 minutes later, Bjorn and Adal arrived at the interplanetary passenger terminal. Bjorn sent his bodyguards and Adal on a lunch break, as he wanted to talk to Keila himself. He also deactivated the security camera in the room before entering. Bjorn entered the room and saw Keila.

Bjorn realised that Keila was the woman from his dreams. But how was this possible? And why did he meet his supposed future wife, while she was being locked up like a criminal? Bjorn's head spun as he sat down opposite to Keila. Before he had the time to talk, Keila spoke.

- You are Bjorn Muller, aren't you? So, it was really you! I have seen you in a lot of my dreams. Together, we shall bring peace, prosperity and equality to the solar system.

Bjorn was struggling for words. How could Keila have the exact same dreams as him? He managed to maintain a professional approach.
Bjorn:

- Keila Eisenstein, we detained you because you tried to travel to Earth illegally. What's your position on the accusation?

Keila:

- I am guilty.

Bjorn:

- Are you aware that the penalty for illegal travel, ranges from a five-year travel ban to indefinite detention at The Kaguya Detention Centre?

Keila:

- Yes, I am aware of that.

Bjorn:

- So, why did you do it?

Keila:

- Because I needed to meet you. Together we can help the downtrodden and set things right.

Keila's words triggered Bjorn's emotions, but he tried hard to not show it:

- You could have requested an audience with me.

Keila:

- Yes, but do you grant audiences to average Martian citizens?

Bjorn:

- Of course not. But I don't interrogate illegal aliens either. So, you were fortunate.

Keila:

- Yet, here we are.

Bjorn:

- Yes... Here we are.

- If you excuse me, I need to discuss your situation with my colleagues.

Keila sighed and replied:

- Okay, I am not going anywhere.

Bjorn got out of the interrogation room. He was panicking and hyperventilating. Confusion blurred his mind, and he did not know what to do. How could the woman from his dreams be the daughter of his late friend, Mahmoud Rashid? How could Keila have the exact same visions as he had? And how was he going to act? Bjorn had three options:

1. To follow his subordinate's recommendation and condemn Keila to detention at the horrible Kaguya Detention Centre.
2. To show leniency and send Keila back to Mars with a five-year travel ban.
3. To risk everything for the woman of his dreams. To run away with her, like his friend Mahmoud Rashid had done in the past. Things had not ended well for Mahmoud, and Bjorn believed that his grandfather, Hans Muller, would act the same way against him.

Crippled by his predicament, Bjorn went to a bar and started drinking. Meanwhile, Rangda was studying Bjorn from the Divine Dimension. Rangda had recently dug herself out from her Zetan prison cell.

Rangda knew that Bjorn's and Keila's premonitions came from Brahma, her former Zetan lover. Brahma wanted Bjorn and Keila to fall in love and have plenty of descendants. Rangda didn't like Brahma's plan and she wanted to ruin his divine intervention. Rangda would give Bjorn fourth option; an option she had foreseen would cause a chain reaction of events that would aid her cause. If Bjorn kidnapped Keila, and used her as his sex slave, he could satisfy his sexual desires without worrying about his father's reaction. Rangda planned to help Keila escaping the sex slavery and fill her mind with vengeance. In Rangda's plan, Keila would cause a massive violent uprising against the Terran Council.

Rangda tried to connect with Bjorn's mind, to intercede with his soul. But she couldn't reach him. How could this be? Bjorn had plenty of Zetan DNA, and given that he was a human, he should be easy to influence. Rangda tried again and again to connect but to no avail. On the fifth attempt, a silhouette of Sabina, garbed in a white robe, appeared and spoke. "You shall not corrupt this man's soul, Rangda. I bid you goodnight." After that, Sabina knocked Rangda unconscious with a psionic blast.

After Sabina's intervention, Bjorn's mind reached clarity, and he felt no fear anymore. He would stand up for the one he loved and had dreamt about. He walked into the interrogation room, and he shocked Adal, as he unchained Keila and spoke. "I'm sorry for the treatment that you have received, Keila. I will escort you to Earth. I will take your hand if you wish to marry me."

Flabbergasted, Adal and the guards watched Bjorn escort Keila to the shuttle that would take them back to his command ship.

Chapter 296: Bjorn and Keila arrive at Europeum Tower.

Joachim Muller was sitting in the CEO's office of the Europeum Tower. Joachim's office was a few levels below the chairman's penthouse, which belonged to his father, Hans Muller. Joachim resented his father. Despite Joachim being over 120 years old, Hans treated him like an ignorant child, as an errand boy.

Joachim feared that Hans might be correct about his lack of ability. Joachim saw no talent or skill in his own three sons, and there was a possibility that he was equally useless. The feeling of inadequacy had tormented Joachim for most of his life. It had started on a Terran Council meeting back in 2785 when Joachim had suggested that the Terran Council should focus on helping the Martians. This suggestion had severed ties with everyone in Joachim's family. After a few decades of bullying, Joachim was a broken man, who blamed the Martians for all his troubles. Hans treatment had converted Joachim from being an advocate for Martian rights to one of the worst oppressors.

Joachim looked at a picture of Bjorn and sighed. What we would he do with his eldest son? Joachim meant for Bjorn to succeed him one day, but Bjorn had turned out to be such an abject failure. When Bjorn was born, House Muller scientists had described Bjorn's genes as perfect. 66 years later, the 'perfect' specimen Bjorn was a whore-mongering drug addict, who was an incompetent Rear-Admiral. Joachim sighed. Bjorn had humiliated House White when he ran away from Alicia at the altar and it would take ages to repair the damage that Bjorn had caused.

Joachim had a sip of coffee, looked up, and speaking of the devil; Bjorn had arrived with an unknown woman in tow. Joachim spat out his coffee in shock. Why had Bjorn come all the way from Mars unannounced? Joachim was about to find out as Bjorn started to speak.

- Father, I realised that you were right. It is time for me to settle down and to get married. Meet my future wife, Miss Keila Eisenstein.

Joachim stared at Bjorn in amazement and disbelief. This was too much even by Bjorn's standards. Showing up unannounced and declaring that he wanted to marry an unknown woman, who appeared to be a Martian! Eventually, Joachim spoke.

- Marriage? What are you talking about, Bjorn? You are a high-ranking member of the solar system's most prominent family. You can't marry someone on a whim! Who is this woman? She looks like a Martian!

Joachim scowled at Bjorn with resentment. Bjorn was going to answer him, but Keila beat him to it:

- Mr Muller, while my origin shouldn't matter as we are all humans, I will answer your question. I was born on Mars, but my parents were not Martians. My father was the prominent Terran, Mahmoud Rashid, and my mother was an Edenite woman named Susanna Eisenstein.

Joachim:

- You better learn some manners around here! Give me a good reason why I should let my son marry you instead of shipping you off to the Kaguya Detention Centre.

Keila:

- Because we both want the same thing. I know about your youth, Joachim. I know how you once wanted peace and equality in the solar system. It's time to pursue that goal now.

Joachim freaked out when he heard Keila say these words. How could she know about his youthful indiscretions, almost 80 years earlier? The Terran Council controlled all the media in the solar system, this episode should have been a well-kept secret.

Joachim acted decisively to hide his weakness. He pressed a button under his desk to alert security. A short while later, the guards arrived. Joachim corrected his tie and spoke:

- Guards, arrest my son and this insolent Martian woman! Put Bjorn under house arrest and transfer Miss Eisenstein to the Kaguya Detention Centre!

Bjorn:

- Please, father, don't do this. I love her!

Joachim walked up to Bjorn and slapped him. Then he spoke:

- Love? You do this to humiliate me.

Keila shouted at Joachim as the guards dragged her out.:

- Joachim! You are making a great mistake. The union of Bjorn and I is the will of the True Maker.

Joachim:

- Then have him smite me, you religious fool!

When the guards had dragged Keila away, Joachim assaulted Bjorn, with a flurry of kicks and punches.

Once Joachim had ended his assault, the guards helped the injured Bjorn to a medical ward. Joachim remained alone in his office to wallow in his bitterness and hatred.

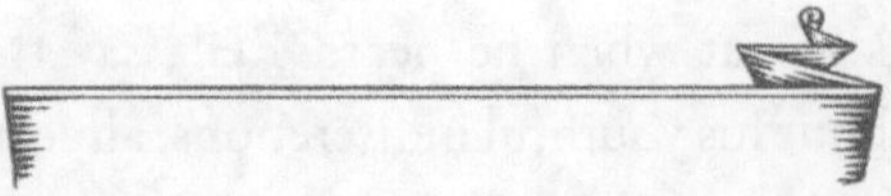

Chapter 297: A Guilt-Ridden Epiphany.

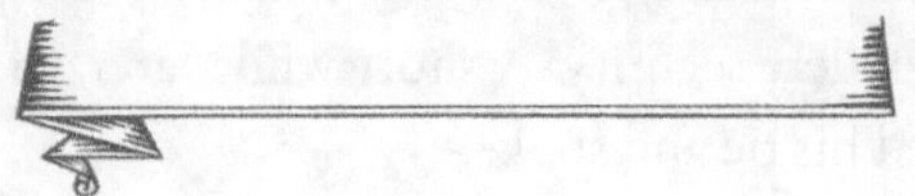

Joachim Muller was lying sleepless, getting flashbacks from his tortured youth. The crucial mistake to invite his dear friend Agnes Bojaxhiu to speak at the Terran Council meeting, back in 2785, had cost him everything. Agnes' tirade had infuriated the rest of the Terran Council. Joachim's father, Hans Muller, had ordered for Joachim to be "re-educated," i.e. tortured and indoctrinated.

After many months of psychological torture, Hans gave Joachim a test to secure his release. Joachim had to kill a dozen of chained Martian prisoners with his bare hands if he wanted to achieve his freedom. Among the prisoners were women and children, but Joachim was so desperate for his torture to end, that he complied with everything.

A gruelling 30 minutes later, Joachim had finished with his task. The Martian prisoners lay dead in the room, and Joachim was blood-soaked and psychologically scarred. After completion, Hans walked up to him and congratulated him upon passing his test. Joachim had asked Hans why they had murdered the prisoners. Hans had answered that the prisoners were innocent, but their deaths were necessary to punish Joachim.

Joachim got up. Why was he thinking about his youth now? It happened so many years ago. He realised that it was because he had treated Bjorn as bad as his father had treated him.

The ethereal mirage of Sabina materialised in front of Joachim. The illusion was the spitting image of Keila Eisenstein, the love interest of his son. Fumbling in fear, Joachim stepped back and fell over. Sabina whispered gently to Joachim.

- Do not fear, Joachim. I am here to help you do the right thing.

Joachim stuttered back:

- Keila? is that you? What is happening!

Sabina:

- I am Keila's daughter, Sabina. I'm speaking to you from the future, by the powers granted by the True Maker.

Joachim:

- What are you talking about? Did someone drug me? Why am I hallucinating?

Sabina:

- Humans will always fear what they do not understand. Realise this! You can either allow the love between Keila and Bjorn to change destiny and build a more harmonious solar system. Or you can stop them, which will lead to the downfall of your entire species and the rest of the Milky Way Galaxy.

- The choice is yours. But remember, darkness is coming.

Sabina granted Joachim a vision of Rangda and the Xenos. After that, she broke the connection with Joachim, leaving him dumbfounded on the floor. Joachim did not understand what had happened, but he did know one thing. He needed to see his father and set things right!

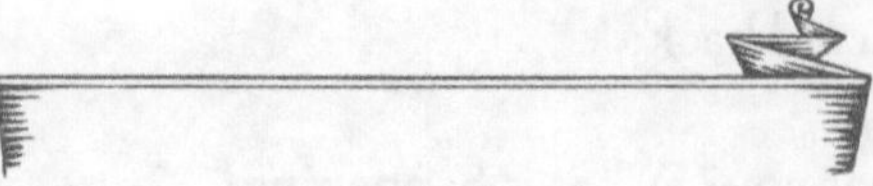

Chapter 298: The End of Hans Muller's Tyranny.

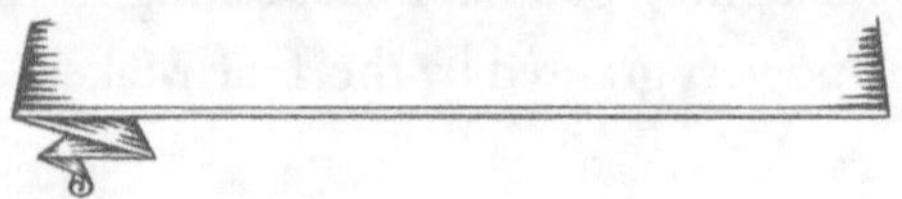

An hour later, the aging Hans Muller, sat at his desk with several bodyguards' present. Joachim had shocked Hans when called him in the middle of the night and required an urgent meeting. The two leaders of House Muller hardly spoke to each other, and when they did, it was always about business matters, with other people present.

Hans disliked Joachim, and he never spent time with him alone. Hans knew that the treatment he had exposed Joachim to would cause a scar between them that would never heal. But what other options did Hans have, being the rightful leader of House Muller and the Terran Council? He couldn't endorse his son's farfetched demands about equality on Mars. Hans couldn't tear down everything his ancestors had stood for in the last 500 years. That was out of the question!

Hans had loved Joachim back then, but things had to be the way they were. Breaking Joachim's rebellious attitude was his only option.

Hans watched the lift as it opened. Hans spotted his son, Joachim, his useless grandson Bjorn, and a Martian who could only be Keila Eisenstein! Hans was uncertain how to react, but he did not want to show weakness. Hans spoke with a commanding and stern voice as he had done during his entire almost 160-years long life.

- What is the meaning of this? A little happy family reunion? I don't allow Martian filth on this level!

Joachim spoke back with a ferocity that shocked Hans:

- This Martian woman has a name. Her name is Keila Eisenstein, and she is a prophet sent by the True Maker to end the hatred and mistrust that have kept humankind divided for too long.

Hans:

- The True Maker? Who gives a fuck about that religion!

- And didn't you order the deportation of this Martian convict less than 12 hours ago?

- You know what? Screw this. I will deal with her myself. Permanently!

After saying this, Hans pulled up a pistol that he had hidden under his desk. He took aim and fired the gun in Keila's direction, but due to divine intervention, the bullet missed. Instead, the bullet ricocheted and hit Hans Muller in the eye, severely wounding him in the process. One of the guards ran up to the injured Hans to stop the bleeding, but Joachim told him off:

- Stop it. As you can see, Hans has lost his mind, firing a pistol against his own family members.

- Dying by his own hand is a well-deserved fate for a man like him.

Since Hans was unconscious, and no-one wanted to argue with Joachim, Hans bled out in his own office, dying by his own hand. Thus, Joachim finally got his revenge on his abusive father and became the leader of his faction.

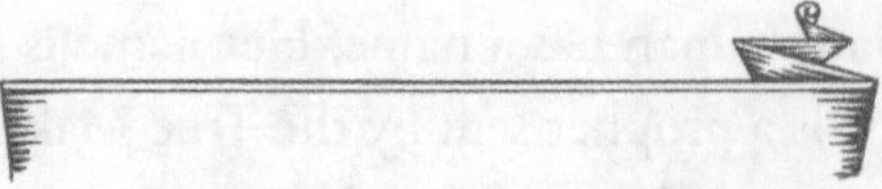

Chapter 299: Joachim Muller Makes New Plans

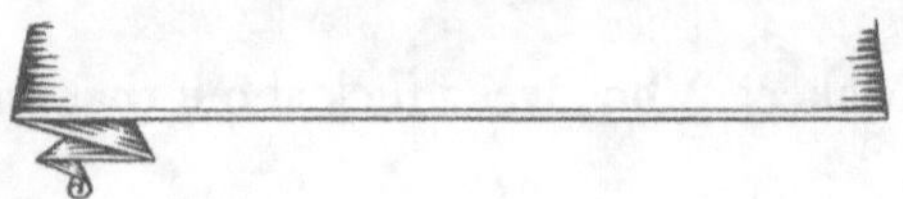

A few weeks later, Joachim had buried Hans Muller, and he became the chairman of House Muller. On Joachim's request, the funeral was a private affair. Joachim didn't want the details regarding Hans' death to become public. Neither did he want to explain why he had refused to revive Hans.

After Joachim had finished with the formalities, he met with Bjorn and Keila in his office.

Joachim:

- Dear Bjorn, my son, and Keila, my daughter-in-law to be. Sorry for being busy the last few weeks. But as you can appreciate, the death of my father has caused upheaval within House Muller.

Keila:

- That is okay, Chairman Muller; we understand that you are a busy man.

Joachim:

- Yes, but now that I am the Chairman of House Muller, I have resources to help you.

Bjorn:

- Great. Are these House Muller resources, or help from the entire Terran Council?

Joachim:

- Only secret House Muller resources, I am afraid. While I know what threat Rangda poses to us, the other factions don't know. I don't dare to risk my credibility by seeming insane to the others.

- If you want a better world, I need to change the Terran Council from within. Seeming insane wouldn't help us.

Bjorn:

- So, what help can we expect?

Joachim:

- Well, there is a portal to the Divine Dimension located in House Rashid territory. It's hidden inside the Cheops Pyramid, and the Rashid's are not exactly our friends. I guess I could send a few special operations soldiers posing as regular bodyguards.

Bjorn:

- Just a few? But we will be up against a dangerous monster. We need to end her life before she causes this apocalyptic catastrophe.

Joachim:

- That is why I am sending another important person, a very capable one, with her own bodyguards.

Bjorn:

- Dad...? You didn't?!

Joachim:

- Well, actually, I did. Keila, meet Alicia White.

Joachim flipped a switch, and the door opened. Alicia entered the room wearing a full combat outfit, smiling a crazed and witty smile, licking her lips and staring at Keila:

- So, this is the woman that Bjorn chose instead of me. What a beauty!

Keila stared at Alicia in disbelief, she had never seen anyone like Alicia. With fangs of a wolf, razor-sharp tiger claws and glowing yellow eyes of a crocodile, Alicia was a sight to behold. While she wasn't pretty, she was most definitely unique. Keila spoke:

- So, how do you guys know each other?

Alicia:

- Our father's betrothed us in an arranged marriage. Unfortunately, a minor hiccup caused us to miss the wedding night.

- I have heard, that you want to open a portal, and fight an evil demon queen in another dimension. And I thought I was the crazy one! Yeah!

Bjorn:

- Father! Why did you bring Alicia here?

Joachim:

- I told you already. I can't send you an army to escort you into House Rashid territory.

- Alicia is the best warrior there is, and besides, she provides an excellent cover-up story for your visit to Rashidium. You'll need to activate four portals, spread across the world, to travel to the Divine Dimension.

Bjorn:

- And what is your cover story?

Joachim:

- The cover is that you you have decided to travel the world together, to get to know each other after the failed arranged marriage.

Keila:

- But Bjorn and I love each other. Why do you want to break us apart?

Joachim:

- You won't be apart. You'll be posing as one of Bjorn's bodyguards. It doesn't make sense to make Alicia, the daughter of John White, appear to be a bodyguard.

- What you do at night, when no-one is watching, is none of my concern.

Bjorn:

- My father is right. It will take us weeks to travel the world and clear the paths to the activation switches. Making it look like a honeymoon is the best way to divert attention from what we are doing.

Keila:

- I don't like this!

Bjorn:

- Neither do I. But sometimes you must look past your own feelings and focus on the greater good. The future of mankind is dependent on our success.

Keila:

- I guess.

Joachim:

- Great then we are all sorted. Sabina has spoken to me, and she ordered that you head to the Sun Pyramid in Central America.

- Jurgen!

Jurgen the bodyguard:

- Yes, sir.

Joachim:

- Show Miss Eisenstein to our armoury and commission her with House Muller bodyguard uniforms and equipment. Make sure to finalise her employment details in our system. I have already given executive permission to allow this Martian to work with our military.

Jurgen:

- Yes, sir. Come with me, Miss Eisenstein.

After that, Keila followed Jurgen to the armoury, trying out body armours and getting weapons training. As Keila weighed the pistol in her hand, she reflected over how familiar the setting was. She remembered training with weapons and wearing body armour, and yet she had never been in the army before.

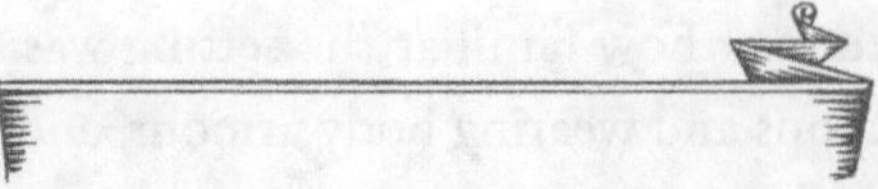

Chapter 300: Jealousy in Central America.

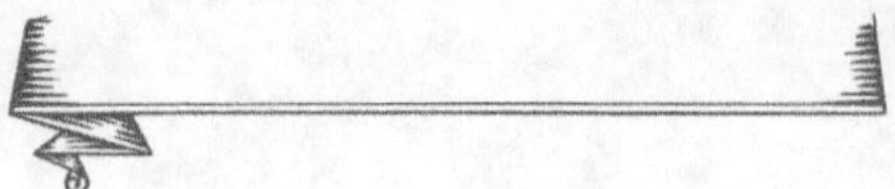

Keila, Jurgen and a few other House Muller operatives were digging in the Sun Pyramid in Mexico. They needed to clear a path to the activation switch. It was tiring work, and they weren't used to such hard labour. Because of the secrecy of the mission, they hadn't brought robots to do the digging for them, so they had to clear the path themselves.

They needed to keep the path to the chamber clear so that they could move quickly. They needed to flip the activation switches at four different locations at noon local time. The only way to do so was to travel fast between the locations. While Bjorn had suggested that they could station one person at each site to activate the switches at local noontime, this wasn't an option. Keila was the only one who could understand the switches, due to her unique genetic makeup.

Bjorn entered the tunnels and spoke:

- Alicia and I have been invited to House Bolivar's fundraising dinner. Keila and Melanie, I need the two of you to come with us as our personal bodyguards.

Keila:

- But why me? And what do I need to do?

Bjorn:

- I will bring you and Melanie to be my bodyguards. Jurgen and others are not very presentable for a fancy fundraising event.

- As for your job, stay in the background and don't say much. I don't expect any threats at the event, and House Bolivar has their own security.

Keila:

- Okay. And you'll be posing with Alicia and speak about your engagement to the press?

Bjorn:

- Yes. We agreed this was the only way. There must be a legitimate reason for me to spend all this time around the pyramids. A reconciliation tour, where we are talking about our love for ancient buildings is a reason that everyone will accept.

Keila:

- I don't like it. It should be you and I together.

Bjorn:

- Look. My father was going to send you to a detention centre on the Moon when he first met you. Although he cannot accept you as my partner, this is a lot better than detention.

Keila:

- You are right. Let's go.

A while later, Keila, Melanie, Bjorn and Alicia arrived at the event centre where the fundraising dinner took place. The venue was beautiful, Bjorn was dashing, and Keila was head over heels for him. It was everything that she had ever wanted. Except that she wasn't his date for the event, she was his bodyguard. Keila felt bursting with jealousy, but there was nothing that she could do. Besides, if her visions were correct, there were more pressing matters on stake than her love life. She needed to stop Rangda, before the universe was in grave danger.

Keila watched Bjorn and Alicia speaking to the press about their renewed engagement. Keila reflected that whoever had done Alicia's makeup had done a fantastic job at hiding her beastly features. Alicia wore contacts to conceal her yellow eyes, she had retracted her claws, and her dress hid her tiny tail. Wearing the makeup, Alicia was a beautiful young woman, unlike the beast Keila had got used to seeing.

A reporter interrupted Keila.

- Wow, you are an exotic one!

Keila:

- I beg your pardon?

Reporter:

- A half Martian, employed by House Muller, as a personal bodyguard to Bjorn Muller. What are the odds?

Keila:

- I don't know. I don't calculate odds. I do my job.

Reporter:

- There is a rumour that your Terran father was Mahmoud Rashid. He was a prominent Terran that Ibrahim Rashid expelled. Do you have any comment on this?

Keila:

- No. My employment contract doesn't allow me to comment on politics.

Reporter:

- But this wasn't a question about politics.

Bjorn noticed Keila's predicament, and he intervened:

- Please don't disturb my bodyguards. They have an essential job to do.

Reporter:

- But this bodyguard, wow! She is a half-Martian. How does that fit in with House Muller's racial policies?

Bjorn:

- My father, Joachim, has relaxed our racial policies after the death of Hans Muller.

- Miss Keila Eisenstein is an exceptional bodyguard who has saved my life on several occasions.

Reporter:

- What about Miss Eisenstein's family ties with House Rashid?

Bjorn:

- Miss Eisenstein's father was my good friend, Mahmoud Rashid. But House Rashid had expelled him before he fathered Keila.

- Now we must proceed to the gala dinner. No more questions!

Bjorn grabbed Keila by the arm, and they entered the event centre; far away from the prying eyes of the press. Once they were in a secluded room, Keila spoke with an agitated voice:

- Why didn't you mention that you knew my father?

Bjorn:

- I didn't know how to bring it up. How do you bring up some-one's long-dead dad when you first meet them?

Keila:

- I never knew my father. How was he?

Bjorn:

- Mahmoud Rashid was energetic. He was an idealist that went his own way and believed more in love than anything else. That's why he ran off with your mum, Susanna, against the wishes of his grandfather, Ibrahim Rashid.

- But he never knew that he would get banished from Earth. I helped him and your mother with money, but there wasn't much else I could do.

Keila:

- I see. So, the mysterious donations that my mother received, were from you?

Bjorn:

- Yes. I had no idea what to do when the woman from my dreams turned out to be the daughter of my dead friend. But, there are more important things at stake than our own lives.

Keila:

- Yes.

Bjorn:

- So, let's play the roles that Joachim has assigned to us. If we get out of this alive, we can worry about our relationship later. Please don't talk to the press. Walk off when they try to interview you.

Keila:

- Yes, sir!

Keila and Bjorn returned to the fundraiser event where Keila had to play the role of Bjorn's loyal bodyguard.

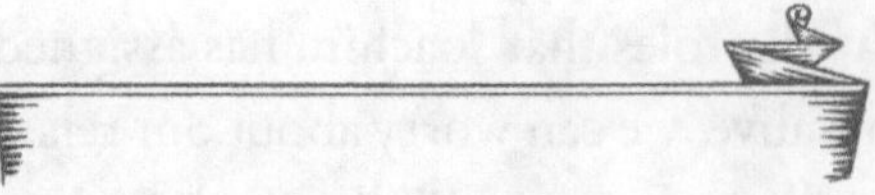

Chapter 301: Involvement in House Rashid Affairs

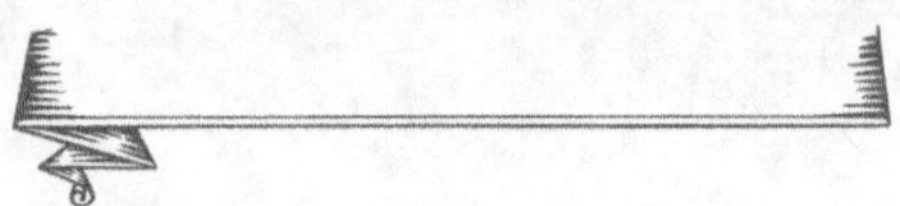

A few weeks later, Keila's group were in Egypt to reach the activation switch in the gilded Cheops Pyramid. It was the hardest one to map as it was a famous tourist destination. Besides, House Rashid was unlikely to provide them with a digging permit. Bjorn and Keila had decided to activate the switch in the Cheops Pyramid first. This way, they would have plenty of time to outpace Earth's rotation speed, to activate the switch in the Sun pyramid.

Before they had the time to set their plan in motion; a group of armed men, led by Khaleel Rashid surrounded them. The prominent House Rashid member walked up to Keila and spoke:

- Keila Eisenstein, or should I say, Keila Rashid. Why have you come to our territory? We banished your father from Earth. You are not welcome here.

Keila:

- I prefer that you to call me by my mother's surname, Eisenstein. My father's banishment has nothing to do with me. I am here as an employee of House Muller, to guard Bjorn Muller and Alicia White while they are on their honeymoon.

Khaleel Rashid:

- Bjorn Muller, why are you insulting us by bringing one of our traitors as your bodyguard?

Bjorn:

- Cut the crap, Khaleel! Keila is my bodyguard, and our business here is our own's. If I intended to use her to claim her father's inheritance, I would have done so over a decade ago. Now go back to your father and don't bother me unless you have something important to say!

Khaleel Rashid gave Bjorn and Keila an ice-cold murderous gaze, and he took off in anger. After the interrupters had left, Alicia spoke:

- They'll be back, and it won't be pretty. We'd better activate the switch at Cheops Pyramid today and get the hell out of here before all hell breaks loose.

Bjorn:

- Agreed. Let's hurry up and go.

Keila:

- But who was that guy and why is he after me?

Bjorn:

- That was Khaleel Rashid. He was the one who inherited your father's share of the family fortune when your father died. He is worried that you will make a claim to your inheritance.

Keila:

- So, I am meant to be a wealthy and prominent person on Earth?

Alicia:

- Only in theory. House Rashid's members are infamous for killing each other to elevate their own positions. A consequence of the many progenies that Ibrahim Rashid's harem has produced throughout the years. As an outsider and a half-Martian, they would kill you if tried to make any claims.

Keila:

- Very well. Let's activate this portal and get the hell out of here.

Having said this, Keila rushed to the room with the activation switch. At noontime, she deciphered the portal switch with the correct sequence of codes, and she activated the switch. They rushed back to their spaceship to outrun Earth's rotation speed so that they would arrive in Central America on time.

Chapter 302: Entering the Divine Dimension.

16 hours later, Keila activated the Zetan portal switch in the Great Pyramid of China, located near the city of Xian.

The Great Pyramid of China was the last of the four pyramids that they needed to activate. To Keila's disappointment, nothing seemed to happen when she activated the switch. Confused and bewildered, she walked up to Bjorn and spoke:

- I don't understand. We all heard Sabina, my supposed future daughter, who warned us of a galactical apocalypse. I have done everything that she has asked me to do. Why is nothing happening?

Bjorn:

- Yes. But she never told us that the portals would open straight away. Let's have dinner and enjoy a well-deserved break. The Xian region is famous for its cured mutton.

Alicia:

- While cured mutton sounds delicious, I will take my leave. Keila is the one you love, and I have plenty of other things to do. With no evil alien demon queen to fight, I don't want to stand in your way anymore.

Bjorn:

- Don't be like that, Alicia. Please stay for another day. There might be a delay on the portals.

Alicia:

- I have waited for too long already. You'll never see me as anything else than a freak, and you will never love me. As will no-one else. But I didn't choose to be born this way. I never decided to have my embryo imbued with predatory DNA.

- But it happened, didn't it? And now I might as well live out my life as the fearsome monster that my father created me to be.

Keila:

- Well, I would be sad if you chose to be that way. The Alicia that I know; is kind and has a beautiful soul. It would be a shame if your father's choices become your destiny.

Alicia:

- Thanks, Keila. I guess it wouldn't hurt to travel to Xian and enjoy an evening of sightseeing and a lot of cured mutton.

Melanie Weber joined in on the conversation:

- Then it's settled. The three of you go to the city for dinner, while I stay here and observe the pyramids. I'll let you know if anything changes.

Bjorn:

- Thank you, Melanie. Let's go, Alicia and Keila.

Having said this, they flew to the nearby city of Xian and they ate the delicious cured meat, topped with a heap of hot steaming rice. As Alicia was helping herself to a fifth plate to satiate her hunger, Bjorn received a message from Melanie. "The top of The Great Pyramid is glowing blue, come as soon as possible!"

The group flew back to the pyramid. As they arrived, it was glowing with a bright blue light, and it had a neon blue laser beam coming out of the tip of the pyramid. It was a magnificent sight, and some of the locals had gathered to stare at it in awe. Keila looked at Bjorn and spoke:

- The portal has opened, what do you reckon is on the other side?

Bjorn:

- I have no idea, but I know one thing. House Cheng's security forces are on their way, so we better move quickly.

- I'll pick up Melanie and Jurgen, and we'll fly straight into it.

Alicia:

- Finally, some excitement!

Bjorn landed the spaceship and picked up Melanie and Jurgen. He noticed that House Cheng's troops were approaching, and he realised there was no time to lose. Bjorn flew straight into the portal at The Great Pyramid of China. Zoom! There was a bright flash of light, and the spacecraft disappeared from the onlookers' sights into thin air.

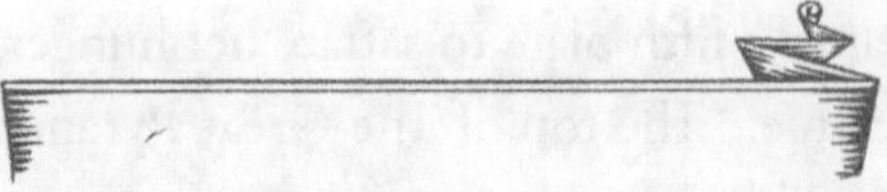

Chapter 303: Meeting Brahma.

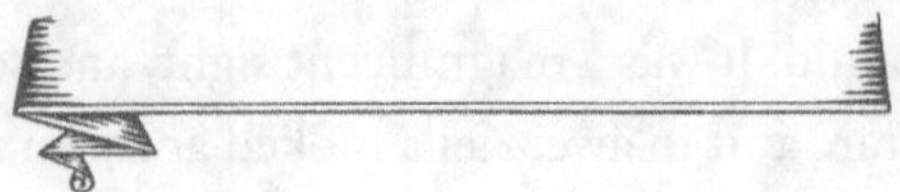

Bjorn opened his eyes as the spaceship hovered over the dusky and featureless plane that was the Divine Dimension. Apart from the shimmering mist of galactical debris in the background, there wasn't much to see.

To Bjorn's surprise, the spaceship's dashboard picked up objects 50,000 kilometres away. It was as if he was on an infinite flat plane. Bjorn saw how planet Earth, as well as the entire Milky Way Galaxy, was zooming out from his peripheral view. It was getting smaller and smaller, as they were leaving the normal dimension. Bjorn turned to Keila, and she opened her eyes.

Bjorn:

- We made it through alive!

Keila:

- Yes, we are alive. Although there is no way to be sure. Then again, is there any way to ever know whether one is alive?

Bjorn:

- That's a philosophical question, and we didn't come here for a mind-boggling debate. What is our next step?

Keila:

- I have seen a kind and old gentleman, the Zetan Brahma, in my visions. Finding Brahma would be our priority.

Bjorn:

- Okay. The ship's sensors are picking up the heat signature from a group of creatures not far away. Can it be them?

Keila:

- It must be. Let's go there and communicate with them.

Alicia:

- Excellent. You do the talking, while I stand ready to save the day if it comes to violence.

Bjorn:

- Keep calm, Alicia; we didn't come to this mysterious place to pick unnecessary fights.

Having said this, Bjorn navigated the spacecraft towards the group of Zetans and he landed close to them. As they approached the Zetans, Odin spoke confidence:

- Greetings, humans. I see that you have finally solved the riddle within the portal in the pyramids, and opened them from your end. Have you brought us any offerings?

Keila:

- We are not here to offer you any gifts. We need to find Brahma and warn him of the apocalypse. Rangda has escaped, and we need to stop her.

Odin's face lost its colour, and he spoke again:

- Rangda? But we locked her up in an inescapable prison, how could she escape? And who are you guys? I sense strong Zetan abilities in you.

Keila:

- I am Keila Eisenstein. I am accompanied by Bjorn Muller, Alicia White, Jurgen Kessler and Melanie Weber. We need to find Brahma at once.

- As for Zetan abilities, I have had strange dreams and visions of Brahma and my future daughter Sabina. Does that count?

Odin:

- I don't know anyone called Sabina, but if Brahma is calling for you, you'd better go see him. He is at the Uluwatu Temple two hundred kilometres that way.

Bjorn:

- Thank you, my good sir. I am looking forward to making your acquaintance when we get back. Now we must hurry.

Bjorn and the others got into the spaceship. A short while later, they arrived at the Uluwatu Temple, where Brahma was expecting them. He nodded as they approached them, and he spoke:

- My premonitions were correct. Pairing the two of you together would open the portals to Earth and free us Zetans from this prison. Have you come to worship us?

Keila:

- Your premonitions are not as good as you think they are. Your ex-lover, Rangda, has escaped. We must stop her before she gathers and corrupts the Zeto Crystals and becomes unstoppable.

Brahma:

- What are you talking about? How do you know?

Keila:

- My daughter from the future, Sabina, told me everything. How you Zetans fooled ancient humans that you were our gods, to make us fight the Xenos.

Brahma:

- You insolent girl. We altered your intelligence to make you what you've become. Without us, you'd be primitive apes and not the "crown of evolution" as you perceive yourselves! For all intent and purposes, we are your gods.

Keila:

- That might be, but that discussion is irrelevant. I need to know where Rangda is so we can stop her.

Brahma froze, and he realised what he had done. The engagement ring he had once given to Rangda, had contained a tiny stone made of a replicated Zeto Crystal. As Zeto Crystals were the hardest material in the universe, Rangda could have used that tiny stone to dig herself out from her prison cell. Brahma had forgotten about this important detail when he sealed Rangda's prison cell. Worse yet, once Rangda was out of her cell, she could have used the Zeto Crystal in her ring to power the portal to her home planet, Xenora. On Xenora, Rangda could find one of the powerful primordial Zeto Crystals.

Brahma:

- Xenora. She must have travelled to Xenora and visited her home planet!

Keila:

- Well, what are we waiting for? Get in the spaceship and lead us to Xenora at once. We got a score to settle and a future to save.

Chapter 304: Travelling to Xenora

Keila, Brahma and the others arrived outside the portal to Xenora. Distances were a lot shorter in the Divine Dimension. Although Xenora was thousands of light-years away from Earth in the regular universe, the trip was quick in the Divine Dimension. They got out of the shuttle and much to their dismay, Rangda had closed the portal behind her, and they had no means of powering it up.

Brahma sighed and spoke:

- So close, and yet so far. I can feel Rangda's presence on the other side of that portal, but we have no way of powering it up.

- I assume none of you brought a Zeto Crystal?

Keila:

- Well to be fair, the word doesn't exist on Earth, so we have no idea what it is?

Brahma:

- In the human language, it would be a sapphire. It's a rare and valuable form of a sapphire.

Keila:

- So, all we need to do, is to go back to Earth and pick up some sapphires?

Brahma:

- In theory, yes. But I can sense unspeakable evil from the other end of the portal. Rangda might be corrupting the Zeto Crystal as we speak, and time is of the essence.

Alicia pulled up a heart-shaped amulet, with a bright blue sapphire.

- Will this work?

Bjorn:

- Alicia! I have travelled with you for weeks, and you have never shown it to me. It's beautiful, where did you get it?

Alicia:

- I got it from my mother before she passed away. After the death of my mother, my father turned insane and deleted all the records of her. The amulet is all that I have left of her.

Keila:

- Your father seems like a complete dickhead. Why would he do such a thing?

Before Alicia had time to answer, Brahma interrupted:

- Look, humans. As intriguing as Alicia's paternal relationship might be to you, we are in a hurry! That amulet is the key to powering the portal. Give it to me now, Alicia.

Alicia had a look at the amulet. For the first time in her life, she shed a tear, and then she handed the charm to Brahma. Alicia spoke:

- Take it; this is what my mother would have wanted.

Brahma took the crystal, and he put it in a slot next to the portal. The portal lit up the door with a sparkling blue light. Brahma shouted out:

- Hurry up. Run into the entrance. We need to stop Rangda.

Bjorn:

- What about the spaceship?

Brahma:

- It won't fit. Hurry up. Run into the portal now!

They all did as Brahma commanded and they ended up in Rangda's temple on Xenora!

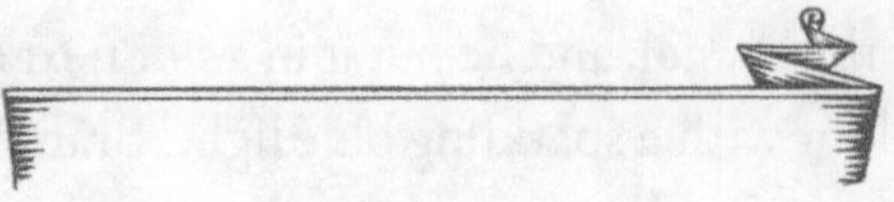

Chapter 305: An Unlikely Hero Saves the Day

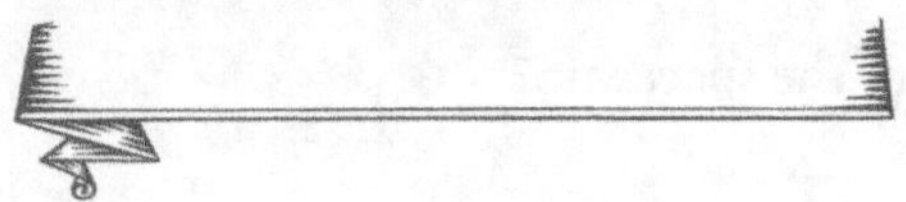

Keila opened her eyes, and she saw the black orb in the centre of the room. The orb radiated with such darkness, so it looks like a black hole, which almost absorbed all the light in the hall. Rangda held the sphere with her hand, and she laughed hysterically. Brahma rushed towards Rangda, and the others followed him. Brahma stopped a dozen metres away from Rangda, and he shouted out:

- Rangda! What are you doing? Stop this madness at once!

Rangda:

- Brahma, we meet again. Earlier than I had planned, but it doesn't matter.

- I was giving this primordial Zeto Crystal its true colour, and the other crystals will follow.

Brahma:

- True colour? You are corrupting it. The crystals are blue: like the sky, like freedom, like life.

Rangda:

- Bah. The air can get polluted, freedom is an illusion and life is only temporary. None of those things last. Black, on the other hand, is the only real colour. It's the colour of the universe and the colour of death. It is the very essence of life.

Brahma:

- Talk all you want Rangda. I am here to stop you, and you won't be a prisoner this time. I will kill you!

Rangda:

- Indeed, I won't be. You have arrived too late, and you will be the one to die today.

Having said this, Rangda blasted Brahma with a psionic blast, powered by her corrupted Zeto Crystal. Brahma tried to resist, but he wasn't strong enough, and he collapsed to the floor. Seeing this, Jurgen ran up towards Rangda and started firing at her with a submachine gun. Rangda's ballistic energy absorbers stopped the bullets. Shortly afterwards Jurgen's head was on the floor, decapitated by Rangda's sharp claws. Rangda licked her claws and spoke:

- Pathetic! But delicious. I don't have time for you now humans, I got to deal with Brahma first.

Having said this, Rangda sent out a psionic shockwave in a circular pattern around her. The shockwave knocked Keila, Bjorn and Melanie to the ground. Keila tried to get up, but she was too wounded, and she could only watch as Rangda turned her attention to Brahma. Rangda pushed Brahma against a wall while draining him with the corrupted Zeto Crystal. Rangda had a long rant:

- I have been waiting to do this for thousands of years. You have disgusted me ever since you first laid your eyes on my "beautiful" Zetan appearance. I was beautiful back then, wasn't I?

- You thought that I loved you and you never saw through my intentions. I guess you couldn't read me as I was only half Zetan. I hated you from the start, but I needed you. You were my tool to advancement within the Zetan society so I could destroy it from within.

- How does it feel knowing that your death is imminent and that your death will power my efforts to take over the galaxy and become its god-queen?

Brahma was powerless and in immense pain, as Rangda was shattering his soul using the unholy powers of the corrupted Zeto Crystal. The pain stopped and what he saw amazed him. Alicia had intervened.

Rangda was feeling immense pain when the sharp claws of Alicia White pierced her back:

Rangda:

- Aarrgh! How did you resist my psionic blast, you feeble human?

Alicia:

- I guess I am not human enough for your magic to affect me! Take this!

Alicia pushed her pistol into Rangda wounds, and she filled Rangda's chest with a dozen bullets. The bullets tore Rangda's organs into shreds but powered by the corrupted Zeto Crystals she didn't die. Instead, she punched Alicia hard enough to send her flying into a wall knocking her unconscious.

Brahma got up, and he chopped off Rangda's arm with his plasma sword causing her to drop the corrupted Zeto Crystal. The Zeto Crystal rolled over to Keila who grabbed it. As she grabbed it, the silhouette of Sabina appeared, and she whispered. "Dear mother, this may be the last time that I will ever speak to you again. Through the power of The True

Maker, I will bless this crystal back to its original purity". Thus, Sabina purified the Zeto Crystal, using Keila's body as a vessel.

Once Sabina had purified the Zeto Crystal, Rangda lost her powers, and her wounds became mortal. As she dropped to the ground, she hissed:

- I lost, but I will live on. There will always be evil in the world.

Brahma looked at Rangda and spoke:

- Yes, there will always be good and bad in people. But your evil ends today. Goodbye, Rangda!

Brahma channelled his powers into his fist, and he struck Rangda in the head. The strike crushed her skull and ended her evil ambitions for the galaxy.

Brahma took out some Zetan healing serum, and he resuscitated Bjorn, Alicia, Keila and Melanie. "Come back with me to the Divine Dimension," Brahma said. Wounded but alive, the group made their way back through the portal.

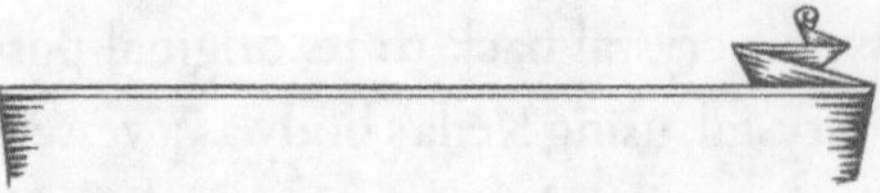

Chapter 306: Alicia gets Rewarded, and Brahma Tells the Truth.

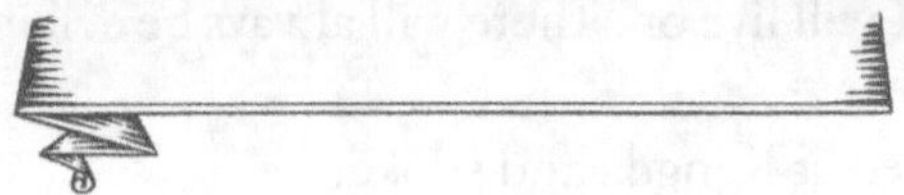

Brahma studied the bright blue light emitting from the primordial Zeto Crystal. Its beauty mesmerised him. Brahma felt relieved that the Zetans had found a new Zeto Crystal to unite their species. But he still mourned the loss of Zetani and Zetani Nova and the end of Zetan civilisation. Unbeknownst to Brahma, primordial Zeto Crystals were indestructible. Thus, they were still floating in space where Zetani and Zetani Nova had existed. That was how Rangda had acquired them in the original timeline.

Brahma turned to Alicia and spoke:

- Alicia, when I first met you, I would never have guessed that you would be the one to save us. How did you do that? How did you withstand the psionic blast?

Alicia:

- It came naturally to me. I didn't feel it much at all, but I pretended that the blast wounded me to convince Rangda that I wasn't a threat.

- I knew that I needed to attack her from behind and take her by surprise. She showed immense speed and power when she killed Jurgen, and there was no way I could fight her in a head to head battle.

- I thought I had defeated her when I unleashed a dozen pistol shots straight into her abdomen. But instead, she knocked me unconscious. What happened afterwards?

Brahma:

- You killed her physical body, but powered by the immense malicious power of the corrupted Zeto Crystal, she wouldn't die. Rangda died when I chopped off her hand, and she lost the crystal to Keila, who cleansed it through the benign powers of The True Maker.

Alicia:

- Cool. It feels good to be the hero for once.

Brahma:

- And for your bravery, I will reward you. What do you want most of everything in the world?

Alicia:

- I want to be normal. To be free of my mutations, I want to love and find someone who loves me back.

Brahma:

- But you are an extraordinary specimen with unique capabilities?

Alicia:

- So was Rangda, and that didn't end too well.

- Being extraordinary is good, but condemnation to a life in solitude drives the mind crazy.

Brahma:

- I will speak to my fellow Zetans. We will cure your ailment turning you into a regular Terran human.

Alicia:

- Thank you, Brahma. I can't tell you how thrilled I am.

Brahma turned towards Keila:

- As for you, Keila, I could sense that you were a Terran/Zetan hybrid with extraordinary abilities. But I could never foresee that you would be this great. You cleansed the Zeto Crystal from Rangda's evil prowess, and you saved us all.

Keila:

- It wasn't me. I was only vessel for Sabina's and the True Maker's holy powers and divine will.

Brahma:

- Well, that kind of humility serves a future queen. I hope that humans will appreciate you as such when you get back home.

Keila:

- Yes. I am so excited knowing that I am to mother the future messiah of humankind with my handsome Bjorn.

Hearing this, Brahma felt deep shame. He blushed and looked away. Keila noticed that something was wrong, and she spoke again:

- What is the matter Brahma? Did I say something wrong?

Brahma:

- I am feeling guilty. You see, you and Bjorn are not meant to be together. I influenced your minds to make you fall in love, because I needed the two of you to be together to open the portal.

Keila:

- Why are you saying these things? Bjorn and I are a great match.

Brahma:

- Tell me, Keila. Except for your dreams and your instant infatuation with Bjorn, what do the two of you have in common?

Keila:

- I... I don't know.

Brahma:

- Well, that because you have nothing in common. You are still young Keila, and Bjorn is old and lonely. Bjorn needs to find love more than you do, and luckily his love is right in front of his eyes.

Bjorn:

- Alicia?

Brahma:

- Yes. The two of you complement each other. You are both outcasts, you both come from prominent families, and together you can change things for the better.

Keila realised that Brahma was correct. She felt heartbroken, and she started crying. How could things end like this for her? How could she lose her hopes and dreams after saving the world? Brahma came up to her and comforted her.

- It might not feel like it now, but there will come a day in the future when you'll realise that this will be for the best.

Keila:

- But can you tell me when that day will be?

Brahma:

- Our destined paths together have come to an end. I can provide you with emotional support, but I can no longer foresee your future. But I know that you'll one day meet Sabina's father and you'll be happy together.

Keila:

- Thank you, Brahma. I guess not everything in life can be perfect.

Brahma:

- No, it cannot. You'll have to deal with what life gives you. Let's head to Earth. There is a lot for you to do.

Having said this, the group set their course towards Earth, and a few days later they were back home.

Chapter 307: Bjorn and Alicia get married and unite humanity.

The following months, came with a lot of upheaval for the future of humanity. Finding out about the Zetans, who were a lot more advanced than humankind, came both as a shock and a blessing. Initially, there was a lot of fear. But as the Zetans brought clarity and peace with their primordial Zeto Crystals, most people relaxed. The Zetans sent an expedition to find humanity's primordial Zeto Crystal, also known as the Holy Grail.

While the Holy Grail didn't end all evil, it stopped most of it. Under its influence most people followed ideals such as unity and peace, instead of pursuing greed, lust, and hunger.

Alicia's father, John White, couldn't handle the change. John blamed the Zetans for taking his daughter away from him. Brahma had turned Alicia from a mutated warrior princess, to a kind-hearted and beautiful young woman. Filled with feelings such a rage, desperation and guilt John took a big leap from his penthouse office to end his life. Alicia succeeded John and became the leader of House White. Everyone respected Alicia, as she had saved the galaxy from the vicious Rangda. Once she was in command, she reversed many of the former House White policies. Alicia's first objective was to send a massive aid package to Mars, to help end the Martian suffering and poverty.

Meanwhile, Joachim Muller, seeing the man that Bjorn had become, gave up leadership of House Muller to Bjorn.

A year later, Bjorn and Alicia got married. Together they united House White and House Muller to improve the solar system under their new doctrines. Bjorn invited Keila to the wedding, but she didn't attend.

Instead, Keila returned to Mars as a House Muller official coordinating the rebuilding effort of Mars. Despite the progress for her home planet, Keila felt heartbroken, and she never wanted to see Alicia or Bjorn again.

Chapter 308: It's Time to Save Eden.

Two years later, in the year 2871, Keila was living in a fancy mansion in her home city on Mars, Pamshal. Keila was a successful official who had reversed the Terran Council's policies towards Mars. Under Keila's supervision, Mars was starting to flourish.

Due to the advanced technologies of the 29th century, the rebuilding process was swift. What was once a toxic and overpopulated wasteland had become a flourishing and peaceful planet, where everyone could get by in peace.

Despite her success, Keila felt broken on the inside. Her visions had shown her a future with Bjorn; and it had all been a lie. Although she had set herself up for life financially, she felt like a failure. It had been years, and she couldn't get her heart mended. Keila's mother, Susanna, who stayed with her, knocked on her door and entered her bedroom. Susanna gave Keila a worried look and spoke:

- Keila darling, are you feeling down again?

Keila:

- It's not fair, mother. My visions showed me the oncoming doom. I set out, and I saved everyone. Yet I am the one feeling lonely, crying myself to sleep at night.

Susanna:

- Life isn't fair, my sweetheart. And besides, everyone loves you. If you stop thinking about what could have been and start enjoying the moment, you'll be happier.

Keila:

- I am doing that every day, and it helps me with my mission to make Mars a better place. But while working for House Muller puts me in a position where I can help others, it also serves as a constant reminder of what could have been.

Susanna:

- Except nothing good would happen if you had married Bjorn. Bjorn's marriage with Alicia worked out for everyone. The marriage united House White and House Muller and gave them the power to advance the solar system. If you had married Bjorn, there wouldn't have been a combined power improving the everyday lives of the people. Besides, Bjorn would face a lot more resistance from his relatives.

Keila:

- Huh. How come?

Susanna:

- Bjorn and Alicia are prominent members of their factions, and together they strengthen each other's positions. But you are the bastard daughter of the exiled Mahmoud Rashid. Your presence would weaken Bjorn's position on Earth.

Keila:

- I guess you are right. But what can I do with my life? I am desperate for change.

Susanna:

- Well, there is one long-overdue thing...

Keila:

- And that is?

Susanna:

- My homeworld, Eden, is still oppressed by the tyrant Abraham Goldstein.

Keila:

- Mum! We have spoken about this. Abraham has a perpetual agreement with the Houses of Earth that gives him immunity. This agreement prevents them from intervening in his business if he poses no threat to them.

Susanna:

- I know. But does Abraham Goldstein have an agreement with you or me?

Keila:

- It doesn't matter. I am an employee of House Muller, and I cannot go on a rogue mission to Eden, to overthrow Abraham.

Susanna:

- Well. You could end your employment. Then you are not bound to follow House Muller's treaties.

Keila:

- But how would we attack Abraham's battle station without any help?

Susanna:

- We don't need to. Your friend Brahma, can give us stealth technology to approach the colony undetected. If we kill Abraham, we can pose as Eden's new rulers and carry out a peaceful transition of power.

Keila:

- I guess you are right. So, what do I need to do?

Susanna:

- Contact Bjorn and tell him about your resignation. Then contact Brahma and get the Zetan technology schematics that we need, to rule over Eden.

Keila:

- I can do that!

Susanna:

- That's the spirit. It's time to save the Edenites at last!

Chapter 309: Infiltrating the Divine Control Centre.

Susanna and Keila were sitting in a small Zetan stealth shuttle. They were observing Abraham's headquarter orbiting Eden. Keila studied a scan of the base. It seemed like the entire crew were in suspended animation, and that the AI ran all the daily operations.

Keila looked at Susanna and spoke:

- Are you sure this is the place? It is so eerie, and everyone seems to be in cryogenic sleep.

Susanna pondered the matter for a few seconds and spoke:

- Well, the cryogenic sleep explains something that I never quite got my head around.

Keila:

- What is that?

Susanna:

- When I grew up on Eden, Abraham's goons, the angels, never aged. I have been thinking about how that could be the case, but extended periods of cryogenic sleep explain it. If they are only awake a couple of days a year, they never have the time to age.

- But this is excellent news. If no one is watching, it will be easier for us to enter the base and dispose of Abraham.

Keila:

- Well. We still must enter the base unnoticed and reach Abraham. Any suggestions?

Susanna:

- Yes. We'll use the Zetan Quantum Computer to hack and reprogram the AI to make it identify us as friendly visitors, and give us full access.

Keila:

- How about reprogramming the AI to kill Abraham for us?

Susanna:

- Too risky. To get the AI to kill someone, you must deactivate Asimov's three laws for robotics. It works for a military application robot with a limited AI. But altering the Artificial Intelligence on Eden might cause it to go homicidal, killing everyone, including us.

Keila:

- Agreed. I'll start the AI Hacking Quantum Computer.

A few minutes later, the Zetan AI hacking device had infiltrated the Divine Control Centre, and Keila's ship was ready to dock. Keila docked with the base, to find Abraham and end his reign of terror over the Edenites.

Chapter 310: The End of Abraham.

Keila and Susanna snuck around inside the Divine Control Centre. They had never seen an installation quite like it. It was a mixture of a top modern research facility and a Bronze-age temple. Passages from Abraham's holy book, the Abrahameon, filled the walls. While walking in the corridor, Keila came across a cryogenic tank and she saw Metatron stuck in suspended animation. Seeing Metatron shocked Keila. She felt like they had met before, and yet she had never been to Eden.

Keila heard the voice of Sabina speaking in her head. "That man is Metatron. He will be my future father. But for now, you must move on."

Keila moved on. Since the breakup with Bjorn, she had felt empty and depressed, but seeing Metatron made her feel better. Keila wanted to study her partner-to-be more closely, but she remembered what Sabina had said, and she carried on.

Keila and Susanna entered the throne room where the robotic body of Abraham Goldstein greeted them:

- Susanna, you came back at last. I must say that I am impressed with you. Altering the AI and sneaking into my base undetected.

Susanna:

- If you saw us coming, why didn't you try to stop us?

Abraham:

- Good question, and one that I cannot answer I am afraid.

- You have fascinated me for many years Susanna; ever since you volunteered for the Edenites selection to get away from here.

- Do you know how lucky you were? Most child brides sold to Ibrahim Rashid didn't survive for long. He didn't want to leave any loose end.

Susanna:

- I never met Ibrahim. Instead, I met with his grandson, Mahmoud Rashid, and together we had Keila before he passed away due to sickness.

Abraham:

- I know. I follow the Terran news.

- From your unlikely relationship with Mahmoud Rashid, sprung your daughter Keila, who turned out to be the saviour of humanity. It is so poetic and improbable that I almost start believing in 'the goodness of love'.

Susanna:

- So you didn't believe in kindness and love?

Abraham:

- Exactly. Humans are animals that need to be controlled

- When I funded the Divine Detector machine, I felt excited. I would achieve what no man had done before. I would be talking directly with God. But once I reached the Divine Dimension, I found out that Yahweh was a Zetan imposter. I stole his Zetan schematics, and I used them to deceive and manipulate my Edenite population to obedience.

- I realised that I could become a god to my people, the god of the Edenites. So, I made a deal with Terran Council. I invested my fortune in buying this asteroid that I call Eden. The Zetan technology enabled me to control the Edenites and smite the unbelievers of the Abrahameon, the dogmata that I envisioned.

Susanna:

- So, do you feel guilty over your atrocities towards the Edenite population?

Abraham:

- What atrocities? I created a safe and enjoyable world for the Edenites to live in. I provided them with the ultimate law and a framework for a happy life.

Susanna:

- You murdered and maimed a lot of Edenite civilians for breaching your immoral laws. You sold innocent children as slaves to fund your madness!

Abraham:

- Those people knew that they were sinning. Those who disobeyed the Abrahameon laws deserved punishment.

- Selling the children was not my original intention, but I was desperate for funding the maintenance of Eden. Sometimes, one must sacrifice a few for the common good.

Susanna:

- But you never considered sacrificing your own power and your self-inflated Godhood for the common good. It was all to satisfy your egoistic hunger for oppression and power!

Abraham:

- I don't claim to be without fault. But I am hoping that you'll realise that I am not the bad guy that you think I was, and that you will spare my life. I am old, and I am nothing without the protection of my super-soldiers, who are now sleeping in their cryogenic tanks.

Susanna:

- You are missing one critical part in your argumentation.

Abraham:

- What would that be?

Susanna:

- That you have been dead for decades. Your kindness left your body when you died. The only thing that's left of you is your wicked brain, and whatever signals your brain receives inside that gigantic android glass cocoon. Your existence is blasphemy on all living beings. Goodbye, Abraham!

Susanna pulled up her pistol and she unleashed a dozen bullets into Abraham's brain. The shots broke the glass cocoon and splashed the clear liquid that contained Abraham's brain. Abraham died within seconds.

Chapter 311: Finding Love at Last.

Metatron opened his eyes, and he looked at Keila. He felt something that he had never felt before. He felt attraction, excitement and passion the moment he saw her. But how could this be? Metatron knew that he was a genetically engineered super-soldier born out of an artificial womb, to serve Abraham. As such, he had never experienced strong human emotions before, as he only knew the dedication to work duties. Unbeknownst to Metatron, Sabina had used her powers to awaken his dormant soul. Metatron studied Keila, the most beautiful woman he had ever seen, and he spoke:

- You freed me. You freed me from my servitude to the evil dictator, Abraham.

Keila:

- You freed yourself. There is nothing that I could have done if you had chosen to take vengeance for your fallen master.

Metatron:

- Abraham's death was long overdue. As a matter of fact, he died decades ago.

Keila:

- So why did you bring him back?

Metatron:

- It was fear of the unknown. We lived to serve Abraham, and we didn't know what to do with ourselves when he was gone. Anyways, I didn't have any say in the matter, but Lucifer wanted to bring our master back. Ironically, Abraham murdered Lucifer for loving a woman more than he loved Abraham.

Keila:

- So, what will happen now?

Metatron:

- I must take my leave. There is no place for me here anymore. I served a villain for decades. I need a fresh start and a new goal for the remainders of my years.

Keila bit her lip. Should she make the leap of faith and proclaim her love for Metatron? It was insane, but her daughter from the future told her that Metatron was the one, so she could not let him go. She cleared her throat and spoke:

- How about coming with me to Mars? I have a lovely house there and influential Terran friends. We could help rebuild the planet together.

Metatron smiled at Keila. Her words filled him with joy and relief. Metatron replied:

- I would like that very much. If nothing else, for the excellent company.

Keila smiled at him and spoke:

- Oh, I am not always this nice. I can be quite a handful when I have my bad days.

Metatron:

- I wouldn't want you any other way.

Keila:

- Good. I'll let my mother know that we are heading back to Mars. We'll have so much fun ahead of us.

Metatron smiled as he watched Keila run off with youthful enthusiasm to tell her mother the good news. Although he was physically only a decade older than Keila, due to extended periods of cryogenic sleep, his soul was that of an old man.

Later the same day, Keila was watching Metatron's naked body in bed. She felt relieved that she had finally got over Bjorn, and she could imagine a bright future for herself and for her people.

Finding peace after several heartbroken years, Keila fell asleep in Metatron's arms.

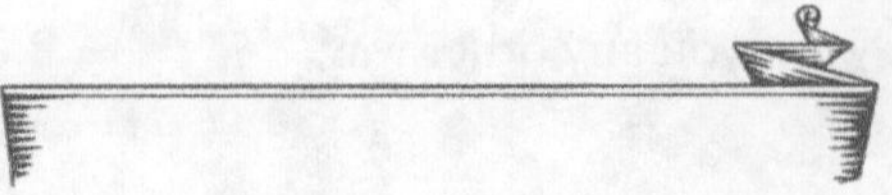

Chapter 312: Sabina Says Farewell to the True Maker.

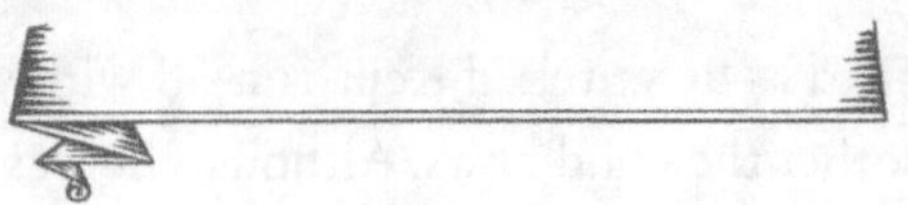

Nine months later, Sabina felt a funny feeling she had never experienced before. She felt like she was about to be born again. While Sabina had been born during the previous timeline, before the True Maker had turned back time, it was different this time. This time, she was going to be born as a sentient being instead of as a baby. Sabina summoned the True Maker to say goodbye.

- I am about to be born again, and I want to thank you for giving humanity and the other sentient species of the Milky Way Galaxy another chance at life.

The True Maker:

- It is I who should thank you. I wanted to save everyone, but the scope of my powers inhibited me from doing so. Only through you, could I set things right.

Sabina:

- I guess we should be grateful that things turned out the way they did.

The True Maker:

- I couldn't agree with you more.

Sabina:

- So, will I see you again?

The True Maker:

- I am the essence of the universe. I am everyone and no-one.

Sabina:

- I'll take that as a yes.

- You have never told me what will happen to my soul when I die. Will we meet in the afterlife?

The True Maker:

- Once you die, the universe will absorb your life force and you'll become part of the universe. Thus, you'll cease to exist and yet you'll live on.

Sabina:

- Wow. I guess I will experience it eventually.
- Farewell, my friend, and thanks again.

Sabina's mind blackened, and she felt a strange feeling overwhelming her. Sabina felt how her mind warped and distorted through space and time. As she opened her eyes, she was in a medical room, naked and covered in slime. After a few seconds, Sabina realised that she had been reborn. Sabina looked at her mother, Keila, who had given birth to her. Sabina's body cried while her heart whispered:

- Thank you, mother. Thank you for giving birth to me.

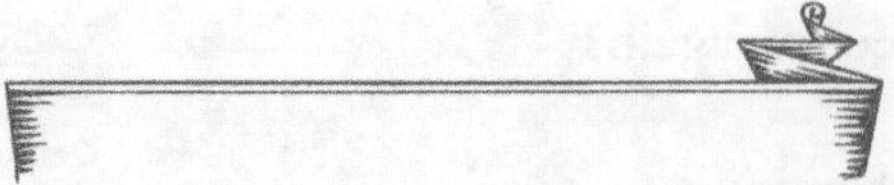

Chapter 313: The Official Ending

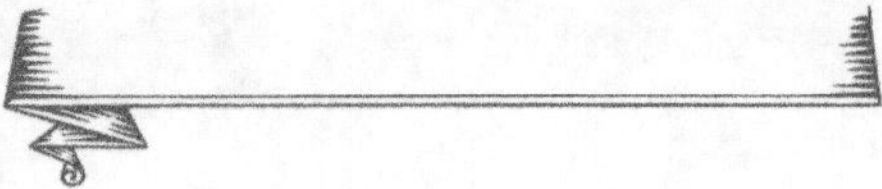

Sabina Eisenstein was a blessed child that turned out to be the Messiah of mankind. Sabina became the Supreme Leader of the solar system, and she utilised the powers of the Zeto Crystals to create a world devoid of suffering and greed. Leading humanity and the Zetans, Sabina initiated widespread space colonisation. Together, humans and Zetans spread across the Milky Way Galaxy, influenced by the benign Zeto Crystals. Having learnt from their previous mistakes, the Zetans left inhabited planets alone. They also stopped playing gods by altering the genome of other organisms.

Sabina refused to use DNA regeneration technology, and she died at the age of 112. When she died, there was nothing left of her body as she evaporated into pure light. Sabina's birthplace on Mars and place of death on Proxima II, orbiting Alpha Centauri, became places for pilgrimage for millennia to come.

Alicia and Bjorn spent a large chunk of their families' fortunes on improving the conditions in the solar system. Due to their wealth and influence, they managed to reduce poverty, war and disease in the entire solar system by 95%, in a couple of decades. When Sabina came of age, Bjorn and Alicia replaced the Terran Council with the Human/Zetan Interplanetary Alliance. Under Sabina's leadership the organisation put an end to war, disease and suffering. The organisation became a great success, and after a few millennia, most star systems of the Milky Way Galaxy was part of the alliance.

Keila and Metatron lived happily together on Mars for many years. They occupied themselves with philanthropy and Martian politics. They were proud of Sabina, although life wasn't always easy being the parents of the Messiah for humankind. Eventually, they moved back to Eden where they could live out their lives away from the press and the social media. Keila died on Eden in 2984 at the age of 134. She died on the exact same day as her daughter did, as the True Maker wanted them to meet in the afterlife.

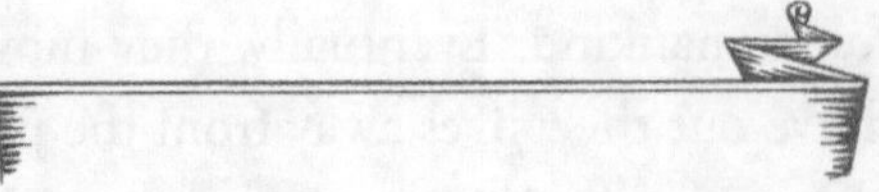

Chapter 314: Ending 2: Rangda Wins and Conquers the Universe.

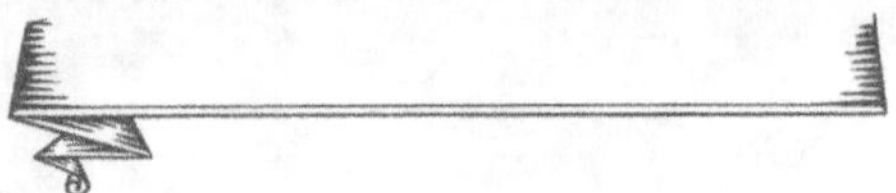

(The following event takes place on the same timeline as chapter 76)

During the apocalyptic battle, Rangda blasted the True Maker with the full force of her seven corrupted Zeto Crystals. This caused her to feel something that she had never felt before. The True Maker felt pain and fear.

The True Maker's physical form manifested in the Divine Dimension, and she was unable to make herself ethereal again. She coughed up some blood and spoke weakly:

- How is this possible...? How can you hurt me when I am the universe? I have created the seven Zeto Crystals in every galaxy, yours are only a fraction of the total.

Rangda:

- You fool. You have underestimated my wrath! Those seven Zeto crystals are the only ones that influence this galaxy. The crystals that you have spread out in the other galaxies won't save you now.

- Any last words?

The True Maker:

- Please spare me. If you kill me, there won't be anyone to reset the universe when it reaches the end of its lifespan. Eventually, darkness and death will replace everything!

Rangda:

- And that is precisely what I want. Ha-ha-ha-ha!

After saying this, Rangda blasted the True Maker with the corrupted Zeto Crystals. The blast caused the True Maker to explode, in an intense explosion of pure light.

Rangda opened her eyes, which were recovering from the intensely bright light. As her vision returned, Rangda felt better than ever. Her powers had increased by several magnitudes, and there was no reason for her to ever stop accumulating power. Rangda saw Sabina, who without the blessing of the True Maker, was just a frightened young girl.

Since Rangda was a sadistic monster, Sabina became her favourite torture victim. Rangda kept Sabina alive for eternity, to fulfil her sadistic desires. Rangda's ravenous hunger for power led her to travel from galaxy to galaxy in a never-ending quest to conquer everything. A few years later, Rangda invaded Earth again. This time she enslaved humanity, turned them into Xeno/human hybrids, and condemned them to forever serve her. Rangda enlisted every human into her army and left before a black hole swallowed the solar system.

Rangda kept increasing her arsenal of corrupted Zeto crystals, which unbalanced the universe. Eventually, the unbalancing, caused by Rangda's endless appetite for Zeto Crystals, reached a critical point. Fuelled by the pure darkness within them, The Corrupted Zeto Crystals collapsed into a Black Hole. The black hole was so large so that it destroyed both the universe and the Divine Dimension. With the True Maker no longer left to reset the timeline, this event led to the end of all life in the universe.

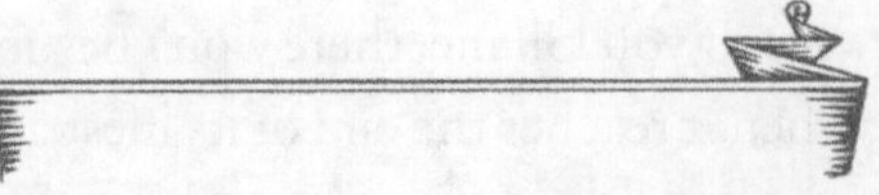

Chapter 315: Ending 3 Time is reset to 10172 B.C. (Preventing the birth of Rangda)

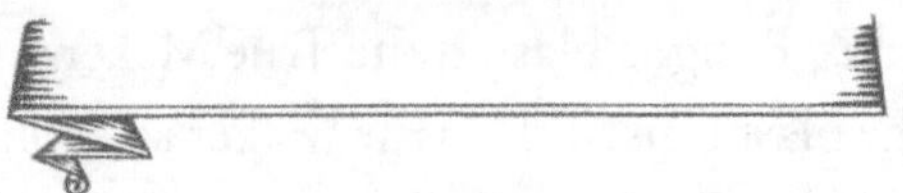

(This ending follows chapter 77)

Sabina was inside the True Maker's mind, and she could turn back time to make things right. But the options were endless and what time should she pick? An idea flashed in her head. What if she could prevent Rangda from ever being born? This way, she would save the Zetan galactic civilisation, and she would avoid all the suffering caused by the multi-millennial war.

Sabina entered the mind of Yahweh who was on research expedition on the Xeno home planet of Xenora. Sabina could feel Yahweh's anger boiling in his head, driving him insane. Kalianka had publicly rejected Yahweh. Yahweh felt humiliated, and he wanted to get his revenge. If Sabina didn't intervene, Yahweh would assault Kalianka, and leave her for dead. The Xenos would find Kalianka and she would eventually give birth to Rangda. The key to saving the future was to stop that from happening. Sabina spoke to Yahweh:

- Yahweh. I know that you are angry, but it's not the right way. Don't do it!

Hearing Sabina's voice shocked Yahweh. He had hidden his intentions to the other Zetan, and he didn't recognise her voice. Panicking, Yahweh yelled out:

- Who are you? Show yourself.

Sabina did as Yahweh requested, and he stared at her mirage in disbelief. Eventually, he spoke:

- A human girl? Utilising telepathy? In a star system very far away from Earth? How is this possible?

Sabina:

- I am a human saint from the future. My soul merged with the True Maker when she destroyed the Milky Way Galaxy to stop Rangda from destroying the entire universe.

After saying this, Sabina showed Yahweh how the Xenos would invade and destroy the Zetans. Sabina showed Yahweh how Rangda was drinking the blood of his fallen Zetan peers. Seeing this gripped Yahweh with panic and he shouted with a desperate voice:

- So, this will happen because I put Kalianka in place for rejecting me?

Sabina:

- Yes. You are in the wrong. You can never force someone to love you. Avenging a rejection makes you a pitiful creature.

At the same moment, Kalianka arrived at Yahweh's location on Xenora.:

- You wanted to speak with me, Master Yahweh?

Seeing Kalianka overwhelmed Yahweh with guilt. During a bout of insanity, he ran up to the top of a cliff. Yahweh jumped off the cliff, and he landed headfirst onto a stalagmite, piercing straight through his brain. This killed him straight away and made his body impossible to resurrect. Shocked over Yahweh's suicide, the Zetan researchers abandoned Xenora and left the Xenos to live as they had always done.

Without the emergence of Rangda and the Xeno hordes, the Zetan galactic empire lasted a lot longer. It was still going strong by the year of 2887 when the timeline of the plot ends.

Without the need for soldiers, the Zetans left humanity alone to fend for themselves. Because of this, humanity never invented civilisation and organised religion. Instead, humans lived as they had always done, as hunters and gatherers, in harmony with nature. Eventually, Sabina was reborn within an Amazonian tribe. She decided to not share her knowledge, and instead, she let humanity live as they had always lived. Humanity lived in innocence and harmony with nature, as the True Maker had intended her creation to be.

Chapter 316: Ending 4: The True Maker Refuses to Reset Time.

(This ending follows after chapter 76)
Sabina cried as the True Maker shouted:

- No, I will not turn back time to save your species. Things happen for a reason, and I am responsible for all the life in the universe, not only the small fraction of it that resided in the Milky Way galaxy.

After that, The True Maker disappeared. She was still there, but she refused to acknowledge Sabina's attempts to communicate.

Sabina sat devastated, and she was crying for eons. Everyone in her galaxy was dead, and the Divine Dimension was also an empty wasteland with nothing living in it. Sabina felt like the loneliest soul in the universe.

But then, Sabina realised something. That the universe was a lot larger than the Milky Way Galaxy. If she kept walking, she would reach other galaxies, and she could study the lifeforms there. The distances in the Divine Dimension was a lot shorter than in the outside world, so she could walk to the Andromeda Galaxy, in a few decades. Sabina studied the lifeforms in the Andromeda Galaxy for thousands of years until she made a depressing realisation. Sabina realised that all the lifeforms in the Andromeda Galaxy were silica-based. Since they weren't carbon-based, she would never be able to connect with them as they ran on completely different wavelengths. While this insight made her depressed, another idea made her happier. Somewhere in the universe, there would exist humanoid creatures, which had evolved independently from those in the Milky Way.

With this insight in mind, Sabina travelled the universe for millions of years until she found humans in a very distant galaxy. There she was born, and less than a cosmic blink of an eye later she was dead. That was her fate, having lived for millions of years, human life was so short to her so she could not even conceive it. On the bright side, once Sabina had been reborn and died, her travels were finally over.

Chapter 317: Ending 5: Time is reset to 2019 AD

(This ending follows chapter 76)

Looking through all the potential timelines, Sabina found 2019 to be fascinating. It had all that she needed to achieve her objectives. There were ancestors to both Metatron and Keila that had very similar genetics to their very distant descendants. If Sabina could get these ancestors to copulate, she could ensure that she was reborn. Once she had been born in the 21st century she could find the primordial Zeto Crystal and stop Rangda who was still in prison at the time.

But first, she needed to be born, and there were a few problems. Her potential parents already had partners and they lived at different ends of the world. Also, her potential father, Marvin Orchard, had a hidden condition that would turn into a very aggressive cancer in a couple of months. The cancer was incurable and Sabina wouldn't be born and able to save him with her divine powers until he had already died. But it was what it was. She would have to deal with the unfortunate loss of her biological father.

For her conception to happen, Sabina had to make her parents meet. The easiest way would be for them to meet on holiday away from their partners. Thus, having fewer interruptions to deal with. But where would she send them? Her mother Ellen Himes was from South Africa, and her father Marvin Orchard was from Australia. The answer came up as a flash for her. She would make them meet in Egypt during a tour to the pyramids.

But time was short, as her father would get his diagnosis in less than two months. Using her powers to influence, Sabina managed to convince both Ellen and Marvin that they were bound to go on a holiday to Egypt straight away. Unfortunately, she couldn't get their partners out of the way, so Ellen and Marvin brought their respective partners to Egypt. While this was a complication, it was also for the best. It would have been difficult for her mother to explain to her partner John, how she got pregnant during a holiday if he wasn't present!

Eventually, the opportunity for Sabina's conception arose. Both Ellen and Marvin were at the same restaurant. Sabina caused their eyes to meet, and she filled them with insurmountable amounts of carnal desire. Marvin and Ellen excused themselves from their partners, and they met up in the bathroom, where they had a tryst. After that, Sabina released them from her spell, and they returned to their respective tables, confused over what had happened.

A few months later, Marvin became very ill, and he died soon after. But this wasn't Sabina's most significant concern. While it would have been nicer to grow up with her biological parents, it was not achievable in this timeline. Sabina needed to convince Ellen to not have an abortion. Sabina was successful, and some months later she was born. One of the first things Sabina did, once she was born, was to tell her mother the truth. That she shouldn't feel ashamed over the tryst, as it had to happen.

Many years later, when Sabina was an adult, she set out to find Earth's primordial Zeto Crystal, i.e. the Holy Grail. She intended to use it to open the portal to the Divine Dimension and confront Rangda.

You can read about Sabina's adventures during the 21st Century in the **Sabina's Saves the Future Trilogy**.

The End!